THE CONSEQUENCE OF ANNA

A NOVEL

KATE BIRKIN
AND MARK BORNZ

For more information about Kate Birkin, Mark Bornz, and their books, visit www.katebirkinbooks.com.

ISBN-13: 979-8-9891841-0-1 (eBook)
ISBN-13: 979-8-9891841-1-8 (Paperback)

In Loving Memory of Crystal and Tarja

Inspired by true events . . .

It had become a thing of legend. Everyone in the Shire of Esperance, Australia, knew the tragedy of Anna May Shahan and her English cousin, Rose Charlotte Moss. The saga of two women—one driven by passion to do the unthinkable, the other plunging into insanity—and a man bound between them.

In recent years, on learning of the tale, two historical writers researched the actual account, attaining all the existing documents, including court evidence, witness statements, medical notes from a psychiatrist about a young mother committed to an insane asylum, love letters, photographs, and a diary dating back to the 1930s. They pieced together the tragic and compelling chronicle, titling it, *The Consequence of Anna*.

This is that story . . .

"Shamed be the woman who alloweth such a sin . . ."

There's something wrong with Anna . . .

Anna May Shahan (née Polston)

Rose Charlotte Moss

She was beautiful.

In a movie star kind of way.

With clear, radiant skin; thick ebony hair; and brilliant, flashing, dazzling green eyes.

Green eyes like two shimmering emerald pools.

Green eyes that spoke with no words.

Green eyes that laughed as you cried.

Green eyes like a serpent, hiding, waiting, slithering, lurching, fangs ready to puncture its prey . . .

The Kalgoorlie Miner Newspaper
Monday, April 10, 1933

ESPERANCE WOMAN ATTACKS FAMILY MEMBER

COMMITTED TO PSYCHIATRIC HOSPITAL

Anna May Shahan, a thirty-two-year-old wife and mother of three-year-old twin daughters, attacked one of her family members with intent to kill, also threatening harm to a newborn infant in a fit of rage. The incident took place Friday morning at the Shahan family cattle station known as Sugar Alexandria outside the town of Esperance, south of Kalgoorlie.

Senior Constable Daniel Higgins stated he was notified but did not arrest Mrs. Shahan, as she suffered a mental breakdown and was committed to the Pleasant Skies Psychiatric Hospital. Sources say she will remain there for evaluation and treatment prior to appearing before a judge. The police gave no other statement.

Immediate family members refused to comment. However, several members of the community were aware of the event and provided their own statements. "It was a love triangle with the most tragic of endings," Father Lothbrok lamented. "Sweet Anna did not deserve such a harrowing fate." Clarion Firestone had a differing opinion, though: "It served her right after what she had allowed. What good Christian wife would scheme such a thing for the happiness of another woman? It just wasn't natural." Yet Hazel Smuckers argued otherwise: "It's all the cousin's fault. Anna was a good girl. If that English tart with the gimp leg hadn't come here, none of this would have happened."

No other information or statements were given.

PART ONE

July 12, 1933

"This is all twisted," I said, narrowing my eyes at my cousin from the other side of the visiting table. "I shouldn't be imprisoned here."

"Anna, please listen to me," Rose pleaded, a sincere kindness in her voice that at one time would have made me move mountains for her.

I shook my head. "I should be at Sugar Alexandria with my husband and daughters. I should be with them, loving and taking care of them instead of here in this asylum." I pointed my finger at her. "And *you* . . . you should be far away on the other side of the Indian Ocean."

"Anna, you're precious to me. You have always been precious to me," Rose said.

"Precious?" I scoffed. "If I am so precious to you, why have you done this to me?"

"I didn't mean to hurt you. You're my best friend; you're like a sister to me."

"No, you're not my cobber, and no sister of mine. You're a liar, a thief, and a trollop," I continued, seething with indignation.

She stared at me in shock, as if looking into the face of a lunatic uttering unholy nonsense.

"As for James, you have bewitched him," I said, thinking how she had poisoned his mind and soiled his sheets.

An eerie silence followed, both of us feeling it. Despite knowing each other all our lives, we were strangers meeting for the first time. The grim reality was that I was no longer the Anna she knew and loved. What had happened transformed me, infected me. Inside and out. As if my bones had been broken and mended back together with pieces of wire.

Sitting there, I studied my cousin, her flapper bob done in perfect finger waves, her lips and nails crimson red—the same hue she always wore. The maternity dress—lavender, her favorite color—silky and expensive looking, bringing out the emerald in her eyes. She reminded me of cool vanilla ice cream, of decadence, of an evil Siren. As her pale hand began to caress her stomach, my eyes gravitated along. It was apparent the bairn within was kicking. "Look, the baby is upset," I said, breaking the silence. "Even your

3

unborn child knows what you have done to me."

"Anna, I never meant to hurt you," she sniffled, wiping her nose with a handkerchief. "I love and miss you." Yet as her words left her lips, she glanced over at the white-uniformed attendants. Was she frightened? Was she shaken that I no longer saw her as I once had? The truth was, I hoped she was scared, as all affection for her had been carved out of me like a gutted pig.

"Love me?" I sneered, appalled at the lie. "You only love yourself."

"Anna," she continued to entreat, trying to assuage my anger. "I do love you, and I came here to make peace."

"You have destroyed me, and now you want peace," I laughed.

"Please, let me explain," she said with desperation. "If you listen, you'll understand, and then maybe you can forgive."

"You want me to forgive? How dare you!" I yelled, choking back my tears. Rising to my feet, I leaned forward across the table and slapped her face. In a rage, I cursed in Danish, *"You once came to me for help, which I gave. And how did you repay me? By killing my soul and abandoning me. I curse you for what you have done to me!"*

"Anna . . . ," Rose said, holding her cheek, weeping.

Her display of emotion meant nothing to me. Once more, I slapped her as the attendants came running to intervene, curling their thick hands around my thin arms, dragging me away from her. *"I curse the very ground you slither on!"*

CHAPTER 1

Anna May Polston
&
Ambrosia (Rose) Charlotte Moss

Fifteen Years Earlier . . . December 14, 1918

"This is your last summer here," Anna said, wearing a white slip, looking at herself in the vanity mirror as a sea of freckles stared back at her. Freckles, freckles, freckles everywhere, she thought. Applying crimson red lipstick, she concentrated on not going over her lip line, just as her cousin had shown her.

Rose had been her mentor, her teacher, and her best friend since they were children, and Anna loved her like a sister, affectionately calling her Lottie at times—a shortened form of her middle name Charlotte. She thought Rose was beautiful, witty, and brave, walking tall and confident with her cane, and she would do anything for her. Anything in the world.

"Did you hear what I said, Lottie?" she asked. "This is your last summer here. I'll probably never see you again after you return to London and marry." Anna frowned, saddened by her certitude. No more knitting quilts together; baking Danish pastries; taking hot, soapy baths at the side of the house, shielded by white sheets hanging from the clothesline; having tea in her childhood secret room, reading and laughing; or spending the day outside, picking mushrooms, herbs, and spices for dinner. "I'd trade my healthy leg for your sick one, if it would make you stay."

Rose, already dressed in her finest chiffon and lace net gown, was waiting for Anna to finish. As she lay on her stomach on the four-poster bed, reading a magazine, she looked up at her younger cousin, so full of quirky bravado. She cared for Anna like a little pet. "Oh, Kitten, don't say such things. I'll be back."

"You pinky swear?" Anna asked, voice cracking, glossy eyes meeting her cousin's in the reflection of the mirror.

Rose lifted her pinky, and Anna walked over, interlinking hers. "I swear," said Rose. The young women remained that way a moment, fingers tightly locked, grinning at each other.

Each summer, Rose would make the long trip from England to Australia to stay at Sugar Alexandria, a remote cattle station outside the town of Esperance. Her mother allowed her to go when Anna's father first suggested it, seeking to soften his tomboy daughter by having her associate with his girlish niece. He was fed up with Anna's behavior, always worried sick whenever his inquisitive and fearless child went missing. Yarrajan, the Aboriginal nanny, usually found her little white rabbit in the neighbor's elaborate garden, playing with her invisible friends among the flowers, trees, statues, and ponds.

"Miss Anna, you come down here right now," the Aboriginal woman would demand, looking up at Anna's legs dangling from the branch of a beech tree. "You be too old to be actin' like this, and your daddy's spitfire mad. It's time you be wearin' a dress and some shoes, learnin' how to be a lady."

Anna would only giggle, dropping leaves or bugs on her nanny. But in truth, she loved the woman dearly. Yarrajan had taught her all about the land and the food that grew on it, enabling her to survive in the wild if need be. Showing her which plants, mushrooms, berries and seeds to eat, and which to avoid. She also shared her captivating stories about her people, their gods, and their customs. To Anna, Yarrajan wasn't just her nanny but her surrogate mother.

"Don't you make me come up there, 'cause if I do, you be gettin' a good beatin' with a switch!"

Anna would eventually crawl down, her feet covered in mud, her pockets full of frogs and other gifts from the land, and the two unlikely yet allied bedfellows—a yellow-haired child and a taller indigene—would walk hand in hand back to Sugar Alexandria to cook dinner.

When Rose first arrived in Australia, Anna was there waiting at the train station with her father. Mesmerized, she stared at her cousin with raven hair that gleamed a hue of blue, emerald eyes that sparkled like shining gems, and pale skin that never saw the sun. She reminded Anna of Snow White. Rose, on the other hand, saw a wide-eyed, freckled little girl in pigtails—spunky, adorable, and full of life. She reminded Rose of a kitten.

Anna ran right up to her, no introduction needed, sisterly love at first sight, wrapping her arms around her and squeezing. "Lottie!" she said, as if officially stamping her claim on Rose.

Rose kissed the top of her little cousin's head. "Kitten," she replied—a pet nickname that stuck ever since.

From the bustling city of London, England, Rose now found herself in the quiet town of Esperance, Australia. Just a flyspeck on the map, Esperance sat on the southwest coast near the Archipelago of the Recherche, or Bay of Isles, that sheltered fur seals, sea lions, and whales which gathered out in the farthest depths of the sea. It was beautiful with its white sands and endless turquoise waters of Lucky Bay, Thistle Cove, Blue Haven, and West Beach. The town itself was named after a famous French ship, *The Esperance*, meaning hope, earning its fame through Bruni d'Entrecasteaux's 1792 expedition of the scenic waterways and estuaries in the area. There was even a glorious pink salt lake—the color of fuchsia bubble gum—where the water was smooth as silk.

The shire exemplified the quintessential land Down Under. A mysterious dimension of red earth, blue skies, and exotic wildlife where the girls went into their own enchanted world together. They spent their carefree days riding horses to the shoreline, having picnics on the beach and searching for mermaids as they ate chocky bickies and drank strawberry lemonade. Or playing inside the ramshackle of a pirate shipwreck that had crashed on the rocks and been abandoned there eons ago, the wood of which had been used by some unknown fisherman to build a small cabin nearby. They walked through the tall cornfield until they found the perfect spot to make corn husk dolls with angel wings, and tiptoed through their agoraphobic neighbor's splendid, statue-laden garden. And they played in the three mammoth windmills in the stockyard, pretending they were in their secret castles. Large-bellied cattle, submissive sheep, horses and camels, vibrant narcissistic peacocks, and various other animals–some tamed, some not–all became companions of the two. The sprawling cattle station in the Outback wasn't just a large farm by the sea anymore but a never-ending fantasy realm of anything and everything they could imagine. Elves, fairies, mythical beasts, a place of dragons and unicorns where they were queens ruling on their thrones made of beech tree branches held together by the gum of eucalypts. Rose's wooden cane–her beast of burden, a necessary evil to support her underdeveloped right leg–would become their magic wand. Whatever they wanted, she would simply point it, and their wishes would come to pass.

Every corner of the endless Outback around Sugar Alexandria was an opportunity to venture out and find some new, unfound treasure. A full day of frivolous fun would invariably end with a swim in the ocean, and hunger would bring the cousins home for dinner. Yarrajan would serve their favorite meals and French braid the girls' damp hair, adding her colorful tribal beads to the braids. Nighttime would arrive, and in their long, matching, white cotton nightgowns, the two best friends would sneak out the bedroom window onto the roof of the farmhouse and stare up at the coruscating luminaries of the Milky Way, pointing at the constellations and whispering about boys and all the things that made young girls giggle. The night would close on a pallet in the attic, where by candlelight they'd tell scary stories to each other, or read from Anna's favorite tales–*East of the Sun and West of the Moon, Alice in Wonderland, The Secret Garden,* or one of her beloved Jane Austen books, most notably *Emma.*

The reality, however, was anything but a fantasy world. Outside the boundaries of Sugar Alexandria were other cattle and sheep stations where red-faced farmers plowed the lands, grew their crops, and raised their livestock. With thick accents–a mix of Aussie and European decent–sounding like a language all its own, stern faces and thin, wiry bodies, slits for eyes from prolonged squinting at the blaring sun, and callused hands from endless work in the fields, the men would afterward pack into the local pub like sardines, drinking too much ale and toasting the land, the sea, and whatever else fed their families.

Wives–sometimes more than one–stayed at home waiting for them, washing the vegetables, the clothes, their babies, and their own bodies in the same outside water trough, then cooked for hours, only to wait some more for their blokes to return. These were the women of Australia. Their mother's mother's mother had lived the same life, in the same house, doing the same chores, barefoot and rawboned, sometimes caught out in the fields birthing children, other times burying a stillborn, or vomiting blood as they pushed themselves to support their husbands any way they could to eke out a living from the land. They didn't have time to nurture a loving family, only to help with the workload. The more children, the more hands to tackle the burden of it all.

Anna and Rose did not see the harsh realities of life on a station in the Outback. Instead, they fashioned their own creative verismo, and over the course of their wonderful visits each summer, from the first day to the last when Rose would return home, the girls became more than cousins and best friends . . . They became close like sisters.

"You two almost ready?" Anna's father asked, poking his head into the room. "We leave in an hour." Clean-shaven, exposing smooth, pink skin—a rarity since he usually wore a full beard—with hair sleeked back, he had replaced his worn-out dungarees with his only suit, a blush-colored carnation pinned to the lapel.

Anna went over to the mirror again and began taking out her curlers. "Rose is ready; I just have to finish my hair."

"Well Lordy, look at you," her father said, admiring his teenage daughter. He was used to seeing his princess in braids, overalls, and muddy boots.

Anna smiled. "I'm hoping to fetch a bloke today, Daddy," she giggled.

Her father only shook his head. "Don't take too long getting ready, love. I'm not going to be late for my son's wedding."

"I won't; I promise." After her father left, she turned to Rose. "You'll be getting ready for your own wedding when you return to England. Except I won't be there."

"Anna, your dad is right. You're too young to travel that far alone."

"It would only be on the way back to Straya. Besides, you traveled here by yourself."

"I'm older than you, though."

"Not that much older."

"Old enough to travel across the sea on my own; whereas you are not."

"Soon I will be."

"Yes, and you can come visit me then."

"Even then my daddy probably won't let me go," Anna said, frowning. "He'll never let me grow up, or leave Straya."

Anna's father had lost his wife during childbirth, and five years later, Anna's twin sister to pneumonia. He kept a tight rein on his only living daughter—the long journey across the Indian Ocean from Esperance to London and back, was out of the question for a seventeen-year-old girl.

"Wish you would just marry a bloke here," Anna said, removing the last curler and unfurling the tight coils in her tresses with her fingers.

"Paul William Montgomery is a nice, kind bloke."

Anna crinkled up her nose, thinking of the photo Rose had previously shown of her fiancé. "If you ask me, he looks like a donkey."

"Don't be cheeky, Anna. This man is going to be my husband in a matter of months."

"Your parents arranged the marriage, Lottie, and only because he's wealthy. You don't even know him, let alone love him."

"He has qualities that I love."

"What kind of qualities?"

"He's gentle and kind."

"How do you know?"

"Umm . . ." Rose hesitated, unsure of what to say. "We've written to each other for a year now. He's an intelligent gentleman, and he accepts me for how I am."

"You mean your leg?"

"Yes."

"Your leg is apples, if you ask me. Besides, it's because of your leg that we have our magic wand."

Rose grinned. "It's a cane, Anna, and I need it to walk most of the time."
"So?"

"So some men don't like that. Some are even afraid our children would suffer the same curse if we married. Remember Triston Miller? I was crazy for him, and he straight out told me I had a beautiful face, but . . ."

"But what?"

"He wanted a woman with two normal legs."

"He was a drongo."

"Paul doesn't seem to be bothered by it, and I consider that a blessing."

"You're marrying a bloke just because your leg doesn't bother him?"

Rose looked away.

"Don't marry because of that, Rose. You're a beauty with a heart of gold; you deserve someone better."

"I'm not a child anymore, Anna. Far from it, even though I get to act like one when I visit here."

"What's that supposed to mean?"

"Just that I'm a woman now." She marked the page of the magazine displaying the wedding dress she fancied. "And that's what women do at my age—get married and have babies."

"I'll only marry a bloke I love, who I'm absolutely mad for," Anna said, clutching her chest.

Rose picked up the locket hanging around her neck, examining it in her palm. Anna's father had bought them both matching friendship necklaces that summer, each containing the other's picture inside. I'll grow to love him, she assured herself.

Anna noticed her staring at the locket. "Every time I look down at mine, I'm gonna miss you terribly."

"I said I'll be back, so you won't have to miss me for long. We pinky swore, remember?"

"That's right, and everyone knows that once you picky swear, it's for life." Anna stepped into her dress and twirled, her mood shifting from melancholy to excitement. "I'm gonna dance with every bloke tonight," she giggled. "How about you, Lottie?"

"I'll dance with some, I guess. Until my leg tires."

Anna glanced over at her cousin's cane propped against the bed. "Does it ever feel like your bone is breaking?"

"My goodness, Anna May Polston, where's your couth?"

She laughed. "Sorry, love."

Rose thought about her underdeveloped right leg, defective since birth. Without her walking stick, it would become painful as it enervated. Like a bad toothache, the small muscle fibers in her thigh spasming if she overworked it.

"Liam is here to see you sheilas," said Yarrajan, walking into the room and placing their clean white gloves on the bed. Both girls put them on. "Want me to tell him you be leavin'?"

"No," said Rose. She loved children and enjoyed their company. "We still have time; send him in."

Liam Herdsman, an eight-year-old boy who lived on the neighboring station across the river, walked into the room smiling ear to ear, holding one of Anna's corn husk dolls he had found on the ground. The deaf, intellectually disabled child had suffered a severe bacterial infection a few years back and almost died, leaving him with his disabilities. He could read lips, however, and his speech hadn't yet changed to the point of being abstruse. Often he would visit Anna and her cousin, hoping they would play with him, whether board games, hide-and-seek, or anything else they would entertain.

"Can we go to the garden again today?" he asked, his words forced and loud. Just the day before, Rose had indulged Anna by playing out a scene from the beloved children's novel, *The Secret Garden*. Anna was Mary Lennox, Liam played Dickon Sowerby, and Rose became the robin—the gatekeeper to the enchanted garden. Though Rose had all but grown out of theme playing, Anna and Liam loved it, so she went along, knowing her youthful days of fantasy lore were fast approaching their end as she would soon be getting married. Besides, the neighbor's garden where they acted out their roles was so grand and lovely that she didn't mind.

"No, Liam, we can't go there today," Anna said, primping in front of the mirror. Her friendship with Liam was both hot and cold, depending on whether she wanted to play or not.

"Why, what are you doing?" he asked.

"Getting ready to go to my brother's wedding."

"Can I go?" He tried to smooth down his dirty blond hair.

Anna shook her head. "No."

"Why not?" asked Rose. "He won't be any trouble."

"Because we'd have to babysit him."

Liam stared down at the handmade doll in his hands. "I wouldn't be any trouble; I promise."

"No," Anna said again. "Not this time."

"What are you going to do there?" he inquired.

"Dance and eat cake," said Anna, brushing her hair.

"What? Let me see your lips." The mentally challenged boy frustrated easily, especially when he could not see someone's lips, or failed to read them properly.

Anna frowned, then turned to him so he could see her enunciate. "I said dance and eat cake."

"I love cake!" Liam exclaimed.

Rose waved at him to get his attention. "I'll bring you back some. A great big piece."

Liam smiled, clapping his hands.

"Anna, have you ever slow-danced with a bloke before?" Rose asked.

"A couple of times. I mean, I did with Daddy and my brothers in the past, if that counts."

Rose got off the bed and put a record on the gramophone. "Come here, Kitten. Let's practice before we go." Pulling Anna in close, they both swayed to the music. "See? It's easy."

Anna gazed up at her cousin as they danced. Rose had the prettiest, greenest eyes she had ever seen, and the kindest smile. "Yes, it is."

"Me next, me next!" Liam chirped, dropping the doll and opening his arms.

Rose let go of Anna and brought the young boy into her embrace. He could not hear the music, but he had an idea of what they were doing. Being small, he leaned his head against her chest, closing his eyes in ecstasy. Anna plopped onto the bed, stuffing two sticks of gum into her mouth, observing her cousin cradle the deaf, mentally challenged boy in her arms. What a strange pair, she thought. Rose, with her flawed leg, lacking muscle and shape; and Liam, intellectually slow and unable to hear. Yet as they danced there in her room, on the hard wooden floor under their feet, they took on such a graceful, beautiful form.

Anna's heart ached. Her beloved cousin would be going back to London right after her brother's wedding, getting married to an Englishman and most likely never returning. Silent tears streamed down her face as she stared at them both, Rose gently swaying back and forth, her lavender chiffon dress softly flowing as she moved, Liam swaying with her to music he could feel but not hear.

─◦◦✦◦◦─

Liam had never seen Anna look so grown up as she did standing in front of her mirror in her ruffly dress, hair flowing and lips stained with red. Where did little Anna go, he wondered? Where was the girl who spat water through the gap in her front teeth, who kissed frogs for good luck, played hide-and-seek with him in the neighbor's garden, and ran barefoot with him through the fields? She was changing, right before his eyes.

As he walked home that afternoon, he thought about how his friend seemed increasingly annoyed with him these days. Over-pronouncing her words so he could read her lips had become such a chore, and she played with him less and less. Even when she sang to the livestock through the haunting, high-pitched sounds of kulning–an ancient Scandinavian herding call she had learned from her Danish grandmother–to summon them home, she no longer let him feel her throat to sense the beautiful vibrations. Everything was now an irritation and a bother to her.

"Checkers, Anna?" he would ask.

But she would only shake her head and want to brush her hair, try on a dress, or listen to a record on the gramophone.

The gramophone. A gadget that was foreign to him. A box that everyone sat around, enthralled, listening to with undivided attention as a flat disc spun on its surface. He had no clue of its magic or thrill. Anna loved the gramophone as all the adults did, slowly slipping into their world–a place he did not belong, nor ever would. At least Rose will always care for me, he thought, unaware she was leaving Australia and might never return.

His mind shifted back to the dance they shared earlier in Anna's bedroom. He could almost taste her perfume, becoming lost in her beauty as they danced, the only music being her heart beating against his cheek. Yes, Rose–one of the few people kind to him, patient with his disabilities–would always have a place for him, he resolved, hoping, longing, consoling himself as he crossed the bridge and climbed the fence, petting the sheep on his way home.

CHAPTER 2

Anna and Rose sat in the pews, waiting patiently for the ceremony to begin. The day was hot and sticky, and as Anna leaned her head against her cousin's smooth shoulder, Rose gently waved a feathered fan between them, cooling their warm, flushed skin.

"What's taking so long?" Anna asked, sitting back up and yawning.

"They're still getting ready, Kitten," said Rose, looking about the room. "It's a big deal getting married. It changes your whole life."

Anna, chewing on her gum, blew a large bubble and popped it, annoying the elderly couple in front of them. Rose apologized for her ill-mannered cousin's behavior, discreetly chastising Anna as she giggled.

"How does it change your whole life?" she whispered.

"Your spouse becomes a part of you," said Rose. "They become your best friend, and from that day forward, they're always with you. Life is more fulfilling when you have someone to share your special moments with."

"Sounds like you're looking through flower-colored glasses. Yarra says marriage is just a bloke being gifted with a hardworking maid and cook."

The elderly woman turned and put her finger to her lips to shush them.

Rose tried not to laugh. "It's rose-colored glasses, Kitten, not flower-colored," she whispered. "And marriage is a beautiful union when you find the right person."

"You'll always be my best cobber, Lottie, no matter who comes into my life."

"It's not the same thing." Rose was going to annotate the difference between a platonic relationship and a romantic one, but the bagpipes commenced, followed by the piano music, and the bride began advancing down the aisle. A shiver ran through her entire body when the bride and groom stood face-to-face in front of the priest, smiling and holding hands, their eyes silently confessing their love for each other before stating their vows. She too wanted to gaze into the eyes of a loving man and glow. To love someone passionately, faithfully, with everything that she was, and be loved the same way in return. But deep down she knew her fiancé was not that man. He did accept her disability, though, and her life would be more than comfortable, even lavish, living in a fancy house in London, dining in the finest restaurants, shopping in the high-end boutiques, enjoying the opera and ballet, and all the other privileges financial security bestowed. Yet somehow it still felt as if she had an open wound festering inside. A woman absent of true love, paying a heavy price for settling. A burden she would have to endure, just like her underdeveloped leg, learning how to live with it.

～⁂～

The wedding reception commenced, and with most of the men more interested in the free grog available, Anna and Rose slow-danced together, just as they had rehearsed earlier in the day.

"You're getting good at this," Rose said, taking the lead.

Anna giggled, paying close attention to her feet. "When I dance later with a bloke, I'm gonna kiss him. You should too, Lottie, with some bloke you fancy. Just for the fun of it."

"Don't be cheeky, love. I'd never do that, and neither should you."

"Because you're prim and proper, aye? An English lady."

"That's right," said Rose, slowly spinning her. "Ladies don't go around kissing strangers."

Several children ran past them to the refreshment table. Rose watched as they eagerly received some cake and soda. "We should have let Liam come. He would have loved it."

"Bah!" Anna fleered, scrunching up her freckle-covered nose. "We would have had to watch him the whole time. He probably would have stuck

16

his face in the cake and ruined it, too, having such a wicked sweet tooth."

"Don't be so hard on him, Kitten. You have a sweet tooth as well, and it can send you into a real tizzy."

"That only happens if I get too excited or upset."

"Or when you've had too much sugar. I've seen it change you."

Anna looked up into her cousin's verdant eyes. "You make it sound as if I'm a werewolf."

"Sometimes you are," said Rose, thinking of her little cousin throwing tantrums so violent and extreme that she had to be held down by her brothers until it passed.

"Hey, let's go get some punch. We can sneak some grog, too, and spike our drinks with it." Anna gave her shoulders a shake. "I wanna get on the tables and kick up my legs. That oughta drive the men crazy."

Rose shook her head. "You are a wild one."

Anna lowered her chin and batted her lashes. "Then I'm gonna pick a bloke and kiss him until he begs for air!"

"Oh, Anna, bold and sinful you are!" said Rose, and both girls broke out into laughter.

Poppy Buttersmith espied the two young women walking across the dance floor to the refreshment table. She was the town gossip, and proud of it, turning it into an art form. Over six feet tall with Argentium silver hair piled up on top of her head in a Victorian-style bun that made her appear even taller, she talked about anyone she fancied, doing so with such zest and charm that one would think it was her profession. Her style was to compliment first, followed by either an insult or a private revelation.

Narrowing her eyes at the two cousins—Anna, excited and animated, pouring a cup of the cerise-colored fruit drink while Rose, shy and quiet, waited for her, leaning on her cane—Poppy motioned in their direction. "There's Anna Polston and her pommy cousin, Ambrosia Moss," she said. "Aren't they looking lovely today in their beautiful chiffon dresses."

All the women at the table turned to stare at Anna and Rose.

"Now here's a story for you . . ." Poppy became sobersides, yet her glistening eyes betrayed her. "Ambrosia comes here every summer to spend time with little Anna. Has now for years. Poor child not having a mother, then her twin sister dying, it's no wonder she whispers to herself and has those fits she throws."

"I heard her mum talked gibberish to herself too," Beatrice Waterloo said, a brooding expression on her face as she sipped from her punch, "and that she'd run barefoot in the cold wearing only her nightgown, wandering off into the bush in the middle of the night. Strange one, she was."

"Too right," said Poppy, feigning a visible shiver. "Crikey, the stories I could tell you about Elsa Polston would make you shudder." She lowered her voice and kept her eyes on Anna. "My Aboriginal nanny is friends with their nanny, Yarrajan, who confided in her that something evil would take over Elsa. Completely different personality inside her."

"My mum said the same thing," added Wednesday Motherland, throwing more fuel on the gossipmongering, "that Elsa was crazy."

Poppy nodded, her stacked steel-wool-colored coiffure wobbling in the air. "Crazy as a loon. Completely mad. Round the twist. All the Aboriginals who worked for them said she had the mulga madness. I'm surprised that bloke of hers kept having children with a sheila not well in the head as she was."

"He had a station to manage–that's why," said Drusilla Esmeralda.

Her sister Lilith supported her. "That's right. He needed sons to help him with it." Lilith was a little person, having been born with achondroplasia. No more than three feet eight inches tall, and more impertinent than her normal-height sibling, the two went everywhere together.

Poppy smirked. "Elsa was a pretty blonde thing, too. I suppose he was in love with her even though she was insane."

"I hope Anna doesn't end up like her poor mother," Beatrice tsked.

Hulga Schaefer scoffed, her tired eyes waking up in a galvanized stir. She was the oldest in the group–in her late nineties–and rarely spoke, but when she did there was always truth in it. "Don't feel sorry for Anna," the near-centenarian muttered, holding her sleeping grandchild in her arms. "Feel sorry for the bloke who someday falls for those freckles and flaxen hair, ending up with a mentally sick sheila."

"Bloody oath," said Poppy.

The quorum of quidnuncs simultaneously nodded in agreement.

With the nuptial vows over, dinner eaten, cake and punch consumed, and dancing well underway, the Aussie wedding between a Danish groom and his Irish bride moved into the customary bouquet toss. Anna and Rose had danced until Rose's leg hurt, and when they stopped the music for the bride to throw her posy into a group of young women on the dance floor, Rose stayed behind, grateful for the break. Besides, she was already engaged.

Hiding in the shadows, leaning against the wall with her cane, scanning the crowd of people in the room, her eyes settled on a handsome bloke sitting at a table with his fellow war Diggers. He was the one who had played several songs on the piano that evening, and his rare talent had made her cry. Homing in on him from across the room, she watched as he laughed and joked with his mates. My, my, she thought, inwardly smiling. Now that's one good-looking Irish-Aussie . . .

James Ragnar Shahan

"Crikey, did all of Straya come to this shindig?" Peachy Jones asked, scanning the extravagant reception hall. "Never been to a wedding this grand; it's like a battalion in here."

"More like a brigade," Slim Stavin said, lighting a cigarette. "I haven't seen this many people together since they saw us off to war."

"Weddings, births, and battles—that's where folks gather," laughed Dewey Silkwood. "And of course, funerals."

The men at the table went silent. Dewey realized his error when he saw them all staring at their drinks with long faces and troubled eyes, each recalling their fellow soldiers and friends who didn't come home. Though the insanity of the Great War had ended, the haunting memories were still raw. Innocent young blokes who marched off to the unknown had come back humbled, wiser men; but also scarred and sullied.

"I wanna make a toast," said Bowie Jenkins, endeavoring to brighten the mood. "To new beginnings and a ripper life ahead of us." A peaceful mien shadowed his features and his voice moderated as he looked at each of his friends. "May the sun always shine on your face, the wind be at your back, and blessings fall at your feet."

All the men raised their glasses and cheered.

The Aussie Diggers, grateful to be home in one piece, resumed celebrating and chatting on endlessly. Especially one: James Ragnar Shahan. His sister Josephine was the bride, and she insisted he be in the wedding party and play the piano as she walked down the aisle.

Originally from Dublin, Ireland, James had moved to Australia with his family when he was a boy, like many families who sought to cash in on the gold rush at Mount Charlotte in Kalgoorlie. Instead of finding gold, however, they settled on the southern coast and found ivory sands, emerald waters, and the biggest fish they had ever seen. Being born in the land of Éire wasn't the only thing that made James unique among his friends. He was meek, slow to anger, kind and articulate with his words. He listened more than he spoke, and most days when he did speak, it was about his music. His love for the piano drove aspirations of becoming an acclaimed pianist, and he possessed the talent to underpin his dreams.

But the war had not left him unscathed. He was now partially deaf—only his left ear still functioned—and his right pupil had been torn after being hit by shrapnel from a bomb. Though he could still see through it, the misshapen iris would never regain its full capacity. For a man who adored music, who was going to be a professional pianist when the madness was all over, it was a severe blow to have both his sight and hearing vitiated. And yet, at the very heart of him, he was still a gifted musician despite his physical maladies. Nothing was going to deter him from pursuing his goals. In fact, even as he sat there, he was thinking of when he would be leaving for London soon to attend the Royal Academy of Music, and all the things he needed to do before he left.

While contemplating his bright future, James let his eyes float around the large, dimly lit room, and that's when he saw her: A young woman leaning against the wall across from them, supporting herself with a cane.

Slim followed his gaze. "Forget it, Shahan. I already asked her and she bloody shot me down."

The other men stopped to look.

"She's a beauty," said Bandy McRoe.

"Look, she's using a cane," Peachy noticed, lowering his voice. "Must have a broken leg."

James descried the young woman looking directly at him, releasing a subtle, soft smile, making him feel as if the sun had just come out.

"Anyone else here brave enough to give it a burl?" Bowie dared.

Maybe it was the strong Irish whiskey he was drinking, or that he was home safe from the war, or that she looked like a lost angel, but the usually quiet and reserved James acted first, deciding to make his move. He stood and walked toward the girl, ignoring the other men jeering him on; before he knew it, he was inches away from her. Her eyes are blue, or maybe green, he thought, and her face as if a light shining in the dark. "G'day, my name is

James. May I ask you for a dance?" he asked, his voice rather shaky.

As they met eyes, something jabbed him in the deepest parts of his gut, and his surroundings blurred. Why is my mind so blank, he wondered? Unable to muster any other words, he stood there smiling like a lovestruck teenager.

"I've been on my feet all night," she said. "Not sure if I can even dance, now that my leg has tired." Yet she too had felt the electricity. Pink, green, and gold sparks flashed through her mind as she slightly trembled.

"Aah, an English girl," he said, recognizing her accent. Leaning forward, he extended his elbow to her. "C'mon, love, let's give it a go."

Her gaze was cautious, yet curious, and she consented, leaving her walking stick behind, stepping into his embrace. He took her hand—how perfectly it fit into his—wrapping his arm around her waist. The song was slow and dreamy.

"So what's your name, love?" he asked, looking down into her face.

As she was about to speak, he tilted his good ear in the direction of her words—a habit that began soon after losing his hearing in the other. "I don't give my name to strangers," she said, her eyes evincing a coquettish grin.

"If you give me your name, we're no longer strangers."

She bit at her lower lip. "Charlotte," she said, conferring only her middle moniker.

"Charlotte, Charlotte, Charlotte," he softly whispered into her ear as they danced cheek to cheek. "It's a lovely name for a beauty of a sheila."

"Thank you." Her heart fluttered. "I was really moved by your piano playing earlier," she said, trying to subdue her butterflies. "One of your songs even made me cry."

"Ta." He was pleased she had noticed.

"Where did a soldier learn how to play like that?"

"I was a pianist before I was a Digger. Played since I was a boy. Now that the war is over, I'll be going to London to pursue a career in music."

"London? That's where I'm from."

"Perfect, I can bring you home," he said, gently spinning her, pulling her back into him. "The only problem is, being in the same city together, I'd never want to attend class."

She blushed, floating on a cloud, her entire body warming to his touch. "I'm actually a musician too."

"Oh yeah? What do you play?"

"The violin. In fact, I noticed you were a little off key during one point in Mozart's *Piano Concerto No.21*," she teased.

"Is that right," he laughed, impressed she knew the opus. Taking her hand, he stripped the glove from it, smoothing over the callus on her string finger. "Yep, there it is."

"What?"

"The sign of a true violinist."

She leaned back, narrowing her eyes at him. "You didn't believe me until you felt my callus?"

"With a face like yours, my sweet Charlotte, I would believe just about anything you said."

She stared back at him, deep into his eyes. I really like this man, she thought, and I can see he fancies me too. But I'm already betrothed to another. Besides, look how lovely he is; he probably already has a girl–a beautiful one with two normal legs. "You must be wondering why I need a cane," she said, timorous over what he was thinking.

"As pretty as you are, I figured you sprained your ankle, running away from all the blokes chasing you."

She smiled so hard it hurt. "Well, no, nothing like that. I was born with a special leg; it's different. The muscles are underdeveloped and weak, so they tire easily."

"I never would have noticed," he said, dipping her, breathing in her scent–Chypre de Coty–intoxicating his senses. The pianist was completely besotted, fancying the violinist so much he never wanted to let her go.

"Most people do."

"I'm not most people," he said, a glint in his eye.

They danced in silence for a moment, the music quickening in pace. She followed his lead, barely aware of her impaired leg.

"Let me ask you something, Charlotte," he said, a flirtatious grin tugging at his lips.

She flashed her green eyes up at him.

"If I asked you to marry me right now, what would you say?"

"You're being silly," she laughed.

"Am I?" He took off his pinky ring, once owned by his great-grandfather–a single band of gold with a Celtic design–and placed it on her index finger.

"You're mad," she said, playing along with his theatrics.

"Look at that—it fits. Whaddya say, love? Wanna spend the rest of your life with an Irish pianist? I'll be traveling the world performing in fancy auditoriums, and a beauty like you by my side would be grand."

"Oh, stop," she laughed again.

As they continued to dance, she relaxed in his embrace, and he gently pulled her close, enjoying her warm, soft body against his. Moving in unison like two lonesome shadows across the room, the world around them faded . . .

"The song is over," she whispered against his ear.

James, transported to another place, gave himself a mental shake and loosened his grip on her. "Sorry, I didn't realize."

"Thank you for the dance," she said, trying to read his expression through the faltering light. They were now standing in a more dimly lit area of the dance floor, and most people had already returned to their tables. James continued to hold on to her hand and wouldn't let her go, and just when he was about to release her, he pulled her in instead, giving her a kiss she would remember for the rest of her life.

Suddenly a young boy waved his arms and yelled, "Fire! Fire! Fire!"

Everyone stopped socializing, scanning the room for evidence of the alarming exhortation. When the banquet hall manager opened the door leading to the kitchen, a billow of smoke entered the reception area. Gasping could be heard and people panicked, rushing onto the dance floor, pushing and shoving to exit the building. In the chaos of the situation, James' grasp on the hand of the Englishwoman he had just kissed broke loose, separating the two. By the time he was outside, she was nowhere in sight.

"Oh, pardon me," Anna Polston said, bumping into him. "I was looking for my cousin."

"No worries," replied James, his eyes sweeping the crowd for the pretty brunette who simply vanished.

"Hey, aren't you the bloke who played the piano tonight? You're James Shahan—Josephine's brother, aye?"

"Yes."

"I'm Anna Polston—Christian's sister. Isn't that funny; we're practically related now," she chortled. Giving him a coy look from the top of her eyes, she twiddled a tendril of her hair, hiding something behind her back. "You know what I did earlier?"

He shook his head.

"I caught the bride's posy; that's what I did," flinging a bouquet up in his face.

He looked down at the arrangement of clustered roses. "Swell."

Anna let out a giggle. "Now that your sister is married to my brother, wouldn't it be something if we got married too?"

James couldn't hold back his laugh.

"What's so funny?" Anna asked, scowling. "Plenty of blokes would want to marry me."

"I'm sure they would; you're a beauty," he said, winking at her, seeing her more as a child.

The banquet hall manager came outside, informing everyone that the fire in the kitchen had been put out. He apologized and invited all the guests back inside, urging them not to let this ruin their night.

"I sure would like a dance from you, James Shahan," Anna said, hearing the band playing again.

Disinterested, James paused, still distracted over the woman who had bewitched him moments earlier. "I would, Anna, but I actually have to go find a mate of mine," he said, taking a step back, intending to search for Charlotte.

Anna's smile disappeared, looking as if she might cry.

"All right, one dance," he said, giving in, rationalizing that he would go find Charlotte as soon as he could break free from freckle face Polston.

Inside the banquet hall, she stood on her tiptoes and wrapped her arms around him so tightly his lungs fought to breathe.

James

Charlotte had simply vanished.

After dancing with Anna Polston, I looked for the pretty English lass who reminded me of the women in the paintings of Alfons Maria Mucha and Gustav Klimt. But I could not find her. Even the people I asked could not tell me who Charlotte was.

Had she been a ghost?

The night before Rose left for the train station, the two cousins went inside Anna's secret hideaway. Her father had built a room inside a room for his daughter to play in as a child, and even now as a teenager, she'd often use it, shutting the door to the outside world to be in her own little sanctuary.

The entrance to the room was disguised as a grand-looking wardrobe made of dark walnut wood. When you opened the double doors and pushed aside the clothing, however, a second door revealed itself, leading to the covert chamber. Inside were shelves with Anna's favorite books; a small, tangerine Victorian velvet sofa; a square table and four chairs, adorned with a rose-covered tea set; and a grandfather clock that tick-tocked in the corner.

Lying on the round, colorful rug on the floor, surrounded by candles, eating lollies and watching Rose as she read from *The Secret Garden*, Anna tried hard not to think of the following morning when her cousin would be leaving to go back to London.

"Lottie, can you read me a different one now?" she asked, rolling onto her stomach, her chin propped up between her hands.

"Which one?" asked Rose, closing the book.

"*East of the Sun and West of the Moon.*"

"Kitten, not again. I've read that too many times to count."

"How about telling me a story, then? Something spooky."

"The *Black Shuck* folklore tale?"

Anna nodded exuberantly. "That one scares the skirt off me."

Rose laughed. "It's pants, Anna . . . It scares the pants off you. And yes, the *Black Shuck* is a creepy tale." She picked up a candle and held it close to her face for dramatic effect, the flickering flame casting shadows on the wall behind her. "The year was 1577," she began, lowering her voice and slowing her speech, "in Suffolk County of East Anglia. A huge black wolf roamed the countryside, terrorizing the people, killing anyone who crossed its path. No one dared to venture out at night."

Already frightened, Anna crawled closer to her cousin, her eyes growing wide. "What did he look like?"

"Oh, but it was not a 'he'. It was a she-wolf, with midnight black hair, razor-sharp teeth, and red shining eyes so terrifying that if you saw them once, you would die of fear."

A tree branch, pushed by the wind, scraped along the small window, sending chills down Anna's spine.

"One early morn, a sheep farmer's wife went outside to collect eggs from the chicken coop, and when she didn't return, he went looking for her. In a panic, he followed the trail of blood on the ground, finding her lifeless body at the edge of the woods. After burying his wife and grieving, the farmer swore he'd find the evil creature and exact his revenge. Day and night he searched the land, setting traps and tracking the beast. Eventually he caught sight of the enormous black wolf standing on a hill, howling at the moon. He shot it, and the animal ran off into the darkness to die."

"What happened next?" Anna asked, engrossed in the story as if hearing it for the first time.

"Satisfied he had killed it, the farmer set off home, and the next day he found a woman lying naked in his field. Oh, she was a stunning beauty, with long ebony hair, skin like white satin, and beautiful dark eyes. He took her home, nursed her back to health, and fell madly in love with her, convinced his life had turned for the better. But then one night, under a full moon again, she changed."

"She turned into the Black Shuck!"

"That's right," said Rose, the candlelight reflecting in her eyes. "And as she was killing him, he cried out, 'But I loved you! I cared for you! Why?' And she replied, her eyes turning bloodred, her teeth now sharp and long, 'I'm a wolf. What did you expect?' "

"Knock, knock, knock!" suddenly came through the hidden door. Both girls shrieked, then laughed.

"You two go to bed soon, aye?" said Anna's father on the other side. "We're not missing the train in the morning."

"All right, Daddy!" Anna replied.

"Good night, Uncle Polston!" said Rose.

"Sweet dreams, girls."

Anna turned to Rose. "How could she do that? He had done so much for her. He loved her."

"Because a snake is always a snake, a scorpion always a scorpion, and a wolf always a wolf. You can't change who you are, no matter how kind the other person is." Rose noticed Anna turning glum. "You look sad, Kitten. What is it?"

"It's just that nights like this are over for me. You'll be gone tomorrow."

"I'm just getting married; I'll be back. We pinky swore yesterday, remember?"

Anna looked as if she were about to cry. "You're going to forget Sugar

Alexandria once you leave. You're going to forget me."

Rose scanned the hidden room, admiring its whimsical charm. "No, Kitten," she said, looking back at her little summer companion who made her laugh and helped her feel like a child again. "I will never forget you, or this magical place called Sugar Alexandria."

Anna smiled, dimples popping, gap between her teeth showing.

"And as long as I am alive," Rose continued in Danish, *"when I need to get away, I will always return to this sanctuary. Always. Remember that, my precious Kitten, because it is my solemn pact with you."* As she said those words, for a flicker of a moment, she thought of the handsome soldier she had danced with and kissed, hoping the life that lay ahead of him would be a happy one.

~⚜~

Rose was leaving the tiny woop woop town of Esperance, with its red earth, blue skies, pink lakes, and turquoise bays. She was leaving the animals she loved—the kangaroos, koalas, and quokkas—and the carefree life she embraced at Sugar Alexandria. Worst of all, she was leaving her sweet cousin Anna.

She would travel by rail to Fremantle, then board a ship and sail across the Indian Ocean, through the Suez Canal, the Mediterranean Sea, and back home to England where a new life awaited her. Standing with her suitcase by her feet, a brilliant purple scarf wrapped around her head, she smiled at Anna through tears under the bright Australian sun. "Kitten . . . ," was all she could get out.

Anna had already sobbed so much her throat was sore, her eyes swollen. She handed Rose her carry-on bag as the train approached. "Chug, chug, chug. Toot! Toot!" it screeched, coming to a halt.

"If you don't write me, I'll come and hunt you down," Anna jokingly threatened, her voice quivering.

"I will; I promise," said Rose. Images of her last day at Sugar Alexandria flashed through her mind. She and Anna had woken up at the crack of dawn that morning, zipping through their chores as usual, milking the cows, feeding the animals, even helping a sow give birth. Soon life would be so much different, living in a big city again, far from the wild and wondrous Outback.

Observing that Anna still had blood and dirt under her fingernails from delivering the piglets—something that always went unnoticed by her cousin, living and breathing farm work, cognizant of little else–Rose smiled at her. "Make sure to wash your hands better, Kitten, like I showed you," she said over the sound of the train. "All the way to the elbows, and don't forget to scrub your nails." She scanned Anna's unkempt locks. "And make sure to brush your hair every night so it won't get so entangled that your dad has to cut it off. Don't fall asleep in the cherry trees at Cassandra's garden, either, for fear of falling to the ground and breaking your arm. Remember, too, that if you accidentally hurt someone's feelings, you have to say you're sorry. And try not to fidget so much, Kitten. Or when you have another one of your whispering spells, take deep breaths to calm yourself. Oh, and tell Liam I said goodbye! And, and, and . . . ," Rose said in a rush of motherly words, trying to remember all the helpful advice she wanted to give before leaving.

"All right, Lottie," Anna kept saying, her chin quivering. "I'll try; I promise," she whimpered.

Rose leaned in and whispered, "And when you see the lady in black, or hear the voices, what do you do?"

"Run to the garden," said Anna, suddenly wide-eyed and looking confident. "It's my safe place."

"That's right." Rose smiled and pulled her little cousin into her arms like a puppy, her cane clanking to the ground. Anna squeezed back with all her might.

"You sheilas finish up, now. No need to make the conductor wait," Anna's father said, standing a few feet away, holding his hat in his hand while drinking a cold soda he had just bought from the dime store inside the station.

Anna picked up Rose's cane, handing it to her, and Rose kissed Anna's damp cheek. "Abyssinia, Kitten," she said, tears now streaming.

"Until then, Lottie Dottie," replied Anna, tears of her own falling at will. "Have a bee's knees time back in London."

Rose walked over to the passenger train.

"Lottie!" Anna called out one last time. *"You'll always be a sister to me,"* she cried in Danish. *"You're my best cobber, and I will always love you. I will count each day until I see you again next summer,"* she said, her father holding her back from running to her cousin as she embarked the train.

Rose briefly turned, parting her lips to say something. But what was there left to say? Instead, she stopped and gave the conductor her luggage, choosing to say nothing and simply wave. Perhaps because she knew, deep down, that she wouldn't be coming back. Not for a very, very long time, anyway.

Anna

That night, I go into my magical childhood hidden room and weep. Feeling like shattered glass, I open one of my favorite books, *The Secret Garden*, hoping it will ease my sadness.

"Would you like me to read that for you, love?" asks a kind voice in the darkness. The candlelight flickers, and a beautiful, feminine hand emerges out of the shadows, unfurling its long fingers at me.

In a daze, I stop weeping and hand the book over, anticipating the story to begin.

The trapper, Glenda Trufflepig, who ironically, bred pigs and sold them to the local farmers, was hiking up the road when she ran into Anna and Liam heading over to Cassandra Fancy's garden. Glenda was the older sibling of Poppy Almira Buttersmith, and lived in a rustic cabin in the bush. Over six feet tall like her sister, she had fire-engine red hair, a stark contrast to Poppy's dark hair that turned silver. There was bad blood between the sisters, too. They hadn't spoken to each other in decades because Glenda's sweetheart left her for Poppy when they were young.

"G'day, Miss Trufflepig," Anna politely greeted. "Where you headed?"

"Lookin' for one of my sows," said the older woman. An experienced trapper and taxidermist, several dead rabbits hung from her shoulder. "She escaped under the fence this mornin'."

"Want us to help you find her?" asked Anna.

"No, you run off and play. I'll track her down." Glenda noticed Rose wasn't with them. "Where's your cousin Lottie? You two never leave each other's side."

"She went back to London," said Anna.

"She's getting married," Liam added loudly.

"Oh, caught herself a bloke, did she?" Glenda smirked. "Men—more trouble than they're worth, and that's no lie."

Anna frowned, fearful their wonderful annual adventures were done. "I already miss her terribly."

"No worries, love. I'm sure Liam will keep you company."

Liam read her lips and beamed, nodding vigorously. He loved Glenda Trufflepig. Sometimes she'd let him tag along when she checked her traps. Other times he'd bring her his own catch—usually just snakes because the rabbits he'd pet and let go.

"Liam's all right," said Anna with a shrug, "but he's nothing like Rose." Pulling on his arm, they ran off toward Cassandra Fancy's garden. "I hope you find your pig!" she yelled over her shoulder.

❧

Anna hoped going to the exquisite garden would help distract and comfort her, but all she found was immense emptiness instead. As she stood among the glorious flowers, the resplendent foliage and greenery, and the impressive ivy-covered statues, she grieved that her beloved cousin was not there. Rather than a place of magic and wonder, the garden was now an abandoned, overgrown coppice, the pond a dirty swamp, the sculptures sad ghosts.

"Let's go home, Liam," she said, walking dolefully toward the gates. "Yarra made chocky bickies this morning; let's go have some."

Liam, with his crown of wildflowers on his head, happily followed close behind his friend.

Halfway there, Glenda Trufflepig's potbellied sow emerged from the bushes, snorting gleefully. Anna and Liam cornered it, grabbing hold of the miniature pig so it couldn't escape again.

"Miss Trufflepig will be rapt when she sees us bring her back," Liam said.

"I'm not bringing her there," said Anna. "She'll just be sold off and become someone's brekkie."

"What are you gonna do, then?"

"Take her home where she'll be happy."

Liam clapped his hands. "She'll make a bonzer pet!"

"Too right. She's lovely."

"She'll need a name, though." Liam thought of the beautiful sunrise that morning. "I know—Lovely Dawn!"

"I like it," said Anna.

Liam clapped again, excited and proud that Anna allowed him to name the potbellied pig.

"Well what are you waiting for? Gimme your belt so I can leash her!"

He obliged, and together they confiscated Lovely Dawn, leading her back to Sugar Alexandria.

The Voices

Soon Anna's loneliness propagates. She knows the anathema well. It is a vicious monster, and sadness is its best friend, sorrow its lover. Like a cancer eating at her joy, it disseminates with a vengeance, bringing with it her undiagnosed delusions of paracusia.

First Genevieve, the lady in a black Victorian dress, appears, motionless beside a tree. Then a little girl who resembles her deceased twin sister emerges, giggling as she dances in the yard. Finally, the whispers begin, faintly, like the first drops of rain from an overcast sky. Building momentum, they encircle her, becoming clear and concise, and Anna does as Rose had instructed, running back to Cassandra Fancy's garden. But the incantations only grow stronger, more familiar. With her cousin not there to strengthen her, the invisible forces she battles with finally win over. Anna stops running and her eyes become glazed.

"Love, come visit me," the many intones say, blending into one.

Anna identifies it as being her mother's voice. "Rose said I shouldn't listen to you."

"Don't turn me away, Turtle Dove. Come visit me."

"Leave me alone!" she shouts. "Rose told me you're not real!"

"I love you, Anna. You're my baby girl," the auditory hallucination cuts through the air. "You're my little sunshine, and I miss you. Please don't hurt me like this."

On hearing her mother's pleas, Anna's trepidation absconds, and she accepts the invitation, slowly walking to the family burial plot overlooking the station.

Inside the low, brick-encased cemetery, with fancy wrought iron gate, lies her Danish grandparents, her mother, two of her brothers who died in the war, and her twin sister. Someday she will be buried there too. Almost in a trance-like state, as she had done innumerable times before over the years, Anna does what gives her comfort, lying facedown across her mother's grave, her stomach adjacent to the earth, her arms spread out, and her head turned to the side with her cheek against the ground as if to touch her mother's face sleeping beneath her. "Mummy, I'm here," she says, eyes brimming with tears.

Just then, a cold breeze swooshes through the air; loose leaves and dried flowers float around before settling back down.

Anna closes her eyes and cries. "If only you would have lived."

"Why are you crying, Turtle Dove?" Elsa's kind voice travels through her consciousness.

"Rose is gone, and once more I'm alone."

Again the wind dances across the ground, rustling the loose foliage.

"Since she's getting married, I doubt she will ever return. Next summer I will ride the carriage down to the train station and wait for her, knowing she won't be stepping out to greet me. I am beyond sad. Heartbroken. She has gone and done what all sheilas do—marry a bloke and his life becomes hers. How will I ever recover from this grief?"

"Find a bloke of your own, dear," Elsa lovingly encourages. "Find a grouse bloke, fall in love, and build a grand life together."

"Yes, Mummy. That's exactly what I'll do."

"Good girl."

"Love you, Mummy."

"Love you too, Turtle Dove."

Anna goes to her secret shrine, her personal altar that no one knows about, deep in the thicket next to the cornfield. Several precious mementos hang from the branches of a tree—her corn husk dolls, Aboriginal beads from Yarrajan, and a couple of photographs. Items of clothing once worn by her mother and twin sister are buried at the roots. She puts on her goose-feathered crown and decorative wings, kneeling before the reliquary to pray. Afterward, she converses with her mother and sister as if they are there. "I've missed you both so much," she says, tears running from her eyes. "And I have so much to tell you . . ."

~c❦ↄ~

Anna indeed does hear and see things that are not there. They come on soft. A gentle murmur. A quiet breeze. Like the hot breath of a lover on your neck, only to turn incredibly fluid, clear, and assertive. They have caused her no harm, though, never telling her to hurt anyone or herself. On the contrary, they love and guide her as no one else can. But the narrative is waiting to become nefarious. Itching to turn on her.

As we hazard deeper into the depths of her mental illness, the light begins to scatter, the shadows deepen, and the whispers grow strong. All indicative of a mysterious and otherworldly existence. Through the voices of her imagination we are learning about a woman who is an adult child, dancing in and out of her own dreamworld, still longing to be loved by her twin sister who died when they were five years old, and her mother who died giving birth to them, as she has been told.

Venturing deeper still into Anna's thoughts, into her psyche a place of strange cogitations and potentially dangerous intentions—a mind touched with madness is unveiled. Unknown, undiagnosed, underestimated, and unwelcome. A mind where everything outside of sane is allowed . . .

CHAPTER 3

"A face with no freckles is like a flower with no bloom."
– Irish Proverb 🍀

After Christian and Josephine's wedding, when Rose had returned to England, Anna set out to cure her loneliness by finding a bloke of her own, just like her mother had advised. Believing she made a connection with James Ragnar Shahan, the pianist she had met at her brother's wedding, she became obsessed with him, following him around like a little bird following its keeper, sneaking around corners and watching him go about town.

At first James didn't pay much attention to the teenage girl who fancied him, pestering him with her questions and adulation. But eventually he found her to be precious and charming. Five years younger than him and quite imperious at times, she had a way about her–a quirky personality that made him laugh–and she pulled him out of his somewhat shy and introverted shell. Instead of spending most of his time playing his piano or reading his books, she would coerce him to the local theater, or to a diner for lunch or dinner. They had been on several dates, but he kept it mostly platonic.

"Show me your Celtic tattoo, James," Anna said one evening as they perambulated along the shoreline. "I wanna see it." She had lured him over by promising he could have any book he wanted from her father's library– he chose Leo Tolstoy's *War and Peace*–then afterward took him to the beach, bringing a bottle of her father's best Irish whiskey.

"How do you know I have a Celtic tattoo?"

Anna laid a blanket on the sand so they could sit and watch the calm waves rolling in. "Bethany Weaver told me. She said she saw it when you changed your shirt before going into the Bijou Theatre last week."

"Did she, now." James indulged her, pulling off his top, exposing an ornate Celtic knot that covered his entire right chest, curving up onto his shoulder.

"I've never seen anything like that before," Anna said, reaching over and touching it. "Where did you get it done?"

"In Turkey, during the war." After being nearly killed by a bomb, sustaining his permanent injuries, James was propitious to doing something else permanent, symbolically reclaiming his body and soul as his own instead of a living weapon of war against another man. The allegorical imprint was a hieroglyph of redemption for him. An ineffaceable mark to remind him of who he was and where he had come from. Even weeks after the insular Celtic artwork had been done, he would often place his hand over it, feeling a sense of comfort, family, and home.

"Did it hurt?"

"Didn't feel good."

"What's it mean?"

"It's a nod to my Gaelic heritage."

"It's rather gnarly looking." Anna glanced down at the bottle of whiskey he was holding, noticing he hadn't touched it yet. "An Irishman who's not drinking—go figure. Who'd have thought I'd have to twist your leg to drink my daddy's whiskey."

He chuckled. "Me arm, not me leg." Opening the glass bottle, James took a swig. "This is pretty good," he said, examining the golden fluid more closely. "Haven't had a whiskey this smooth in a while." He handed it back to her.

Anna took a sip herself, coughing at its strength. "Here, keep it," she said, shoving the bottle into his hands. "Drink as much as you like."

James grinned. "Are you trying to get me blotto, Anna Polston?"

"I just want you to have a good time, that's all."

He looked down at the liquor again "Won't your dad miss it?"

"No, he's got plenty. He makes his brew in his hidden distillery."

"Aah, good on 'im. My uncle in Ireland does the same. He calls his little operation Ugly Agnes."

"James . . . ," Anna said, pouting her lips. "Don't you like me?"

"Of course I do, love."

"Don't you wanna get married and have a family?"

He laughed. "In the future, yes. Right now, I have big plans for myself."

"Your piano music?"

"Yes."

"Can't you do both?"

James threw her a side glance. How could he explain it wasn't so much he didn't want to get married as it was he didn't want to marry her? "I just don't have the time for a wife right now," he said, giving her a soft smile. "A career like the one I'm pursuing takes years to become successful at, and there's no room for anything else. Not for a while, anyway. Does that make sense, love?"

"What about having someone by your side at night? A warm sheila to share your bed with."

"In due time," he chuckled.

Anna persisted. "I would make the best wife for you. I wouldn't even care if you were away a lot, being a pianist, as long as you came home."

"No, love, I'm just not that bloke. You need a man who loves station life, and that's not me. I'm going to tour the world playing the piano."

But Anna May Polston was not one to take no for an answer, her determination brewing into a festering, iniquitous plot. She could hear the whispers in the back of her mind again—the ones that directed her, guided her, always there when she needed help. "All you have to do is get him drunk," the voice postulated. "Really pissed, and he won't even remember. Get yourself pregnant, and he'll have to marry you."

Going forth with her stratagem, Anna tried to make James relax so he would imbibe until inebriated. "Tell me all about your dreams, James. I want to know everything."

He smiled up at the sparkling diamonds in the sky. "Well, the Royal Academy of Music in London has accepted my application to advance my studies there."

"Ripper," said Anna, maintaining her masquerade of polite interest.

"Too right. I'm going to train with the best, learn new techniques, and sharpen my skill so I can excel in my craft. I hope one day to play professionally, touring the world with a symphony orchestra. Crikey, Anna, I'm so excited. I have so much to look forward to, so much ahead of me. I can't wait."

Totally wrapped up in chatting about his career aspirations, James slowly began to consume the alcohol, without even noticing how much. Anna watched in delight as the tea-colored liquor went from full bottle to half empty.

"Look at you," James said, smiling at his date through glazed eyes, now slurring his words. "With the moon shining on your face like that, makes me wanna kiss every freckle."

"You like my freckles?" Anna beamed.

"Tá aghaidh gan uimh freckles cosúil le bláth gan uimh faoi bhláth."

"What's that mean?"

"A face with no freckles is like a flower with no bloom. That's what my grandfather always said about my grandmother."

Anna knew it was time, and she started to kiss him. He reciprocated. Passionate kissing turned into heated touching. At one point, James pulled away, trying to focus his eyes under the moonlight, but Anna continued to kiss him, touch him, seduce him.

And then it happened . . .

Like a bull to the slaughter, he rolled on top of her, and so easily it was done.

Genevieve

"Well you're no longer an innocent now, are ya."

Anna sits up in bed to find the lady in the black Victorian dress standing there in the dark, her face hidden in the shadows. Genevieve is her name—a hallucination Anna has seen since childhood. Dressed in proper 1800s attire, she seems to care about Anna, looking out for and nurturing her, acting as if her nanny.

"I'm still innocent," Anna defends. She lights the candle on her bedside table, making the room swell with a warmth of honey-colored light.

"Not after what you've done with that bloke," Genevieve tsks.

"We'll be married soon, though. He'll marry me once he finds out I'm carrying his child."

"What makes you so sure you've conceived?"

"I just know. A woman knows these things." Anna snuggles back under her blanket. "Tell me a story, Genevieve."

"Which one, Sweet Pea?"

"The *Black Shuck*."

The woman from the 1800s sits in the rocking chair beside Anna's bed.

"The year was 1577 in Suffolk County of East Anglia," she began, just as Rose always had. "A large, black wolf with bloodred eyes and razor-sharp teeth was terrorizing the village . . ."

Anna listens to the story as the dramatic words from her imaginary friend lull her back to sleep. Slipping into her slumber, she mumbles, "Genevieve, I'm so thankful I have you . . ."

"You'll always have me, Sweet Pea," says the illusory woman. "I'm here to protect you."

Anna was very pleased with herself, how she had cleverly seduced the pianist. Who would have thought that would be so easy, she laughed? She could not stop thinking about that night James took her virginity down by the shoreline, her hair tangled from his hands, her neck sensitive as he feasted on her skin. He had been so gentle with her, almost as if it were one long, passionate kiss. Yet it wasn't just a kiss. They had made love, and it lifted her spirits, offering tremendous hope for the future.

The days turned to weeks, and as Anna waited for her body to give her the wonderful news, she went for a long walkabout to the shoreline one day, even letting Liam tag along.

"You seem different," he said as they moseyed down the beach, noticing her cheery mood and overly pleasant disposition toward him.

She picked up a seashell, ignoring his observation.

"You're keeping secrets, aren't you," he added. "Secrets, secrets."

Still she didn't answer, a perma-smile on her lips.

Liam didn't persist further, just happy she had let him come along. "This is how it used to be—you and me," he said, skipping a rock across the calm ocean surface. "Remember all our adventures?"

Anna rolled her eyes. She didn't have time to reminisce about childish escapades. No, she was a grown woman now, and she'd soon be getting married and having a child of her own. A child with the handsomest and smartest bloke in the entire Shire of Esperance!

Seeing how happy she was, Liam tried his luck: "Sing to the animals, Anna. I wanna feel your throat when you make that noise you do."

She hesitated.

"Pleeeaase?"

Anna reluctantly agreed, and as the haunting, high-pitched sounds resonated from her vocal cords, Liam held his fingers gently across her throat, smiling with excitement. Anna wondered if the baby inside her could hear her kulning too. She sang so loud and strong that several wild horses approached from the bushes up ahead.

When it was over, they both teared up for different reasons . . . Liam, ecstatic she had let him once again feel her mellifluous kulning, experiencing the vibrations deep within his bones; and Anna, blissful in her belief she was pregnant.

Alas, however, she was not.

The very next morning while she bathed, she saw the bathwater turning pink. The unfairness of it! The travesty! As the water removed the blood of her menses, she sobbed. James would be leaving for London soon, and she had lost her chance to cure the heavy plague of forsakenness she wore like a second skin after her mother and sister were taken from her.

Yet not all was lost.

Lying on her bed, sulking, it dawned on her that she could still tell James she was. After all, they had indeed been intimate; she could just fib and speak contrary to the truth.

A lie.

But it would be a sugarcoated lie that would better her life. Help her. Give her what she desired.

⚜

Nervous and excited, Anna was on her way into town. Not to buy lollies, a magazine, or material for a dress like she usually did, but to tell James she was carrying his child.

Well, his imaginary child.

He would never have to know that, though. Once they were married, she would get pregnant for real, and then it wouldn't matter anyway.

What would James say, she wondered? What would he think once she told him she was pregnant? As Anna drove the horse and carriage down the long dirt road, she anxiously bit at her nails. She did not see the beautiful blue sky above, the enormous plush gum trees dominating the landscape, or the kangaroos hopping on by. She only saw James' face and tried to imagine how he would react to the news.

Pulling up in front of the music store, Anna commenced her flagrant ruse . . .

"You're pregnant?" James asked, his complexion paling under the warm Australian sun. Everything around them seemed to go strangely quiet as they spoke in whispers beside the carriage.

Anna nodded.

"Are you sure? I mean really certain?" Never had he been so afraid in his life, pinioned by words coming from this young woman's mouth.

"Of course I'm sure. This isn't something you guess about. I haven't had my period since that night on the beach, and I've been feeling crook most mornings lately."

"Have you been to the doctor, though?"

"Um . . ." Anna quietly panicked. She hadn't thought of him asking that. "Where do you think I just came from?" She lied.

His shoulders visibly sank; his mouth went dry. "Crikey, I don't believe this!"

"I'm a good Christian girl, James. I can't have a baby on my own."

Holding a roll of several sheets of his music, he tapped it against his thigh. "To be honest, I barely even remember that night. I was so sloshed."

Anna put a hand on her hip. "I certainly remember. And don't you dare ask me if I'm sure it's yours. You know you're the only bloke I've been with."

James appeared as if a deer caught in the bright lights of a car. Frozen. The sardonic thing was, he still had another girl on his mind—an English violinist named Charlotte he had met at his sister's wedding. Just earlier in the week, when he couldn't get her out of his mind, he had decided he was going to try to find out who and where she was. He thought of her in that moment, too, with Anna leering at him, recalling her green eyes and angelic face. There would be no prospect of searching for her now.

"I'll be ruined, you know," Anna lamented. "No other decent bloke will have me now. And my father will kill me when he finds out . . . He'll kill you too."

His eyes flashed up at her. "Bloody hell. I'm sure he and your brother will hunt me down, skinning me alive for this."

Anna slowly nodded.

James raked his hands through his hair. "I'm supposed to be leaving for London next week to find a place to live," he said, distraught.

Anna folded her arms across her chest. "You're going to abandon me and our child?"

He looked astounded. Physically ill.

Anna studied his face. Before her eyes, he appeared to be shrinking. Slowly vanishing. Guilt enveloped her for lying, but with her mother, sister, and now Rose, gone, the hollowness inside her was so vast and starved for love she just couldn't tell the truth. James was the remedy to fill the void.

"Buggers, I don't know what to say or do!" he exclaimed. "I've worked so hard for this, too. I've always wanted a career in music and teaching."

"I'm not asking you to give that up."

"It would have to be put on hold, though."

"So you'll do the right thing, then?"

"Buggers, I don't know what to do!" he repeated, giving her a serious look. "Crikey, what should we do, Anna?"

"What should we do? . . . What do you think we should do!" she almost shouted "Get married as soon as possible!"

James stared off into the distance, far away, until his eyes watered. Or were they tears? Anna couldn't tell. Looking down at the roll of papers in his hand, still tapping against his thigh, she asked, "What is that, anyway? Those papers."

"Music I have written."

"You write music, too? I didn't know that."

He locked eyes with her. "There's a lot about me you don't know."

Anna gave him a wide smile. "I guess I will know soon enough. You're gonna be my bloke, aye?"

James crumpled up the handwritten sheets of music, throwing them inside the carriage. He reached over and grabbed her hand. "Yes."

"We're gonna get married?"

Stunned, he had no idea what he was getting into with a girl he hardly knew. Nevertheless, he surrendered, accepting the honorable thing that came next. "Yes, Anna, it's the right thing to do."

The Voices

Anna's late mother calls out in her mind again, demurring over her daughter's egregious trickery . . .

"Oh, Anna, I told you to find a bloke of your own, but not through a crook lie.

"You're stealing his life from him.

"His talent.

"His dreams.

"You're playing with his heart, manipulating his world.

"You're denying him, deceiving him . . . and yourself."

But Anna doesn't listen.

～≈✦≈～

"What are you still doing here, mate?" Peachy Jones asked, drinking a longneck at the pub with Dewey Silkwood. "Shouldn't you be in London by now?"

James sat next to the two men and ordered a whiskey from the bartender. "Plans have changed. I'm getting married this month. You and the rest of me mates are invited."

Peachy gave him a congratulatory handshake. "To that pommy sheila you kept talking about, I reckon?"

"That pretty brunette with the broken leg, aye?" added Dewey, leaning back on his stool, flashing his crooked smile at James. "You lucky bastard!"

"No, I never saw her again after my sister's wedding."

"That's a pity," said Dewey, taking a swig of his beer. "You two seemed smitten."

"We were." James downed his shot and asked for another, inwardly frowning, wishing he had tried harder to find her.

"Who's the skirt, then?" asked Peachy.

"Yeah, who got James Shahan to give up his precious London dreams?" Dewey asked.

"Anna Polston," James said with little enthusiasm.

Peachy laughed. "Her? Freckle face Polston? I would have thought you'd nab a tall poppy, with how debonair you are." He looked at Dewey with surprise, then back at James. "Instead the pianist is marrying the daughter of a station owner—go figure."

"I'd marry her," said Dewey. "I've been looking for a sheila ever since we got back from the war."

"Good luck with that, mate, 'cause you've got a face not even a mother could love," Peachy joked.

Dewey laughed. "I think Anna's a beauty of a lass. A little strange at times, maybe, but she'll make a grouse cook."

"I've worked at Sugar Alexandria before," Peachy said. "It's a grand property but bigger than most, which means nonstop work."

"I know," said James.

"You'll be slogging those fields for the rest of your days, mate. And I'll tell you another thing . . ." With his beer he pointed at James' fingers. "You can kiss those baby soft hands of yours goodbye. That's no lie."

James tossed back his drink. "It'll only be for a short while. I plan on pursuing my music again later."

Peachy shook his head, imagining all three of them sitting there years from now, covered in red dust and drinking side by side. "With as good as you are on that piano, though, it's kind of a shame, don't you think? Can't you two wait until you get back from London?"

James only stared down at the bar, and from the look on his face, Peachy understood. His cobber didn't want to get married . . . He had to.

"Well, it happens to the best of us, mate. Every single one of us eventually walks that plank," Peachy said, clicking beer bottles with Dewey.

James ordered a third shot. "Walk the plank . . . Fair dinkum, mate. That's a beauty of a way of puttin' it, too," he said, tossing back his whiskey."

Anna felt as if the entire world were cheering for her, and the heavenly angels were smiling down. For some odd reason, however, she thought of Rose's folklore tale, the *Black Shuck*, and how the man trusted the she-wolf, only to suffer her betrayal. *I might have lied, but I will never betray him,* she promised herself. *I will never hurt James Shahan.*

As she promenaded the pathway to the ocean that evening, she became lost in her happy thoughts over her future with him. Oh, how lucky she was! She was going to be the most perfect wife, too! She'd cook stacks of yummy pancakes for breakfast, make him hearty sandwiches that would choke a horse, and bake all kinds of fancy Irish dishes like his mother did. And after a long workday, she'd rub his aching feet while he relaxed and drank his longneck by the warm fire. They'd be the happiest couple in all of Esperance!

"But you got him through a lie, Anna! A bold-faced lie!" a voice shouted from nowhere.

"Who's there!" Anna asked, panicking, thinking someone had found her out.

"How could you scheme such a thing? You're a pretty enough girl, too, with your flaxen hair and deep blue eyes. You could have easily gotten a bloke without the falsehood."

"Who's there!" she demanded again, squinting into the tall grass. "Is that you, Genevieve?" Anna looked around for the woman wearing the black Victorian dress who often appeared from thin air and followed her everywhere. "He's mine! All mine! I own him now, and you nor anyone else can stop me!" she shouted, throwing her fist up at the sky.

But there was no answer. The voice simply vanished, carried off with the wind, back into the fields from where it came.

"Wanna go to the garden?" Liam asked the next day as Anna held a little lamb with white curly fur in the paddock.

"No, I really shouldn't anymore. I'm getting too old to play there now."

"Aww, c'mon, Anna. Pleeeaase?" He pulled on her arm. "Let's go to our secret place."

Anna kissed the furry baby sheep. "I'm getting married soon, and I have to start acting like a mature adult." She put the tiny lamb down on the grass and ran with Liam to the enchanted garden anyway.

Genevieve

"If you come to the wedding, you can't wear that dress," Anna says, sitting in front of her vanity, looking at the woman only she can see. "No one wears black to a wedding."

Genevieve doesn't answer. She only picks up a brush and begins brushing Anna's golden hair.

"Can you imagine the looks you would get?" Anna laughs. "Victorian dresses are out of style, too."

"Tell me about your plans, love," says the woman from the 1800s. "Tell me everything."

In a rush of words, Anna excitedly chatters all about her hopes and dreams, how she's marrying a handsome Irishman and they'll be raising a family together, and how she'll never be lonely again. "Genevieve, he's tall and handsome with blue gray eyes, a soft-spoken demeanor, and he's super smart. Oh, I just love him so."

Genevieve continues brushing Anna's long, flaxen-colored tresses. "But does he love *you*, Sweet Pea?"

Anna, staring at her reflection in the mirror, her braids undone and framing her round, cherub face, her countless freckles dotting her skin, her scarlet lipstick glistening in the natural light, responds confidently, "He will learn to."

~·⊂♦⊃·~

James Ragnar Shahan married Anna May Polston at Sugar Alexandria, the glorious cattle station owned by Anna's father outside the Shire of Esperance. James waited until a week before the wedding to notify the Royal Academy of Music in London—the hardest telegram he ever sent—canceling his invitation to the esteemed conservatoire. He did it, though, and promised himself that when he was situated, he would arrange to pursue it again.

He had a conversation with his parents, too, the night before he got married. His mother Beulah, who spoke no English, disliked Anna, telling him there was something not right with her. His father Riordan, however, saw things differently. Smoking his corncob pipe, he said to James in Gaelic, *"Anna will be good for you. You need some responsibility to save you from these silly dreams of playing and teaching music."*

"Music is a part of who I am, father. It will always be there, one way or another," James replied in the Goidelic language. In his heart he was forever a pianist, always waiting to play the next song. *"It's what makes me happy."*

Riordan exhaled a billow of smoke, frowning at his son. *"I see you still have a hard time letting go of the boy inside you. Real men don't play the bloody piano, lad. They get a decent job and get on with life. It's time for you to grow up and be a real man."*

James filled with indignation. It had always hurt him how his father said he wasn't a real man for wanting to pursue a career in music. *"So I'm just supposed to sacrifice my happiness now? Is that it? Give up on what I love?"*

Riordan pointed his pipe at him. *"After tomorrow, you're going to be married with a bairn on the way. Your happiness is of no mind. Taking care of your family is what's important now, not chasing some cockeyed dream."*

On their wedding day, James watched Anna Polston saunter down the aisle in a borrowed dress too tight and too long, proceeding through the motions of exchanging vows with a girl he did not love but felt responsible for. Following the nuptials, he was numb. He stood off to the side, watching the festive celebration, loosening his bow tie, holding a longneck and staring into nihility. In his mind he heard two things: Anna's voice telling everyone she had landed James Shahan, and the priest saying, "Till death do you part . . ."

CHAPTER 4

I t was the Roaring Twenties–a decade on fire.

A period in which a sense of cosmic order prevailed. When the earth was full of sugar and spice, and all the flavors between. Exuberant. Prosperous. Unrestrained. Pushing and yearning, stretching into the dawn of a new era.

The War to End All Wars had just come to an end, and the people, the cities, the towns, and even the sky full of twinkling stars above lit up in an extravagant surge of blazing promise. A time of passion, change, and innovation, bursting with delicious possibilities. Women earned the right to vote; mass media was born; Art Deco style flourished; the newly formed League of Nations vowed peace and security worldwide. The stock market skyrocketed; bankers and traders became wealthy. Prohibition began; bootlegging gave rise to organized crime. Americans called it the Jazz Age, Germans the

Golden Twenties, and the French, *Années Folles* (Crazy Years).

And it *was* crazy.

Uninhibited. Wild. Free. Socially exploding, culturally dynamic, and artistically genius. Women cut their waist-length hair into short, severe bobs, styling it sleek and straight as a razor, or in intricate Marcel waves. They traded their corsets and floor-length skirts for spangled satin dresses, doing the shimmy on top of tables while kicking up their bare, thin legs. They wore fake eyelashes, beaded headbands, waved colorful feathered fans, smoked cigarettes in jeweled opera length holders, and made sure their lipstick was bright bloodred to match their dancing shoes. Farmers' daughters became babes, dames, broads, Shebas, bearcats, flappers, and choice bit of calico. Quiet evenings spent at home changed to swing dancing all night, doing the Foxtrot, the Charleston, the Black Bottom, the Lindy Hop, and various others at the local nightclubs and juke joints. They were liberated, and they loved it, giggling and flirting, drinking champagne until zozzled, celebrating whenever they could, living each day as if it were their last.

Oh, and let's not forget the men. Economic prosperity boomed; mass consumerism thrived. They traded their boots and overalls for silk shirts and tailored suits—pinstripe, plaid, or linen. They wore raccoon fur coats, two-tone shoes, and fedoras tilted across their brows. They flocked to the cities, bought homes, replaced horses and buggies with Henry Ford's Model T, or if they had the cabbage, a Rolls-Royce Phantom I Jonckheere Coupe, a Bugatti Type 35 Grand Prix, or a Duesenberg Model J. "Swing dance with me, babe," they would say to their dates. "Let's drink some giggle water and neck in the back of my new Model T, and maybe, just maybe, I will buy you some ice to put on your little finger."

James Ragnar Shahan was one of those men who wanted to partake of what life had to offer a young bloke in this new golden era. He had dreams. Big ones. His goal was to become a professional pianist and music professor—something he had aspired to since childhood—but instead of residing in London and pursing his career, he was now tied to his new wife, Anna May Shahan, and the burgeoning cattle station she inherited in the Australian Outback when her father passed away, succumbing to a long battle with tuberculosis.

Living at Sugar Alexandria was as if he had opened a door by accident, only to be locked inside. Trapped, like an insect caught in a spider's web. And in truth, he was. Fooled into marriage; yoked together through moral chicanery; the product of Anna's lie and his own virtuous belief that he was doing what was right. Collectively, those irrevocable verities shackled him to the land, and a life Anna worshipped yet he despised.

During this stretch of time, late at night as he lay next to his wife, his body aching from the rigorous day's work, red earth staining his callused hands, his mind would sometimes wander to a different place. A place laden with dark, lyrical notes on alabaster paper, freshly ironed dinner jackets, and a stage with a black grand piano where he'd play for the masses. He would think of other things, too, like the sheila he had met at his sister's wedding— the beautiful stranger from England with bright green eyes who used a cane. He wondered what became of her, and hoped the life she had chosen for herself made her happy, as the life he had been forced into had not.

PART TWO

Sugar Alexandria Cattle Station
Shire of Esperance, Australia

CHAPTER 5

Ten Years Later . . . November 15, 1929

Ten years had come and gone since their wedding, and James had transformed from a cultured would-be pianist into a rugged, red-skinned, blond-bearded cattle station owner, all thanks to his wife's caper. Shearing sheep, branding cows, feeding livestock, fixing machinery, and tending the unruly land were now his daily life. He was different from the other station owners in the territory, though. Kinder to the animals and fairer to the stockmen and ringers who worked for him, including the Aboriginals. Unwilling to exploit them, he treated the natives the same as the other men, even learning to speak their language of Nukunu so they could communicate with each other more effectively. Likewise, he would teach them and their families English, setting up a makeshift classroom in the back of the barn.

After a long workday, James would often sneak out to his Ford Model TT Huckster pickup and head down the road to visit a pub called the Blue Lizard Cave. There he would socialize with other locals in the area—miners, fishermen, lumberjacks, and graziers—all congregating to enjoy the fruits of their labor. Despite the worsening economic climate, the regulars at the Blue Lizard Cave always seemed to find enough coin for their grog.

Inside the pub was an intricate oak bar with twisted posts that ran the length of the room, facing a wall-to-wall mirror. Several paintings of the nineteenth-century bourgeoisie hung on display throughout—the previous owner was a Frenchman—accompanied by an oil painting the new owner had commissioned of his wife. In the corner rested a Steinway piano that a barmaid used to play to entertain the guests; these days, it usually sat quiet, unless James was there—after a couple of shots of whiskey they couldn't drag him from it. The centerpiece of the room was a striking ballerina fountain, surrounded by a dozen wooden tables and chairs. But most of the men, sweaty and dusted with red earth, sat in succession at the bar, drinking grog and discussing their day's work, their families, and their concerns over the Great Depression now sweeping the land like a deadly virus.

The pub was owned by James' good friend, Casper Cotton Fancy—an older unconventional man and a free-spirited maverick. Casper traveled the world to seek his fortune when he was young, and when he returned to Australia, he bought a small mine near Kalgoorlie that struck gold. With his earnings he bought the Blue Lizard Cave for fun, and renovated an old castle near a cliff overlooking the sea into a home for his new bride Cassandra. For the next thirty-plus years he spent his days loving his wife, who for some unknown reason after giving birth to four healthy babies, developed agoraphobia, never leaving the large estate. Ever. But that didn't stop Casper. Genuinely one of the most easygoing chaps around, a natural expression on his face of continual amusement, he ventured out daily, visiting friends, smoking his favorite cigars, and telling stories in his pub about all his travels around the world.

The double doors of the Blue Lizard Cave flapped open, and in walked Anna Shahan, a flash of outside light illuminating her entry. Curious eyes looked up from their mugs and the voices hushed for a brief moment, agitated to see a sheila—women weren't allowed in the pub.

Anna scanned the room for her husband. Wearing her lavender velvet cloche hat tight over her ears and her new dress that had just arrived in the mail, she elatedly waved something in her hand when she spotted him.

"Jimmy, your cook is here," Casper Cotton Fancy said from behind the bar, puffing on a stogie as he handed James another mug of beer topped with frothy foam like shaving cream, "and she looks like she has fire in her eyes."

James looked over to see his wife approaching, ignoring the sneers and grumbles from the male patrons as she beelined toward her husband.

Tilly Barlowe, a tiny Irishman and the town drunk, shook his head. "The poor bloke's c'mere to wet his whistle and forget his problems, and his cook's c'mere to remind him of 'em," he slurred, trying to focus his double vision on James.

"Aah, ya bloody larrikin, you're just sour 'cause you miss havin' a cook yourself," teased Casper Cotton.

Tilly's wrinkled face scrunched up into a funny, toothless grin. "Smelly, hairy beast, she was."

"Didn't she run off with your brother?" goaded another man at the bar.

Tilly feigned heartbreak. "Bloody oath, she did. And I sure do miss . . . me brother!" he exclaimed, bursting into laughter and slapping the bar.

"G'day, Casper Cotton," Anna greeted when she reached them, giving James a quick kiss on the cheek.

"Anna, you know you can't be in here, love," said Casper.

"That's right," James said, surprised to see her there. "You should be with the twins." After Anna's blatant lie about being pregnant, a decade later they indeed had a child. Two, in fact. One-month-old twin girls–Scarlet Rose and Mabel Blessing.

"They're with Yarra, Sugar Bear."

He could see the glee in her face. "Well what's so bloody important that you had to drive all the way over here, aye?"

Anna handed him a telegram with an excited giggle. "My cousin Rose sent me this!"

The pale, small missive, originating from the metropolis of London, England, had been transmitted across a riotous ocean and the red, unending Outback, hand-delivered to its final destination at Sugar Alexandria. James took the paper and read it . . .

```
THE WESTERN UNION TELEGRAPH COMPANY
December 20, 1929

From:                        To:
Rose Charlotte Moss          Anna May Shahan
7089 Willowbrook Ave.        501 Abbey Rd.
London, England              Esperance, Australia
NW1 4NP                      11529

Dear Anna,

I write to you from a convent in London. My hus-
band Paul has committed suicide after the terri-
ble stock market crash. I was hoping to find
solace with the nuns, but I still feel so empty
here.

Please let me travel to you.

Love,
Rose
```

"Crikey, that's terrible," James said. "Her bloke killed himself."

"And she's wanting to come live at Sugar Alexandria." Anna beamed underneath her hat. "You know how much I love her, James. How much I miss her. She needs our help now."

"No sheilas in the pub!" someone shouted.

"Yeah, that's right! Git 'er outta here!" a second voice demanded, followed by the men murmuring among themselves.

"Ohhh, go eat your grubby shoe, you dirty horse!" Anna fired back, feisty and ornery as always, shaking her balled fist at him. "All you blokes care about is whiskey and whores!"

James pulled his bantam wife into his arms and covered her mouth.

She pushed his hand away. "I'm not afraid of a bunch of filthy drunks."

"You know the rules, love," Casper Cotton said.

"Since you're here, we might as well eat tucker at The Flame Tree Grill," said James. Christian and Josephine owned the small diner in town, named after Australia's beautiful Illawarra Flame Tree, with its bright coral-red blossoms that grow in clusters at the end of its branches. "Let me finish my drink, and I'll meet you there, aye?"

Anna scowled at the men.

James gave her a pat on the bum. "Go on before you get into a fistfight," he teased.

Anna headed for the door, and just before she stepped through the exit, she stuck her tongue out at the group of men sneering at her.

Casper Cotton and James laughed.

"How's Anna and the little ones doin', mate?" Casper asked, cleaning shot glasses.

"Babies are grand.," said James. "Anna, on the other hand, has her good days and bad."

"I had a fear her spells would get worse after the babies arrived." Casper Cotton was the one who had found Anna running down the dirt road a year earlier, naked and crying. He had put a blanket around her and taken her back to James.

"Me too."

"She seems all right now, though."

"That's just it. She's fine for a while, then suddenly it hits, and she gets bloody hysterical. Then she goes right back to being Anna again as if nothing happened."

"How often does it occur?"

"Hard to say. Could be days, weeks, or even months before she has another relapse."

"The doc ever give a name for it?"

James shook his head. "And now her pommy cousin wants to come stay with us." He was less than thrilled with the idea.

"I remember her as a teenager," said Casper. "She used to come visit Anna in the summers, and the two of them would play in my wife's garden. A sweet lass she was; it's sad to hear she's a widow now." He served drinks to a couple of other men before returning to James. "You gonna be all right with another sheila under your roof?"

"Not sure I have a choice in the matter. You know Anna when she sets her mind on something."

"Don't worry, mate. From what I remember, she wasn't just sweet but pretty too. Dark hair, green eyes 'n all. She'll find a bloke soon enough and be married off."

James thought of the English violinist he had danced with at his sister's wedding years ago. It had been a while since he thought of that night. She too had dark hair and the greenest eyes he had ever seen, and he wondered whatever became of her.

"I can help ya, mate," slurred Tilly Barlowe, leaning too far to the left.

James pushed him upright so he wouldn't fall over. "How's that?"

"When the sheila gets here, just introduce her to me and I'll sweep 'er off her feet."

"How you gonna do that, mate?" asked another man, egging him on.

"I'd show 'er what a true bloke is, not like all these boys nowadays." He squinted his squinty eyes at James. "And the stories I could tell her 'bout me youth—I was like thunder. She'd hear 'em and fall in love, and that's no lie."

All the men at the bar roared with laughter.

Anna held the telegram close to her chest as she sat in the booth at The Flame Tree Grill, waiting for her husband. Unlike the pub, it was scarcely busy, and Christian and Josephine were not there, leaving the diner in the hands of an employee. Overwhelmed by the news, Anna's mind wandered to the time when she was a young teenager, listening to her daddy explain to Yarrajan why Rose was coming to the station that first summer . . .

"Anna needs female companionship to help her grow out of this tomboy stage," her father had said.

"She be a free spirit, Mr. Polston. That's all it be," Yarrajan replied. She liked Anna the way she was.

"The girl won't wear shoes, dresses in her brothers' overalls, and rarely brushes her hair. Crikey, half the time she's covered in mud. No, she needs a female cobber now. Someone who can influence her to become a lady. That's why I've sent for her cousin Ambrosia from London. She'll come and stay the summer, and it'll do Anna a world of good."

Mr. Polston was so right. Rose coming to Sugar Alexandria did change Anna's life, and from that first summer to the last, Anna always cherished those memories she had with her beloved cousin. Every night since then, she included Rose in her prayers, hoping that someday life would reunite them.

And now her prayers had been answered . . . Rose was coming back!

In that moment, a brilliant idea materialized in Anna's head. Something magnificent. Something so grand her beloved cousin would never leave her again!

James came into the restaurant, and they both ordered their dinner.

"You've got that twinkle in your eye, love," he said. "Like you're up to something. Should I be scared?"

"Always," Anna giggled, grinning at him as she sipped on her soda through a straw.

⁓⧉⧉⧉⁓

"So you'll build it, aye?" Anna asked when they were home, a wide smile flaunting the gap between her front teeth. "Or do I have to twist your leg?"

"It's arm, Anna. Twist your arm," said James. "I've told you that countless times, now."

"Bah, same thing."

Anna and her husband stood in front of the center windmill—the largest of the three Goliaths that resided at Sugar Alexandria. She had come up with the marvelous idea to convert the regal edifice—a sacred entity that represented her grandparents, her mother, her childhood, and her beloved cousin, all within the walls of the complex wooden formation—into a maisonette for Rose. Inside the massive structure was a great deal of room, and if James agreed, he and the men could do all the carpentry work in time for her arrival. What a wonderful gift that would be!

James touched his beard, thinking. Though he was fine with Rose coming to Sugar Alexandria, he was against his wife's idea to renovate the center windmill into a home for her. The last thing he needed was more work, not to mention destroying a good, functioning windmill. Nevertheless, fearful of Anna spiraling into another emotional episode, he reluctantly considered it. "I've never done such a thing," he said as they stood there, staring up at the spinning sail.

"Yeah, but this way she'll have her own place. Something to call her own. Oh, Sugar Bear, please?"

"Couldn't she just stay in the spare room down the hall?"

"No, that's too small."

"Not if you add the space in the secret room."

"You can't be serious. You'd have her walk in and out through a door at the back of the closet and stay in a room with one small window? Like in a dungeon? Absolutely not; that was just a playroom when I was a child."

James was still unconvinced. "Even if I agreed, I'm not sure it would be

61

ready in time, love."

"You patched up the second floor of the house pretty quick after the fire, and it looks grand."

"I only fixed the outside. The inside is still a bloody mess."

Anna looked deep into his eyes. "I won't ask for anything ever again; I swear. This would be so wonderful for her, like her own private castle."

"A castle in the bush, aye? In the Outback of Straya. I don't think she'll be expecting something that extravagant, Tin Tin." James had nicknamed her Tin Tin from *The Wizard of Oz* story—another one of Anna's favorite books—teasing her that she was like the Tin Man character with no heart because she could be so insensitive, ornery, and stubborn at times.

"Think of it this way: If she has her own place, we'll keep our privacy," Anna reasoned. "Pleeeaase?"

"I just don't know, love," he said again, unsure if he was skilled enough to do the job. "Let me think on it."

❦

The following evening, Anna prepared a delightful meal for her husband, being overly attentive and pampering toward her bloke. She wanted to butter him up so he'd be more willing to move forward with her plan to renovate the center windmill into a home for her cousin.

"Thanks a million for tucker, love," James said after dinner. He kissed Scarlet Rose and Mabel Blessing, sleeping in their bassinets, then put on his Akubra hat and headed for the door.

"Where are you going?" Anna asked.

"The Blue Lizard Cave."

"What? You're always going over there."

"C'mon, don't get onto me about that again, aye?"

"But I thought we could start planning how we're going to renovate the mill."

"I told you I needed to think on that. It's a waste of a windmill, for one, and not an easy thing to do."

Anna became angry. "You're a waste of a bloke if you don't build that for my poor widowed cousin!" she shouted, balling her fists and glowering at him. "That's what you are!"

James sighed. "Stop talking rubbish, Anna."

She began whispering to herself, wringing her hands as she paced around the kitchen, engaged in a trance-like conversation with someone not there. The susurration became more agitated, growing into a vociferous argument.

A sinking feeling settled in the pit of James' stomach. This was not the first occasion he had witnessed such peculiar behavior in his wife, yet he never grew used to it. He simply made himself pretend that Anna was normal and would have emotional outbursts like everyone from time to time. That is until she would have one of her more severe episodes.

With her back turned to him, the ire toward her husband continuing to build, Anna grew more animated in her conversation with no one. Even her pet cockatoo, Moby, appeared nervous and aware of the change in her deportment, bristling his wings and his crest as he watched from his cage. James stood there listening carefully, trying to discern the manic whispers flowing from her lips. Was she going to mollify this time, or fly into a rage? The wind pushed against the house, its sad, lonely whistle mixing with her haunting undertones creating an eerie atmosphere.

Anna turned to face him . . .

Her visage, distorted from madness, and her breathing, labored from anger, incited him to action, running to get the medication Dr. Crawford had prescribed to keep her calm. Just as he opened the cabinet drawer, a dish flew past his head, barely missing him. "Bloody hell!" he exclaimed, ducking as the second one followed close behind. "Anna, the babies! For God's sake, you could have hit one of them! Don't you dare throw another!" No sooner had he said it than a third plate zoomed past, this time clipping the side of his head, almost knocking him to his knees. He winced in pain as he barreled forward, grabbing hold of her while she fought him, pounding his chest with her fists. Her screaming became so loud and fierce that he tried to cover her mouth, but she only bit his hand. Wrestling his out-of-control wife to the ground, he pinned her there. "Anna, calm down!"

"Jeg kommer aldrig min vej!" she screamed in Danish, her lungs hyperventilating. (*"I never get my way!"*) Extremely upset, Moby screeched and thrashed about in his cage.

"Listen to me, Anna! You need to calm yourself, right now!"

"If you love her, James, you'll do it!" Anna yelled, acting as if speaking in her mother's voice, her face warped into a heavy frown.

"Stop that!" he demanded, holding her in his arms, aware that under extreme stress, excitement, or anger, his wife would sometimes take on other personalities. "You're Anna, and you know I love you!"

"My daughter wants Rose to have her own place!" she screamed into his shoulder.

James held her tighter. She hadn't had a spell this eldritch in a while, speaking as if she were Elsa Polston. He had no idea what caused the delusions; he only knew how to calm her, console her, until it passed.

"The shadow people will help me build it if you don't!" she screamed out. "They do anything I ask!"

He had heard her speak of the shadow people in the past, how they followed her and sometimes she would follow them, only for the mysterious figures to vanish, just like Genevieve. "Who are the shadow people, love?"

Anna began to laugh through her tears, staring up at the light from the kerosene lamp, unblinking and disoriented. "They know me better than I know myself," she said. "And there are many."

A shiver ran down James' spine. He said a quick prayer, hoping she would snap out of her paroxysm of delirium, and moments later she pacified, her breaths calming, her pulse rate regulating. James tenderly kissed her sweat-laden forehead. "I'll build it, love," he said, sitting her up on the floor, rocking her to keep her placated, as he always did. "I've never built something like that before, but I'll do it. Crikey, consider it done."

Both physically and emotionally exhausted, they sat there for a long while as the shadows crept along the floor and stretched up the walls, a deafening silence settling in.

Anna

Doesn't he know by now, I always get my way?

That night as he lies next to his wife in bed, a strange sensation creeps up on James while a thousand words accumulate in his mind, wanting to be released into sentences that convey how her illness worries him. Terrifies him, even. There are times when he doesn't know if he'll be able to conciliate the next ebullition, and that exacerbates the fear. What if her condition worsens? What if someday he has to commit her? How can someone with such a vexatious mental ailment raise children, as they are now doing? Dr. Crawford has said it's a harmless condition, prescribing medication that will calm her, but James isn't so sure. Under the right circumstances, one day she may snap and become dangerous to herself or others.

Perhaps even lethal.

Anna's affliction—unforeseen and undiagnosed, yet clearly there—manifests when she is stressed, eats too much sugar, doesn't get her way, or becomes overly emotional about something: Whispering to herself, throwing truculent fits, and most discomfiting of all, hallucinating. Generally her boutades and odd proclivities are benign and disappear as fast as they occur, but there are moments when she frightens him. As if demon-possessed, her words and behaviors in that state are obstreperous and petrifying, sending chills down the spine of a grown man who has even experienced the horrors of war.

Her sickness has no logical reason or explanation for it, either. Like the time he found her kneeling at an extraordinary and bizarre—if not freakish—shrine in the bush, crying and talking to a tree that hung colorful beads and numerous corn husk dolls from its branches. At first he could only stare, seeing his wife wearing a crown of white goose feathers on her head and matching wings on her back. Never before had he seen such a thing. "What on earth are you doing?" he had asked, grabbing her up from the ground and almost shaking her. She swore the tree held the souls of her mother and sister, and there she could visit them whenever she wanted. James, of course, tore the altar down, but no matter how many times he did, Anna only built it back up.

James wants to express his concerns, discuss things further with his wife, but she has already fallen asleep. Only the candlelight remains, giving off a warm glow in the room. He stares at their two shadows cast against the wall—the curve of her body on the left, his head and shoulders on the right—then looks at the space between them. It seems larger than normal, as if the distance is growing by the second. Rolling onto his side, he stares at the candle. It is low, and he watches it burn until the wick is no more.

Then the light extinguishes.

Anna

There are three of me. Three persons in one. A farmer's wife, a wild woman, and something else that has no name . . .

As the devoted wife and mother, I scrub the wood floors, polish the furniture until it shines, wash the clothes down at the river, knit quilts of different patterns and colors, and bake fresh bread and bickies. Things that any wife and mother would do.

As the wild sheila, my free-spirited nature rules, and I become a nymph inhabiting the woods, a queen of the elves and fairies, a maiden in my secret garden. Often I wear no shoes and dance naked under the stars.

And there is another part of me, as well. A darker side. The part of me I hide. The part of me that, if I were to tell you all about, you might be afraid.

<hr>

With work done the following afternoon, James rode his favorite black stallion named Ireland to the top of the hill overlooking Sugar Alexandria. Gazing down at the station, his eyes zeroed in on the livestock, the Danish-style farmhouse, the large barn, the three colossal windmills, and everything that surrounded the property. From where he stood, the parcel of land resembled a miniature model—a tiny gingerbread house with adjacent structures and animals that all appeared like mere toys. Such a contrast to the reality of what was actually involved in running the station. Once inside the gates, everything was as large as life. And as heavy.

In many ways, the oil from his soul lubricated the wheels of life at the station, as if an unholy theft from his body poured into the land. Day in and day out, a continuous taking, giving nothing back but aches and pains and ridicule the minute he dreamed of something more. And now to add to the weight of his responsibilities, James was also a father to twin girls. He thought of that night his daughters were born, when he laid on the bed next to Anna, their babies sleeping between them. It reminded him of when his mother had given birth to his sister when he was a little boy, and how his father had laid beside his wife too, with their newborn between them. For a moment James felt as if he had traded places with his dad, and that his father's life was now his. It made him shudder. Regardless, whatever reservations he had about his marriage to Anna before, after the birth of his daughters, those dubieties were annulled.

Anna's voice belted out from the front porch–a high-pitched sound that faintly reached his ears–bringing him back to the present. It was time for dinner, and a welcomed sign that he had made it through another day. He rode Ireland back to the barn and went inside to eat.

Back to her normal self, wearing her favorite homemade apron, Anna busily worked in the kitchen. Her lime green jadeite dishes were already set on the table, and as she completed the finishing touches to the dinner she had prepared, she spoke to her pet parrot on her shoulder.

James sat patiently waiting for her, bottle-feeding little Scarlet in his arms. He stared at his wife with candid eyes, bewildered over her transitional moods and what seemed like honest-to-God possessed behavior, influenced or controlled by something unknown. "We need to talk about last night," he said to her.

Anna took Scarlet from James and placed her in the bassinet next to Mabel. "Is this how we're gonna start dinner–you chastising me?"

"I'm not chastising you. I'm just . . . concerned, is all. Concerned for you and our girls."

"I'm all right, James. No different than the sheila you married."

He disagreed. "It seems to me these fits are getting worse. They trigger more easily, too, and when you have them, it's like you're losing your mind."

Anna flashed her dark blue eyes–the color of the bottom of the sea–on her worried husband. "I'm not insane, James. I just get too riled up sometimes, that's all."

"Insane!" Moby squawked, ruffling his feathers. "Bloody bogan!" The two-year-old pet cockatoo, hot-tempered and feisty like his owner, adored Anna but had a disliking for James, often jumping on the kitchen table, puffing up his chest and calling him names.

Anna kissed her bright pink galah's beak and put him back in his cage.

"These are more than mere tantrums, love."

"It was just another spell," Anna insisted.

"Well these spells you have . . . something's not right."

"Sugar Bear, I'm sorry about last night; I really am. But there's nothing to worry about. Genevieve says all women get stressed from time to time."

Aware of his wife's imaginary friends, James went silent.

"She was rather talkative today. I asked her to stay for dinner but . . ."

"Stop it, Anna. Stop that rubbish right now," he said, setting stern eyes on hers.

Anna's demeanor changed.

"She's not real, and you know it. You're a mother now, and those silly delusions need to stop."

In her moments of clarity, Anna knew the woman in the black Victorian dress and the voices she would hear were not real. "I imagined her again, didn't I," she said, on the verge of tears. "But she always seems so real to me when she appears."

James got up and walked over to his wife, kissing her on the forehead and wrapping his strong arms around her, letting her know that everything would be all right.

"I remember the first time I saw her," Anna said, feeling safe and secure in her husband's firm embrace. "I was just a little girl, and Yarra had taken me outside to play in the yard. Genevieve appeared from behind a tree, and we played hide-and-seek. I thought she was my second nanny. Ever since then, she has always kept a watchful eye on me."

"What did Yarrajan say when you told her about this woman?"

"She had the elders from her village come and pray for me."

"Did it help?"

"No, I still saw her. Yarra said if I talk about her again, though, she'd take a switch to me, so I never spoke a word of it."

"Were you ever hit on the head, love? Maybe it's from an injury. After the war, I would see things sometimes too."

"No, I was never hit on the head."

James studied her face a moment, as if searching for a diagnosis in his wife. "Aside from last night, you've been doing grouse lately, Tin Tin. Let's just keep taking it one day at a time, aye?" Kissing her on the forehead again, he went over to the bassinets to see his two Sleeping Beauties.

"Don't wake them, James. I have a terrible time getting them back to sleep."

Picking up little Mabel this time, James gently cradled his daughter in his arms. "They're identical, yet I can easily tell them apart."

Anna agreed. "From the day they were born, I could too."

"Was it like that with your sister, love? Could people tell who was who?"

"Most times, no. We looked too much alike," Anna said, taking the baby from him and putting her back in the bassinet. "But Yarra could always tell."

"It's that sixth sense of hers, aye?"

"Too right. I think Liam has it too. He's always been a little special in that way," Anna said, placing the food on the kitchen table.

James settled down to eat. "He was over by the family burial plot today."

"Really? Why?"

"He likes to put flowers on the graves," James said, digging into his food. "He even puts flowers on the one with no tombstone."

Anna flashed her eyes up at him. "I thought we weren't going to talk about that. Ever. That was our promise to each other, remember?"

"We're not." He paused, his expression shifting from relaxed to something more cumbering. "But maybe we should. It bothers me how we act like it never happened. It bothers my conscience, Anna."

"It was a wolf, James. The Black Shuck."

He stopped eating and stared at her. If only that were true, he thought. He would like to think it was just a wolf, to pretend along with his delusional wife, allowing the lines of reality to blur.

"Anyway, enough," she said, pointing her fork at him. "I prepared a grand meal for you; let's enjoy it in peace."

But James wasn't done with their tête-à-tête. "Hold on; we're not finished yet."

"What is it now, Sugar Bear?"

"A couple of times last night, you spoke as if you were your mother. You've done that before, too," he said, recalling the occasions he had seen and heard her take on a different persona. "To be honest, it scares the bloody hell out of me."

"Imagine that–li'l ol' me scaring James Ragnar Shahan."

"I've seen some things in my life, having been to war 'n all, but nothing like when you . . . change like that."

Anna seemed disinterested, taking a bite of corn bread.

"You also mentioned the shadow people again." It always elevated James' fear of her disorder when she spoke of the enigmatic beings. "How long have you been seeing them, anyway?"

"Since I was a girl."

"Did your dad know?"

Anna didn't answer.

"Tin Tin, listen to me."

"I *am* listening," she said with irritation.

"Did your father know about these hallucinations?"

Anna nodded.

"And what did he say?"

"To ignore them."

James was thinking, trying to piece things together. "Are these shadow people also the voices that you hear?"

Anna found his question amusing. "No," she chuckled.

"Are you sure?"

"I think I would know the difference, James."

"Are they always just shadows or do they sometimes change?"

"Just that once."

James again recalled that mortal day from the past, about what had happened and what he had to do. The unspoken secret cast a pall on his mood. "So who do you think these shadowy creatures are?"

"I don't know who they are. I just see them sometimes," she replied, as if it were perfectly normal. "Don't you ever see things that are not there?"

"Flashbacks from the war, maybe. Now and again."

"Then why am I any different?"

"Because you haven't been to war, Anna," he said, putting his cutlery down, having lost his appetite.

"No. But my mother and sister were taken from me, and that's worse than war."

James stared at his wife with curiosity. There was such an innocence about her; yet at the same time, a darkness. He knew, deep down, that someday–maybe years from now–her hidden demons would let loose. God help him then, he thought. "Love . . ."

Anna looked up from her plate. "What."

"Your dad was right. When you see the shadow people again, ignore them. Pay them no mind."

"James," she said, consonance in her eyes. "That's what I've been trying to do my whole life."

James

And so I go on pretending.
I pretend I am in love with my wife.
I pretend I enjoy the work at Sugar Alexandria.
I pretend Anna is sane . . .

When Anna May Shahan smiles, anyone looking upon her melts. Such a precious woman, they think. Batting eyelashes, round angelic face, lips turned up into a charismatic grin with an adorable gap between her front teeth. Yet underneath that cherub exterior is a woman with deep layers of complexity. Signs that our little Anna is not well. A sweet adult child with random emotional outbursts and perplexing mental issues, living with several false personalities that exist on the inside waiting to be introduced, if not rule. It is almost incomprehensible that a woman so small and harmless could become so ferocious, but she can . . . And she will. At Anna's core there is a storm brewing, strong enough to level a town.

But there is another side to Anna, as well. Her face of normality, where she desires a loving family, a nice home, and a thriving cattle station. Once her housework is done for the day, she often inspects the farm, the stockmen, and even her own husband, making sure everyone is doing their job. And if anyone isn't, they will experience firsthand the wrath of a tiny female Napoléon. She rules Sugar Alexandria like a diminutive tyrant carrying a loaded six-gun on each hip.

Beyond the boundaries of her empire, however, Anna can be quite different. Howbeit still feisty, she lacks the same autocrat confidence she wears like a garment at the station, appearing awkward and maladroit in the outside world. Nervous and fidgety, offended easily, she will curse in Danish if someone upsets her. James finds it rather endearing, seeing her vulnerability as the true Anna—soft and sweet inside the despot patina.

There is no one quite like Anna May Shahan. Depending on her mood, she can be sweet as a cherry or a fractious bitter bane. James has learned this the hard way, knowing to always let her win.

Or else . . .

CHAPTER 6

U p before the sun, James splashed cold water on his face to jolt himself awake—a morning ritual—and trimmed his beard. Breakfast with his wife was next—apple pancakes, scrambled eggs, crispy bacon, and coffee. Then he bottle-fed the girls before heading out to work.

"Look at you," Anna said, leaning on the doorframe, her coffee so sweet and creamy it made her smile. "You were made to be a father."

James held his daughter close to his bare chest, relishing how the tiny infant felt like a warm sack of fresh dough. "They're so fragile and innocent," he said, smiling down into the child's face. "All I want to do is love and protect them. With my life, if necessary."

"I feel the same, Sugar Bear."

After a quiet moment, Anna whispered, "We made them, James Ragnar Shahan. Me and you."

He gave his wife a tender look. "Quite a creation, aye? You had twins, and you yourself were a twin." Putting little Scarlet back in her bassinet, he asked, "Do you remember much about your sister, love?"

Anna's face softened. "Yes, I do." Her eyes suddenly looked darker, more desperate. "We had this amazing bond that I can't explain. As if we shared one soul. Without her I am half a person—something I've had to learn how to live with."

"But you have us now. We're your family."

Anna still appeared downcast. "It's not the same, James. You wouldn't understand. The closest thing I ever had to it again was my cousin Rose, and I never heard from her soon after she married."

"I thought you two used to write."

"We did, and then she moved and my letters were returned undelivered."

"Well now she's coming back," James said, kissing his wife and daughters goodbye. Grabbing his Akubra hat, he left out the door.

Looking out the open kitchen window, Anna gazed at the three windmills of Sugar Alexandria. Something about the mammoth structures was healing, calming to the soul. Quiet, efficient, intelligent in their design, they confidently captured the wind with great authority. What if I were a windmill, she wondered? I too would stand proud, harnessing God's breath and spinning it between my arms and legs for infinity.

As the smell of honeysuckle wafted through the window, Anna noticed Genevieve smiling at her in the stockyard, wearing her accustomed, high-necked, black Victorian dress and her hair in an elegant bun. "Why don't you come into the house for some tea," she said to the woman in a low voice, waving her over. "We can talk about Rose returning to Sugar Alexandria."

"Don't you sass me, James Ragnar Shahan," Anna chided later that afternoon. She was scrubbing clothes on the washboard outside while reprimanding her husband for going to the pub too often lately.

James pumped more fresh water onto his handkerchief, placing it on the back of his sweaty neck. "What else do I have but my piano and the Blue Lizard Cave?" he riposted, wishing he were there now, drinking a cold one.

She stopped and glared at him. "Me and newborn twins, that's what. And a station to manage. It's not gonna manage itself, aye?"

"As much as you nag me, I'm surprised you haven't banned me from my piano, too," James said.

"Don't get me started on that," scolded Anna. "That's all you want to do is play that bloody thing, then go to the pub in town. Lord, I fear I married a sissy boy."

He shook his head. "You can be one irritating sheila, you know that?"

"Well . . . well . . . you're the most irritating bloke in the universe!"

Lovely Dawn, their pet potbellied pig and the daughter of the original Lovely Dawn stolen from Glenda Trufflepig, trotted over, wanting affection. James knelt and rubbed the sweet-natured sow that roamed all over the station as if she owned it. When the pig had enough and ran off, he stood and scanned the land as far as he could see. An abundance of cattle and sheep grazed peacefully in the distance, countless chickens clucked nearby, and arrogant peacocks proudly flared their feathers like decorative fans.

"Crikey, are you listening?" Anna barked, annoyed that her husband's attention now seemed to be elsewhere.

James' eyes moved from the horizon to his wife. "Don't you ever have a kind word for me, love?"

"Not as long as you keep wasting time in that boozer house or on that blasted noisemaker." She shook her finger at him. "And I'll tell you another thing: Those blokes at the pub only care about whiskey and whores. Not good company for a family man."

He held her gaze, smiling with a glint in his eye. "My piano and the pub make me a better bloke."

"Oh yeah? And how's that?" asked Anna, putting her hand on her hip.

"'Cause they make me happier, that's why. A better lover, too."

Anna tried hard not to smile, but she lost that battle and her dimples popped, the gap between her front teeth showing. They grinned at each other until a distressed voice cut through the air, ending the sweet moment between husband and wife.

"Help! Help!" Liam yelled, jumping the fence, running in a panic toward them. "There was an accident on Abbey Road!"

"Who was it?" asked James.

"Abbey Road! Abbey Road!" Liam shouted.

"I know, lad. Who crashed on Abbey Road?"

"Herman Marshall and Bandy McRoe!" the teenager answered, exasperated. "They were racing again!"

James jumped into his Ford Model TT Huckster pickup and rushed to the scene. It was complete mayhem. Casper Cotton Fancy was already there, trying to extricate Herman from the car on fire.

James ran up to help. "Where's Bandy!"

"Dead!" said Casper. "His body flew clear into the field!"

The two men frantically worked to free Herman from the burning vehicle, and finally succeeded, dragging him to safety. Seconds later, Herman's car exploded, and they both stared in shock, realizing how close they all came to dying.

"You sure Bandy's dead?" James asked.

Casper nodded. "And don't go look at 'im. You don't wanna remember him in such a state. I can bloody guarantee he died before hittin' the ground."

"What happened?"

"Damn fools were racin' again. Bandy lost control and flipped his car, landin' right in front of Herman's."

Herman was barely conscious, bloodied and in excruciating pain. "I need to talk to Maxine," he groaned.

James knelt beside him on the road and held his hand. "We need to get you to a doctor now, mate."

"No, I'm not gonna make it," he said, tears rolling down the side of his face, mixed with blood.

Casper Cotton and James exchanged glances.

"Please go get her." Herman winced in pain again, and his breathing turned shallow. "I need to say a proper goodbye," he moaned. "I think I can hold on till then."

From the severity of his injuries, Casper knew that Herman was done. "Jimmy, go get her. Hurry."

James sped off in his truck to Herman's house. Maxine was out front when he arrived, planting flowers, and when she saw James screech into the driveway, she immediately knew something bad had happened. With fear in her eyes, she dropped the flowerpot in her hands and ran up to the truck. James drove her to her husband.

"Sorry, baby," Herman cried, barely holding on. "We had so many plans, too. So much life ahead of us."

Maxine was crying hysterically.

"I love you . . . ," he whispered, voice fading, eyes closing, life force leaving his body.

Maxine put her head on his chest, and he was gone.

～⁓≈✧≈⁓～

Both funerals were held at the same time, as Herman Marshall and Bandy McRoe attended the same church. "Too young to die," all the towns-folk kept muttering that day, shaking their heads in disbelief. But it was what Maxine had shared through her tears that really struck a chord with James: "At least I knew love," she said with conviction. "What it means to have and give love. God Almighty knows what a wonderful gift that was."

James played the piano while they waited for the priest to begin his eulogy. As everyone settled into their seats, the congregation had nary a dry eye.

"That bloke plays like an angel in God's orchestra," Poppy Buttersmith whispered to Hazel Smuckers sitting next to her. She wiped her nose with her silk handkerchief. "It's a shame what happened to him."

"Being tricked into marriage by Anna, you mean?" Hazel whispered back.

Poppy nodded. "He was supposed to go to some fancy music school in London years ago. That is until Anna told him she was pregnant." Poppy leaned into her. "Turns out she wasn't; can you believe that? The poor bloke did the honorable thing, but it was all based on a lie."

"Well, they have two daughters now."

"Took ten years."

"He seems to be doing all right."

Poppy shook her head. "You listen to him play and tell me if he shouldn't be playing for crowds of people. It's a pity, is what it is. A sad pity."

Hazel listened for a moment, then turned to Poppy. "I love Anna, but you're right. It's a shame what happened to him. A bloody shame."

As if on cue, Scarlet Rose began to cry, triggering her sister Mabel Blessing to join her, their wails intermixing with the beauty of their father's music.

The priest, a gray-haired, long-bearded man named Joseph Bartholomew Kohan, commenced his eulogy. Once a humble fisherman, now a man of God, he resembled Abraham Lincoln, the people often referring to him as Father Abe. Standing tall at the pulpit made from the bowsprit of an old English merchant ship, his gravitas commanding attention, he began his bold and emotional homily by quoting from the Holy Scriptures . . . *"O death, where is thy sting? O grave, where is thy victory?"*

The congregation went silent, hearing the powerful words from the imposing man, his deep voice resonating, his austere gaze scanning the audience as if searching for someone in particular. He continued, *"And I heard a voice from heaven saying unto me, 'Write, blessed are the dead which die in the Lord from henceforth: Yea, saith the Spirit, that they may rest from their labours; and their works do follow them.' "*

After the funeral service, James and Casper Cotton stood outside the church, smoking rolled cigarettes while talking among themselves.

"That was a beauty of a song you played earlier, Jimmy Boy. One of your finest, and that's no lie."

"Ta, mate. I knew that piece would be fitting."

"What's it called?"

"*Requiem*, by Wolfgang Amadeus Mozart."

"It has a melody that's . . . haunting," said Casper, glancing at his friend. "Felt it right in me bones."

James nodded.

"Isn't there a story behind that song?"

"Indeed there is. Mozart had received an anonymous commission to compose a Requiem Mass for a man who had lost his wife. But Mozart's health was also deteriorating, and he believed he had been cursed to write a requiem as a swan song for himself, certain he too was about to die."

Casper Cotton shook his head. "Imagine that—believin' you're writin' about your own death."

Several children burst through the church doors, laughing and running about, guileless to the solemn event. Casper chuckled. "I knew Herman and Bandy when they were just ankle biters," he said, his eyes becoming watery.

James' fought back the tears too. "I used to run with them in this same courtyard, just like those wee lads over there." He paused, trying to steady his breaking voice. "Then I fought beside them in the war, and celebrated with them when we all came home."

The two men went silent, staring at the children playing, fearful that if either said any more, they'd both start crying and be unable to stop.

Anna

At the funeral today, I saw the stranger again, quietly sitting in the pews. I nearly screamed in fright. Usually he hides behind a tree, or in the barn, or lingers in the shadows, staring at me from a distance, and yet there he was only a few feet away.

As Father Abe delivered his eulogy, I stared back at the stranger staring at me, his appearance destitute, his chest covered in blood, his face devoid of life.

Why was he here?

What does he want from me?

When James played the piano, the bloodied man turned and watched him instead, lifting his arms in the air, waving them to the music. What an odd sight to witness!

Sometimes I am in awe at what I see that others don't.

Other times it scares me to tears.

I suppose I am gifted.

When Anna crawled into bed that night, James pulled her in closer than usual, tight against his belly, until her heartbeat vibrated into his own. The funeral had left him lugubrious, and he sought comfort from his wife, pressing up against her, kissing her neck and touching her inner thigh.

She brushed his hand away. "James, please, not tonight." Anna loved her husband, but sex was just an irritation to her. An obligation that she had as his wife. "We just came back from a funeral, too."

"I know," he whispered, still kissing her neck. "That's why I wanna feel closer to you. I need some tender love and affection."

"Not tonight, I said."

He stopped, grumbling, "Not any night."

"We have two babies, so how could it not be any night? And you know full well we tried for years before I got pregnant."

The look on James' face soured, and he became quiet. Her comment had conjured up memories from a decade past when she first told him she was pregnant, only to discover months later once they were married that she was not. He recalled having the caprice to flee on finding out the truth, to leave in the middle of the night, to pursue his dreams in London after all. But upon talking to his priest, he realized his fate had been sealed. Marriage was a holy union, and he had made a vow before God. An oath that decreed he stay, despite it feeling forced, and even malevolent.

Countless times over the years since then, he would stop what he was doing in the paddock and wonder where he would be right now if he hadn't met Anna Polston. Playing his piano for a crowd of people in England, no doubt. Teaching music the next day at a prestigious university, dispensing knowledge to shape and sharpen the hungry minds of those eager to learn. But that dream had been stolen from him.

"What is it?" Anna asked, noticing the change in his comportment.

James hesitated, leaning back on his pillow, then decided to speak his mind. "I love you, and I love our girls . . ."

"And?"

"But you were supposedly pregnant ten years ago, too. Remember that? That's why we got married in a rush."

"I thought I was; I swear," she protested, lifting her chin.

"You weren't, though," he said in a low, calm voice.

"It was a false alarm."

"Anna, you told a sugarcoated lie, and you know it," he alleged, clipping his words.

An awkward hush followed, and within the couple's long, catechizing stare was the quiet acknowledgment of Anna's successful manipulation. He had been hoodwinked, falling into a life-changing snare.

"You didn't marry me just because I told you I was pregnant, anyway. You married me because you loved me and you thought my freckles were adorable."

"I married you because I thought you were pregnant with my child, and

I was doing what any decent bloke should do under those circumstances."

"Then why didn't you leave me when you found out I wasn't?"

"We were already hitched; I was locked in," James said, giving his wife a mordant look. "Your convenient oversight changed my life. I had my entire career planned out ahead of me, and I had to abandon it."

"Crikey, don't sound so glum. You make it seem as if you received a death sentence."

His umbrage broke through: "Music was supposed to be my career, Anna, not some after-work hobby. I could have been a professional pianist. Or a music professor at a university. I was even accepted into the Royal Academy of Music in London, but meeting Anna Polston changed all that."

"You regret marrying me?"

"That's not what I said."

"Then what?"

"I just resent having to give up my music career, that's all. It was all I thought about once."

Anna shook her head. "A musician's fantasy, aye? And what would that life have been like?"

Plundered aspirations filled his head. "Performing concerts in auditoriums. Playing benefits for charities and fundraisers. Entertaining music lovers around the world. Many doors would have opened for me."

"Well now you have two daughters and a station to manage. That's what you should care about."

"That's the thing, Anna—I love our girls but not the land. Not like you, anyway."

A Mona Lisa smile born of pride and contentment dallied across Anna's face, thinking of the silky red earth outside that stretched on for miles, and how every inch of it she owned. To her, she was just as much a part of Sugar Alexandria as the animals, the crops, the water that fed them, and the blue sky that hovered above. All of them one. "You're right—I do love it. With all my heart. Maybe someday you will too," she said, making sincere eye contact with her husband.

He kept silent.

Anna ran her fingers through his hair, as she often did. "I know things didn't turn out as you hoped for in life, and I may not be the sheila you dreamed of, but I love you, Sugar Bear, and you love me. Till death do us part, aye?"

"Yes, love. Till death do us part."

Though they were both annoyed with each other, they found themselves grinning. James leaned over and whispered into her ear, "Can I please have a root tonight?"

Anna heaved a heavy sigh. "Crikey, James, if you have to, go ahead. But turn off the lamp first."

"Ta, love." As he went to put out the light, his hand hovered above the kerosene lamp switch, hesitating, not wanting to turn it off. He yearned to see what his mind imagined–the visualization of his body merging with hers was just as erogenous as the act itself. But he knew Anna, and her aversion to intimacy. He knew the limited and controlled rhythms she was comfortable with. Turning off the light, he reached for her in the darkness.

James

That night after I make love to my wife, I fall asleep, giving rise to my guilt, my subconscious mind recalling another tragic death from long ago. The dream is always the same, unnerving and in black-and-white . . .

I am reading in my den when a shotgun goes off.

The aftermath is ghastly and macabre.

I build a casket, and as I saw the wood, the fibers bleed as if I'm cutting through flesh.

When I hammer the nails, the wood screams.

I dig a grave in the Polston family burial plot and lay him to rest.

No name, no marker, never discussed, a secret between husband and wife.

And the secret goes on and on . . .

Maybe it was my mates' funeral that made my subconscious remember, but what kind of man would I be to forget? No, I cannot, and it will haunt me the rest of my days.

Often as I lie awake in the comfort of my warm bed, I think of him not far from me in his cold grave. It is a mystery I am a part of, and by association amenable for. An unsolved riddle. But I know the answer, and not revealing it may cost me my soul.

CHAPTER 7

Rose replied to Anna's return correspondence with another message that sent her cousin to the moon, describing their friendship in a way that touched Anna's heart. James was familiar with the quote she had used by the famous philosopher Aristotle, and it intrigued him . . .

My Dearest Anna,

"Friendship is a single soul dwelling in two bodies."

Thank you for allowing me to come to Sugar Alexandria. I am on my way!

Love,
Rose

As Anna stirred the stew that evening, her pet cockatoo rested on her shoulder like a prince on his throne. The crimson-breasted galah proudly held Rose's last telegram in his beak, somehow knowing it gave his owner great joy.

Yarrajan sat at the large wooden table in the kitchen cleaning fish. She had scaled, skinned, gutted, cut, and filleted so many fish in her lifetime that she now did it by rote, as easily as one would peel the husk from a cob of corn. The smell, texture, slime, and sight of it all made no difference to her, either.

Fish was never in short supply at the station, as the family lived by the sea. Either James went fishing on the weekends, or the fishermen he was friends with would share their catch, and almost every night they would eat different kinds—tiger flatheads, mahi-mahi, pigfish, King George whiting, snapper, and several others. They ate it fried or baked, preparing it in different ways, using local herbs and spices to flavor the seafood. If they had an overabundance, the women would pack the fish in salt tubs to cook later.

"Yarra, tell me about my mum again," Anna said, adding more potatoes to the stew. She loved hearing the stories about her mother whom she never met.

The older woman who had been the family's nanny and housekeeper for years, thought for a moment. Yarrajan was a salient Aborigine, with curly hair, dark eyes, dark skin, and an intricate tribal tattoo athwart her cheeks that had been given to her as a child. Her native language was Nukunu from the tribe that lived around the Spencer Gulf, but she spoke several other Aboriginal dialects as well, handed down to her from her ancestors. A proud, stern woman, whose common sense, insight, and wisdom were razor sharp, she had known Anna's parents when they were first here in the beginning. When they were young, before the tragedy struck them. After Elsa had passed, she raised Anna as if she were her own.

"C'mon, Yarra, tell me about my mum," Anna begged.

Yarrajan grinned. "I be tryin' to think of somethin' new, Miss Anna. Somethin' different from the same stories I be tellin' before."

"I love the story about how she looked, and how she reminded you of a white rabbit."

Yarrajan's smile grew wide. That was Anna's favorite, and the Aboriginal woman enjoyed indulging the little girl in her. "Your mum be like you, Miss Anna. Small and blonde with deep blue eyes. And yes, she be like a wild, pale rabbit, runnin' around in the bush. The Outback be her playground. Barefoot in her worn-out dungarees, with her hair down and messy, she be goin' walkabout everywhere, sometimes sleepin' under the stars. She'd ex-

plore the bush all day and find herbs and berries and all kinds of wild mushrooms to eat, comin' back home with a basketful. She also talked to the
moon, and she learned all 'bout the animals of the land. Your mum be a
white woman from Europe, but inside she be a true Aborigine."

"Tell me about her laugh, too."

"Yes, she laughed like a wild sheila. Ain't met anyone else like her. She
laughed from her soul."

"And the last thing she said was . . ."

Yarrajan's ebon eyes glazed over. "Take care of my sons and daughters
as if they be yours."

"And you have, Yarra."

"I tried. I couldn't save your sister, though. When she died, it be like I
lost one of my own."

"But I lived, and you raised me."

"From the moment you were born, you be a fighter, Miss Anna," Yarrajan said, picking up another fish to clean. "And you still be."

Content with the story she had heard a hundred times by now, Anna
changed the subject: "Yarra, can you believe Rose is coming back to us?"

The Aboriginal woman slowly shook her head as she scaled the fish.
"Miss Anna, you best be listenin' to me when I tell you somethin'. She needs
to go stay with her own family."

"I *am* her family. Rose is like a sister to me. The sister I lost."

"Sisters—that's rubbish. A woman is a woman—always," Yarrajan said,
her sable eyes gleaming. "And she be a single sheila with no children. She
has no business comin' here." Her eyes seemed to darken a shade, and the
furrows in her brow deepened. "The Rainbow Serpent told me in a dream
that she be no good."

"The Rainbow Serpent, aye?" Anna smirked. She pretended she didn't
care, but she knew the Aboriginal people and their beliefs. When the Rainbow Serpent spoke, it was not to be ignored.

"He be showin' me a snake comin' out of the most beauty of a flower I
ever seen. A green-eyed female snake."

Anna's eyes flashed up at the older woman, and the mood in the room
changed. "You're worrying yourself over nothing, as usual," she said, dismissing the augury. "Rose is my cousin. I love her, and she loves me."

"That dream be a prophecy, Miss Anna." Yarrajan pointed her finger at
her. "Somethin' bad be comin'. I can feel it. This will only cause trouble for

you and Mister."

"Oh, Yarra, you and that third eye of yours."

James walked in through the back door, exhausted from the day's work. "What did you see this time?" he asked, having heard the end of their conversation. "A flood? A drought? Is the house gonna burn down, or is someone gonna be murdered?" he teased.

Yarrajan's bearing remained foreboding. "Maybe," she said, looking him directly in the eye.

Anna placed a bowl of hot stew and a cold iced tea on the table. "Don't encourage her, James. She's suddenly being an ornery, cranky sow."

He chuckled and sat down to eat.

Anna put Moby in his cage and joined her husband.

"Well, Tin Tin, are you excited about your cousin coming back to Straya? Won't be long before she's here, aye?"

"Counting the days," Anna said with stars in her eyes, giggling in her seat. "Rose is going to change our lives."

I hope for the better, James thought, taking a drink of his iced tea, smiling affectionately across the long wooden table at his wife.

Yarrajan shook her head again. *"You never be listenin' to me, Miss Anna,"* she mumbled in Nukunu, leaving the room. *"Your mum never listened, either. Just don't forget: I warned you."*

Yarrajan

I have a sixth sense.
A heightened ability to see things before they happen.
This Rose sheila will bring nothin' but ruin to the Shahan family!

It was another day at Sugar Alexandria, like any other, except now Anna could barely contain her excitement. She did the household chores in a daze, and as she swept the back porch, she thought of all the things she was going to talk to Rose about when she arrived, and all the fun they were going to have.

James interrupted her quiet ruminations, hollering from the paddock that some of the sheep had strayed. He could go look for them, of course, but it was always easier to get his wife to do her kulning to beckon the animals home. Anna enjoyed it, too, having this special skill: The livestock whisperer.

As she stood in the field releasing her evocative tune, Anna sensed someone watching her. She stopped singing and looked around, expecting to see the bloodied stranger again. Instead, she caught Liam staring at her from behind the barn. He smiled and waved, but she only ignored him, resuming her kulning.

Liam lived not far from the Shahans. The only son of Travis and Cybill Herdsman, an Australian sheep station owner and his American wife, now a widow, he and his mother lived alone—his six sisters had all married and moved away. A frequent visitor to the Shahans' station, albeit incognito, the shy and timid young man kept to himself, hiding in the bushes, watching the daily activities unfold. When no one was around, though, he would approach the animals and pet them. He liked James, too, and often came to see what he was doing, but his feelings toward Anna were mixed, her comportment sometimes amicable and other times unkind, treating him like a pest.

This saddened Liam. Many years ago, as a small boy and she a young teenager, they were good friends, and he missed those days when they would frolic together. He missed her chubby face, and the gap between her teeth that she would spout water through to make him laugh. He missed her little notes with words and pictures, as if pages from a comic book, that she would use to communicate with him since she had not the patience to learn sign language. And he missed playing all day with her in Cassandra Fancy's marvelous garden.

When Anna became a young woman, however, she started to withdraw from him, not answering the door when he knocked, and not waving to him when he visited the station with his pet dingo, Boomerang. "I'm not a child anymore, Liam," she would say as he read her lips. "I need new cobbers. Women cobbers like me, not you." Liam was devastated. I am not a child anymore either, he would think. But inside, he was still very much so.

When finished kulning to the animals, Anna walked back to the farmhouse to resume her chores. Liam waved again, but Anna refused to indulge the teenager, turning her back to him. Then he whistled, trying to get her attention, and yet still she ignored him.

"You see me," he forced out in a strangled, incoherent utterance. Though he could speak, his voice had now changed, becoming inscrutable at times, causing a disinclination toward speech. He knew it sounded strange to others, and that embarrassed him. If emotional enough, however, he would let his words loose, or if he wanted to communicate with someone who couldn't sign, he would carefully try to enunciate his articulations to get his meaning across.

Anna heard his obnubilated words and stood still. He was trying to verbally express himself, and for a moment, it moved her. But her stubbornness got the better of her; her superiority complex kicked in. She was too good for Liam to be friends with him anymore. Putting the broom aside, she disappeared into the house.

"Anna," he garbled again, tears glistening in his eyes. "Anna . . ."

Liam

I love seeing Anna sing to the animals. It is an ancient sound born from the mountain people in another land far away where Anna's family is from, is what I've been told. I cannot hear it; I can only imagine what it's like. The livestock know the sound, too, and they magically respond, returning home to her.

Anna used to let me touch her throat as she sang, and I would feel what the animals could hear. But that was a long time ago. Before Anna became a woman. When she used to run barefoot through the mud like me, cavorting and laughing without a care in the world.

Now I can only watch.

I miss that feeling of the kulning sound on my fingertips.

I miss my friendship with Anna.

CHAPTER 8

A great anticipation swelled over Rose coming to Sugar Alexandria. For weeks, each day after the station work was done, all the men stayed late, taking instructions from James to transform the womb of the center windmill into a beautiful home for their soon-to-be guest. Anna excitedly watched in wonder as it gradually molded into the gift she had planned for her beloved cousin.

First the inner mechanics and machinery were taken out. Wood flooring and framework for each room were installed next, along with a winding staircase that led to a large loft with a skylight, serving as the bedroom. A cozy fireplace was installed to keep the interior rooms warm during the damp winter months, and Anna artistically adorned it with countless seashells and seahorses hand-glued all the way up the mantel. Entrance to the mill opened up to the living room, and James enlarged the window three times its original size to ensure the farmhouse was in plain view. Off to the right was the kitchen, fully equipped with an icebox, stove, and table with four chairs. The bathroom was situated to the left, and had a freestanding Victorian-style clawfoot tub, wash sink, stained glass window, and red tapestry wallpaper. James also built a pleasant nook close to the fireplace where Rose could sit by a small window and read.

The last task was the wooden double doors that would serve as the impressive entrance to the unique abode. James knew exactly what he would use. Taking two Aboriginal stockmen with him, they rode their horses down to the shoreline where the old pirate shipwreck had run aground during a previous century. Though the vessel was mostly gone, the doors to the captain's quarters were still there. James and the men removed the massive pieces and tied them to a flat board to drag behind his horse.

"It's not wise to use something from a shipwreck," Mandawuy said in Nukunu. *"It will bring bad luck."*

"Superstitious rubbish, mate," replied James in the Aboriginal man's native tongue. *"Besides, look at those doors—they're a beauty."* And away they went, giving the center windmill a distinguished face.

When finished, the entire maisonette was cleaned, painted, and decorated. Anna was moved to tears when James brought in an antique brass bed, once owned by her mother, in from the barn. A plush love seat, a bookcase, and a large patterned rug completed the living room, with three colorful oil paintings that had been passed on from generation to generation hanging on the walls. Various other necessities, conveniences, and knickknacks were added to each living space as well. The final detail was the hybrid tea roses, crimson waratahs, and golden wattles—Australia's national flower—that Anna planted outside the mill on both sides of the door.

James enjoyed the process of renovating the windmill more than he liked to admit. When completed, he and Anna christened it with a bottle of Yarrajan's blackberry wine, spending the night inside, listening to the sound of the blades spinning in the wind. Keeping the sail functional was something Anna had insisted on, knowing how much Rose loved the constant hum it generated.

"I think we can call it a day. The windmill is finished—a bona fide maisonette," James said, holding Anna in his arms.

"It's a beauty, James. Just a beaut. Good on ya for doing such a ripper job."

"I did it for you, Tin Tin. I love you, and I want you to be rapt."

Anna lightly poked him. "You put up a bit of a fight in the beginning, you bugger," she joked.

"I did, but I had good reason. The sheila will probably be married off again soon, and it'll be a waste of an ace windmill."

Anna frowned, not wanting to believe his prediction. "She could end up staying longer than you think."

"With as much hard yakka as that was, I hope so. Be a shame if we did this all for nothing."

"Oh, stop. Rose is going to love her new home, and she will stay here forever."

"How old is she now, anyway?"

"Thirty-three; same age as you."

"When was the last time you saw her?"

"Eleven years ago at Christian and Josephine's wedding. I was seventeen; she was twenty-two. That was the last summer she visited because she met that bloke from England and got married. We used to have so much fun during those summers. I wish she would have just stayed here and started a life in Esperance."

"I didn't realize she attended my sister's wedding."

"Yes, she was there."

"Hmmm," was all James said.

Snuggling closer to him, Anna listened to the swoosh of the turning blades, noticing a pause between each turn. Like the steady cadence of a pulse. She lay her head on her husband's chest and slowly dozed off, the blades turning in sync with each beat of his heart.

Anna found sleep easily that night, ensconced in the safety of her husband's arms. Floating on a cloud, she fantasized about her life to come upon Rose's arrival. Images of them happy and laughing under the warm Australian sun, drifted through her subconscious. Her beloved cousin's presence was going to be the benefaction she had been waiting for.

James had a vivid dream too. An odious dream. A strange woman tried to gain entrance through a window in their home. Curious, he let her in, desiring to know who she was and what she wanted. She was drenched from the rain and shivering; he started a fire and put a blanket across her shoulders.

Slowly they began to talk, and James became fascinated with the conversation and the story she was telling. She said she was lost, trying to find her way home, then dropped the blanket and hovered next to him, across from him, all around him. He reached out to touch her, yet no matter how hard he tried, she only evaporated before his eyes, then reappeared.

Engrossed in their conversation, Anna found them and began to scream. Her scream was shrill, strident, piercing to the ears. She picked up a knife and lunged after him and the woman, but stabbed at her own flesh instead, an alien expression on her face, blood covering her arms and clothes. The grisly image abruptly woke James from his nightmare, heart pounding, mouth dry.

"Crikey, James, what is it?" Anna asked, half sitting up in bed, rubbing her eyes. "Nightmares of the war again?"

He took a deep breath. "No."

"Go do what you do—get a whiskey and come back to bed."

"I said it wasn't about the war."

"What did you dream about, then? The unmarked grave?"

"Not that either," he said, hands still shaking, heart still pumping, Anna's scream still ringing in his ears. "Go back to sleep, love."

"Tin Tin, I want some pancakes with those eggs!" James yelled out from inside the bathroom. He had a towel wrapped around his waist and was shaving his neck.

"All right, Sugar Bear," said Anna. She came into the bathroom, put his coffee cup on the sink, and watched as he shaved. "Your beard is getting long."

He smiled, his teeth a flash of white underneath his dark blond mustache. "You like it?"

"You look like a Viking. Like that Viking named Skarde in that story you tell me."

James chuckled.

Anna slapped him on the bum. "Well finish up in here, aye? Breakfast is almost ready." As she left the room, she turned and added, "Oh, before I forget, I need you to clear the walkway from the back porch to the windmill."

"Why's that, love?"

"Because Rose uses a cane to assist her weak leg. I don't want any rubble getting in her way."

James abruptly stopped shaving, the razor pressing into his skin midway down his neck as he stared at his own reflection. "You never mentioned she used a cane, before."

"I didn't think it mattered," Anna shouted from the kitchen.

The girl he had danced with and kissed at that wedding used a cane too, and she was also English. Was the Charlotte he had met all those years ago possibly his wife's cousin Rose? The sudden realization of what very well could be jolted him, causing a nervous excitement to tickle at the very pit of his navel as he dipped the brush into the foam, slathered his skin, and continued with his shave.

⁓⧉⁂⧉⁓

News traveled fast in the Shire of Esperance, and as word got out among the Aboriginals that a white man at Sugar Alexandria had turned a functional windmill into a home for a single sheila, they were more than curious. Especially since they would put ten women in one adobe.

"We have come to see the mill," a deep, distinctive voice resonated in Nukunu.

James and Liam looked up from the calf they were branding to see Banjora, a perspicacious Aboriginal man James had hired ten years back, with five others in tow from his village.

"They did not believe me when I told them," Banjora said, *"and wanted to see it for themselves."*

All the other men nodded.

Banjora was the one who had taught James how to speak Nukunu. The good-natured, laconic man was now over seventy years old but could still put in a decent day's work, although these days he usually just tended to the sheep, ate lunch with the stockmen and ringers, and roamed the station at night. *They said who in their right mind would do this for a woman,* he added.

I did it for my wife, James replied in the man's dialect. *To make her happy.*

Your cook has you whipped, said one of the men. *How sad for you to be under her thumb.*

They all laughed, including James, knowing there was truth in it. He was used to their deeply ingrained misogynistic humor and attitudes, though he did not subscribe to their views.

James took the Aboriginal men into the now-furnished mill for a tour. As they inspected the unique dwelling, they spoke among themselves in Nukunu, impressed with the layout and workmanship, pointing and nodding in approval. Yet still, none of them could understand why Mister James would destroy such a bonzer, working windmill for a sheila he had never met.

Banjora tilted back his Akubra hat, a single ostrich feather sticking out from it. "You do a lot for your cook," he said, switching to English.

"I do."

"You ever say 'no'?"

"She's not a sheila you can easily say that to."

"It would be good for her to hear 'no' sometimes. 'No' teaches you."

"Teaches you what?"

"To accept the word 'no'."

James chuckled.

Banjora looked up at the skylight, rays piercing through the clouds in large silver shards, illuminating the entire living space. "At night, when I go walkabout, I hear you play your piano," he said, his characteristic tone slower than usual, almost a drawl. "For years, now."

"And what do you think?"

The sapient old Aborigine patted James on the shoulder, switching back to Nukunu. *I think you should be playin' for many people, not just an old Aboriginal man and the midnight moon.*

Sometimes I play for the men in the pub, said James.

Liam became frustrated trying to read their lips, unaware they were going back and forth between English and Nukunu. "What's he saying?" he signed.

"Banjora thinks I should play my music for many people," James signed back. He had learned Australian sign language from Cybill a few years earlier to better communicate with her son. "I told him I play for the men at the Blue Lizard Cave."

Liam flashed a mischievous grin. "Whiskey and whores!" he yelled out in his recondite voice. "Whiskey and whores!"

"Liam!" James scolded, shocked at his sudden vocal burst. "You can't say that, mate."

The Aboriginal men all laughed.

"Who taught you such a crass thing?"

"Anna," Liam signed. "She said that's what's at the pub."

James shook his head, thinking of his ornery little wife and her choice set of words. "Don't repeat that again," he signed.

"Why not?"

"Because it's crude."

"How come they laughed, then?" Liam signed, pointing at the Aboriginal men.

"They shouldn't have."

"Whiskey and whores! Whiskey and whores!" Liam shouted out again, laughing along with the Aborigines.

"I'm disappointed in you, lad," James signed. "A gentleman doesn't talk that way."

Liam immediately became solemn. "I'm sorry, Music Man."

"You're a gentleman, aren't you?"

The teenager nodded.

"Then act like one," James said, frowning at the lad.

At the end of the tour, everyone went outside, and one of the Aboriginal men extended his arm to shake James' hand. *"You did a fine job with this home,"* he said, speaking in Nukunu. *"The sheila will be pleased when she sees it."*

James thanked him.

"Two sheilas to warm his bed," another Aboriginal teased. *"Mister James is a lucky bloke."*

"No," said James in their native tongue. *"Anna is my cook; her cousin is just going to stay with us for a while."*

"But what if they were both yours?" the man asked, raising his thick eyebrows in amusement.

95

James' face flushed red. *"Only one cook for me."*

"Why not consider it, Mister James?" asked Banjora. *"Many blokes in my village have more than one cook."*

"Because . . . ," he began, finding himself at a loss for words. *"Just because."*

Mandawuy, who had helped build the maisonette, walked up to join the men from his village. *"Mister James could not handle two sheilas, that's why,"* he said. *"Look at him—all lean and wiry. It would break him in half. Now me, on the other hand, I could handle three."*

"Should I tell that to your cook?" James fired back. *"Maybe Kareela has something to say about it."*

"No, no, no! She would have my hide if she knew I thought such things."

All the men laughed.

With only days to go before her long-awaited reunion with her cousin, Anna absorbed herself in the remaining minutiae of final preparations. She spent hours inside the windmill, adding her finishing touches to every room, placing scented soaps and candles, dishes and cutlery, sheets and towels, and other conveniences in their proper places. That's when she discovered a glaring imperfection, a fatal flaw. As if finding a crack in a rare, expensive vase, she realized the closet in the loft was too small for Rose's bedding and clothing. More of a cubbyhole than a practical space for one's personal items.

How did she not notice this before, she bemoaned?

How could she miss such a critical blunder?

Thinking long and hard, knowing her husband would never spend any more time or coin on it, a wonderful idea conceived in her head to correct the error. James had previously told her that Cybill's piano had recently given out, no longer able to play a single tune. Anna knew that must have saddened Cybill because her deaf and intellectually disabled son loved to place his cheek and palms against the lid to feel the vibrations from the musical notes. With the deleterious effects of the Great Depression now reaching Australia, though, she had not the money to fix or replace it. She did, however, have the most stunning antique armoire Anna had ever seen. A splendid, imposing piece, with elaborate carvings and artwork on the wooden double doors.

Anna straightaway went to talk to her neighbor. Wearing her nicest dress, her long white gloves, and her favorite cloche hat, she knocked on the door with one of Yarrajan's delicious berry pies in her hands. Cybill, gracious and sprightly, always exuding a happy face that looked as if she were on the brink of laughter, welcomed her in. Then, after tea and pie, Anna told an egregious lie. Cybill believed it . . .

On a firm handshake, she agreed to the great exchange, and it was done.

James would sometimes play his piano into the early-morning hours, where instantly there was no past, present, or future but only a heavenly space between. A blissful domicile all his own, where the emptiness filled with the ardor of his music.

Anna was a deep sleeper, and usually her husband's music didn't wake her. That night, however, he played more passionately than usual. Boister-ously. As she roused from her slumber and heard the melody reverberating through the walls, she wrapped herself in a shawl and quietly went to the living room where he sat at his treasured instrument, eyes closed, head turned slightly to the right, his good ear facing the sound.

Silently she watched as her husband's fingers mastered the ebony and ivory keys, laying down bass, skipping across melodic intervals and arpeg-gios, landing on high notes, then starting low again, only to build back up to a boom and a release. He played loudly (fortissimo), his right hand closely following his left, crossing each other in a wild, rhythmic motion, muscles tensing, head thrown back, lolling side to side. Possessed, enthralled, in lust with the song. The sound grew thunderous and vivid (strepitoso), as if a light becoming too bright, then peaked with an explosive finale. And then there was calm (placido). A bittersweet softness that trailed away and dissipated into a dying vibration (perdendosi). Though James had stopped touching the keys, the powerful resonance still circulated the room like a fading fragrance.

"Have you come to listen to me play?" he asked, opening his eyes, feeling his wife's presence behind him.

"No. Your piano woke me," she answered, unmoved by his tremendous skill and the sheer beauty of his music.

"Sorry, love. I couldn't sleep."

Anna stared at him a moment. "The way you play sometimes scares me," she said. "As if something possesses you."

He tossed back the measure of whiskey from a shot glass sitting on the edge of the piano, opening his arms wide as he spun around on the bench. "Perhaps I am a possessed station owner, and a free soul only when I play at night."

Their eyes met in a dual stare, neither backing down. A continuous clash between husband and wife, whether spoken or unspoken, about how James' true destiny had been permanently altered by Anna's lie.

"You're playing a sad song tonight," she said, breaking the stalemate.

"Am I?"

"Sounds sad to me. If you love playing that silly box so much, why such a sad song?"

"Because there's beauty in the expression of the sadness."

"Would you be sad if you no longer had your piano?"

"Why would you even ask me that?"

Anna walked up to the instrument, touching its lacquered surface, observing its bodacious elegance. "You have me and the girls; why would you need it?"

He watched as she caressed the top of the piano, envisioning her dragging her nails across its surface. "This is a ridiculous conversation. My love for you and our daughters has nothing to do with my piano."

"At times I feel like your precious instrument is another sheila."

James laughed, but inside he knew she was jealous of it from the beginning.

"It's true. The way you are with it; the way you touch it. It's an opulent distraction for you."

"No, Anna. It is a cherished conduit to the life I was supposed to have."

"If your piano vanished tomorrow, what then?" she asked, a strangeness in her mien.

A part of James was afraid of his tiny wife. Not just of her mental insta-
bility, but of her odd quirkiness and controlling behavior. She had a modus
operandi that intimidated him, and he often wondered exactly what was going on inside that small, golden-colored head of hers. "Where is this all coming from, love?"

"Enjoy playing your music tonight," Anna simply said. Kissing her husband on the cheek, she left the room, turning at the bedroom door and adding, "Till death do us part; aye, Sugar Bear? That's what we always say. Nothing else could break us apart. No matter what, we'll always be together."

He nodded, not understanding his wife's anomalous ways, knowing he
likely never would. And maybe he didn't want to . . .

James returned to his music for comfort and succor. Laying his fingertips
affectionately on the keys, he began to play another soft, rueful song, written
by Beethoven—*Piano Sonata No.14 (Moonlight Sonata)*. Instantly the piano responded, filling the room with exquisite sound as the musical notes swelled
and burst into sweet highs and haunting lows. It was as if the piano owned
him, and while he played, the fears of his wife's illness and the beast of burden that was the station faded away, replaced by a musician immersed in
what he loved. Closing his eyes, the opus consumed him, as if diving into the
sea. Such a sweet sound emanated from the house that the moon lowered
from the night sky to better hear it.

The next day when Anna sent James into town to run some errands,
three Aboriginal stockmen carried the massive wardrobe into the windmill
and up the stairs to the loft. *"Is this a white man coffin?"* Mandawuy joked in

Nukunu so Anna wouldn't understand.

"*No, fool, it is a closet for a white woman who is coming to live at the station,*" Warragul said.

"*At least it's not as heavy as Mister James' piano,*" the third Aboriginal, Tarka, chimed in. "*Getting that into the bed of the truck and over to Miss Cybill's house almost killed me.*"

"*You're both getting fat and lazy,*" said Warragul. "*That's why they're too heavy for you.*"

"*Miss Anna traded this wooden box for Mister James' piano, and he doesn't care?*" asked Mandawuy.

"*He doesn't know yet,*" Warragul answered.

All three men laughed.

Anna turned to them. "What are you laughing at? What's so funny?"

Warragul spoke up in his broken English: "I say I wish I could give my wives beaut box like this, Miss Anna, but they only fight over it."

"It's an armoire, not a box," she corrected, directing them to place it by the window.

"*When Mister James finds out, he is going to be mad as a cut snake. He'll make her trade it back, and we'll have to carry it down again, then go pick up the piano,*" Tarka predicted.

"*No, she is the boss,*" Warragul said.

"*His piano is sacred to him.*"

"*I know, but he does everything she says.*"

Anna, oblivious to their conversation, began to clean and wax the fancy armoire.

With the wardrobe now in its final position, Warragul pointed at the intricate design carved and painted on the double doors. "See this maiden and unicorn?" he asked Anna. "This represent good in people." He moved his finger to the right. "But wolf hidin' over here represent bad."

Anna focused on what he was pointing at. "Huh, look at that. I saw the princess and the unicorn, but I didn't even notice the wolf until you pointed it out."

"It means good and evil exist in all, and even the most beauty of things can have fangs."

She smirked. "How do you know it's not just a maiden, a unicorn, and a wolf?"

Warragul shook his head. "They all have same golden heart on their chest. It means they are one."

Anna paid no mind to his notion. Superstitious musings, she thought.

"My people believe artwork like this is urgent warnin' of somethin' to come."

Anna resumed polishing the new addition to the windmill, the portent of his words lost on her.

When James found out what Anna had done, he was furious. "Goddammit, son of a bitch!" he said through clenched teeth. "I can't believe what you have done!"

Anna only giggled, always enjoying when she angered him enough to curse.

Storming out of the house in a rage, he beelined straight to the center windmill that was now a maisonette. He wanted to inspect the armoire that had been traded for his venerated piano. Emotions aside, how could it possibly have been a fair trade?

The great exchange sat near the window, and as he laid eyes on it, surprisingly he found it elegant and impressive. Glorious, even. The wardrobe was enormous—much larger than he had imagined—at six feet wide, three feet deep, towering over his own six-foot frame. Well taken care of through the years, its rich, dark mahogany, though antique, still held on to its original luster. Standing in front of the piece of furniture was almost intimidating, and as he stared at the intricate detail, similar to the craftsmanship of the small Danish-style bar Anna's grandfather had built in the farmhouse living room, he couldn't help but admire it.

Carved and painted into each door was a flaxen-haired maiden, dressed in a white gown, sitting next to a unicorn with a rose wreath. A cunning, black wolf hid mendaciously behind a tree, and paisleys resembling lace filled the background, adding to its charm. "So you're the beast that was traded for my piano," he said out loud.

Of Germanic heritage, the antique armoire had originated with Cybill's great-grandmother in Europe, made its way across the Atlantic Ocean to her parents in Tennessee, only to cross the great sea once more to its final destination in the Outback of Australia. But Cybill valued what James' piano would do for her son more than she valued the history and antiquity of the family heirloom. After all, it was only a piece of furniture, she reasoned, and the joy her disabled son would receive from the trade was worth so much more.

"Well, at least you're an extraordinary looking beast," James again said aloud, his anger cooling, "and the exchange will do Liam good." Besides, he thought, I can still go over to the Herdsmans and play my piano whenever I want. And when Anna's cousin leaves, Cybill and I will do the exchange again.

Closing the double doors of the armoire, he backed out of the room slowly, his eyes lingering on the imposing wardrobe that would soon house the clothes and personal items of a woman he had never met, yet whom his wife dearly loved.

James

In my head, I make a list.

I write down all of Anna's unusual tendencies I have become familiar with since I married her.

The list is quite bizarre.

I know it by heart.

I know she is wired wrong, with some unnamed causal syndrome.

Often I feel as if I'm beating my head against the wall, enduring her condition, and because of this, my spirit has dimmed.

Some vagaries are small, scarcely noticeable.

Others extreme, hard to tolerate.

She can be sweet to a fault, and make me laugh with her quirkiness.

Yet she can also be manipulative, stubborn as a mule, and childish in her response.

At times she will talk continuously, barely letting anyone get a word in edgewise.

Or else she will go into a silent trance and won't say a word for hours.

Her fidgeting, compulsiveness, and whispering appears for no reason.

Sometimes she sees and hears things that are not there.

Like Genevieve, a woman from the 1800s who floats in and out of her life; or the mysterious shadow people; or a mute, nameless stranger, covered in blood.

She speaks to her dead mother and sister, too, even speaking as if she were them.

When she does this, it terrifies me.

Where do the hallucinations come from?

What kind of sickness would cause such things?

And still there is more . . .

Physical intimacy is a bother to her, a chore.

She thinks of love as ownership.

The worst of all, though, is her inability to have empathy for others, or even recognize their feelings.

Including mine—trading my piano away is proof of that.

But I am her husband, and she is my wife.

I must love and take care of her, even though I cannot bond with her, or even understand her.

Despite it all, I have to be patient with her.

Thank God I am a patient man.

Anna

Yarra left Sugar Alexandria this afternoon and will not be returning for several weeks. Her daughter recently gave birth and needs her help. It's probably for the best, too, as Yarra does not trust Rose.

"I still don't feel right 'bout this, Miss Anna," she had said to me. "I get this jab of dread when I think of that green-eyed sheila comin' here."

"Oh, Yarra," I rebuffed. "She's just a widow who uses a cane to walk. What harm can she cause?"

"I remember her well. She be a *pretty* widow, with a look outta her eyes like she be poison. A quiet and cunning curse."

Those were the words Yarra left me with. Such a silly goose she is, thinking Rose will cause us trouble. By the time she comes back, though, she'll see how happy I am and realize she was wrong.

Rose is a blessing not a curse . . .

⚜

The night before Rose's arrival, under a silvery full moon, Anna sees the Black Shuck and shudders. The she-wolf is growling in the tall stalks of wheat, mouth open, teeth shining, eyes glowing red. Anna gasps, stumbles back, and prays.

As her skin prickles, she hears the voices calling her to the soul tree. Gathering her courage, she gets up and kills another goose for the feathers to make a new crown and wings—the dogs had found her old ones and carried them off—and places violets among the feathers, as purple is Rose's favorite color.

With her brand-new crown on her head and wings on her back, she walks the pathway to her shrine, her mind twisting and turning, going into a trance, deeper and deeper with each step closer to her private altar that connects her to the other side. She sits on her knees on the silky earth in front of the tree with the corn husk dolls, colorful Aboriginal beads, and old photos. Closing her eyes, she smiles and says, "Rose will be here soon, Mummy and Blessing. I'll have a sister again. Once more we'll all be together as a family. As a family should be."

CHAPTER 9

Anna and James were driving to the train station in Esperance. Both nicely dressed—Anna insisting—James even wore his bow tie and his favorite fedora. A few times along the way, James reached over and squeezed his wife's hand, giving her a wink, knowing how elated she was to see her cousin again.

As they continued on their drive, Anna watched the darkening sky. Gray clouds swelled, hanging low as if too heavy for the air, looking fierce and gloomy with an imminent storm while the smell of impending rain filled her nostrils. Storms were bad luck, her father used to say. A sorceress would cast a spell on a farmer, riding in the clouds, directing the storm over his crops. "Be wary of witches and necromancers," he once told her when she was a little girl. "They are forces not to be trifled with." When she asked him if he had ever met one, he said that he had, but it was not a story for the ears of a young child.

"It would have to rain the day she arrived," Anna said, frowning. "What crook luck."

James couldn't help but grin. "Perhaps Yarrajan is right—bad omen 'n all. There could be a flood on the way," he teased. "Or maybe someone's gonna be murdered today."

Rose

Finally my journey from England to Australia has come to an end. I'm off the train, after sitting adjacent to a woman who never stopped talking for hours. Even when I feigned being asleep, it made no difference. Then when I actually did fall into slumber, she was gone when I woke, and I missed her presence. Probably due to traveling alone for so long.

I'm so tired. Feels like I've been on this voyage for years instead of weeks. Drained. Exhausted. And not just from the journey but also from my terrible marriage, my husband's suicide, and the convent with the nuns who prayed with me and for me.

All of it a blur.

Now that I am here, I want to forget all that I was and start anew. I want to eat a hot meal, take a warm bath, read my books all day, and sleep in the farmhouse in a bed with clean, crisp sheets. I want to wake up in the morning refreshed and alive, and walk to the shoreline, aimlessly traipsing along the Australian sandy beach for miles.

Swimming in the sea sounds so good to me right now, with all this humidity in the air. The mugginess is so bad my clothes are sticking to my clammy skin. To add to the discomfort, I have started my period, the blood even running down my leg as I got off the train. I cleaned up as much as I could in the ladies' room, but the rest I will have to abide.

Sitting on this bench, awaiting my cousin to arrive, I watch the angry gray clouds move across the infinite sky, and it triggers the strangest of thoughts, remembering the wedding I had attended the last time I was here, and the young soldier I had danced with and kissed that night.

The pianist.

I wonder whatever became of him . . .

~ased~

They saw her right away when they entered the train station–a sheila sitting alone on a bench, pet carrier and luggage by her feet, staring straight ahead, wearing all black with a diaphanous lace veil covering her face. Anna figured she would immediately run to Rose upon seeing her, but it didn't happen that way. Instead, she hesitated, as if two arms had wrapped around her and held her still. Looking at her cousin sitting there so quiet, so thin, face forward and motionless, an unsettling sensation came over her. A coldness. She had no idea why she was feeling that way and could make no sense of it, and inexplicably she had the urge to grab James and run to the Ford Model T, never looking back.

It was a premonition of the strongest kind, reaching down into Anna's very bones . . .

"What are you waiting for, love? Go to her," said James.

She nodded and slowly approached. There, in the flesh, was her beloved cousin—the other part of Anna that at one time made her feel whole. The cure that somehow remedied the overwhelming emptiness that often plagued her as a child through to a young woman. "Rose . . . ," she said.

Rose's neck turned—a mannequin come to life.

Her skin too pale—ghostly even.

Her hair a shade darker than black—the color of tourmaline.

Her body as thin and wispy as the growing stem of a fledgling tree.

"Jeg kan ikke tro at det er dig! Jeg kan ikke tro at du er tilbage!" Anna exclaimed in Danish. *("I can't believe it's you! I can't believe you're back!")*

"Også mig," Rose replied, standing from the bench with her cane. *("Me too.")*

"Det har været så længe! Ti år! Sidst vi så hinanden, var vi bare unge piger der sagde farvel," said Anna. *("It's been so long! Ten years! The last time we saw each other, we were just young girls saying goodbye.")*

"Ja, det er rigtigt," said Rose, lifting her lace veil. *("Yes, that's right.")*

When Anna saw her cousin's eyes, it reassured her, and she reached out to hug Rose. Holding on tight, the scent of Chypre de Coty perfume filled her nostrils, mixed with a hint of black licorice—Rose's favorite candy—and the disquieting sensation in her gut fled as quickly as it had come. She imagined being embraced by her late sister and mother, and after the hug, they both stepped back and stared at one another for the longest moment—a feeling of family, intermingled with uncertainty and newness.

"Look at you, all grown up," Rose said, taking in the presence of husband and wife who stood before her. They reminded her of a couple in a painting from Swedish artist August Hagborg, both towheaded with cherry-colored, sunburnt skin. "You're not a little girl anymore. You're a wife and mother."

"Yes, we have newborn twins!" said Anna. "Can you believe that, Rose!"

"That's wonderful," she replied, her words seeming forced rather than joyful—another peculiar moment in the day. "You were a twin."

Anna briefly looked away. If her twin sister had lived, no doubt she would be with them there too, welcoming Rose back to Straya. But all Anna had were foggy memories and stories. Memories of her holding hands with a little girl who was her mirror image, and stories of how inseparable they were when they played together. "I miss Blessing," she said. "If she had lived, it would have been grand."

James observed them both as they spoke, and it began to dawn on him that his wife's cousin looked familiar. Very familiar. Though he had never met her before, his mind kept telling him different.

"Oh, I'm so sorry," Anna said, "where's my manners? Rose, this is my husband James."

He stepped forward. "Good to meet you, love."

Rose took off her cloche hat and smoothed back her hair, removing her spectacles and flashing her aquamarine eyes at him. "Yes, you too."

In a rush, it hit him, as if being struck by lightning. The way the light reflected off her face caused a flood of memories to invade James' mind. Memories from right after the war, the night of his sister's wedding. The dance. The kiss . . .

It was her!

Rose now fully recognized him as well. She had to look past the thick beard and unruly blond hair, but he was the handsome, clean-cut soldier who had kissed her that night before she left Australia—an encounter she had never forgotten. How ironic! Not thirty minutes earlier, she had been thinking of him, and where his fate had landed.

"James, don't you think her eyes are cat-like?" Anna asked. "Look at them—they're a beauty."

Rose blushed. "Oh, Kitten."

Anna beamed. "That's right, you called me Kitten when I was younger. And I called you Lottie."

"Lottie," echoed Rose. "I haven't heard that nickname in years."

Anna turned to her husband. "I called her Lottie because her middle name is Charlotte."

James nervously played with the rim of his fedora in his hands. He was still in shock, flummoxed, trying to process the wild thoughts racing through his mind over the identity of his wife's cousin.

"You still have our friendship locket," Anna said, marveling at the heart-shaped pendant around Rose's neck, as if it were glowing. It pleased her a great deal that she was wearing it. "I have mine too."

A fugacious smile fought to grace Rose's lips. She too was struggling with her own untrammeled thoughts, trying to assimilate how that soldier from long ago became her cousin's husband.

Anna reached over, lifting Rose's locket, and a small ring slid down the chain. James recognized the ring . . . It was the Celtic band he had given her that night at the dance. She had not only kept it but also wore it around her neck.

"What's that?" asked Anna.

"Oh . . ." Rose quickly tucked the necklace down her neckline. "Just a relic from a long time ago."

"Must be important to wear it around your neck."

Rose gave no response, nervously shifting her weight on her walking stick.

Anna noticed. "How's your leg feeling after such a long journey?" she asked, staring down at her thinner-than-normal ankle and calf. "Has it gotten worse?"

"It tires when I'm on it too long, just like before."

Anna leaned down and lifted Rose's pencil skirt to the knee. "See James? It isn't so bad; just a little skinny."

Rose blushed, jerking her skirt back down. "Anna, please."

"Good God, Anna, stop," James said, tugging on his wife's shoulder, trying to quell her impudence.

"I'm sorry," said Anna. "I just wanted to show him it's not . . . not that bad." She turned to James. "I shouldn't have done that, should I."

"It's all right," Rose said, her cheeks returning from flushed to ivory, remembering her cousin's propensity for odd behavior. "I'm used to people being curious about my leg and my finger."

James observed she had a slight deformity on her right pinky as well. Her pale, slender digit curved at the knuckle, and she would often massage it when anxious.

Now upset with herself and unsure of what to say, Anna wrung her hands while they all stood there, a brief quiet washing over the interlude. The train started up, releasing charcoal-colored smoke into the air, and the large iron wheels began to turn. A few passersby greeted each other with a hug, then continued on their way.

"I speak for both me and my wife," James said formally, "when I say we are very sorry about your husband."

Rose nodded. "Thank you; yes, Paul is gone." She momentarily glanced up at the sky, her expression appearing lost, her eyes glazed and bereft. She was thinner than Anna remembered, her face drawn. If she had not known that Rose was a grieving widow, Anna would have assumed her cousin was ill. Still watching the shape-shifting clouds, Rose reached up with her delicate hand and touched her chapped lips. She was remembering. Or reminiscing. Maybe both. Once she's at the station, it will do her good, Anna thought. All that fresh air and sunshine, she'll be rosy and radiant before long.

"Across the Indian Ocean by ship, then the Outback by train. Quite the voyage," James said, trying to diffuse the awkwardness.

"I saw nothing but blue water for weeks, followed by red earth and trees for days. At times I wondered if I would ever get here."

"Are you knackered, Rose?" Anna asked. "You must be."

"Yes, I am. I didn't get much sleep on the train. If you don't mind, can we head to Sugar Alexandria now?" No sooner had the words left her mouth than the first few drops of rain began to fall. James gathered her things together and they all went to the car.

At first Anna chattered on endlessly about how thrilled she was that Rose was there, but soon it became apparent the colloquy was one-sided. Rose was mostly quiet. Controlled, even. Somewhat sad and distant, she stared out the window as they drove, watching the sky shift colors. She had changed. No more the happy-go-lucky young woman, she was now reserved, mature, prim and proper. Anna inwardly frowned. She yearned for the bubbly girl who had left Australia all those years ago. Hopefully, in time, Rose would revert to who she once was.

The rainstorm began with a vengeance. James flipped on the windshield wipers, turned on the headlights, and for the rest of the trip they each remained sequestered with their thoughts on the long ride home.

Anna

I love my husband James.
I love him dearly.
His calm voice.
His moral compass.
His gentle hands.
His dedication to me, doing everything I ask.
I love so many things about him.
It's just . . . well . . . in all honesty, in a guileless, sisterly way . . .
I love my cousin Rose more.

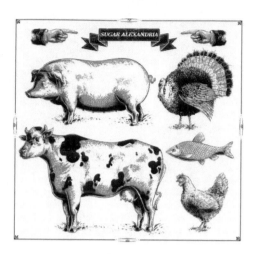

The rain subdued to a soft but steady pace by the time they arrived at the remote cattle station outside of Esperance. As they pulled into the driveway, several hens hopped out of the way, running around clucking, protectively chased by a rooster, and two pigs and a small pony looked up from foraging on the grass in the front yard. Hundreds of lofty sunflowers, smiling on their stalks, gazed heliotropically heavenward, searching for warmth in spite of the rainfall, and domineering sheepdogs barked their commands in the paddock.

James and Slim took the luggage from the vehicle while Anna and Rose stayed behind, shielded under matching black umbrellas, scanning the prodigious landscape of Sugar Alexandria. Omnipresent fields of red and yellow terrain, rolling green hills resembling humpbacked giants marching shoulder to shoulder, and massive outcrops in the far-off distance guarded the valley. Innumerable cows grazed the land, countless sheep scattered about like fluffy white grains of rice, and a fence line streaming out in both directions for miles enforced the livestock boundaries. Rose smiled as she took it all in. The bush was everything London was not. Truly breathtaking. An oil painting come to life.

"Is everything how you remembered it?" Anna proudly asked.

"No. It's far more beautiful," said Rose. "As if time has stood still, waiting for my return."

"Du er hjemme, Lottie," Anna said in Danish, squeezing her cousin's hand. *("You're home, Lottie.")*

Rose's eyes came to rest on the large, two-story farmhouse with white-washed walls and green ivy and ferns stretching up the front left side. Though the second floor had been damaged by a fire years ago, you'd never know it—James and the stockmen repaired the exterior as if it never happened. Little hearts chiseled into the wooden window shutters reflected the Danish heritage of their grandfather who built it, and the unique, intricately carved front door still maintained its welcoming charm. The oversized front porch extended the full circumference of the farmhouse, and a porch swing along with four different-colored rocking chairs gently rocked back and forth in the breeze.

Inside the noble home, decorated with red and green velvet sofas and chairs, exquisite multicolored Tiffany-styled kerosene lamps, and other European themes, the architecture was impressive, exhibiting their grandfather's love of ships. He had been a fisherman in Denmark before moving to Australia to start over as a station owner. Even the handmade beds had been crafted to resemble the design of a Viking ship, and many other details throughout each room embodied the allure of a vintage Danish vessel.

Reddish-brown Tasmanian oak covered the floors, and two stone fireplaces—one in the living room and the other in the master bedroom across from the kitchen adorned with hand-painted Danish tiles above the stove and sink—kept the farmhouse pleasantly warm and cozy. A cobblestone wall separated the large living room from the kitchen, and a handsome, ornate wooden bar sat against the divider, welcoming its guests with a refreshing libation. Down the hallway was the nursery, James' den, and Anna's small childhood bedroom. Access to the upstairs was closed off after the fire happened, though—James locked the door shut rather than spending the time and money on it, seeing as how it was just the two of them living there and they didn't need the extra rooms above. Now that their family was growing, however, he'd soon have to repair that too.

The enormous barn in the stockyard was off to the right in the near distance, the stockmen quarters beside it, a small homemade distillery behind it. What immediately caught your eye, though, were the three gigantic Danish windmills—white with red tops and red sails—standing as if mighty soldiers surrounding the station. Their blades spun in the wind, reminding all who watched them how powerful the air could be.

"I missed the windmills," Rose said. "I forgot how imposing and lovely they are."

Anna smiled, looking up at the towering structures. "I know, aye? A beauty, they are."

Both women continued to walk the grounds, and an inquisitive baby sheep that had wandered off came up to them. Rose picked up the little lamb, kissing it, holding it close.

"They're so tiny and precious, aren't they?" Anna asked.

Rose nodded, pressing her cheek against the baby's satiny wool.

Arriving at the fence line, they returned the lamb to its mother and stopped to watch some cows being branded. Rose noticed the stockmen were Aborigines and must have recently had a ceremonial rite due to the white dots and red markings still painted across their faces. As they observed the procedure, three sheepdogs and their faithful companion—a potbellied pig—ran up to greet them.

"The one with the dark patch on his eye is Bluebelle," said Anna, "the spotted one is Catalou, the one with golden fur is Beauty, and the pig that runs with them is Lovely Dawn. She's James' favorite and thinks she's one of the dogs." Just then the pig snorted, and all of them ran off again to pester the sheep. "She's also the boss and tells them what to do."

James approached them on his horse Ireland, surveying the women huddled together—two feminine silhouettes under a light shower of rain, shielded by the opaque umbrellas that hid their faces. "Anna," he said as he got near.

"Did you put her things away and let the cat out?" she asked.

"Yes. You gonna show her the mill soon?"

Anna smiled. "We're headed over there now; I was saving it for last."

"The mill?" inquired Rose.

"I have a surprise for you, Lottie," Anna said with a girlish giggle. She had exercised a great deal of patience to not divulge it right from the start. Before she could bring her cousin to the renovated windmill, however, the stockmen and ringers—both Aussie and Aboriginal—started walking up to them, hats in hand, introducing themselves to Rose.

"It's been all the talk 'round here, you comin' to stay at Sugar Alexandria," said Koa, one of Yarrajan's many nephews. "My cook make you this gift." He handed Rose a straw-colored, broad-brimmed hat, plaited from the fibrous leaves of a cabbage tree and pointed at the sky. "She know white sheila need protection from burnin' Straya sun."

"Thank you," said Rose.

As the men returned to their work, James said, "What are you waiting for, love? Go show her the mill." Pulling on the reins, he threw a glance at his wife's cousin as the black stallion turned and gallantly trotted off.

Rose watched him ride away into the paddock, his Akubra hat low over his brow. He seemed older than his age. Battle-weary. Much different from the clean-cut, fresh-faced, flirtatious soldier who had danced with her and kissed her eleven years ago. The charming, gregarious young man once full of life and promise, enamored of her at that wedding long ago, was gone.

∾⛇∿

"*Det er dit eget private slot, Lottie,*" Anna said in Danish. *("It's your own private castle, Lottie.")*

"*Killing, hvad har du gjort?*" Rose asked, eyes wide and mouth agape, gazing at the living space in awe. *("Kitten, what have you done?")*

"I wanted you to have a special place of your own. I want you to be so happy here you'll never want to leave again."

Mesmerized to the point of tears, Rose walked through the renovated windmill that had been wonderfully crafted into an incredible abode for her. She ran her hand across the maroon velvet love seat, noticing the Belknap velvet curtains on the window to match. The lovely patterned rug softened her steps on the wooden floor, and the warmth from the fireplace chased away the damp. Tiffany-styled lamps—annexed from the farmhouse—gave the rooms a playful flair, and a lonely bookcase begged to garrison some tomes.

The kitchen left nothing to want, either, with its white stove, black icebox, and table with floral linen tablecloth. The bathroom was her own private spa with Victorian clawfoot tub, swanky wallpaper, and dazzling stained glass window. And the bedroom was an inviting place of respite with goose down duvet on the bed, skylight to gaze at the stars, and eye-catching armoire for clothing. Nothing in any room was missing; everything was perfect.

When the grand tour was done, Rose hugged Anna, looking down into her little cousin's beaming face. "You have created an unbelievable sanctuary for me, Kitten. A priceless jewelry box to live in. Thank you so much."

Anna couldn't smile any wider, her dimples popping and gap between her teeth showing.

115

Once they left the windmill, the high-pitched ring of an infant's cry oscillated through an open window in the farmhouse. Then a second one joined in, intensifying the wail. Rose stopped where she stood, homing in on the ululation, her skin prickling from the sound. It seemed to rapidly spread inside her in a strange and brand-new way, as if something had awakened deep within. "I can hear babies crying," she said, suddenly feeling a desperate desire to hold and console the infants.

"I know, you silly goose," said Anna. "That's Scarlet Rose and Mabel Blessing."

"You named one of your daughters after me?"

"Of course—you're my best cobber. Mabel got Blessing's name."

"Kitten, that's so sweet," Rose said, affectionately touching her cousin's cheek. "I love that you did that."

Anna grinned. "Are you ready to meet them? You can hold one while I breastfeed the other."

"I'm nervous."

"Nervous to meet an ankle biter?" Anna laughed. She grabbed Rose's hand, and together they walked arm in arm to the farmhouse. Oh how happy she was in that moment!

They entered the kitchen to find a pensive Moony Jagger, the oldest stockman on the station, buried in a crossword puzzle. Tall and skinny, bowlegged and red-skinned, with striking turquoise eyes that at one time, in his younger years, the women had swooned over, he had been at Sugar Alexandria from the beginning, working side by side with Anna's parents. Nowadays he mostly supervised the workers and kept them in line, and sometimes babysat the twins for the Shahans—something he enjoyed. "What's a four-letter word for passion, Miss Anna?" he asked, staring at the last question. "What could that be?"

"Lust," Rose answered.

Moony looked up, somewhat startled, even though he knew Rose was coming. "Well g'day, Miss Rose!" he greeted with a broad, genuine smile. "Fancy seein' you again after all these years, aye?"

"Hello, Moony," Rose said, flashing a warm smile in return. "My goodness, you haven't changed a bit."

"And you're as pretty as a picture," he said with a flirtatious wink. "A true beauty."

"How were the girls?" Anna asked.

"No trouble at all, Miss Anna. I think they be needin' their mum's milk now, though," he laughed, motioning toward the nursery where Scarlet and Mabel kept up their hungry cries. "They were fast asleep until a few minutes ago."

"Ta Moony. We'll take it from here."

He tipped his hat and said, "Gonna be grand havin' you around again, Miss Rose. Just grand," walking out the back door.

Anna brought Rose into the nursery to meet her daughters. The newborns stopped crying as soon as they saw their mother, aware that food was on the way. Rose stared down at the precious new lives, cooing in their cribs. The sight was absolutely beautiful, and she drank it all in. "May I?" she asked.

"Of course, Lottie. You don't even have to ask. My babies are your babies," said Anna, picking up Mabel to breastfeed her.

Rose cuddled little Scarlet. As her fingertips touched the soft, doughy chubbiness of the child, a warmth covered her from head to toe. She tingled everywhere. So powerful was the feeling that it seemed as if she spontaneously grew fresh, new skin. This was in fact all she had ever wanted—to be a mother—and yet they were not the thoughts of a blossoming young woman whose life lay before her but a crestfallen, beautiful tree whose fruit had seemed to have died.

"Are you crying, Lottie?" Anna asked, noticing her cousin get emotional.

Rose wiped away her tears. "Sorry, Kitten. Babies always have that effect on me."

"Well like I said—my babies are your babies."

Sitting in the rocking chair next to her cousin, Rose continued to coddle little Scarlet, and the neonate began to suckle on her neck. In that moment, all the sights and sounds around her disappeared, the child desiring nourishment from her own body eclipsing everything in the room.

<hr />

That evening, Rose smelled the raw fish packed in salt in the kitchen, ready to be cooked, and became ill. Running outside, she hunched over at the back of the farmhouse, vomiting as Anna held the hem of her skirt to prevent it from getting soiled.

"Sorry, Kitten," Rose said, tossing up one last time. "All that traveling must have made my stomach sensitive."

"It's all right, love. No harm done; you get it all out," Anna replied.

Rose leaned against the house, one arm holding her stomach, the other hand on her forehead. "What a way to start a visit."

"Shoo!" Anna yelled at the three sheepdogs that ran up with their surrogate canine friend, Lovely Dawn. The four-legged residents, curious to see what was happening with the new visitor, playfully surrounded them until Anna threw rocks to make them flee.

Both women went over to the water pump, and Rose washed her face and hands.

"Do you wanna go lie down?" Anna asked, handing her a clean cloth to dry off with.

"No, I just need some of my black licorice and something cold to drink." The dark candy made from licorice root always soothed her stomach, and she ate it often.

James was sitting at the kitchen table when they went back inside. "Could she be expecting?" he asked his wife without thinking, concerned for the family's reputation, and the station, if a single sheila who was pregnant were living with them.

Anna looked at her cousin. "Rose, could you be?"

Her eyes grew large. "I was living in a convent, Anna," she said, digging through her satchel for the licorice.

"Oh, yes, of course. Sorry, Rose. It's just when you're pregnant, that's the first thing that happens."

"It's the smell of the raw fish," Rose said, sitting down at the table, glancing at the pigfish and snapper in the sink. "I forgot how prevalent it is at Sugar Alexandria, living by the sea. I'll get used to it again soon enough, though."

"Yes, love. In time you'll be right as rain," Anna replied with a wink, handing her a tall glass of mint iced tea sweetened with honey.

⁓ܢܝ≍ܢܝ⁓

During dinner, James and Rose listened while Anna, sitting at the front of the table, giggled and yabbered on about anything and everything. She was electric. A little squirrel entertaining her guest in a tree. Rose, who had recovered from her nausea, personified a graceful praying mantis, striking and slow moving, sharply clever with a quiet charm; and James embodied an intelligent, lone wolf, not sure where to cast his eyes—at his wife who had the vim of a buzzing bee, or her decorous cousin who was as gentle and calm as a clear summer day.

And as intriguing.

With her underdeveloped leg as it was, James thought of Rose as an exquisite word with a single letter missing. Her imperfection did very little to distract him from her overall beauty. Yet still, he felt conflicted over her being there, hoping it wouldn't make Anna's condition worse and upset the balance he had tried so hard to create.

Rose kept stealing subtle glances at James too, noticing things about him, especially how he would touch his beard when deep in thought, his hand reaching up and ever so gently caressing his chin. He was a man with an easy smile, an air of class, a dignified bearing and a dash of elegance that one would think a grazier would not have. As if beneath the station owner's costume was something hidden. Something sophisticated and refined.

Strangely, Anna abruptly stopped talking, as if a new persona came to the fore. It triggered an uncomfortable silence among the three. A powerful, quiet calm, encircling them, causing a peculiar undercurrent to rise from the midst of the table and turn wildly as if a glass soda bottle spinning on the ground. They could all feel it—a pulling of sorts. A tug of war between three energies. Anna flouted the feeling, cutting into her Danish *forloren hare (meat-loaf)*; Rose nibbled at her vegetables; James continued to drink.

As he tossed back his whiskey, he still could not wrap his head around the astonishing revelation that the girl he had often thought about over the years was the same woman now sitting across the table from him. His wife's dear cousin. While she sat there politely smiling and nodding, memories of that night continued to wreak havoc in his mind. "What did you think of the windmill?" was all he could come up with to ask.

Rose looked at him with eyes large and mesmerizing. "It's beautiful. I'm incredibly grateful you did that for me."

James motioned toward his wife. "It was all Anna's idea. I thought you should just stay in the guest bedroom."

"That's right; it was my idea," Anna beamed. "But I couldn't have done it without James—he and the stockmen worked on it for weeks."

"What even gave you the idea to build it?"

"When we were younger, we would play in there, remember? You said

119

you wished you could live in the mill because you loved the sound of the sail spinning in the wind."

Rose smiled.

"And the antique armoire is a beauty too, aye Lottie?"

"Yes. Stunning."

"I traded James' piano for it," Anna said as if it were nothing.

Rose gave her a look, eyebrows raised. "You did?"

"Yep. A wonderful exchange."

Though Rose loved the gorgeous wardrobe, it troubled her that it cost a man his music. Especially one as gifted as James, having heard him play before. "I don't have to have it, Kitten. You can trade it back."

"Nonsense. He can still go over to the Herdsmans and play it any time. Tell her, James."

He forced a half smile.

Rose spoke to her cousin in Danish. *"I would prefer to give it back, Anna. Please, it's only a closet."*

Anna shook her head. *"Don't be a galah. He was happy to do it."*

Rose turned to James. "It was a wonderful gesture, but I'd feel better if you still had your piano."

He glanced at Anna glaring at him. "It's all right. Like she said, I can go play it any time."

"Well thank you very much, then," Rose said, giving him a heartfelt smile. "And maybe someday I can hear you play it at the Herdsmans."

"Lottie, that's an ace idea!" said Anna. "We can all go visit Cybill, and James can play for us. You should hear him, too. He's a master pianist. No one can play like my Sugar Bear."

James looked at his wife with surprise. She had never complimented his music like that before, at least not in front of him.

"Right, love?"

He locked eyes with Rose. "Yes, I would like to play for you sometime."

Rose's pulse quickened and her pupils dilated. "Looking forward to it," she softly said.

"Lottie, wanna hear a dreadful story that happened here last year?" Anna asked. Before her cousin could answer, she continued, "One of the stockmen raped an Aboriginal woman."

"Oh my God, that's awful," Rose said, wondering why Anna would bring something like that up.

"Yep, Henley Rome raped her, and she hid in the barn. Tell her, James."

He looked away, uncomfortable with his wife's lack of couth.

"James found her and took her to Dr. Crawford. When he got back, he grabbed Henley and tied him to a tree, then let her husband beat him." Anna laughed. "Nearly killed the bloke."

"Anna, that's enough," said James.

She ignored him. "Afterward, James ripped Henley's gold pocket watch from his waist and gave it to the husband. Moony removed Henley from the property, and James took the husband to the sheriff's office to report it."

"Did he end up in jail?" asked Rose.

"Constable Higgins locked him up for a few days, but the woman and her husband refused to testify for fear of reprisal from the white folk, so the dirty scoundrel walked free. I bet he never does that again, though."

"Poor woman," Rose said, her eyes welling with tears.

"Too right. She got pregnant, too, and had a creamie."

"Creamie?"

"A half-caste with lighter skin. They're now raising the boy as their own. Isn't that a wild story?"

"It's a sad story, Kitten, but I'm happy the woman recovered and they kept the child."

"Would you have, Lottie?"

Rose too felt uncomfortable, but she answered anyway. "Yes, of course. I've always wanted a baby of my own."

~··⚜··~

After helping Anna with the dishes, Rose said good night and took her leave. Anna walked her cousin outside, and they both stared up at the full moon fighting through the nimbus clouds.

"Want me to walk you to your door, Lottie?"

"No, it's all right, Kitten. It's only a few yards away."

"Still, it's raining and it's so dark out there."

Rose noticed her peering intently into the blackness of the night. "What is it?"

"Last night, I saw a wolf. But not just any wolf . . . The Black Shuck."

Rose almost laughed. "That's just folklore, love. The Black Shuck doesn't exist. And even if it did, it's long gone, dead and buried in Suffolk

121

County, England. There's no legend of the Black Shuck in Australia."

"I saw it, though. I know I did," Anna insisted. "I even killed it once," she wanted to add but didn't. "Killed it and James buried it in a shallow grave," her inner thoughts continued.

"What you likely saw was a large dingo. Besides, there are no wolves in Australia—you know that. The moonlight was playing tricks on your eyes."

"Perhaps," Anna said, her face projecting deep concern. "There's also a strange man that lurks around our property sometimes."

"He's probably looking for food. An economic depression is happening worldwide now, and a lot of hungry mouths are wandering about."

Anna wanted to elaborate further about the bloodied man. "I think he's been injured."

"Really? Did you tell James?"

"He doesn't want to talk about it and said to ignore him."

That surprised Rose. "But if the bloke is hurt, shouldn't we help him?"

"No, Rose, no! Please, you have to promise me! If you see him, come and get me!"

Rose slowly nodded.

"And be careful, too. Keep an eye out for him. Now that you're back, I'd hate to see any harm come to you."

"I'll be watchful, Kitten. I promise."

With umbrella in hand shielding her from the drizzling rain, Rose ventured out into the darkness, slowly walking with her cane across the stockyard to her new home. Once inside, she sat in the living room, staring catatonically at the fireplace while smoking a clove cigarette, mesmerized by the dancing flames. Thoughts of her cousin's husband danced around in her head, wondering whether he had recognized her, and if he had mentioned it to his wife. She doubted it, since Anna never brought it up with her. Neither would she tell Anna about the encounter unless it was mentioned to her first. What would be the point? It was only one dance, and one kiss. Better to leave it be.

Looking out her window, Rose noticed their bedroom light was on, illuminating the room. She could clearly see two shadows thrown up against the wall—a small silhouette brushing her long hair and a taller one getting into bed. Minutes later, the light snuffed out, slaying the silhouettes with it. She crawled into the middle of her own bed and stared up through the skylight at the dark Australian sky. The empty space on both sides of her felt as if it went on for miles as she closed her eyes, her body still rocking to the slow motion of the ship she had arrived on.

"You're gonna be proud of me, love," Anna said, snuggled up close to her husband in bed. His skin was still warm from the heat of the day, and he smelled of spicy soap and Irish whiskey.

"Oh yeah? Why's that, Tin Tin?"

"Because Genevieve was staring at me through the window tonight at dinner, and I ignored her the whole time."

That same uneasy feeling gripped James, as it always did when she mentioned her hallucinations. "That's grand, Anna. Now that your cousin is here, you don't need anyone else, aye? You won't be seeing the lady in black or the strange man anymore. They're all gone now."

"No, they're not. Genevieve is always watching over me, and the strange man wants me to figure out a riddle."

"Don't be mentioning any of this to Rose, love."

"Why not?"

"Because it will scare her," he said, listening to the rain tap dance on the roof. "The good Lord knows it scares me, and I'm a grown man."

"She already knows I'm . . . different. That I see things others don't."

"You mean you see things that don't exist."

Not liking the conversation, Anna changed the subject: "You sure were

KATE BIRKIN AND MARK BORNZ

cold to Rose at dinner."

"It's not that I meant to be cold. I'm just in shock over learning who she is," James thought but did not say. "I was polite and respectful," he replied instead.

"No you weren't. You acted strange."

He gave no response, unsure if he should divulge that they had met before. Or if Rose had even recognized him.

"You better be nice to her while she's here, and I mean it. For goodness' sake, James, she's a cripple and just lost her husband."

"She's not a cripple; she just uses a cane."

"Even still. She needs our love and support right now."

"Maybe if I still had my piano, I could play something to console her."

"James Ragnar Shahan, don't you sass me," Anna admonished. She thought about what her poor cousin had been through, living in a convent with nuns after her husband's suicide, followed by the long journey across the ocean from England, resulting in the frailty in her posture. "She does look a little crook, though, don't you think? When I first saw her at the train station, I was worried she was ill."

"Just give it some time. A few of Yarrajan's meals when she gets back, and a month of Straya sunshine is all she needs."

Anna agreed and snuggled back into her husband's arms, content and happy her beloved cousin was home. "I wanna tell you something, Sugar Bear."

"What's that, love?"

"I saw the Black Shuck yesterday. It's still alive."

⁓⧼⧽⁓

James had trouble falling asleep, staring at the ceiling, thinking of the Aboriginal woman who was raped last year by Henley Rome. Anna's recounting of the gruesome event had brought back the strong emotions that made him sick that day, witnessing what he did. He could tell the story had made Rose uncomfortable, too.

Finding Isley hiding in the barn, clothes ripped, naked and afraid, was an unspeakable sight to see. Face beaten, thighs bloodied, body bruised and broken. It reminded him of things he had seen during the war, and when he kneeled to cover her, softly speaking in Nukunu, she wept uncontrollably in his arms.

Now Isley and her husband—a good, understanding man—had a twelve-month-old son with lighter skin than their own. Despite the stigma of a half-caste child, they were a family, finding peace in an unjust world.

Why on earth did Anna tell that horrible story tonight, he pondered? Unable to comprehend his wife yet again, he waited for sleep to find him.

The Voices

"Mummy, she's home," Anna whispers, kneeling at her secret sanctum in the thicket by the cornfield. She had woken in the middle of the night to go visit her favorite spot. "She's not herself right now, but she'll get better soon. And when she does, it will be as if you are here with me again, Blessing."

"We're happy for you, Anna," the familiar voices reply in unanimity.

Anna takes one of the corn husk dolls from the tree and cradles it in her arms. "I'm safe again, Mummy. I'm so happy." Before she leaves, she places her palms against the tree, and as if staring in a mirror, sees a little girl—her twin sister—pressing her hands back against hers.

CHAPTER 10

The next day it once again pours. A strong, hard, thunderous down-pour with excruciating humidity. Rose stares out the window, the drops so heavy she can almost taste them, the ground fat with mois-ture, turning to mushy, reddish, clumpy, brown clay. She opens the double doors of the windmill, the fresh smell of unyielding rain rushing in, and leans against the frame. As she watches the small pond kitty-corner to the mill fill with water, preparing itself for the small birds and multicolored frogs that will visit later, she senses someone observing her. Glancing over her shoul-der, she catches James on his horse, motionless, gazing at her with intensity. The look in his eyes, fixated on hers, and the expression on his face reveal to her his thoughts. He knows. He knows she is the young woman he danced with over a decade ago at his sister's wedding. The same one he had kissed, just before the fire separated them.

Instead of looking away, they each hold their stares in an awkward, in-tense dual. Can you believe this, they both think? I thought I would never see you again.

I never forgot you, James continues in his mind, squinting through the rain. How much time would have to pass before I ever could? That dance, the way you made me feel when you smiled at me, the passionate kiss—I have relived those memories over and over in my mind until they nearly drove me mad. Why did I let you out of my sight? Why did you have to leave right after?

I thought of you often over the years, Rose's internal dialogue adds. I left to marry a man I didn't love, regretting it ever since. So many times that handsome soldier in my memory, the one who kissed me the way he did, pulled me from a ruinous place. I always dreamed I would someday see him again, hoping against hope. And yet here you are.

Anna steps out onto the back porch to greet her husband. James and Rose break eye contact, going their separate ways.

Rose

I lay awake in bed the following morning, thinking of the story Anna had told about that poor Aboriginal woman who was raped. She didn't seem as bothered by it as James. I love my dear cousin, but she has trouble empathizing with people, responding inappropriately at times. How James handled the horrible situation is also quite telling, letting the husband beat the man and giving him the rapist's gold pocket watch as a form of compensation. It reminds me of the Biblical story of King Solomon and his wisdom.

Oddly enough, it makes me think of another story, too—Anna's favorite childhood book, *East of the Sun and West of the Moon*. I can remember our grandmother reading us that magical Norwegian tale when we were children, listening wide-eyed in total delight about a young woman married to a white bear, only to find out he is a prince, and she must save him from a life controlled by a wicked witch-queen. Curiously, it is one of the few stories where the female saves the male, rather than the reverse. Why am I thinking of that tale now, I wonder?

From the open window in the loft, I hear evocative singing resounding through the air . . . Anna is kulning to the animals. I remember her doing this when I used to visit Sugar Alexandria every summer, and the hypnotic, sweet song puts a smile on my face. Looking up into the skylight above my bed in my new home, listening for a moment, the high-pitched tones with the beautiful and haunting notes convey a feeling of sadness, resonating with my own.

Then I remember why I am here, and who her husband is. Corybantic thoughts again run rampant through my head about how we had met before, and how astounding it is to have met him again. He was smitten with me once, and I with him, and now he is married to my kin.

How is this even possible?

Rolling over and gazing out the window, I think about how he had stared at me yesterday through the rain. Then the morning light streams in, making the room aglow, and somehow Anna's singing becomes more intense in my ears and the image of James' face more clear in my mind.

~⚜~

The sun had come out in full force, drying the red earth, and the men were busy shearing sheep in the woolshed.

"Your wife's cousin is a beauty," said Declan Dunn with a ribald tone to match his lascivious grin. "A grouse addition to the scenery around here, aye?"

"Yeah, pretty little thing," Lucas Fox concurred. He had a harsh scar from a bull's horn that had ripped him open from his lip to his ear. "I wouldn't mind snuggling up to a sheila like that at night."

Valentine Finnigan wiped his brow. "A cold beer and a pale lovely between the sheets–sounds like heaven."

All the men chuckled.

James, shirtless and sweating, released his grip on the sheep he was shearing and turned to face the men. "She's a recent widow," he said, a sternness in his voice, "so none of that, aye? The last thing she needs is a bunch of randy blokes gawking at her like a starving dingo staring at a piece of meat."

"But she's single, ain't she?" asked Declan. "We can ask her out, right?"

"No, you can't."

"Why?"

James' temper flared. "Because I said so, that's why! Leave her be! If any of youse blokes bother her, you'll no longer be working at Sugar Alexandria! Understood?"

The men exchanged looks and nodded.

Rose went to the farmhouse that afternoon to have tea with her cousin. With great excitement, Anna brought her into her childhood secret lair–the hidden room where they used to play as young girls. The rose-covered tea set and cucumber sandwiches were waiting for them.

"Oh, Anna, it looks exactly as it did the day I left," Rose said, looking around, bringing back fond memories.

"I know, aye Lottie? Isn't it grand?" Anna spun with her arms open wide. "Sometimes I still read in here, or take a nap."

Rose picked up *The Secret Garden* from the bookshelf, flipping through its pages. "You must have had me read this to you a hundred times," she said. "*Alice in Wonderland* and *Emma*, too. Oh! And *East of the Sun and West of the Moon*–that's such a brilliant Norwegian tale. I was just thinking earlier how unique it is."

"Too right. I love that story."

"A girl doesn't know she's married to a wonderful bloke until it's too late," said Rose.

"She even thinks he might be a troll, when he's actually a prince," added Anna.

"Those carefree days seem like yesterday, don't they? Now you're a grown woman with a family of your own. You'll be reading these books to your daughters soon."

Anna poured them both a cup of Yarrajan's Aboriginal tea, then pulled out a lavender box. "I have something for you, Lottie," she said, again with great excitement.

Rose opened the box, lifting up a shimmering green velvet cloak, long and flowing with a protective hood.

"Do you like it? I ordered the fabric from Woolworths and made one for each of us."

"I love it, Kitten. It's beautiful. But you've already given me so much; you're spoiling me now."

"Never," said Anna, smiling effusively. "Your friendship is everything to me."

Touched by her sweet, generous cousin, Rose hugged her, kissing Anna on the cheek. "I'll wear it often, Kitten. On those cold days, it will keep me warm."

"Too right. And I'm making you a beauty of a dress, too. When you're feeling up to it, we'll get all fixed up and go into Esperance for some shopping. We'll spend the whole arvo there, and afterward eat at The Flame Tree Grill."

Rose nodded, her despondency yet again returning, thinking about her life, the past, the future.

"What's the matter, Lottie?"

"I'm still grieving everything, that's all." She looked at her cousin's dollish face, seeing how desperately Anna wanted her to be happy. "Think of a deer struck by an arrow, Kitten. Instead of dying, the deer hides away for a while to heal. That's me. Just give me some time before I'm Lottie again."

CHAPTER 11

Rose

I spend most of my time inside the windmill, resting, trying to figure out what it is I must do next. I don't really feel up to farm chores yet, so I nap or read, and Anna brings me meals with delicious hot soups and salty buttered bread. At night, I open the windows and listen to the sounds of Australia.

The other evening, James had worked late, and as he walked past my place, I heard him hum. It's this sad little song that reminds me of a lost doe out in the forest. I must admit, though, it has a beautiful, captivating melody.

I must know the name of this song, and when I feel up to it, I shall ask him.

~~~⚜~~~

For an entire month, Rose slept long and deep, hiding inside the windmill she used to play in as a young teenager. Anna would bring her breakfast in the morning, and she would eat in bed then go back to sleep. The afternoons and evenings weren't much different, and it worried Anna, seeing Rose in a depressed state of mind. She didn't know what to do.

"You should come to church on Sunday," Anna said one afternoon. Both women had their hair curled in pins as they hung the freshly washed clothes on the clothesline. The babies slept in their wicker bassinets next to them. "Everyone wants to meet you."

"I'm not ready to socialize yet, Kitten."

"No worries, love. Well let's do something fun today, aye? Wanna go into town for a soda?"

Rose lifted her face to the sun, letting its rays warm her skin. "It's been over a decade since I've seen the turquoise waters of the Southern Ocean. Let's go there instead and get some fresh sea air."

Anna agreed, and while James looked after the girls, the two cousins went for a walkabout to the shoreline. Halfway there, at the outskirts of the golden wheat field, Rose stopped to retrieve some black licorice from her bag, and that's when she thought she saw something move from within the stalks. Squinting from the glaring sun, she focused and waited, and sure enough, a strikingly thin young man, disheveled and rawboned, with curious, childlike eyes, slowly showed himself. Definitely not one of the stockmen or ringers. She stopped and gasped.

"What is it, love?" Anna asked.

"That strange man you mentioned earlier–he's following us."

Anna turned to look. "No, that's not him. That's Liam, the deaf boy. He's harmless."

"You mean little Liam?"

"Yes, but he's not so little anymore."

Rose stared back at him. Her mind was having a difficult time conceiving that the child in her memory was indeed the young man now leering at her. She wondered if he remembered her too, and if that's why he was following them. Slowly she lifted her hand and waved; he mimicked her and smiled.

"Liam likes to spy on everyone, watching the goings-on around here as if he's watching a moving picture show. He runs all over the bush barefoot; he won't wear shoes."

"Did his mental capacity ever improve?" Rose asked.

"Some, but he's still slow."

"He was such a sweet child. I remember he would follow us everywhere."

"Yes, we all played together back then. But now I don't even talk to Liam much anymore."

"Why?"

Anna shrugged. "I grew up, I guess; and he stayed the same. James spends time with him, though. They're good mates."

"How is the Herdsman family doing?"

"The sisters have all grown up and married off. A few winters ago, the father died of a long illness, and now it's just the mother and Liam. Their sheep station isn't what it was, but she still has some head."

Rose nodded.

"James goes over there sometimes, especially after Mr. Herdsman died. He used to play their piano for Liam and his mum before it broke, and now he goes more often to play his own." Anna smirked. "He's always doing silly things like that for people. He's a time waster, he is. If it wasn't for me, he'd be a bludger, spending his days playing for any stranger who'd listen, no doubt."

"I don't understand—Liam can't hear it."

"No, he can't. But he can feel the musical vibrations through the lid with his hands. I suppose it gives him some impression of what music sounds like. That's what James says."

As Rose pictured the scene in her mind, she turned to look at the deaf young man again, but he had already disappeared into the stalks from whence he came.

❧

Liam was not the only one they encountered that day. Returning home from checking her traps was Glenda Trufflepig, holding another slew of dead rabbits. "G'day, Anna!" she greeted, happier than usual due to her abundant catch. It took her a second to recognize the visitor. "Crikey, is that you, Rose?"

"Sure is," said Anna, beaming with joy. "My cousin came home."

Glenda smiled. "Welcome back to Straya, love. What brings you after all these years?"

"Her husband died," answered Anna.

The older lady frowned, thinking of her own heartache and misfortunes in life. From the expression on her face, it seemed as if they had occurred only yesterday. She shrugged and said, "Blokes, aye? More trouble than they're worth, and that's no lie." Though she had been single herself for many years, an older Aboriginal man lived with her. She swore he was only her helper, but rumors to the contrary abound.

"Rose has been sad lately," Anna disclosed. "I can barely get her out of her house."

"Anna, please," Rose said, finding her voice.

"It's all right, love. This life cuts you open, only to stitch you back up. In a month or so, you'll be grand."

"Thank you, Miss Trufflepig," Rose replied with a weary smile. "I appreciate your kind words."

Glenda nodded. "Come by the house sometime, aye?" She started walking away, continuing over her shoulder, "There's always rabbit stew on the stove, snake pie in the oven, and plenty of whiskey to wash it all down. Would love the company."

133

CHAPTER 12

C aught in an unhappy labyrinth for many years, culminating in the catastrophic event of her husband's suicide, Rose found herself settled in at Sugar Alexandria, defenestrated from the past and landing miraculously on her two feet. Like yarn crossing over to make a stitch, the days were now interlacing with each other, one in tandem with the next, in unfamiliar yet welcoming cycles for her: Anna calling out to the chickens in the morning to feed them, then collecting their eggs, milking the cows and goats, and kulning to the livestock to lure them home. James and the men busy working around the stockyard, the paddock, and the barn. The stockmen and ringers gathering around a bonfire at night, laughing and drinking their grog. She still rarely left the windmill, though, a crab inside her carapace, sipping at her new life instead of swallowing it whole. Living at the center of Sugar Alexandria, Rose was like the sun, and everyone else, including the animals, were the planets rotating around her as she stood still in her moment of solstice.

During this time, Anna relished treating her cousin like a sick doll, staying by her side when done with her diurnal chores, eager to help her convalesce. "I'm going to boil some more water before you get in," she said one afternoon.

"No no, Kitten, let me get in now," Rose insisted, walking over to her Victorian-style clawfoot tub. Anna had prepared a hot bath for her, steam rising from the water inviting her in. As the burgundy silk robe slid off

Rose's shoulders and onto the ground, exposing her naked, lithe form, Anna's neck did not turn. Rather, her eyes flickered a furtive glance, processing what she saw.

Rose was so pale, her skin like the petal of a white oleander, a stark contrast to her short, coal black hair. Her body too thin, yet possessing a winsome curve at the hip. Her right leg, underdeveloped from the mid-thigh down was her only blemish, and in that moment, Anna pitied her cousin. More than that, as always, she wished she could heal her defective limb.

Rose stepped into the tub, the warmth of the water permeating her skin. She closed her eyes, leaned her head back, and relaxed, her body becoming limp. Anna did not leave; instead, she sat beside her, submerging a sponge and gently cleansing her cousin's décolletage. Earlier, the two women had been conversing for hours about the life her cousin left behind, with Rose chain-smoking and drinking homemade blackberry wine as she spoke. The alcohol made her tender, melancholy, and she began to cry for no particular reason.

"What's wrong; why are you crying?" asked Anna.

"Just feeling sorry for myself," said Rose. "One day I'm living in a convent with nuns praying with me. For me. The next I'm here, back in Australia, like a lost and abandoned child, with my little cousin taking care of me."

"I don't mind," Anna said, dipping the sponge, squeezing the soapy water over Rose's skin. As her cousin lit another cigarette, exhaling a billow of smoke that surrounded them like a faint aurora mist, she probed a little deeper: "Can I ask you something personal?"

"Yes, Kitten. Anything."

"It's about Paul."

"You want to know how he did it."

Anna nodded ever so slightly, as if she hadn't nodded at all.

"He . . . He shot himself."

"I'm so sorry, Rose . . . And you found him?"

"Yes."

"Good God."

"When you see something like that, you can never unsee it."

"Unsee?"

"The image is engrained in your mind. You can't wash it off; you can't erase it. It's an indelible scar you carry forever." In a flash, Rose saw the whole scene de novo—a gunshot wound to Paul's head, blood gushing from his temple, a blank expression on his face and a smoking revolver in his hand.

Anna dipped the sponge into the soapy water again, dispensing its warmth over her cousin's skin. "I understand, love," she said, having her own flashbacks of when she had shot and killed the black wolf.

Rose navigated her thoughts from Paul's suicide to her stint at the nunnery. "After that I went to the convent."

"That was Aunt Irma's idea, wasn't it."

"Yes, I went at my mother's behest."

"What was that like?"

Rose recalled the small, cold cubicle they gave her as a living space at the motherhouse, with its tiny bed, icy floors, and flickering candles for light. The murmurs and prayers of the nuns that sounded like soft chants and disjointed whispers. The nights when she cried herself to sleep, feeling as if she were in purgatory, wondering if Paul had shot her too and she was just now realizing it. Though it was calm and quiet inside the nunnery, internally she was shrieking in terror. Screaming silent screams, wailing unuttered wails, moaning inaudible moans. Living in the convent, she felt as if she had one foot in the grave, caught between life and death. "The nuns are kind women," Rose finally said. "They truly want to help you, but it's so lonely there. So quiet. A stillness that goes right through you. At times I thought I had died and was placed there as a form of punishment."

"Punishment for what?"

"Who knows? I have always felt that way about my leg, too. Punished for something I've done."

"But you were born that way. It was a birth defect."

"Then punished for something my mother did. I don't know—something. Because why me? This curse has held me back my entire life. A disfigurement that changed everything, chaining me to a cane and branding me a gimp forever. With two normal legs, things would have been so much different. So much better."

Anna had no answers. "Well I don't mind your leg," she said, trying to comfort her cousin. "If you ask me, it's quite lovely. So delicate, like the limb of a fallow deer."

The corner of Rose's lip turned up a fraction.

"And I will tell you another thing, Lottie: I'm here to take care of you now. Heart and soul."

"At least someone wants to take care of me," Rose said, slowly dipping her head halfway into the water, leaving her face exposed before quickly coming back up, slicking back her hair and resting her neck on the rim of the tub. "Of all people, I'm glad it's you, Kitten."

Anna smiled. "Didn't Paul take care of you when you were married?"

"Financially, yes. Emotionally, no." In the beginning, Paul had been erstwhile charming, conferring on Rose a sense of love and security. In time, however, the façade waned, transmuting him into a Dr. Jekyll and Mr. Hyde—verbally abusive, emotionally distant, cold.

Anna thought of how James often repined about her being emotionally unavailable too—an ironic coincidence. "Why didn't you two have children?" she asked, dunking the sponge into the bathwater before caressing Rose's shoulder with it.

"After we were married, I found out he couldn't have them."

"Oh . . . And you didn't want to adopt?"

"He told me he didn't want children unless they were his own." She laid her arms along the rim of the tub, releasing a long exhalation. "I suppose some things aren't meant to be."

"You mean children?"

"Yes, with someone I love . . . Isn't that something, though? The last time I was here, I had my whole life ahead of me, getting ready to marry Paul. I already had names picked out for our children. And now here I am again, just as I was: Alone."

"You will meet a grouse bloke and start a family here, Rose. You'll find your happiness."

She only stared up at the skylight.

Anna followed her eyes. "That was James' idea, you know."

"The skylight?"

"Yes. He said it would be ace to see the moon and stars at night, lighting up the heavens." Anna dipped the sponge into the water and wiped her cousin's long, slender arms. Rose leaned forward so Anna could tend to her back, as well. When finished, she applied shampoo to Rose's crown, massaging the soap into her scalp, pouring warm water over her head to rinse away the suds.

"Thank you, Kitten," Rose said, leaning back against the tub again, closing her eyes.

Anna stared at her. There was such a demure quality about Rose. An ingenuous elegance. Something about her looked so right, as if Rose were posing in the bath while an artist painted her, strands of wet hair stuck to her forehead and neck, lips the color of a scarlet bruise, skin free of freckles and blemishes, like the inside of an ivory shell. Poetry personified.

"What is it?" Rose asked, flashing her eyes up at her. "You're so quiet."

"Oh, I was just looking at you. You're so pretty," Anna said, lowering her head. "And I'm . . ."

"You're adorable, is what you are. With your cherub face covered in freckles, those dimples of yours, and that cute gap between your teeth."

Anna paused. "I'm not a beauty like you, though."

Rose reached over and touched Anna's chin. "You *are* a beauty, Kitten. And you have always said such sweet things to me; I missed that. I missed you, Anna."

"I missed you too, Lottie," she said, smiling, filling with joy. She had missed Rose so much that it felt like another death in the family when Rose never returned. But now her beloved cousin was home again.

After a moment, Rose brought the conversation around to James. "You have spent so much time with me since I've arrived. Sometimes from morning till night, making meals, cleaning up, reading to me, even bathing me," she said. "Doesn't James miss his wife being there for him?"

"You don't feel well right now; you need me. Besides, he has a lifetime with me; why should he complain?" Anna answered, knowing that her husband did have an issue with it. In fact, he had already mentioned his annoyance more than once about her constant absence from the house.

"Yes, he does have a lifetime with you," Rose agreed, once more closing her eyes, sinking lower into the tub, enjoying the heat of the bath. "And a lifetime is a long time."

⁓ↄⲉ✺ⲇↄ⁓

After Rose finished her bath, Anna went back to the farmhouse to prepare dinner. Rose stepped out of the windmill, welcomed by the fresh air on her newly cleaned skin, allowing the late-afternoon sun to warm her face.

Like bees to nectar, a gaggle of geese waddled over to her, seeking food, attention, or both. Rose smiled at how well-behaved they were, petting their long necks and feathered lores. When she went back inside to retrieve some

138

bread for them, they followed her in single file, as if trained schoolchildren following their headmaster. She laughed as she shooed them back outside, tossing their treats in the yard.

The white sheets on the clothesline swayed gloriously in the wind, and Rose decided to take one down for herself to use that night while she slept. Walking over, she removed it from the line, surprised to find James standing on the other side. Once again, they stared at one another in an awkward, uncomfortable moment.

"I see you have your fishing gear," Rose said, forcing a smile. "Off to get us some dinner, are ya?"

James appeared stoic, giving no response, his aloofness stemming from his fervent attraction to her. He didn't like being alone with Rose. He felt as if she were examining him—his eyes, his thoughts, the way he stands—mentally scrutinizing his every move. He was used to Anna's detachment, looking at him but through him, her mind somewhere else, always fixated on some task or chore requiring attention at Sugar Alexandria. Yet when Rose looked upon him, her gaze demanded instant intimacy.

"Good luck out at sea," she offered again.

"Ta," James said, his tone and demeanor rather inimical. Turning away, he left in the direction of the shoreline.

Frustrated at his inhospitable behavior, Rose hit her cane on the ground, the alcohol from earlier, still in her veins, rallying her boldness. "Is it because of your piano? That wasn't my fault, you know. I had nothing to do with that exchange," she said, hitting the ground with her cane again, this time so hard the soil slightly vibrated under his feet.

He stopped for a second, standing there, his back to her. She thought he was going to say something. Argue, even. But instead he continued on his way.

That night, Anna had a frightening nightmare. She dreamed the Black Shuck was chasing her through the fields, its hot breath on her neck, its razor-sharp teeth about to puncture her skin.

"Anna, wake up," James said, gently shaking his wife.

She suddenly woke and started crying in his arms. "Something is out to get me! Oh, James, I just dreamed about my fate! The Black Shuck was here to get me!"

"It was only a nightmare, love. That's all it was," he said, kissing her sweat-laden brow. "Nothing is out to get you."

"Yes it is! Yes it is! Just like last time, I had to kill it, and now it's back again!"

"Anna, do not talk like that! You are never to do that again! Do you hear me?" The unmarked grave in the family burial plot entered his mind, robbing him of any more sleep.

⁓⌁⟡⌁⁓

Rose too had a nightmare. One she had never had before in her life. She dreamed Anna had died and was buried in the Polston family burial plot. Weeping above the grave, she placed flowers on the soil, and when the bouquet touched the ground, Anna's hands came up through the dirt and pulled her under.

Waking up screaming, Rose found herself in the quiet bedroom loft of the windmill, her cat Matilda by her side and the whir of the Australian gale spinning the sail in the wind.

⁓⌁⟡⌁⁓

Anna went into town to meet Drusilla and Lilith Esmeralda the following day for some shopping and lunch. The sisters had invited both her and Rose when Anna last attended church, but Rose was not up to going out in public yet, so Anna went by herself, leaving James to watch the babies.

Rose was looking forward to the time alone, too. Though she adored Anna, there were moments when she felt smothered by her overly attentive cousin, as if the life were slowly being squeezed out of her. She felt guilty for thinking that, especially since she was beholden to Anna who had provided this beautiful place to recuperate, but it was a fact. Anna didn't just

140

love–she devoured.

The weather was glorious that day–crisp, fresh air and clear, blue skies–and it galvanized Rose into action. She wanted to clean, organize, and rearrange things inside her windmill, adding her own personal touch to her new abode. Letting Matilda out to play with the other farm moggies in the barn, she went to work, and by late afternoon she was done.

Proud of her accomplishments, she needed some water to freshen up, so she made her way to the water pump in the stockyard to fill her bucket. The cool air kissed her skin as the faltering light stretched across the valley, and she took a deep breath and exhaled, admiring the pulchritudinous scenery–a fuchsia sunset bleeding through a cobalt blue sky covering the reddish yellow landscape. No one was around, Anna hadn't yet returned, and she had Sugar Alexandria all to herself.

It felt good.

Peaceful.

Splashing water on her face, she dried it with a cloth and sat down on the rock table near the pump, scanning the horizon of the wondrous Outback. It wasn't just what she saw but what she heard . . . the bombinating insects, the rummaging animals, the rustling wind–all of it a divinely synchronized orchestra. So deep in thought at what she was seeing and hearing, she didn't notice James approaching from behind. When he gently touched her shoulder, she wasn't startled, either. On the contrary, she felt oddly calm by his presence.

"I kept waiting to see if you were going to say something," he said, "but I guess it'll have to be me." He removed his Akubra hat, his searing blue eyes staring intently at her. "Do you remember me?"

Rose blushed. "Yes, I do. But I wasn't sure if you remembered that encounter."

"How could I forget? It was a special night."

They stared at each other, unable to look away. Memories from the past, rushed to the fore. Something powerful still lingered, the chemistry they shared all those years ago still alive.

"You told me your name was Charlotte," he said. "Why did you only give me your middle name?"

"James, I was already engaged at the time," Rose answered, a little abashed at her quondam social artifice, "and I didn't see the point in giving my full name. I thought it would complicate things."

"And yet you took my promise ring."

"We were just being silly." Suddenly she felt panicky. Cornered. Unsure of the conversation and guilty for having it. "I was going to return it, but the fire caused so much commotion that we got separated. Do you want it back now?"

He shook his head. "Anna would wonder why I have it. Just keep it." The tension between them kept building. "After the fire, you vanished; I couldn't find you. Where did you go?"

"My leg was hurting. I asked my uncle to take me back to Sugar Alexandria."

"After the way I kissed you? Seeing how much I fancied you?" He lowered his gaze from her eyes to her mouth, then back to her eyes again. "You should have stayed."

Rose wished she had. "It doesn't matter much now, anyway, does it," she said, trying to dispel the fervid sentience between them. "You married my cousin and have two children together. I'm just a widow looking to start over."

"You're right," he replied, brio absent from his voice.

A quiet moment passed between them, and James subconsciously began to hum again—the same tune that caught her attention before. "What is that song you're humming?" she asked, intrigued by the melody.

"Oh . . . Nothing, really."

"It's such a sad, yet pretty sound." Looking over at the trees in the distance, she watched as they swayed gracefully in the wind.

He followed her eyes. "See how the tops of those trees don't touch? If you were standing underneath them, you'd see a canopy of channel-like gaps. It's a natural phenomenon called crown shyness."

"They're actually shy?"

James smiled. "No, it's just a term used to describe the occurrence. No one knows for sure if the trees are trying to reduce the spread of harmful insects, protect their branches from collision damage with adjacent trees when it's windy, or maximize photosynthesis."

Rose was impressed. "Not something I thought a station owner would know."

"I've done a lot of reading in my spare time. Over the years, I've accumulated a fair number of books, too. It's like a small library in my den. You're welcome to peruse through them any time you like."

"Thank you," said Rose. "I'm surprised with your sudden hospitality, though."

"Why's that?"

"Because ever since I arrived, it seems as if you don't want me here." Notwithstanding that magical night from long ago, her intuition had told her she wasn't welcome.

"What makes you think I don't want you here?"

"I can tell."

"You're misreading it. I just wasn't expecting to ever see you again, that's all. As far as I'm concerned, you can stay as long as you like. Besides, why else would I have converted that windmill into a maisonette for you?"

She softly smiled.

James tried to lighten the mood. "The wooden double doors on the mill came from an old pirate shipwreck," he said, motioning over to them. "I thought they were a bonzer touch, especially since the farmhouse has a lot of Viking themes."

Rose agreed. "Yes, they look grand. They're from that wreck down by the shoreline, right? Anna and I used to play in that when I'd visit her in the summers. In the old cabin nearby too."

"I go there myself, now and again."

"Why?"

"To compose music. I find it a place of solace where I can think creatively."

"I remember you playing the piano when we first met at the wedding. You were brilliant."

He released that arresting grin that made her feel faint. "Ta."

As they stood there in the gentle breeze, their minds racing, both knew that if circumstances were different, they'd so easily pick up where they had left off. But of course, they couldn't. A wedge laid between them as far and wide as the ocean itself. And that large body of water was Anna.

"Do you think we should tell Anna we had met before?" Rose asked.

"No," was all he said.

Another gust of wind hit them, harder than the last, making Rose's hair dance around her face and shoulders. James watched in pure fascination.

"Anna will be home soon," Rose said. "I better head back."

As she went to pick up her water bucket, James grabbed it from her, their arms briefly touching in the process, and began walking toward the center windmill.

"It's all right; I can do that myself," she said, feeling awkward.

James didn't listen. Pushing her front door open with his shoulder, he walked in and placed the bucket on the kitchen counter.

The tension in the room was palpable. Or was it chemistry again? James' Celtic tattoo peeked from underneath his shirt, half unbuttoned to cool down from the rigorous day's work, and Rose tried to avert her eyes but failed. Catching sight of the intricate markings etched across his skin summoned a kaleidoscope of butterflies in the lower half of her stomach. Slowly he looked her up and down, and she wondered what he saw. He had called her beautiful once; did he still feel the same? Without saying another word, he left.

Rose poured some fresh water into a Victorian bowl that once belonged to her Danish grandmother, triggering a memory of her and Anna washing their faces in it as little girls. Their grandmother, a petite yet strong woman with bright blue eyes and golden silver hair, always had a kind word for them. She had the same dimples and gap between her teeth as Anna, too, and that's what Rose remembered most.

Damping a cloth, she cleaned her face and neck again, along with her arms and bosom, thinking about when James' skin had touched hers when he grabbed the bucket from her. An electricity ran through her when it happened. She thought about his lazy grin, too, how it fascinated her as much as it frustrated, and she thought of his ornate Celtic tattoo, fighting to be seen from underneath his thin cotton shirt. She wondered what it looked like when he was bare-chested, and what it would feel like to run her fingers over it. "Oh, dear," she said to herself. "What have I gotten myself into?"

CHAPTER 13

Rose

I'm quite perplexed about my cousin's husband James. The messages he gives me are mixed, inconsistent, and confusing. Often I catch him staring at me, only to quickly look away. Other times he's sarcastic with me, or avoids me altogether. And then occasionally he's warm and friendly, like the other day when he said I could peruse through his books.

I can sense he still has feelings for me, yet why does he seem to dislike me so?

What have I done for him to resent me?

It's making me insecure, wondering if I should leave, because the longer I stay the more difficult it will become.

Anna's attachment to me, and the feelings I have for James, will only form deep roots and grow.

With Anna gone shopping in town, Rose becomes restless and wants out. Out of the windmill, out of her problems, out of her head . . . Anywhere but in. Her destination makes no difference.

She goes for a stroll without her cane, reasoning it will only be a short saunter, but the farther she goes the farther she wants to go. Past the farmhouse, past the crops, past the animals that pay her no mind, their large eyes disinterested, heavy bellies full. She feels as if she could meander forever, and her mind barrels forward while her body tries to keep up.

Dingoes cavort on the horizon, quokkas rummage in the bushes, and kangaroos stand perfectly still like trees, only to hop off when she gets too close. So many of them, large and small, some with babies poking their tiny heads out from the safety of their mother's pouch, others in pairs, leisurely chewing and eating grass. She identifies Poka among them—the unique spots on her fur give her away—and the semi-tame marsupial who frequents the station looking for food recognizes her too, staring back a moment, trying to decide if she should visit the visitor before hopping off in the other direction.

Continuing until she sees Neptune's treasure in the distance, Rose wants to dip her feet in the surf, now regretting not having her walking stick. It's only a little farther, she thinks, and then I can rest my leg. Though the familiar burning in her thigh has begun, she ignores it, pressing on to the water's edge. The day is bright and beautiful; she wants to relish in it, selfishly claim it, refusing to turn around in defeat. Taking off her shoes, she lies down on the sand, the warmth of the sun suffusing her skin, the rhythm of the waves barely lapping at her toes, and drifts into a hypnagogic state. As if at the center of the universe, her body humming to its ineffable tune, a sense of peace envelops her like a cocoon. The squawks of seabirds, the rolling waves, the faint voices of fishermen on their boats come in and out of her subconscious, caught between reality and a dream.

An hour later, Rose wakes to the sights and sounds around her, somewhat befuddled by the somniferous state she had entered, as if another Rip Van Winkle, asleep for twenty years. As she stands to her feet, her underdeveloped leg begins to spasm. Having no choice but to persevere, she begins the long trek home, her thigh on fire, her limp severe, knowing she will not make it back any time soon . . .

~୦ଓଚ୍ଚ~

The sun was starting to set, a cool wind channeling through the valley. Dusk was coming, and with it, all the wild animals that hunted in the Outback at night. Rose had not yet returned to Sugar Alexandria; every time she attempted to walk, she succumbed to the pain in her impaired limb and had to stop, finding a tree to sit against and rest. Waiting for the throbbing to subside, she cursed at how foolish she had been, going for a long jaunt to the shoreline without her walking stick. She knew better, too, but her burning desire to get out of the windmill earlier deceived her, replacing common sense with adamantine, temerity, and denial.

While making another attempt to stand and resume her trek, Rose heard something that resonated with her fears: A spine-chilling squealing. Unnerved, she looked around, and that's when she saw them . . .

Wild boars!

Dozens of them!

The sounder of swine was heading straight for her, and in a panic Rose tried to run, but the small muscle in her underdeveloped leg gave out and she fell to the ground. Helpless in the open field, she watched in horror as they drew near, galloping at full force. They'll rip me to pieces, she thought, adrenaline surging through her body! James and Anna will find me torn apart, bloodied and half eaten! God help me!

In her moment of sheer terror, Rose somehow heard a whistling, faint yet audible. Seconds later she saw James in the distance, walking through the fields. "James!" she screamed out.

He stopped and scoured the area, looking for the source of the scream.

"Over here! Help me!" she yelled, frantically waving her arms in the air.

James saw her on the ground, then saw the feral pigs barreling toward her, now only yards away. He ran as fast as he could, withdrawing his rifle and shooting into the sounder. The wild boars veered off and fled, sensing they were no longer the hunters but the hunted.

Upon reaching her, James knelt down to calm her. "It's all right, Rose," he said. "They're gone."

She threw her arms around his neck, burying her face in his chest. "I thought I was going to die," she sobbed. "I thought they were going to rip me apart and eat me." Her whole body shook.

"It's all right now," he repeated. "They know what a gun is and they won't be back."

She stopped crying and let him go.

"What happened?" asked James "Why are you out here by yourself, lying on the ground?"

"I became too confident with my leg," she said, still trembling. "I foolishly went for a long walk to the shoreline without my cane, and the muscle started to cramp badly. Now I can hardly walk." She grimaced as she rubbed her thigh, letting out a whimper from the painful muscle spasms still rippling through her flesh.

Without hesitation, James reached out and grabbed her exposed leg, massaging the muscle with greater intensity.

"Please stop," she said, discomfited.

He didn't. Instead, he kneaded more vigorously to the point where he completely took over. Finally the pain began to subside, and she leaned back, allowing him to continue massaging her entire limb. "Is this helping?" he asked, noticing the long, vertical scar–evidence of the surgery she had had as a young child.

"Yes," she said softly. For some unknown reason, she wanted to laugh, or rather cry, as new emotions swelled inside her. No man had ever touched her flawed leg in such a compassionate, tender way before. Not even her late husband, who even refused to be intimate with her unless it was covered by the sheet, insulting her, hurting her, making her feel ashamed and ugly as a result. Yet at that moment, as James expertly manipulated her limb, she felt exhilarated. Aglow.

As if she had no flaw at all.

"Don't leave the station without your cane ever again," he said, still kneading her small muscle fibers. "You got lucky this time."

"They would have killed me, right?" she asked, still shaken by it all.

"With you on the ground like that, vulnerable and alone–yes. Usually they don't attack unless they feel cornered or threatened, but when they're hungry enough, they can be unpredictable and predatory," he said, holding her gaze.

In the evening light his eyes were bluer than Rose realized. A fathomless sapphire blue. Stonelike in their appearance–like cracked glass. Yet she also noticed an imperfection. An ocular abnormality. One of his pupils took the form of a teardrop, and was a shade lighter than the other. His misshapen pupil bestowed his face with a touch of sadness, meekness–a detail not lost on Rose–imparting the most unique expression, as if a million feelings were being spoken through his eyes.

"It was only supposed to be a short walk," she said, now embarrassed, "and I wanted to believe I didn't need my cane as much as I do. Pride got the better of me."

"Just remember there are all sorts of wild animals out here," replied James. "You get stranded like this all alone, pride could take you to an early grave."

She only watched as he adroitly continued to work her leg up and down, his long fingers pressing into her epithelial tissue as if a sculptor molding clay. When his hands moved all the way to her mid-thigh, her insides warmed. Then he stopped and looked up at her. "Better?"

"Yes," she answered. "I'm ready to go home now."

He helped her to her feet, and slowly they walked back in silence, Rose leaning on him, James holding her up, stabilizing her gait. Side by side she could smell his scent—a mixture of the sea and Anna's spicy homemade soap. He could smell the sweet black licorice on her breath.

At the front door of the windmill, James released his supporting hold on her. "Like I said, don't go for a long walkabout without your cane again, aye?" His vivid, aberrant blue eyes rested on her face a moment, staring longer than he should have. Longer than he would have if his wife were there. "And I wouldn't mention anything to Anna, either. She'll just get upset and become even more protective of you."

"I won't. And thank you for your help, James. Thank God you were coming home when you did; you saved my life."

"Of course—you're my wife's cousin." Tipping his hat, he left her standing there.

"Right," Rose said . . . And that's all I am, she silently continued. That's all I will ever be to James Shahan: Anna's widowed cousin.

As it should be.

~ecfofesr~

James' peculiar infatuation with Rose's leg begins . . .

Pale. Thin. Underdeveloped, yet still so lovely.

The images in his brain perplex him because she is a woman he somewhat resents, yet is fascinated by.

He thinks of the length of her limb, and the smoothness of her skin as he ran his fingers along its slender form.

Why am I seeing these images in my head, he wonders, feeling slightly guilty over it?

It dawns on him why he is so perturbed by the encounter: His wife's cousin had reacted to his touch. He could tell. A tacit knowing. Where Anna was emotionally unavailable, Rose was not. No deficiency, no holding back, responding with her eyes, cheeks flushing, tiny goose bumps spreading over her flesh. Not only had she been relieved by his touch but also stimulated by it. How long has it been since a woman responded to my touch, he questions?

Over ten years.

In the beginning, he had tried every possible way to connect with his new wife. To bond with her, seek and nurture intimacy, develop a close and loving union. Yet to no avail. Anna was a warm body to hold, but internally she was hollow, and it soon became apparent that hugging and kissing were a chore, and sex only an itch his wife would help him scratch.

Again he thinks of the physical reaction Rose had to his touch, and he closes his eyes, wanting so badly to go inside that feeling once more . . . and stay there.

Early the next morning, James rides Ireland to a picturesque cove in Indigo Bay, carved out over the millenniums by the constant erosion of the sea. A small island floats close to the mainland, and there an abandoned cabin still stakes its claim. Built by a fisherman of years gone by from the scrap wood of a pirate shipwreck, its onetime owner had named it the Barracuda Hut, engraving the moniker above the door. Now it serves as James' treasured place of diversion.

Taking his boat to the vacant bothy, with pencil on paper James begins to draw what he sees in his mind, sketching Rose from different angles and dimensions, drawing for hours until his fingers become sore and covered in lead. The images soon accumulate—all of Rose and her tarnished wing. Some pictures he draws her leg as it should have been; others as it is. Those are his favorite, and he sits back staring at them, marveling at what he has created. The drawings of her are perfectly imperfect, and he adores them but has no conception why.

James

I remember intimacy with a woman before I met Anna.
The closeness, the reciprocated affection.
I have since grown to live without it.
But Rose has reminded me of how it could be . . .

Rose hadn't seen Cassandra Fancy's exquisite garden in over a decade, and Anna was thrilled to be taking her cousin to visit it. Matilda, now more confident in her new habitat, trailed behind her owner, and Lovely Dawn tried to sneak behind them too until Anna shooed the potbellied pig back home.

The enchanted, archaic grounds on the Fancy estate were a good walking distance from the neo-Gothic castle with towering circular stone wall and massive wrought iron gates. Two giant male angels with swords and spears guarded the entrance to the domestic citadel, and gargoyle creatures stared menacingly from its rooftops. Tall spires and stained glass windows, pointed arches and vaulted ceilings, all added to the authenticity of the medieval home.

The castle itself was once owned by an exiled British duke who had been banished to Australia after committing crimes against country and king. The duke's wife was so distraught at their disgrace and excommunication that he had the garden made for her as a gift, endeavoring to provide a place of solace for his beloved. When Casper Cotton bought the old castle after his mine struck gold, he renovated it for his own bride Cassandra, and expanded the garden to include life-sized statues of lions and dragons, knights and maidens, cherubs and seraphs, fountains and ponds.

Though the garden had been neglected over the last several years, luxurious cherry trees and cherry blossoms still grew alongside the stone statues, seasonally blooming frothy masses of pink and white flowers. A low-hanging swing attached to a thick branch of a lonely beech tree oscillated in the breeze, and an eighteenth-century Georgian carriage sat beside it in the middle, rusty and withering away in the Australian sun. Vines and shrubs grew around its wheels and frame, but the apparent decay only added to its anachronistic charm.

Anna sat on the swing as Rose walked about with her cane, staring at the overgrown, unkept garden that looked so different from when she was a teenager.

"What do you think, Lottie?" asked Anna.

Rose put her hand on her hip, scanning the garden one last time. "It needs a bit of work to restore it to its former beauty, that's for sure."

"You think we can use our green fingers to get it back to how it was?"

Rose laughed. "It's green thumb, Anna. Not green finger."

She rolled her eyes. "Same difference."

"Well, with a little love and some good old-fashioned hard work, I'm sure we can do it."

"And a little magic!" said Anna, scrunching her nose and smiling.
"Yes, Kitten. A little of that too."

Rose

It's going to feel amazing to stick my hands into the soft soil, dirty my fingernails, and immerse myself into nurturing Cassandra Fancy's garden. In London, I had a marvelous greenhouse that was absolutely stunning, with an arched ceiling, Art Nouveau stained glass, a fountain in the middle, and flowers and plants of all kinds. It was there I would escape from my husband and go into my own private world.

Now I'll be doing the same thing in a much larger garden. A much more impressive, grandiose, and palatial one, despite its current state. Anna and I will spend hours here, our faces stained with dirt, our hands covered in mud, digging, planting, pruning, dreaming of what it will soon become.

The funny thing is, the more the garden comes to life and thrives, I know the more I too will heal.

CHAPTER 14

On Sunday morning, Rose was finally ready to venture out in public, and they all attended church. Anna made sure they sat right up front, a permagrin on her face, knowing all eyes were on them. The more the congregation whispered and stared, the more she bubbled inside.

James surreptitiously observed his wife's cousin that day. Though she was using her walking stick, she still carried herself with an elusive grace, holding her chin up high. She didn't look for her reflection, either, nor shy from the eyes of others, insouciant about their extended stares. Perhaps the years of using a cane had left an unintentional legacy for her, developing a strong self-possession.

Rose wasn't vivacious, open, and sweet like Anna, James thought. On the contrary, she was rather solemn, introspective, and secretive, as if part of a shadowy cabal, and yet kind in a way that was for the good of all and not just those whom she favored. If Anna was the bumblebee, her cousin was the spider. Her quiet elegance and wickedly beautiful smile gave her an air of intrigue, never really letting you know what she's thinking, or what's lurking behind those haunting, large green eyes.

Despite his cogitations and being acrid about his wife's adoration of Rose, James had not forgotten how he himself had felt when he first laid eyes on her at that wedding over a decade ago, besotted by her unique and alluring image. How different things could have turned out if he had been more aggressive then. If he had kept looking for her. Searching. Asking others who she was. Sitting next to her in the pew, mulling this over while Father Lothbrok delivered his sermon, the familiar scent of Rose's perfume—Chypre de Coty—faintly touched his senses as a feather touches the ground.

After the service, the sticky beaks flocked over, agog about the new visitor, each one introducing themselves and welcoming Rose to Esperance.

"A pommy; how lovely," said Fiona Blacksmith. "We don't get many visitors here in Esperance, let alone an English lass."

"Rose used to visit me every summer when she was a teenager," Anna proudly stated. "That was before you and your husband moved here from Brisbane."

"Best decision we ever made, too," Fiona replied. "We love our church, and of course, the fishing here is the finest in all of Straya."

Poppy Buttersmith, standing like a tall ostrich among the women, couldn't help herself and boldly said, "I heard you're a widow now."

Everyone watched as Rose slowly nodded.

"How did he die?"

Rose saw the image of her husband's cold, lifeless body on the floor, and thought of the ensuing nights where she would stare at his empty favorite chair, or his side of their matrimonial bed, or his clothes meticulously organized in his closet. "He took his own life," was all she said.

The older woman's face transformed into a mask of geniality. "Sorry, love."

As the circle of women went atypically quiet, Rose looked over at the tiny detailed designs artistically painted on the tiles lining the church walls. Though the building itself showed signs of its age, the vivid colors in the overlays did not. She remembered as a girl seeing one of them on the floor and picking it up to keep as a memento of her carefree summers there, and in that moment she spotted the empty square on the wall where it had once lived. Now it was lost forever . . . Like her.

"Let me look at you, dear," said Beth Clydesdale, elbowing her way through the crowd. Putting on her spectacles, she examined Rose closely. "Green eyes with ebony hair; how precious. If any of my sons were still single, I would do some matchmaking, but I've already found them wives."

"Yeah, and now they're miserable," Clarion Firestone snickered. Motioning at Rose's cane, she asked, "Did you break your leg, love?"

"No, it's a birth defect," Anna answered on her cousin's behalf. "She has little muscle in her right leg, making it very weak."

Rose blushed as the small gathering focused on her leg, until Hazel Smuckers said, "I had an aunt born with six toes once."

"Saint of a woman," added Beth.

"Yes, these things happen sometimes," said Hazel with a wink.

"But what's different can also be advantageous," Beth comforted. "It can make you stronger than others—on the inside, anyway." She gave Rose a motherly pat on the back.

Poppy raised her nose. "Definitely nothing to whinge about, I'd say." She herself would use a cane from time to time, having been thrown off her husband's prized Arabian stallion a few years back, tearing the ligaments in her knee.

"My name is Mazie Winters," said a short, plump woman. "I'm a widow too. We'll have to have lunch sometime and get to know each other."

Anna inwardly frowned. If anyone was going to have lunch in town with her cousin, it would be her, not one of these sticky beaks.

"How long are you staying, dear?" asked Wednesday Motherland. "Long enough to meet a grouse bloke, perhaps? Wouldn't that be a beauty, aye?"

"Wednesday, she just lost her husband," Anna chided. "She needs time to heal."

"Oh, yes, yes. In due time, in due time." Wednesday continued, "I knew Elsa—Anna's mum. Of course, I was only a teenager back then, but I remember her well. You resemble her."

"But the eyes are different," said Gretchen Holland, stealthily appearing, almost unnoticed. Her husband had been deathly ill for years, they'd lost everything they owned, and the stress of it all had taken a heavy toll on her mental health.

"How so?" Fiona asked.

"Elsa's eyes were happy and joyous," Gretchen said, coming right up to Rose. "And hers have a chill behind them. A coldness that brings misery."

All the women went quiet again.

"What are you hiding behind those emerald eyes, love?"

Rose forced a smile, painfully calm and polite, as always. "Gretchen, it's so nice to see you again. How have you been?"

"And she's skillfully charming, too," Gretchen answered. "Charming people are dazzling, aren't they? They also scare the bloody hell out of me. What exactly are they after?"

"That's enough!" said Anna, pushing the other women aside to come to her cousin's defense. "What on earth has gotten into you!"

Gretchen scoffed, gripping her purse with two hands, holding it close to her chest. During the sermon, she had sat at the back of the church and witnessed James admiring Rose, with Rose stealing glances at him as well. "I have found in life that the whole world is a hungry stomach with teeth," she said, looking at Anna, then Rose, then over at James who was socializing with the men. "One person is the teeth, the other the meat, and that is how it is." She started cackling hard, but it quickly turned into a cry. Father Lothbrok escorted her to her car as she sobbed to the priest.

⁓ᴄᴇᴘᴉᴄᴇ⁓

The whole world is a hungry stomach with teeth.

⁓ᴄᴇᴘᴉᴄᴇ⁓

"We're lucky James came with us today," Anna said, grinning. They were now in the Ford Model T, driving home.

"Why's that?" asked Rose, sitting in the back seat with the twins.

"He doesn't approve of how they segregate people. He thinks all races should attend one church, and because they separate the dark-skinned from the light, he doesn't like attending."

"Well it's true," said James, lighting a cigarette, blowing the smoke out the car window. "People are just people, all made by one God."

"For now it is what it is, and it's proper to attend church," Anna said, unpinning her cloche hat. "Anyway, how did you like the service this morning, Rose?"

"It was nice," she said, staring down at her gloved hands. "But the attention afterward was a bit overwhelming."

Anna giggled. "The worst was Gretchen Holland. Lord, she's lost her ever-lovin' mind."

"What was that all about?"

"Her husband is sick, and the bank foreclosed on their home. They had to move in with her mum, so she's a bit out of sorts right now."

"You could hear her cackling through the whole bloody church," James said.

"I know. And she said something rather strange, too—that the world is a hungry stomach with teeth. One person is the teeth, and the other the meat."

"Maybe it's true."

"You think the world is a stomach with teeth?" Anna asked.

"It can be," said James, his eyes flashing from the road to his wife.

"What about Rose's eyes? Gretchen said they have a chill behind them. A coldness that brings misery." Anna sneered. "You believe that too?"

James met Rose's eyes in the rearview mirror. "A bit icy, they are. That's no lie," he said, teasing her.

"I was thinking the same of yours," Rose fired back.

"Stop, you two," Anna butted in, letting out a laugh. Oh how she loved them so in that wonderful, light-hearted moment. How exciting the future was in front of her. "There will be no quarreling between the two people I adore the most in the whole wide world."

They drove for a while in silence, James with one arm hanging out the window, Anna happily musing over the attention her cousin had received in church, and Rose staring at the back of their heads. Two flaxen domes. She thought James' was rather nicely shaped. The kind of bonce a woman would like to cradle between her breasts while making love, his hair a silky, buttery blond, his neck thick and reddened by the sun. Anna's cranium was tiny by comparison, small even for a petite woman, her golden locks done up in Danish braids, her thin neck and narrow shoulders resembling the back of a child's wooden chair. How did you lasso that handsome soldier, she wondered, glancing between their two crowns? It wasn't that she thought Anna deserved someone less than James; it was just that they seemed so emotionally and intellectually different. Polar opposites.

Focusing on her cousin's husband, Rose began to fantasize things she ought not. Things that were wrong and a sin. She wondered what it would be like to be intimate with James, her lips kissing his, her legs wrapped around his bare buttocks, her olfactory receptors intoxicated by his 4711 Eau de Cologne, their bodies becoming one. Moving her cane aside, she slowly inched forward to where she could pick up his scent and study his profile, and the romanticism intensified, her body responding, tingling at her center.

Anna swiveled and said, "I hope Gretchen didn't scare you off from coming back to church with me," catching her cousin staring hard at her husband.

"Oh, I . . . I . . . ," Rose stuttered, turning beet red, pulling herself from her chimeric fantasy. "No, she didn't."

"And don't worry about the sticky beaks asking so many questions. They're just curious about you."

"You mean nosy," James corrected, slowing the car down to let a family of quokkas cross the road. "Hope we don't have to go through that every time we come into town."

"They're like a bunch of hens, they are," Anna laughed.

"More like vultures—staring, whispering, firing off one question after another." The animals finished crossing, and James picked up speed.

"Let them stare and whisper and ask what they want. It's good for them to have a bit of excitement in their boring lives once in a while."

Rose gazed out the car window, the Australian scenery passing by in a consistent rhythm of rolling red, yellow, and green earth, chaperoned by flashes of massive Weeping Peppermint trees. Again she thought of Gretchen Holland's words: "The whole world is a hungry stomach with teeth." Even as she stared at the beautiful countryside, the stinging sentiment she could not shake from her mind. What did Gretchen see that made her say such a thing?

"Just let me know if they do bother you, Lottie, and I'll take care of it," Anna said, her happy smile exposing the gap between her teeth. "After a while, they'll get used to you and pay you no mind."

"Anna, you make it seem as if she's going to be at the station forever," James caught himself saying out loud. He knew the longer Rose stayed, the more distant his wife would become toward him. "I . . . I just mean . . . eventually she'll find a home of her own. You do want a home of your own, aye Rose?"

Rose met his stare in the rearview mirror again. "Isn't that what everyone wants?" she asked, never breaking eye contact with him. "A family and a home of their own?"

～⁓❦⁓～

After the commotion Rose engendered in church, Anna had another wonderful idea. She wanted to look more like her cousin, so she requested

Rose cut her long, Danish-styled braids into a stylish bob like her own, dying it from blonde to brown as well. When it was done, she gazed in amazement at her reinvented self in the mirror, smiling ear to ear as she touched the tips of her new, chestnut-colored tresses. The style she had worn like a uniform since childhood had been shorn, now replaced with a modish cut that barely touched past her chin.

"Please tell me you love it," Rose said.

Anna had tears in her eyes. "Of course I love it, Lottie! It's grand! Let's go to Cassandra's garden to celebrate!"

Donning their green velvet cloaks, the two cousins walked arm in arm to the enchanted botanical place and sat down on the bench.

"Can you imagine the duke and his bride here, lounging about, enjoying the day like we are now?" Rose asked, looking around at the greenery. "I can still feel their presence."

Anna harkened back to the time when they were young, when together with little Liam, they would come here to play, investigating every inch of the inimitable grounds. The garden wasn't just a cluster of unique and alluring flora but an enchanting realm of mystery and whimsical magic where the statues came to life, elves and fairies lived in the trees, and they themselves were the queens. "Look, Anna; look, Liam," Rose would say. "Don't you see it? Right over there . . ." She would point to an area where the mushrooms sprouted from the ground, and add, "That's a pixie ring where the fairies dance while the elves sit on the mushrooms and watch. And over there," pointing at Casper and Cassandra's stone castle, "that is where the great wizard lives. He's a dragon charmer, and his pet dragon with diamond eyes lives in the mountain near the ocean. The wizard uses a giant conch horn to summon the beast and rides him all over the world."

Smiling coyly, Anna turned to Rose and said, "The presence you feel is the elves and fairies, love. Or maybe even the dragon charmer. Remember?"

Rose smiled. "Yes, Kitten, I remember. We had our own private fantasy world in here, didn't we. Those were wonderful times."

"Too right, and we're gonna bring them back, Lottie. We're going to reawaken that fantasy world." She grabbed Rose's hand. "All we have to do is believe."

The Voices

Anna lies awake in bed that night, thinking of the glorious day she had with her beloved cousin. She wants to tell her mother and sister all about it, so when James is fast asleep, she quietly gets up and goes to her secret shrine.

With her goose-feathered crown on her head and wings on her back, Anna begins her ritual, kneeling at the base of the soul tree, a curious moon watching from the heavens above. She reaches out, touching the bark, and waits.

"We missed you," the voices slowly drift into her consciousness.

"Oh, Mummy and Blessing, there you are!"

"I like your new hairdo, Turtle Dove," Elsa says.

"Ta, Mummy. Isn't it lovely? Rose did it for me today, and then we went to Cassandra's garden. We're going to use our green fingers to bring it back to what it was. I'm so happy, I never want her to leave!"

"She has to eventually, dear. No man wants to share his wife's love, not even with another sheila."

"It's true, Anna," says Blessing. "James is jealous of the attention you give her."

"Far too much attention," her mother agrees. "James is your bloke, your better half. The man whose children you bore."

"But Rose is my best cobber," Anna replies to the voices in her mind. "She's the only one who can help me when I'm sad, pulling me from the heartache, making me whole again when I miss you both."

"If you must have your way, we'll tell you a secret," the voices say in unison. "A way to keep her here for eternity."

Anna leans into the soul tree and smiles, listening fastidiously.

⁓ ❦ ⁓

For weeks on end, Anna and Rose visited Cassandra Fancy's garden and worked long hours to restore it to its former glory. Casper Cotton had agreed to the project, and the women used their horticultural skills and love for the lush garth to cultivate a collage of different flora that would soon bloom.

The men helped too. James refurbished the eighteenth-century Georgian carriage and fixed its wheels, painting them a deep red. Casper Cotton repaired the large fountain and restored the statues of Venus de Milo, David, Discobolus, and several winged angels, sealing the cracks and polishing the stone. And Liam helped where he could, doing odd jobs and removing the refuse. To him it was all a wonderful game, one in which the end result would be his own paradisiac playground.

With weeds pulled out, fresh grass laid down, seeds and bulbs planted, the favorable Australian climate took over and did the rest. Soon decadent, vibrant shades and hues from pink kangaroo paws, royal bluebells, yellow flame grevilleas, raspberry waratahs, fuchsia correas, lavender Cooktown orchids, scarlet spider flowers, and many others, all blossomed with stunning beauty, shouting out their praises to God. So beautiful was the colorful verdure that even Cassandra would sometimes muster the courage to overcome her agoraphobic angst, leaving the safety of her home to roam the garden in the early morn or late eve.

"Oh, Anna, it's so lovely here now," Rose said one afternoon, basking in the garden glory. She brought her nose close to a variety of flowers to smell their transcendent bouquets.

"Like that story in *The Secret Garden*, aye?" said Anna, smiling widely. "A magical place."

The two cousins laid down on the soft grass holding hands, surrounded by the imposing stone statues, resplendent flowers, and manicured shrubs. Staring up at the cerulean sky above, cottony clouds leisurely floating by, a soft breeze tussling their hair and ruffling the hems of their dresses, it seemed as if they had found Pan's Labyrinth.

"We did this, Kitten," said Rose. "Together we made all this happen. I'm so happy I left London and came here."

Anna's heart melted hearing those words. "Me too, Lottie. No one is ever going to separate us again," she said, trying hard to ignore the hallucination in her peripheral vision. "Not ever."

"Not ever," echoed Rose.

Unbeknownst to her, Genevieve stood behind one of the cherry trees, watching, listening, and smiling.

Rose

My cousin Anna often wants to have tea in the secret room we used to play in as children. She has me read her favorite books to her while she breastfeeds her babies. In so many ways, she is still a child who pretends to be an adult, and I am an adult who pretends to be a child, for her sake. It is a curious situation, but I do not mind, for even the Bible says, *"Truly I tell you, unless you change and become like little children, you will never enter the kingdom of heaven."*

But then I see James, and the child in me flees while every part of me that is a woman opens like a flower on a warm spring day.

CHAPTER 15

Something peculiar happened to Rose's body one morning: Her breasts became tender, and her nipples sore. Upon bathing, she realized she was lactating. Rose knew it was possible for a woman who wasn't pregnant to lactate; she had even read about it in a medical book. But she never imagined it could happen to her.

When her breasts first secreted the small amount of liquid, it was somewhat discomfiting to her. A bizarre manifestation that left her dizzy and bewildered. But then she saw it as fascinating, and she wondered if she should tell Anna or just keep it to herself. Staring at her swollen breasts in the mirror, she smiled.

"Anna . . ." Rose was holding Scarlet while sitting at the kitchen table. "Did you know that a woman can produce breast milk even if she hasn't had a baby?"

Anna held Mabel over her shoulder, patting her back until she burped up air. She wiped the baby's mouth with a towel. "Seriously? How?"

"If you're around a newborn long enough, certain hormones and glands can slowly activate spontaneously. It's rare, but it happens."

Anna paused. "Lottie, are you producing milk?"

She bit at her lower lip and nodded.

"My goodness."

Rose's eyes began to water. She looked at little Scarlet and smiled as the baby's gaze danced around her face while cooing and gurgling. Then Scarlet became fussy, wanting to be fed. She squirmed against Rose and started to cry.

Rose looked up at Anna, and the two women stared at each other. Would her cousin allow this? Without saying a word, Anna got up and went over to Rose, pushing her blouse aside, allowing her baby to find a nipple. At first the child seemed confused, but soon she began to suckle.

Shock came over Rose's face. With wide eyes, she stared at Anna. Then she relaxed, cradling the infant in her arms. It was the closest thing to her knowing what it felt like to have her own child, and the feeling was pure heaven. Nothing she had experienced in life compared. Tears ran down her cheeks, and as the baby nourished, she gently smoothed down Scarlet's hair. Scarlet closed her eyes, within seconds falling asleep, content and feeling loved.

Anna returned to the other side of the table and breastfed little Mabel. There they sat for the longest time, both feeding the babies in silence, until James walked in. Initially he didn't notice anything as his eyes casually flickered around the room, taking in his wife and child, then Rose and child. Then he looked again, making sure he wasn't seeing things. Quickly he made a drink and went back outside.

Anna and Rose looked at each other and smiled.

～੬੭ৡୄ੭ৄ～

"Are you sure there's no issue with her doing that? Seems wrong to me," James said. He was already in bed, reading one of his favorite books about the military exploits of Alexander the Great.

Anna finished washing her face in the washbasin, patting her face dry. "She's producing milk. It happens to some women when they have regular interaction with a newborn."

"Still doesn't seem right."

"How is it bad? I want to share the experience with her."

"Anna, you share a baby by letting her hold it and love it. This is going too far."

She crawled into bed beside him, pulling the covers up to her chin. "It's no different from when a cow gives birth to twins, and we sometimes get another mother to help feed them."

"Cows are animals; babies are not."

"It's the same thing, though."

"No, it isn't. I don't want to see that again."

"It's not up to you."

"It's not her baby; it's our baby, love. I just can't wrap my bloody head around this."

"Then don't think about it. If she can breastfeed, it only helps me out. Having to feed twins around the clock is knackering. If you ask me, it's a godsend."

"How far are you willing to take this friendship, Tin Tin? It's not natural."

Anna thought it was wonderful. "Stop meddling, James." She rolled over and tried to get comfortable in bed. "You wouldn't understand, anyway. Besides, what my cousin and I do is none of your beeswax."

"My children are none of my business, aye?"

"I just mean with something like this. It's a bonzer gift to give to another woman who's never had a child."

James closed his book and looked over at his wife. "You know who you two are like?"

Anna rubbed her sleepy eyes. "Who?"

"Alexander the Great and Hephaestion."

"Who are they?"

"Alexander was a powerful king in the Greek kingdom of Macedon during the fourth century BCE. He and his best cobber Hephaestion were so close that he gifted his wife's sister to him in marriage, making Hephaestion part of the royal family. Their friendship was even compared to that of Achilles and Patroclus from Homer's *Iliad*."

Anna yawned. "You and your silly books."

"They would do anything for each other," James continued, "just like you and your cousin."

Anna was drifting off to sleep. "I *would* do anything for Lottie. Anything."

"But there's a line you shouldn't cross, love. You can't live for someone else's happiness." The irony of his own words hit him as he turned off the kerosene lamp. Closing his eyes, the image from earlier in the day of both women breastfeeding his children irradiated in his mind as he pulled his sleeping wife into his embrace.

~∙c৩⧉৩৩∙~

Every day, Anna and Rose shared in breastfeeding the twins. At first Rose's breasts had only slightly swelled, but now they would ache until she fed one of the infants. In the nursery, both cousins would sit across from each other, smiling and rocking in their chairs, allowing the babies to feed. Sometimes they would even take them to Cassandra Fancy's garden and sit on the wrought iron bench, enjoying the day while feeding them. Rose would feel the small heartbeat against her chest and gush with love, holding the sleeping beauty's tiny hand as the baby curled her fingers around her thumb and suckled. Such a gift. Such a wonderful gift, and a bonding experience for them all.

Recessed in the back of her mind, the desire to have her own child was now growing strong, like a constant hunger. The longing stretched and yawned inside herself as if a shadow, pushing past the boundaries of her flesh and becoming real. How could she possibly shut this desire out, this powerful instinct to create a life from her own womb?

"When you have a child, you play God for a while," she said one morning, looking down into the radiant face of the tiny soul in her arms.

"You play God? How so?" Anna asked.

"Because you create a life. Your own body magically produces another."

Anna studied her cousin, observing how enchanted she was with the little human being she held. A dread washed over her. Rose would be seeking a man soon in order to have her own child. "My children are your children," she quickly said.

Rose looked up. "I know, Anna, and I love them very much. But to have my own baby, to play God for those nine months—it is something I dream about."

Anna inwardly frowned, jealous of the baby that didn't exist, the man who would take her away, and the love Rose would give them both.

~∙c৩⧉৩৩∙~

Anna leaves the nursery to make dinner, and Rose stays behind, staring at the Shahans' treasures with amazement. Gently she places the back of her cool hand against the warmth of their cheeks that feel like soft dough, in awe of these miracles of life, their diminutive shape and delicate form still curved from being freshly plucked from her cousin's womb. Every time they breathe, each subtle turn of their heads, or the faint noises they make while they sleep, is a thrill. Having waited so long for a child of her own, she feels as if her heart is outside her body, shared between the two tiny lives lying before her in their cribs.

As Rose watches the babies sleep, Mabel brings her thumb to her mouth, trying to part her lips. She struggles a bit, so Rose assists using her own pinky finger; instantly the thumb inserts and the infant begins to suck. "Are you still hungry, Mabel Blessing?" she whispers as she leans into the crib to pick up the child. Sitting down in the rocking chair, she lifts her shirt to allow the baby to nurse some more.

Mabel is so happy that she slightly jumps in Rose's arms, and as she finds the nipple, her eyes drift back to sleep, only to quickly open again to make sure Rose is still there. Satisfied, she falls into a peaceful ecstasy.

Rose leans back in the rocking chair, and within minutes, Mabel collapses completely forward into her chest. She again feels the tiny heartbeat adjacent to her own, smiling as love spreads through her like sun-warmed honey. As the baby suckles, she daydreams the twins are hers, and that one day when they are old enough, they will call her Mummy. She imagines James is her husband, and this is her family, not Anna's. The fantasy expands to where her twin daughters grow up happy and healthy, learning to walk and talk, running around the old farmhouse playing while she cooks dinner. James comes in after work, embracing her, kissing her breathless.

It is a sordid, cruel dream for a woman who has never been in love, never had a child of her own, and fears she never will.

Genevieve

"I watched you two in Cassandra's garden the other day, breastfeeding your children on the bench. I'm not sure I would allow that, Sweet Pea," Genevieve says to Anna. "I agree with James–seems odd to me."

"Rubbish," replies Anna to the hallucination. "Rose is like a sister to me. I would certainly let Blessing do the same if she had lived."

"She didn't, though. And Rose is not Blessing."

"I know, but it allows her to feel what it's like to have a child."

"She needs to have one of her own."

"Rose hasn't met another bloke she fancies enough to marry."

"What about James?"

"What about him?"

"Remember the secret your mum and sister told you at your special place? How James could give Rose a gift?"

"He would never."

"Wouldn't he?"

CHAPTER 16

"Oh, sorry James," Rose said, surprised to see him in his den so late. "You had said before that I could look through your books if I wanted. I thought maybe I'd borrow one."

"No worries," he replied, sitting at his desk, absorbed in a book himself, a single kerosene lamp illuminating his face as he read. That night, he was researching mental conditions and psychological issues–a subject he studied often–trying to find a diagnosis for his wife. A bottle of his latest Irish whiskey and a shot glass sat in front of him. "Take what you like, aye?"

"Thank you," said Rose. As she turned her back to scan the numerous titles lining the bookshelves, she felt his eyes all over her. "You have a beautiful collection."

"Ta. Took ten years to acquire them all." He watched as she slowly glided left to right, her slender fingers lightly touching the spine of each book she passed, the same way his affectionately caressed the ebony and ivory keys of his piano before playing.

Rose stopped at an old leatherbound book written in Latin, its title embossed in the ancient language. "You can read Latin?" she asked, recognizing the vernacular.

"Some, yes, but I'm not fluent. That book of phrases in your hand has four of my favorites."

"What are they?" she asked, not looking up as she flipped through the pages.

"The first is *Post nubila, solem* . . . After the clouds, the sun."

"And the second?"

"*Luceo, non uro* . . . I shine, not burn."

"The third?"

"*Per aspera ad astra* . . . Through hardships to the stars."

As she looked up at him, he smiled, and her insides warmed. "And the fourth?"

"*Dum spiro, spero* . . . While I breathe, I hope."

"Which one is your most favorite?"

"The last one—while I breathe, I hope," he said, his eyes reflecting the power and depth of that apothegm.

"Lovely," she replied, a kaleidoscope of butterflies once again going wild in her lower stomach.

"Anyway, I want to thank you for what you've done for Anna," he graciously said. "I haven't seen her this rapt in years."

Rose returned the compendium of Latin phrases and pulled out another leatherbound book—*The Time Machine*, by H. G. Wells—turning to face him. "Anna isn't the only one who's rapt. Returning to Sugar Alexandria has brought me back to life."

"Indeed," he said.

She smiled and looked around the den. The large, daedal desk—the centerpiece of the room—was made of luxurious cherrywood, with a spinning copper globe sitting on its corner. Behind the desk on the wall, an impressive oil painting depicted a scene from *Moby Dick*, where a burly man with a harpoon stood courageously on a boat, facing down a mammoth white whale emerging from a thrashing sea. Floor-to-ceiling bookshelves lined two of the other walls, barely a space left for another tome.

James glanced at the second book she had picked. "*The Time Machine*. That's a grand book. What a blessing it would be if we could go back in time and right the wrongs, aye?"

Neither of them spoke as their eyes met, both thinking the same thing . . . If only.

James began to hum that sad but pretty melody again.

"There's that tune you keep humming," said Rose. "You must be composing a new song."

"No, it's just a familiar hum I do. Most of the time I don't even realize I'm doing it. Does it annoy you?"

"No, not at all. I like it."

He smiled.

Rose stopped at the door. "Good night, James. Thank you for the book."

"G'night, Rose. Sleep well."

~≪⊹≫~

Upon entering their bedroom that night, James noticed his wife in sleep distress, having another one of her nightmares. "Anna, wake up," he said, gently shaking her.

She abruptly woke and sat up straight, sweating from the subconscious trauma.

"It's all right, love. You were just having a nightmare again."

Her nocturnal incubi were so real they always made her cry when she woke. "Oh, James, I dreamed about the Black Shuck again! It's after me! The wolf is still alive and it's going to kill me! It's going to kill all of us!"

~≪⊹≫~

The sound of the windshaft turning the sail woke Rose the next morn. She had spent half the night reading, and the book still laid on her chest. Looking up, she watched as the metal gears engaged, transferring the force of the gusty breeze to the blades. When the summer zephyr briefly slowed, the mechanics stilled, and she could hear Anna calling her outside the mill. They were going to have a picnic and spend the day at the shoreline. Jumping out of bed, she quickly dressed, excited to go visit the turquoise waters of the Southern Ocean again.

When they reached the beach, they put Scarlet and Mabel—already asleep in their wicker bassinets—down on the blanket along with the food, and held hands as they ran to the water, diving into the waves, just as they had done many times years before.

"This feels wonderful!" exclaimed Rose, floating in the liquid silver, frolicking about like a baby seal.

Anna was so happy, so full of bliss, watching her cousin laughing and splashing in the cool water, her nose and cheeks flushing pink. This was the Rose who used to visit her every summer. "Remember when we used to pretend we were mermaids?" she asked, spurting water from the gap between her front teeth.

"Yes!" said Rose. "And your brothers were the pirates."

"That's right. They would try to catch us and take us prisoner, and if they caught us . . ." Anna stopped and looked toward the shoreline. One of the babies had started crying. "I better go check, Lottie."

Anna swam back; Rose stayed behind.

With the taste of salt rimming her mouth, the sound of the seabirds ringing in her ears, her hair sleeked back and her green eyes shining, Rose watched from afar as Anna went to her babies in their bassinets and began breastfeeding them. It caused an unfamiliar envy to stab at her inner self. An unpleasant revelation that she could feel the sting of jealousy toward her cousin.

While the ocean pushed her to and fro, she thought about how she was only a small part of James and Anna's lives, and nothing more. Their world was their marriage, their station, and their newborn children. Their bond was sealed by means of their babies, and this was sacred. Sacrosanct, even. Yes, James Shahan very much belonged to Anna and his daughters.

With this reality in her mind, Rose leaned back and stared up at the heavens, her body weightless, succumbing to the will of the sea. James' familiar hum then surrounded her, as if the sound came down like a dove from the sky, the sweet, gentle melody fluctuating with the waves. Closing her eyes, a memory flashed through her mind: "If I asked you to marry me right now, what would you say?" James had teased that night they first met. Or had he been serious? "Whaddya say, love? Wanna spend the rest of your life with an Irish pianist?"

"Lottie," Anna called out, scarpering the memory. "Let's have some tucker; I'm starving."

Rose returned to join her cousin, and together they sat on the blanket eating Vegemite sangers and fruit, sticking their toes in the sand and enjoying the warmth of the sun on their faces.

After Anna was done breastfeeding, she handed one of her daughters to Rose. "Scarlet and Mabel are going to grow up to be just like us," she said, smiling at them with pride and joy. "They'll be the best of cobbers too."

Rose coddled little Scarlet, and her eyes misted over with fresh tears.

"What's the matter, Lottie?"

"I'm sorry, Kitten. I've wanted a baby of my own for so long, and when I hold one of these little ones, that craving consumes me. It's like I'll die if I don't have one."

"There's still time, love. You could meet a bloke tomorrow and be married off before you know it."

Touched by how her little cousin was always looking out for her, Rose gave a weary smile, kissing Anna on the cheek. *"Åh, min dyrebare lille Killing. I lvor jeg forguder dig så,"* she said in Danish. *("Oh, my precious little Kitten. How I adore you so.")*

James had been riding Ireland in the area, and when he descried his wife and her cousin on the beach, he came over to say hello. He tried not to stare at Rose, how her bathing suit clung to her slim figure, unveiling a sensual suggestion, until his eyes traced downward to her exposed legs, clearly revealing why she needed a cane.

With her left leg long and lean—perfection—and her right leg lacking muscle and form—almost skin and bone—the walking stick was a necessity. James wondered what Rose must have gone through growing up, knowing how cruel children can be, making fun of those who are different. Perhaps it was one of the reasons her parents sent her on the long trip from England to Australia each summer, allowing their daughter to escape it all by spending time with her cousin on a remote cattle station in the Outback.

After he left, James watched them from a distance while they packed up and headed home. As Rose walked, he observed that she had a rhythm to her gait. It was obvious her limb had tired, putting all her weight on her good leg, then shifting it to the bad, using the wooden device to support herself. Though he could not hear it from where he stood on the hill, it made a slight scraping noise on the earth as she moved forward with each step.

He wondered if she was in pain when she walked, and how difficult it would be to transition from walking without the cane, to depending on it when her leg grew weak. She tripped and fell suddenly; Anna leaned down and helped her up, giving her embarrassed cousin a hug. In that moment, James realized more than ever that Rose was simply a woman who needed time and a place to recover from her loss, and if his wife's ubiquitous affection for her left nothing for him, so be it. It made him somewhat ashamed of himself, at how he had been acting toward her, resentful over something that wasn't her fault. While she is here, I will endeavor to be more friendly and welcoming, he decided. Just as I should have from the beginning.

When they returned from the shoreline, windblown and skin rosy from the fresh air, the two women went inside the windmill for some apple and pecan bickies with tea. Afterward, Rose pulled out her violin and began to play.

Anna studied her cousin as she conjured the musical notes from her stringed instrument, homing in on Rose's hands. So lovely they were, she thought, even with one of her digits crooked and curved. Her long fingers pale and slender, with flat, oval nail beds turning pink when pressed against the strings. Anna envisaged many things as she kept looking, of how Rose's hands most likely resembled her mother Elsa's when she was young, and how they were linked through blood. How inside their bodies, what made Anna who she was, was also the same with Rose.

Cousins.

Different but the same.

Now that Rose had returned, there was hope for a greater sense of family than ever before. I can now be who I was supposed to be, Anna thought as she watched her cousin play. Rose is the other part of me that was missing; her friendship completes me.

Together we are one.

Rose became immersed in her music, face flushed, strands of hair in her eyes, fingers dancing across the strings as the bow sharply stroked. She was a musician, a woman, a widow, caught somewhere between sorrow and rebirth. Someone who had drowned but played her music as if she were still swimming, gasping for air toward the watery surface of the sublime sea.

James was working on his Ronaldson Tippett tractor with Tarka when he heard Rose's violin. The window in the mill was open, and the wind carried the music through the air. *"Hold on,"* he said in Nukunu.

"What's wrong?" asked Tarka.

James touched his ear. *"Listen."*

At first the sound was faint, similar to when whales communicate with each other in the depths of the ocean. Then the sound grew stronger, undulating and becoming clear.

"I hear it," Tarka said. *"What is that?"*

"It's a violin," James answered. For a moment he closed his eyes, his fingertips tingling, yearning to play his piano alongside her stringed instrument. Then he recognized the sound. Rose had mirrored his humming on her violin! The sad yet beautiful melody sung out like a nightingale, touching James' soul.

Tarka nudged him, pointing at the sky. The sun was getting low, and the day was coming to a close.

James opened his eyes, and they went back to work. Still listening to the music, he quietly hummed the familiar song.

Anna and Rose accepted Glenda Trufflepig's recent invitation and went to her cabin for an early dinner. The older woman had cleaned up, having brushed her long, wild hair into a tamed bun, and exchanged her rawhides and furs for a feminine, flowered dress. She raved about James' whiskey, asked about Moony whom she always had a crush on, and even inquired of Lovely Dawn, knowing that long ago Anna had stolen the potbellied pig's mother.

They had a wonderful dinner of rabbit and snake potpie with creamy mashed potatoes grown in Glenda's own garden, served by her Aboriginal male companion. It was such a nice visit, but as always, when Anna asked about the bad blood between Glenda and her sister Poppy, the older woman frowned, saying she'd never be in the same room as that wretched woman again, alive or dead.

What could make a woman hate her sister so much, Anna wondered?

She could never imagine feeling that way about Rose.

Never.

※

That same evening, after the two cousins returned home, Rose retired to her maisonette while Anna sat on the couch with her husband listening to the radio, Lovely Dawn napping on the floor in front of them, the babies sleeping soundly in the nursery. With the light from the fireplace illuminating her appearance in the dimly lit room, James observed his wife, her red lipstick glimmering and her new hairstyle framing her cherub face. "You're a beauty tonight, love."

Anna smiled. "I was wondering when you were gonna notice. Rose did my makeup today. I fancy the way she does her own, so I asked her to do mine the same."

James polished off the rest of his drink. "Rose seems to be settled in now, aye? Has she told you how she likes it here?"

"She loves it. Why wouldn't she?"

"Just curious."

"I don't know who's happier, though—me or her. Every morning I jump out of bed and can't wait to see her. Today we had a ripper time, just like we did when we were younger." A worried look then crossed Anna's face.

"What is it, love?"

"When we went down to the beach today, she started to cry when she held Scarlet. She told me she wants a baby of her own."

"Of course she does. Most sheilas do."

"When she remarries, I will lose her all over again, James."

"Now Anna, we talked about this. Just enjoy her while she's here."

Anna mentally stirred, desperately wanting to secure Rose at the station permanently. Biting her nails, she mulled over the secret her mother and sister had told her about how to keep Rose at the station for eternity. "I wish there were a way we could keep her at Sugar Alexandria," she said—a segue to the bomb that would come next.

James was tired and began to nod off, no longer paying attention to the conversation.

"Too bad you couldn't bed her once and give her a baby. Then she would stay forever."

176

He jolted awake. "Crikey! What did you say?"

She blinked, unsure of her words to follow. "I was just saying that if you were to root her once, she could have a baby of her own and stay with us to raise it."

"What in the bloody hell! Anna, you're talking crazy now. I know she's your best cobber, but this is too much. Don't ever say anything like that again." He looked at her nonplussed and bewildered. "Makes me think your mind is not the full quid."

"It was just a thought."

James turned off the radio and went to the bar, pouring himself another measure of whiskey. "Crikey, woman. The things you come up with." Shaking his head, he took a large swig.

"It's not that crazy of an idea," Anna muttered to herself. "It would only be once. What could it hurt?"

"What decent Christian wife would ever offer up her husband for such a thing? Even the idea is obscene," he said in disbelief.

"I just care about her, that's all."

"Listen, Tin Tin, don't be telling any of this to Rose, either. She'll think you've gone mad."

"No she won't. She'll be happy I'm trying to help her."

James rubbed his eyes; he was exhausted. "She's going to meet a bloke and have her own family, as it should be." Taking his drink with him, he headed to the bedroom, again shaking his head, flabbergasted over his wife's outrageous notion.

"She can't leave, James," Anna said, turning her back to her husband. "I won't let her."

James

Bed my wife's cousin so she too can have a child?
Anna and her ideas!
Someday her schemes and outlandish behavior will be the end of her.
And of us . . .

Hours later, James opens his eyes to darkness. Pulling the covers off his body, he goes to get himself a glass of water. As he stands over the sink, bare-chested, he unintentionally sees Rose through the window, reading the book she borrowed from his den. While turning the page, she looks up and notices him staring at her. He wants to smile and wave; instead he looks away, partly due to the conversation he had earlier where his wife suggested he could give Rose a child.

As he crawls back into bed, he lays his hand gently on the curve of Anna's hip. Closing his eyes, he tries to blank his mind and will his body to find sleep, but try as he may, he cannot. Thoughts fill his head, past and present—experiences from the war, men crying to him for help, images of the blood of castrated bulls, the smell of horses he had to break in, the red dust that covered his skin, and the Australian wind that rocked his body like the waves of the sea. The sights and sounds of the workday haunt his sleep, but when he thinks of his music, his mind finally rests. It is a lullaby for a man who hides his gifts and lives a life he did not choose, all for the happiness of his wife.

❧

"You said what to him?" Rose asked the next morning. They were in Cassandra Fancy's garden, pulling weeds and trimming hedges.

"I made a comment about how badly you wanted a child . . . and well . . . I suggested he could give you one."

Rose stopped and stared at her, wide-eyed. "What did he say?"

Anna, surprised at how tame her cousin's reaction was compared to her husband's, replied, "Some rubbish about me talking crazy."

"Great, now I won't be able to look him in the eye."

"Would you go for something like that, though?"

"Anna, it would never happen. Ever."

"I don't think it's that crazy. Some men have more than one wife, and no one blinks an eye. Why is it so wrong to help someone you love have a baby?"

"Because I want my own family, that's why."

"It was just an idea."

"It's a ridiculous idea," said Rose. Yet her eyes said something contrary.

The two women remained silent for a moment. Anna, discerning that her cousin was thinking about it, looked intently at her and said, "Rose, he does everything I say. It would only be one time, and you could have a baby of your own. You could raise it here at Sugar Alexandria and stay with me forever."

Rose imagined James' body blanketing hers, and instantaneously Anna's idea vividly oscillated through her mind. Her inner thoughts went wild, drowning out her cousin's voice in the background. James, alone with me, she imagined. Touching me, kissing me, making love to me, all for the sake of giving me a child. Closing her eyes, she became lost in the fantasy.

"Rose? . . . Rose?"

"Oh, sorry. What?"

"You all right?"

Rose's green eyes seemed brighter than usual. "I'm grand, Anna. Why wouldn't I be?"

Rose

Anna offering me such a gift?
Incredible.
Yet it's a sin, for one.
Some would say an abomination.
I have underestimated the magnitude of her affection for me.
The sweet tenderness.
Her need to be loved by me, making her willing to do anything for me.
She sees me as a replacement for what she has lost.
Her mother . . . Her sister.
But I am not them.
Nor will I ever be.

Somewhere in the posterior of Anna's mind, she sees love as ownership, where James and Rose are her prized possessions. James does whatever she wants at the station, and Rose is her porcelain doll. But the truth is far different. James is a man who hopes one day to be free from the obligations that tie him to the land, and Rose is no inanimate doll, but a young widow who is very much a vibrant woman. A woman who wants sunshine in her life, and more than anything, a man to passionately love and have his child . . .

CHAPTER 17

J ames had run into some of the local fishermen by the pier a few days later, two of them his old war buddies and their fathers. He asked them for dinner, and all four men came home with him that evening.

Before they went into the farmhouse, James showed them his small distillery—one of his favorite pastimes living at the station. He had been brewing Irish whiskey using a three-hundred-year-old Gaelic recipe from his great-great-grandfather, and had just finished his latest batch. Pouring each of the men a dram of the previous batch, now aged for three years to tease out the desired result, they all stuck their noses in it, inhaling a deep breath. The oak barrel had slowly infused the liquor with lignin and vanillin, lactones and tannins, imbuing the rich, distinctive flavors and color James was seeking. Vanilla-like, buttery, spicy, golden-brown, smooth. It was perfect.

James spoke to the drink as if it were a goddess come to life. "Look at you," he said, brimming with pride. "What a beauty."

Each of the men agreed, savoring the libation as it went down.

Moony walked in, interrupting the fulsome moment between product and maker. He nodded at the visitors.

"C'mere, Moon Pie," James said, waving his friend over. "Taste this."

Moony smiled. "You opened the barrel, aye?"

"It's been sealed up for three years now, maturing. Here, give it a go."

Moony was about to toss back the dram of whiskey, but James stopped him.

"Smell it first, mate. Take in the rich aroma; let it intoxicate you without drinking."

Moony brought the glass to his nose and breathed in. "Corker," he said, nodding at its delectable characteristics.

"Too right. Now drink it, but let it sit on your palate for a second before swallowing."

The older man did as his boss asked. "Crikey, mate, you outdid yourself this time. Is this Irish whiskey or milk and honey from the Promised Land?"

All the men laughed.

"I've always fancied your way with words, Moon Pie," James said, patting him on the back. He served the men a few more rounds while Moony shared one of his long-winded stories about how he had caught the once wild black Arabian stallion James' named Ireland.

An hour later, Anna and Rose walked into the distillery.

"Tucker is ready, love," said Anna.

Rose's eyes danced around the room, resting on the bottle in James' hand.

"Wanna taste?" he asked her, lifting the amber-colored glass bottle. Slightly inebriated, he was now more comfortable and relaxed in her presence, gazing at her without looking away.

"Give it a burl, love," Anna said. "I'll have one too." She walked over and took two drams from her husband, handing one to her cousin.

Rose hesitated.

"Come now, Rose, don't be shy," said James, a twinkle in his eye. "It'll put some hair on your chest."

Rose accepted the drink, lifted the glass, and proclaimed, "Here's to Sugar Alexandria!"

Everyone cheered.

⁓⁓⚜⁓⁓

The women had cooked Danish *karbonader (breaded pork patties)* that evening, serving it with boiled potatoes, grilled vegetables, and corn bread. James of course brought along a bottle of his latest batch of Irish whiskey from the distillery. As everyone sat around the table, Rose studied the appearance of the four visitors. They looked different from the men who worked the land. You can always tell a fisherman by his skin, she thought—

red like the stockmen, but also chapped and scaly. Fishermen were happy blokes, always smiling, grateful to make a living off the sea. They spoke about it with passion, as if it were a woman they were in love with, soft and giving, yet also ruthless and deadly if you crossed her. That is how they saw it.

While eating their food, the men shared their experiences during the Great War, and speculated on the Great Depression now threatening the industrial world. Bowie Jenkins was eyeing Rose, grinning and trying to flirt with her. Rose managed a smile, though not reciprocating his affections, and Anna inwardly cringed, annoyed with the man's chutzpah. She wasn't ready for Rose to start fancying a bloke and be married off so soon. Whenever Bowie tried to engage Rose in conversation, Anna would jump in and interrupt.

"You were at Christian and Josephine's wedding," said Bowie. "I remember now. You were the sheila James kissed."

Rose's face flushed. "I was there, yes, but I didn't meet James. You must be thinking of someone else."

"No, it was you, all right," Bowie said, simpering over his discovery. "Me and me mates saw it. We figured Shahan had found his bride that night."

"Sorry, it wasn't me," she insisted.

Anna laughed out loud. "Those two kissing? Now that's a hoot!"

James and Rose exchanged awkward glances; he quickly changed the subject: "Anna, where's your famous blueberry pie, love? Bring it out and let's have at it."

After dessert, the men thanked the Shahans for their hospitality and left. Bowie had kissed Rose on the cheek, whispering something in her ear, and it angered Anna. "Why did you invite them," she said to her husband, banging around in the kitchen as she cleaned up.

"They're my cobbers, love. I hadn't seen them in a while."

"Trying to set Rose up, aye? Get her married off."

"That's rubbish. Besides, you just told me the other day that Rose wanted a child. How's that gonna happen if she doesn't meet a decent bloke?"

"You can't stand that I'm finally happy, can you."

"Like I said, if she wants a family, she needs to find a bloke."

Anna whirled around, holding a cutting knife in her hand. "Rose just got here, and you're already trying to get rid of her!" she yelled.

James was now taking her anger more seriously. "Put down the knife, Anna."

"You make me so crook sometimes! You knew Bowie was single, and you told him to make a move on Rose!"

"That's nonsense." He cautiously walked up to her, taking hold of her wrist and removing the knife from her grasp, placing it in the drawer. "This obsession you have with keeping Rose here permanently is mad."

"She's mine," Anna said, as if a child possessive of her doll.

"She's not a toy, love. You don't own her. And when she's ready to leave, you're gonna have to let her go," he said, turning in for the night, shutting the bedroom door.

Anna picked up the knife again, sharpening it until both sides shined.

James

That night as I lie in bed, the wild dingoes begin to howl. I know the young calves and lambs are in danger, so I get up and retrieve my shotgun, preparing to go outside.

But Anna stops me.

Instead, she heads to the fields alone, and soon I hear her kulning to the beasts. This mysterious type of song does not just call the desired animals home but also scares the unwanted ones away. She vocalizes a deeper, more ominous pitch and tone than usual, and my skin prickles. It is, in fact, an awesome thing to hear. I wish so badly that the way her kulning makes me feel, I could feel about her as well. Yet I cannot, as she is unable to bond.

Then I think of my wife's cousin and how open and emotionally available she is. Two different women—my wife being the earth where my feet are firmly planted, her cousin being the galaxy where my head is in the stars. I'm going to admit it . . . I still have strong feelings for Rose. Like a possession, slowly taking over my soul. To add to this dilemma, Anna has asked me to give her a child. She has no idea of the Pandora's Box that would open. To make love to Rose would be akin to diving into the sea and never returning.

The spellbinding melody of Anna's kulning gets louder, resonating across the valley. Before she returns and crawls back into bed, I fall asleep.

Anna

I scare the dingoes away, yet see the large Black Shuck, her red eyes staring at me through the tall grass. She is not afraid, nor threatening, and has come to listen to me kulning. So I sing louder for her, until my lungs tire and my throat hurts. Then I see the shadow people and Genevieve. They too have come to listen to me kulning.

"Doesn't she sing like an angel?" I hear my mother asking them all. And as I sing, I cry.

Then I say to the great black she-wolf hidden in the bush, "The shadow people and Genevieve are my friends. What about you? Are you friend or foe?"

CHAPTER 18

"I heard you playing your violin the other day," James said, carrying a box into Rose's windmill. Her missing belongings had finally arrived from England: A Wurlitzer spinet piano, a gramophone, a large trunk containing the rest of her clothes–satin and sequin dresses, shoes and hats, jewelry–and several miscellaneous boxes including her books, records, champagne, and her easel, oil paints, and brushes. The shipment lifted her spirits, nudging her former personality to further recrudesce.

"Did you recognize the tune?" Rose asked, pleased that he was listening.

"I did. The same one I always hum."

She smiled. "That's right. It's such a lovely, sweet melody, and I was itching to create something with it."

"I hear song too," said Tarka in his broken English, placing the last of the boxes in the living room. "It sound like beauty of a bird from the bush, singin' Mister James' tune."

"Indeed it does," concurred James, winking at Rose. With everything now inside the windmill, he looked around, noticing the easel. "I see you like to paint, aye?"

"Yes, it's another passion of mine," she said. "I can't wait to start." Rose wasn't just a violinist but also an amateur artist, and enjoyed painting with oil on canvas because of the flexibility and depth of color oil paints offered, along with the many ways they could be applied—from thin glazes diluted with turpentine to dense, thick impasto.

"What will you paint?" James asked, impressed by her multifaceted artistic aptitude.

Rose looked out the window, her lucent green eyes reflecting shades of aquamarine and gold in the brightness of the natural light. "I'm going to paint life at Sugar Alexandria."

⚜

There was something special about Rose's artwork. It held a sadness, a mystery, a longing that, if you stared too long at the piece, made you feel as if the pathos were crawling inside you. Her style was redolent of the French artist Paul César Helleu—albeit unintentional—best known for his numerous portraits of beautiful society women of the Belle Époque, and she had even sold a few while she was in London.

Situating her easel out in the field in front of the station where the entire grand estate was her vista, or taking it down to the shoreline, waving at the fishermen as they sailed by, the spectacular seascape her panorama, she completed a couple of landscapes—something different from her usual work. Then she returned to what she did best—portraits.

Her first was of Anna. The vignette took several days, but Anna didn't mind; she enjoyed the attention from her cousin. Rose painted her in a pink dress, even though the one she had on was light brown, and she made her eyes a brighter sapphire blue compared to the darker deep ocean topaz that they were. The backdrop was a glorious red Victorian wallpaper with a gold vase full of lilies sitting on a small table. Anna would frequently ask, "Is it done, Lottie?" And Rose would reply, "No, Kitten, not yet."

Until it actually was . . .

Anna stood before the painting in absolute awe. "There's two of me," she said, unable to pull her eyes away.

"Yes," said Rose, pleased at her reaction. "I painted you with Blessing, as if she had lived."

Anna started to cry, hugging her cousin. "Oh, Lottie, it's just grand! I love it! It's magically haunting, and I love how it makes me feel when I look at it!"

"How does it make you feel, Kitten?" Rose asked.

187

Anna kept staring at the portrait, her eyes fixated on her deceased sister. "Like she's alive again. In the flesh. As if she could step out of the frame and hug me right now." She looked back at her cousin, an eerie expression in her eyes. "Rose, you've resurrected the dead."

Anna

We hung Lottie's painting of me and Blessing on the cobblestone wall that separates the kitchen from the living room. Such a grand sight it is to see my sister as a grown woman next to me. But I have to share something with you. A secret. One I can never tell another soul . . .

In the middle of the night, I got up alone and went to look at the bewitching painting, as if it had summoned me. Then it happened . . . I saw myself and Blessing move! Blessing smiled, stepped out of the frame, and walked down the hallway to the very room we had once slept in as children.

Can you imagine my horror!

This is something I will not share, as no one will ever believe me.

I fear James would even take the artwork down and burn it.

Genevieve

"Did the shadow people tell you?" a bevy of unfamiliar voices whisper simultaneously in Anna's mind as she goes back to bed that night, her husband snoring beside her.

"Who's there?" Anna asks.

Genevieve appears at the foot of the bed. "Did they give you the answer to the riddle?"

"No, what is it?"

"Something quite incredible, dear."

"Tell me."

"Come with me and I'll show you."

Anna gets out of bed and follows . . .

"Good morning, James," Rose said, tightening the belt on her burgundy silk robe as she opened the door to her maisonette. The rapid knocking had woken her.

"Is Anna here?" he asked, tension in his face.

"No. Everything all right?"

"She wasn't in bed when I woke up this morning, and she's nowhere in the farmhouse."

"Have you checked her secret room?

"Yes."

"What about the barn and the chicken coop?"

"I've checked everywhere. She's gone."

Anna had not been seen or heard from in hours. James and the stockmen searched every inch of Sugar Alexandria and beyond. The paddock, the wheat and corn fields, the bush, the shoreline, Cassandra's garden—not a trace of her. Was she really gone? James felt a strange mix of panic peppered with something else he would not admit. He would never want anything bad to happen to the mother of his children, and yet why when she disappeared like this was there always an undercurrent of emancipation? Maybe it's finally over, his subconscious would whisper. It's over and no one else will get hurt by her again.

"James . . . ," Rose said, motioning behind him as they stood in the yard talking.

Two Aboriginals rode up on their horses, one of them holding Anna, her face stolid and unresponsive. James and Rose ran across the stockyard to meet them.

"We found her wanderin' around the bush, Mister James," Banjora said in Nukunu, his baritone voice a quicker pace than usual. *"She was talkin' gibberish to herself."*

"Ta, mate," James replied, reaching up to take hold of his wife, still in her nightgown. Anna's hair was matted and in knots, her face dirty, her bare feet covered in mud.

"Oh my God," Rose said under her breath.

James carried her to the house.

"Do you think she was drunk?" the other Aboriginal asked as the two men rode back to their village.

"No, this is not from grog," Banjora said. *"And it's not the first time she's done this, either."* The deep wrinkles in the older man's ebon face seemed deeper that morning. *"One of these days the mulga madness will take Miss Anna and not let her return."*

Rose

Anna has been out all night, God knows where. Coming back in her torn nightgown, head to toe covered in dirt, acting irrational, she swears that some woman named Genevieve promised to reveal an important riddle to her. James carries his wife to bed and holds her until she calms, curling up in the fetal position and hugging her pillow.

Soon after, Anna suddenly sits up and begins to shriek, frantically swatting and scratching at her skin, hallucinating bugs crawling all over her. She begs me to run and get Genevieve, who apparently knows how to get rid of the insects. Again James holds her as her hysterics perpetuate, this time pinning her firmly to the bed.

In all my life, I have never seen anything like this. It has shocked me to my very core, and I now question my decision to come here. Have I made a grave mistake? Was my mother right all along, warning me about Anna?

And yet, if I do leave Sugar Alexandria, where will I go? I have little money besides what the nuns have given me, and going back to the convent is something I cannot bear. For the time being, I am trapped here.

⚜

Locked away safely inside her windmill that evening, Rose made a cup of tea and started a fire in her seashell-covered fireplace. Her cat Matilda sat next to her on the velvet love seat, purring with each stroke. As she sipped her hot, sweet concoction, she mulled over Anna's frightening behavior that morn—wandering off into the bush in the middle of the night; returning almost in a trance; speaking of a mysterious woman from the past; hallucinating insects all over her skin. Much worse than the minor oddities Rose remembered her cousin having when she used to visit each summer. Her mind wandered further, and she recalled the conversation she had with her mother before she left London . . .

"There's something wrong with Anna," Irma had warned.

"Something wrong? What do you mean?"

"The poor girl has inherited my sister's mental problems, God rest her soul. She suffered them until her dying day."

"What mental problems?"

"Bizarre and unpredictable behavior."

"You've never mentioned that before."

"I've never had to. But now that you're intent on moving there, I thought you should know."

"Anna may be a bit different, but mental illness? And Aunt Elsa too?"

"Yes, love. It's a dark family secret that mental disorders plague the women in our lineage. Goes all the way back to my great-great-grandmother. Maybe even further. Some were sent to psychiatric hospitals, others committed suicide, and a few even killed someone in a fit of rage. All kinds of tragic stories. Thank the good Lord you and I have been spared."

"Mum, I've visited Anna every summer for years, and aside from being a little spoiled at times, she's fine."

"No, Ambrosia, she's not. She's not right; she has problems. You know

191

she whispers to herself all the time."

Rose couldn't deny it, remembering little Anna having conversations—even arguments—with herself on a regular basis. "Doesn't everyone talk to themselves once in a while?"

"Not to the extent that child did. I'm warning you, dear, be careful. Mental illness is a disease of the worst kind. Don't stay there too long."

Rose laughed. "Why, you think she could hurt me?"

"Maybe."

"Oh, Mummy, I know Anna—she's harmless. She used to be my little companion, and I adored her."

"People don't grow out of mental disorders. They don't go away; they get worse. And as a full-grown woman, she could now be dangerous."

Rose returned to the present. Anna is as sweet as can be, she reassured herself. Yes, she has some strange behaviors; so what? That doesn't make her insane. She's my cousin and my best friend, and it's ludicrous to think she would ever try to hurt me.

Or would she?

To quell her unbridled fears, Rose pulled out her violin and began to play Tchaikovsky's *Swan Lake* over and over, thinking of Odette and Odile, the white swan and the black, anthropomorphizing them as her cousin Anna—a woman with disparate sides to her—symbolizing the battle between good and evil that rages within. Or perhaps she herself was one of the swans, thrusting herself uninvited into Anna's world, imposing her own problems on her sweet cousin. The question is, which one? Vulnerable and pure Odette, or audacious and deceptive Odile?

<hr />

The music flowed like a fragrant summer breeze into James and Anna's bedroom as they lay side by side—James still holding his wife, now placated—and they both silently listened. Plush, supple, velvety notes, the melody tender and soft. As the song progressed, it transitioned to where the instrument was weeping—dramatic, sharp chords spilling out an exquisite vibration of longing and sorrow. The music soothed Anna; but for James, a chill ran down his spine.

Moved. Riveted. Dumbstruck by her ability, he felt as if someone had just slapped him. Realizing her talent on the violin matched his own on the piano, it made him feel different about Rose. Much different. Any vestige of his initial envy over the kinship she shared with his wife swiftly dissipated, the weeks of unease and resentment dissolved, and a feeling of something else swelled within him. While the poignant, emotive notes disseminated through the air, the center windmill appeared to be closer. As if a small, intangible line connected the house to the mill, like two ends of a rope, and he was holding fast to one end.

"I had a really crook one this time, aye?" Anna asked, her head laying against her husband's chest.

"No worries, love," James said.

"I had too much sugar, that's all. No more pies and sodas for me."

If only that were true, James thought, knowing it was much more serious than that. Mental health issues were behind the veritable dynamics of his wife's oddities.

"Want me to close the window to drown out the music?" Anna asked, back to her normal self.

"No, love," said James. "The sweetness of it will lull us both to sleep."

❧

A cool wind, chilled by the sea and transported to the station, blew against both women as they ambled along the fence line the next day. The matching velvet cloaks Anna had made kept them warm, and as the gust picked up, the sleeveless garments billowed in the breeze.

"Does it make you regret coming here?" Anna asked.

"What, Kitten?"

"How I acted yesterday."

"I'm just concerned for you. That was frightening, and I worry that my presence may be making things worse."

"No, Rose. A thousand times no. I'm just different, that's all. Besides, remember what Grandmother used to say about your leg and your finger when you'd get upset about them? Or about having to wear glasses? 'Different is good,' she said. 'Different is interesting. Without our differences, the spice of life is bland.' "

"You're talking about physical ailments, though. Mental issues are more serious. Maybe you should see a specialist about it."

"I will if you stay."

Rose nodded.

Anna scanned the land to the farthest point on the horizon. "See all this? It's all mine . . . My land, my animals, my crops. Just looking at it makes me so proud."

"I would be proud too."

"Well, what's mine is yours, Lottie."

"Oh, Kitten," Rose said, putting her arm around Anna's shoulder as they walked.

"No, it's true. I would give you anything to make you rapt." Anna looked intently at Rose, feeling bad and embarrassed that her cousin had witnessed such a severe, unnerving incident. "Even the stars, if I could."

Rose smiled.

"So let that be something that will help you in your quest to feel whole again. This land you now live on, and everything else that is mine, is also yours."

Rose gave her a squeeze. *"Min kære lille Killing . . . ,"* she said in Danish, as she often did when using expressions of endearment. She plucked a wild-flower and stuck it in Anna's hair. *"Hvad ville jeg gøre uden dig?"* (*"My dear little Kitten . . . What would I do without you?"*)

"Og hvad ville jeg gøre uden dig, min søde Lottie?" Anna affectionately responded, watching as the morning sunlight lit up her cousin's blue-green eyes. (*"And what would I do without you, my sweet Lottie?"*)

Rose observed how dollish Anna looked, with her innocuous features, scattered freckles, and flower in her hair. She raised her camera and took a few shots; Anna giggled with each click. "C'mon, Kitten, a serious one," Rose said. "Look at me the way you just did before I took your picture."

Anna regained her composure, staring into the camera with an innocent, childlike cast.

"Yes, like that," said Rose, snapping a few more shots. "Now smile for me."

She smiled, her hair messy from the breeze, her cheeks flushed from the cool air, the gap between her teeth prominent.

Rose slowly lowered her camera. "This is how I want to remember you, Kitten. Exactly like this."

Anna's brighter-than-life smile faded as she homed in on someone hiding behind the trees in the near distance. "See Lottie? There he is—the strange man who follows me. Out of nowhere, he appears, and for the longest time he'll only stand still and stare. I think he has me confused with someone else. A case of mistaken identity."

Rose quickly searched around the nearby trees but found no one there.

⌘

"James, who is this strange man Anna sees?" Rose asked the next evening in his den. She had returned a book and was now perusing his others, looking for her next interesting read.

"You know Anna sees things," he said, sitting behind his desk, immersed in a book on ancient history. "The bloke's not real."

"I was hoping this wasn't another one of her hallucinations."

"Sadly, it is."

Rose turned and stared at him, trying to comprehend how he could so easily dismiss such a serious issue with his wife. "James, I think she needs help."

"I've already gone to several doctors, seeking answers. They say it's a harmless condition that shouldn't get any worse."

Frustrated at his unwillingness to persist in helping Anna, Rose continued her search, retrieving her selection off the bookshelf and tucking it under her arm to read inside her windmill later. "How long has she been seeing this stranger, anyway?" she asked, turning back to face him.

"I'd rather not talk about it," said James in a quiet voice. "I have it under control, and Anna's doing all right."

"But what if I see him too?"

"Do you?" He knew full well she didn't.

"No, but what if I did? How do you know he's not real?"

"Because I know," he said, slowly turning the page in his book. "She's been like this throughout our marriage. These hallucinations come and go; most of the time, Anna is good."

Anna came back from retrieving the mail, and they could hear her singing in the kitchen.

"Thank you for the book," Rose said, leaving to go help her cousin prepare dinner.

"No worries," replied James. Only when she turned to leave did he glance her way, his eyes flickering from the passages in his book, lingering where she had just stood.

In the weeks that follow, Rose paints more portraits. Sometimes she paints inside the windmill, other times outside in the field, by the shoreline, or in Cassandra Fancy's garden. She portrays her subject on plush velvet furniture, fancy wallpaper in the background, transforming her muse into a regal socialite with a touch of Victorian or Edwardian. The artwork is beautiful, mounted in decorative edgings, some small in a round or oval frame, others on larger canvas in a square or rectangular frame. Each painting depicts someone on the station wearing bright, vivid clothes with intense colors—popsicle orange, cherry red, emerald green, indigo blue, shining amethyst—and Anna hangs them on the walls throughout the farmhouse.

Often in the dead of night, Anna rises from bed like a thick fog from the surface of the sea, her husband asleep beside her, and walks through the house, a lantern lighting her way, her bare feet gentle on the floor so as not to make a sound. Raising the lantern to each painting in each room, with excitement she beckons the images to come alive.

And they do.

Every one of them steps out of the canvas and surrounds her, talking to her and hugging her, making her feel blessed. Even Liam, in a blue crushed velvet suit, steps out from the painting Rose has created. He can hear, too, and he talks to Anna, his voice strong and confident, his bearing dignified and intelligent, as if he never knew disabilities at all.

What a fright!

What a miracle!

All the images are her beloved family and friends. To her they are the souls of the dead and the living who are trapped, and who only come out for her in the paintings. Unlike the insects that suddenly appear, the puritanical woman from the 1800s and the Black Shuck she often sees, and the bloodied man and mysterious shadow people who follow her, she again keeps this bizarre anomaly a secret.

She tells no one.

"What are you doing?" James asked, standing in the doorway of the bedroom, catching Anna staring at one of the paintings in the hallway in the middle of the night. It was a portrait of her mother Elsa—another painting

Rose had done, using a black-and-white photo of her late aunt as a guide.

Anna didn't answer.

"Love? What are you doing?"

"Don't tell him we're all talking to you, Turtle Dove," the image of her mother warned. "He won't believe you because he doesn't have your ability. You're special, and he's not."

James walked up to the vignette on canvas, examining it, wondering why his wife was so captivated by all these portraits in the house. "I don't like these paintings," he said.

Anna moved the lantern from the artwork to her husband's face. "Why?"

"There's no arguing they're a beauty, but they're also . . ."

"Also what?"

"Haunting."

"Yes, beautifully haunting," Anna agreed.

"I dislike how their eyes follow you everywhere. Almost as if they're alive."

"They *are* alive, James," Anna wanted to say. Instead she held her tongue, keeping her secret.

"Good girl," Elsa said to her, smiling.

"I want Rose to paint our family portrait. A huge painting of us all, and we'll hang it above the fireplace. Oh, Sugar Bear, it will be grand!"

"All right, love; we'll talk about it later, aye? Let's go back to sleep," James said, picking up his wife in his arms.

"Good night, Anna," the images in all the paintings throughout the house echoed concurrently.

"G'night, everyone," Anna replied as her husband carried her to bed.

CHAPTER 19

Rose visited Cassandra Fancy's garden again, this time by herself as Anna stayed home to look after Scarlet who had a cough. Liam was already there when she arrived, fishing for crawdads in the pond. Boomerang watched by his side, and a splendid fairy-wren sat on his shoulder. He had recently found the injured electric blue warbler along the riverbank and nurtured it back to health like he did when he found Boomerang as an abandoned dingo pup. Naming the bird Contessa, it now went with him and Boomerang everywhere.

"Hello, Liam," Rose said, walking up to him. "How are you doing?" She had several photographs in her hand that she just got back from the developer in town. Her plan was to create a photo album of life at Sugar Alexandria—a collection of images, frozen in time—and give it to Anna as a gift.

The teenager grinned. "I'm fishing for crawdads," he said, reading her lips.

"Did you catch any yet?"

Liam opened his sack to show her his bounty.

"Wow, your mum will be happy."

He nodded enthusiastically, then pointed at Mrs. Swan basking in the calm water. The pond appeared metallic that day—anodized titanium faintly rippling under the draft.

198

"I know. She's lovely, isn't she," said Rose.

"She reminds me of you," Liam bashfully replied.

Rose smiled.

"What do you have in your hand?" he asked in his arcane, inchoate voice.

She barely grasped his cryptic words. "Photographs. Wanna see them?"

Again, Liam nodded with alacrity.

Rose pulled out the one she had recently taken of him, where she caught him staring into the lens with a sepulchral look, a wayward stare, his gray eyes tenebrous and haunting. Curious as to what he had been thinking when it was taken, she handed it to him.

Liam marveled at the image, staring down at his own face, examining the picture closely.

"Haven't you ever seen a photo of yourself before?" Rose asked, noticing his reaction.

"Yes, but not like this."

"What do you mean?"

Liam momentarily crushed his eyes shut as he tried hard to speak coherently, forcing his amorphous words out. "Your camera . . . it caught . . . how I feel inside."

"And how is that?"

"Lost," he said, his voice high-pitched, cracking.

"Why do you feel lost, Liam?"

"Because I can't hear, and I keep trying to feel things differently." He clenched his fist in frustration, unsure if she was understanding his vestigial ability to speak. "I keep trying to hear other ways . . . to feel more because . . . because I know I am missing something so wonderful."

Rose wanted to say something to him, to make him feel better about himself, about his lot in life. But what could she say? Hearing is a priceless gift, and it had been stolen from him before he had a chance to fully experience the true miracle of it. "There are many beautiful things in life, Liam," she finally said. "Draw from those you can, not the things you can't."

Liam's eyes glazed over as he read her lips. Reaching out, he covered her ears, intentionally cutting off the sounds around her, trying to give her an idea of what it was like to be deaf. Rose played along. With his palms pressed firmly against her ears, she stared at the birds perched in the cherry trees, but she could no longer hear them singing. She looked at the fountain in the middle of the garden, but there was no sound of trickling water. She imagined not being able to hear herself talk, or others talk, or even her own music when she played her violin, and her heart began to race. Her breathing quickened; the world seemed to be closing in on her, and immediately she pulled his hands away, gasping for air. They only stared at each other in bewilderment over what Liam had accomplished. As if he had literally drawn her into his solitary world, and there she had come to know exactly how he felt . . .

Isolated. Alone. Desperate.

Rose said the first thing that came to her: "You're not alone, Liam." She spoke slowly and deliberately to ensure he would understand each word. "I hear you, and I see you. You matter."

Emotion and relief washed over his face, a catharsis so powerful, one that Rose had never witnessed before in her life.

"Music Man understands too," Liam said, feeling better about himself. "He's like me."

Rose wasn't sure if she understood his obscure utterance correctly.

He touched his ear. "One ear don't work."

"You're saying James is partially deaf?"

Liam bobbed his head up and down. "He's just like me."

"Hmmm," was all Rose said. She gave him a hug, and he insisted she take half of his crawdads, placing them in another sack. Then he left.

As she watched the young man make his way across the garden and exit the gates, Rose contemplated James being deaf in one ear, and how it would affect a musician who loved to play the piano. She mulled over sweet Liam trying to get her to understand what it meant to be deaf, and yet proud to bear some semblance to James whom he looked up to; and she thought of her own defective leg and deformed finger. In that moment, she too felt connected to James in a strange and unusual way. And to Liam.

The silent, ineffable bond of the imperfect, the flawed, the irreparably damaged.

~⚜~

That night, the two women cooked crawdads and served them with all the fixings. Afterward, the three of them went into the living room and sipped on Coke and Irish whiskey, listening to the radio. James was always grateful when Anna acted normal and behaved like the woman he had first met–jovial and full of spunk. It fostered confidence that everything with her was all right, allowing him to relax.

After putting the babies to bed, Anna opened all the windows to let the fresh country air sift in and out of the house, the wild and wondrous Outback adding its familiar exotic sounds. They then livened things up and put a record on the gramophone, pushing the furniture aside to dance awhile. James swung Anna; Anna swung Rose; then James swung Rose. Again and again, they took turns, dancing the Foxtrot, the Charleston, the Black Bottom, and the Lindy Hop, until each of them flopped back down on the couch, sweating and out of breath.

Anna, feeling feisty, lit one of James' cigars. "I love to dance," she said. "I'm like a fish in water."

James and Rose exchanged amused looks.

"It's a fish *out* of water, love," said James. "Not a fish *in* water."

"And you're only supposed to say it about something you're not good at," added Rose. "When you're out of your element."

Anna took a puff from the cigar, exhaled a billow of smoke, and proudly said, "Bah! Fish in water, fish out of water–same diff if you ask me!"

They all laughed out loud, harder than usual because of the alcohol. The laughter continued all night, at times until they cried. This would be one of many golden moments for the familial triad. Treasured times, before the heartbreak would show itself.

Before the gift.

Before the betrayal.

Before the madness.

⚜

At dawn the following morning, James walked along the knee-high newly sprouted wheat. He inspected the rows with careful interest, hoping the rains would continue, as the crops were producing generously. When the heavens fed the fields, it made his job easier.

A steady hum began to vibrate through the ether, throwing his attention toward the east. The Aborigines were playing their didgeridoos and drums again, chanting as they often did, but today a ceremonial blessing was taking place for the coming change of season. The hum rose and fell, similar to the rhythm of his heartbeat, as the raw, guttural tumult, mixed in with the wind, sounded as if giants calling to their gods. Strange, yet simultaneously haunting.

It was early still, and in the distance, a red-orange glow was slowly emerging from the center of a dark blue horizon. James continued to walk, grazing his hand across the top of the wheat stalks, when all at once several feral cats popped their heads up out of the strands of long grain. Holding still, they watched him with both fear and fascination. Was it his imagination, or were they growing in number these days? He stopped and looked at them—all different colors, delicate features and piercing eyes, speaking to him without words—while his wife's voice echoed in his mind about Rose: "Don't you think her eyes are cat-like?" As swiftly as they came, the cats then disappeared back into the wheat field. Except for one. It held his gaze. With the hum from the Aborigines still circulating in the air, the cat's stare grew more intense, and James' heartbeat quickened.

"Mornin', Mister James!"

James jumped, turning around to meet the voice that appeared out of nowhere. "Yarrajan, you gave me a spook. What are you doing here?"

"Sorry, didn't mean to startle you none. When I come to help Miss Anna, I sometimes bring leftovers from my house and feed the wild cats."

"I was wondering why they were all together here in the field, as if they were expecting someone."

Yarrajan had a red scarf around her hair, wearing a multicolored dress—a bright contrast to her dark skin. She opened up a small cloth and began tossing food into the wheat field. "They're too beautiful to let starve, you know."

James was slow to nod.

"They be all shy and sweet, quiet and pretty. Hard to not fall in love with a creature like that. I think God made us that way on purpose so we would care for his creations and keep 'em safe. The heart does fall for what the eyes see . . ."

James began to walk toward the paddock. "Well, it's grouse to see you back. Have a g'day, Yarrajan."

"Miss Rose be back too," she said, looking over at the rising sun—an ever-changing fireball in the sky.

James stopped walking.

"It's a shame what happened to her husband. Guess now she be lookin' for another man soon. I hope she be, anyway."

He moved forward again. "See you at dinner, Yarrajan."

"G'day, Mister James," she replied, throwing crumbs to the hungry ferals.

Yarrajan

I be seein' past her beauty.
I be seein' beyond the pretty eyes and smile.
She does not care for Miss Anna as Miss Anna cares for her.
I be afraid for Miss Anna.

Rose tossed and turned in bed that night, ruminating on her new life at Sugar Alexandria. Rolling over, she blankly stared at the antique armoire Anna had acquired for her.

The great exchange.

With only the moonlight streaming in through the window, illuminating the impressive wardrobe, she studied every inch of it, top to bottom. Such a deep, dark wood—like amber chocolate—and intricate details that hypnotized without fail. She admired the painting, too, that seemed to pop out of the wood, as if a 3D image. The wolf, half hidden. The maiden and the unicorn, sitting unsuspectingly in the tall grass. With the semidarkness playing tricks on her eyes, she saw the painting come to life. The wolf stepped forward with a duplicitous grin, the maiden naïvely smiled, and the unicorn nervously threw back its head. Rose narrowed her gaze and saw the maiden's face become her own, while the wolf resembled Anna. Then in the blink of an eye, the image transformed. Now she was the wolf and Anna the maiden . . .

In the hush of the night, Rose drifted off, only to be awakened by the sounds of James and Anna's lovemaking. Though the noises were soft, the wind carried them through the open window into the mill, into her ears. A mixture of feelings swelled inside her: jealousy, excitement, resentment, sadness. She closed her eyes and imagined she was Anna, with James above her. When Anna breathed heavily, so did she; when Anna moaned, Rose did the same. In the privacy of her windmill, it was as if James were there with her.

Then the breeze kicked up, spinning the sail, and the sounds from her cousin's open window drowned out. Rose listened to the blades hum as they carved through the night air, grateful the wind turbine hid the intimacy she so wished were hers.

The windmills spin constantly. Day and night, the blades cut through the Australian air effortlessly, graceful in their movement, yet fierce nonetheless. They do not sleep. They stand like quiet giants, warlords, overseeing everything, but saying nothing.

What *would* they say if they spoke? What stories would they tell? Would they reveal whom they loved? Would they acknowledge the wind that gives them life, or the sun that keeps them warm? Would they protect their owner, or would they betray his secrets? . . .

CHAPTER 20

A very touching and special thing happened at the Herdsmans one evening. After that day in Cassandra Fancy's garden, when Liam had poignantly shown Rose what it was like to be deaf, she thought of a novel approach to help Liam better understand the vibrations coming from the piano, heightening his enjoyment of what he could feel but not hear. She and James decided to teach him this technique. By training Liam how to connect different sensations, images, and colors to sounds and emotions in music, they postulated it would complement his sense of touch, changing his entire experience of sound beyond what he's known up until now, elevating it exponentially. It appeared to be working, too.

Removing an ice cube from his iced tea, James placed it in Liam's hand. "This is cold," he signed, "like a sad sound on the piano. A sad and lonely melody." As he usually did when Rose was around, he spoke the words as he signed so she could follow.

Liam nodded, making a frown face. He was familiar with loneliness, and suddenly he could feel a sad song vibrating from the piano.

Rose took Liam's hand and pressed it against her coffee mug. "Warm," she said, "like a beautiful, welcoming sound on my violin."

He read her lips, holding the ice in one hand while touching the mug with the other. "Cold and warm are like sad and happy music," he signed.

"Too right, me boy!" James exclaimed.

"He understands?" Rose asked.

"Of course I understand," Liam answered. "I'm not dumb."

James chuckled as he pointed at the sky, shifting the lesson to colors. "Blue," he signed. "Blue is calm, like a calm sound, or a weak vibration."

"But blue can also be sad, just like cold," said Rose.

James nodded. "Yes. When you feel a weak vibration from the piano or from Rose's violin, it means the music is calm, quiet, tender. And maybe even sad or melancholy. Depending on the type of song, blue can be either."

"What color is happy?" Liam asked.

James looked around, then pointed at Cybill's dress. "Yellow . . . Yellow is a lively vibration from a happy song."

"Yellow is happy," Liam signed, clapping his hands.

Rose added to the imagery: "Think of a bright, sunny day, Liam. Or laughing with Boomerang and Contessa. Or even a slice of cake."

"I love cake!" Liam exclaimed.

Rose laughed.

James finished the lesson with red, pointing at the setting sun. "Hot. Intense. Angry," he signed. "Red is booming, thunderous, loud—the strongest vibration you will feel."

"Or it can also mean love," said Rose, glancing at James. "Love is red too. The most beautiful and vivid red there is."

Liam thought for a moment as he read Rose's lips. Grinning, he signed, "Like Music Man and Rose. They are red for each other."

James blanched, choosing not to respond.

Cybill smiled, enjoying the kindness and patience displayed toward her son. Delighted with this new way of teaching him how to experience music more fully, she said, "Think of all the various colors in Cassandra Fancy's garden, love. Each one is like a different vibration, a different sound."

The countless flowers blossoming with unmatched splendor filled Liam's thoughts. "Cassandra's garden is a symphony!" he shouted out, not caring if his nebulous words sounded funny.

"Yes, love, exactly!"

And so it went . . . With James' musical direction and Rose's methodology of connecting different sensations and colors to sound, Liam not only learned how to associate the vibrations he was feeling to the music but also how to play the piano. Slowly. Very slowly. But each step forward was a huge triumph, especially for the disabled teenager. It wasn't just a vibration anymore but the awareness he was attempting to make music for other people—

despite its simplicity—even though he couldn't hear it himself. Eventually, and with much practice, the succession of keys he pressed began to resemble music. Music he could feel but not hear.

Except in his mind.

Rose

Over the last several weeks, a beautiful kinship has developed between James, Liam, and me. When time allows, James and I visit the Herdsmans, and together we teach Liam through the lens of life what music sounds like. Sometimes the three of us will even leave Cybill's house—taking long drives, going horseback riding, or fishing in Indigo Bay—to explore the natural world around us, relating it to music.

Last Sunday, a peculiar and beguiling thing happened: Fishing far out at sea, we became caught up in a great murmuration of migratory starlings. Thousands of them. The passerines performed spectacular aerobatic displays of intriguing patterns, so well-coordinated that they looked and behaved as if a single being, twisting and swirling and swooping in the sky in tight formation, constantly changing its shape.

Each of us looked at each other, saying nothing, yet knowing how special it was. Otherworldly. For Liam it was something he didn't have to hear to feel, or feel to hear. He turned to James and signed, "This is what you mean when you teach me what music sounds like."

James nodded, touched by his comment. "Yes, lad. This is exactly what I mean," he signed back.

I am learning from Liam.

It is a strange awareness to absorb the beauty of life through the eyes of a deaf and intellectually challenged young man.

Nonetheless I am learning, and I find the experience quite lovely.

Liam

When Music Man and Rose come over, I watch as they lock eyes, unable to hide what I so easily see. They believe that because I cannot hear, I am not aware. They believe that because I am slow, I do not understand. But I am aware, and I do understand. I also see. I see things that others who can hear and who are not slow do not. Like the way Music Man looks at Rose, and how Rose smiles back. Yes, I am aware, and I understand quite well.

Just as I long for my ears to be opened, Music Man and Rose long for each other . . .

⌘

"Anna, what do you think about James giving me piano lessons?" Rose asked. They were in the farmhouse working on a patchwork quilt together.

Anna looked up from the half-finished comforter. "Why would you want piano lessons from James? You already play ace on the violin."

"That's exactly the point. I have a piano; I just can't play it like the violin. James could teach me how."

"Have you spoken to him about it?"

"Yes. He told me to ask you."

Anna thought about the idea as she threaded a needle. "I suppose it would be all right. If it makes you happy, Lottie, give it a burl, aye?"

"Thank you, Kitten. I've always wanted to play my piano better. Now I'll learn from the best."

"But you two can't be getting too friendly," Anna half-joked. "You're *my* cobber not his."

Rose smiled. "No worries, Kitten; you'll always be my favorite."

Later at the dinner table, Anna eyed her husband with a pensive glower. "You didn't tell me Rose wanted piano lessons. I wasn't too keen on that, but I agreed anyway."

A long, gaping pause settled in as husband and wife cut into their food. James knew what this would mean, and Anna was aware too: Her husband and cousin would be alone together for a period of time without her supervision. James wondered if she would really allow it.

"Well, if you're gonna give her lessons," Anna finally said, pointing her fork at him, "don't be hard on her. Teach her songs easy to learn, not those horribly hard ones you always play."

"The songs I teach her will be ordinary and elementary, love," he assured, wiping his mouth with his napkin.

Anna took another bite of her food, talking with her mouth full. "And they end the minute she tires of them."

James was slow to nod, picking up his drink and surveying his wife over the top of the glass.

Genevieve

"Piano lessons for Rose? You're a confident sheila to let another woman be alone with your bloke," the lady in the black Victorian dress says as Anna does the dishes.

"She uses a cane, Genevieve, and she's a tender soul. She would never betray me."

"Remember what Yarra told you, Sweet Pea? . . . A woman is a woman—always."

"Rose isn't just any sheila; she's my cousin and I trust her with my life," Anna says with fierce conviction to the hallucination.

Rose was a mediocre pianist at best. She had taken lessons in her youth, and throughout the years had taught herself a few easy pieces, but she hadn't fallen in love with it like she did her violin. Paul would sometimes ask her to play for him, only to fall asleep on the sofa when she did. Now, however, she had the opportunity to sharpen her skills by someone incredibly gifted.

A *true* pianist.

Wednesday night arrived, and James found himself surprisingly nervous as he stood before Rose's door, though he wasn't sure why. They had been visiting Cybill and Liam's together for quite some time, and it never bothered him before. But now they would be alone. He knocked, and Rose welcomed him in.

"I brought music to play," he said. "Wasn't sure if you had any."

"I do, but if you don't mind, I'd prefer it if you chose the song," she replied, the piquant scent of her black licorice wafting through the air.

With his hair sleeked back and his beard trimmed, Rose observed how James' appearance was a stark contrast to the rest of the week on the station where his hair was dirty, rumpled, and windblown, and his work clothes covered in red dust. Now, the Australian dirt had been washed off, and he smelled of mint soap mixed with Anna's perfume that no doubt rubbed off on his shirt when she hugged him goodbye. The faint fragrance was a constant reminder he was a married man. A reminder that James belonged to her cousin Anna, lay next to her at night, and had two daughters with her, their lives intertwined as if trees rooted in the earth.

They sat down on the bench, millimeters separating their shoulders. While James rummaged through his sheets of music, Rose couldn't help but notice the irregularity in his eye again, staring at it longer than she should have.

"What is it?" he asked, throwing her a glance.

"Sorry, I was just looking at your eye," she said. "The one with the teardrop pupil."

"I was hit by shrapnel during the war. Almost lost it."

"It gives your face a certain countenance."

"Anna calls it my clown eye," he softly laughed. "Liam tells me it's a tear from my soul."

"I find it quite lovely, myself," she said, picking up a sheet from the collection on his lap. "Because of it, your eyes hold this alluring sadness."

Neither said a word; neither looked at the other, until James took the sheet of music back from her and placed it on the rack. "I think it makes me look crook, if you ask me."

"There's nothing crook about you," said Rose.

From the expression on his face, he found her compliment amusing or flattering–she couldn't tell which. Lifting the fallboard to expose the ebony and ivory keys, he said, "I will play the entire song first, with you only observing, and then we'll break it up into several sections and go through them separately. Once you've mastered a part, we'll move on to the next, and so on until finished."

She nodded.

Just before he started, James reached over and gently uncurled her thrawn pinky finger that, out of habit, she kept hidden. "You need to try to keep all your fingers stretched out. Don't be shy about it; look at the scar I have," he said, showing her the jagged cicatrix on his own hand that ran from his thumb down to his wrist.

"As you feel about your eye, I feel about my leg and finger. They look crook, and I've always been shy about it."

"There's nothing crook about you," he said, giving her a wink and a smile. Turning back to the keyboard, he readied himself to play.

And so it began . . .

The back of James' fingers grazed along the top of the piano keys, caressing them as if skin, without applying enough pressure to make a sound. After a brief pause, Rose saw his torso straighten and swell with air, followed by exhalation as he began to play. The nuanced way in which he touched the keys and the mannerism of his fluid movements made Rose feel as if she were watching someone spin gold. How easy he made it appear. At one point during the music, she did not know where James ended and the piano began. Seemingly one piece. Two parts of the same whole. James was the piano; the piano was James.

His fingers danced across the keys, one hand following the other. The beginning was slow, dulcet, almost sad, the melodic, euphonious notes tumefying around her. Then the song erupted into the most beautiful sound Rose had ever heard. Letting himself go, James immersed himself in the classical work of one of the great Renaissance masters, and the result was awe-inspiring. As if a caged bird, finally set free. Closing her eyes, emotion overwhelmed Rose, and she struggled hard not to cry.

When the song was over, the sound yet hovered in the air, and all she could do was sit there, numb, attempting to regain her composure. The expression of the song and the stirring way it was played had touched her inner core where scars, tenderness, and pain still resided. It opened an old wound, and she felt as if she were bleeding. "I'm sorry, I don't know what's wrong with me," she said through tears. She had fought the emotion and lost—she could not stop crying.

His talent and ability had moved her in such a profound way she did not understand. The experience did something to her; changed her. Her soul felt lighter and her surroundings more vivid and clear. But there was something else. Her feelings for James were changing too—from friendship to something that would only cause trouble . . .

For her.
For James.
For Anna.

"You play so beautifully," Rose complimented after regaining her equanimity. But what she did not say was, "I could sit beside you for hours and listen to you play." She did not say, "My past years of suffering heal when I hear your music." She did not say, "How lovely you look as your fingers undulate across the ivory keys." No, those words were withheld. Her own private conversation. Words that sat on her tongue, yearning to be released to the pianist, yet not shared.

After his next song, Rose asked, "What is music to you, James?", her voice breathless. "How would you explain this magic?"

He smiled. "It's the universe talking to you. It's God's spirit running through your veins. It's the unsurpassed connection to everyone and everything beautiful in the world. The ultimate universal language."

The lesson went on longer than expected—three hours, nonstop. They were both in a trance, until it finally broke when Anna banged on the other side of the door. Rose let her in.

"Three hours, Jiminy Cricket!" Anna exclaimed as she entered, holding a twin on each hip.

"Sorry, Anna. It was me," Rose apologized. "I kept wanting to play another song. I didn't realize how much time had passed."

Anna smiled. "No worries." Looking at her husband, she asked, "How did she do?"

"She did well. She already has some experience, so it made the lesson go much smoother," James replied, lifting from the bench. "Well, I'm turning in, sheilas. G'night."

"Thank you for the lesson, James," Rose said as she watched him walk away.

He gave a slight nod, not looking back at her as he left.

Rose

The way in which he plays the piano is as if his soul catches fire.
To witness such a thing, right before my eyes, is mesmerizing.
His elegant hands, oscillating over the ivory keys.
His pneuma, mastering the great masters.
If he were mine, I would make sure his talent did not go to waste.
I would make it my life's goal to support him.
To allow him to immerse in his beautiful music.
But he is not mine.
He is Anna's.

Inside the farmhouse, James laid alone on the four-poster bed. He felt numb, extinguished, unable to move past what transpired that evening. His spirit, his psyche, had been dormant for so long that to experience some form of emancipation felt liberating. The lesson was no ordinary session, but an intimate and blissful interlude. I love to teach, and I adore the piano; that's why I feel this way, he assured himself. But he had taught before, and never had he had such an encounter.

Gazing through the open window of his bedroom, listening to an army of crickets stridulating ceaselessly, James stared at the center windmill glowing with light from within. He noticed what appeared to be two shadows cast against the wall, sitting close together on the love seat. One larger–Rose. The other smaller and almost childlike–Anna. Although related, the two women seemed to him as if from different species. Rose–tall, thin, and pale, with jet black hair and vivid green eyes; and Anna–petite and curvaceous, with sun-kissed skin, golden locks beneath the dye, and dark blue eyes resembling the sea at night. But the differences did not end there. Rose was an aesthete as he was, having intelligence and profundity beyond her years, and the ability to give warmth as well as receive it. Anna, though humorous and jovial, lacked empathy for others, and did not desire to stretch her intelligence, comfortable in the ways and teachings she had known since childhood, destined to remain that way her whole life.

Acknowledging the extraordinary differences between the two women–both still wonderful in their own right–James closed his eyes and rolled over, his body still pulsating from the music he had played at length that night for his wife's cousin.

The next day, James inspected the station with Lovely Dawn, checking the fences, the animals, and the crops before breaking for lunch. As they walked the length of the cornfield, he became lost in thought over how much he had enjoyed Rose's piano lesson. Her sound was different from his–a softer touch and tone–and although she was still learning, the vibration continued inside his head for hours afterward. Seeing the way she was moved by his music was powerful to him, too. It made an impact. Not because he was looking for admiration or praise, but because she had such depth and feeling for the music.

When he got to the edge of the vegetation, he glanced into the stalks, and there, only a few feet away, Rose stood in the tall corn, leaning on her cane. Earlier she had gone for a walk, and she was now coming back through the field. Both somewhat startled, they stopped and stared at one another without saying a word. Something had begun between them, and they both knew it. The piano lesson had initiated it, as if some unknown force binding them together. What it was or where it was going, they were unsure.

But it felt good.

It felt right.

Smiling at each other, they continued on their separate ways.

⌒�>⌒⌣

"I hope James wasn't showing off last night, trying to impress you with his playing," Anna said. "He's supposed to be teaching you, not enjoying himself."

The two cousins and the twins were having lunch in Cassandra Fancy's garden, with the women sitting at the white wrought iron table and chairs while the girls played with their dolls on a blanket beside them. The sun was shining, the wind gentle and warm, and Mrs. Swan swam gracefully in the pond waiting for crumbs, adding to the ambience of the glorious scene.

"No, not at all," said Rose, smiling as she thought of sitting so close to James, making prolonged eye contact with him, spellbound by his virtuoso skill. "He's a great teacher."

Anna pulled a small box from her purse.

"What's this?"

"A prezzie," said Anna, handing it to her.

"Another gift? Oh, Anna." Rose opened the box, and inside was a family heirloom—an exquisite comb previously owned by their Danish grandmother. Made from white tortoiseshell, it had four long teeth and intricate flowers carved into the base. "Kitten, it's beautiful. But I can't accept this. Grandmother gave it to you."

"Don't be a goose, Lottie. I want you to have it. You're my best cobber, and you help me so much around the homestead and with the girls. I want to give you something special; please take it." Anna removed the comb out of the box and placed it securely in Rose's hair.

Rose hugged her. *"Tak skal du have,"* she thanked in Danish. "You alone are a wonderful gift."

Anna blushed. Her cousin's words touched the very heart of her. She loved Rose dearly, and would do anything for her, having no suspicion of Rose's inner feelings and how she was slowly falling in love with her husband James.

Anna

After visiting Cassandra's garden, I decided to do the laundry, and I saw the bloodied man again, hiding behind a tree.

I tried to ignore him as I scrubbed the clothes.

Suddenly the water turned crimson red, and it was *his* clothes I was washing.

Blood overflowed the washtub, running through my fingers, and in terror I dumped it on its side, only to find the water crystal clear . . .

It was all in my mind.

Rose's piano lessons continued. Always on Wednesdays, right after dinner. James would clean off the grime from the day, change out of his work clothes, eat his food quickly and head straight to her maisonette. He so looked forward to this one day a week that everything else leading up to it seemed as if an obstacle he must overcome to arrive at his destination.

"I like this, you know," James said one evening, scratching at his beard after their last song. "I really enjoy coming here, giving you lessons." He smiled. "Maybe a little too much."

"Me too," said Rose, smiling back at him.

He thought for a moment, taking a piece of black licorice from the small bag she kept on the piano, splitting it in two and eating half.

Rose reached over and took the other half.

"It's grand having someone to chat with about things other than just the station, too, aye?" Most days after the lesson ended, they would converse about art, music, places they'd love to travel, and even social issues and politics.

"Yes, it certainly is," she said, her face aglow.

That night they talked about Ireland and how they'd both love to visit the small country someday. James shared that he often dreamed of the place and had family there, but admitted the station work would never allow him to leave. Rose swore she would go no matter what, alone if she had to, teasing that she'd send him a postcard from Dublin.

When James finally left the windmill to go home to his wife, Rose stepped outside into the darkness for some fresh air. As the cool breeze kissed her skin, a swell of light illuminated the spot where the Aboriginal stockmen sat around a blazing fire, drinking their grog and relaxing after another long workday. She heard them speak in Nukunu, play their primeval instruments, and chant their ancestral songs. The earthy sounds of the didgeridoo filled her ears, intermingled with the romantic piano music James had played for her earlier in the windmill, and somehow the combination of the two penetrated deep within her soul, circulating through her blood, causing the strongest of sensations in her.

A desire she was fighting . . .

She came to Sugar Alexandria a recent widow to seek refuge, to find herself and move on, not to fall in love with her cousin's husband. And yet that's exactly what was happening.

God help her.

 Anna.
His daughters.
The station.
His values that define the life he lives . . .
And divide him from the life he desires.
His music.
Rose.

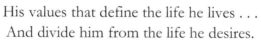

Wednesday arrived again—James' favorite day of the week. As they situated themselves on the piano bench preparing to begin the lesson, their shoulders briefly touched—a pleasant hap James savored. That and Rose's scent. She always smelled of Chypre de Coty, with a hint of licorice from her breath and clove from her cigarettes. Later, when at home and changing for bed, he would often smell his shirt where the fragrance lingered.

They played Bach's *Well-Tempered Clavier: Prelude No.1*, working on certain points of weakness in Rose's musical interpretation. James was patient and instructed her with kindness and skill. Every so often, he would lay his hand over Rose's, positioning her fingers correctly, his touch lingering longer than it should.

"You're so easy to teach," he said, releasing a slow smile. "Someone must have trained you before."

"I had lessons as a child," said Rose. "And Paul knew a little piano; he taught me some songs."

"You don't speak of him much."

Rose paused. "I don't have many good memories."

"Surely there were some."

"In the beginning there were. We went to Egypt on our honeymoon, and that was lovely. But soon after, he became another man. The same face on a different soul."

"How do you mean?"

"Overnight he became very controlling and cold."

"A loveless union."

She nodded.

"I'm sorry," was all he said. They sat there for a long moment, and then he touched her arm. "You'll meet a grouse bloke here, Rose, and this time it will be true love."

"Thank you, James. I appreciate your kind words."

After the lesson, he inadvertently rubbed the prominent scar on his hand, and Rose noticed. "That scar you got in the war," she said, pointing at it. "What happened?"

James hesitated. His own wife didn't want to hear any of his experiences from the war, and yet her cousin was asking him to share. And he wanted to. During his time on the battlefield, he had witnessed things no man should witness, leaving behind indelible memories forever ingrained in his brain like haunting nightmares. He saw death's cruel intentions and wicked, faceless smile. No rules, no mercy, no allegiance, no alliance, sneaking in quiet as a whisper, rushing in loud as thunder, acting quickly and taking its time. Fellow soldiers—husbands, fathers, sons, and brothers—all taken right before his eyes, some screaming, some begging, some embracing their fate, others caught un-awares, as if watching a flower bloom, only to fade and crumble in the blink of an eye.

"An injured soldier was caught in some barbed wire on the battlefield one day," James began. "The enemy was shooting at us as I tried to release him, but I couldn't get him loose. Bullets were whizzing by my head so fast, and that bloody barbed wire would just not let him go, entangling him as if in a web. I thought for sure we were both going to die." He paused as a wave of emotion swept over him. "I had ripped my hand open while struggling to free the man, and that's when a grenade landed close by, throwing us both back from the barbed wire. Miraculously neither of us were badly hurt from the blast, and I was able to carry him to safety without being hit by any bullets."

Rose put her hand on his shoulder. "My goodness, James, you're a hero. You saved a man's life."

He stared at her, a desperate expression assailing his features, his eyes searching her face. Yet he said nothing. Desperately he wanted to tell her how the real story ended. What would happen years later. But he couldn't, choosing not to share the secret.

Sensing something else tragic and sad in his countenance, Rose gently nudged him. "What is it?"

"There's another story I would like to share with you," James said, his voice breaking. "Can I?"

She nodded.

"Our ship had been bombed, and all the men were scattered. I was one of the lucky ones who managed to get into a dingy while the sea was literally on fire. Flames and bodies were everywhere. I was trying to grab anyone around me to get them into the dingy, but they were all dead. Then I heard Chance Dillon screaming for me. I got to him as quickly as I could, and when I pulled him aboard, his skin came off in my hands." James' eyes completely glazed over as he recounted the horrific ordeal. "The fiery water had burned him alive. He was unrecognizable and moaning in severe pain, begging me to put him out of his misery. I did the only thing I could think of: There was a medical box in the dingy, and I gave him a large dose of morphine. He closed his eyes, and that was it." Silent tears ran down James' face.

Rose was crying too. "James, I'm so sorry. You poor man."

"I had no other choice, the shape he was in. His bones . . . The boy's bones were showing!" James cried out. He turned and wept into Rose's shoulder, shaking in anguish. "Rose, his face haunts me to this day! His scream! His bloodcurdling scream for my help, and all I could do was put him out of his misery!"

"Shhhhhhhh . . ." Rose rocked him. "It's all over now. You're here, and you're safe."

James cried for only a moment, then pulled back, wiping his eyes as he regained his composure. "Sorry, I don't know what came over me."

"It's all right. You have been holding those tears in for a long time."

"Too long."

"Does Anna know?"

He shook his head. "You're the only person I've ever told."

"I'm honored you felt comfortable enough to share that with me, James. And if you ever want to talk again, I'm right here." She reached over and wiped away the moisture under his eyes.

He caught her hand, holding it fast, kissing the back of it before releasing. "You're very kind."

"I'm your friend. Friends are kind to each other."

"Yes, cobbers. Of course," James replied, wishing there could be more. But there couldn't be. He was strapped into a life that had grown around him as thick as the underbrush of the unforgiving Outback. A solid barrier stood between him and anything else he might desire, and that infinite stone divider was his wife. "You know, when you eventually find some lucky bloke and leave Sugar Alexandria to start your life with him, I will miss you," he said, glancing over at her with a melancholy grin on his face.

"You will?" Rose asked, his words making her feel like a star shining in the night sky. She had to fight the urge to throw her arms around him and kiss him. "What exactly will you miss about me?"

He smiled widely, his light blue eyes searing into hers. "Everything, Miss Rose Charlotte Moss. Everything."

~~❦~~

Continuously the weeks roll by, and James, Anna, and Rose become inseparable. They work, they eat, they sleep, only to get up again to repeat the day that resembled the day before and the day before.

Life is hard but never boring, variegated by picnics on sunny afternoons where they ride the horse and carriage to some paradisiac spot and eat lunch made by Yarrajan, or race horses down to the shoreline and swim in Indigo Bay, or linger in Cassandra Fancy's magnificent garden, or simply visit with each other after dinner and listen to the radio—all of it a blissful ritual. When they go to church or into town, they feel as one unit, one family. As if a knot were pulling them together, interlaced through their ribs and tied at the heart.

Anna's whispering episodes have lessened, too, the hallucinations less frequent, the disturbing fits calming like a sleeping giant. For her the days are wonderfully happy, and often as Rose leaves the farmhouse to return to her windmill, Anna shouts from the back porch for her to do the jig. Rose at first resists the dare, but then quickly tosses her cane aside and does her best to oblige. Anna joins in on the porch, doing the little dance, laughing so hard she cries.

There are stolen moments, though, when both James and Rose become quiet, lost in thought over each other, a tenseness shadowing their expression. Both wanting the same thing—something they cannot have. This goes unnoticed by Anna, caught up in her own rhapsody, her own seventh heaven, despite the overlaying that begins. Layers of hidden emotions, where her husband and cousin pretend. Pretend that they don't have feelings for each other. Pretend the long looks across the dinner table are as innocent as looking at oneself in the mirror. And when Rose later begins a short courtship with a local fisherman, and then a gentleman in town, James pretends he doesn't care about that either.

Soon the twins take their first steps. Rose's piano lessons continue; James perseveres his kismet; Anna revels in her joy. Though they are very much a ménage, lives interlinked, interwoven by blood, circumstance, and fate, the truth is also laden with fallacy.

Life, like the Australian wind, pushes forward, the days blowing by like leaves in the autumn breeze.

Anna

I'm so happy now, I could fly.
If I hear the voices, I try to ignore them.
If I see Genevieve or the shadow people, I look away.
If the bloodied man follows me, I let him.
I can be normal just like James and Rose.
I can pretend for the sake of our family.

PART THREE

CHAPTER 21

One Year Later . . . February 28, 1931

Summer is over.
Winter is looming.
Another year gone.

It was harvesttime for the sugarcane again. They set it on fire that evening as the sun was setting, cottony clouds dragging along the horizon, the sky an infinite milieu of intense sapphire with orange and red bleeding down in feathery strokes. Anna and Rose both watched from a distance, a baby on each hip, their hair still in pin curlers and wrapped in a colorful scarf, while James, Moony, and a few other stockmen walked along the stretch of field with a torch, periodically igniting certain areas aflame. Within seconds, the wind caught it, and the produce blazed an orange-red to match the sky, removing the outer leaves and tops from the stalks, and at the same time killing the snakes.

Each year, the sugarcane harvest gave rise to a joyful celebration, and with the burning of the crop well in hand, everyone would sit around a bonfire to eat, drink, and dance as the Aboriginals played their didgeridoos, beat their drums, and sang their autochthonous ceremonial tunes. James and Anna would even paint their faces as the Aborigines did—red and yellow with white dots scattered across their cheeks. This year Rose also followed the tradition and joined in.

As the exotic sounds of the unique instruments made from the hollowed-out trunks of a eucalyptus tree vibrated in low, husky pulses, hypnotizing all who heard them, Rose stared in wonder at the indigenous men with intriguing streaks and markings decorating their faces, each pattern representing some ancestral story or tribal significance. Inhaling the burnt cinnamon smell, she sat back and relaxed, enjoying the curious spectacle and wild atmosphere surrounding her. Her whilom life in London had expired, everything her existence had once been now gone—ashes, as if by the fire that burned the sugarcane—and she was grateful her cousin had allowed her to come to Sugar Alexandria.

The evening wore on, and James rolled up his sleeves, picking up a didgeridoo, blowing forcefully into the mouth of the hollow, creating his own distinct sound with a warm, resonant hum. He had too much to drink, and as he played the ancient instrument, he smiled and laughed with all his mates, the flames reflecting his face in the darkness.

Rose quietly watched him. It had been a year now that she lived at the station, and the infatuation with her cousin's husband had become almost unbearable. Of course she kept it hidden, and every time she witnessed an expression of affection between James and Anna, another pang of jealousy would cut through her heart, seasoned with guilt knowing she had no right to him. Yarrajan knew, though. The sapient Aboriginal woman could see it, her eyes shining odium and disapproval.

"What did you think of the sugarcane celebration this evening?" James asked, approaching Rose as she stared at the dancing flames of the blazing bonfire. Anna was preoccupied with something, the stockmen were chatting and drinking, and the Aboriginal wives and children sat in chairs in a circle, pointing up at the stars.

"It was lovely," said Rose. "The Aboriginals put on quite a show, and their wives are good cooks."

"Too right." As always, when they were alone, James stared at her so absorbedly she felt stripped bare.

"Do you have a durry?" she asked, breaking the intensity of his gaze. Gabbing the longneck in his hand, she took a quick drink and handed it back.

He gave her a cigarette and lit it.

"Ta."

"Look at you, smoking and drinking," he teased. "What would the nuns at the convent say?"

Rose exhaled a stream of smoke as she laughed. "They wouldn't be happy, I'm sure."

"I bet they miss you."

"They do. I get letters from them still, and just recently a postcard."

"What did it say?"

"Be good, Rose. God is always watching."

"And are you being good?"

She gave him a coquettish grin. "Not tonight."

James laughed. "Pray tell, what would being bad mean to Rose Charlotte Moss?"

Her eyes shined, but she had no reply.

"Some of the fishermen were asking about you the other day," he said, trying to quell the undeniable chemistry between them that was like electricity. "Down by the pier."

"Were they, now."

"Jack Bennington was particularly interested, pestering me with questions."

Rose only laughed.

"Would you marry a fisherman?"

"If I met one I liked, why not?" She nicked his beer again, taking a drink and handing it back. "I suppose I'd have to get used to the taste of salt, though," she added, pausing to observe his reaction. "That's what a fisherman's lips taste like when you kiss him—salty like the sea. As you know, I've already courted one."

"That's right—you've broken a few hearts in the last year, aye?" he teased, fully aware of whom she had courted and for how long, thrilled when each courtship ended.

"Something about being on the ocean all day makes them quite passionate." She wanted to bruise him a little. Seeing James and Anna show affection in front of her hurt Rose more than she would ever show. "And I hear they're rather good at other things, too."

Her frankness surprised James, but it only made him smile. "Ambrosia Charlotte Moss, a prim and proper English rose living by the ocean with a red-faced seaman who scales and cleans smelly fish every day. Doesn't seem to suit you."

"Oh yeah? What *does* suit me?"

"I would say a musician or an artist."

"Profession doesn't matter, as long as I like the bloke."

James finished off the last swig and threw the bottle into the bonfire. "You should wait for someone you more than like. Someone you're absolutely mad about."

She wished he wouldn't say things like that, as it was him she was mad for. "Time marches on and takes no prisoners. I'm going to have to settle for someone if I'm ever going to have a family of my own."

"Don't ever settle, Rose," he said, resting his gaze on her face again, his piercing blue eyes searing right through her. "You deserve better."

"The way you look at me sometimes . . . ," she began, stopping short.

His gaze turned bemused, that grin she adored playing at the corner of his lips.

"It's like you're studying me." Feeling awkward, she looked away into the flames of the bonfire that appeared to touch the sky. "As if you're about to paint me," she said, looking back at him. "Are you?"

"Would you mind?"

Holding each other's stare, they both smiled.

Rose

During this past year, something profound has happened to me. Something that cannot be disclosed to anyone—not even whispered to a priest. Slowly, gently, quietly, secretly, almost unknowingly, I have fallen in love with my cousin's husband James. A deep and amorous love that keeps me up at night.

I think he feels the same, too. The way he speaks to me, acts around me, and lingers when I am near.

I like the way he looks at me.

I wish all men saw me the way James Ragnar Shahan does. Like I'm an attractive, sensual woman instead of a skinny widow with a cane. Sometimes at night while I'm lying on my bed gazing up through the skylight, I imagine him staring at me like he does as I lay naked beneath him. My skin fresh and exposed to him, my nipples sensitive and yearning.

Alas, what will become of all this?

What will become of me?

～✦～

Anna had turned in early that night, putting her daughters to bed. Hours later, she awoke from a deep sleep, perpetrated by the Australian wind rattling the window. The space beside her was empty–James was gone. Like an apparition searching for its shadow, she rose and walked through the farmhouse, greeting the images in the paintings along the way, asking Elsa and Blessing how they were and if they wanted to have tea with her in the morning in her childhood secret room. Her mother and sister only blankly stared at her, refusing to come to life. Tonight they were just paintings.

With a kerosene lantern to guide her way, Anna searched for her husband outside, her cornhusk-colored hair glistening in the moonlight and her long white cotton housecoat appearing luminescent in the umbra, summoning a ghostlike persona in the gusty breeze. Intuition told her he was in the distillery. Sure enough, he was there.

James had his back to her, and between drams of whiskey, he diligently worked on something, so engrossed in his activity and inebriated from the alcohol that he didn't notice his wife had walked in. For a moment Anna only stood there, watching him indulge in his task, oblivious to her presence, and that irritated her even more.

"Good grief, James, it's nearly 3 a.m.," she finally said, lifting her lantern up at him, "and you're doing God knows what while tossing back that blasted whiskey. Didn't you drink enough during the celebration?"

James froze, only to quickly regain his composure and attempt to conceal the article in his hand. But he wasn't quick enough for his wife.

"What is that you're working on?" she demanded, scurrying over, grabbing it from him before he could hide it away. "What is this?" She scowled at the object she clutched–a small carving of a woman in fine detail. Anna moved the lantern right up to its face to inspect it closely, realizing it was a figurine of Rose. Yet he had created her with two normal legs. She kept studying the piece, mesmerized by the exact likeness of her cousin, while James only watched, his heart racing.

Anna looked up from the statuette, glaring at her husband's face aglow from the lantern, then again at the carving, trying to understand why he had created it. When James tried to grab it back, she held it close to her body and glowered at him. They were like two children fighting over the same toy. Anna slowly walked backward out the door without saying a word, her eyes never breaking from his, leaving him alone with his chisel in his hand and his whiskey by his side.

The carving of Rose had been disposed of. Or at least that's what James presumed. Why would his wife want to keep it, he reasoned? The next evening at dinner, however, to his surprise she pulled it from a drawer and said, "Look at this," placing the figurine in the middle of the table. "James carved a statue of you, Rose. He gave you two normal legs. He was curious to see what you would look like."

All three of them stared at the sculpture as if it were alive. Rose focused on how perfect her two legs were. Identical, with no defect at all. It was the first time she had seen a physical representation of herself in that way.

"I found him in the middle of the night in his grog hole, drinking the devil's elixir while carving it," Anna continued. "And he calls *me* the quirky one."

James almost snatched it off the table. He was embarrassed by not only *what* he had made but also *how* he had made it, giving Rose two normal legs when he should have created them as they were.

"It's lovely," Rose said with a tremor in her voice. She looked directly at James, excusing herself and abruptly leaving, her dinner unfinished.

Displeased, James turned to his wife. "Why did you have to show her?"

"Why did you bloody create it?" Anna fired back. "Why in the middle of the night is my husband sculpting an image of my cousin?"

"As you said, I was curious to see what she would look like with two normal legs." He lied.

"Why?"

"I don't know."

Anna stared at him, unconvinced, then picked up the figurine and placed it back in the kitchen hutch drawer. "Wasting time on rubbish, as usual. If you're not carving some object, you're writing some worthless piano music," she chided, shaking her head. "Acting like a useless bludger when there's real yakka to do."

"Useless bludger!" Moby squawked on cue, ruffling his feathers. The galah always seemed to know when Anna was berating her husband, never missing an opportunity to support her. "Irish whacker is what he is."

Anna laughed. "Too right."

James

I check the kitchen hutch drawer later, and the sculpture is no longer there.

"What did you do with it?" I ask Anna in bed.

She turns her back to me, pulling the covers over her shoulder. "I threw it in the fireplace and watched it burn into nothing."

Closing my eyes, I envision my carving of Rose turn black, then disintegrate into ashes in the orange-blue glow of the flames.

The statuette is forgotten, and each person continues in their expected role, dedicated to the part they must play: James, the hardworking husband who loves his wife and family. Rose, the widow who cherishes her little cousin. And Anna, the symbolic intertwining root, immuring them all conjointly. If it had been an opera, it would be dramatic, plausible, and even commendable, if it were not for the stolen glances, prolonged looks, and obvious yearnings. At the heart of it all is a naïve young woman with severe hidden mental illness, in complete denial of the passion growing between two people, right under her nose.

CHAPTER 22

"What a beauty of a day, aye?" Anna said, positioning herself to luxuriate in the bright sunshine. She and her cousin had walked to the beach after finishing their morning chores. "To live right by the ocean is so grand."

Rose closed her eyes and tilted her head, letting the rays between the fluffy white clouds tan her face as she dug her toes into the warm sand. "It's like heaven here."

"Too right. The fishermen call this stretch of beach Heaven's Gate."

"Yes, Heaven's Gate indeed. You really arc lucky to have grown up here, Kitten."

After lunch, Anna laid back on the blanket, listening to the sound of the water crashing against the rocks, enjoying the warmth of the sun on her skin. Scarlet and Mabel collected tiny seashells, fascinated by the different shapes, colors, and striations of the calcium carbonate exoskeletons, their chubby faces scrunching in bewilderment as they separated them into small piles on the sandy beach. And Rose tweaked the strings on her violin, preparing to play.

Tuning the instrument in perfect fifths to attain the desired pitch, she placed her chin on the rest and slowly slid the bow across the strings, twisting the peg of each one until achieving the right sound—an interval of a perfect fifth from the string next to it. When finished, she played an emotional Irish ballad. The twins sat down beside their now sleeping mother, staring in awe at the sharp and quick movements Rose made as she conjured the haunting music, their young minds completely unaware of the pain, frustration, and longing hidden in each and every stroke of the bow.

Rose

Whenever I play my violin now, I find myself communicating through the music what I wish were so.

What I long for.

Even to my own ears, the music is heartbreaking.

Oh, how I yearn to have a life with James Shahan–so much so it frightens me.

To touch him, kiss him, lie next to him, the rhythm of his heartbeat next to mine.

But these pleasures belong to my cousin.

His wife.

What God has yoked together let no man put apart, I remind myself.

He is a married man, as if a covenant handed down from heaven, and I dare not attempt to break it.

James belongs to Anna as the sun belongs to the sky.

Anna

The things that surround me . . .

Sugar Alexandria
The Australian gale
The Southern Ocean
My darling daughters
My beloved cousin
Rose's paintings
Chypre de Coty that lingers
The strong aroma of black licorice
Vanilla crème soap on her alabaster skin
Her violin
The piano
The scent of James' whiskey
The voices
My mother
My sister
The soul tree
The shadow people
The Black Shuck
The bloodied man
Genevieve watching over me
Lottie's desire to have a child . . .

CHAPTER 23

Rose had been spending more time at Cassandra Fancy's garden lately. Just like the duke's wife from a bygone era, she too needed a place of solace where she could think clearly about her untenable situation, having no idea how to escape, lost over an apposite resolution for her conundrum. She wanted to leave Sugar Alexandria but couldn't. She wanted her cousin's husband but knew she would never have him. She wanted a baby of her own but only through James.

Visiting the enchanted garden was the perfect place for Rose to ruminate, because at least she could enjoy its divine pulchritude in the process. Mrs. Swan often visited too, swimming in the pond, which only added to its beguiling charm.

With a gradual chill in the air and hunger pangs ensuing, Rose decided to return to the station. Walking across the paddock, she encountered a sudden, frenzied rush of cattle, stampeding straight toward her. In fear of being caught up in the mayhem, she accidentally dropped her cane as she darted out of the way. She saved herself, but her cane was not as fortunate, trampled underfoot by the spooked animals.

When Anna told James, he did something special. Visiting Cybill's, he took the original lid prop from his piano and fused it together with another piece of wood to create a new cane for Rose. One that had sentimental value for him.

The head of the walking stick he made from smooth pearl white quartz with a hint of Berlin blue. Along its length, he hand-painted Art Nouveau flowers in purple, pink, red, and gold, continuing the pattern top to bottom with such intricate detail it resembled lace. Afterward, he lacquered it to bestow its shine. Pleased with his handiwork, he headed over to Rose's maisonette.

As he walked across the stockyard, James' eyes remained fixed on the center windmill. Though no longer a working machine for the benefit of the station like the other two, the blades still spun in the wind just the same, as if an illusion where the outer shell hid the inner reality. From the outside, it was just a normal mill, but like a pearl within the oyster, inside was a rare jewel.

"Oh, James, it's beautiful," Rose said as she examined her new walking stick.

"A part of my piano is in it," he said.

"Your piano?"

"Yes. I started out with a piece of karri wood for its durability. But then . . . it just didn't feel right. It wasn't enough. And that's when I thought of the lid prop from my piano. I wanted to incorporate something significant to me as a gift to you, so I went to Cybill's to get it." James grinned, proud of the history behind the wood in his treasured instrument. "There's actually quite a story behind that piano," he said. "Goes back to the land of Éire. My great-grandfather built a boat from a two-hundred-year-old tree, calling it Whiskey Sails because he ran bootlegged whiskey to the local fishermen out of it. During a bad storm one night, the boat hit rocks and capsized. He clung to a portion of the wreckage, making it safely to shore, and later built a piano out of the wood that saved his life."

Rose was intrigued. "The same piano that now sits at Cybill's and is played by a deaf boy."

"And a piece of it has now become a cane for a beauty of a sheila to help her walk."

They both smiled.

"That piano must be precious to you," said Rose. "It should be in your possession. Why don't I give Cybill and Liam mine, and you can take back yours?"

James shook his head. "I can get it later."

They both went quiet for a moment, knowing what "later" meant . . .

the day Rose would be leaving.

She brought her attention back to her new walking stick. "You really outdid yourself on this. It's not just a cane but a piece of artwork. The flowers you created even have the essence of Gustav Klimt's *Flower Garden* landscape."

"When I first laid eyes on you that day at the wedding, you reminded me of the women in his paintings, along with those of Alfons Maria Mucha," James did not say but wanted to. Instead, he said, "Yes. He's one of my favorite artists."

"Mine too." She walked over to her bookcase and pulled out a large hardcover. "Here's a collection of Gustav Klimt's work. You can have it; it's my gift to you for making me such a wonderful cane."

"Ta," James said, opening the book. Flipping through the pages, he stopped on an image of *The Kiss*, staring down at the glossy sheet displaying the famous painting of a man and woman locked in an intimate embrace against a shiny gold leaf background.

"Stunning, isn't it?" said Rose.

"Outstanding. It's been rumored that it's a portrait of Gustav himself and his companion Emilie Flöge."

"And yet others suggest the female was the model known as Red Hilda, bearing a strong resemblance to the woman in his *Lady with Hat and Feather Boa*."

James nodded. It always impressed him how much he and Rose were alike, both so cultured and interested in the arts.

"Anyway, thank you again for the beautiful cane, James. I'll think of you every time I use it," she said, giving him a warm embrace.

"You're welcome. You're very good to my wife and my children; it's the least I could do." Pausing, he wanted to say more . . . And then he did . . . "You're also a dear cobber to me. My life has changed profoundly since you came to Sugar Alexandria."

In that moment, nothing else mattered to Rose, and she wanted to confess her feelings for him, to tell him everything that had been going on in her heart over the last year. But of course, she could not. As Liam was deaf, she had to remain mute about her true feelings, like a songbird whose voice had been stolen.

James was the first to break the enchantment. "Let's go outside and give your new cane a burl, shall we?"

"Yes, let's go show Anna."

The seventy-seven steps to the farmhouse could have been seven hundred as they took their time, chatting while they walked. With the sunlight directly on his face, Rose noticed James appeared worn and tired. Eyes bloodshot from the dust in the wind, his light Irish skin burned red from long hours in the sun, deep cracks lining his eyes, dry lips, strands of gray prematurely feathering out around his temples. Though still a handsome man, he seemed as if a lost and exhausted animal, searching for its home for far too long.

Rose looked away, unsettled by what she saw. Despite being blessed with great musical talent, he had been forced into an ineluctable bastille, giving up his dreams and enervating himself for the happiness of his wife. The pianist and teacher was imprisoned by the grazier, and the keymaster had yet to be found.

"There's my bloke!" Anna exclaimed, a happy smile on her face as she opened the screen door, Scarlet and Mabel holding each hand. She gave James a squeeze, and the image once again made Rose think of an August Hagborg painting of a young Scandinavian couple, this time with their children. "He's mine you know, Lottie," Anna teased, dimples popping, gap between her teeth showing.

Rose watched husband and wife embrace. "Yes, Anna. I know James is yours."

Rose

Here I am, coveting her husband, and all Anna wants is my love . . .

These are my secret thoughts—thoughts that go through my mind every time Anna hugs me, or invites me over for tea and bickies, or takes me to the shoreline for a picnic.

I care tremendously for my younger cousin, but I have grown to love her husband James more.

Such a problematic situation; such an impasse!

I should leave, I keep telling myself. Move tomorrow, start over in some small town, and never look back.

But if I tell Anna I am leaving, she will cry. She will follow me around like a hurt puppy until I change my mind. She will barter with me, plead with me, beg me. She will want to come with me.

This could go on for the rest of my life, allowing her to control my world.

Why can't Anna see what's happening and tell me to go? To save her marriage, protect what's hers.

And yet, not seeing James on a regular basis will come at such a great cost to my heart.

Hence, I continue to wage this war within myself, only to succumb to defeat.

I have lived without love for many years when I was with Paul; I can at least embrace this love for someone at arm's length.

I deserve at least that.

CHAPTER 24

Backbreaking work at the station, Rose's piano lessons on Wednesdays, girls' night in the windmill on Fridays, occasional church on Sundays, and picnics by the shoreline or visiting Cassandra Fancy's garden—life goes on as usual at Sugar Alexandria. Anna longs for the station to become more successful and make them wealthy, James for a life where he can teach and play the piano every day, and Rose for a child she can call her own. Their desires seem like the sea—without boundaries, unattainable, a hunger that cannot be satisfied.

There are moments while James is working when he thinks of the dance he had shared with Rose that night of his sister's wedding, when he felt as if time had stood still and transported him to a faraway place. Too often, he catches himself daydreaming about her, vivid images dripping with color, thinking about a different life in a different time in a different world. One of the stockmen inevitably hollers and brings him out of his daze, and the long workday continues.

Anna

Late at night, the voices summon me again. At first unfamiliar, then all too familiar. Quietly I dress, take the kerosene lamp, and visit the paintings, then my shrine.

I live inside a world within a world, where the veil has been lifted and I see what others do not. I am gifted in this way.

I live where paintings are alive and trees hold souls. Where shadows protect me and voices guide me. Where strange men follow me, wanting me to solve their evil riddles.

As I put on my goose-feathered crown and wings, kneeling at my special tree, I smile. I live where secrets rule, and I am the queen over this land.

Rose

On the way home from Cassandra's garden today, I took a different route and came across Anna's clandestine shrine. The eerie-looking tree startled me, and I almost stumbled back, staring at the numerous Aboriginal beads and corn husk dolls hanging from its branches. At its base sat a scull of a dead animal with fresh flowers coming out of its eye sockets, tied together with a piece of fabric from one of my dresses. That too almost made me stumble back.

I remember Anna confiding in me once that the little animals she favors on the farm that are unique in some way—a smart chicken, a black lamb, a runt piglet—she buries in a special place and they come back as birds, flying out of a soul tree. No doubt this was that tree. The entire aberration drove a horrifying chill right through me.

I know my sweet cousin needs professional help, but instead James and I ignore her bizarre idiosyncrasies and indulge her like a child. Why, I wonder?

As I continued on my way, I saw another curious sight: Liam was putting flowers on the grave with no marker inside the Polston family burial plot. I wanted to ask Anna about it, but she had gone into town to have lunch with the Esmeralda sisters—an invite I too had been given but declined. James was in his den, so I asked him instead: "I noticed Liam places flowers on the unmarked grave in the family burial plot," I said, scanning the books on his bookshelf. *Wuthering Heights* by Emily Brontë caught my eye, and I tucked it under my arm for later. "Who's buried there?"

James looked up from his desk where he had been reading and nervously touched his beard. "No one," he said, his eyes both haunted and hunted. "There's no unmarked grave. Only Anna's family members are buried there."

Dinner that night was awkward for everyone, as Anna had served raw, uncooked meat, seemingly unaware. Sitting there, staring down at their blood-soaked jadeite plates, precipitated a peculiar confluence of shock and droll. Anna had done that in the past, too, and when James questioned her about it, she appeared addlepated. He didn't press the issue; he just took the bloodied pieces of meat and cooked them himself. When Anna finally realized her blunder, she apologized profusely, embarrassed. James and Rose told her not to fret about it, knowing it was another manifestation of her innominate illness.

Later, while in bed, Anna said, "Remember when we first got married and you would read *Alice in Wonderland* to me?"

He caressed her cheek. "I remember, Tin Tin."

"Rose used to read it to me too when we were girls."

"I know; you told me."

She snuggled closer to her husband. "I always feel safe with you, Sugar Bear."

James smiled. "I'm glad, love."

Anna looked up at him, and with a saccharine voice, whispered, "In fact, I wouldn't mind it if you wanted a root tonight."

James turned to face her in the darkness, the only light a soft illumination from a candle still burning on her vanity. It surprised him she offered; usually he was the one who initiated intimacy. Crawling on top of his wife–she smelled a mixture of sweet chocolate and spice–he pushed her thighs apart. With her face turned to the side, she made no sound as he mechanically went through the motions she would allow. Even when her own body responded to his, she only tensed, waiting for him to finish.

Music drifted in through the open window, disrupting his routine. Rose had begun playing her violin. The sound touched the very heart of him, slowing his body down, as if hypnotized.

"James, hurry up," Anna said.

He quickened his movements, trying to concentrate on her, but the sound kept distracting him. It was the melody of a bleeding heart. Only a true musician would understand the language of such a sound.

As he continued to make love to his wife, James felt confused, selfish, even lost. He was saturated with so many emotions–irritation and resentment for Anna, mixed with excitement and lust for her cousin. Still, the violin music encircled him as he thrusted in and out, intoxicating him with melodious notes coming from the center windmill. Envisioning Rose's face; her thin, bare neck; slender, lissome frame; arms open wide, welcoming him into her soft embrace; he immediately spasmed, letting out a loud, raspy moan, shuttering and shaking. Then he collapsed.

Anna pushed away from him, settling in bed, dozing off to sleep.

Awake with his thoughts, James stared at the ceiling, fearing that Rose might have heard the sounds of their lovemaking. He tried hard to hold back, knowing the window was open, but failed. Perhaps the music had drowned him out, he hoped.

As he laid in the darkness, a silence unfurled. An earsplitting silence so powerful the beating of his own heart echoed in his ears. The music had stopped, and it seemed as if the whole universe had paused to take a deep breath. In that same moment, James felt connected to Rose as if she were lying right next to him . . . Even though he had just made love to his wife.

Rose

Everything is strange now. Tense. Creepy. Dirty. A strong sense of perversion inoculates me. A growing sense of fear, too. I know what it is: I'm too fond of James Shahan—a man I cannot have. No, that's not it . . . I'm in love with him with all that I am, and it hurts me as much as it excites. Stings worse than my leg when it spasms and the bone aches down to the marrow.

I heard them making love last night, and it nearly broke me. Not because I don't know what husbands and wives do but because James knows I care for him and didn't have the respect and consideration to shut the window. My jealousy is so ripe it's turning into hate for my dear cousin. Hate for how she clings to me like a child, as if I were her doll. Hate for how she tries to look like me, smell like me, sound like me. Hate for how she's always seeking my attention, my approval, my friendship, trying to fill an emotional hole that never seems to fill.

All of this has left me completely imbalanced, unsure of what to do. I cannot go on like this any longer, harboring such deep antipathy. It isn't healthy. I am frustrated constantly, with no cognitive acuity on why I cannot start my own life without it somehow being attached to Anna's. As if I were another Rapunzel locked in a castle, unable to escape.

Today I tried to explain to Anna that I must go and find my own life, pursue my own dreams, start my own family.

She panicked. "Give it time, Rose," she pleaded. "You will eventually meet a grouse bloke; I'm sure of it. Then you can both live here at Sugar Alexandria, and we'll still be together."

That frustrated me even more, and I lashed out at her. "Ohhh God, Anna, it's not about you!" I rebuked. "You'll never understand! Just leave!"

Aghast, her mouth dropped open.

"I said go! I don't need you! I don't want you!" I screeched, my pent-up jealousy, longing, desire, and resentment bursting forth.

Anna fled in tears, ululating uncontrollably, while I collapsed on the floor, clutching my cane to my chest and crying.

～⚜～

"Anna, what are you doing!" Rose's heart raced as she woke up the next morning to find her cousin standing above her, a rum look on her face, watching her sleep.

Remaining motionless, as if in a trance, Anna didn't answer.

"Did you hear me? . . . Anna!"

Suddenly she snapped back from wherever her mind had been. "Are you still mad at me?" she sheepishly asked, looking as if she were about to cry.

Rose sighed, running her fingers through her messy morning hair. "No, Kitten. I'm sorry I lashed out at you yesterday. I was just frustrated with my life, and you didn't deserve that."

Anna's girlish smile slowly formed on her lips, exposing the gap between her front teeth–the same gap Rose always thought adorable and that reminded her of a kitten. "But you can't come in here unannounced like this. You have to knock first. You gave me a fright."

"Sorry, Lottie. I won't do it again."

The two cousins made up, and Anna convinced Rose to have breakfast in her childhood secret room. Though it appeared everything was back to normal, Rose still felt the need to leave Sugar Alexandria to finally start her own life. Then something tragic happened that reinforced her decision, making her want to flee with only the clothes on her back . . .

CHAPTER 25

The weekend arrived, bringing with it a heartrending sadness for Mandawuy and his wife Kareela. Anticipating the joyous birth of their first child, Kareela delivered a stillborn. Anna and Rose held hands during the Aboriginal burial ceremony that followed, deeply saddened and weeping as the inconsolable parents lowered their child into the cold ground.

Later, at dinner, Anna whispered, "I could go get it and bury it at the soul tree."

James and Rose looked up from their food.

"What did you just say?" he asked, always taken aback by Anna's strange notions.

"I could go at night, and no one would know. Then the soul tree would . . ."

James abruptly stood and walked over to his wife, grabbing her by the shoulders and shaking her. "Don't you touch that child!" he warned. "You hear me! That's sacred Aboriginal land, and that baby has been laid to rest!"

Rose came to her cousin's defense, protectively wrapping her arms around Anna, trying to push him away. "Don't you touch her!"

But he kept his firm grip on his wife, staring down at her.

"She doesn't mean any harm, James." Rose gently removed his hands. "She just thinks that by putting the baby there, it will in some way live on. She would never follow through with it, though. Never."

Anna was now wailing. "But the birds that fly from the soul tree come from its roots," she cried. "And I can talk to Mummy and Blessing there."

"I have had enough of this madness!" James yelled, his eyes blazing at both women. "If I hear she's gone anywhere near that burial place, I'll take the belt to her!" he threatened. "I'll take the belt to both of you!"

"My shrine is holy!" Anna argued. "It has power!"

"That bloody abomination is rubbish child's play, and it needs to be burned!" In his anger, he let loose on Rose, too. "I've always feared you coming here would make her worse, and I was right! Bloody oath, she's gonna end up in the insane asylum soon!" Grabbing his Akubra hat, he stormed out the door.

Rose was in shock, hurt beyond words. But maybe it was true. Maybe her presence was making Anna's condition worse. Though she loved her cousin, she didn't want to become a part of her illness, nor did she want to cater to it anymore.

This was the final provocation.

Rose attempted her escape.

On Sunday, when her cousin had gone to church, she left the mill when no one was watching and quickly prepared the carriage to leave, attaching it to the horse. The train station was her destination. Dressed in all black–the same outfit she had worn the day she arrived–her gossamer lace veil covered her eyes, Matilda meowed in the pet carrier by her side, and her luggage sat stowed in the back. But James caught her before she fled.

"You're going to leave without saying goodbye to Anna?" he asked.

She froze, her heart pumping wildly.

"Or your piano teacher either? Shame on you."

Instead of shrinking back, Rose mustered her courage to stay the course. "That's right; I'm leaving. There's something wrong with Anna, and like you said, I'm making her condition worse." Besides, the dysfunctional circle must come to an end, she thought.

"So you're going to run and hide in the nunnery again?"

"It's none of your business what I do."

"I didn't mean what I said to you, Rose. If anything, you've helped Anna by making her happy. I just get frustrated with her illness sometimes. Scared, even."

"Regardless, these feelings between us . . . It's too much for me." His vitreous blue eyes met hers, fervent and evocative, softening her mien into a desperate look. "James, I came to Sugar Alexandria to recover, and I have. What am I supposed to do now, live the rest of my life here? I want what you and Anna have—my own family." Watching Anna and James raise theirs, living vicariously through them while she languished, had become a cruel torment for her.

James knew what she was feeling and saying was true. Though he wanted to convince her to stay, in that moment he felt like a caretaker of a haunted mansion, and Rose was the maiden trying to flee with her life from all the monsters. Who was he to keep her trapped in such a place?

They stood there in silence, endeavoring to assimilate their cerebral cogitations in the face of the insoluble emotive quandary, the theme always the same: James and Rose wanted to be together, and the reality was they couldn't. A platonic relationship was the only option.

"Trying to escape the monsters, are we?" he asked.

"Maybe *I* am the monster," she replied, feeling like the real enemy.

"Impossible."

Rose stared at him, and with the fight returning in her eyes, she said, "I need to find a place where I can lock myself in and figure out what I'm going to do with the rest of my life."

"You can't do that here? I built you a beauty of a maisonette for that very purpose."

"No, I can't, and you know exactly why."

James slapped his leg with his Akubra hat. "I don't want you leaving like this, Rose," he said, dreading the thought of not seeing her around the station anymore. "And you owe it to Anna to tell her in person."

She looked past him into the illimitable fields as if searching for the right answer. Cows and sheep grazed peacefully, little calves and lambs by their mothers. Ambrosial fragrance from the hybrid tea roses, crimson waratahs, and golden wattles outside her windmill permeated the air. And a light breeze tantalized her skin, chasing away the sun's heat. In spite of the stressful situation, it seemed Sugar Alexandria wanted her to stay. "But I *have* to leave, James," she replied, almost a whisper. "Please believe me."

He took her hand in his and slowly removed her silk glove. Rose thought it peculiar, until he tenderly felt over the callus on her string finger, exactly the way he had done on that magical night they first met. "With a face like yours, my sweet Charlotte, I would believe just about anything you said. But don't leave, aye?" he pleaded, his voice low, his eyes glossy. He had no idea what he was saying, or what would come next; he simply spoke from the deepest parts of his heart, struggling to control the maelstrom of feelings rampant inside him. "I'm begging you, Rose. Don't take my smile away just yet."

She wanted to hold her ground but found her posture elusive. Then it hit her, dissolving her willpower, her logic, into liquid. His earnest plea had surfaced what was deep down inside her, that no matter where she went, how much time had passed, what distractions she could embrace, or how many men she would meet, it would not change her yearning for her cousin's husband. Nothing would banish or even fade the imprint he had made on her.

Rose exhaled as she held his gaze, and James knew he'd won. Retrieving her luggage, they walked back to her maisonette in silence.

Fate was not done with them yet . . .

At the entrance to the mill, Rose turned to James and said, "During that argument with Anna, you threatened that if she went anywhere near the Aboriginal burial place, you'd take the belt to her. And me too."

"And?"

She grinned. "I'd like to see you try."

Anon everything went back to the way it was on the station, and Rose, still feeling trapped, wanting to leave but not wanting to leave, remained stagnated under the hegemony of her mentally unstable cousin and her love for her cousin's husband.

Her Wednesday night lessons with James resumed, as did their visits to the Herdsmans where she would watch him patiently teach Liam how to play the piano. The three of them would often spend time together in the outdoors where they'd continue relating the sights and feelings of the world around them into expressions of music. Liam absorbed it all in. He was improving, applying what he was learning, gaining confidence and overcoming his need to feel the sound to produce the music. To Rose, he was playing Beethoven.

Many a time, her flesh would cover with goose bumps, knowing how rare and beautiful it was for a deaf individual to learn to play a musical instrument. An intellectually challenged young man, no less, living in his own private shell, forced to adapt to the restrictions and boundaries of his disabilities. Yet James was teaching him how to break through those fettered thresholds and come out on the other side, experiencing things he would not otherwise. As if attaching wings to a bird born without them.

Liam

I close my eyes and feel for the keys.

I cannot hear the sound, but I have memorized the steps as one does a dance.

There is a rhythm I follow, and I count as I play, each song having many numbers.

In between, like deep breaths, I glance over to see Music Man encouraging me to continue.

And I do.

"Imagine something bonzer as you play," he signs to me. "Imagine a beauty of a day."

Rose joins in: "Think of the ocean," she says. "The roar, the power, the endless waves."

I used to think music was simply the vibrations I could feel through the wood of the piano.

A delightful resonance infusing into my skin.

Now I know it's much more . . .

Music is what emotions sound like.

"Seeing Liam play the piano and be so immersed in it is very touching to me," Rose said. She and James were walking back from the Herdsmans' house, taking the long way home, along the river and over the bridge to Sugar Alexandria. "He tries so hard to play it right, always looking at you for confirmation. What you're doing for him is extraordinary, James."

He gave her a soft, boyish smile, and Rose let her eyes linger on his face. She didn't just see a handsome man but a powerfully compelling one. Notwithstanding the resplendent sunny day, he seemed to have a bright aura about him, as if he generated his own light. She often noticed it when he played the piano, too, how the light would become radiant.

Their walking had slowed, and when they came upon the long winding fence that stretched the length of the paddock, they both leaned against it, staring out at the vast green meadow—cows, sheep, and horses roaming the land.

"Look at this place," he said.

"It's a beauty."

"Takes a lot of hard yakka to keep this ship on course."

"You do a great job, too. Never a harder-working bloke."

He seemed to find that humorous for some reason, letting out a laugh.

"What's so funny?"

"It's just when you say how hard I work, it's true; but thinking back, I would have never guessed this would be my life. I honestly thought I was destined to be a professional pianist and music professor."

"Perhaps someday you will be."

His face took on a soulful, sad expression, his gaze moving past her, looking beyond at something far away. Or maybe something in his mind. "That's kind of you to always say, but I doubt it," was all he said.

Rose glanced over at the large farmhouse in the distance, the red barn, the center windmill where she lived, looking deeper still, discerning what hid behind the walls of each structure. The stories of Sugar Alexandria and its people, including hers. A woman who had traveled across the sea to live with her cousin, only to fall in love with her cousin's husband. Madly in love.

"I want to tell you something," he said, "but you can't ever tell Anna."

The wind had kicked up, causing a chill on her skin, yet Rose felt surprisingly warm. "I won't."

"Promise."

"To the grave." She leaned in closer to him. So close that his misshapen pupil took on its full teardrop appearance.

James paused, touching his beard, thinking. Long and slender were his fingers, strangely elegant hands covered in calluses, nails dirtied from the soil he travailed in each day. He continued, "I never courted Anna. Never had any intention for it to be anything serious. At the time, I was dating a handful of girls, actually–just all for fun. Then I had too much to drink and . . . well . . . let's just say I barely even remember that night. After that, it was all a blur, and I found myself married to a sheila I didn't even know."

"A rushed wedding," said Rose, holding his gaze.

"Yes. She told me she was pregnant. That one severe lapse of judgment on my part forced me to cancel going to England to pursue my studies, changing my whole life's course to marry her. Then she ended up not even being with child. Not until ten years later, at least."

"I know."

"What you don't know is, there was another reason it was extremely difficult for me then." He looked at her intently, regret in his eyes, staring as if a looming, thirsty tree staring at a river from afar. "There was a sheila I had met at my sister's wedding, and at the time, I was still thinking of her. Never forgot her," he said, his words cutting deep, piercing her over what could have been. What should have been. His features softened, and a gentle smile appeared. "I told you I dream of Ireland, aye? And that once or twice you flashed into my dream? The truth is, over the years, even before you arrived, you were *always* there with me in that dream."

Rose suddenly felt light, as if her cane were not needed at all, and if she didn't hold on to the fence she would fly away.

He broke eye contact with her, scanning over the paddock again. "It's true. I never forgot you, Rose. If I had only been more aggressive and kept searching for you after that wedding, things would be so different for us now. I would be married to you, not Anna. My daughters would be yours, not hers."

Rose was stunned; her mouth went dry; her hands trembled. Why am I shaking so badly, she wondered? Even her teeth began to chatter.

"And isn't that something–you end up coming back here a decade later and showing me how it could have been." He noticed Rose was shivering. "Here, take my jacket," he said, removing it and putting it around her shoulders. "Hope you're not coming down with a fever."

"Oh, but I am," she did not say. "A fever of the worst kind," she thought as he reached over, rubbing his hands up and down her arms to warm her.

꧁ ꧂

Rose

Being in love with the pianist, yet unable to have him, is torture.

Wanting to leave, but emotionally extorted to stay for the health and welfare of my mercurial cousin, is impuissance.

How does one escape purgatory?

I am but Alice in Wonderland, a real-life woman in Anna's favorite fantasy, and I have fallen into the rabbit hole with no way out.

꧁ ꧂

James and Rose play a duet during their next piano lesson—he on the keyboard and she on the strings. The notes from his piano, mixed with the sweet, long chords from her stringed instrument, vibrate into the air. They go inside the music. Around it. In and out. Beneath and beyond. Exact, complex, punctilious. James follows the mood Rose creates with her violin, reciprocating the same emotional esprit through his piano, and the juxtaposition of the two creates a beautiful, graceful harmony, becoming one.

"I will create this music for you since I cannot touch you," James does not say.

"I will express how deeply I feel about you with this piece," Rose wishes she could say.

They both experience an intimacy with the music they cannot experience with each other, communicating through a musician's vernacular. An unspoken dialect of creativity, depth, and inseparability. As the music encircles them, resonating through their bodies inside the windmill, James feels exhilarated, happy, alive.

And so does Rose.

꧁ ꧂

Rose lights candles around the bathroom in the windmill the next evening and steps into the hot water. As she lays in the tub, she meditates on what James had confided in her on the way back from the Herdsmans the other day. He had been thinking of her the whole time since they first met, even dreaming of them together in Ireland, despite being caught in Anna's grasp, finding himself trapped in a situation he could not escape, wishing he had married and had children with her instead. Instantly she herself feels cornered by her cousin's love again. Tied, unable to move forward because of Anna's dysfunctional need for her. The resentment starts building once more. Everything Anna has should actually be mine, she laments. He had picked me once, before he met Anna, before Anna schemed and manipulated him to be bound to her.

As the light from the candles fleet, Rose's wild musings escalate. She thinks of Anna's idea from a year ago, her mind still hearing the words: "Rose, he does everything I say. It would only be one time, and you could have a baby of your own. You could raise it here at Sugar Alexandria and stay with me forever."

The light finally goes out. Darkness and the insatiable desire to be with the pianist encapsulate each other until Rose cannot separate the two. As if she no longer knows right from wrong. Closing her eyes, she slowly submerges into the bathwater, James' music in her mind and a plan of her own in her heart . . .

CHAPTER 26

"Anna!" Rose called out, waving from the entrance of the windmill. "Anna!"

But Anna was too far away in the paddock and couldn't hear her cousin. Wearing her denim dungarees, she stood in the open field, kulning, beckoning the cattle and sheep home. The high-pitched sound floated into the air, carried by the wind for miles, and soon the first few cows and sheep began to appear.

Rose listened for a moment. Under the late-afternoon sun, she watched this sweet and trusting farmer's wife calling to the livestock. As Anna continued to sing the ethereal song to bring the herds in, goose bumps sprouted all over Rose's skin. It would be so easy to keep living here, she thought. To be subdued by her situation, grateful and content for the blessings she's been given, rather than bemoaning the curses she must bear. "Kitten!" she called out louder. This time, the wind carried her voice.

Anna turned and smiled. She headed back toward the windmill, and when in earshot yelled, "It's Friday, Lottie! Want me to put the twins to sleep early and come over later for our girls' night?"

Rose smiled too, nodding.

Anna loved their weekly girls' night where they would get together in the windmill and stay up late, sometimes until dawn. This was the one night a week she could be a kid again, laughing and playing with her best friend.

It always made her feel liberated, regaining a measure of personal freedom—time to do with what she wanted.

After eating dinner with her husband, Anna headed over to the windmill, leaving the twins with James. She and her cousin did as they always did: They opened up Rose's trunk and pulled out her finest sequin dresses and feather boas, dressing to the nines, just to enjoy sweet mixed drinks out of Rose's expensive Italian wine glasses while listening to their favorite programs on the radio. They played records on her gramophone and danced the Foxtrot and the Charleston. Or they simply chatted away on the love seat, conversing about this and that.

"For goodness' sake, girl," Rose said, "would you sit still? I can't finish this if you keep fidgeting." The two best friends had rolled down their stockings that night and were painting wildflowers with tiny hearts on their kneecaps.

"Remember when you used to draw those little fairies?" Anna asked, watching Rose finish the last flower from behind a fringe of false eyelashes. "I still have those. I keep them in a photo album under my bed."

"Really? You loved those fairies," Rose laughed. "I must have drawn you a hundred of them back then."

"Paint one on my knee."

Rose obliged, and as she began to paint the fairy, she thought of what she was going to say to Anna. She had something weighty and private to ask.

Taking out two bottles of sparkling wine that had arrived with her things and that she had been saving, Rose poured them both a glass, took a sip, and raised hers up. "Tonight, I am tasting the stars!" she exclaimed, drinking the rest in one shot.

Anna laughed and asked, "Made that up just now, did you?" downing hers as well.

"No," said Rose, running her finger methodically over the rim of her wineglass. "The story goes that when Dom Pérignon, a seventeenth-century monk, first created his delicious bubbly champagne, he called out to his fellow monks, 'Come quickly! I am tasting the stars!' "

The two women finished the first bottle quickly, and Rose, almost covertly, opened the second. Keeping her eye on Anna, she discreetly kept filling her cousin's glass.

Late into the visit, an inebriated Anna giggled in delight, "This is the happiest night of my life!"

"You say that every Friday," Rose laughed, attempting to do the Charleston despite her cane.

Anna, in turn, did the shimmy.

Rose laughed even harder, watching little Anna shake. "You're not conducting yourself like a good Christian mother and wife, Anna May Shahan," she teased, shaking her finger at her.

"These Friday nights in the windmill make me a *better* mother and wife, if you ask me."

Rose pushed some loose strands of hair out of her eyes. "Can you imagine if the folks in church saw us right now, wearing all this makeup and these sequin flapper dresses lit up like fireflies, dancing these wild, immoral dances? They'd probably burn the barn down and run us out of town."

Anna tossed back the rest of her bubbly. "That's a bloody oath," she laughed.

They both stopped dancing and sat on the floor adjacent to the love seat, out of breath. "I can't believe it's been over a year since I've been here," Rose said, pouring more sparkling wine into Anna's glass.

"I know. But you're rapt, aye? You love it here."

"I do. It's wonderful at Sugar Alexandria, Kitten."

"And I'm certain you'll meet the right bloke in time, Lottie," Anna reassured, her speech slurred.

Rose took a puff from her cigarette holder, blowing the smoke over her shoulder. Turning to directly stare at Anna, she said, "But what if I don't want a bloke? What if I just want a baby?"

"How can that be?"

"Remember when I first moved here and you were afraid I would leave to start a family?" She narrowed her eyes and lowered her voice an octave. "Remember what you said?"

"What did I say?"

"Oh c'mon, Anna, you remember." Leaning over, she whispered into her cousin's ear, "What you said about James, and what he could do for me."

Anna coughed, instantly sobering some. "You mean giving you a baby?"

"Yes. Not long after I got here, you said if I don't meet someone,"–her words so faint Anna could barely hear–"that James could provide me that gift."

Anna became momentarily speechless.

"Remember?"

"Yes, I remember," Anna said slowly.

"Well, what do you think of it now?" asked Rose, clear as a bell, as if she hadn't drunk a drop of alcohol all night.

"Are you being serious?"

Rose nodded.

Anna pursed her lips, her mouth becoming dry, realizing her cousin wasn't joking. She blinked hard as her mind tried to conceive the unthinkable, while Rose remained motionless, fixated on her reaction. "James has such high morals, and he believes our marriage vows are sacred. And, and, and . . . ," she stuttered. "I don't think he'd ever do such a thing."

"Are you sure?" asked Rose, a twinkle in her eye.

Anna hesitated. "I would have to convince him."

"He usually does what you say."

Anna twisted a lock of hair between her fingers. "What about the single stockmen?" she asked in a small, quiet voice. "I know a couple of them are sweet on you."

"I just want a baby, though. No ties."

"No ties, aye?" Anna echoed.

"None."

"I dunno, Rose. I just don't think he'll go for it."

"It would only be once."

Anna stared down at Rose's underdeveloped leg, noticing the contrast between it and the healthy one. So thin and frail. She wished she could reach out and with one touch, heal it, removing the abnormality. Pitying her dear cousin, she thought of how Rose may never find a suitable husband to love and give her a baby. And as Rose had said before, some men were too afraid their children would inherit the defect if they married. This could be her last chance for a child of her own, and at the same time, keep her here at Sugar Alexandria forever. They would be bound by a secret that would secure Rose at the station for the rest of their lives.

"Anna, did you hear me? I said it would only be one time."

"Just once?"

"Yes," said Rose, the wonderful aroma of black licorice mixed with wine fanning Anna's face.

"What if you didn't get pregnant?"

"What if I did? I could raise my baby here, and we would be one big happy family." Rose could see her cousin weighing the idea in her mind, mulling it over. "That's all I really want, is a child. Not necessarily a husband."

Anna kept thinking, then once again tossed back the wine in her glass. "Just one time."

Rose seemed to glow in the dimly lit room, her dark hair shimmering, her ruby lacquered lips glistening, her green eyes shining. "Yes, Anna, just one time."

An immoral abomination?
Or a gift?

"You have got to be out of your bloody mind!" James emphatically said.

"Keep your voice down," Anna fired back. "The window's open."

"You mentioned this when Rose first arrived, too. I told you then, and I'm telling you now, it will never happen."

Anna frowned and balled her fists at her sides.

"What in the blue heavens made you think of that obscene idea again, anyway?"

"Rose brought it up last night."

Silence . . .

James looked at his wife with disbelieving eyes. "Rose asked for me to bed her so she can have a child? I don't believe you."

"She did."

"Then you have both gone mad," he said, an incredulous half smile breaking through.

"Look at you; you're smiling."

"Yes, because it's so preposterous."

"We're only asking for you to do this one time with her. Just once." Anna clasped her hands together. "If she doesn't get pregnant, that will be the end of it."

Dumbstruck, James' body began to tingle, his head reeling to the point of feeling feverish. "First off, Rose getting pregnant and not being married would tarnish her name. And then having a child out of wedlock would tarnish the child's name. Not to mention the disastrous repercussions for our family. The whole bloody town would completely shun us, creating a scandal that lived on for years."

Anna refused to listen. "You'll do as I say, James Ragnar Shahan."

"Not this time, love. I'm not doing that to her, or to us. It's morally wrong, and I will take no part in it."

"You'll do as I say!" she repeated, this time more aggressively through clenched teeth.

James stared at her, yet again shocked at her irrational ideas and behavior. "Crikey, this whole bloody rubbish is only because . . ."

"Because what?"

"You're different, Anna."

"Not that again."

"Well it's true. Just like Liam, there's something not quite right."

"I am nothing like him!" Anna snapped. "How dare you even say such a thing!"

James grabbed his Akubra hat and walked out the door.

Anna scowled as he left. Who was he to judge her, telling her she's not normal? And who was he to preach to her right from wrong? He was only a former war Digger who drank too much whiskey and got pissed with the Aboriginals. He never had a friendship like hers and Rose's, and he'd never known what it's like to have someone closer than a sister. As she mulled over his offensive notion, she cursed in Danish. And yet, she could not shake the inconceivable idea that she was not normal, forcing her to consider that there may be something wrong with her, and everything she hated about Liam—strange, weird, unusual, odd, alien, disabled, broken—was only a reflection of how she felt about herself.

※

Anna and Rose sat in the windmill, two cups of hot tea between them. But they weren't alone. Matilda had recently given birth to a litter of kittens, and the adorable little moggies were climbing all over the two women as they visited. Their exhausted mother took advantage of the babysitters and retreated upstairs to rest on the bed.

"You haven't asked me what James' response was when I told him our idea," Anna said, kissing one of the rambunctious kitties.

Rose's breath caught in her throat. "What did he say?"

"He said he would do it."

"Kitten, are you telling the truth?" Rose asked, her pulse quickening. The idea of James kissing her, touching her, flashed through her mind.

Anna nodded.

"I have a hard time believing he would agree."

"He also said he wanted you to stay here with us while you raise the baby."

As Anna spoke, the images in Rose's mind became clearer, more vivid. She had to shake herself from her thoughts. "James really said that?"

"Yes. He even said he hoped it would be a boy."

Rose continued to listen—numb, yet excited.

"So what do you think?"

"I don't know what to say."

"Say something."

"What about when I started showing? People would talk."

"Let them think what they want. It's no one's business, anyway."

"Anna, an unmarried woman having a baby is a disgrace, especially in a small town like Esperance." Rose began to reconsider the idea. "The gossip could be brutal."

"The sticky beaks are always going to gossip."

"We'd have to come up with something. A convincing story everyone would believe."

"We will; don't worry."

Rose stared at Anna, shaking her head. "This is all crazy talk. Pure crazy talk." But as she spoke, a flutter of happiness tickled her stomach. She could not deny that she wanted a baby, and as insane as the idea was, it offered her hope. "Tell me again what James said."

"He said he understands, and he's willing to give you this gift. Rose, you could finally have the baby you always wanted, and no man to have to bother with."

Rose's green eyes suddenly looked brighter, more alive. She couldn't help but smile. "This is crazy, you know."

Anna laughed, then reached out and held her cousin's hand. "A baby of your very own, Lottie. A beautiful baby."

Is Rose the unscrupulous one?
Or is Anna?

"She said what?" James was bathing, scrubbing the day's dirt from his body.

Anna walked into the bathroom with Moby on her shoulder. "She said she thinks it's a brilliant idea and she'd be so grateful if we gave her this gift." The galah rubbed his crest against Anna's neck as if to express his approval of the plan.

"I don't believe you," said James. The hot water in the tub suddenly felt hotter.

"That's what she said, love."

He continued lathering his skin. "Like I said before: It's rubbish and I refuse to take part in it."

Anna frowned. She bit at her nails, thinking hard on what to say next to convince her husband.

"Don't bring this up with me again, either."

"When I tell her you're not grouse with the idea, it's going to break her heart."

"Strewth, Anna! Stop what you're doing!" he demanded. "Stop it right now!"

"You stop it!" she fired back, stomping her foot.

"You stop it!" Moby squawked. "Bloody bogan!"

James ignored the bird. "Listen love," he said, trying to defuse things and reason with her. "The moral law of the land forbids what you're asking. Do you understand what I'm saying?"

Anna folded her arms over her chest and tapped her tiny foot. "You want our Rose to find some stranger instead? Some bogan we don't even know? Is that what you want?"

Stupefied, discombobulated, James again tried to reason with her. "Anna, I'm a simple man. I'm not the kind of bloke who can do such a thing. I can't even wrap my bloody head around what you just said." His resoluteness came back to him. "What I do know, though, is that you're my wife.

We may not always get along, but you are my spouse, and we have two children together. Rose is your cousin and my cobber. That's what I know, and that's how it's staying."

She clenched her hands into a fist. All he had to do was bed her once, and the bloody drongo couldn't even do that. An anger rose deep inside her soul. "If she marries some bloke just to have a baby and then leaves, when you could have given her one, I will leave too." Anna's obdurate determination would not be thwarted. Rose would have a baby in her arms by this time next year, or else, and he was the bloke to facilitate the grand gift. She left and slammed the door.

Now seething, Anna walked out into the stockyard, her temper boiling over. How dare James repudiate her beloved cousin's dream. I don't understand him, she thought. I don't know why this would be such a wrestling for him. A real man would do this!

In that moment, Anna remembered James confiding in her what his father Riordan always used to say, that James wasn't a real man because of his love for music and teaching. She remembered him confiding in her how much that hurt him, making him feel worthless and even ashamed of his natural-born talent. Looking up at the turning blades of Rose's windmill, she smiled.

It was an epiphany that would change the course of her life forever . . .

❧

In contrast to Anna acting as if it were nothing but just a simple solution to her cousin's problem, Rose was living in emotional turmoil over what she should or shouldn't do. She declined to go for lunch with Anna and her cobbers on Wednesday afternoon, and instead, went down to the shoreline, intending to go for a long walkabout until her leg tired and her mind found peace.

Perambulating along the calm waters of Indigo Bay, she came across James' small rowboat sitting at the ready on the beach. The adjacent island with the unobtrusive fisherman's hut was only a short jaunt, and it had been many years since she last saw the place where she and Anna once played in as children, so she ventured out in the boat to take a look.

What a surprise when she walked inside! The rickety old cabin she remembered as their childhood magical lair now resembled a humble home.

The open concept structure had a kitchen with a tiny sink fastened to a freshwater bucket, a cabinet made of inlaid wood with laminate countertop, and a small table with two chairs. In the center of the room was a dilapidated couch, against the wall a bookshelf filled with several of James' favorite books, and in the corner a double bed. The mermaid bust—once mounted to the bow of a vessel—still claimed its prominent position above the fireplace, as if the proud owner of the dwelling.

Rose rummaged through the small domicile. Scanning all the titles of James' books, she pulled one out, and that's when she noticed a worn leather folder concealed at the back of the shelf. It was personalized with his initials, Gaelic words and Celtic symbols decorating the front cover. Curious, she opened the folder to find James' handwritten compositions, flipping through the elegant sheets of music, the dark ebony symbols appearing as if ancient cuneiform syllabary. And then she saw them . . .

Drawings of a woman.

Intimate. Artistic. Erotic.

At first the curves on the paper appeared as a cluster of long, feminine lines; but then the lines grew more apparent, frighteningly familiar, the semblance more visible until they became clear.

It was her!

Within the stack of papers were James' creations, beautifully portraying Rose and her underdeveloped leg. She stared at them—enthralled, excited, aroused. He draws me because he cannot touch me, she thought. Just like with the statue he had carved. He wants to be with me, and he's struggling with his emotions as I am. Rose returned the drawings to the folder and placed it back on the shelf. All except for one. One she kept—her favorite—depicting her likeness so accurately it resembled a photograph.

~c🙖🙖ᴐ~

James sat beside Rose on the piano bench. She had taken great care with her appearance that evening, her hair done in shiny Marcel waves, her look more seductive than usual. She wore a cream satin dress, no glasses, a hint of shadow smudged above her large green eyes, and Chypre de Coty floated through the air, adding to the enticement. Her walking stick was nowhere in sight.

Though she was stunning to him, James knew she had done it because of Anna's idea, and it saddened him seeing her lower herself to that level. He had picked three pieces for their lesson that night, but as he looked over the first sheet of music, he did not see the notes. His mind was preoccupied with gathering the right words.

Noticing the small bag of black licorice on the piano, he said, "You really love the sweets, aye?" grabbing the bag and eating a piece.

"Yes, I do," said Rose. "When I left the convent, the nuns gave me enough to last a lifetime."

"It leaves a strong aroma."

"Does it bother you?"

"No, not at all. It's a wonderful smell, actually."

"It's calming to me."

"How's that?"

"As a child, when my leg would hurt, my mum would give me licorice to eat." Rose reached over and took a piece herself, chewing on the soft candy. "It soothed me, and even now as a grown woman, the effect is the same."

"We've never really talked much about your leg before. How's it doing?"

"If I walk on it too long without my cane, it starts to ache. Otherwise, it's fine." Rose knew he was stalling, preparing to tell her what he thought of the proposition, and the wait was brutal.

"About Anna's idea . . . ," he finally began.

Her heartbeat quickened.

James put down the bag of licorice. "You are my wife's cousin, and my good cobber. To do such a thing would instantly blur those lines."

She gave him a flummoxed look. "Oh . . . Anna had said . . . something different."

"I figured as much. I'm sorry." James drummed his fingers on the fallboard of the piano, thinking of his next words. "Anna isn't well. You know that. Day to day she seems all right, and is even functional, but we can't take anything she says like this seriously."

Rose bit down on her lower lip, fighting hard not to cry.

"And another important thing is your reputation–having a baby out of wedlock would taint that. People here might even shun you."

She stared down at his wedding ring. Although the band was only a thin piece of gold, it seemed incredibly strong and unbreakable–a constant reminder he belonged to her cousin. "Why didn't you let me leave that day?"

she wanted to say. "I could be living my new life by now had I left for that train," she almost said but didn't. And yet she found herself reaching up and touching the promise ring he had given her all those years ago.

"Anna doesn't always think clearly on things," James said, trying to be the voice of reason, "and you're just confused right now, alone out here, wanting companionship."

Rose tried to remain unemotional, but inside she was bleeding. She felt extinguished, mortified that the idea had even been given life.

"I have to think logically here for the benefit of us all," he continued. "Anna is my wife, and I have two young daughters to consider. If something like this got out, it would wreak havoc on our lives. The station would probably be blacklisted, and that would make it difficult to put tucker on the table, not to mention keep the blokes employed."

"I understand," Rose said in a feeble voice.

During all his years on this earth, James had never once imagined having to tell a sheila, let alone Rose, that he could not give her a child. "You deserve better than this, Rose. A lot better. Look at you—you're a beautiful soul, inside and out. Not to mention a gifted violinist, a talented painter, and even a bonzer photographer. You're going to meet some amazing gent, and when you do, it will happen the right way. The honorable way."

She did not speak, staring straight ahead, glassy-eyed.

"It's not that I don't care for you, Rose. You know I do, very much. It's just that it would confuse me. It would confuse both of us . . . Crikey, say something; say anything."

Rose had lost her voice from the emotional upheaval inside her. She turned her face away from James, not wanting him to witness her in such a state. It wasn't so much that he didn't want to follow through with the idea as it was knowing everything he was saying was true. A strong dose of reality, and rejection, hit her.

A hush came over the room, swelling into a great chasm, expanding between them until it was deafening. Rose got up and retrieved the drawing of herself that she had taken from the fisherman's cabin. "This is me, isn't it," she said, handing it to him, palpitant of his reaction.

James' face turned red . . . "I see you went to the Barracuda Hut. That's a private place, you know."

"Anna and I used to go there when I'd visit in the summers."

He stared at the drawing—Rose's image staring back. "Please don't mention this to her."

"The way you drew me is beautiful," she said, a quiver in her voice.

A smile touched at his lips.

"James, you drew me that way because you have feelings for me, and I for you."

He didn't disagree.

So badly she wanted to express what she was thinking—how she wanted a child, and she wanted it with him—that the words just burst out of her: "We could be together, if only one time. We could experience all these feelings we have for each other, that we've always had for each other, in a way that only two people in love can." She was pleading now, shocked at the words coming out of her mouth.

"Rose . . ."

"We could, James. Anna will allow it. What harm could come of it?"

"Harm?" His brow grew tense. "I just finished telling you the harm. You and Anna clearly don't understand the gravity of all this. If something of this nature got out, it would be brutal, Rose. People judge this kinda thing harshly in these parts, and our reputations would be destroyed."

"It would only be one time, and Anna is allowing it," she repeated.

"Are you listening to me?" He wanted to grab and shake her. "The whole bloody world is going through an economic depression right now, and if folks boycotted the station over this, it would get real bad for us too. You wanna see Anna have to sell Sugar Alexandria?"

Rose stared deep into his eyes, focusing on his irregular teardrop pupil, loving him all the more for his imperfection. "But what if they believed the story we tell? We'd come up with something plausible."

His eyes transitioned from her face down to the drawing of her. "Then what, Rose?"

"Well . . . We would go back to how it was . . . Good cobbers, our Wednesday night lessons . . ." The despair in her voice was salient, wanting more but knowing it would be forbidden. When she saw he wasn't arguing, she pressed further. "I want this, and I know you do too."

He gave her a pensive, calculated look. "You're living in a bloody fantasy world if you think we could just go back to normal after that."

"Please, James, listen to me," she entreated, clutching his arm, her nails nearly puncturing skin. "No one but the three of us would have to know."

He gazed fervidly into her eyes and saw an unnatural coalescence of desperation and longing. It bothered him, perhaps because it resonated with his own proscribed desires. "My conscience would know. God would know." James said nothing more; yet deep down he was thinking. As much as he wanted to say yes, he didn't want to taste something so coveted unless he could have it for a lifetime. That was his true nous for not giving in.

"It's my leg, isn't it," she said, looking in disdain at her cane. "If only I were normal, right?"

"That's bloody rubbish, Rose, and you know it."

"I wish I had never met you," she said, embarrassed, ashamed. But most of all sad. "I wish I had never come here." Finally her tears broke loose, the hurt expressing as anger: "You could have let me leave! I was almost free, but you stopped me! Why! Why! Why!"

James did the only thing that seemed natural to him. Putting his arm around her, with the other he gently pulled her face toward him, embracing her head against his chest as she sobbed hard into his shoulder. They sat like that in silence until Anna's voice came through the walls of the windmill, calling her husband home.

～くンℯℱ᠅ℛℯ᠍ᑌン-

Rose

If I can just figure out a way for him to be with me one time.

If I can, and we do, he'll want to be with me from then on, and nothing else will matter.

Until then, I am trapped here living in this windmill.

Trapped by Anna's love for me.

And trapped by my love for James.

What an imbroglio!

From where does the wind originate? Does it come from the forces of the earth pushing against each other, or does it come from the nostrils of God? What source brings such a dynamic and mysterious energy that cannot be seen, yet makes the sea push forward, the seasons change, and the windmill blades spin tirelessly? Unyielding and unwavering, it is a constant reminder that the air is very much alive, just as much as we are.

An unusually strong gale had hit Sugar Alexandria that night, and the following morn James is on the farmhouse roof replacing shingles. He looks down to see Rose walking toward her windmill, her slender arms swaying close to her body in unison with her feet stepping blithely on the earth. Instantly Anna's voice rings in his ears: "I'm only asking for you to do this one time with her. Just once." His wife has implored him to be intimate with this woman–her cousin, and his good friend–in order to give her a child, and for a moment he thinks of sitting next to her on the piano bench, her Chypre de Coty suffusing the air, her blouse open a fraction, exposing her cleavage, her legs slightly apart as if a flower on the verge of blooming.

He knows it will never happen, immoral and outrageous as it is, and yet his mind wanders further into the verboten, envisioning himself moving Rose's hair aside, kissing her neck, and then ravaging her. Anna should have never planted such a seed, he thinks, shaking himself back. She never should have voiced such a forbidden thing, as if it were as simple as making a cup of tea.

The whole premise goes against everything James has ever been taught about morality—by his parents, by his priest, by God—which defines his conscience and all the beliefs and values that make him the man he is today. A sudden dissolve grips him. A separation. An otherworldliness. A shift in consciousness, as if another man is trying to reformulate his virtues and decide his choice. "What unfolds, unfolds," he hears the man saying.

Rose is at the entrance of her windmill. Right before she steps inside, she turns and sees him, timidly raising her hand and waving. He waves back. She smiles at him, just as she had that day at his sister's wedding all those years ago, and once again it feels as if the sun has just come out and shone upon him.

Anna

Rose, Liam, the twins and I, were all in Cassandra's garden today. Such a beauty of a place! I was planting more flowers with my girls, Rose was sitting in the Georgian carriage, and Liam played on the swing. As I looked up, I could see the sadness in my cousin's eyes. "He's never going to allow it, Anna," she had said to me. "Just let it be."

In that moment, a marvelous idea came to me. A sort of game. "This is childish," Rose protested, but I made her follow my directions anyway. With the babies sitting in the middle, the three of us linked hands and danced around in a circle. "Let it happen!" I called out to the garden fairies. "Oh please, let it happen! Please grant Lottie's wish!"

And then the wind blew, and a wonderful feeling befell us all. It was magical, and I knew my wish would come to pass.

Because I, Anna May Shahan, can make things happen . . .

CHAPTER 27

James found himself lying in the dark alone. His wife would not return to the matrimonial bed until he agreed to do the deed she demanded. A prisoner of his own values, his unassailable judgment of right and wrong under attack, he felt pigeonholed, cornered, and frustrated.

Thinking of his wife's argument, how she had said it was for the greater good of all–for Rose, for her, for the family–he struggled to find common ground. How could this irrational, implausible contrivance possibly end up on the right side of decent, blameless, and respectable, he wondered? No matter how he approached the idea, or from what angle he considered it, it could not be made honorable. As if a man lost at sea, the poser pulled him to and fro.

In that moment, lying on his bed, nothing made sense to James. Though his countenance appeared steadfast, on the inside he was lost, not knowing what to do. The only thing he knew for sure was that the responsibilities in his life–the demands of his wife and the station–were on him like a catcall on the way to the gallows, itching at his ears, intensified by Anna's intonation, inflection, pitch, and tone. Always wanting something from him. Wanting, wanting, wanting–a constant tick that never stopped. Tick, tick, tick . . .

And now Rose had added to his distress, pleading with him in the windmill, her face evinced with sorrow, twisting at his resolve, knowing he wanted very badly to give her what she desired, yet would not. He closed the book he was reading, turned off the kerosene lamp, and placed his hand on the bed where his wife should be lying. "Tin Tin!" he called from their bedroom. "Will you please give up this nonsense and come lay with your bloke? I miss your little body next to mine. Lovely Dawn misses you too."

But Anna only covered her ears, lying in bed in the spare room down the hallway, her daughters on either side of her, still livid over her husband's refusal to acquiesce to her will. She was not one to give up on anything, even when it was for her own good.

Anna heard James get up and shut the bedroom door, and for a glimmer of a moment, she wanted to go to him in spite of it all, to crawl up into bed next to him and feel the comfort of his arms embracing her, listening to the humorous snore of Lovely Dawn on the floor. But she stood her ground and only turned on her side, her eyes dusting her childhood room under the muted glow of a low flame from a kerosene lamp.

Staring at her old closet, still full of Edwardian skirts and blouses, then over to her dresser with little hearts and roses intricately carved in the wood that her father had made and been so proud of, a nostalgia took hold of Anna. The old posters of her favorite silent movies—Mary Pickford in *Johanna Enlists*, Douglas Fairbanks in *American Aristocracy*, and Charlie Chaplin in *Shanghaied*—still hung on the walls, their paper curled up at the corners, accompanied by a couple of Rose's new paintings.

Gazing out the window into nothingness where only a long dirt road traveled on endlessly, she remembered herself as a child, staring out at that very road as the loneliness consumed her. She knew if Rose left, the isolation would return. Though she had a station to manage, a husband and daughters to love, nothing replaced her mother and sister like Rose. Her beloved cousin filled an empty space in her heart that no one else could.

Or ever would.

But still, maybe pushing James to offer such a thing was wrong.

The mellifluent sound of Rose's violin drifted in through the open window in the kitchen and traveled down the hallway, finding its path to Anna's room and up into her ears. The melody was soft and sweet, yet held a steady anticipation in its chords. A strong yearning. A joyous ripple that continued to rise like a helium bubble. Anna's mood brightened, imagining her cousin talking to her through the music, like a Siren out at sea. She continued to listen, smiling, the sereneness of the sound calming her inner turmoil, making her think of all the delightful times her cousin had played for her and her girls on the beach. Whilst the lullaby lingered, her conviction grew stronger and her doubts relinquished, as if the notes were a sub rosa key, unlocking an iron vault, the inside of which contained the secret to grant her cousin's wish . . .

It is a warm night, and Rose has her window open, just as the Shahans do in the farmhouse. Leaning on the windowsill to smoke a cigarette, she recalls overhearing James call for Anna to come back to their bed. She knows her cousin is making a stand for her, and once more the excitement tempered by guilt overruns her.

Rose feels the same pulling that James feels, but only worse. I know he wants to do this, she thinks, so why is he fighting it? Closing the window, she retires to bed.

Only Matilda waits for her.

James

I go to the Blue Lizard Cave almost every night these days. Drinking whiskey with me mates and playing the piano while all the blokes cheer me on. I play for hours, until Casper Cotton is the only one left and touches my shoulder, telling me it's time to go home.

I am trying to avoid Anna as much as I can, because all she talks about is me giving Rose a baby. Badgering me, belittling me, threatening me, igniting into a fit when I tell her I won't do it. "It would be so easy," she says to me. "Rose will stay with us forever if you give her a child, but you're ruining everything."

Putting on my Akubra hat, I stagger to the pub door. "See you tomorrow night, mate," I slur to Casper Cotton.

"All right, Jimmy Boy. See ya then, aye?" he replies.

When I get home, I stumble to the bar in the living room and drink some more. She's breaking down my conscience, I fear. My moral fiber, my scruples, my ethics. As I stare at my reflection in the mirror above the bar, my image blurs . . . As does my sense of right and wrong.

~ᴄᴇᴘ⚜ᴑᴠᴢ~

Genevieve

'The lady in the black Victorian dress paces at the foot of Anna's bed in her childhood room, worried for her Sweet Pea.

"Genevieve, remember all our wonderful lunches in the secret room when I was a child?" Anna asks. "When it was just you and me and our long talks? I loved you so much then. You were my whole world before Rose arrived. But then you would hide when she started visiting. Why?"

The woman gave her no response.

"You're giving me the silent treatment because you disagree with what I'm doing, don't you. You think it's wrong."

Genevieve stops and turns to her. "Yes, I do, Sweet Pea . . . Shamed be the woman who alloweth such a sin."

~ᴄᴇᴘ⚜ᴑᴠᴢ~

It was a morning bursting with light, not a single cloud in the azure sky. Rose watched from the entrance of the windmill as little Anna hung the clean white sheets, a small figurine–petite and ingénue yet possessing a powerful spirit befitting a giant–busily moving back and forth as she clipped the wash to the line.

Bluebelle, Catalou, and Beauty ran by, eager to harass the grazing cattle and sheep. Lovely Dawn considered joining them, instead choosing to stay by Anna's side. Even when the gaggle of geese marched superciliously in front of her, she remained loyal to her Homo sapiens friend.

Anna began to whisper, and Lovely Dawn looked up at her in curiosity. Fascinated, Rose too quietly listened, yet with a tinge of fear, concerned over what ailed her cousin. At first it sounded like tiny fairies chatting, but as the undertone grew louder, the conversation became clear . . . Anna was talking to her late mother and sister again. A prickling covered Rose's skin.

"He's going to give in any day now, and I will be able to grant Rose the gift she desires," Anna said to the wind.

"Too right, sister," she replied in a different timbre. "He appears to be buckling; you have him right where you want him."

Yet another voice, more motherly and sincere, departed Anna's mouth:

271

"All this is a sin, dear. Rose should find her own bloke and start a family the right way."

"No!" Anna argued with herself. "James can and *will* give her a child, and she's going to raise it here at Sugar Alexandria!"

Rose stepped back into the windmill, ashamed and contrite over what she had incited. What am I doing, she asked herself? Anna is not in her right mind to offer such a thing. Nor am I to accept.

But then again, it would only be one time.

Is Rose the perpetrator in this love triangle?
Or is Anna?

"I keep hearing you and James fighting because of me," Rose said one morning. They were having tea while Scarlet and Mabel played with their dolls on the rug. "I feel bad, and I'm not even sure what to think anymore."

"Just tell me you want this, Rose. Tell me it will make you happy and that we can raise our children together, here at Sugar Alexandria."

The two women met eyes, holding fast in a long, intense stare. Anna could feel Rose's pain, identifying with it, assuming it mirrored her own permanent scar of loneliness that she endured before her cousin came back into her life.

As they sat in silence, Rose's eyes glazed over. She too went to that place of isolation within herself—a place of craving and need. Once there, she tasted the yearning, the despondency, the emptiness, dismissing the notion that she should end this wicked dance. Maybe it was the fear that she would never find another man she loved again, and this was her last chance to have a baby, knowing that there were seasons to a woman's life, and her childbearing years would someday approach winter. Or perhaps it was because her cousin didn't care that it was her own husband; in fact, Anna's the one who came up with the original idea. She embraced it.

Finally Rose spoke the words Anna was waiting to hear: "I do want a child, Kitten. Regardless of how."

That was all that needed to be said . . .

CHAPTER 28

The Voices

"**M**ummy, I have wonderful news!" Anna says, wearing her green velvet cloak while kneeling before the soul tree at her surreptitious altar in the thicket by the cornfield. Sunlight breaks through the leaves, shining on her goose-feathered crown and wings. "I think James is going to give Rose a baby!"

The tree branches sway in the gusty breeze. "This is a sin, Turtle Dove," whispers through her consciousness.

"Is it?" Anna asks. "But you and Blessing were the ones who told me how to keep Rose at the station for eternity."

"We've changed our minds."

"Why?"

"Because we no longer trust Rose."

"Oh, fiddlesticks! I have the power to do this for her, and I will. Besides," Anna reasons, "how could creating a new life for someone you love ever be wrong?"

A throng of unfamiliar voices encircles her, laughing. Anna laughs with them, dancing joyously around the tree. Then Genevieve and the Black Shuck appear.

"It's going to be so grand!" Anna shouts up at the sky. "We'll all live together. All of us. Grandmother, Mummy, Blessing, Rose and her new baby, James, Scarlet and Mabel. You too, Genevieve."

"No, Sweet Pea, you're wrong," says the woman in the black Victorian dress. "If you continue to pursue this, it will not end well for you."

Her warning does not register with Anna. "You can help when the baby is born, too. We're going to be one beautiful family. As a family should be."

She raises her arms to the heavens and spins and spins and spins until reality and fantasy merge into one glorious glow of colors.

Liam watches from afar, keeping his distance as Anna twirls and sings and chats away like a small child, entranced in her own little world, engaging with someone or something not there. He has seen her do this since he himself was a child, and when she does, he knows to leave her alone . . .

Anna

Sometimes now when I do my kulning, Rose does the loveliest thing: She'll take out her violin and play alongside me as I call to the animals. It is a beautiful feeling to sing from my heart and have my beloved cousin next to me, playing her instrument. I am so happy in that moment. Proud and joyous all at once. The sound of us together is quite grand, too. Even James stops what he is doing, listens, and smiles. It only proves she was meant to come here. To live . . . To have a child.

Anna decides to go to extremes to force her husband into granting Rose's gift. She has now stopped cooking his meals, washing his clothes, cleaning the house, and doing her daily chores, arguing with James nonstop. He goes about his workday, as always, hoping his wife will eventually give up on her louche idea, but instead she is more invigorated, having a sense of determination that can cut glass.

James is also drinking more, either at the Blue Lizard Cave or in his distillery, often staggering to the bedroom in the dark, emerging the next morning hungover and unkempt, his beard growing wild. Anna is wearing him down, and she knows it.

For the rest of the week, James hides in his distillery, sitting in the corner of the room on the worn-out leather sofa, sipping the Irish whiskey he had made for himself—probably his best batch hitherto. He is not drinking alone, either, as he has his demons with him. His internal struggles. The whole situation Anna is trying to dragoon him into is overwhelming him, and he's at the edge of a steep precipice, with his own wife pushing him off the cliff.

And yet . . . he cannot deny he wants to fall.

Tossing back the last of his drink, he looks down at his wedding ring, and even through the darkness it catches light from some faint source, momentarily twinkling. He is a man torn between doing what is right and what he desires . . .

Loyalty over lust.

Commitment over passion.

Responsibility over love.

Anna

"Y eeuuck, I can smell that nasty grog on your breath!" Anna said that night. "I'm so sick of that bloody smell!"

It was now late, James had come in from the distillery, and once again she refused to sleep in their bed. "Yes, I drink whiskey. You're driving me to it."

"You've been living in that blasted distillery way before all this."

James didn't debate with her. It was true. The distillery was a place where he could temporarily hide, just like the Barracuda Hut. Years of living with an insensitive wife with mental illness had forced him to find a locus of succor, for his own sanity.

"You're a drunk," Anna said. "You know that? Leave me alone."

"And you're a cold sheila who has no normal affection for her bloke. You have obligations as a wife to give me my due."

"You have obligations as a husband to make me happy. That's what you promised my daddy you would do, remember?"

"That meant loving and taking care of you. Taking care of your bloody needs, Anna, not bedding your cousin so she could have a baby."

Anna stamped her foot like a petulant child and headed to her childhood room.

"Why are you doing this?" he asked, following behind her.

She stopped. "You know why. My best cobber wants a baby, and you won't do the right thing and give her one."

"The right thing is to sleep with another sheila?" he mocked.

Anna turned around to face him; she was crying. "It's just one time."

"I'm a married bloke!" James yelled, his voice a thunderous boom. "My vows mean something to me!"

Anna's eyes grew large, startled by his abrupt anger. Staring up at him, his face reflecting his defiance to her wishes, she realized she was losing this battle. In her mind she saw Rose meeting a new man, having his baby, and leaving Sugar Alexandria with him forever. Or alternatively, never having a child at all, becoming sad, perhaps even sick, and eventually going back to England. Without the help of her husband, what she had fought so hard to keep would soon be gone. Just like her mother and sister. Indignation burned up her spine; her expression changed. She would make him do this. Scowling at him, she bit out, "A real man would do this, but I guess you're not a real man. That's what your father used to say, wasn't it? That you had a hard time letting go of the boy inside you."

Silence . . .

"What did you say?"

"You're not a real man," she repeated, given no choice but to deliver the blow. She had rehearsed those words in advance for days, practicing exactly how to say them, ever since that day she had the great epiphany. She knew how deep it would cut him. Pierce his soul. Emasculate him. Just as it had when his father always said it many years ago.

"I confided in you what my dad had said, and now you throw it back in my face and use it against me?"

"It's the truth, isn't it? What real bloke wouldn't give a beauty of a sheila a child if she's asking and he's able?"

A cynical smile crossed his lips. "I'm not a real man, am I?" He glared at her so long she felt uncomfortable, as if he were looking through her, not at her. Stabbed with those acidulous words from his wife, internally bleeding and tired of the fight, James was finally ready to capitulate to her illicit ploy. She had created the perfect storm, her sharp-tongued utterance twisting into a deadly dagger, and he buckled under it. "All right, Anna," he said, infuriated. "You win."

She remained mute; inside she was rejoicing.

"You will get your way, as always. But afterward, we will not speak of this night ever again. Do you hear me! Not ever!"

Anna nodded. She tried to say something, but James only yelled at her to go to bed. Closing her mouth, she retreated to their bedroom and crawled onto the mattress, staring at the door, expecting James to burst back in and tell her he had changed his mind.

He didn't.

Instead, he went to the living room and grabbed the whiskey bottle, pouring himself another drink.

After several more shots, James' vision began to blur. Exhausted, his body wanted sleep, but his anger kept pushing him forward. He stared at his reflection in the mirror above the liquor cabinet; an image red with ire glowered back. Setting the whiskey glass down, he took off his wedding ring and dropped it in the shot glass. It made a clinking noise as it bounced around, settling on the bottom. A deafening silence followed. James stared at the ring for what seemed an eternity, then prayed for forgiveness for what he was about to do. In a haze of disorientation and stinging rage, he headed out the door to Rose's maisonette.

James has left Anna to go to her cousin.
An unsettling disquietude churns in his gut, forsaking his wife.
Or has his wife forsaken him, from the moment she asked him to do such a thing?

Genevieve

"It's not too late, dear," resounds in Anna's mind. "You can still stop this, but you have to act now."

Anna turns around to see the lady in the black Victorian dress standing a few feet away. "Why would I halt something I have worked so hard to attain?"

"It's going to change things."

"Yes, it will. Rose will finally have a little one."

Genevieve's tone becomes more solicitous. "You could end up losing it all by loving someone more than your own husband. More than yourself."

"I can't have Rose leaving me again, Genevieve. I just can't."

"God help you, child."

～ぐかふ～

"James, what's wrong?" asked Rose, holding a lantern, her burgundy silk robe shimmering under its glow. "Why are you here so late?"

He blankly stared at her, his heart thumping in his chest, trying to figure out how to tell her he had finally agreed to Anna's plan. But now that he was face-to-face with his wife's cousin, the courage driven by the rage started slipping. Unable to find his next move, he remained taciturn.

"You're scaring me. I'm going to get Anna."

She went to leave, but he quickly grabbed her arm. "No," he said, releasing her. "She's all right. She knows I'm here."

Once inside, James locked the door. Hearing the click of the lock, Rose instantly realized why he was there, and she blanched. How did Anna finally get him to break, she wondered? What words pushed him over the edge, getting him to agree to the salacious idea, igniting the flames of the unthinkable? She narrowed her eyes at him and asked, "Can I make you a drink?", feeling slightly dizzy, as if she herself had just consumed several shots of whiskey.

"No," he said, frenzied thoughts racing through his head . . .

What now?

How do I begin?

Where do I begin?

Should we talk first?

Maybe we should drink.

Maybe we should drink so heavily that neither of us remember in the morning.

No, I want to remember.

All these questions bombarded him, stalling his actions, impelling him to do the only thing that felt innate in the moment—he sat down at the piano and began to play. To Rose's utter surprise, it was the very tune he had been humming all along! The melody she had grown to love, composed into a beautiful song.

The piece was titled *Sùilean Uaine* in Gaelic, which, when translated into English, meant *Green Eyes*. He had written it in the fisherman's cabin about Rose. Deep and low, bitter yet sweet, never becoming thunderous or loud, just tender and soft, the song had a specific, ardent rhythm. It meant a great deal to James, and he played it with such emotion that it moved Rose, opening up her soul.

She walked over to him, placing her hand on his shoulder, and instantly Anna's voice rang in his ears, jarring him back to why he was there. "A real man would do this," ricocheted in his head. All of James' thoughts instantaneously converged into one swift motion as he stood, turned to face her, and moved aside her hair. Delicately he began to kiss up her neck, just as he had imagined doing many times before.

Rose tingled from his hot breath, goose bumps covering her skin. Gently he removed her glasses, putting them in his back pocket, then held her face in his hands, gazing at her, absorbing her delicate features. Leaning down, he kissed her mouth; the kiss was soft as he brushed his lips against hers. He tasted of whiskey, of a hard day's work.

He tasted like heaven.

And she like the sweetest, darkest licorice he had ever had.

"I have thought about this moment endlessly," he confessed against her ear, one hand on the pulse of her throat. "And now here we are, and yet I don't know where to begin."

"Just kiss me," she whispered breathlessly. "Please, James, just kiss me."

He opened her robe, exposing warm, silky skin, and as his hands touched her, she shivered. This was only supposed to be a coital act to give a woman a child, yet it was so much more to James. He was given a free pass to enjoy a night of passion with someone who could reciprocate affection and intimacy in a way his wife could not. "Rose, help me to remember who I was before," he pleaded. "Help me to look into the mirror again and recognize the man I once was." His words came from the deepest parts of him, from a place of desperation, confusion, and raw yearning. Could he still make love the way it should be, without the restrictions and controls his wife had always imposed on him? Could he overcome the lack of physical and emotional bonding he had grown used to, and enjoy the erotic pleasures of a woman?

Rose cradled his head as he kissed her bosom, pulling him closer, her entire body opening up to him as if a Venus flytrap seducing its prey. His lips returned to her mouth, becoming aggressively passionate, punishing, boring down with such fervor that she forgot where she was. Or who she was.

Or even her own name.

They became lost in their kissing. Intense, eager, and yearning. Vertiginous, as if the whiskey in his veins had entered hers through osmosis. Somehow they found themselves upstairs in the bedroom, clothes vanished. He lay her on the bed and took her underdeveloped leg into his grasp, gently caressing the weak muscle, kissing up her thin calf, knee, and inner thigh.

She moaned.

Running his hands over the smoothness of her body, his mouth hungrily found hers again and again. She reciprocated, consumed by wanton desire. Consumed by not just carnal lust but also the puissant emotional connection they had already forged. Who they were and what they were doing mattered very little as they let go of everything they had held on to for so long. They were like the sea—tossing, turning, crashing. Laying his full weight against her—stomach to stomach—there was no part of their flesh that didn't touch. As his tongue explored her mouth, his member entered her femininity, and the rapturous dance of sexual union commenced.

The deed had begun . . .

Time passed; the world around them disappeared. It all seemed like a dream. They made love, in every sense of the word. James spoke in Gaelic, sexually passionate things in husky whispers, and Rose, not understanding, ran her hands through his hair, listening to his concupiscent words while his mouth ravaged her body. Lolling her head and arching her back as he sucked on her nipple, she looked up at the small skylight in the roof. Clouds floated by; a single star winked at her before disappearing behind the white, fluffy mass. She was aware of her breathing, his breathing, the sensual motion of their hips. They were fusing together, becoming one.

James felt as if he were drinking fresh water for the first time in years. Alive and on fire, he thrust into her with vigor. The sight, the feeling, and the smell of her surrounded him, intoxicating his senses. She closed her eyes and softly moaned. He felt like a tool, a hammer, embedding her into the earth, nailing her deep into the Australian ground.

Anna paced around the room while Lovely Dawn snored peacefully on the rug. Excited and nervous, she couldn't sleep. After all that time and effort of begging, coercing, and fighting with her husband to give Rose a baby, it was finally happening! She clasped her hands and squealed, imagining her cousin having her own child by next spring. To Anna, it was a certainty. They would raise their children together, go on picnics, and live as one felicitous family. Rose would never leave her now; she would stay at Sugar Alexandria forever. Anna had sealed her cousin's fate through the gift of a newborn given by her very own husband. She smiled. No more having to worry if Rose would run off with some bloke, or if she was sad. All those days were over now.

To pass the time, Anna flipped through magazines and listened to the radio. Her eyes flickered over at the clock on the wall; he had been gone a while. She looked out the window and noticed the light was still on in Rose's bedroom. What was transpiring over there? Were they talking things over, debating what they should do? Frowning, she drummed her finger on the side table, wondering if James had backed down and was reasoning with Rose that it was a sin. No, James would follow through. The look in his eyes confirmed it, too. He would bed Rose quickly and come home, and soon they would all live happily ever after.

Anna grabbed a blanket and curled up on the chaise longue, gazing out the window until her eyelids became heavy.

"Shamed be the woman who alloweth such a sin," whispered into her ear as she slowly dozed off.

"A child is a gift, Mummy," she mumbled to the voice. "A child is always a gift."

Hypnagogia settled in, and suddenly, for no reason at all, Anna heard a faint sound rise into the air. The soft, sweet melody of her grandmother's singing developed, advancing into full Scandinavian kulning. Angelic, bewitching, an unearthly melody growing louder and louder with each note, it resonated all around Anna. She wondered if James and Rose could hear it too, and for a moment her glassy eyes opened from her lucid dream, staring out the window at the center windmill where her beloved, loyal cousin lay in the arms of her devoted, faithful husband.

Anna

I wake in the middle of the night, and James still isn't home. Drifting back to sleep, I dream I am walking through the fields at night with the Black Shuck by my side. We walk until the ground turns to water, and suddenly I am flailing helplessly in the deep, drowning out at sea. The black she-wolf grins, her razor-sharp teeth glistening under the moonlight, her bloodred eyes watching from the shore as the waves take me far and away . . .

CHAPTER 29

James roused the next morning disoriented.

The room was spinning.

He needed to dunk his head into a vat of ice water to jolt himself awake. Glancing over at Anna lying beside him, he almost said, "Grab me a cold glass of water, will ya love? I drank too much at the pub last night," but just as the words were on the tip of his tongue, he saw that his wife was not by him. What's more, he was not even in the farmhouse.

The woman who lay naked next to him, their skin still touching, her back pushing adjacent to his ribcage, was Rose. Instantly his memory knocked him over like a powerful wave out at sea.

He had spent the entire night with his wife's cousin!

A scandalous tryst . . . Or was it?

Realizing where he was and what he had done, he dared not move. Yes, he remembered now. Pushed to his limit and maneuvered by egregious wiles, acting out of anger, like a moth to the flame he partook of what he had fought so hard to deny, at last savoring the warm, sweet embrace of the woman he loved.

Sunlight illuminated the room as he stared at a sleeping Rose, her dark hair cascading around her pillow, his gaze sliding from the top of her silky crown all the way down to her toes peeking beneath the white sheet. He was hyperaware of her every physiognomy—even her lungs as they softly inhaled and exhaled. Bare shoulders. Feminine curve of her neck, a mark of passion still bearing witness. Her long, slender arm draped across her nude torso.

Oh, Anna, what have you made me do, he thought? What tangled web have you forced us all into? She had finally gotten to him. Or he had finally given in. Or he had done what he had wanted to do since first laying eyes on the singular Englishwoman. Maybe all three had happened.

Trying to rein in his wild meditations, his gaze seared through the small window in the loft. There on the other side of that curtain, through the thin pane of glass, his life that had been extant for over a decade was waiting for him to step back inside.

The station.

His daughters.

Anna.

What will happen now, he wondered, staring up at the skylight, watching the white clouds sail by beneath a teal blue opus? If Rose has a child and stays at Sugar Alexandria, will this precipitate closure for his wife, allowing her to finally move on from the loss of her mother and sister? Perhaps this was all for her happiness in the end, rather than her cousin's. Or maybe it was the beginning of something else for him and Rose.

But the beginning of what?

Incontinently, a craving for Rose enveloped him, being so close to her naked form, inhaling the sweet scent of her perfumed skin. A deep, canine lust, wanting to taste once more what he had experienced the night before. Rose rolled onto her back, still asleep, and he fought the urge to touch her inner thigh. Her entire body was basking in the morning light, her expression peaceful, her small breasts exposed to the open air. One nipple had puckered–the one he favored while making love to her–and he wanted to reach over and caress it, despite knowing he could no longer do so. Now, sober, in the broad light of a new day, she was Rose again–his wife's cousin.

Guilt pummeled his conscience.

Heavy, nagging guilt.

James abruptly felt the need to apologize, to repent for what he did. But apologize to whom? Rose? Anna? God? Maybe himself? Never before had he felt such a mental turmoil. Getting out of bed, he slowly dressed; the movement woke Rose. She pulled the sheet closer to her body, covering herself as he buttoned his shirt. Their eyes met in a long, wordless stare.

As James left and closed the door, Rose simultaneously closed her eyes. What had she allowed to happen? There was no turning back now.

The deed had been done . . .

Next door in the farmhouse, the morning light awoke Anna. Lovely Dawn was still snoring on the rug beside her, and Moby—she had forgotten to put him to bed in his cage—was strutting on the vanity, wings flared and crest erect, admiring his reflection in the mirror. Blinking, Anna rubbed her eyes and stretched on the chaise longue near the window where she ended up sleeping through the night, waiting for James to return.

Yet he had not returned.

She drew her knees up and hugged them close to her body, chewing on her nails, wondering why he had stayed with Rose all night; it should have taken no more than an hour at most. But at least it was done. Hopefully, Rose would soon be blessed with a child, and life would go on as she planned. Ebullience again overwhelmed her at what the future now held. Rose could have a baby, and Anna would be the benefactress of that precious gift.

Hearing her husband come in through the door, she jumped up and went to meet him. Her mind pulsated with so many questions.

James reached into the shot glass on the liquor cabinet and put his wedding ring back on.

After flittering around, cooking eggs, pouring juice, and making coffee, Anna laid a plate of breakfast down in front of him, sitting on the other side of the table and anxiously watching him fork his eggs and drink his coffee. Finally, she said, "You didn't have to stay with her all night."

James slammed his fist on the table. The plate fell on the floor. "It never happened!" he yelled. "Do you hear me! It's done, but it never happened! Do you understand!"

Startled, Anna jumped.

James stood and glared at her, leaving the kitchen.

Anna cleaned up the mess and made another plate of breakfast for him, placing it on the table. An hour went by. When James reemerged, he ignored the food, walking right past it. Anna tried to hug him; he only stood still, arms to his sides. She gave him a squeeze, but he freed himself from her grasp, exiting out the door.

Rose lies in her bathtub, letting the hot water dull the sensations on her skin that James had left behind. She does not think of Anna, or the corollary that will follow. Instead, she feels blissfully numb. Diaphanous, and even a touch of sanguine. The instrumental music on her gramophone meanders in from the background, and as she listens, a sereneness lights up her face. She is in complete reverie, lost in thought over her cousin's husband.

James Ragnar Shahan had made love to her—softly, aggressively, almost painfully.

Making love to him was like the rising sun—warm, then hot, then scintillating—and she can still feel herself melting into his arms as the entire room luxuriates in a luminous glow. Though he hadn't taken her virginity, in so many ways he had. Never before had a man been so tender, assiduous, unselfish, percipient to her needs, lustful for her body. Rose Charlotte Moss is forever changed by the experience.

Bringing her hand up out of the water, she runs her fingers along her mouth. He had bitten her lower lip, and the skin is still sensitive there. As she leans back against the basin and closes her eyes, Anna's voice echoes inside her head: "Rose, you could finally have the baby you always wanted . . . A baby of your very own."

· · ✦ · ·

James drove aimlessly around the station in his Ford Model TT Huckster pickup. Coming to a clearing at the edge of the wheat field where the view of the Australian skyline was like a painting of a beautiful bouquet, colors running down the canvas, he parked his truck and took a deep breath, exhaling heavily.

He felt chaotic.

Disembodied.

Surreal.

More than anything, a plenary detachment from Anna, and an instant bonding with Rose.

"Dear God, I made love to her last night," he said under his breath. "How could this happen?" He rubbed his face with both hands, trying to make sense of it all. Shaking his head, he could hardly believe the quagmire he now found himself in.

Several kangaroos hopped by in the distance, capering toward the trees. James wished he could go with them, run away from this place, away from his reality. Away from both women and the calamitous concomitants that would follow. But he couldn't. What was done was done—it could not be taken back.

The floodgates had been opened.

~⚜~

Anna and the twins went over to Rose's maisonette, Bluebelle, Catalou, and Beauty nipping at their heels as they walked, looking for leftovers. Anna just shooed them away. Despite how James had acted that morning, she was thrilled over what transpired the night before. When she knocked on the windmill door, there was no answer. She knocked again and waited.

Rose slowly opened it. She was dressed, but her hair was still wrapped in a towel from a fresh wash in the bath.

"Can we come in?" Anna asked, trying to gauge her cousin's demeanor.

Rose gave a small nod.

Anna placed the twins on the rug with their dolls while Rose poured them some coffee, and the two women sat on the love seat to talk.

"Can I ask if it happened?" Anna needed confirmation from her cousin, even though her husband had already told her.

Uncomfortable, Rose hesitated before slowly nodding.

"Good. It's done. And with any luck, you'll soon be pregnant," Anna said, a confident smile on her face.

Rose's posture stiffened, and she started to cry.

"What's wrong? Why are you crying?"

"I'm so sorry, Kitten," she sobbed. "I should have never let him do it. It was a mistake."

Anna's voice softened. "Did he hurt you?"

"No, he didn't hurt me." Tears streamed down her face.

"Then why are you sorry? This is what we wanted, aye? What we planned and talked about for weeks. We schemed this together."

Rose covered her eyes with her hands as she cried. "I shouldn't have let this happen; I should have stopped him," she repeated. "I know you have been pressuring him about it, and I could tell he was pissed."

"But Rose, don't you want a baby?"

A silence encased them until the sound of the windmill spoke. Rose listened to the haunting hum while she searched for the appropriate words. "You don't understand, Anna. You have an innocence about you, and a childlike love for me. I cherish that, but I had no right sleeping with your husband."

"I allowed it, though." It was true–Anna didn't understand, shaking her head, confused.

Rose looked so distraught, yet sincere. "I just wanted a baby so badly that I went along with it, but it was wrong. I'm sorry."

Anna reached over and held her cousin's hand. Her eyes started to water. "I'm glad it happened, Lottie. I want you to have a baby; that was my dream too. I want us to raise our children at Sugar Alexandria, and stay together forever."

Rose forced a smile, knowing that Anna meant well despite her inability to see the gravity of it all. "Let's talk about something else."

Anna nodded, leaning in to hug her, feeling nothing but warmth and love. "Rose, everything is going to be grand. You'll see. And if you're not pregnant, we'll figure something else out. As long as we're together, that's all that matters."

The two women embraced, and as Anna put her head on her cousin's chest, a surge of guilt and regret gnawed at Rose. So strong and vivid were the sensations and sounds in her mind from the impassioned night before, she had to bite down on her finger as Anna held on to her for dear life.

Rose

All day long, I hide in the windmill, afraid of seeing James, afraid of what I've allowed.

Afraid of myself.

I eat dinner alone, listening out my open window as my cousin, her husband, and their children enjoy the evening together–the perfect little family.

I feel like a spider caught in my own web . . .

The following morning, James felt wholly different about the situation. Having had the time to think it over, it revitalized him. But more than anything, he could not stop thinking about the sights and sounds of their lovemaking, wanting to do it again, but even slower.

At the crack of dawn, there was a knock on the windmill door. Rose was already up—the ponderous situation she now found herself in engendered a wakeful night. When she opened the door, James was standing there. Reaching over, he took her hand and placed her spectacles into her palm, not letting go. How do you feel, he wanted to inquire? Are you all right? These were the questions in his mind—questions he didn't ask.

A rooster crowed loudly in the background, breaking the silence between them. "Thank you," Rose said, a breathy whisper.

He nodded.

Rose glanced beyond him at the morning light barely breaking through the darkness. She was looking to see if Moony or any of the stockmen were up yet; they weren't. Throwing a glance at the farmhouse, looking for Anna's presence, she found no evidence of her cousin as well. They were alone in the early-morning hour, searching each other's face, trying to discern what would happen next. Rose had no answers. Neither did James. But he held her hand for the longest time, and she allowed it. He was talking with no words, and yet she understood.

Had the sun not broken through the horizon, edifying the dawn of a new day, he would have been more brazen and taken her into his arms and kissed her. Instead, he stepped back, heading off to begin another long workday. Rose watched him all the way out to the paddock where Bluebelle, Catalou, and Beauty ran up to him, jumping all around. With her eyes never wavering from James, she slowly closed the door.

⚜

Dinner that night was awkward for James and Rose, neither sustaining prolonged eye contact, barely speaking to one another. Several times he quickly looked at her, though, watching her every move, noticing the plum-colored passion mark he had left on her neck. Rose, too, purloined her own furtive glances—short stares at James when her cousin was distracted—forcing her gaze away before being noticed. Anna, on the other hand, had slipped right back into her chipper, jovial self, chatting away endlessly, serving food and laughing at Moby who was showing off at the dinner table again. The entire scene was as if nothing had happened at all.

James barely touched his food, absorbed in the unknown, still pondering over all the variables of this new corporeality. Sitting at the same table with both women—the architect of the venereal encounter, and her female lead—was surreal to him, and he felt sensations he ought not for another woman while sitting right next to his wife.

～ぐぎこゝ～

James could not get Rose out of his mind. When the craving became too intense, he followed her to the henhouse one morning. She was fetching eggs for breakfast when he brazenly grabbed her—eggs falling to the ground and cracking open—taking her by the hand into the small distillery beside it. It was the first time they were alone since the night of intimacy, and now that the barrier of forbidden desire had been broken, the initial shock worn off, James was losing all self-control.

Pulling her in close, he smoothed over her bottom lip with his thumb, staring at the full, luscious perimeter of her mouth before assailing it with his own. Kissing her, tasting her, breathing heavily the whiskey-infused air.

She did not resist.

"I need to be with you again," he demanded, his mouth on hers with a carnal appetence.

Lifting her up onto the workbench, the osculation became more heated, spirited, her legs wrapping around his waist. In the semidarkness of the distillery, kissing passionately, wildly, Rose finally pulled away, straightening her clothes and escaping back to the windmill, leaving James breathless, hot, and yearning.

～ぐぎこゝ～

The next day, Rose kept herself busy by finishing a painting her cousin had requested a while back. When done, an elegant lady from the 1800s wearing a high-necked, black Victorian dress stood proudly on the canvas, her companion she-wolf sitting obediently by her side.

Having no reference to work from, Rose painted the woman as a combination of Anna and herself—deep blue eyes like her cousin's, raven hair like hers, height and weight an average of them both—the perfect blend.

The wolf she painted exactly how Anna had described: Large, with midnight black fur. Long, razor-sharp teeth. And bloodred eyes.

"It's a beauty, Lottie!" Anna exclaimed. "I love it!"

Rose too was pleased with how her work turned out. "Why did you want me to paint this, anyway?" she asked, helping Anna hang it in the hallway among the others.

"It's for Genevieve. She needs a place to rest when she gets tired. Otherwise she walks the grounds all night."

Rose played along. "And the Black Shuck?"

"The wolf is docile when it's by her side." Anna stepped right up to the beast, staring into its menacing eyes. "Genevieve knows how to keep it tame."

"Oh, Kitten, you are such an imaginative soul," Rose said, not realizing her cousin meant every word.

Anna

Black Shuck!
Where is Genevieve's companion?
Where are you?
Oh, you lovely, beautiful beast!
You are a wonder to behold.
A strange breed.
A mystery and enigma.
The stories you would tell if you could speak!
Traveling the world, there is nothing you have not seen.
What lies behind those bloodred eyes of yours?
Tell me who or what you truly are; tell me your secrets.
Because I am no longer afraid!

CHAPTER 30

The days went by agonizingly slow after that approbated night of intimacy between James and Rose. The mundaneness of everyday life ticked by in long stretches of time, punctuated with a quiet knowing that all three of them were waiting to see if that instance of passion had resulted in a child.

"Have you gotten nauseated yet?" Anna asked one morning. "Any signs of being pregnant?" She was helping Rose clip her clean wet clothes to the clothesline.

Rose glanced at the two stockmen working nearby. "Anna," she said in an undertone, bemused at how her cousin could be so comfortable speaking of the subject. "You can't just blurt things like that out. Someone could hear you."

"Oh, sorry," she giggled. "Any signs, though?" she asked again, this time whispering.

"No, it's too early." Rose clipped a sheet to the line, and the three sheepdogs ran underneath it, chasing each other in a game.

"Not true, Lottie. I started feeling crook after a week."

"Well I doubt I'm pregnant, anyway," said Rose, nervously touching her neck. "It usually takes more than once to conceive."

Anna suddenly looked distressed. "You think it was all for nothing?"

Rose moved a hanging dress aside to look at her. "What I think is that I don't want to talk about it anymore. All right? If it happens, we will face it then."

Anna grinned. "You mean we will celebrate it then. We'll break out the champagne and taste the stars!"

Rose picked up the wicker basket, gesturing to go back inside. "Yes, Anna, we'll celebrate it then and taste the stars."

Rose

After dinner, we all go into the living room, and James puts a record on the gramophone. For a while, we drink and dance, and when it's my turn with James, a mutual electricity reverberates through our bodies–two souls speaking an arcane language only we can understand.

Keenly sentient of his hand on my waist, fully aware of the sexual tension between us, the music seems to stop, and we are no longer in the farmhouse, or the windmill, or even at Sugar Alexandria, but far away in a different world, his thighs brushing against mine so intimately as if we are about to make love. Wanting to kiss him, fighting my desire to kiss him, wishing he were mine to kiss . . .

After the festive intermezzo, Anna hands me a pretty box, nicely wrapped with a bow. She can barely contain her excitement as I open it. "To match your eyes," she says as I lift up the striking emerald dress.

I force a smile; I act grateful; yet my mind is elsewhere. Not with my sweet cousin, but with her husband, and to where this trifecta is all going, knowing it cannot continue like this indefinitely.

Anna insists I try on the dress. Numbly I indulge her, changing in their bedroom and re-emerging to her sitting in her favorite chair by the fire, with James drinking his whiskey on the sofa. "Oh, Lottie, you look so lovely," she says to me. "And it fits you so well." Turning to her husband, she adds, "Look at her, love. Isn't she stunning?"

I walk over to him, my face away from my cousin. "What do you think, James?" I ask. And yet, it seems as if another woman is asking. A woman with two normal legs who knows how to seduce a handsome man, who has no relation to Anna. Yes, as I speak, I am someone else, standing in front of my lover in that glorious emerald dress.

James' eyes slowly rake over me—from my feet, to my waist, to my breasts, to my face. His smile is libertine, matching a licentious one of my own.

"You ever feel like leaving the life you have and starting over?" James asked the following evening, sitting in the passenger side of Casper Cotton Fancy's brand-new cherry red Tin Lizzie he named Sophia. The two men had just left the Blue Lizard Cave and were headed to Sugar Alexandria for Yarrajan's special stew and corn cakes.

"Where would you go, mate?" Casper asked, keeping his eyes on the road.

James, inebriated, pointed at the rather large and milky-looking celestial body orbiting the earth.

"The moon, aye?" Casper Cotton laughed. "That's pretty bloody far from here."

James glanced over at his friend. "You've never had a craving to leave this place?"

"Nah. I have my sons and daughters, my lovely sheila, my castle, my pub, and my new girl Sophia. What else would I need?"

"I've been thinking about it lately."

"Sellin' Sugar Alexandria and movin' to the city, aye? Anna finally givin' in?"

James closed his eyes and pulled his Akubra hat over his face, leaning back in the seat. "Yeah, something like that."

⁓ᴄᴇ☙☀❧ᴐᴝ⁓

Early the next morn, Rose went to fetch water from the pump. James was just leaving the farmhouse, fresh from a bath, his dark blond hair sleeked back and his beard trimmed. When they crossed paths, she flashed a devilish smile.

"That's a wicked smile you got there, Ambrosia Charlotte Moss," he said, whistling loudly, making the birds fly into the morning firmament.

⁓ᴄᴇ☙☀❧ᴐᴝ⁓

An entire month passed since the event. Rose's small breasts became tender, fuller. Oddly, she began to have vivid dreams of a child crying for her. When she missed her period and started feeling ill in the morning, she went to see the doctor.

The nurse in the pink uniform led Rose into the examination room, giving her a smock to change into. Rose fidgeted in her seat until Dr. Crawford opened the door, scanning his clipboard.

"Miss Rose, how are you doing today?"

"I'm good, just not feeling that well these days. I throw up almost every morning."

"Crook, are ya?" He surveyed her appearance, noticing her coloring seemed to glow. "Could you be pregnant?"

Rose paused as James' face flashed through her mind. In that moment, she could taste his mouth and smell his scent as if he were there in the room. "Yes, it's a possibility."

The doctor instructed her to lie down on the examination table and felt around her abdomen. He gently pressed in several areas, then sat back in his stool. "When was the last time you had your menses?"

"I missed the last one," she answered, biting at her lip.

"Well, let's do the test, then. We'll know in about a week or so when the results come back."

It is a calm and uneventful evening after Rose returns from the doctor's office. James, the two women in his life, and his twin girls are all in the windmill—he on the piano playing Chopin's *Nocturne Op.9, No.2, in E-flat major,* Rose on the love seat listening intently, his wife and daughters sitting on the living room floor. Rose is wearing her favorite sapphire dress, and as she sits there listening to the melody of the song, she steals amorous glances at James, watching Anna in her peripheral vision, careful not to stare too long at her cousin's husband. Anna is preoccupied, as always, braiding Scarlet and Mabel's hair, and when finished, she laughs as the girls twirl around to the music, coming together to hold hands, only to break apart again and twirl once more.

As James continues to play the composition, a peaceful ambience surrounds the three adults. A protective bubble of joy, each of them happy for different reasons: Anna, thrilled that Rose may soon be raising a child at Sugar Alexandria. Rose, hoping a miracle happens, gifting her with a baby. And James, excited for the future.

If only it could have stayed this serene.

This wonderful trinity.

Anna's perfect little world.

Something unbidden is happening to Anna, and James and Rose are balefully unaware. A slow simmering is brewing within her psyche. A festering has begun. The sickness is yawning and stretching, blossoming into something new, like a snake getting ready to shed its skin . . .

CHAPTER 31

Seven days later, Dr. Crawford confirmed what Rose's body had already told her. She was with child.

"I'm pregnant?" she asked, the room suddenly swaying.

"Yes," said the doctor.

Rose appeared in shock.

Dr. Crawford smiled, thinking her reaction was based on this being her first child. "Oh, don't worry, love. With nature how it is, everything will be apples," he said, lifting her white smock to gently feel around her lower abdomen.

Rose, still at a loss for words, felt anesthetized.

The doctor lowered her smock and wrote a few notes on his clipboard. "Drink lots of milk, all right? And get your rest and some daily sunshine, aye? I want to see you again in four weeks." Before he left to attend to the next patient, he added his warm felicitations. "Congratulations, Rose. You're gonna be a mother this winter."

Rose's face paled and her hands went clammy. As much as she had always wanted to be a mother, the reality of it now happening hit her. On driving to the doctor's office—a humble home that he worked out of—she had reasoned with herself that if she wasn't pregnant, she would leave Sugar Alexandria at once and never come back. She'd say goodbye to Anna and James and the entire love triangle for good, not letting either of them stop her. But now that she was indeed with child, this would force her to stay. Of course she could still leave and have the baby by herself in some other town, or country, or continent, but an unwed woman with a growing belly would not fare well on her own no matter where she went.

"You look faint, love," said Nurse June. "Would you like some water?"

"Yes, please," Rose answered, still trembling.

297

Dr. Crawford's wife, Iris, who worked as his receptionist and bookkeeper, stepped into the room. "Congratulations, Rose. I didn't know you had married."

"I'm . . . I'm not married," she replied, her nervous smile never quite reaching her lips.

"Oh . . . I didn't know you were engaged, then. Who's the lucky bloke?"

"I'm not engaged, either."

Iris and Nurse June exchanged glances.

Rose ran her fingers through her hair, searching both women's faces, discerning what judgments were being made. "When I told him I might be pregnant, he left town."

"One of the Shahan's stockmen?" Iris asked.

"No." Perspiration accumulated on Rose's upper lip. "Just someone I met from Perth. He sweet-talked me and . . . well . . . I foolishly fell for it."

Nurse June softened toward her. "Sorry, love. It's a grouse thing that cousin of yours has taken you in. Anna is a good girl; she'll help you through this."

"Too right," said Iris.

Rose nodded as her insides tightened. It was the beginning of the lie she and Anna had hoped everyone in town would believe.

Iris tsked in disgust, patting Rose on the back. "The good Lord knows a clean-shaven bloke with a box full of promises is hard to resist. But no worries, love. You'll have your baby, and everything will be grand. Then you can go find a worthy bloke and start fresh. You've just stubbed your toe, that's all. Happens to the best of us."

On the drive home, Rose was in a daze. Exhausted, exhilarated, terrified, emotional beyond anything she could imagine. There was no denying what had happened, nor what would happen next.

Just as Anna had planned.

And she had dreamed.

However, a devastating facet existed about her new reality. She felt as if she were trampling on her cousin's body to achieve that dream. The perception was enough to make her regret the whole thing, until she got past the initial shock of it all, whence came a sense of triumph and shining joy. She radiated, remembering the night the baby had been conceived—an impassioned experience that changed her as a human being.

How would Anna react, Rose wondered, when her cousin found out she was pregnant? Even more important, how would James respond? He was somewhat forced into the situation through his wife's conniving manipulation, and now Rose was going to have his baby.

Anna's idea at first seemed ludicrous, laughable, even unconscionable. Yet it worked out seamlessly. Elation filled Rose, imagining what her baby would look like, hoping it would be a lovely blend of both mother and father. As she turned down the long dirt road to Sugar Alexandria, all she could think about was how she was pregnant, and James Shahan was the father.

Anna was folding clothes on the couch, her little pink-breasted companion on her shoulder, singing and keeping her company while Lovely Dawn napped at her feet. Usually she didn't give laundry a second thought, but as she separated James' garments from her own, she noticed the long length of his trousers and the width of his shirts, breathing in the smell of the soap while her mind dwelled on her husband—his sincere eyes, kind voice, and how nice it felt to lie next to him at night. Funny, she had never contemplated those things before. Mostly all she cared about was how hard he worked on the station to make it a thriving success. She didn't want him thinking about music, or teaching, or his silly books she would find lying around. Yet at that moment, those things didn't really bother her anymore.

Anna frowned. James had been distant with her since the night he had spent with Rose. But it was understandable. He needed time to adjust, for things to get back to normal. And things *would* return to normal, she assured herself. It had been over a month already, and Rose hadn't mentioned anything. It's likely that night was for naught—no fruit produced from the encounter. Surprisingly, Anna felt a sense of relief over it. Not meant to be, she thought. Rose will just have to persevere until she finds herself a bloke, and as James said, have a family the right way. The honorable way. At least I tried my best, and Rose will always love me for that. But it's done now, and I have to concentrate on enjoying the family I have.

Rose opened the front door, and with glossy eyes, walked over to the couch, sitting down slowly. "I'm pregnant," she announced, almost a whisper. She simultaneously squeezed Anna's hand.

"Oh, Lottie!" Anna squealed. "Goodness gracious, you've been blessed! This is the most ripper news!" She hugged her cousin tightly.

"I had symptoms, and I missed my period, but I wasn't sure. I just didn't want to get my hopes up and be disappointed. But Dr. Crawford told me I was definitely pregnant."

Anna kissed her on the cheek. "You're gonna be a mummy!"

Rose started to cry, placing her hand on her stomach. "I already love the baby so much, Kitten. It's such an incredible feeling."

Anna couldn't stop smiling if she tried. She was so ecstatic that the idea had worked and everything was going as planned. And yet, a strange stinging sensation arose in her stomach. An extraneous pang of insecurity. She ignored it. She would not allow herself to consider anything other than happiness in that precious moment. She loved Rose, and her gift to her cousin would bind them together for life.

That is what she wanted.

The burden of a human being is that we are weak when it comes to what and who we love.

We are also a product of our sins, transgressions, and iniquities.

We reap what we sow.

The question is, what will little Anna reap from what she has sown?

By early afternoon it started to rain, and with the sheep wool soaking wet, it was too difficult to shear. The men did other work instead, until the downpour became too mighty, halting everything. The Blue Lizard Cave was the only option left—a welcome one at that—and most of the men left for the pub.

As James sat at the bar drinking his beer, he thought of the many families now suffering through the Great Depression, without food, without shelter, without money. Cold and hungry, land sold off or foreclosed, hopes and dreams destroyed. The men in the pub were the lucky ones. Despite their muddy boots, worn-out clothing, and smeared, dirty faces, they could at least feed their families and pay their mortgages, having a little left over for some grog.

Taking another swig of his beer, James' thoughts turned to Rose, as they often did. The chatter in the pub disappeared, and so did the men all around him, as his mind relived the passion they had shared. He wondered whether or not Rose was with child, and what each outcome would mean for him, for his wife, and for her . . .

~~~

That night in his bedroom, propped up against his pillow, James' eyes were closed. Too much grog in his veins from imbibing at the pub earlier had induced that sweet, floating feeling in him, yet also carried that vengeful augur that he'd pay dearly for it in the morning.

Anna entered the room with a big smile on her face.

"What is it?" James asked, opening his eyes. Lovely Dawn was sprawled out beside him, relishing the rare privilege of sleeping on her owner's bed.

Anna clasped her hands and sat on the corner of the mattress. "I have ripper news . . . Rose is pregnant!"

He didn't respond, but his heart began to race, in shock, unsure of how he should feel. Then the room began to spin. Was it from the revelation or the alcohol? Probably both.

"Aren't you rapt?" Anna asked. It sounded more like a demand.

James' mouth went dry, his expression unreadable. "Crikey," he barely got out, his body electrifying.

"That's all you have to say?"

"It doesn't make any difference to me." He lied. "This was all your doing, not mine. It's what you wanted, what you pushed for. I never wanted any part of it."

She looked away, disappointed in his reaction.

"Have you two decided what you're going to tell folks when she starts showing?"

"Yes, we already have a story prepared."

"And what's that?"

"She was being courted by a bloke from Perth, and when he found out the news, he left town."

James sighed. "The story you tell won't make any difference–people are still going to shun her. We'll probably be shunned too."

"I give you wonderful news about something sacred to me, telling you that a miracle has transpired, and this is your response?" Anna asked, sincere in her delusion. "James Ragnar Shahan, I demand you say something kind.

Rose is going to have a child!"

"Yes, my child."

Anna clenched her fist, aggravated by her husband's lack of buoyancy. "This has nothing to do with you, James! This was about Rose and fulfilling her dream to have a baby!"

He scoffed. "Nothing to do with me, aye?"

"You're not his father. Period. The baby's father abandoned them, and I want you to swear an oath."

"An oath about what?"

"About the truth. No matter what happens, the truth stays with us and dies with us."

A bewildered expression traversed James' face, as if the entire situation were absolutely insane, like some kind of extraordinary theater playing out in his bedroom where he was one of the actors. He thought of the disastrous consequences for them all if the truth got out, and conceded to his wife's wish. "Fine," he said, his heart pounding with incertitude. "I will take the oath, and the truth to my grave."

"Yes, to the grave," echoed Anna, her face a mask of solemnity.

James stared at her, the light in his eyes fading even as hers grew brighter. He was in love with Rose—he was certain of that—and to have a child with her only felt natural, but it troubled him how it was done. Things were happening in reverse, and he was breaking every rule he had been taught in life. His grandfather, who spoke only Gaelic, had often said to him when he was alive, *"Ná briseadh lámh briste,"* (*"Don't break a broken arm."*) meaning don't make a bad situation worse. And yet that's exactly what they were doing by following through with Anna's plan.

Turning off the lamp, he said, "You got your way, Tin Tin. Rose will raise the child at Sugar Alexandria and be here for quite some time. I suppose you both got what you wanted, really."

A heavenly expression came over her face. "Yes, now she'll be with us for the rest of her life."

"The rest of her life, aye? You don't think she'll ever want her own companion still? Her own home and family?"

Anna didn't answer.

James studied the outline of his wife's silhouette in the shadows, with her tiny feminine neck and narrow shoulders. Such a small woman, he thought, yet with so much stubbornness and determination. She had no idea what she had done. "Anna, it's getting late," he said. "I'm knackered and morning comes early. We can talk about this some more tomorrow, aye? Although there's not much more to say. It's done, and now let's hope all goes well." He reached out his hand for her. "Come lay next to me and we'll have a good night's sleep, love."

Anna remained at the edge of the bed, staring at her husband reaching for her through the darkness, deciding if she should crawl up and lie next to him or go see how Rose was feeling. Grabbing her sweater, she headed out the door to her cousin's maisonette.

Anna

As I walk to the windmill, something is watching me.
Bloodred eyes gleam in the darkness.
What is your concern with me, wolf?
Have you come to help me or kill me?
If you're here to harm my family, I will skin you alive!

Anna found Rose sitting on the floor in the windmill, drinking hot tea and rummaging through her trunk. "What are you doing?" she asked.

"I know it's early, but I'm looking for dresses I can wear during my pregnancy."

"You can wear mine."

Rose laughed. "Anna, you're a good six inches shorter than me. And you have those fetching curves that I don't."

"We could make you some, then."

"That would be lovely."

Anna sat next to her, lifting a sequin dress from the trunk. "I suppose we won't be having our dress-up days and cocktail parties for a while."

"No, not for a while. Close to eight months."

"Are you excited?" Anna asked, beaming.

"I'm just beside myself. When I walk, it's like I'm floating."

"Det fungerede, Lottie," Anna said in Danish. *"Jeg sagde til dig; før eller senere ville han gøre som jeg siger."* They held each other's gaze. (*"It worked, Lottie. I told*

you; sooner or later he would do as I say.")

"Ja, Killing, det fungerede," Rose said, sticking out her pinky finger. Anna quickly did the same, and the two cousins interlocked digits, smiling widely, almost wickedly. *("Yes, Kitten, it worked.")*

The Voices

"You can come out now, Mummy," Anna whispers when back inside the farmhouse, lifting the kerosene lamp at Rose's painting of her mother. "I have something special to tell you."

"I already know, dear," Elsa replies, stepping out of the picture frame. "Isn't it wonderful?"

Elsa walks over to the bar mirror, primping her golden hair and straightening her dress.

"I'm so excited, Mummy. This is what I have fought for. What I have wanted all along."

Returning to her daughter, Elsa's kind eyes convey grave concern. For a moment she puts her hand on Anna's cheek and holds it there.

Anna places her own hand over her mother's. "Look at what Rose has given me," she says, tearing up. "I have my mum back."

"Us too," Blessing and her grandmother say from inside their paintings.

"Yes, I have all of you. Not just your voices in my head, but the real you. How could I not be gracious with her? How could I not allow this?" Tears stream down Anna's face.

"This will shake the very ground you walk on, love," says Elsa. "It will be a grand test for you."

"Test?" Anna questions, wiping her eyes.

"Yes." Her mother's voice becomes more ominous. "A test of endurance. Faith. Sanity, even. It's not going to be all peaches and cream like you think."

"I wasn't wrong to allow this, Mummy," Anna replies, watching as her mother walks back to her painting.

"Oh, but you *were*, Turtle Dove," Elsa's voice says, fading away as she steps inside the frame, "and you will regret what you have allowed until your dying day," her mother's sweet, lyrical whispers vanishing like a flowery fragrance in the Australian breeze.

CHAPTER 32

"A nna told me the news," James said the next day, sitting down on the love seat inside the windmill. His face was open and relaxed, and he had the slightest smile touching at the corner of his lips.

Rose, nervously polishing her violin, met eyes with him. "Feels like a dream," she said, her voice breathless.

James touched his beard, thinking. "There are so many thoughts running through my head right now. It took so long with Anna that I didn't think one could . . ."

"Produce a child so easily?"

He nodded.

Sifting through her mind for just the right words, she added, "You said before that you didn't want any part of this," a woebegone expression on her face as she pretended to be fixated on cleaning her stringed instrument. "And you still don't have to. I'm all right by myself. I'm ready to raise this child on my own. I knew from the beginning what this was, and that your real family is with my cousin Anna."

James walked over to her, taking her violin and putting it down, wiping a tear that had run down her cheek. Gazing at her, he contemplated how he felt as a jolt ran through his chest, propelled by a change. A slipping away of his old life, precipitated by the awakening of a new. He welcomed it, pulling her in for a long embrace. Then he kissed her. A long, passionate kiss—intense, unrestrained, perfervid.

"For the first and last time in my life, I am in love," he confessed against her cheek. "And I don't just want to be a father to our baby, but a husband to you."

Rose put her arms around his neck. "I too am in love for the first and last time in my life," she said, eyes brimming with tears. "And I don't just want to be a mother to our child, but a wife to you."

There they both stood, holding each other inside the windmill maisonette he had built for her, feeling strangely, deliriously happy. He lifted her from the ground and spun her around, and she laughed. At that moment, they were not thinking about how it would all work out. They were not worried over the future knots and ties that would have to be untangled. Instead they only celebrated, knowing that in the most unconventional way, they had found love.

That night, neither James nor Rose played the piano. Instead of having their lesson, Rose only played her violin. *Swan Lake.* She began Tchaikovsky's composition, stringing out the musical score with as much passion as she could, while James evaluated her performance.

"Slower," he said, engaged in her interpretation. Then, "Slower still."

She obliged, performing it as unhurried and temperate as she could. He walked around her as she played, hands behind his back and a solemn expression on his face. When the song was finished, he would tell her to play it again, each time drawing nearer, until his breath fanned the nape of her neck. Putting his arms around her waist, he gently pulled her close to his body; she leaned into him. Quickly he spun her around to face him, kissing her, fiddle still in hand.

Neither one held back.

Genevieve

"Anna, you can't be such a fool, girl. Men cheat and women lie; men lie and women cheat."

"They didn't lie or cheat," Anna replies to the lady in the black Victorian dress at the foot of the bed, darkness hiding her features. "I allowed it."

"You're being naïve, dear. Gullible, even."

Anna sits up and looks over at her husband, sound asleep. "Who are you to judge me? James says you don't even exist."

"Tsk, tsk, tsk," Genevieve utters. "You used to listen to me, Sweet Pea."

"Whaddya want me to do, throw Rose out and divorce my bloke? Never! They're my family, and you're nothing but a figment of my imagination, so leave me alone!" Anna yells, throwing her bedside Bible at the hallucination.

"Wha . . . wha . . . what's going on?" James asks, abruptly waking from his deep slumber.

"Nothing," says Anna. "Go back to sleep."

* * *

"During your piano lesson last night, I noticed you only played the violin," Anna said. The two women, both wearing their matching velvet cloaks, had taken the twins to Cassandra Fancy's garden to play.

"We sometimes perform a duet—he on the keyboard and me on the strings," Rose replied. Opening the door to the eighteenth-century Georgian carriage, she stepped inside.

Anna followed, sitting across from her. "I know, but I could only hear *you*."

Rose bit at her lower lip, knowing what she was doing was wrong, continuing an affair with her cousin's husband. "He wanted me to play that song solo, to give me advice on how to perform it better."

"What's it called?" Anna asked, glancing out the carriage window to check on her daughters. Scarlet and Mabel were sitting on the ground, playing with some flowers.

"*Swan Lake*."

"Is it about swans?"

Rose weighed the moral of the story behind the famous composition. "It's a ballet about love and longing, betrayal and despair, using a white swan and a black one in a symbolic way to represent good and bad."

"Oh, goody," Anna said, tapping her feet on the carriage floor. "I love stories about the battle between good and evil."

Rose felt over the red, cracked leather covering the seat as her eyes inspected the inner structure of the antique carriage. "The white swan, Odette, symbolizes purity and vulnerability, while the black swan, Odile, symbolizes shameless deception," she said, the irony of her synopsis twisting her insides into knots.

Anna, too, scanned the inside of the carriage, remembering the many times they had played in the retired contraption as children, pretending they were traveling all over the world. "What happens?"

"Odette is under the spell of an evil sorcerer, only able to take on human form at night. One evening a prince witnesses her transform into a beautiful maiden, and the two fall in love. But the curse can only be removed if one who has never loved before swears to love Odette forever."

As always, her cousin's exotic tales fascinated Anna. "Was the spell broken?"

"No. The queen tells the prince he must select a bride at the royal ball, and that's when the deception occurs. The evil sorcerer makes his daughter, Odile, look like Odette, and the prince is fooled into choosing her, proclaiming to all in attendance that he will marry the imposter."

"What a crook thing to do. Does it have a happy ending at least?"

Rose looked deep into Anna's eyes, seeing only naïveté and trust reflecting back. "No . . . The prince finds out who Odile truly is, and is now grief-stricken. Since the spell can no longer be broken, he and Odette, in utter despair, drown themselves together."

"Crikey, why would they do that?"

"They shared a boundless intimacy for each other they couldn't live without," Rose said, daring not to look her cousin in the eye for fear of culpability overwhelming her. "Their love was absolute."

Anna frowned. "I can't imagine dying for a bloke."

"I can," Rose almost said, sitting back in the carriage, her hand on her stomach, thinking of the very moment James had passionately kissed her, telling her to help him be the man he once was.

Anna leaned out the window, staring out into the garden. "Just look at this place, Lottie. By our touch, it was resurrected to something magical again. We made it happen." She looked back at Rose. "And that's how I knew you were pregnant. I willed that to happen too."

"You are a little Aussie battler, Miss Anna. That's what you be, ever since a little girl," said Yarrajan that evening, not looking up from the food she was chopping. "But I fear you have started somethin' that will end dark." Her eyes gravitated over to Rose's windmill. "Not sure what it be, but it ain't gonna end grouse for you."

Anna gave her an inquisitive look, sitting down at the kitchen table.

"For centuries, my people had no written language. To record our stories beyond oral tradition, we be usin' symbols and artwork. Shapes and colors, beads and animals—from these a person's life story be told."

Sipping her tea, Anna stared at the Aboriginal woman, listening attentively.

"If I were to create your story, Miss Anna, it be sad. A vulnerable rabbit, left behind by a beautiful deer."

Anna smirked. Yarrajan was always talking in metaphors, similes, and parables, trying to convey life's lessons to her; or omens, warnings, and premonitions, trying to keep her safe. Nothing the older woman ever said made any sense. She dismissed Yarrajan's stories as just amusing mumblings.

Later that week, Yarrajan left a piece of indigenous artwork on the kitchen table. It was a striking picture, made with beads of every color. A small, white rabbit sat abandoned in the corner near a dark hole, and far in the distance, not one but two deer were running together into the blue horizon . . .

CHAPTER 33

In the dead of night inside the windmill, it was pitch black. With no lit candles or kerosene lamps to illuminate the interior shell, and the curtains drawn to block out the moon, it was so dark that one would stumble if they tried to walk across the room. That was how James and Rose continued their affair, inside the windmill, kissing amorously at 1 a.m.

As he touched her, James thought of the leviathan he initially hesitated to convert into a maisonette, and how it was now a lifeline for him, housing the woman he loved, embodying everything he wanted for the future as if a gateway to another dimension.

"We can't keep doing this," Rose said. Yet as she spoke, she smiled.

"If I were to kiss you then go to hell, I would," he whispered in the darkness. "So then I can brag with the devils I saw heaven without ever entering it."

She let out a soft laugh. "Where did you hear that?"

"Shakespeare. The bloke knew what he was talking about." Propping her against the door, he started kissing up her neck. "Meet me at the Barracuda Hut today at noon," he said, his hand slowly traveling up her thigh. "I will leave the motorized boat at the shoreline. Promise me you will meet me there."

"James . . ."

"I want to be alone with you without having to worry if someone will knock on the door and interrupt us. That's all I'm asking." He kissed her again. "Meet me there." She tried to protest, but he put his finger against her lips to hush her. "I won't take no for an answer."

A knock startled them both . . . It was Anna!

Rose panicked, her heart pounding, her body pressed up against James with her hand covering his mouth. "Goodness, Anna, it's so late. What is it?" she asked without opening the door.

"I woke up and James was gone. Do you know where he is?"

"Why are you asking *me*?" Matilda traipsed over to them, purring and rubbing her head against James' leg.

"I dunno. I can't find him."

"Have you checked his distillery?"

"Yes."

"Maybe he's drinking grog with the men in the stockmen quarters."

"You're probably right; I bet he's in there. Sorry I woke you."

"No worries, love. Go back to bed."

"All right. G'night, Lottie," Anna said, completely unaware of the Trojan horse that had entered her life, nescient to its wooden walls that were destined for fire and war.

"Good night, Kitten," Rose said against James' lips.

Anna

Back in the farmhouse, to my delight, everyone from Rose's paintings is visiting with each other, smiling and laughing, hugging and conversing.

What a sight!

What a joy!

I visit with them—oh, how I love them all!

Afterward, I cannot sleep, so I run to Cassandra's garden. Under the moonlight, twirling and dancing, whispering to the elves and fairies, I collect flowers from the garden to put on Mummy, Blessing, and Grandmother's graves. Raspberry waratahs, fuchsia correas, yellow flame grevilleas, and pink kangaroo paws, all tied together in a beauty of a bouquet.

And then something horrifying happens when I go to the family burial plot . . .

The air turns icy, prickling my flesh, and the ground trembles as a fog lifts from the unmarked grave where my husband buried the Black Shuck! Like a belly splitting to expose its entrails, the ground opens up, and out steps a skeleton man!

"You think me a beast, do you?" it asks. "A demon? A creature of the night?"

"Yes," I say, falling to my knees. "You're a demon wolf, and you deserved to die."

"If I am a beast, then why do I have the bones of a man?"

I run from the cemetery, stumbling and falling, scraping my knees, blood running down my legs.

"Did you hear me, woman! If I am a beast, why do I have the bones of a man!"

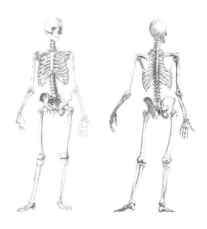

"James is out fishing again," Anna said the next day as she was baking pastries. Strawberry rhubarb, banana cream, and lemon meringue pies sat on the table, ready for the oven. Moby strutted on the counter, flaring his wings and pink crest, trying to get his owner's attention.

"Fish for dinner tonight?" asked Rose, helping her cousin.

"Yes, along with *flæskesteg med persillesovs og kartofler*." *(roast pork with parsley sauce and caramelized potatoes)*

"It's going to be a lovely meal," Rose said, getting anxious. She was supposed to meet James at the Barracuda Hut.

"Every night, we'll make scrumptious meals for you, Lottie. You have a baby now that needs nourishment." Anna gave her cousin a warm smile. "Have you thought of any names yet?"

Rose stared at her, blank-faced, always amazed at how far removed Anna was from the reality of the situation. "I don't want to jinx anything. I'm going to wait until after the baby is born to pick a name."

Anna nodded, placing another pie on the table. "Can't wait until the baby is here."

"Me too." Rose looked down at her watch; she was already late.

"I have a bunch of baby clothes from Scarlet and Mabel stored away in the trunk," Anna said, smiling. "Wanna look through some of them now? You can pick out what you like; it'll be fun."

Although Rose was sitting there with Anna, her mind was already in the arms of James. "Maybe another day. I was thinking of taking a walk to the shoreline."

"A walkabout? Now?"

"Umm . . ."

"You sure that's a good idea, considering your condition?"

"I'm not that far along yet, Anna. Besides, exercise is good for me."

"All right; just be careful and get home before dinner. You're eating for two now."

Rose hastily leaves the farmhouse with her cane and her best walking shoes, the hood of her cloak hiding her face and the tail billowing behind. Ignoring the compunction growing inside her with each step, she scurries down the path to the shoreline as if both legs are strong and healthy. As if she's in a race, like people in London jostling for a cab. She does not look left or right, up or down, only straight ahead, fixated on her destination. Nothing else matters but to get to the man she has waited for her entire life, enduring an emotional war to attain. Though she is not there yet, she sees his face, his smile, his strong hands all over her body. Quickening her pace, faster still, even faster, using her cane to catapult herself forward, she walks to the point of sprinting.

Sprinting to her cousin's husband James.

The boat was right where he said it would be. She jumped in, starting the motor and directing it over to the small island where the abandoned fisherman's cabin stood. As she approached the small house, her heart accelerated. Again, she did not see the vast ocean that spread out around her, or the cloudless blue sky above, or the bright, yellow sun warming her skin. Only the impending touch of the man she loved and the sound of his voice in her ears monopolized her thoughts. And as always, his hands. Every detail, front and back, and how they would soon be all over her skin.

Tying the boat to the dock, she hurried to the door. James let her in, kissing her face, her lips, hugging her, picking her up into his embrace, spinning in a circle.

"Sorry I'm late," Rose said. "Anna was in a talkative mood, and . . ."

He kissed her into silence.

The bed in the corner had been prepared with clean white sheets, and soon they were there, consumed in their mutual pleasure, thirsting for each other like fresh water from a cool stream. They did not feel separate, but one. The same person, tenderly making love, as their past heartaches and present troubles evanesced.

James caressed Rose's body, feeling down the length of her thigh as he thrusted in and out. It wasn't just the sex they craved but the intimacy they had never before experienced. "I can't get close enough," he kept whispering into her ear. "Come closer to me," tucking her body into his. "Closer," everything around them melting away.

⚜

Anna's existence is much different. In her realm, her loving and devoted husband is out at sea, fishing in his small boat under the blazing sun, catching an abundance for dinner. Her best cobber and cousin is on a long walkabout, taking time for herself, getting a good stretch of her legs as she beats down a slender pathway. She'll be walking that same trail she has created even decades from now, Anna muses.

Mechanically she goes about her afternoon routine—now done by rote—giving her daughters their bath, feeding her pet cockatoo, washing and preparing the vegetables for dinner. She sharpens the knife beforehand—both sides—until the metal shines, and as she slices through the cucumbers and squash like butter, she revels in her glorious life. How I love my husband and my cousin, she cerebrates, who love me in return and complete me along with my children. I am so blessed; I need not for anything in the world.

The Australian sun, once in the midday sky, began to cast long shadows across the room as the two lovers, intermingled with the bedding, peacefully rested in each other's arms after their amatory escapade.

"I should go," Rose said, kissing James on the cheek. "It's been hours; I'm going to have to tell Anna that I walked all the way to Kalgoorlie."

"She would believe anything you said," he replied, kissing her lips.

"I know, and I don't feel good about it." A tightness gripped her chest. "We're taking advantage of her love for us, James. We're betraying her trust."

Her words hung heavy between them, and he felt the same lack of rectitude.

"It almost feels as if we're hurting an innocent child, considering there's something not right with her."

James recalled the first time he found out there were issues in Anna's family. "Her mother had something not right with her too."

"You knew about Elsa?"

"Yes."

"How?"

"Anna's father told me. After we were married, he took me aside and confided in me about it, telling me how Elsa had some kind of mental disorder. They didn't know what it was, but he said she suffered a great deal with it, and he wanted me to know that it could be hereditary."

"My mother told me the same thing. She said mental disorders exist in our family tree, going back generations." Rose was grateful she had been spared, suffering instead only a physical malady. "Did my uncle say anything else about my aunt?"

"He said he would often find her wandering around in her nightgown, her feet covered in mud, whispering gibberish to herself. Arguing with someone not there about nonsensical things. When he would shake her back to reality, she would throw a horrendous fit, then go into a trance-like state, staring at nothing for hours."

"Sounds like Anna, only much worse."

James nodded.

"I've seen her shrine," said Rose, "with the beads and corn husk dolls hanging in the tree branches."

"It's disturbing, aye?"

"It is."

"Have you seen her praying to it while she wears her feathered crown and wings? That's even more ghastly."

Rose shook her head.

"She thinks she can talk to her deceased mother and sister there. I tried to reason with her that it's not normal, but she wouldn't listen. She only told me that she's gifted and sees and hears things others don't."

"She told me the same thing."

James thought for a moment, remembering all the strange experiences he had with his wife over the years. "All I could do is try to be a support for her. To love and protect her, like I vowed I would." He looked over at Rose. "I really did try to be a good bloke to Anna."

"That must have been hard for you, marrying a woman who wasn't pregnant after all, then finding out she has mental issues."

"Yes, it was. But we do what we have to to survive. Those were the cards I was dealt with, and I tried to play my hand the best I could."

"James, I honestly think Anna's condition is more stable because of you."

"Possibly. I know her triggers and the remedies to calm her."

"You've been her foundation for so long. She'd probably be completely mad without you."

"I've thought of that too. But I can't stay here anymore just because she has mental issues. For God's sake, I'd end up losing my mind *with* her."

❧

On the way back to Sugar Alexandria, Rose hears Anna kulning. The distinct, characteristic sounds pulse in the air, beautifully echoing across the land. Anna's calling me home, she thinks. As always, the quarter tones and half tones reverberate through her, the crisp inflections and eerie cadence prickling her skin. The same skin Anna's husband has just touched, kissed, and caressed.

⚜

"Did you hear me calling to the animals?" Anna asked, standing over the stove, stirring the parsley sauce in a large metal pot. Lovely Dawn was by her feet, patiently waiting for food scraps.

"I did," said Rose, kneeling to pet the potbellied pig. "It's amazing how far that sound travels."

"James has his piano music, you have your violin, and I have my kulning."

"It's an impressive and unique talent, Kitten."

"Grandmother used to say I was better than anyone she's ever heard."

"She always liked you better than me," Rose admitted. "I think because you reminded her of herself in her youth."

Anna didn't disagree, proud that she was her grandmother's favorite. "That was a lengthy walkabout you took," she said. "You're pregnant, now, Lottie. I don't think you should be going that far."

Rose picked up little Scarlet, giving her a peck on the cheek before sitting her back down. "The sauce smells wonderful," she said nonchalantly.

"And your leg," Anna continued, pointing at it. "Not good to strain it like that."

"I always have my cane with me, and it's good to get some fresh air," Rose replied. She took off her cloak and hung it on the back of the chair.

"You certainly have gotten good use out of that gift, aye? The highest quality velvet I could find," Anna said with pride. "When we're both wearing them, I feel as if we've stepped back in time, living in a quaint village somewhere far far away."

Rose studied her cousin, noticing her eyes glaze over, an enigmatic smile crystallizing on her lips. She wondered where Anna's mind went in those momentary lapses of reality.

James came in through the back door, holding a string of fish. Unbeknownst to Anna, he had paid an Aboriginal fisherman to catch them for him.

"Crikey, James, I thought you'd never come home," Anna said, snapping back from the unknown. "How many did you get?"

He lifted the fish stringer, showing his catch. "Six. Tiger flatheads and mahi-mahi."

"Good on ya, love!" Anna chirped.

Moby wasn't impressed. "Irish whacker!" he squawked.

The two women laughed, and even James couldn't help but chuckle.

"See? I don't mind when you go fishing, love, as long as the station yakka is done, and you bring back the goods."

"It's going to be a lovely dinner," Rose said, adding garlic cloves to the sauce. She glanced at James as he walked past her to hand Anna the fish.

"Danish *flæskesteg* served with seasoned pan-fried fish in extra virgin olive oil," said Anna with delight. "A swell dinner with two people I love the most in the whole wide world."

Genevieve

Anna!
You should have told Rose to leave!
You should have saved yourself, your family!
Now it is too late, Sweet Pea . . .

For weeks on end, whenever the situation allowed, the two lovers met at the island, as if two lost souls who had finally found their way home. When Anna went into town, to church, or to visit a friend, Rose would find a reason to decline accompanying her, and together with James, they would swiftly make their way to the abandoned fisherman's cabin. Clothes tossed aside, deep kissing rapidly progressed into heated lovemaking. Even as the fever between them soared, their lustful hunger for each other never satisfied. Nothing in their intimacy was rehearsed; each touch, kiss, taste, thrust, was as natural as breathing the air.

Rose felt confused, yet more herself than ever before. Their passion seemed to strengthen their identities and polish their souls, making them hyperaware of their desperate need for one another.

"I am not whole until I am with you," James whispered one day as they laid in each other's arms.

"I feel the same about you," she whispered back.

Warm skin on skin, breathing in tandem, a calm peace weaved through them both as they rested.

"In Europe, there are areas where it's common for men to have more than one wife," Rose said. "It's illegal, but it happens anyway."

"Yeah, polygamy. It's illegal here too, but they don't do anything about it. Russ Wyatt has three wives—two of them sisters, the other one a migrant from Poland. They live deep in the Outback. Middle of nowhere with a bunch of ankle biters and dogs."

"We could do something like that," Rose suggested. "We can make this work—both me and Anna as your wives. I believe she would allow it, especially when she sees the baby. James, she loves me so much, I honestly think she'd go for it."

He only shook his head. How could he possibly go back and forth between two women who were like night and day? How could he be intimate with the love of his life who longed for his passionate touch, then return to another who simply fulfilled her conjugal duty? It was possible, even manageable, despite the gossip and scorn that would catalyze in town, but it would not be fair to his wife. Or to himself. He was a man made to be with one woman, and he wanted that woman to be Rose. "I don't want two wives; I only want you," he said. "Besides, if I wanted to stay here at the station and remain married to Anna, it would be different. But I don't, Rose. I don't want to be a grazier any longer, and I don't want to be married to her, either."

"What should we do, then?"

"Run off together. Just take our things, throw them in the Tin Lizzie, and go."

Rose contemplated his solution. "We can't do that, James. Not now. Let's wait until after the baby is born before doing anything."

"That's months away, love."

"It doesn't feel right to leave now."

"We should go."

"After what she has given me?"

He rubbed his eyes. Everything in his gut was screaming at him to flee with Rose.

"She wants to see the baby born, too. We owe her that."

"All right," he said with a sinking feeling. "Once the baby arrives, you will move to Perth, and I will follow soon after. I'll put Moony in charge and have Yarrajan watch over Anna and the girls until the dust settles." He turned to her, pulling her body closer to his, kissing her eyelids. *"Tha gaol agam ort,"* he softly said in Gaelic. *"Is breá liom gach rud fút."* *("I love you. I love everything about you.")*

Rose kissed his crown as he nestled into her breasts. "What are you saying?"

He looked up at her. "I love you with all that I am."

"I love you too," she replied against his lips.

"Now promise you'll leave with me right after our baby is born."

"I promise."

Anna

While James is out fishing again, and Rose for her walk, I look out the window and see the mute stranger, bloodied and in dire straits. I now feel pity for the injured man who wanders around Sugar Alexandria, instead of animosity.

Making him a nutritious meal of steak, eggs, biscuits and gravy, I take the plate to where he hides. It is a peace offering for a bloke who is continuously suffering, and I think he wants my help.

By coincidence, later that week, James had to make a trip out to Russ Wyatt's station. Russ had bought two heifers from him, and he had to deliver them. The ride took the better part of the day, and when he got there, all three of Russ's wives were out in the field, working as the children played around them like kittens. Their blondish red hair was long and uncombed, their dresses tattered and worn, and their faces gaunt and dirty. Two of the women were heavily pregnant; all three looked up from their work with wild and untrusting eyes.

An uneasiness crawled up inside James. This could be his life—two wives and countless children. Anna and Rose deserved better than that; he deserved better as well. He vowed to himself that any earlier discussions about having two wives would no longer be entertained, and the notion fled his mind.

"G'day, James. How ya be?" Russ asked.

James shook the man's hand. "Been swamped, mate."

"Ya gonna be a tall poppy one day with that station of yours."

"I reckon, if Anna has her way."

"How is that sheila, anyway?"

"Happy and healthy."

Russ smiled and patted one of the cow's belly. "Gonna be ripper to have some fresh milk soon." He then pulled out several bills.

James took the money and nodded. "Nothing like fresh milk in the morning."

"Yep. Bacon, eggs, and bickies with cold milk—brekkie for a king."

After more small talk, James looked over at the women again. Though they were busy with their chores, they appeared lost. He envisioned a hypothetical future with both Anna and Rose as his wives, simultaneously pregnant and working side by side in the fields with their countless children all around. The image made him shudder.

"You want one of my sheilas?" Russ joked.

James laughed. "No ta. One sheila is enough for me." He tipped his hat and left.

CHAPTER 34

James

My whole life I have done the right thing. Always. Without fail. This was expected of me from a very young age, too. To everyone around me, I was the bloke to lean on, to believe in, to trust. Honor before glory. Or even happiness.

But you see, once you taste happiness . . . I mean *really* get a good bite of it . . . it's very difficult to go back to what you were.

———※———

Later that week, James saddled Ireland and rode to the shoreline. The small motorized boat that Rose would use to get to the island was already there; she was waiting for him. Smoke floated from the chimney of the cabin, creating a cozy attestation of the warmth inside. James smiled; he was only moments away. Our flesh is our soul, our touch a gateway to that soul, our love a validation of the soul, he thought as he rowed his boat vigorously. Rose is my earthly connection to heaven. A connection I have never felt before.

Hastily tying the rowboat to the dock, he rushed inside, closing the door so the intimacy could begin. The two lovers merged with each other, inside and out, forward and back, lost and found, becoming one. The level of intimacy they now shared had been foreign to them before Rose. Before James. Lovemaking in the broad light of day—an experience new to James—felt as if they were shining. Shining brilliantly, conjoined in a euphoric entanglement of arms, legs, and lust . . .

What are we doing?

Who are we to do this to Anna?

What are we becoming?

Guilt-ridden thoughts raced through Rose's mind as James pulled her into him. Such a bitter casualty, knowing that to sustain this pleasure, another must suffer. But too quickly the passion burned the voices into oblivion.

No part of her did he not touch, inspect, devour. Where once his fingers made love to his piano, they now made love to her skin. Unfamiliar was she to his senses, yet uncannily familiar. Afterward, as they lay in each other's arms in wonderment, dazed, as if they had been spliced together, the voices in Rose's head returned. First faintly, then loud and blaring . . .

What are we doing?

Who are we to do this to Anna?

What are we becoming?

Rose didn't want to think about the future in that moment. It scared her, knowing that this love triangle would end badly for someone. James, on the other hand, could think of nothing else but the future. The chains and burdens of the station owner were crumbling in front of the pianist's eyes. All the possibilities ahead of him clouded any repercussions that waited.

～✺✺✺～

At the cabin entrance they stand, interlaced in hugging and deep kissing. Rose keeps trying to open the door to leave; James only shuts it. "How did I ever live without you?" he asks, touching his forehead to hers, running his fingers through the silkiness of her hair.

Rose's heart flutters from his words, as if a tiny bird caught in the center of her chest. "James, I have to go," she whispers.

Out of the hut and several steps across the sand, she is back in the boat returning to the world where Anna and her twin daughters live. Her cousin is waiting for her, and Rose can feel it as if a lure pulling her by the lungs.

James waits until the sound of the boat is a faint buzz in the distance. Barefoot and bare-chested, he walks outside, letting the evening air kiss his skin. The wind off the Southern Ocean is exhilarating–crisp, salty, a breathtaking, regenerating rush of cool. He stands there, eyes closed, sun on his face, and enjoys the delightful breeze as it blows past him. I never thought I had the right to feel such love, such joy, he thinks. I always figured I needed to seek Anna's approval first, and only her happiness mattered, just as my father had told me.

But he was wrong.

I was wrong.

Kicking off his trousers, he dives into the waves, howling as he emerges. He throws his arms up at the sky and yells in Gaelic, *"Cad a mothú! Cad a mothú!"* *("What a feeling! What a feeling!")*

So this is what love feels like, Rose inwardly says as she guides the boat to shore. She smiles and sighs, lost in her own world, beatifically unaware of her surroundings as the intense emotion courses through her veins.

Liam, sitting on a grassy dune nearby, polishing his collection of sea glass, looks up from the colored stones. He watches with curiosity as Rose steps out of the boat, humming while she secures it to the shoreline before heading back to Sugar Alexandria.

~⚜~

That evening, Rose came in flushed and windblown. "Sorry I'm late," she said, striding past Anna to retrieve the jadeite dinner plates from the cabinet. "Such a beauty of a day; took a longer walk than usual."

Anna removed the dish from the oven, placing it on the table. "No worries, Lottie. But being pregnant now, you shouldn't be on your feet so much."

Rose distributed each plate on the table. "It's healthy for me to stay active. Besides, a good stretch of the legs is good for the spirit."

Anna laughed. "That's what James always says . . . Hey, you two weren't on a walkabout together, were ya?"

Rose's face flushed. "Anna, what would make you ask such a thing?"

"It's a joke, you galah." Grabbing the gravy from the stove, she asked, "Where's your cloak?"

Rose nervously played with a lock of her hair—she had left it at the cabin. "I didn't wear it today, Kitten."

"You wear it every time you go walkabout, now."

"Not today."

"But I saw you leave in it."

Rose panicked, licking her dry lips as her heart thumped in her chest. "You must be thinking of yesterday."

Silence . . .

Anna slowly sharpened the cutting knife for the chicken, her back to her cousin. "I suppose I was."

"Yes, it was yesterday," Rose repeated, silently praying Anna wouldn't go check the windmill for the garment, realizing it would be that simple to expose everything that was going on.

Thankfully, Anna changed the subject: "James sure is working hard these days. He's been putting in long hours, and without a fight. What a blessing." She looked out the window to see her husband in the near distance, walking with one of the Aboriginal stockmen. Opening the back door with a longneck for him in her hand, she waved the bottle and yelled, "Get your heinie home for dinner, my Irish bloke," then waited for him on the porch.

As he stepped up to greet his wife, James took the longneck and wrapped his arms around her, kissing her on the cheek.

Rose stopped preparing the table and watched through the screen door, a tinge of resentment splintering up her spine.

When dinner was ready, they all sat at the table and began to eat. Suddenly that same strange energy that surrounded them when Rose had first arrived at Sugar Alexandria encircled them again, gyrating in the middle of the table, electrifying them all. They each felt it, but none spoke of it.

Spinning.

Faster.

Faster still . . .

"No one can hold a candle to your cooking, Tin Tin," James said, breaking the alien élan. He was sitting at the head of the table, the women on either side, his eyes dancing from his wife to his mistress. From the energetic spunkiness of the flaxen-haired, sun-kissed Anna, to the calm, quiet nature of the dark-haired, alabaster-skinned Rose. A mischievous rabbit and an elegant, exotic bird. They were, in truth, like the yin and yang, and though James cared deeply for them both, he wanted a future with only one.

"I was thinking, Lottie," said Anna, spreading butter on a piece of bread so fresh from the oven it steamed, "we could still have our weekly girls' night. We just won't drink Yarra's blackberry wine, that's all."

Rose smiled as she too buttered her bread. "Of course we will, Kitten. Nothing has changed except I'll have a little one soon."

James sat back in his chair, continuing to observe both women. "No, that's not true," he thought but did not say. "*Everything* has changed."

"I made both apple and pecan pie, Sugar Bear," Anna said. "Which one would you like?"

"Tonight I'm hungrier than usual; I think I will have both," he replied, catching the irony in his own words.

～◦⋛⋚◦～

With dinner finished and dishes washed and put away, Rose goes home to her windmill, leaving husband and wife the rest of the evening alone. As she opens the door, she notices James had brought her velvet cloak back, draping it on the love seat with a note tucked inside . . .

Rose,

Something surreal has begun to stir in me. For the first time in my life, I wake up in the morning and burst out of bed, heart pounding, my mind excited, my body so alive.

And then I see you . . .

You are as if a room I want to enter and never leave; a river to swim in for the rest of my days; and if I drown in you, I drown a happy man. I love you, Rose.

I am forever yours,
James

Her heart filling with joy, Rose climbs up the spiral staircase and lies on her bed, staring at the skylight, reminiscing about the earlier interlude she had with her lover. She touches all the places he had kissed–her lips, her breasts, her stomach, her thighs. His scent still lingers everywhere on her body.

Turning on her side, she crushes her eyes shut. How difficult it was to see him go back to Anna after they had made love earlier. She wants him to come home to her, instead. She wants to be the one to greet him at the door, kiss his face, and spend the evening with him. He had suggested they leave, that they run off together, but after what Anna had orchestrated—for her to conceive, and it worked—how can she abandon her so coldly? How can she hurt her precious Kitten, the same woman who fulfilled her perennial dream—a treasure that will enrich her life forever? And yet, that's exactly what she is doing, continuing this affair with her cousin's husband after that one sanctioned night.

Rose stares at the antique armoire in her room.

The great exchange.

The trade Anna had made with her neighbor, taking something sacred from her husband in return.

As her eyes rake over the intricate German wardrobe, she whispers, "I love him, and he loves me. I'm sorry, Anna. I am so sorry . . ."

Rose

How bizarre. As I close my eyes, it dawns on me that James is now mine, and no longer Anna's. It feels as if the sun and moon have traded places.

Is he mine?

He feels like mine.

Yes, he is mine now.

So be it . . .

CHAPTER 35

Being alone with Rose inside the Barracuda Hut wasn't enough for James anymore. He wanted to take her somewhere else, anywhere but close to Sugar Alexandria. They made their plans, and on Friday morning, Rose left a note for Anna, explaining she needed a day away, taking the Tin Lizzie to a neighboring town. James inconspicuously followed soon after in his Huckster pickup.

Sneaking into the local movie theater, they sat at the very back, touching and kissing passionately. James chose a dimly lit Chinese restaurant for lunch, and like in the theater, found a private, intimate table near the back to enjoy themselves. They ate egg rolls, egg foo young, chow mein, orange chicken, and sticky rice, talking and laughing, wonderfully happy and carefree, while Anna and the station slipped out of their minds as if a weightless leaf blowing by in the street. Rose realized, with a start, that perhaps she was having the best day of her life. Afterward, they leisurely strolled outside, window-shopping, and when no one was looking, held hands.

When it was time to return to the station, they sat in James' truck for a while, in such deep thought they said very little, knowing days like this were going to be few and far between. At one point James took her hand, pressing it against his cheek and closing his eyes. Very badly he wanted to run off together, right then and there. But it wasn't the time, and they both knew it.

"As right as this feels, it's still wrong," Rose said, staring straight ahead. "I know we plan to leave together, but the guilt over what we're doing to Anna is killing me." A man and woman walked nearby, and she lowered her head, hiding behind her hat.

James waited until the couple had passed. "Do you want to tell her now, then?"

"No. Not until after the baby is born, like we agreed."

"But if we left now, by the time our child is born, I could be divorced from Anna and we could be married. We'd be starting out fresh a lot sooner."

Rose contemplated it. As perfect as that sounded, however, she quickly dismissed the notion. "Anna's so happy, so excited about seeing the baby, it would be cruel to shatter that."

"I'm not so sure. It might be even more cruel for her to see it, and then find out we're leaving."

They said nothing more, kissing goodbye, and the pretense and mendacities resumed.

James went straight to Sugar Alexandria, but Rose drove to Esperance first to ensure her alibi was airtight by being seen in town. Lingering a little too long, she ran into Hazel Smuckers and the Esmeralda sisters at Woolworths. They chatted up a storm with her, then invited her to eat dinner with them at the café. She reluctantly agreed, thinking it would only add to the proof of her whereabouts.

It wasn't until after dark that Rose arrived home. As she pulled into the driveway, she saw her cousin on the porch in her housecoat, waiting up for her. It made her cringe. Just as James was tied to Anna, in many ways so was she.

"Rose! Where have you been!" Anna barked as soon as she stepped out of the car.

"I told you—I was taking the Tin Lizzie into town today."

Anna tightened the belt on her housecoat. "It's so late, though. I was worried."

"I shopped most of the day, took in a movie, and afterward ran into Hazel Smuckers and the Esmeralda sisters. They asked me to dinner, and time just flew by."

"If I had known that, I would have gone with you."

"I like my alone time too, Anna. I don't always want to spend every minute with you."

She narrowed her eyes at Rose in the darkness of the night. "What's that supposed to mean?"

The wind had kicked up, and the two women stared at each other while the breeze pushed against them. "Nothing. It doesn't mean anything," Rose said, throwing a nervous, quick glance at James behind the screen door. "Look, I don't want to quarrel, Anna. I'm sorry I worried you."

"It's late you two," said James, shirtless and wearing only his long johns. "Get to bed." He returned to bed himself.

"I'm glad you're home now," Anna said in a motherly voice. "How was the movie?" Her demeanor instantly switched from worried and annoyed to calm and happy.

"It was good. I'll tell you about it tomorrow, though. Sorry I kept you up."

Anna smiled. "It's all right. I'm excited to hear about your day," she said. "Sleep well, Lottie."

"Good night, Anna."

As Rose walked to her maisonette, she thought of how Anna had been almost angry at her absence, only to become merry upon her return. It should have softened her toward her cousin, knowing Anna's reaction was only out of concern for her well-being. Instead, it severely irritated her. She found herself fighting not to scold Anna for waiting up for her, to tell her how she was her own woman and wanted the liberty to do as she pleased without Anna's imprimatur or permission. But she only said good night, and both women went inside. Anna to her warm and safe bedroom she shared with her husband, and Rose to the windmill where only her cat waited for her.

As she stepped into the mill, the crankshaft shifted, creating that wonderful sound she loved of the blades spinning in the air. But tonight the hum sounded unholy, and the windmill seemed ghostly. Slowly she walked up the spiral staircase to her own bedroom, thinking of the image of Anna waiting for her on the farmhouse porch, a tiny silhouette in the middle of a vast cattle station. If things didn't change, she could see herself years from now—her cousin still waiting up for her, still reprimanding her if she stayed out too long—coming back to the windmill from wherever she had been, undressing, crawling into bed alone, while Anna and James lay together only seventy-seven steps away.

Except now there *had* been a change . . .

Though Anna was the one lying next to James, Rose was the one carrying his child.

James

Stealing away to be with Rose in the Barracuda Hut,
Or to be with her in a nearby town,
Or sitting beside her in the windmill during our lessons,

Or playing music together at Cybill's . . .
These are the things I think about.

What gets me through the brutal days,
When my lips are chapped and my face covered in dirt,
When my callused hands are bleeding,
When my body is bone-tired . . .
Is when my mind wanders and I think of her.
My wife's cousin.
Ambrosia Charlotte Moss.

***

A mother bird will build its nest gradually, one piece of straw at a time. A tiny creature spinning her gold. Then one day, an empty nest is no longer empty but full of eggs. This natural phenomenon created by God seems so simple to our eyes, but is truly miraculous. The quiet occurrence goes unnoticed by most, yet ensures the cycle of life continues.

Similar to how the mother bird's eggs magically appear, Rose's stomach magically begins to swell. She stands naked in front of her mirror and smiles, staring at her once flat stomach, now fuller and taut from the child growing inside her body. A feeling she cannot describe overwhelms her.

***

My Dearest James,

You are going to laugh as you read this and think it silly of me, but this morning I stood in front of my floor-length mirror, caressing my small baby bump, speaking to our unborn child. Our priceless gift. I said, "My precious little one, I can feel you now. You are so wanted. Unborn, yet already so loved. I can't wait to hold you," and as soon as I said it, to my surprise a slight tickle fluttered in my stomach. As if hummingbird wings, oscillating ever so gently. A tiny life that thrives.

I am in awe of it all, marveling that a new life exists inside me. Now I, too, am bound to you by blood. I used to see Anna and you together, thinking that you shared the same vein by virtue of your children. And now we do as well, by virtue of ours.

I love you, James, and the feeling is indescribable. Please be mine forever.

Kisses to the moon and back,
Rose

◦◦◦❦◦◦◦

"It's exciting to see how your stomach is growing," Anna said as she was making corn husk dolls for her daughters to play with. "Watching you blossom is quite amazing."

Rose was sitting on the couch in the farmhouse, preparing to paint her nails. "I can even feel it move now."

"Soon you'll have what you've always wanted, love."

Rose smiled at her cousin. "I know. Time goes by so slowly, though, when you're anticipating something special."

"I hope when the baby arrives, it looks just like you," Anna said. She grabbed a broom and began to sweep the living room floor.

"It could also look like James."

Anna stopped sweeping and flashed her eyes up at her cousin. For some reason, the comment stung.

"Well he is the father," said Rose, matter-of-factly, noticing the expression on Anna's face. She opened the nail lacquer and began gliding the blood-red pigment across each cuticle.

"No, I know." A tension began to build in the room between the two women. "But not in the sense of him acting like the actual father, though."

"Why not?" asked Rose, looking up from her nails.

Anna contemplated the question a moment. She hadn't thought that far, and perhaps should have. Her sole focus was to gift Rose a baby, and now that it was coming to fruition, she wasn't sure of the right titles and roles to be played. "To be honest, I hadn't thought of that part too much."

"Anna, every baby needs a father in its life. We're not talking about a puppy here. It's a human being that needs as much love and direction as we can give it. Were you thinking I would just raise it all by myself?"

Anna nervously resumed sweeping. "I guess . . . I dunno . . . Yes . . . I mean, just you and me."

"Why would it bother you if James was involved in the baby's life?" Rose asked, blowing on her cuticles.

"It wouldn't. But in my mind, the bloke you had an affair with ran off on you, and you and I are going to raise the baby. James is my husband and a father to *my* children. I thought that was our understanding."

333

"That's what we've let everyone else believe," said Rose. "But between us three, there was no one else. No affair. James is the father, and he will play a part in the child's life."

Anna's sweeping became hurried, anxious. "I know, but he'll be like an uncle, and that's all."

Rose looked up from her glossy, crimson fingernails again, a curious cast in her eyes, giving no response.

The Voices

Elsa's voice calls out from the painting of her in the farmhouse. Anna stops to listen, but is unable to make out the faint auspice . . .

"Oh, Anna, how can you not see what you have done?

"Are you really that naïve?

"I fear it will be the ruin of you."

James opened the second neatly folded love letter Rose had written him that week. Sitting on his Ronaldson Tippett tractor at the edge of the field, he grew excited as his eyes scanned the page. Transcribed in black ink, her penmanship resembled calligraphy, and he delicately grazed his fingers over the paper as if it were braille.

My Dearest James,

Can we really leave soon after the birth of our child, as we talked about? Will we have the courage? Or will I have to be content with you fathering my child, watching from a short distance as you raise a separate family with my cousin?

I might have to.

Yet just to see you, be next to you, have a baby boy or girl that resembles you, will bring me so much happiness. What lays in front of us is a roaring lion I am afraid to approach. So let us enjoy the orchard for now, protecting the happiness we have . . . No matter how short-lived.

Love,
Rose

Everything she expressed in both letters, he felt as well. Falling in love with her had saved James' soul, and for the first time in years, he could see glimpses of a life he might get to have.

But what now? They could never go back to how it was before; they could only move forward. The proverbial roaring lion would eventually have to be provoked. One thing was for sure, though . . . He was in love with Rose, and he no longer wanted to be with Anna.

"What are you reading?" Anna asked, walking up to the tractor.

James' heart thumped in his chest. "Notes on supplies I have to order."

"Staring pretty hard at it. You might be ordering too much; lemme see."

"Anna, good God, I think I know how much we need by now!" He stuffed Rose's letter into his breast pocket.

"Crikey, just trying to help."

"Well I'm a grown bloke, not a child, and I've been working this station for over a decade."

Anna put one hand on her hip, shielding her eyes from the sun with the other. "I wanted to see the crib you're making for Rose's baby, but it's not there in your workshop."

"Moony took it; he's lacquering the wood," James said, his mouth parched and dry. His pulse throbbed in his neck.

"I wanna see it soon."

"When it's ready, I will bring it into the house."

"All right." Anna smiled up at him, standing there for a long moment. "Remember when we first got married? I used to sit on your lap, and you would drive that tractor all over the place," she said, reminiscing. "We laughed so much, then we would find a private spot and pash."

"Those were grouse memories, aye?" James said, trepidation imploding in his stomach.

"Yes, they were. And many more to come; right, love?"

He nodded, starting the tractor, waving goodbye to Anna as she stepped back and watched him leave, heading to the golden wheat field.

❧

Rose stands at the entrance of the windmill, about to walk over to the farmhouse, when she sees James and Anna talking out in the paddock. Her cousin is smiling up at her husband as he sits on the tractor, affectionately looking down at his wife.

But Rose no longer sees them as she used to. Now it appears her cousin is talking to *her* bloke. *Her* love. I'm carrying that man's baby, she says in her mind. And someday soon, it will be me he comes home to, kisses, and lays next to at night.

James rides his tractor far away from the station, flanked by several kangaroos hopping along the rugged terrain. Above him, a flock of birds swarm before landing on the beech trees that surround him. Even though he is now miles away from Anna, he steals a glance over his shoulder, finding only outstretched land. Pulling out pencil and paper from his pocket, he begins to write to his wife's cousin . . .

The woman carrying his child.

My Dearest Rose,

I have been reading both of your letters so much that the papers are starting to wilt at the corners.

Yes, of course I am yours. We might as well share the same heart now. Did you know there is a fish deep in the sea that, when finding its mate, clings to her, embedding himself with her, eventually sharing the same bloodstream? That is how I feel about us. We are no longer two, but one.

And you are right, Rose—this feeling is sublime, heavenly, unlike anything I have ever known. Who was I before Rose Charlotte Moss took me into her embrace and healed me? A lost and sad soul, I was. I have faith we can be together soon. Hold on a little longer.

Your breath is my breath. Endlessly yours,
James

"These letters we're writing, I think we should stop," Rose said inside the windmill that night when James snuck over. "It's too brazen. If Anna ever found out, it would be a disaster."

"No," said James. "With your pregnancy further along, we'll soon have to stop your piano lessons, and our visits to the cabin too. These letters will be the only personal connection we have left."

"But Anna almost caught you already."

He nodded. "I know; I'll have to be more careful."

"I dunno, James."

"How about this: I'll put my letters in a book I'm loaning you, and when you give it back, your response will be inside. Anna never pays attention to my books."

Rose smiled.

Opening Leo Tolstoy's *War and Peace*, Rose unfolds the next letter that falls out . . .

My Dearest Rose,

I want to touch every inch of your skin, every part of your body. That night of making love to you, my hand on your throat, feeling your pulse while I was deep inside you, was the most intense moment of my life. I felt like a god.

When I kissed you last, I left a love mark on your inner thigh. A mark of jealous ownership. I have branded you in a way that will remain long after the bruise fades. I want to break rules with you, break boundaries, break laws.

Tell me what you want me to do to you.

Tell me what you're going to do to me.

Love,
James

James discreetly removes the reply letter from Leo Tolstoy's *War and Peace* before returning the book to the shelf . . .

My Dearest James,

I too remember that night of passion, lying underneath the weight of your body, submissive to your will. Your mouth everywhere, your hands all over me. The erotic sensations I had dreamed about for years overwhelming me. You were my air; I was your fire. You were my fire; I was your air.

The things I want to do to you cannot be put into words.

Wait until we are at our private place, and I will show you . . .

Love,
Rose

Anna busily cooks while her husband is working in the paddock and her cousin napping in the mill. "It's going to be a lovely dinner," she says aloud, cleaning the fish, preparing the vegetables, and baking the bread.

An odd atmosphere pervades the air, her eyes are glazed over, and she can sense the shadow people surrounding the house, peering at her through the window as she cooks.

"Genevieve, I was thinking the Victorian era was such a beauty of a time. Can you think of any popular baby names from that period? Maybe Theodore, Rudolph, or Edmond if it's a boy? Or Amelia, Eleanor, or Harriet if it's a girl?"

The woman in the black Victorian dress sits down at the kitchen table and smiles. "How about my name?"

Anna pauses. "Hmmm . . . Genevieve . . . Yes, perhaps."

Elsa, Blessing, and Anna's grandmother leave their paintings and enter the kitchen, sitting down at the table to join them.

Anna keeps talking to everyone . . . Talking to no one.

One cannot stop the hours from passing by, or the days from overlapping each other until they become a lifetime. Flowers bloom, then die. Food grows, only to be eaten. Seeds are cast back to the earth, only to grow more food to be eaten again. The universe, the sky and the sea, the spirit beings that reside in the heavens—these are the only entities that remain unchanged. Everything else dissolves and turns to dust.

Time passes at the station. Rose's stomach continues to grow as each day folds into the next. Yet Rose isn't the only one changing; James and Anna are too.

All three are evolving in their own way.

Their inner circle is constricting. The existence they live in—their world—will not hold three for much longer. The trinity in which they have thrived for so long at Sugar Alexandria is now quickly vanishing. Though unseen, the cracks are crawling up the walls of their reality and changing the fate of these three lives forever . . .

CHAPTER 36

AUSTRALIA *The First Fleet* $1

June 1787 : TENERIFFE

Barefoot, Rose stares out at the ocean. She had a yen that day for not only the taste of its salt but also its smell. With one hand on her lower abdomen and the other on her cane, she looks across the deep blue sea, gazing at its beauty, searching for the mammoth whales. Sadly, she sees none and is left with an empty feeling–the cetaceans must be sleeping. But then all of a sudden, as if a ghost rising from the deep, a rare white albino breaches high out of the water like a torpedo, twisting in the air in a spectacular display of power that would frighten Poseidon himself, slamming back down in a tidal wave of splash. Seconds later, a black one does the same. The magnific titans spew a showering blast through their blowholes, then disappear into the murky, dark nadir of the sea.

Rose cheers with glee, clapping in a standing ovation, waiting to see if they'll return for an encore performance. She recalls a story her grandfather had told her about fishing in Denmark when he was a boy. A pod of whales surrounded the boat, and though it was an unnerving event, he instinctively knew that everything would be all right. After their inquisitive visit, the marine Goliaths disappeared back into the sea. It was a fond memory he retold over and over.

Reaching down, Rose grabs a handful of sand and opens up her fingers, watching the grains speedily slip through. She does this several times, entertained by the simple pleasure of the velvety soil passing through as if her hand were an hourglass. Before she knows it, a small pile accumulates at her feet—the beginnings of a sandcastle—and she molds it, decorating it with seashells. Someday soon, my child and I will make sandcastles together, she muses.

Walking over to the water's edge, Rose examines the waves, thinking about her situation. Relentless, unyielding, completely loyal to its own consistent rhythm, the ocean's dedication brings a promise of absolution to her. She tries to remain inside that feeling, despite the troubling quandary she finds herself in.

Despite her insecurities.

Despite the unknown of what's to come.

~꧁꧂~

James cuts out early from work the next day, rushing over to the fisherman's cabin, just as he and Rose had planned. Once there, he slams the door closed and pulls his lover into his arms, carrying her to the bed as their lips meet, igniting the passion. Heated lovemaking follows, zealous and uninhibited, releasing pent-up Eros for each other. These are the stolen moments when they stare deep into one another's eyes and say and do all the things that are forbidden in the real world. Dramatic, intoxicating, all-encompassing, neither having been in love before. It is all wonderfully, blissfully new to them. The only thing that matters is each other, and finding a way to exit Sugar Alexandria in the most graceful, decent way possible, for Anna's sake.

With the libidinous cacoëthes fulfilled, James says, "I have this heavenly feeling when I am with you."

Relishing the rapture of being zestfully in love, Rose replies, "It's such a strange sensation to care so much for someone. I am now more alive than I have ever been." She grazes her lips against his cheek, softly whispering, "More vibrant . . . More vivid . . . More woman . . . More everything," kissing him between each phrase.

~꧁꧂~

After the rendezvous, Rose left the cabin first and went back to the station. James soon followed, and midway on his trek home, Liam emerged onto the pathway. "You haven't been over in a while to play the piano," he signed. "I came looking for you to ask if you could visit tonight."

"Maybe tomorrow, lad," James signed back.

Liam appeared displeased. "You go to the Barracuda Hut a lot," he signed, pointing in the direction of the dwelling. "Why?"

"Why are you noticing?"

"I notice everything."

"Perhaps you shouldn't."

"You used to come visit my house, and we would play our music. Now you go to the cabin all the time and hide."

"It's my special place, Liam; you know that."

"A special place where you take Rose but not Anna," he signed, looking up at James on his horse, studying his reaction. "You only meet Rose there because you wish she was yours."

Taken aback by Liam's blunt statement, James stared uneasily at him. Though Liam was intellectually disabled, a hidden defiance had sparked in him out of nowhere, cognizant that James cared for Rose, notwithstanding that he had a wife. Perhaps the young man's condition made him hyperaware and sensitive to what most people could not see. "No, Liam."

"Yes you do! Yes you do! Yes you do!" he insisted, nodding his head aggressively up and down.

Dismounting Ireland, James stepped forward until inches away from him. "These thoughts about me and the cabin and Rose—stop thinking them," he signed.

Liam backed away, almost tripping.

"Do you understand, lad?" he asked, verbalizing his question for emphasis as he signed. "If Anna ever found out what you're thinking, it would hurt her. Is that what you want—to hurt her?"

Liam looked down at James' boots, still wet from the ocean brine. He shook his head no.

"You haven't seen anything," James signed. "Nothing to tell another soul about."

"All right, Music Man. I have seen nothing." He lifted his hands and covered his eyes. "Nothing, nothing," he forced out, his coarse, distorted utterance rife with indignation.

James, mindful of time, remounted his horse. "Good on ya, lad. Good on ya," he said, galloping off.

"I saw nothing!" Liam yelled at the top of his lungs—hermetic words he could not hear—watching Music Man barrel down the pathway. "I saw nothing!" Louder still, he shouted, "Secrets! Secrets!"

CHAPTER 37

Wednesday Motherland caught wind of Rose's pregnancy from Nurse June, and from there the tittle-tattle spread quickly. She told Fiona Blacksmith, Beth Clydesdale, Drusilla and Lilith Esmeralda, Clarion Firestone, and Hazel Smuckers, all whispering together at church. The minute Father Lothbrok finished his sermon and said "Amen", all seven women beelined to Anna.

"Who's the father?" Fiona asked. "Anyone we know?"

Anna straightened her shoulders, ready to elucidate the explanation she had practiced countless times in her head. "No, he's some bloke from Perth. He sweet-talked Rose about marriage, then when he found out she was pregnant with his child, he vanished like a ghost."

The nosy busybodies shook their heads in unison as they stood in a circle around little Anna. Poor Rose, they thought. What will become of a widowed sheila with a disfigured leg, a bastard child, and no man to call her own?

Anna knew these sticky beaks so well she could read their minds. "But no worries, aye? Rose is beautiful and still has time on her side. She'll be apples."

"Arntie Rosie's getting fluffy," Scarlet said, staring at Rose's stomach. Anna and the girls had come over for a visit the next day, and everyone was eating licorice inside the windmill.

"Because she's eating too much," Mabel explained, placing her tiny hand on Rose's baby bump.

Rose smiled. "But this black licorice is so good, I just can't stop," she teased, tickling both little girls as they squirmed and giggled.

Anna laughed, watching her cousin engage with her adorable daughters. "You can tell them, Lottie. It's time they know."

Scarlet crawled onto Rose's lap and kissed her cheek. "Tell us what?"

"Can I have some more?" Mabel asked, black licorice stains covering her mouth.

"No, love; you've had enough," said Anna. "We don't want your tummy to start aching, aye?"

Rose looked at both little girls. "You know why my belly is fluffy?"

They simultaneously shook their heads.

"It's because I have a beauty of a flower inside me, and it's starting to bloom. When the petals fully open, a baby will come out."

Scarlet looked shocked. "What kind of flower is that? Can I have one?"

Anna and Rose laughed.

Genevieve

I see them laughing and trying to be a family.
All lies!
That pommy sheila wants what Anna has.
I've tried to warn her, but she will not listen.
Oh, poor Sweet Pea . . .
Woe to you and what you will become!

The men were shearing sheep at the entrance of the woolshed, shirtless and sweating in the heat of the day, when Valentine Finnigan espied Rose walking across the stockyard to her maisonette. "I see Miss Rose has gotten herself into trouble," he chuckled.

Slim Stavin looked up. "Too right. Which one of us is the father?" he asked, laughing.

"It ain't me, but I wish it were," said Dewey Silkwood. "She's a beauty, cane 'n all."

"That's enough," James intervened. He let go of the sheep he was holding down and stood up.

"But she's preggers, ain't she?" said Slim. "Who's the daddy? We never saw her with anyone."

"It's none of youse bloody business, that's who." James watched as Rose entered the windmill, and when he looked back at the men, they were all staring at him. "The bloke ran off on her, all right? And that's it. There's nothing more to say. It was a brief courtship that ended with a child, and I won't have her being gossiped about in my presence. Understood?"

They all nodded.

～⚘～

Rose was heading back from James' den. Usually she would only go in there when Anna left for church or went into town, but that day she was more confident, a bit too bold with the love triangle.

Anna snuck up and stepped in front of her. "Boo!" she playfully giggled. "You wanna have tea tonight? We could have it in the secret room again."

Rose held the book with James' letter in it tighter to her chest. "I'm a little tired, Kitten. I just want to go home and read."

Anna stared at the book in her cousin's embrace. "You sure are reading a lot, lately. By the time the baby is born, you'll have read all of James' books."

Rose's heart slammed against her chest; her mouth went dry. "That's impossible; his collection is endless."

"Remember when we were young girls and you would read me all my favorites? We would light candles and stay up all night."

Rose nervously smiled, hoping James would walk up and interrupt the conversation.

"What are you reading tonight, anyway?"

"A poem by Edgar Allen Poe."

"What's it called?"

"*The Raven.*"

"Can I see?" Anna reached out for the book.

"I don't feel well, Kitten," Rose quickly said, walking away, looking like she might faint.

"Oh, sorry, Lottie. Can I get you anything?"

"No thanks; I just need some rest," she said over her shoulder.

Perplexed, Anna watched as her cousin briskly made her way to the windmill, clutching the book in her hands as if it held the secrets of the universe inside its pages.

～⌒⊙⌒～

R̲ose shuts the door to the windmill and opens Edgar Allen Poe's *The Raven*, letting James' letter slide out . . .

My Sweet Rose,

This morning I woke and rode Ireland to the edge of a cliff overlooking the sea, and all I saw was your face.

Everywhere.

Your scent permeated the air; your laughter tickled my ears; your love filled my heart. I know we cannot show a blithe disregard for our plight, that the nature of all this is crucial and life-changing, but please remain brave and optimistic. I will build a path for us so we can be together as we should have been from the beginning.

I will figure out a way.

Love,
James

～⌒⊙⌒～

J̲ames shuts the door to his den and opens the same book, now returned, letting Rose's letter slide out . . .

My Dearest James,

I want to touch you; I want you to touch me.

I want to kiss you everywhere, and everywhere be kissed.

When our baby moves inside me, I again think of that first night of passion we shared, conceiving a child. A child who will be born into this world through

love. And I do love you, James Ragnar Shahan . . .
With every fiber of my being.

Love,
Rose

In the months that follow while Rose is pregnant, an anomalous period ensues for James. Unbeknownst to his wife, his time is shared between her and her cousin. Split in two—physically, emotionally, and clandestinely, intimately. The mornings he spends with Anna, and the afternoons he looks for opportunities to be with Rose, often cutting out early from work to meet her at the Barracuda Hut, or to visit the Herdsmans.

The evenings seem normal enough, eating dinner with both women, but when bedtime arrives, he's amorous with his wife, waits for her to fall asleep, then sneaks out to Rose's windmill to finish what he started, returning to his own bed early the next morn before Anna wakes up.

The masquerade is exhausting.

James mulls things over. His wife's cousin had previously suggested polygamy, and he categorically rejected the idea, yet here he is acting as if he indeed has two wives. Though he has sworn to Rose they will leave together, he often wonders if this will be his life indefinitely. Half of him yoked to Anna, the other half to Rose. Can he continue on like this, living a double life? Or will he really be able to unearth the courage to break free from Anna's grasp . . .

Genevieve

Anna watches as the Black Shuck stays close behind Genevieve, head down, eyes searching, looking for its next prey. "Why does the she-wolf always follow you?" she asks on her way to the soul tree. "Have you tamed it?"

"Its rage is only sleeping, Sweet Pea," says the woman from the 1800s in the black Victorian dress.

Anna puts on her feathered crown and wings and kneels before her shrine. "What will happen when it wakes?"

Genevieve seems to go pale. "Woe to the flesh who awakens its madness, for its ferocity is like no other!"

Beginning her ritual, Anna prays, sings, and dances around the tree. In her mind the elves, fairies, and spirits are watching her, blessing her, loving her, protecting her . . .

CHAPTER 38

Rose

I am now just shy of nine months along, and the charade marches on. I spend my days lounging at Cassandra Fancy's garden, ambling along the shoreline, or drinking tea with Anna in her secret room. To her I am a doll with a smaller doll growing inside.

At the family dinners, I try hard to avoid lingering looks at James. If I do, my breath quickens and my cheeks flush. I notice James averting his eyes too, quickly dusting my face, trying to circumvent prolonged stares throughout the night. We wrestle with this, and inside we yearn to do what feels so natural—to interact, to smile and laugh, to touch each other and express ourselves as all couples do. Yet we refrain, knowing we cannot let Anna suspect our true feelings. The irony is she herself struck the match that set our love affair ablaze.

By her hand alone, this has transpired.

Or maybe we were always meant to be together, and now fate has finally stepped in.

The Voices

Anna watches a heavily pregnant Rose water her flowers outside the windmill. When finished, Rose leans back and stretches, seeking temporary relief from the weight of her pregnancy on her lower spine. She lifts her face heavenward and smiles. How lovely she looks, Anna thinks, observing her cousin under the warm Australian sun, her creamy face aglow and her dark hair—the color of her black licorice—glistening like ebony silk. That's my best cobber whom I love and cherish, who'll be with me the rest of my days.

Elsa interrupts the visionary image. "That child she carries is your husband's," she says in Anna's mind.

"I know, Mummy," replies Anna, annoyed by the intrusion.

"Doesn't it bother you that his blood now runs through her veins?" Blessing asks.

"You're both just jealous of the bond we have now. Jealous that Rose and I are closer than sisters."

The voices only laugh.

It is not always *what* we see,
but what we *want* to see,
that defines our reality.

"The flowers are so lovely outside the mill," Anna said. She had cut a dozen of them, putting them in a vase and setting it on Rose's small kitchen table. "Every morning as I cook brekkie, I like to look at them blooming."

"They ought to be beautiful—I water them enough."

"It's a shame they can't bloom all year."

"Wouldn't that be grand."

Anna noticed James pass by the mill window and look inside before continuing on his way. "That's odd," she said, tensing her brow.

"What?"

"James just peered inside the windmill, then left."

"I'm close to giving birth, Kitten. He checks on me daily."

Anna nodded, walking closer to the window to watch her husband. "Look how tall and strong he is," she said, smirking. "And so smart, too. You would think nothing could buckle him, yet I was able to. Li'l ol' me. I have always made that bloke do as I please."

Rose sat on her love seat, her hand on her enlarged stomach, observing her cousin stare out the window. They were miles apart in thought—Anna basking in her triumphant control over her husband; Rose holding fast to her secrets, truths, and lies.

Anna turned from the window and smiled. "He'll always do as I say. I own him and always will." She paused for a moment, thinking. "In a way, because of what I allowed, I own you too, Lottie," she said in an unco, unfamiliar voice.

Rose only stared at Anna, trying to remember her as she once was—all freckles, excitement, and giggles. But that look was gone, replaced with a foreign canvas of irrational delirium.

The Voices

That night, Anna gets out of bed and tiptoes through the quiet farmhouse, holding a kerosene lamp to light her way. She wants to chat with her loved ones in Rose's paintings. "I don't want to wake James, so I'll meet you at the soul tree," she whispers.

"All right, Turtle Dove," Elsa replies. "We'll be waiting."

"Hurry," adds Blessing.

Anna slips out the door into the darkness.

Genevieve follows close behind, the Black Shuck by her side.

The weather was changing, carrying with it a chilly breeze. The two cousins, draped in their matching velvet cloaks, visited the garden the following day, knowing how different it would soon look with winter fast approaching. Liam tagged along, Boomerang by his side and Contessa on his shoulder. He relished those moments that harkened him back to the time when they were children enjoying that same magical place.

"It's sad that winter is coming," Anna said. She and Rose were lying on the grass by the pond, Mrs. Swan floating nearby. "The garden will look different."

Rose squeezed her cousin's hand. "Springtime won't be far behind, Kitten. And with the change of season comes the gift of life."

Liam walked over and handed them each a crown of wildflowers, clapping as the women sat up and put them on.

Anna looked around the garden. "Can you imagine if the statues came to life too?"

"That would actually be frightening," said Rose. She smiled as a western spinebill hovered over a flower a few feet away, feeding on its sweet nectar.

"I believe there's a world within a world," Anna said, gazing at the sculpture of Venus de Milo. "And sometimes I am able to see that world."

Rose looked over at her cousin, a sense of unease creeping up on her. Anna was always trying to rationalize her illness as nothing more than her being different, if not gifted. As she stared at Anna staring at the statues, the baby inside her womb moved, and then kicked. "Ouch!" she let out.

"What is it, love?"

"The baby is kicking me."

Anna put her hand on Rose's stomach, and the baby kicked again. "There it is! It's ready to come out and meet you, Lottie!"

Rose smiled, and Liam ran over, wanting to feel it too.

Soon the wind picked up, growing colder, and the threesome collected their things to go home. Glenda Trufflepig intersected them along the path, several dead snakes slung over her shoulder. "G'day, folks," she said. "Comin' back from Cassandra's garden, I reckon?"

Liam read her lips and nodded with a big smile.

"Well best you be gettin' home, now. There's a nasty storm brewin', and the sheila's headin' our way." Though the sky had yet to reveal its telltale signs, the older woman always knew.

Anna noticed the jug of James' whiskey in her hand. "Were you just at Sugar Alexandria?"

"Sure was. Your bloke makes the best grog in the shire." Glenda looked directly at Rose's distended belly. "He seemed awfully stressed, though," she said, as if talking to the unborn child. "Strangely so."

Rose gave Anna a nervous glance.

"Reminded me of that bastard bloke of mine when I was preggers and about to deliver. He had that same face of worry only a new father could have. It was the only time he acted like he truly cared for me." Right on cue, as always she added, "Men—more trouble than they're worth, and that's no lie," continuing on her way.

"What do you think about what Glenda said," asked Rose, "that James had the face of a new father?"

"I don't care what that coot says," answered Anna. "She's just a nutty trapper who lives with a bunch of dogs in the bush. No one's gonna pay her no mind."

Now inside the windmill, the women were warming themselves in front of the fireplace, sipping hot ginger tea while Yarrajan still babysat the twins.

"What about the sticky beaks at church?" Rose asked, adding sugar cubes and stirring. "I bet it's killing them not knowing who the father of my baby is."

Anna grinned, loving that they shared such a secret. "Too right. They were all prying for information, trying to get me to spill the beans."

"What did they say when you told them our story?"

Anna poured more tea into her cup. "They called him a vile creature, a bogan, and a scoundrel, leaving you in such a state."

"Sounds like they believed it." Rose was starting to hate the lie. James would never abandon a woman pregnant with his child. On the contrary, he had married Anna for that very reason, sticking by her even when he found out she wasn't. And though concealing the truth was a necessary evil, she still loathed hearing hateful comments about the real father whom she was desperately in love with.

"Of course they did. What else would they think?"

"Perhaps that James fathered the child."

Anna's eyes grew wide, her mouth dropping. "Why on God's green earth would they think that?"

"Because, Anna, it's the truth, and people have a way of finding out," Rose said, speaking from the part of her that resented the dishonesty.

Anna's lips tightly pursed. "I won't let it. Not now, nor ever," she said with a fierce, stern stubbornness Rose had never witnessed before in her cousin.

Looking around the maisonette, Rose thought of when they were young girls, hiding and playing in there when it was just a windmill. "We used to spend hours in here," she said, "pretending the outside world doesn't exist. That it was just you and me and our dreams. But the world outside does exist, Anna, and it's always waiting for our return."

Anna seemed somewhere else again, her eyes glazing over—another cognitive lapse.

Rose studied her cousin's face reflecting the light from the fire, reminding her of something. "I see you at night sometimes, walking through the house with your lantern," she said, breaking her cousin's mental hiatus. "What are you doing in those moments?"

"Nothing," said Anna. She got up from the love seat and placed another log in the fireplace.

"Through the window it looks as if you're talking to the paintings."

"No I'm not," Anna said, lying to protect her secret.

"But it looks like you are." Rose glanced out the living room window where she had drawn the curtains and could see the farmhouse in full view. "When the light from the lantern reflects off your face, I can clearly see that you're talking to someone. Quite enthusiastically, in fact."

Anna too glanced out the window at the farmhouse, then back at her cousin. Both women stared at each other, Anna contemplating whether or not to share.

"Kitten, you can tell me anything," Rose assured, reaching out to touch her hand.

"If I do, will you promise not to tell James?"

"I promise."

"Remember a while back when I told you Mummy and Blessing talk to me? That I hear their voices sometimes?"

Rose thought of her cousin's disconcerting shrine, and how she felt their presence there as well. "Yes," she said, getting a little nervous.

"Well, if I'm lucky enough, and it's a very special night, they come out of the paintings and visit with me." Anna became animated. "Oh, Rose, it's just glorious! It's always been only the voices before, but now Mummy and Blessing are back in real life! Grandmother too! I couldn't believe it myself when it first happened, but it's true! I'm so happy, Lottie, and it's all because of you!"

Speechless, Rose's eyes grew wide.

"Your paintings are so grand, so full of magic, that they actually come alive! And just as you created them, too, wearing those beautiful clothes 'n all! Can you believe it?"

"You're joking," Rose finally said, a shiver running down her back. "You can't mean any of this."

Anna saw the fear in her cousin's eyes, stopping her from confiding anymore. "I um, um, um," she stuttered, panic setting in. "Of course I'm joking, you silly goose! I'm just trying to make you laugh."

Rose subconsciously held her stomach, not sure of what to say or do. It dawned on her that Anna might be telling the truth about hallucinating her paintings come to life, and that her cousin was far sicker than she could have ever imagined. She wanted to continue investigating the topic and ask Anna more in-depth questions about this bizarre, far-fetched anomaly she knew was pure fantasy, but there was no time . . . Suddenly she felt odd, clammy, dizzy. As if an earthquake were coming, but the tremors were inside her body. Looking down at the floor, she saw a puddle forming by her feet.

Her water broke!

"Anna . . . ," she said, a new look of dread on her face. Slowly she stood, supporting herself with her cane, her other arm holding her swollen stomach. "Go get James. It's time."

⁓⋆⁓

Outside, a rancorous storm had materialized just as Glenda Trufflepig had warned. Already the trees were swaying, bending to the will of the wind, red dust kicking up and launching through the air. The horses dashed about nervously in the corral, sensing what was pending, while the cows and sheep huddled in groups, instinctively moving to higher ground. In the darkening sky, a billowing mountain of clouds had turned from ivory white to slate gray.

Anna helped her cousin to the farmhouse just as James came in through the back door. "We're in for some fierce weather, sheilas. Someone let out a wicked banshee, and she's spitfire mad," he said, the wind bashing the screen against the wall. "Might even see some hail or a rare twister. We'll have to go into the cellar if it gets too nasty." He noticed the anxious expression on both women's faces. "What's wrong?"

"I was just coming to get you; Rose is going into labor."

And just as Anna said it, it began. In unison they all stared out the kitchen window at the thick waterfall that deluged the station, as if Zeus had decided to bring a second flood to the earth. The Asgardian god of thunder joined in, slamming down his Mjolnir with each bolt of lightning, angrily smashing his hammer against the churning Australian sky.

Hours passed, and the fever of the storm only escalated. The once sprawling cattle station in the tranquil Outback, with miles of rugged terrain surrounding them, was now but a small island, threatened on all sides by an acrimonious Mother Nature. As James stood on the back porch, staring into the twisting, turning gale, he imagined invisible demons responsible for the mayhem, relentlessly thrashing about, throwing tantrums and wreaking havoc, causing the wind to become furious and out of control, only to go oddly still in what seemed like a quiet surrender before returning worse than the last.

Inside the farmhouse, Rose was now in the throes of labor, hunched over on the bed, groaning and wincing, sweating profusely. The contractions were occurring stronger and faster. "Feels like I'm splitting open!" she moaned in agony, the waves of pain tearing into her lower pelvic region so viciously she would cry out for God's help.

When a sheila gives birth, death holds her hand for a spell, Yarrajan thought, the furrows in her brow deepening. She started humming an old Nukunu song she used to sing to Anna and her cousin when they were young girls.

The tempest continued to fulminate without mercy, intensifying its on-slaught—an apoplectic kraken rising from the abyss, hurling thunder, light-ning, and hail from its mouth, making the farmhouse walls creak and whistle and the three windmill sails spin rapidly until the blades appeared to vanish. There was no way to get Dr. Crawford there in the storm.

Anna and Yarrajan did their best to coach Rose, conjuring up accoucheuse skills to assist with the birth. And then it happened . . . The baby finally crowned, and within minutes, exited the womb . . .

A boy.

The infant shined with birthing fluid like the first snow covering the ground at the outset of winter, but he was pinkish-blue and wouldn't move.

"Is the baby all right?" Rose asked, her lips dry and cracked, her voice hoarse and raspy from the screaming. "Shouldn't it be crying?"

Yarrajan flipped the baby over, tapping its back, rubbing up and down its spinal column. Not a pin drop could be heard in the room. No one even breathed . . .

What is a moment in a day but a grain of sand . . .
until that moment means everything in the world?

The Aboriginal woman tapped the baby's back again. Seconds later, the Force of Life broke through and the baby lifted its small head, exhaling a copious, booming cry.

"Thank God!" Anna exclaimed. Immense relief palliated everyone.

Yarrajan smiled at the energetic newborn as she cut the umbilical cord and wiped it down, pleased it was so full of life. She couldn't help but laugh as the neonate wriggled in her hands, expanding its lungs to breathe. *"Little white rabbit,"* she said in Nukunu. *"That's what you be."*

"Rose, it's a boy!" Anna cried. "You have a beautiful baby boy!"

Exhausted, Rose cradled her newborn, guiding him to her breast. "I did it," she said breathlessly.

Anna smoothed back her cousin's sweat-soaked hair. "Yes, love, you did. You're a mummy now!"

James watched the scene with tears in his eyes as the new miracle of life struggled against Rose until finding a nipple, attaching to it and closing his eyes in ecstasy. I have a son, he thought. The realization swept over him in warm, steady waves. A woman, not his wife but whom he loved, had given birth to his child. Regardless of the complexity of the situation, he had a son . . . A beautiful, healthy son.

As she tenderly held her gift, gazing down at her precious baby, an intense sensation ignited inside Rose's heart. Never before had she felt such a feeling. There was no denying she had found a new level of love: The love of a mother for her child. This was what she had been praying for all these years, waiting for all this time. Watching as his tiny lungs inhaled and exhaled, and without removing her eyes from her beautiful newborn, she slowly reached for his father. James took her hand, gently kissing the back of it, not caring if anyone saw.

They named their son Joshua.

~⊱✦⊰~

Dr. Crawford came later as soon as the storm had calmed.

"They're both normal," Rose cried, overjoyed at her son's two chubby legs. "I was worried, afraid that he'd have my condition. He doesn't. He's perfect."

"Too right, Rose," Dr. Crawford confirmed, examining the baby's extremities. "He's as healthy as can be."

She smiled through her tears as the infant gazed up at his mother in wonder. "No cane for him."

"No cane," ratified the doctor.

Rose kissed Joshua's silky head and cradled him close to her bosom, cherishing the neonate as if a sparkling gem emanated from the heavens. The beginning of a new life had come into existence because of what her cousin had done. Anna manipulated the events leading up to this day, playing God, and the results turned out favorable. Without her providence, the child would not be taking his first breaths.

Anna was thinking this too as she watched the new mother and child. She knew at that very moment that her plan for her husband to bed her cousin, no matter how preposterous, how illogical, was the right thing to do.

~⊱✦⊰~

My Sweet Rose,

I write this letter in the dead of night, sequestered in my distillery, the only light a low flickering candle. I am thinking of you and our newborn son, and the yearning is indescribable.

How can I not go to you?

How can I spend the first night of my child's life away from him?

I should be in bed with you as he lays between us, but this special moment is stolen from me.

Know that in spirit I am always with you, holding you, cuddling our son, embracing our love no matter where I am. We must leave together soon, for the sake of my sanity.

I am blowing a kiss out into the night, hoping the wind delivers it to you and our newborn child at sunrise.

Love,
James

M*y Forever James,*

You are always on my mind too, as I hold our tiny treasure. I think of nothing else. As Anna chats away about how amazing the birth was, and how ecstatic she is for the future to have him raised at Sugar Alexandria, my attention drifts off, envisioning us together. Let us pray for strength at this time. For patience.

We will leave as soon as it feels right.

Love,
Rose

P.S. The wind delivered your kiss, and when it did, our son smiled.

Rose

My son . . .

I have loved you before you were even born. When you were only a seed in my womb. A twinkle in my eye. Now I hold you and smell your sweet scent, listen to your adorable coos, and watch you move and smile.

You amaze me.

Even your miniscule hands that I kiss while you breastfeed are beyond precious to me. Your tiny, pink, scrunched-up flower buds, waiting to open their petals and cling to their mother's finger.

Joshua was baptized almost in secret, with only Rose, Anna, and James in attendance. Father Lothbrok thought it peculiar that James held the child during the christening, but he didn't ask any questions. While he sprinkled water on the infant's head, one thing troubled him, though. As beautiful as this innocent baby boy was, he couldn't help but notice how much the child resembled Anna's husband . . . Resembled him a great deal.

For the first few weeks after Joshua was born, Anna could hardly contain her excitement. Every morning she would make a wonderful breakfast for Rose and bring it over on a platter, holding the baby while her cousin ate.

"Just look at him," Anna said one particular visit, staring down at the tiny pink bundle of joy securely wrapped in a soft cotton blanket, snug like a caterpillar wrapped in its cocoon. "He's the most precious baby boy I have ever seen."

Rose took a sip from her tea, ardently agreeing as she watched Anna rock him in her arms. "Oh, Kitten, isn't he beautiful? How can something so small be so amazing?" she rhetorically asked, her heart overflowing with love.

Anna glanced up from the infant. "He certainly is, Lottie. You have a beauty of a son, and he's all yours."

The two cousins smiled widely at each other.

Rose walked over to them. "If I were to kiss you then go to hell, I would," she whispered, kissing her baby's chubby cheeks. "So then I can brag with the devils I saw heaven without ever entering it."

"What's that mean?" Anna asked.

"I suppose that you've kissed an angel."

"Read that in one of your books?"

"No, James told me," said Rose without thinking. As soon as the words left her lips, she realized her error, locking eyes with Anna. "I mean . . . he was telling me all about Shakespeare and his famous quotes."

An uncomfortable buzz of electricity stirred between the women, as if two magnets with like poles repelling each other.

"Didn't that bloke also say, 'Hell is empty and all the devils are here?' I've heard James quote that one too, when he was upset about something."

"Yes," said Rose. She quickly tried to diffuse the unpleasant energy, looking back down at her son. "His little legs are adorable, aren't they? I was so worried he would inherit my defect, but he didn't. I'm so thankful."

Anna's eyes lingered on her cousin, knowing she was purposely changing the subject. It gave rise to a confusing sense of unease in her. "Even if he did have a special leg like you, he'd still be apples. You do all right with yours."

"No, Anna. Surgeries as a child, made fun of, difficulty running, having to take a cane everywhere you go—I'm grateful he doesn't have to endure any of that."

"Lemme see 'im," little Scarlet said, losing interest in her doll.

Anna lowered the baby for her daughter to see.

Scarlet gently touched him, smelling around his head.

"What's he smell like?" Anna asked, curious over what she was thinking.

"A baby, you goose!"

Anna and Rose laughed.

"Lemme smell," said Mabel, wanting to know what her sister discovered.

Anna brought Joshua's head to Mabel's nose.

"It *does* smell like a baby! I love it!"

Again Anna and Rose laughed.

"He's your little brother," Rose said.

The smile faded from Anna's face. "They're second cousins," she corrected.

"True, they are. But they're also siblings."

Anna looked perplexed. "You're saying Joshua is Scarlet and Mabel's brother?"

"Well of course, Kitten. You hadn't thought of that? They're half siblings."

"I just think of them as second cousins," Anna said, walking over to the morning light streaming in from the living room window, letting the rays illuminate the child to get a closer look. "That's how we will raise them."

The baby blinked as it studied Anna's face, lifting its hand, reaching up to her. Anna kissed his chubby fingers, and that's when she noticed something. "Huh, look at this," she said, gently flipping his hand over to expose his inner wrist.

Rose leaned forward, inspecting her child's skin. "It's a birthmark."

"Not just any birthmark—it's a strawberry heart-shaped one. Lottie, do you know what this means? He's been kissed by an angel and it left its mark! It's a sign that what we did has been blessed from above!"

Rose took Joshua from Anna and cradled him tightly, kissing his forehead, his cheeks, and his tiny hand with the crimson nevus. "James has a birthmark just like this," she said. "It's on the front of his lower hip."

Anna looked puzzled. "Um . . . I don't think so," she replied, nervously starting to fidget.

"Yes, I'm sure of it. Same shape and color." Rose pointed to the exact spot on her own body. "It's on him right here."

Anna thought long and hard, trying to remember, and an odious awareness hit her, having to swallow the hard truth of how Rose could know such a personal detail about her husband. "Come to think of it, you're right," she admitted. "He does."

James

I have inadvertently become an incidental polygamist, waking up every morning to this unwanted fate. Living with them, eating with them, working alongside them, caring for two wives, two daughters, and a newborn son.

One woman I love; the other I want to be free from.

With each I share a separate abode; a symbolic barrier that divides the trinity.

The farmhouse is where I conceal and pretend; the windmill is where I celebrate and rejoice.

Two domiciles; two realties; two men I have become . . .

Yet one and the same.

"I told you we'd have to bring this white man coffin back," Tarka said in Nukunu as he, Mandawuy, and Warragul carried James' piano across the stockyard to Rose's windmill. Anything large, heavy, and made of wood that the white folks owned, the Aboriginals called a coffin, no matter what it was.

"Miss Anna gave it away, and now her skinny cousin is bringing it back," said Mandawuy.

A few Aboriginal children ran past the piano, dogs nipping at their heels. *"Does Miss Anna know?"* asked Tarka.

"No."

"What about Mister James?"

"He doesn't know either," Warragul said. *"It's a surprise."*

Rose had made the arrangements with Cybill and didn't tell James or Anna, waiting for them to go into town together for supplies. She wanted to do something special for him by returning his treasured instrument, intentionally keeping it a secret from her cousin for fear she wouldn't allow it.

"Both coffins are the same, anyway," Tarka said. *"I don't see the point."*

Warragul disagreed, looking at the intricate Celtic designs carved into the wood. *"No, this one is special to him. Look at these markings on the lid. They come from the ancient people in his homeland where the ground is green as far as the eye can see. This coffin has been in his family for many moons and seasons."*

"Why does the skinny sheila care so much?" asked Tarka.

"Why do you think, you drongo?" said Mandawuy. Gossip about James bedding his wife's cousin and fathering her son had started buzzing through the Aboriginal village. *"Some say he's the father of her newborn."*

"She's too skinny for me," Tarka said. *"Bony and plain with ghost eyes. His cook is better—she can keep you warm at night, and her hair is like gold."*

"True, Miss Anna looks like a little yellow flower, but she has the mulga madness," said Warragul. *"You'd have to sleep with one eye open."*

The three Aboriginal men laughed, just as Rose opened the double doors to the windmill. She had a full smile on her face, excited to be making the exchange.

Once James' piano was in place, Warragul said in his broken English, "Yarrajan startin' to like you, Miss Rose. But I still don't think she trust you."

Rose was wiping off the thin film of dust on the piano that had accumulated during the move; Matilda jumped on top of the smooth, sleek surface and laid down. "Maybe I *shouldn't* be trusted," Rose replied with a wink.

"Yarrajan thinks you be bad omen," Warragul elaborated. "She feels evil energy from a killer. Have you killed a bloke today?"

Rose, knowing he was teasing her, played along. "No, but the day's not over yet."

~≪≪✥≫≫~

The following week, Yarrajan was sitting very still in the living room of the windmill. Rose had convinced the Aboriginal woman to let her paint a vignette of her.

"I want the paintin' to be regal, Miss Rose," Yarrajan said, uncomfortable with the idea, yet also excited, despite trying hard not to show it. No one had ever painted a portrait of her before. "Paint me as you did Miss Anna's mum, sittin' in a velvet chair with fancy clothes 'n all. And don't be forgettin' that jewelry and the beauty of a wallpaper you put in the background."

Rose smiled. "Don't worry, Yarrajan. You're going to look like a queen when I'm done."

Though the older woman still had misgivings about the pommy sheila, she put her distrust aside and mustered a paradoxical smile.

Anna, too, was inside the windmill, holding baby Joshua as Rose did her artwork. Cradling the infant close to her bosom, rocking him as she walked about the room, she suddenly realized something . . . Rose's Wurlitzer spinet piano was gone, replaced by James' venerated one! The very piano she had traded with Cybill Herdsman to get Rose's antique armoire!

"What's the matter, Kitten?" Rose asked, glancing at her cousin, noticing her changed demeanor.

"What's James' piano doing in your living room?" Anna questioned, incredulous over her discovery. "You exchanged yours for his?"

"Yes."

"When?"

"Last week when you went into town for supplies. Cybill was happy to do the trade, knowing how much James loves his piano."

Anna looked at Yarrajan sitting perfectly still. Only the Aboriginal woman's eyes moved, making contact with hers. "Didn't know nothin' 'bout it, Miss Anna," she said, repudiating involvement.

"That piano has been in his family for generations," Rose explained, justifying her actions, "and was made from the wood of a boat that saved his great-grandfather's life. It was time for him to have it back."

"But you didn't ask me," said Anna, now feeling hurt. "And you always tell me everything."

"Sorry, Kitten," Rose nonchalantly replied, returning her attention to Yarrajan's portrait. "I didn't think I had to."

"Why didn't you have the stockmen move it into the farmhouse, though?"

"I wanted to surprise him, now that we've restarted our piano lessons. Besides, you don't want me and James having our lessons in the farmhouse from now on, do you?"

Anna walked around the piano, inspecting it. It still looked grand, its lacquered surface and bodacious elegance withal pristine. Then she looked even closer, discerning something. "The lid prop is different."

"Yes," said Rose. "James used the original prop to make my new cane, remember?"

"No, I don't. He didn't tell me."

"Oh . . . well . . . he must have forgotten."

That too bothered Anna. Now she had been shut out of two significant decisions. Attempting to ensconce her feelings, she said, "Well that's a fine thing you both did. He made your cane out of something special, and you gave him something special back."

"Yes, exactly, Kitten."

Anna didn't know how to react over the revelation. Should she be angry, especially since her cousin didn't tell her about exchanging James' piano first? Or rather, ask her permission? And what about her husband? Why would he use a piece of his treasured instrument to make her cousin's cane, and not even tell his wife about it? The prevarications were very unsettling.

Still unsure of what to think, or feel, or say, Anna sat down on the love seat and quietly watched Rose paint Yarrajan's portrait, all the while cradling her husband and cousin's son closer to her chest.

Rose

I put Joshua in a sling and went for a walk to the shoreline today. Along the way, I saw Anna, her feathered crown on her head and wings on her back, praying in front of her private sacrarium. James had hitherto told me how ghastly it was to behold her wearing her sacred emblems while kneeling before that eerie tree. And now that I've witnessed it for myself, I most certainly agree.

"You know how in that story, *The Secret Garden*, a key was needed to enter the garden," Anna explained to me when I asked her about her bizarre insignias. "Well, my crown and wings are the key to Mummy and Blessing," she said. I just held her and told her that I love her.

I accept Anna for who she is.

I accept the situation for what it is.

I accept the madness I have become a part of . . .

CHAPTER 39

Life carried on at Sugar Alexandria, and Anna exulted in what she had accomplished. She gloated over how she had made her loyal husband grant her beloved cousin's gift, and rejoiced over her triumphant gambit to keep Rose at the station forever. She was a woman brimming with happiness, having created her own personal nirvana. A queen sitting on her throne, with a jeweled staff she would hold and point when directing her servants.

Rose, however, had an antithetical view. A psychological warfare was going on inside her heart, comparable to the earth shifting below the abyssopelagic ocean floor. Lately, when Anna would smile or reach out for her, she found herself recoiling, her affection for her cousin under attack. Anna had a power over her and James, a type of dominance over them, laden with the strict laws that govern marriage. But now that those vows had been broken, the nonverbal expressions of animus were beginning. The emotional tremors. It wasn't intentional; she loved Anna, yet her protective instinct for what was hers was rearing its formidable head. She had had James' child. His blood coursed through her veins for nine months while she carried it, and after giving birth to this new life they created together, she felt so different than she had expected. She felt James was hers.

And only hers.

To frame her legacy on canvas, Anna begged Rose to paint a family portrait. Rose obliged. She painted James sitting in a large, cherry red wingback chair, cradling baby Joshua, the twins sitting by his feet, with Anna and her standing on either side of him. All of them were dressed to the nines—Anna and her wearing pearl necklaces and diamond earrings–the backdrop a Victorian-style, dark blue wallpaper with paisley designs. Very opulent and lavish looking. A stark contrast to the real life they lived at the station–cooking, cleaning, knitting, baking, washing, feeding livestock, and cleaning out stalls.

When the painting was completed and hung in the farmhouse above the living room fireplace, Rose stood back and admired her work, a wicked grin tugging at the corner of her lips, knowing something her cousin did not: She had painted herself standing closer to James, with Anna further to the right. If you examined the painting carefully, you would notice another detail, too . . . Anna's ring finger was bare, whereas hers was adorned with a shining gold band.

Rose sits on the edge of the bed in the Barracuda Hut the next day, waiting for James. She's wearing the emerald dress Anna had bought her, and a sweater she had knitted her. Thinking of this, her shame grows.

The sunlight streams in through a break in the sheet covering the window, shining on her skin, and its warmth reminds her of the touch from her cousin's husband, arousing her senses. Where is he, she wonders?

Did Anna stop him?

Did he change his mind?

Should I just go home?

A shadow crosses the window, and the door swings open . . . It's him!

They embrace.

"Too much drink in the distillery, and I lost track of time," he softly apologizes, the smell of whiskey fanning her face. "The stress is getting to me," he whispers against her ear, "and the anxiety of it all is like wrestling a demon because I want us to leave today, but I know we can't just yet." He touches her gently, caressing her silky skin as if she's made of fragile glass.

"Oh, James, I thought you weren't coming," she whispers back breathlessly. "I thought you had changed your mind," she says, running her fingers through his unruly dark blond hair.

He picks her up, walking over to the bed, kissing her into silence as she drops her cane and it clatters on the ground.

That night, Anna snuggled up to James in bed. "You'll always be my bloke, love. You know that, right? Till death do us part."

James' arm wrapped around his small wife.

"Don't think because of what I made you do that you're not mine. I own you. The Bible says, 'What God has yoked together, let no man put apart.'"

The couple hadn't ever spoken of that carnal union, and it surprised James she brought it up. "I know, Anna. What's done is done," he said—a phrase he often used. Tension started to build.

"Too right. And now Rose has a beauty of a baby, and everyone's rapt about it, aye?"

"Yes, Anna, we're all rapt," he said, his eyes flickering out the window toward the center windmill.

"Sugar Bear, tell me one of your Viking tales, like you used to when we first got married."

"Tin Tin, I'm tired."

"Please?"

He mumbled in Gaelic. "All right . . . Centuries ago, there was a beloved Viking named Skarde. Not only was he the strongest among his people but also the wisest. During one bloody battle, when invaders stormed a neighboring village in the night, he saved the clan from being slaughtered. As a reward, the clan leader bequeathed his daughter to be Skarde's wife."

Anna leaned into her husband and closed her eyes, envisioning Viking ships, warriors, shield-maidens, swords and spears, painted faces and horses.

"The Viking leader he defeated heard about the wedding and sent his brother, Tyr, to charm the would-be bride away from Skarde. Tyr was successful, and she left to marry him instead."

"She left, even though she was promised to Skarde?"

"She did."

"What did Skarde do?"

"In his anger, he pillaged the same clan he had previously saved."

"He went mad."

"Yes, with jealousy."

"I thought you said he was wise."

"He was, but vengeance can blur the straightest of lines," James said.

Anna's eyelids became heavy. "Sugar Bear, I noticed your breath smells of licorice these days. I thought you didn't like sweets," she mumbled, dozing off to sleep.

"Well," he said, knowing it was from kissing Rose, "I now have a craving for it."

At the entrance to Sugar Alexandria, on both sides of the wrought iron gate, sunflowers grew in abundance. Tall and wild, if not trimmed regularly, they would proliferate and take over the driveway. One afternoon, Anna was cutting some of them down, keeping the blooms to later harvest their seeds. Her daughters played next to her on a blanket, Lovely Dawn sprawled out beside them bathing in the midafternoon rays, and Poka stood off in the distance, trying to decide if she should come visit.

Eight-year-old Marmalade Murphy and her six-year-old sister, Pepper, rode up bareback on a horse. Their dresses were stained, their hair knotted and unruly, and their bare feet and ankles dangling over the horse's belly were muddied to the knees after playing all day down by the river.

Anna put down her gardening shears and greeted the girls. "G'day, lovies. How's your mum?"

"We're not supposed to talk to you," Marmalade said.

"That's right, we can't talk to you," Pepper echoed, shaking her head vigorously.

Anna put her hand on her hip. "How come?"

"Mummy says Miss Rose is a loose sheila and has an ankle biter with no daddy. She says your family has no mooruls and we ain't gonna associate with the likes of those who ain't in the right way with God," Marmalade said loudly all in one breath.

"Is that so," Anna replied, holding back her temper.

"Yep. And Mummy says, Mummy says," Pepper stuttered, rubbing her eyes, "Mummy says you're always whisperin' to yourself like a kook, and your cousin is a tart." Pepper nodded, proud of herself for getting it all out.

Anna had heard enough. "You tell your mum to mind her business and keep her eye on her own bloke who lives at the pub and visits that floozy Emma Boggs for unspeakable purposes." Stepping forward, she slapped the black-and-white spotted Appaloosa on the arse as hard as she could. The horse took off like the wind, both little girls hanging on for dear life.

"Agatha Murphy," Anna said, wiping her hands on her apron after opening the front door. She looked the woman up and down.

"Anna Shahan," Agatha hissed back, a baby on her bony hip. She was wearing a pretty raspberry-colored cotton dress, but her feet donned men's brown worn-out dress shoes.

Both women stood there a moment, staring at each other in distaste.

"What brings you to my property?" Anna finally asked, swatting away a horsefly.

Agatha and her husband Henry owned a cattle station in the Shire of Esperance, not far from Sugar Alexandria. The Great Depression had hit them particularly hard, and they were struggling. Though the wiry woman with eyes too big for her face, a small chin, and naturally white hair the color of vanilla was only in her early thirties, her appearance added at least a decade. She had had a crush on James when she was younger, like most of the girls in the territory, and resented Anna for marrying him the way she did. The two women barely spoke to each other since.

"It's been a while," Agatha said, pulling her baby higher on her wide, childbearing hips. The infant stared at Anna with big hazel kaleidoscope eyes like her mother's, wearing only a homemade diaper and a small pink bow in her hair.

Anna nodded, crossing her arms over her chest. "Last time I saw you was at my wedding where you spent most of the evening crying in the loo over my husband." She looked over her neighbor's shoulder at the rusty Tin Lizzie in the driveway, where little Marmalade and Pepper were frowning at her from the safety of the back seat.

"My daughters told me what you said," Agatha scolded. "Tellin' my little girls that my bloke goes to the pub too much and visits that trollop Emma Boggs afterward."

"And she hit Sadie, Mummy!" Pepper shouted from the car. "She hit Sadie and we almost fell off!" Pepper quickly ducked below the window after saying her piece.

"Yeah, she was mean to us!" Marmalade added. "You're just plain mean, Mrs. Shahan!"

Pepper's eyes slowly peeked up again, nodding in agreement with her brave sister, and the two of them stuck their tongue out at Anna.

She ignored the little girls. "So Henry doesn't visit the pub too much, aye? And he never stops by Emma Boggs house? Well that's funny, 'cause

Moony told James that his truck is outside her place practically every Saturday night."

Agatha scowled at Anna. "You have no right judgin' anyone after lyin' like you did."

"About what?"

"You lied to get that good man to marry you, and everyone in the whole territory knows it."

Anna became defensive. "What does it matter; we have a family now."

"A family born of deception. The worst kind, created from selfishness. Everythin' you have is based on a lie."

"Get off my porch, Agatha."

She didn't move. "Don't you ever be tellin' my babies nothin' tripe 'bout their daddy again. You hear?"

"You threatening me?"

"I'm warnin' you. And you best heed my words, too, lest I tell your daughters how you tricked their daddy into marriage, sayin' you was preggers when you ain't."

Anna narrowed her eyes at Agatha but didn't deny it.

"And I'll tell you another thing," Agatha continued. "That cousin of yours is no better than you, unwed with a bastard ankle biter. It's an abomination, is what it is."

Anna's anger flared, hearing her insult Rose and Joshua. "Agatha Murphy, shut your bloody mouth!"

"You probably told her to do the same thing you did to snare a husband, but this time it didn't work. Can't blame the bloke, either, whoever he be. Who wants to marry a thornback with a crook leg?"

Anna had enough and slapped Agatha. Hard. Agatha held her cheek, glaring while the baby jerked in her arms. Her two little girls, watching from the car, gasped.

"Rose is a sight better looking than you, Agatha, and you know it. She has the face of an angel."

"Ha! An angel of darkness, maybe."

Anna was done arguing and went to shut the door, but Agatha stuck her foot in the entrance, pointing her long, bony finger at her. "All this sin is gonna come back and bite you one day. Nobody gets away with nothin'. Nobody."

Anna tried to slap her again, but this time Agatha caught her wrist. "With your wicked ways, you're gonna end up just like your mum."

Anna's anger turned to shock. "Is that what you're wishing on me? Death? How dare you!"

Agatha blinked hard, about to unleash a blaze of fiery words. For some unknown reason, however, she changed her mind. Turning abruptly, pulling her baby closer to her body, she left Anna speechless at the door.

Genevieve

"Agatha is right, Sweet Pea. What you have allowed will be the end of you. You must send her away. Send her away now."

"No! What I have allowed will keep Rose with me forever!"

"In the Holy Book, Sarah told Abraham to expel her servant girl after she bore them a son. Into the wilderness he sent her, and you must do the same. God will provide for Rose, just like he did Hagar."

"Get away from me! You're not even real! Leave me alone!"

"I'm trying to protect you, child."

Anna shakes her finger at the hallucination. "Mummy and Blessing come out of the paintings and visit me at night. James, Scarlet, and Mabel are with me during the day. And my cousin has her own child now and will be raising him at Sugar Alexandria. I have all I ever wanted!"

CHAPTER 40

On Sunday, Anna took Scarlet Rose and Mabel Blessing with her to church. Rose instead went for a walk to the shoreline—they had decided it was for the best she not attend until Joshua was older. When James saw the Tin Lizzie disappear down the long dirt road, he stopped his work in the paddock and saddled his horse Ireland, riding to the beach to find her.

"We need to leave soon," he said, dismounting the black Arabian stallion. "People are starting to talk, and this could escalate."

Rose too was concerned about the nasty gossip. Aside from a few who were sympathetic toward the disabled widow's situation, most of the judgmental townsfolk and whited sepulchers reacted harshly. "Anna's gotten a couple of anonymous letters, as well, saying it's an abomination to let me stay here."

"I know," said James, shaking his head. "Self-righteous Bible-thumpers."

"We can't just abandon Anna, though."

"Rose, we said we'd leave after the baby was born. Remember?"

"But the sticky beaks will tear her apart."

"On the contrary, she'll look like a saint because of us. We'll take the blame. People will think we planned it all, having an affair from the start, and that Anna was naïve to it."

Baby Joshua laid securely in a sling, draped across Rose's chest. She anxiously rubbed his back. "I want to leave, James. I do. But this sounds more like an escape."

"It is."

Without thinking twice, James interlaced his hand with hers, and they promenaded along the calm ocean waves, both realizing how right it felt.

Then, as if the last two pieces of a complex puzzle coming together, they stopped and embraced, softly kissing.

Off in the distance, atop a jagged outcrop, Liam was once again watching. Mesmerized. Shocked by what he had just witnessed, he dropped his fishing pole. It clunked down the rocks, falling into the deep abyss of the dark blue sea.

Liam's thoughts race . . .

Confusion. Hurt. Jealousy.

He understands, and yet he doesn't. Some things make sense to him; others are confusing, lost to him.

Did he really see what he saw?

At times when he's alone, thinking, Liam looks down at his hands. No more are they small and fragile, but large and strong like his daddy's. He knows they are capable of holding on to the hand of a woman, to love and protect her, but what he does not know is how to attain one. Envy over his neighbor having Anna and a family sometimes eventuates, despite James being his friend, because Music Man has everything Liam wants but does not have. It frustrates him. He doesn't know how to express his feelings, or communicate as the others so easily do.

And now he has seen Music Man kiss Rose. Although his childlike mentality keeps him unaware of many things, he does know right from wrong. His mother has taught him that a husband only kisses his wife, and no one else.

Liam continues to watch as James and Rose walk along the shoreline. When James takes Joshua from the sling and holds him close, tenderly kissing him, a revelation takes hold of the deaf young man. His thoughts turn wild and rampant. He thinks of them meeting at their hidey-hole, and of what they do once inside the small structure. Then he thinks of Anna, realizing he knows a secret she does not.

⁓ܢܐܓ⁓

Liam spent the rest of the day walking and thinking, trying to process what he had seen, to make sense of it all. The sun was setting, his hunger pangs stirred, his knees bled from falling twice, and his skin was filthy from the long hike through the bush. But still, he didn't head home. Instead, he headed to the pier where the fishermen were returning with their catch. He liked visiting with the men, curious to see their day's bounty, even helping them skin and clean the guts of the fish at times.

Sitting on the pier, Liam turned his face to the sunset and thought of Anna. How he loved her so. *I could say nothing about seeing Music Man and Rose kiss,* he thought, *or about them coming and going from the Barracuda Hut. Anna doesn't like me, anyway. She hasn't in years. All she'll do is push me away and scream at me to leave her alone as she did before. So why bother?*

Randy Mocker, an elderly fisherman with a long white beard and sea blue eyes like Anna's, came up to him and touched his shoulder so Liam could read his lips. "Whatcha thinkin' 'bout, lad? Seems you're deep in thought."

Liam nodded.

"Wanna share with an old bloke?"

"What makes a man a man?" Liam forced out in his esoteric voice.

Randy paused to think. "Good question." He turned and asked the other fishermen on the pier. Soon they were all surrounding Liam, giving him their advice.

Vedder Salzenstein patted Liam on the back. "Probably no different from what makes a sheila a good woman," he said, lighting his corncob pipe. "Just doin' the right thing, I reckon. It's about being a good, honest soul—man, woman, or child."

All the fishermen nodded in agreement.

Liam smiled. That was his answer. Yes, he would do the right thing.

⁓ೞ⊰⊱ೞ⁓

"Is James coming over too much to visit the baby?" Anna asked the next morning, sitting on Rose's love seat. She was knitting Joshua a sweater. "I can tell him no more visits for a while."

"Of course not, Kitten," replied Rose, holding the newborn. "Why would you even ask that?"

"It's just that he visits almost every night now."

"He read somewhere that a baby needs to hear its father's voice in the first months. It's healthy," Rose said, smiling at her son and kissing his cheeks.

"I don't want him to be a bother."

Rose sat down next to her cousin. "Does it bother *you*?"

Anna blanched. "No. Why would it bother me?"

"Well, I'm fine with it. I find it rather cute, actually. He holds the baby, sings to him, plays the piano for him; he even changes his diaper. I think James is really taking to Joshua."

"Of course he is. That's his son," Anna said, the magnitude of it hitting her as her own words reached her ears. "But I mean, later they will become like a nephew and uncle."

Rose nodded ever so slightly, as if she didn't nod at all.

Anna put down the half-finished sweater, and the two sewing needles intercepted each other, sticking straight up into the air. Staring at the exactness of their slender shape and symmetry, she thought of how one could not do the job of knitting without the other—a perfect complement. If a third were introduced, it would be nugatory, unless one of the other two were broken. Rose was like the third needle, she thought. Or maybe she herself was the third needle. It was a strange musing that crossed her mind as if a cold breeze, causing a chill to run down her spine.

"This is certainly a peculiar situation, that's for sure," she said to her cousin. "But such is life, aye? You have a baby now, as you've always wanted. I wanted that for you too. James will come over for a while, but as soon as Joshua is older, everything will go back to normal." Anna sounded as though she were trying to convince herself more than she was Rose.

The door opened, and James walked in. Surprised to see his wife there, his eyes flickered between the two women.

"Why aren't you out in the paddock working?" Anna asked. "You couldn't have waited till tonight to visit?"

He pushed his Akubra hat up. "Just thought I would stop by and see Joshua."

Rose walked over to James, handing him their baby. Anna watched as the exchange took place, noticing how their bodies briefly touched. That interaction bothered her, poking at the nerves under her skin, as if the edge of a razor blade had punctured her flesh. But she only dismissed the agitation.

James lifted Joshua into the air, staring at the child before cradling him in his arms. "Look, Rose, his crown is starting to get thick and dark. He's gonna have that beauty ebony hair of yours—lucky bloke."

Rose stood close to them, watching her baby smile and coo at his father. "Yes, but he has the Shahan sky-blue eyes and that slight cleft in his chin like yours." As she gently caressed Joshua's cheek, they both met eyes, not wavering from each other.

"He's gonna be a heartbreaker, for sure," James added.

Anna wanted to order her husband back to work, but she held her tongue, allowing him this moment with his son. "An infant doesn't stay small forever," she recalled him saying. Nervously she played with her wedding ring, observing the entire scene.

Anna

Deep down, I'm starting to feel a sense of regret.
Am I slowly losing control?

CHAPTER 41

Days mesh into weeks as an invisible web spins between the three. The proteinaceous spider silk draws James and Rose closer together while separating Anna from the fold. This goes unnoticed by Anna. She is too busy with household chores, the station, and her own children to realize James is pulling further and further away from her, preparing to fully open Pandora's Box . . .

Everyone strives for love.
For happiness.
To reach their dreams.
But sometimes what is right is wrong and what is wrong is right.
Sometimes the road is not always so clear . . .
When the desire outweighs the cost.

One evening after dinner, Anna took Rose onto the roof of the farmhouse to stare up at the coruscating luminaries, just as they had done many years ago as young girls, pointing at the constellations and whispering about boys and all the things that made them giggle. Now they were grown women, and the mood was quite different. Rose wasn't feeling right—it was possible she was pregnant again. And though her first pregnancy was a joy for both her and Anna, this one would have to be concealed, along with her intention of leaving Sugar Alexandria with James to start a new life.

A new life without Anna.

"Remember when we used to come out here at night?" Anna asked, lying back, gazing at the sable velvet sky sparkling with billions of stars.

"We would sneak out the bedroom window and hide from Yarrajan," Rose laughed, opening a bag of black licorice for them to share. "She would get so mad at us."

"Little devils is what she'd call us," said Anna, biting into a piece of the sapid candy.

"If memory serves, she'd call *me* the little devil for being a bad influence on you. I think she still feels the same, too."

"Yarra means well, Lottie. She loves you in her own way."

"I don't think she does," said Rose. "She trusts me just about as much as a mouse does a cobra," the irony in her own words pricking her skin.

"I could always talk to her. Straighten her out."

"Oh, don't do that. Yarrajan thinks of herself as your mum and you her daughter, and it'll just make things worse." Rose chewed on another piece of black licorice, thinking. "I suppose she's wise not to trust me, though."

Anna turned to look at her. "Why would you say that?"

"I just mean it's wise not to always expect the best from everyone. We all have our faults and our secrets, and it's good to be . . . cautious."

"But I trust you with all that I am, Rose. I trust you with my life."

"Please don't say that," Rose said, a painful and lost expression shadowing her features as she tried to hide her unmistakable emotion in the darkness. Anna would be finding out the truth soon, how the precious gift she had offered had turned into the ultimate betrayal. "I'm human, like anyone, Anna. But we're family, and family will always forgive and find a way back to each other. Promise me you'll remember that. Promise me."

"I promise," said Anna, not having the faintest idea of what her cousin was referring to. Nor in that moment did she care. "And yes, love, we're family," she added, reaching over to hold Rose's hand.

Rose squeezed her hand back, fighting hard not to cry. She desperately wished they could split James in two and share him, but that was mere fantasy. Pointing at the brightest heavenly body in the sky, she said, "Anna, stare at that star for as long as you can without blinking."

"Why?" she asked, nescient to the crack in Rose's voice and the silent tears streaming down her cheeks.

"Just try it."

Anna did as she said, and within seconds felt as if she were flying. So real was the sensation that she grabbed on to Rose for support, and that's when she detected another aroma layered with the black licorice–the strong, familiar scent of the soap she had made earlier for James. "Lottie," she curiously asked, "did you bathe with one of the soap bars I made for James? I thought your favorite was the vanilla crème."

"The vanilla *is* my favorite," Rose answered, wiping away her tears. "The scent you're smelling must be on my clothes from helping you make the soap and candles all day, that's all." She lied.

"Oh," replied Anna. Not giving it a second thought, she stared up at the stars again, seeking the weightless sensation of flying to usurp her once more. "Remember when we were children and I asked you who made the stars?"

Rose smiled. "Yes."

"You said there's a beauty of a woman with long raven hair who sits on the moon, swinging on it, and all night long she creates diamonds, sprinkling them across the night sky. And that's how the glittering stars are born."

"I remember, Kitten."

Anna leaned her head on her cousin's shoulder, her soft hair caressing Rose's skin and tickling her chin. "I'll always believe God sent you here because he knew how much I missed Mummy and Blessing. I love you, Lottie."

"I love you too, Kitten," Rose said, feeling the weight of the universe on her shoulders. Dreading the moment she would have to single-handedly shred apart Anna's perfect little world.

Anna wasn't the only one who had noticed the scent of James' soap on Rose. Yarrajan could smell it too. Her sage perception and discernment told her that the pommy sheila had chosen the mint, oatmeal, and whiskey bars because she loved the man they smelled like.

But that was not all. Though Anna was guileless to it, the Argus-eyed Aboriginal woman could also see the lingering looks, the audacious smiles, and the unnecessary interactions between James and Rose. Deceit at Sugar Alexandria was thick, and it didn't take the astute older woman long to figure out who Joshua's real father was.

With Anna oblivious to everything, or in denial of it, or both, Yarrajan felt she had to finally speak up. The Rainbow Serpent was angry, and there was little time left to make things right.

"You have a moment, Mister James?" she asked as he worked in the barn, her stern, level gaze somewhat intimidating, even for him.

"Of course, Yarrajan," said James, cleaning his saddle. "What's on your mind?"

Her visage seemed to cloud over. "Many years ago, when my father be a young man, they held him in one of those Aboriginal camps in Queensland," she began. "A slave camp. The white men forced him to work for nothin', chainin' his ankles, his wrists, and even his neck at night, treatin' him like a beast. He be lucky to be alive, survivin' what he did, only by the grace of the gods."

James looked up from his work, curious about her story and why she was telling it. She had not mentioned it before.

"One day, when he saw his chance, my father broke away and ran to the lake, tryin' to swim across to his freedom. A fisherman saw what was goin' on and took him into his boat, hidin' him from the bad men lookin' for him. He risked his own life for my father, and together with his wife, took grouse care of him and helped him start over far away. That fisherman be a kind bloke, just like you, Mister James."

James smiled.

"You be givin' yakka at Sugar Alexandria to all these Aboriginal folk, with fair wages, when the white men in the territory pressure you to only hire whites. And you teach my people English, too, riskin' further backlash from those takin' exception. You showed 'em respect. Loved 'em, really, and for that I be grateful."

"Ta, Yarrajan," James said, wondering where she was going with her kind words. "Men are all equal in God's eyes–says so in the Bible. We're all brothers. From one man, all nations."

"Yes. And because you be such a good man," the Aboriginal woman continued, "I'm not gonna tell Miss Anna about you and Miss Rose."

James froze, locking eyes with her.

"Don't look so bloody surprised, son. Don't have to see everythin' to know everythin'."

His heart began to pound.

She glanced over at the farmhouse; Anna and the twins were inside. "You gonna be found out anyway; best you be on your way with Miss Rose."

"Yarrajan, please don't say anything right now."

"I said I wouldn't. Not unless you don't. But there be one thing I wanna know, Mister James."

"What's that?"

"Joshua."

James hesitated. "Yes, he's mine."

"I knew it." She shook her head. "It be a gift from Miss Anna to Miss Rose, I reckon?"

He was slow to nod.

"That sheila thought she had it all figured out. What woman would do such a thing for another woman?" Yarrajan appeared lost in thought for a moment, a deep frown etched across her ebony face. "Then afterward, you two fell in love."

James wanted to say, "I have been in love with her from the beginning." Instead, he only agreed.

"Well, the sooner you get it over with and move on with Miss Rose, the better. Miss Anna still be young; she will meet another bloke. Just hurry; don't stretch it out so long that she catches you."

Again, he agreed.

"I tried to tell her to get rid of Miss Rose. Send her off. But I see she'll never do that. And since I gather you be leavin' us, I might as well finish my piece: You were never rapt with station life; were you, Mister James."

"No."

Yarrajan's eyes turned dark and ominous. "I could see the sadness comin' from the start," she said. "I told Miss Anna never to bring a sheila like Miss Rose into her marriage, but she never be listenin' to me." Her face became sullen, and she walked off, mumbling to herself in Nukunu, shaking her head.

James leaned against the stall, shaken by the Aboriginal woman's words. He had to tell Anna their marriage was over. No matter how difficult and painful, it would have to happen sooner than he thought.

Yarrajan

The Rainbow Serpent is near now.
Very close.
It is inside the house.
It is enraged.
And it be comin' for Anna . . .

Inside the windmill, James and Rose huddled on the love seat, serious expressions on their faces. They were discussing things of a pressing and secretive nature. Two new realities had now changed the dynamics of everything at Sugar Alexandria, and there could be no more waiting for the perfect moment to leave together . . .

Rose had just told James she was pregnant again.

Yarrajan knew about the love triangle, giving James an ultimatum: Either he told Anna, or she would.

They had to plan their escape quickly. James leaned in closer to Rose, his forehead grazing hers, her sweet breath fanning his face. "We'll leave when Anna goes into town next Saturday with the girls," he said in a low voice. "She'll be taking the Huckster pickup, and they'll be gone most of the day."

"James, I'm scared," Rose whispered back.

"I know you are. But just trust me."

"Where will we go? Where will we stay?"

"We'll find a hotel in the next town and stay there until the dust settles. A couple of weeks from now, I'll come back alone and get everything situated. By then she'll have had enough time to get over the shock and digest it all."

Rose's demeanor appeared irresolute over what they were planning.

Holding her chin in his hand, James gazed deep into her iridescent green eyes, an entire world he wanted reflecting back at him. "Everything will be all right, Rose. I promise."

News of the pregnancy and alarm from the ultimatum made dinner very uncomfortable that night. As James sat at one end of the table, Anna at the other, Rose and the children surrounding them, the conversation was dry and perfunctory.

James stared down at his food, barely eating, deep in thought over leaving the station on Saturday and all the final details he would have to tend to later. Like petitioning for divorce. Explaining things to his young daughters and establishing visitation with them. Informing the stockmen and ringers of his departure and ensuring Sugar Alexandria would keep running without him. And a plethora of other items. The list was long and arduous but not impossible.

Rose, on the other hand, felt torn. Part of her wanted to tell Anna everything and beg for her forgiveness. The other part loved James and couldn't wait to lie next to him in a more wholesome, permanent situation. With difficulty, she swallowed her food and smiled at her cousin.

After dinner, Rose wanted to go back to her maisonette, and James needed a drink, pouring himself a shot of whiskey. As he looked at his reflection in the mirror above the liquor cabinet, it caught him off guard–the beard, the shaggy hair, the steely gaze–and he thought of how he would soon look nothing like himself when he trimmed away any remnant of the station owner, washing it clean.

"Wait!" Anna called out, running to her cousin as she walked across the stockyard, baby Joshua on her hip. "You're still happy here, right Lottie?" she asked, an insecure smile on her face. "This was all a good idea, and no regrets, aye?"

"Anna, why are you asking?"

"Because you were so quiet and glum tonight. You looked kinda sad."

"I'm just tired, Kitten. New baby 'n all."

"A baby you're gonna raise here at Sugar Alexandria."

Rose nodded.

"You pinky swear?"

"Oh, Anna, we're not children anymore."

But Anna lifted her pinky anyway, waiting.

Rose forced a smile and reluctantly latched hers on.

Anna searched her cousin's eyes for a glimmer of dishonesty but found nothing. Only the shine of Rose's aquamarine gaze she had always known and admired stared back. Letting go, she said, "I love you, Lottie," feeling reassured. "G'night."

"I love you too, Kitten. Sleep well."

My Sweet Rose,

I am in my distillery right now, hiding in the shadows, drinking whiskey and writing you this letter. I want to tell you what's going on in my heart, my mind, my soul. Rambling on like a mad man, inscribing how I feel.

Too sloshed.

Too honest.

Too emotional.

Bloody hell, I want to hear your voice right now. I want to hear you breathing against my ear as I touch every part of you and kiss every inch of your skin while I'm deep inside you.

Would you lie in bed with me for days on end, making love day and night? Thirsty. Hungry. Exhausted. Yet just feeding off each other. Living off our lust. And it's true—you nourish me in ways food and water never could.

This is such a convoluted and trying situation, yet with a beauty of a future. I've been married to Anna for over thirteen years and she is a stranger to me. And though I have known you for only three, you are my other half. Thank you for coming here; thank you for saving me.

I was dead before you.

Love,
James

My Dearest James,

Reading your words, I find myself trying to catch my breath. The room is slowly spinning. My love, I am addicted to you, drowning in a sea of passion and yearning.

I want to fly to you.
You hold my life in your hands.

Love,
Rose

Saturday rushed upon them, and James and Rose fretfully waited for Anna to leave with the twins. He paced back and forth in the barn, keeping his eye on the Huckster pickup in the driveway, while Rose remained in her windmill, packing up the last of her belongings. As fast as a flame bursts alive from a struck match, immediately after Anna left, they tossed their things into the back of the Tin Lizzie, and in a blaze, headed in the opposite direction down the dirt road. James reached over and held Rose's hand. She was crying, holding Joshua in her lap. Even Matilda could sense the drama, meowing in her cage on the floor.

"Where did you leave the note for Anna?" Rose asked.

"On the kitchen table."

"Was it a kind letter?" Tears streamed down her cheeks.

"Yes, of course, love. Very gentle and compassionate."

"What did it say?"

He squeezed her hand. "I explained that we have fallen in love, and we thought it was best to leave first and discuss things later. I told her I would be petitioning for divorce."

Rose stared straight ahead. "We're running away, abandoning her."

He didn't deny it, but what other choice did they have? Being with the woman he loved meant leaving the woman he didn't.

They drove for a while in silence. James had no regrets, and in his mind's eye he was already laying out all the necessary plans for the things he needed to take care of. Rose, on the other hand, was tense and dithered, suffering a crisis of conscience. Finally, she broke. "I can't leave like this. I can't do it."

"What do you mean you can't do it? We're on our way."

"We need to sit down with Anna and talk this out. What we're doing is cruel; it will kill her. We need to just tell her we have fallen in love and want to be together."

He kept driving. "And she'll be all right with that? You don't think that will kill her too? No, we should keep going as we planned, make a clean get-away, and I'll return and talk to her later."

"This is Anna we're talking about. My cousin and dear friend, and the mother of your children. Where is the clean getaway? How is that even possible?"

"If we wait, it's only going to get worse."

"James, go back."

"Go back to what? Rose, you're pregnant again. And I don't want to live that life with Anna anymore."

"I can't do her like this. And what if she ends up hurting herself or the girls?"

"She'd never do that."

"How do you know?"

He gripped the steering wheel tighter. "She loves our daughters. She'd never harm them," he repeated.

"We both know Anna has mental problems, James. Abandoning her like this, leaving only a note, could push her over the edge, and who knows what she'd do? We'd be culpable, too. If we're physically there when we tell her, it will soften the blow, and we'll prevent anything tragic that might otherwise happen."

He shook his head in disbelief, yet the thought of it gave him pause.

"You told me that day I was about to leave Sugar Alexandria that I owed it to Anna to tell her in person. How is this different now?"

He had no answer. Again, she was right.

"I didn't realize I would feel so horrible doing it this way. Turn around, James. Go back."

"Bloody hell!" he exclaimed, throwing his fedora on the dash. He stopped the car, staring at the bare, endless road ahead of them. So close to freedom. "You do realize all hell could break loose, aye? She throws fits for no reason and goes into weird spells. I can only imagine what she'll do when we try to talk to her about this."

"We'll be kind and gentle with our words, just like your note. She'll understand. Anything is better than simply vanishing from her life."

James circled the vehicle around with a heavy sigh.

"We're doing the right thing. Anna deserves that, at the very least."

When they arrived back at the station, James turned to her in the Ford Model T. "Tomorrow morning we will tell her everything, just as you said."

She nodded.

He looked at baby Joshua in her arms. "God help us, then."

James

Before Anna gets home, I take the note I had left her on the kitchen table and go hide in the Barracuda Hut, my private place of easement. There my eyes rake over my own words, explaining why we had left. I know Rose is right–Anna is mentally unwell–and I would never forgive myself if she did something to herself or our daughters upon finding out the truth. And she does deserve to be told in person, just as I had lectured Rose that day when she tried to leave for the train station.

Yet still, somehow this terrible feeling washes over me that returning was a grave and lethal mistake . . .

The next day came and went with no taking Anna aside to divulge the truth. Both James and Rose lost their courage in the moment, unable to find the emotional strength to tell her. One thing after another prolonged the disclosure, whether some work required on the station, or Anna acting so happy that Rose couldn't bear to break her heart.

"I was thinking about you earlier today, love," Anna said the following weekend, lying next to her husband in bed.

"You were, were you? All grouse things, I hope."

"Of course, you silly goose. I was thinking how grateful I am to have you." She was uncharacteristically amorous that night–probably from Yarrajan's blackberry wine at dinner–and began to kiss him while rubbing his thigh.

At first James recoiled and wanted to stop her, but he feared she might suspect something if he did. A man at the mercy of his own circumstances, to get what he truly wanted, he had to navigate sagaciously through the last of the land mines, so he turned and crawled on top of her instead. It triggered a perturbing mental struggle for him–he felt as if he were cheating on Rose–giving rise to an anger. With every thought of resentment for the past thirteen and a half years—the excruciating work, the redacting of his talents, the constant badgering to make the station a success—he thrust into his wife. Frustration, loathing, regret. Thrust, thrust, thrust. Anna began to moan. James cringed, knowing that Rose might hear through the open window again, and pulled himself from his acrimonious trance, slowing his movements, hoping to quell the sounds. To ensure Anna didn't get pregnant, he rolled off before finishing.

Afterward, James woke in the middle of the night. Beside him, a sleeping Anna lay passed out. Slowly he got out of bed, careful not to wake her, and pulled on his trousers, quietly leaving the bedroom to head over to Rose's windmill. He could not wait until morning to see her.

"If it wasn't for Rose, Mummy and Blessing would never have come back to life," Anna mumbled in her sleep. "Rose did that for me with her paintings. She was meant to come here."

Outside the air was fresh and clear; the myriad stars glittered like diamonds. James ran to Rose's front door, let himself in, and went upstairs to the loft, crawling into bed beside her. She turned to face him, staring into his eyes through the darkness, aware of what had occurred earlier that night. As James held her, she cried.

He said nothing. What could he say? How could he explain this unpleasant reality they must endure until they can leave? A conversation better left unsaid. No elucidation, no rationalization, no justification, no annotation, no words.

Simply wordless.

Without the ability to articulate those words, however, Rose felt trapped. Mute, as Liam was deaf. Unable to fully express herself, to vent her pain. James noticed she was shivering, though not from being cold. She was shivering from distress, from worry, from jealousy, from hurt.

He could not warm her.

He could not stop her quivering.

He only hushed her tears with his lips, and as they started to kiss, so easily the lovemaking began. And yet, Anna's scent still emanated from James' skin—a sad reminder of their reality. A dichotomy between fact and fiction, between what is and what could be.

As he entered her, Rose took a deep breath. Anna's fragrance only seemed to get stronger, filling her nostrils; she could not escape the aroma. It seemed to engulf her. James could smell it too, as if his wife were in the room with them. He focused on Rose's face, not letting the unspoken disturbance distract him. After several more moments, what he held back earlier with Anna, he now released into Rose.

Lying in the darkness, staring up through the skylight at the twinkling stars, James felt strangely triumphant, having been intimate with two women in one night—one out of obligation, the other love and passion. Vivid images of his naked wife on their bed, mixed with images of her naked cousin on hers, filled his head. It made him feel somewhat guilty again, knowing he should have told Anna months ago that he and Rose were leaving. But he just couldn't muster up the courage. After that night of lovemaking, however, James made a resolute decision. No more intimacy with Anna in any form, he promised himself.

It was time to end this lie.

CHAPTER 42

It was a bright and beautiful morning, hot with an assuaging breeze, the leaves of the trees quietly clapping as the birds sang their happy songs. The heavens were a translucent blue, and the moon, still present, was a white sickle hanging on nothing, refusing to say goodbye. Rose strapped baby Joshua to her chest in an Aboriginal sling Yarrajan had made for her, and mother and child headed down to the shoreline of Indigo Bay for a swim. She bathed her son in the shallow end of the lagoon, holding him afloat as he kicked his chubby arms and legs in delight, laughing as her little treasure reveled in the silky waters. Afterward, they leisurely strolled back to the station, detouring through the wheat field.

James had built a miniature teepee at the edge of the field for the twins to play in—a combination of beech tree branches, blankets, and a wool rug on the ground—and Rose decided to rest there a while. The little makeshift fort would be coming down soon, as the season for reaping the harvest was nigh, so this would be the last time for them to enjoy its charm.

Lying on the fertile earth, she looked out the entrance of the teepee at the wheat stalks softly swaying in the breeze—a bevy of brush strokes painting across a lazuline sky. Such a calm day, she thought, mesmerized by the graceful serenity. Too calm. As if the entire universe were waiting for something to happen. Baby Joshua snuggled closer to her, nestled into her side with his face against her chest, listening to his mother's heartbeat as he did in the womb, and the two of them drifted off to a soporific place between consciousness and deep slumber.

"There you are," James said, peeking into the tent, his face covered in soot from smoking out a swarm of locusts that had infested a section of crop on the east side. "I looked for you earlier. Where'd you go?"

Rose sat up, shooing a fly away from her face. "We went for a swim."

"Good on ya; it's a scorching day," he said, wiping his brow while smiling at his son. "Listen, I want to tell you something."

She lifted Joshua into her arms. "What is it?"

He gave her a quick kiss on the lips. "I'm telling Anna today."

"Today?" she asked. "Why today?" surprised by his sudden imperative.

"Made up my mind, is all. Especially after reading your last letter again. Besides, if not now, then when? We can't keep stalling. Last week we were on our way, and we came back to make things right, so that's what I'm gonna bloody do."

Rose thought it over. "I wish there were a way we could be together without hurting her."

"Me too, but we can't go on living like this anymore. None of it is real. We're both pretending for the sake of Anna's happiness, denying our own."

She looked over his shoulder at the golden wheat stalks still swaying. Although she wanted to leave, she would miss living at Sugar Alexandria. The vastness of it with its rolling hills and open fields. The animals that lived off the land. The jovial stockmen and ringers that worked it. The station itself was alive and breathing—Anna being the heart of it—and by leaving, Rose knew a part of her would never be the same again. "We could tell her Monday," she said, looking back at James, her resolve weakening. "Give it one more week."

He shook his head. "No more waiting. We already stayed until Joshua was born, like you wanted, and now it has been months. We could have left while you were still pregnant, but we allowed her to experience his birth with us."

"I had to let her be a part of it, James. It was her idea from the start—she gave us Joshua."

He didn't disagree.

Joshua became fussy, and Rose pushed her shirt aside. The baby instantly latched on. James watched the woman he loved breastfeed his son, caressing the child's plump, sun-warmed cheek. "We're leaving," he said. "You're going to start showing soon, and Yarrajan won't wait forever–she'll tell Anna if we don't. The sooner we leave the better."

"All right," Rose said, frightened at the very thought of it all. Saddened there was no other way. "After I put Joshua to bed, we'll tell her together."

James stared into nothing for a moment. "No, it's best if I talk to her alone, first. Then afterward, you can help me explain it better."

"I don't think there's any good way to explain this."

"I know it's going to be bloody bad, but what choice do we have? I have to just tell her. She'll probably have a fit, but after she calms–and she always does–you can hold her hand and we can explain together how we'll always be in her life in some way."

"What do you think she'll say?"

"Honestly, once she realizes how serious I am, I think she'll demand I marry you and have two wives."

"Maybe we should think more about that."

"Is that what you want, Rose? To share me?"

She didn't answer.

"Listen, we've gone over that idea before, and it's not what either of us want." He took off his hat and wiped the sweat from his neck, narrowing his eyes at her. "We'll get through this, Rose. I'll talk to Anna gently and with kindness. There are lots of things for her and I to discuss, too, that don't involve you. Like the station and the girls. You just stay in the windmill until I come get you to console her if need be."

"She's going to be heartbroken," Rose said, kissing the crown of her child.

"Bloody hell, she loves you more than me, anyway. I'm sure that's the part that will hurt her the most–you leaving, not me."

Anna honked the horn in the Tin Lizzie as she came up the dirt road–a signal to her husband that she was home and wanted his help to carry in the supplies. As James went to leave, Rose grabbed his hand, squeezing so tightly her knuckles paled, angst oozing from her pores.

"It's either tell her now, or we wait until Sunday and leave like before when she's at church," James said. "No goodbye, no explanation, we simply go and I take care of everything else later." He threw a glance toward the farmhouse as his wife pulled into the driveway. "I'll let you decide."

Rose still held fast to his hand, thinking. Wild thoughts ran through her mind a mile a minute as she contemplated what to do. Both choices were impossible, each with their own set of hurtful ramifications. Do they make their escape the next time it's clear? Or does James elucidate to Anna forthwith what will be happening to their trinity? "No, tell her now," she finally said, slowly letting go of his hand.

James put all the supplies away, quietly excogitating. He was finally prepared to tell his wife the truth. "I need to talk to you about something, Anna, and it can't wait."

"Not your silly piano school idea again, I hope," she said, shaking her head. "Always thinking of how to get away from the station yakka, aye?"

"No, it's not about teaching the piano."

Anna looked up from a box of supplies. "Look at your mug, all covered in filth. If you're gonna talk to me about something important, at least go clean up first."

He did as she asked and went to draw a bath, realizing it would probably be best to have a clean face while speaking to her about a serious and life-changing matter.

While soaking in the soapy warm water, practicing his words in his mind, Anna surprised him by walking into the bathroom with a sharpened blade in her hand.

"What's this?" he asked as she sat down beside him.

"I thought I'd shave your neck for you as you soak, love."

"Not today, Anna," he nervously replied.

"Why? You usually let me."

"It's not grown out enough, that's all. My skin will chafe."

"All right, no shave," she said, casting him a cool, level gaze. "So what's happening with the locusts?"

His mouth was incredibly dry, hyperaware of the razor still in her hand. "The smoke worked," was all he said.

"Good."

Silence . . .

"What do you need to talk to me about, anyway?"

"Huh?" His peripheral vision remained focused on the blade.

"In the kitchen you said you needed to talk to me and it couldn't wait.

What is it?"

With Yarrajan gone for the day—he had hoped she'd still be there to help quell Anna if need be—the timing didn't feel right, and he was now sitting naked in a tub with his prone-to-fits wife holding a straight razor in her hand. "I don't remember now, love."

"Don't remember?"

"Nope."

Anna stood and stared at him a moment, hovering above his head, the blade glistening under the light streaming in from the window. Only the sound of the bathwater as he moved cut through the uncomfortable silence. She knows, he thought. Good God, she knows. She had stolen my life from me once before with a lie; she will not be doing it again with a razor. In one swift movement, James grabbed the blade out of her hand, quickly snapping it shut.

Anna only let out a small giggle. "You're such a silly goose; you know that, James?" she said, turning to leave. "You say I'm the one with strange ways, but you're just as odd." Shutting the bathroom door, she left him clutching the razor.

~✺✺✺~

"You didn't tell her," Rose whispered that night as James slipped into the mill. "I was so sure you were ready."

"I'm gonna tell her tomorrow. It will be better if Yarrajan is there. She's like a mum to Anna, and when Anna throws a fit, Yarrajan can help calm her." He drew Rose in for an embrace, kissing her forehead. "Unless you've changed your mind and we just flee without saying a word when she goes to church on Sunday."

Rose shook her head.

"All right. I promise you by sunset tomorrow, Anna will know every-thing."

CHAPTER 43

Rose

I awake to the sound of Anna's kulning to the livestock, as she often does in the morns. It causes a great stir in me, and I roll over in my bed, my baby lying near me. As I stare into his innocent, sleeping face, I think of my dear cousin and what she will find out today. I imagine James sitting her down and gently telling her that we are leaving, and how she'll no longer be a part of the fold.

But then I think of my suitcase under my bed, and how I am ready to leave and start anew. Anna's singing intensifies, waking my child. We both lay in silence, listening to the emotive, powerful sound as it encircles all around us.

❧

James was out in the paddock but could not keep his mind on his work. He was deliberating what he was going to say to his wife, rehearsing his words over and over. Tonight I tell her, he kept saying to himself, watching the sun in the sky, eyeing it as it moved painfully slow toward the horizon. Rose was fretting in the windmill with baby Joshua, distraught over the certain heartbreak of her cousin, trying to figure out a way around the inevitable but finding no answer. And Anna, living in her own private dreamworld, finished her housework, fed Scarlet and Mabel lunch, then went for a long walk while Yarrajan took her girls to the paddock to play with the lambs again.

After making her way down the beaten path to the shoreline, Anna kicked off her shoes and lifted the hem of her skirt, letting the cool water kiss her feet. The peaceful moment made her smile, and as her eyes searched the skyline along its infinite boundary with the sea, she settled her gaze on the abandoned fisherman's cabin in the distance, staking its claim to the small island. Then her peripheral vision caught sight of Liam walking up the beach. She thought he would wave and veer off, as usual, but instead, he approached her.

"Anna," he garbled, using his own abstruse voice.

"G'day, Liam."

"Music Man and Rose are being bad," he said, his utterance hoarse and inscrutable. Anxiety underscored his features.

She let the hem of her skirt drop, shaking her head that she didn't understand.

"Music Man made drawings of Rose, and they're both writing bad letters," he forced out, trying hard to be coherent.

The waves kept rolling in, caressing their bare feet. "I don't understand what you're saying, Liam," she mouthed.

He became frustrated, reaching out and grabbing her wrist, pointing at the Barracuda Hut. "Over there."

Anna jerked away. "What is wrong with you! Get away from me!"

Exasperated, Liam balled his fists and closed his eyes, concentrating as hard as he could to articulate his words. "I saw Music Man and Rose pashing. They're keeping secrets from Anna."

Anna finally understood what he was trying to say. She pushed him away. "You're mad."

He pointed at the cabin again. "Music Man and Rose," he repeated, then kissed the back of his hand.

A cold, sharp prickle covered Anna's skin. "You saw James and Rose pashing?" she asked, wanting to ensure she understood him correctly. She didn't believe it, even as she said it.

He nodded as he stood there, squinting with the sun in his eyes, feeling bad for Anna, feeling bad for Music Man, feeling bad for Rose. But he had to tell.

Anna grabbed ahold of his shoulders and shook him, slapping him hard. "You're crazy! You're crazy and you're seeing things!"

He ran away, not looking back.

Anna knew how difficult it was for Liam to speak. He had gone to great lengths to do so, trying desperately to communicate with words, despite his usual aversion to them. The stress on his face had been almost tangible. Mulling over what he had said, a worrisome fear gripped her. She could dismiss it all as the verbal nonsense of a deaf and intellectually disabled young man and go home, or she could go over to the cabin to investigate the veracity of it. A voice in her head pleaded with her, "Leave it be; look the other way; you're happy and that's all that matters; you've worked so hard for what you have." But the interaction with Liam summoned a curiosity in her.

Stepping forward, not back, she headed over to James' boat waiting on the beach.

Liam

I have been watching them, hidden behind the rocks.

Music Man takes the rowboat to the island, and Rose takes the boat with the small motor.

Sometimes Music Man arrives first, then Rose. Other times Rose, then Music Man.

They stay inside the Barracuda Hut for hours.

I know what they are doing in there is wrong.

When they both left one day, I went inside and found the drawings and letters in a small box.

Some of it confused me, but most I understood.

Music Man wants to be with Rose, but he's already married.

He is my mate, but it's not fair what he is doing to Anna.

It's not fair he has two sheilas when I have none.

It was the right thing to tell Anna what I saw.

Wasn't it?

Anna stood in the center of the cabin, her eyes dusting the entire room. It surprised her how clean and organized it was. Floors swept; the bed made up in the corner, layered with white sheets and a quilt; the counter clean and uncluttered; canned food and dry goods in the cabinet. Even the old couch in the middle of the room looked like it had been cleaned and given new life. The fireplace, too, gave evidence of its frequent use, holding remnants of black, charcoaled wood.

Taking a deep breath, Anna caught Rose's scent. Chypre de Coty, mixed with clove, permeated the air. It befuddled her. Why would Rose have been here? As if by instinct, she walked over to the bed and smelled the sheets—the scent was even stronger.

Her heart began to pound, pulsating all the way up her neck. Homing in on the bookcase against the wall, she noticed a bag of black licorice among James' books, as well as a framed picture of Rose, smiling and holding baby Joshua in her arms. How bizarre, she thought, feeling faint. Were they playing house together?

Anna inspected every inch of the room—under the bed, under the rug, behind the cabinet, between the books, anywhere that looked like a potential hiding spot. She turned the entire place upside down but found no real evidence of Liam's accusations. Perhaps Rose's scent on the sheets could be explained; and as for the photo, where was the harm in that? Joshua was James' son, after all.

Anna heaved a sigh of relief. She tidied up her mess, and as she turned at the doorway to take one last look at the room before she left, she noticed a small decorative box on top of the mermaid bust mounted above the fireplace, barely visible from where she stood. Hmmm, she thought.

Using a chair, she reached up and grabbed hold of the box, placing it on the table. Her heart thumped again as she removed the lid . . .

What's this, she thought, finding James' sensual drawings of a woman? Why would my husband be creating these? Her mind raced. It doesn't look like me, so who . . .

Oh my God!

It's Rose!

In a manic frenzy, Anna whipped through the drawings—numerous creations of her cousin—some merely a silhouette, others more distinct and defined. Shapes and lines, smudges and shadows, light strokes and dark, some depicting only Rose's face, some her underdeveloped leg, others her entire body. Standing, sitting, lying down . . .

Even naked and exposed.

Each drawing became more and more provocative and erotic, the last few showing James standing next to her, reclining beside her, and lying on top of her.

Yet that was not all.

Anna found the letters, too.

Countless letters.

She began to read, her eyes scanning the words, absorbing each written expression. Passion, lust, and longing—these were the emotions poured out on every page. He spoke of the life he hated, a wife he did not love, and the excitement of beginning anew with Rose, anywhere else but Sugar Alexandria. In shock, and with eyes blurred from tears, Anna almost fainted when she read the last letter from her husband . . .

My Dearest Rose,

> *You are carrying my child again.*
> *I dwell on this at night as I lie next to her. Her a woman who trapped me into marriage, making me give up what I love: music and teaching. Forcing me to work on a station that is gradually killing my soul. The years I have burned with her, the time I have wasted, it angers me.*
> *Then you arrived like a beautiful song, a song I was yearning for.*
> *We have Joshua; we have our baby you are now carrying; we have each other. Very soon, we will fly free. Hold on just a little while longer, my love. Fate will show us the way; the future is ours.*
>
> *Forever yours,*
> *James*

It was damning testimony of their scandalous love affair, and Anna felt as if she were falling off a cliff. The last letter from her cousin thrust the knife even deeper . . .

My Darling James,

> *I cannot wait to start our new life together with our children. When I am not with you, I am thinking about you, obsessing about you, wanting to be next to you, wanting to make love to you.*

I know you are mine, and I am yours.
When we are together, the universe is us, and we are the universe.

Love always,
Rose

"They're in love with each other, and Rose is having his second baby!" Anna painfully cried unintelligibly. "They're both leaving me!" Falling from her chair, she wailed on the floor.

Rose was in denial.

As she packed her things to leave, she reasoned that Anna would be upset and heartbroken, but would eventually come to terms with them leaving. She imagined sitting Anna down, telling her nothing was really going to change except that she and James would be living elsewhere, and they'd come and visit her at Sugar Alexandria often. She visualized Anna being calm and reasonable, and that as long as she and James promised they'd always be in her life, everything would be fine.

She was wrong . . .

While Joshua slept in his crib, Rose decided she could use another suitcase and went to the farmhouse to search for one, knowing Anna was down by the shoreline to collect clams for dinner, and Yarrajan had taken the girls to play with the lambs. Unable to find a valise in the master bedroom, she went to her cousin's childhood room next, and found nothing. Anna had previously told her that she sometimes stored items that weren't frequently used on the fire-damaged second floor, so Rose retrieved the skeleton key from the kitchen and unlocked the door leading upstairs.

That's when the horror struck her . . .

On pushing open the door to the first room at the top of the stairs, she found numerous corn husk dolls scattered about, just like the ones at Anna's morbid shrine, along with countless drawings of faceless figures taped to the black, soot-covered walls. Dark images, pernicious and disturbing, created by a mind that had inexorably moved out of reality and into macabre territory.

Anna had been drawing the shadow people that she had seen!

Yet there was more. She had also been writing things on the floor. Numbers and letters in all different colors, strange words that made no sense or were too scribbled to understand. She even wrote down the names of her favorite stories, changing their titles from *The Secret Garden* to *My Secret Garden*, *Alice in Wonderland* to *Anna in Wonderland*, and *Emma* to *Anna*. On one of the blackened walls, "Kitten owns Sugar Bear and Lottie" was scratched repeatedly into the charred wood.

The sight was so overwhelming that Rose staggered backward, falling to the floor. With her hand over her mouth, petrified, she realized in that moment that both she and James had completely underestimated the extent of her cousin's illness. "Oh my God," she whispered. Anna was not sane enough to handle what was about to be disclosed. Scrambling to her feet, Rose ran downstairs to look for James before he could tell his wife the truth.

~ᴄᴇ🙨ᴏ~

James was in his distillery, sipping his whiskey and pondering where he and Rose would go once they left the station. Notwithstanding his anxiety over having to tell Anna the truth, the anticipation of a new life at his fingertips filled him with vim.

"What is this!" Anna yelled, barging through the door. Now enraged, she shook the collection of letters in his face.

His stomach dropped. How on earth had she found them when they were hidden so carefully!

"You don't love me? I trapped you?"

James' heart pounded against his ribcage, completely unprepared for his wife's discovery.

"Answer me!" she shouted.

"Anna . . ."

"I said what are these letters!" Suddenly Genevieve appeared next to Anna with the Black Shuck snarling by her side.

Shell-shocked, James did not know where to begin. His mind floundered until the speech he had prepared a hundred times began to materialize in his thoughts. "I don't love you, Anna. I never have," he was going to say. But now, with her standing in front of him, sadness and distress behind the anger, those words seemed too harsh and obtuse.

"Tell me this is a bloody mistake!" she demanded.

He took a deep breath and exhaled. "I'm sorry, Anna. It's not a mistake. I'm in love with Rose and we want to be together." His answer came out in a rush of words, and as they left his lips, relief swept through his body.

Her eyes became wide and confused. "No! No! No!" she yelled, wringing her hands violently. "I own you and Rose! I own you both! I own you for what I allowed!"

"That's right, Sweet Pea. You own them," Genevieve hissed. The Black Shuck bared its razor-sharp teeth.

James maintained his granite and stayed the course. "You'll always be the mother of my daughters, but our marriage is over, Anna. I wanted to tell you for months now. I'm sorry."

"You've been planning to leave me for months?"

"I was going to tell you today. I was going to sit you down and explain everything."

Anna trembled. The utopian existence she had fought so hard to build was in fact a mirage. Its fruitage a sickly, prickly toxin.

"Rose and I have been in love for quite some time," he continued, "and we didn't know how to tell you. But since we just found out she's pregnant again, the truth has to come out now."

"So it's true, then?" Anna asked. "She's pregnant again?"

"Yes," he said calmly.

Outside the windmill blades spun and the wet clothes on the clothesline swayed. If you listened very carefully, all the familiar sounds of life on the station were extremely clear: The stockmen and ringers chatting, the peacocks and chickens in the yard, the cows and sheep in the paddock, the horses and camels in the barn. All very much alive. Within those sounds loitered the life Anna had been so happy in. The same sounds James wanted to now flee. Suddenly baby Joshua's cry sliced through everything, and in an instant husband and wife were thinking the same thing . . . That child was James' son, and it was Anna who made it happen.

"Do you hear that, James?" she asked. "The cry of that child?" The look on her face gave him a chill. "That baby has the breath of life because of me." Her expression vacillated between anger, sorrow, and lunacy, settling on sorrow. Lowering her head in despair, she began to cry. "I'm the one who made it possible for her to have a child in the first place," she sobbed. "And now you two are in love, she's pregnant again, and you're gonna leave me."

He gave no response.

Anna looked at the Black Shuck—still growling, teeth still showing, eyes glowing red—then back at her husband, her anger returning, giving him a scowl so astringent he did not recognize his wife. "It was only supposed to be once!"

James prepared himself, ready for her to fly into a fit of vexation. He knew there would be turmoil—there was no escaping it.

"Did you hear me! One time! I only allowed it once!"

For a glimmer of a moment, so accustomed to always capitulating to Anna's will, James almost withdrew from his avowal about him and Rose. But he was a different man now. His comportment had changed considerably after Joshua was born. "Calm down, Anna, or you'll descend into one of your spells."

"You're bloody telling me to calm down after what I found out? Rose is pregnant again, you say you're in love with each other and you're both leaving, and you're worried I'll have another fit? The bloody hell with you, James Shahan!" An intense heat rose up Anna's throat. She wanted to scream, and almost did, yet somehow held it, continuing to listen in shock as her husband explained why their marriage was over.

"I did what I thought was right back then. But you lied to me, saying you were pregnant when you weren't, just so I would marry you." He stared down at his hands. "And even over the years, things didn't change much for us. I was always your main stockman more than I was your husband."

As Anna glared at him, the room dipped and spun, until James' image obscured and became foreign to her. She did not see her husband anymore, but a man who looked like him, sounded like him, yet was not him.

"And now that I'm in love with Rose, it's time we admit the truth and end this lie," he said, attempting to reason with her. "Divorce is the only way."

Her mind panicked. "Divorce? What about the station? What about our daughters?"

"You know how to manage this place in your sleep; you don't need me. And I will visit Scarlet Rose and Mabel Blessing on the weekends."

Anna stared at him wide-eyed, as if he were on fire. "You can't leave me!"

He held firm. "Yes, Anna. I'm leaving, and Rose is coming with me."

"We can fix this! Whatever's wrong, we can fix it!"

"No! What's done is done!"

"You can have two wives!" she pleaded. "Please!"

"I don't want two wives. I only want Rose."

A thick, dark sensation crept up on her. Seeing nothing but red, she felt as if she were walking through the catacombs. They were leaving without her . . .

Pain. Heartache. Terror.

Deceived and abandoned by the people she loved the most.

Anna lost her senses as the world around her became a blur. A surge of emotion erupted inside her, and as James looked away for a second, she grabbed a mallet and hit him on the back of the head as hard as she possibly could. He fell to the floor. Attempting to stand, stumbling forward, she hit him again and he collapsed. Dropping the mallet, she then grabbed a knife off the tool shelf and ran to the windmill.

"Tell me it's not true!" Anna pleaded as her cousin opened the door.

When Rose couldn't find James earlier, she had retreated to her windmill to wait for his return.

"The letters in the box at the fisherman's cabin–tell me it's not true!" Anna repeated.

Rose saw the anger on her face. And the knife. Her heart raced and her mouth went dry, realizing the secret she and James had been hiding for months was now exposed. Instantly she remembered James telling her they should just leave, and in that moment, she regretted her decision to stay.

"Rose, please tell me it's all lies," Anna begged.

Rose remained silent. Words eluded her, seeing that Anna had lost her mind. She looked over at the farmhouse, desperately searching for James to rescue her from this nightmare, but he was nowhere in sight.

"You're my family, my best cobber," Anna cried. "I let you sleep with my husband so you could have a baby, and we were supposed to raise our children together. Now you're both leaving me!"

Rose began to tremble, gripping her cane tightly, preparing to protect herself.

"For God's sake, I even let you breastfeed my daughters!"

"Anna, please calm down," Rose implored. She was crying now too.

"You can't leave me!" Anna screamed. "Not after all I have done for you! You can't do this to me! I love you! Please, I'm begging you!"

Yarrajan was watching from the back porch. *"I told you, child! I told you!"* she cried out in Nukunu, falling to her knees, wailing in her native tongue. The twins were listening to the screaming, standing in the doorway with horrified faces. They both began to whimper and crouched to the floor, hugging each other for protection and comfort. Yarrajan pulled herself up, gathered them in her arms like a mother hen, and brought them to their room before running back outside.

Anna was now hysterical. "You're pregnant again; aren't you," she sobbed.

Rose dared not answer.

Anna shook as she glared at her, while the shouting prayer of an old Aboriginal woman echoed in her ears. Who was this woman whom her husband now wanted and was leaving with? In her right hand, she clutched the knife, and the light from the late-afternoon sun reflected off the metal, causing a silver shine to flicker into the eyes of her disloyal cousin. "Answer me!" she yelled.

Rose was too frightened to even move.

"And you're leaving with James," she said, sobbing even harder.

"Anna . . . ," Rose entreated, her voice quivering. "They're just letters; they mean nothing. We're not leaving you. No one's leaving anyone."

Anna looked up at the sky and screamed, "Liarrrr! I saw how he drew you! I saw those disgusting images! You're both going to hell!"

The Black Shuck looked up at the sky too and howled—a spine-chilling wail.

Suddenly Anna was no longer Anna, but her mother Elsa. She had left her body and was watching it all happen from some high, far-off place. "How could you do this to my daughter," she growled in an outré, raw voice, her face deranged and demented. "Anna did everything for you, and yet you betrayed her! I won't let you get away with this!"

As Rose stared at her unhinged cousin, her own mother's portentous words rang in her ears, yet again, caroming about in her head: "There's something wrong with Anna . . . Mental disorders plague the women in our lineage . . . A few even killed someone in a fit of rage . . . I'm warning you, dear, be careful."

Anna became Anna again, turning her head to the left and whispering to someone. No longer was she just hearing voices; she was actually seeing her mother and sister incarnate, just as she did when they came out of the paintings. Elsa stood only a few feet away, and she was holding a five-year-old Blessing's hand, personified from a picture Anna had in her drawer. Wrathful indignation enveloped her like a corona, and a commensurate scowl marred the little girl's face.

"You need to discipline this Jezebel for what she has done," Elsa said.

Blessing nodded in agreement.

"I know, Mummy," Anna replied to the hallucination. "I know."

"Kill her, Turtle Dove! Kill her and protect your family!"

"Yes, kill her for betraying you," Genevieve concurred, the black wolf with the bloodred eyes standing next to her. "I warned you, and you didn't listen. Now fix what you have done."

"Kill her! Kill her! Kill her!" all the hallucinations chanted together.

Anna only screamed.

Terrified, Rose tried to shut the door; Anna forced her way in. Bunching up her skirt, Rose prepared to run past her, but Anna spread out her arms, knife in hand, letting her know that if she did, she would only intercept her. Releasing her hem, Rose slowly withdrew the tortoiseshell comb from her hair that Anna had given her as a gift. Glossy white, with four long teeth, the striking comb was able to hold up the thickest of hair; yet with its solid base, it could also be used as a weapon. She pointed the comb at Anna as her dark locks loosened, disseminating about her face, resembling wings unfolding.

Rose would defend herself at all costs.

It was a come-to-Jesus moment for them both. A day of reckoning and regret. They continued to stand their ground, hearts pumping, fear and anger mounting in a perpetual circle. The energy locked them together in a motionless dance, a silent duet of sadness and choler. With each second, they were closer and closer, and with each second, Anna's rage grew hotter and hotter.

"Anna, it's me!" Rose pleaded through her tears. "Please put down the knife!"

She gave no response. In her fury of temporary madness, transmuting back and forth between herself and her mother, Anna no longer knew the woman who adjured and cried before her. She was her cousin, she reminded herself. Her beautiful cousin whom she loved more than life itself. But as she narrowed her gaze at her once best friend, Rose's green eyes no longer looked so pretty and cat-like. Instead, they seemed wild and foreign. More like a strange, rabid feral that had bitten her and wanted to run away.

For some odd reason as Anna glared at her, the image of Joshua's birth flashed across her mind. Even the smell of the blood was still fresh in her memory. It was a spiritual moment, almost ceremonial, as if the red ichor from the birth–the bequeathed gift she had given her beloved cousin–had bound them together for life. Crushing her eyes shut, she no longer wanted to think of it, or to see this woman, or be where she was.

Everything was now in ruin. Nothing would ever be the same again. All that once was, was now lost, and as her mind continued to race, the voice of her husband rang in her ears: "What's done is done!" A searing wave of heartache swept over her, and with a sharp intake of air, Anna opened her eyes again, pointing the knife at her cousin while screaming in Danish, *"Hun stolede på dig! . . . Min datter stolede på dig!"* *("She trusted you! . . . My daughter trusted you!")*

"Anna, you're talking crazy. You're scaring me," Rose cried.

"Anna? . . . No, you trollop, it's Elsa!" she screamed, frothing at the mouth. "And I will kill you for what you have done to my daughter!"

Rose dropped the comb and fell to her knees, raising her arms up to the heavens, pleading for mercy and begging Anna for forgiveness. But Rose wasn't Rose anymore, either, as Anna watched her cousin slowly transform, her eyes turning bloodred, her teeth growing long and sharp, her body morphing into a black wolf . . .

Was she the Black Shuck all along!

James regained consciousness in the distillery. Within seconds, his mind cleared, and the dire situation came back to him. Wasting no time, he ran outside; Yarrajan yelled that Anna was in the windmill with Rose, and she had a knife.

Anna heard them outside as she kept pointing the weapon at the Black Shuck kneeling at her feet. James' heavy footsteps pounded the ground as he charged toward the mill, and she knew her opportunity to kill the beast would anon be lost. She made her choice. Lunging, she stabbed at the air; she stabbed at the wolf. Several times.

There was blood.

James hurled himself onto Anna. Husband and wife rolled on the floor. Anna screamed, crying uncontrollably, thrashing about until James was able to restrain her.

Rose, in shock, held her throat while blood seeped through her fingers. Her face paled, and as she tried to stand, her knees buckled. "My son needs me," she cried out, attempting to stand once more before collapsing to the ground.

The scene looked like something out of a horror movie.
Or a war.

Anna, deranged and hysterical, had fought back with all her might until two Aboriginal stockmen ran over and were able to hold her down. The dogs scampered in a circle in the yard, confused by the commotion, barking and yelping. And Yarrajan kept crying and praying in Nukunu, distraught over her little white rabbit and what she had done.

James picked up Rose, his shirt covered in blood from her neck, and frantically ran to the house, fearing he had lost the woman he loved. Laying her on the kitchen table, he tore off her blouse and quickly examined her wounds. She had been stabbed in two places in the neck, passing out from shock and fear.

Relieved that the lacerations had missed her carotid artery and jugular vein, James bandaged her neck and applied pressure to the area until the bleeding had stopped. He then laid her on the couch in the living room, waiting for her to regain consciousness.

"James . . . ," Rose softly said, slowly opening her eyes.

"I'm here, love."

"Where's Joshua?"

"He's with the girls in the nursery. Yarrajan's looking after them."

She started to cry. "I can't believe Anna stabbed me. I thought I was going to die."

"Me too," James said, smoothing back her hair, his face tense and pale. "But the wounds are superficial. You're going to be all right."

~~❦~~

Anna had finally subdued and was taken to her bedroom in the farmhouse. Staring catatonically at nothing, she lay curled up on the bed in the fetal position. When James entered the room, however, she began to sob. "You can't leave me; you can't leave me; you can't leave me," she cried over and over, then screamed hysterically, "You can't! You can't! You can't!"

James cursed in Gaelic, furious about what just happened and inwardly kicking himself for turning around that day he and Rose had left–they should have kept going. He paced the room, unsure of what to say or do.

"I'm here, Turtle Dove," Elsa's consoling voice said to Anna. "Your sister is too."

Anna stopped and looked at the foot of her bed. Elsa was sitting there, a warm motherly smile on her face, and little Blessing sat on the floor by her

410

mother's feet, legs crossed and hands folded in her lap.

"We both love you, dear. We'll never leave you; I promise."

"I love you too, Mummy," Anna said. "Thank goodness you're here."

James looked around the room, realizing she was hallucinating again.

"Don't be rude, James. Say hello to my mother and sister; they're right there in front of you."

A shiver ran down his spine.

"Tell him he can't leave me, Mummy. Tell him." Anna began to sob again, curling back into the fetal position, burying her face in the pillow.

Compassion took hold of James as his soon-to-be ex-wife continued to mumble and cry to her mother. Though his anger over what she had done had still not dissipated, he hated seeing her in such a state, and he felt pity. A part of him wanted to fix everything. He wanted to make Anna's pain go away by telling her it was all a mistake and everything would be ok. But he couldn't–it wasn't the truth. He loved Rose, and she was carrying his second child. "Anna, calm down. I'm here, and I'm not going anywhere," he said, sitting next to her, gently touching her forehead, trying to soothe her.

Anna mollified when she heard those words, closing her eyes and allowing him to caress her hair.

"That's it; easy, love . . . Everything is good as pie . . . Relax . . . Good girl."

With Anna drifting off from pure exhaustion, James left the room, quietly shutting the bedroom door. He walked back into the living room to check on Rose.

"How is she?" Rose asked, still holding her bandage.

"She's doing better. I don't know for how much longer, but at least she's not hyperventilating anymore."

"I need some air, James. Walk me out to the front porch."

"You need to stay lying down."

"No, I need some fresh air," she repeated. Putting her arm around him for support, she stood, and they both went outside to talk on the porch.

The mailman pulled up, making a late delivery, and they both stopped talking. Discerning by the look on their faces that something was wrong, he hesitated, then waved, sticking the letters in the box instead of hand-delivering them. James waved back, frowning as the man left, knowing that the Shahan name would soon become fodder for juicy gossip in town. Salacious stories were sure to spawn like wildfire.

"James, what do we do now?" Rose asked.

"Moony went to Casper Cotton's to call Dr. Crawford. We wait for him before doing anything."

Still suffering the aftershock of what had just taken place at the station, both James and Rose tried hard to assuage their rampant thoughts. Brows furrowed, lips dry, faces pale, neither one could fathom how Anna was capable of such injurious intent. It seemed as if an earthquake had just hit Sugar Alexandria, splitting open the ground beneath them, swallowing them whole into its fiery depths.

Yarrajan burst open the front door. "Mister James, she's got the baby! She's got Joshua, and she's gonna kill him!"

Rose let out a bloodcurdling scream.

James sprinted through the house, but she was gone. Only his twin daughters were there, looking up at him in confusion. In a panic, he raced out the back door to find Anna holding baby Joshua near the refuse fire that the stockmen had made earlier. Glassy-eyed, she stood right next to the immense blaze, holding the tiny infant, rocking the child in her arms as she spoke to him.

"Anna, give me my son," James said in a calm voice, slowly walking up to her with his arms extended.

She ignored him, talking to her incensed mother again. "Throw it in," the hallucination demanded.

Genevieve agreed. "You brought this child into the world, now take it out," she said, the Black Shuck growling ferociously by her side.

Rose and Yarrajan ran onto the scene. "Anna, my baby!" Rose cried out. "My baby! Please!" She fell to her knees; the cut on her neck began to bleed again.

Anna looked up from the infant, glaring at them all, this time transitioning into an adult Blessing. "If it wasn't for my sister, this child wouldn't even exist," she snarled.

"Miss Anna! Dear Lord, give the child to his mother!" Yarrajan ordered.

She smirked. "Anna's not here. You're dealing with me, now." Staring into the flames, she then looked down at the baby. All it would take is one simple toss, and Joshua would be gone. She glared at her beloved cousin again and said, "You both think you're so bloody important, but Anna's the one who gave him life. And what she gave, she can take away!" She was speaking like an insane person. A walking incendiary.

"Anna, your mum is watching in the heavens," James said.

She scowled at him, changing back to Elsa. "I'm not in heaven, son. I'm right here, and I say throw the child in the fire!" The baby let out a scream.

Rose wailed, begging on her knees as the flames of the refuse fire grew higher and higher like a demon licking at the clouds. "Please, Anna, don't hurt my son! My baby! My baby! My precious baby! James, stop her!"

Anna stepped closer to the fire; Joshua cried even louder from the heat of the flames. Her identity and thoughts kept altering, transmogrifying between her mother, her sister, and herself. "You think I would allow such a thing to happen–giving you this gift, only to have you both leave me?" she asked. "Never!"

Rose grabbed on to Yarrajan's leg, burying her face into the Aboriginal woman, unable to watch what would happen next . . .

Warragul had been observing nearby, aware that Anna had lost her senses. She could not see him signal to James as he stealthily approached behind her. In a rapid maneuver, he grabbed her, clenching her neck with his forearm, just as James caught the infant.

With Joshua back in Rose's arms, she cried hysterically, kissing the child's face over and over. James returned to Anna and slapped her so hard she saw stars, wrestling her to the ground, holding her down as she screamed until she passed out.

"An evil spirit got into her," Warragul said in Nukunu. *"The elders say the mulga madness comes from the dark side."*

James looked up at him, still restraining Anna's arms. *"Yes, she has gone mad,"* he replied in the Aboriginal man's tongue. *"She's definitely lost her mind."*

Anna

I didn't want to hurt Rose.
And I would never hurt her baby.
It wasn't me!
I stepped outside my body for a moment . . .
And something else stepped inside.
Please forgive me.
Please, I beg of you!

~꧁꧂~

Dr. Crawford entered the house, unnerved by the message Casper Cotton had left his receptionist earlier. It read: *"Urgent. Please come to the Shahans' station. There has been an accident."* Without asking questions, he had driven right over. He was anticipating that one of the stockmen had been injured, which had happened in the past, but instead he found Rose on the couch, crying, holding her injury with a bloody cloth. "They're both just surface wounds, really," he said, inspecting the lacerations. "I'll close them with some stitches."

"There was so much blood," Rose replied.

"The neck, face, and head are very vascular. Minor cuts often bleed profusely because the blood vessels are so close to the surface of the skin." After suturing the wounds, the doctor turned his attention to James, examining his head. "Now this bump is something else. Are you seeing double vision at all, mate? Do you feel nauseated?"

"It hurts a bit, but I'm all right," he answered.

"That's to be expected. If the pain increases or you get any of those symptoms, though, you should go to the hospital."

James appeared unconcerned, remaining focused on Rose.

"I'm serious. With a blow like that, you could have a concussion. Symptoms can be subtle and may not show up immediately, so keep an eye on it, and let me know if anything changes."

James led the doctor into the bedroom. Yarrajan was in the room with Anna, sitting by her side, holding her hand. Scarlet and Mabel played apprehensively on the floor.

Dr. Crawford flashed his penlight into Anna's eyes, waving his hand in front of her face. No response. She only laid there in a catatonic gaze, staring into space with an elegiac expression. "Now what the bloody hell happened to all of you?" he asked, holding Anna's wrist while checking her pulse.

James stood in the doorway, exhausted. His face was phlegmatic, but internally, he brimmed with guilt.

Yarrajan spoke up, scowling at him: "Mister James and Miss Rose bin messin' around, and Miss Anna found out today."

The doctor looked up at James. "I see."

"After she go and attack Miss Rose, she grab the baby. We thought she gonna throw him into the fire," Yarrajan added.

"What! Where's the baby now!"

"Joshua is all right," James assured. "He's asleep in the nursery."

"Crikey!" Dr. Crawford exclaimed, shaking his head. "I can't believe Anna would do any of this."

"These two drove her to it," the Aboriginal woman said.

"Yarrajan, please take the girls to their room. Ta."

She kissed Anna on the forehead, then did as James asked, taking the twins to their room, closing the door behind her. Once there, she sang a sad, lonely song in Nukunu. The hum of the emotional Aboriginal ballad vibrated into the air, seeping through the entire house. Compunction crept over James as the sound caught between his ribs.

Dr. Crawford searched through his medical bag. Withdrawing a syringe and a vial, he administered a sedative into Anna's arm. "She will sleep for about eight hours now. Plenty of time for the psychiatric hospital to come and get her."

"Psychiatric hospital?" James asked.

"James, let's go outside where we can talk."

He followed the doctor outside. In the near distance, he could hear some of the stockmen conversing about the incident. Again, James frowned, realizing that soon the whole town of Esperance would know, bringing judgment and shame. As they continued to walk, a memory crossed his mind of when the twins were born. How different things were then. He was very much Anna's when his daughters came into the world. Now he was Rose's. James recalled giving Dr. Crawford a piglet that day for his assistance during the birth.

The doctor must have been thinking the same thing: "That little piglet you gave me is huge now."

James nodded.

"My wife ended up keeping it as a pet. We call her Sally. That sow walks around my entire property like she owns the bloody place."

Both men stopped at the dividing fence encircling the farmhouse, leaning against it. After a long moment, the doctor glanced over at James. "I'm going to have to report this to Constable Higgins, mate. Attacking someone with a knife and threatening to kill a baby—the proper authorities need to be notified."

James' heart raced. "Can't we just let the hospital deal with her?"

"I'm obligated to report it. I could lose my license if I don't. I am going to recommend a full evaluation based on her current mental breakdown, and also note her past mental issues and behaviors that she's been treated for. The emotional fits and such. Whispering to herself, wandering off, and so on. Either way, though, she'll still have to go before a judge. He'll render a decision on her actions based on her mental state at the time of the offense, and whether she should be left in the care of the hospital or receive some other punishment."

James paled; his knees weakened.

"I know this is difficult, mate, but it's the only way to handle a situation like this. The fact that no one was seriously hurt works in her favor, though. Otherwise, it would be much different."

Distraught and anxious, James stuck his hands in his pockets while giving the doctor a somber look. His wife had just suffered a severe mental breakdown, losing all control of her faculties in a paroxysm of rage, knocking him out with an iron skillet and attacking her pregnant cousin with a knife. If the worst had transpired, he would have lost both women—one to death, the other to certain prison. And what if in her moment of madness she had injured Joshua, or even killed him? Or hurt the twins? His mind raced with so many morbid thoughts.

"I'm not here to judge you, James. But as your doctor, you have to tell me exactly what happened."

James exhaled heavily, his shoulders dropping. "It all started when Rose wanted to have a baby, and Anna pushed the idea of . . . of me giving her one."

Dr. Crawford looked at James with surprise. "Joshua is yours?"

James slowly nodded. "Yes."

Everything started to become clear to the doctor. "And after that, you and Rose continued?"

Again, James nodded.

"Quite an ordeal, mate. Don't have much experience with affairs like this."

"Now Rose is pregnant again, and we were planning on leaving Sugar Alexandria."

"And Anna found this out today."

"Through some hidden letters we had written each other."

"Not hidden well enough." Dr. Crawford appeared baffled by what he heard. "What are you going to do now?"

Despite the sadness of the grievous situation, it surprised James to find himself so open to discussing it, wanting to be free from all the deceit and denial of living a life he no longer wanted. "Our plan was to sit her down and explain everything. I have never been rapt here, and Rose and I want the same things in life. I've always wanted to pursue a career in music in the city, rather than be a grazier. But now, after this, I don't know what to do."

The doctor's tone lowered, becoming more authoritative. "Well, for now, Anna needs to be committed."

"Committed?" James echoed.

"This is for her own good and the protection of your family." A dark shadow cast across Dr. Crawford's face, imagining the worst. "James, she's not going to be herself for a while. She could even have another episode and hurt someone again, this time fatally. What are you gonna do, just keep the sheila locked away in a room?"

"Are you certain we have to involve the police, though? Couldn't we just say she had a nervous breakdown and had to be taken to a mental health facility?"

"I have been Anna's doctor her whole life; she's like a daughter to me. But this has to follow the correct protocol. Besides, the hospital has to know the full extent of what she did in order to effectively treat her. By law, they will then be obligated to inform the authorities themselves, even if I didn't. There's no way around it, mate."

"Is it possible she'll get jail time?"

"With the report I'm going to write, and the subsequent evaluation by the assigned doctor at the psychiatric hospital, not likely. But it's still going to be up to a judge."

James' head spun; the entire situation was devastating. "All right; what happens next?"

"I make a few phone calls, and the medical attendants come and pick her up. They'll take her to the Pleasant Skies Psychiatric Hospital south of Kalgoorlie where she can be properly treated by a cadre of physicians."

"What do I have to do?"

"Sign a release."

"And when will she appear before a judge?"

"Once she's evaluated, the court will set a date. Hopefully he'll find her criminally not responsible, unfit for trial, and she'll remain in custody at the hospital."

"For how long?"

"Until they see that she is well again."

"How long will it take to recover from something like this?"

The doctor looked up at the sky as if the answer were written in the clouds. "Only the good Lord knows that, mate."

~⚜~

The men in white uniforms arrived a few hours later. Anna was still in a medicated sleep, completely unaware she was being escorted to a psychiatric hospital miles away from everything she knew. Away from Sugar Alexandria. Away from her husband and daughters. And away from Rose.

As they placed Anna into the ambulance, James and Rose watched, while Yarrajan hurried the twins back inside the farmhouse so the sight of their mother being taken by strange men would not scar their young minds. When the medical team drove off, James turned to Rose and said, "Let's pack and leave as soon as possible. The truth is out now, and Anna's under proper medical care. There's nothing more we can do for her."

"Leave right now? After what just happened?"

James threw a glance at several stockmen nearby, then took off his Akubra hat, forking his fingers through his hair. "To be honest, I think it's for the best."

"Tonight, though?" She stared back at the farmhouse, the three windmills, the barn. On this evening, it all looked eerily different. Almost haunted.

"Rose, we should have kept driving that day we first left, but you changed your mind. Now it's all out in the open, and the sooner we leave, the better. I'm going to tell the men to keep working the regular schedule until I get

418

back. And I'll ask Yarrajan if she can stay and look after the girls until we get settled into our new place."

"Why not take them with us?"

"This is their home, what they're used to. Their beds and toys are here; it's better they stay for now. Besides, Yarrajan is like their grandmother; she'll take good care of them."

"This is all happening so quickly . . ." Overwhelmed, Rose stood in the front yard with him, debating their next steps in the aftermath. She began to tremble.

James grabbed her hand, pulling her into his embrace, holding her close. He kissed her cheek, then her forehead, locking eyes with her. "Let's leave this place, Rose." Instantly, she too wanted to be as far away from the station as she could. She didn't want to wait another day, another hour, not even another minute standing on the red earth of Sugar Alexandria.

Rose finished packing the last of her things in a tremulous hurry, as if Anna would come barging through the door at any moment, halting their getaway. Closing her suitcase, she recalled when she first arrived in Australia—with the sights, the sounds, the smells of the Outback—and how her excitement for her new life and future overflowed. Now she was leaving with James, her cousin's husband. She cried as she left the mill.

Outside the fresh air dried her tears, and she felt strangely intoxicated. Was this actually happening, she kept asking herself? She surveyed the station one last time, letting her eyes linger on the center windmill that had been her home. Her Shangri-La. Her place of healing and solace. It had turned into an intimate haven where her love for James grew, but now it seemed dark, as if a hole that would suck you in, keeping you for eternity if you stood too close. The feeling was discomfortingly sad.

"Let's get out of here," James said. Lovely Dawn came up to him, raising her snout to be petted, seemingly aware that something was wrong. He kneeled down and hugged her.

"Did you speak to Yarrajan?" Rose asked, holding Joshua on her hip. A suitcase and valise sat by her feet; Matilda crouched nervously in the pet carrier.

"Yes. She's going to watch the girls as long as needed, and the men agreed to keep working in my absence until I can arrange things properly." He gave Rose a weary smile. "Did you pack everything you need?"

She nodded.

"Grouse," he said, opening the car door.

Rose stepped into the Model T with baby Joshua while James put Matilda in the back seat along with the luggage. "I'll come back for the rest of our things after we find a place to stay."

"James, hurry. Let's go," Rose urged. For no apparent reason, they both felt an anxiousness to leave. He hastily got in and started the car.

Rose squeezed James' hand as they passed the front of the farmhouse and made their way down the long dirt road. Both remained quiet as he drove. A few hours later, they saw the city lights, and that's when he looked over at her. Rose's hair was blowing in the wind; baby Joshua slept against her chest. Leaving one hand on the steering wheel, he reached over with the other and picked up hers, gently kissing the back of it. "Crikey," he said. "Never thought I would get out of that place alive."

CHAPTER 44

Arrival at the hotel felt malapropos. Incongruous. Both numb, neither James nor Rose knew what to say or do after checking into their room. They were still in shock, and it would take time to digest what had just happened, despite having known, and even planned, that this day would come.

James went back to the lobby to fetch two bottles of Coke. A disheveled teenager approached him, asking if he could spare some change, hitting him with another wave of melancholy as it evoked thoughts of Liam. He gave the lad what he had; the kid rejoined his younger brother and sister, parents nowhere in sight.

Back in the room, Rose was sitting on the sofa, eyes welling with tears. James handed her the Coca-Cola. "Drink it, love," he said, putting the bottle in her hand.

She took a sip. "Thank you."

He sat down and put his arm around her, and for a moment they just sat there, drinking their sodas in silence.

When they were finished, Rose stepped out of her shoes, hung her jacket in the closet, and looked around the room. "This is our new home for a while."

"Yes, at least until I get things smoothed out," he said. "You all right staying here? Might be a few months."

She took in the green carpet, the blue velvet furniture, and the pinup photos on the wall of wartime beauties. Such a stark contrast to the Danish-style farmhouse at Sugar Alexandria, with the beautiful multicolored Tiffany-styled kerosene lamps, the reddish-brown Tasmanian oak floors, and the unique, handmade furniture—an ode to the Viking era. She thought of her paintings that adorned the walls in the house—another extreme diver-gence from those in the room—and her lovely renovated windmill she inhab-ited for three years. And of course, she thought of little Anna, with her bright smile and cherub face that always beamed when she looked up at her. Strangely enough, it felt like Anna should be with them. "It's actually quite nice," she said, her face bereft of joy. "Under different circumstances, I would love being here with you and Joshua."

James kissed baby Joshua good night and guided Rose to the bed. They crawled under the clean sheets; Rose wept on his chest until sleep found her.

⁓ɔ꠱ɔ⁓

The following morning, James and Rose woke up feeling like outlaws. It was the day after Armageddon, and they had survived. Upon showering and getting dressed, they went downstairs to the hotel diner. They were in a new city, far away from Sugar Alexandria where nobody knew them, and to any onlooker, they were just a regular family having breakfast in an eatery.

As they sat in the booth, still feeling the tremors of yesterday, the wait-ress brought their food, but they found they had little appetite, both blankly numb. A conspicuous woman walked into the diner, looking at them a little too long, making the couple wonder if they had been recognized. Fortu-nately, however, the woman looked away and joined her cobbers at another table.

James read Rose's mind. "We're in the city, hours away from Esperance. You can relax, love."

"For a minute, I thought she knew us."

"I know. But to everyone here, I'm not Anna's husband, and you're not her cousin. We're just a couple eating brekkie with our son." He turned his attention to his eggs and toast, forcing himself to eat.

"I just keep thinking about what happened," Rose said. "I keep thinking about Anna."

"She's being taken care of at the hospital; they'll give her the help she needs. Next week, when things calm down, I'll go visit her."

"I feel like we should go see her now . . . Or go see a priest . . . Some-thing."

"Seeing her now is out of the question," James said, taking a drink of his coffee.

422

"But how can we just go on while she's in there? We need to . . ."

"There's nothing we can do for her."

"I wish I could tell her everything will be all right. I wish I could hold her; talk to her. Anna and I always talked about everything."

"Rose, after what she just did . . ."

"I know . . . She got so enraged. Taking the baby, even. James, how could she change so much? She turned into a monster. She could have killed Joshua."

"And you too." James thought of when Anna had killed before, and a mix of guilt and shame washed over him. To a certain degree, he himself was responsible for that person's death by protecting Anna from her actions. But not this time. Not ever again.

"That wasn't Anna, James." Rose took a sip from her coffee. "Something else went inside her."

"No, it was her. That was just the part of her she hides. The part of her both of us tried to appease for far too long."

Rose's eyes dusted the restaurant—people coming and going, eating and talking, cars passing by outside the large window of the diner. Life continued on, unabashed. "It still feels so surreal to me," she said. "A tragedy has taken place, yet everything keeps moving forward as if nothing has happened."

"I know it feels chaotic right now. But try to relax; the worst is over. Eat your brekkie, love."

She took another sip of her coffee. "She was talking so crazy, too, thinking she was her mother, and then her sister. I pray the doctors help her now."

"They will. And as I said, I'll visit her next week and make sure she's all right."

❧

Anna heard the doctors talking to each other as they examined her, reading the admissions paperwork and taking notes as they discussed what they knew and what they suspected . . .

Emotional breakdown.

Psychotic episode.

Mood disorder.

Obsessive-compulsive disorder.

Schizophrenia.

Multiple personality disorder
Other unknown mental issues.
"Stop talking about me!" Anna screamed.
"Leave my sister alone!" Blessing shouted.
"Please help my daughter!" Elsa pleaded.
All from Anna's mouth as the nurse sedated her.

The Voices

"They have me locked up in a room," Anna says the next morning, "with my arms strapped to my body." She is having a conversation with her mother and sister, both now in the room with her, their voices in her head manifesting out loud through her. "It's floor-to-ceiling white, and the walls are padded. They keep me drugged up, too, and they're always watching me."

"Well what did you expect, dear?" says Elsa. "You tried to kill your cousin and almost threw her baby into a fire."

"I didn't mean to, Mummy. James and Rose abandoned me, and I lost all control of who I am."

"I tried to warn you, but you wouldn't listen."

"All she was trying to do was give Rose what she wanted," Blessing says, defending Anna.

"Don't worry, Turtle Dove. Your sister and I are here, and always will be."

"That's right," Blessing chirps. "James and Rose have left you; we never will."

"Ta, Mummy. Ta, Blessing," Anna says, hanging her head down and crying. "I have lost everything, but at least I have you."

"Who are you talking to, Anna?" a male doctor asks. He and another female doctor have entered the room without Anna noticing.

"My sister and my mother."

"Are they here with us?"

"Yes, I'm right here," says Anna in her mother's voice.

"Me too," says Blessing, again through Anna.

"How often do they visit you like this?"

"Whenever I need someone to talk to."

"I see." Both doctors look at each other, the female doctor taking notes. "Can I talk to them?"

"Sure. My mum's name is Elsa; my sister is Blessing."

"How are you today, Blessing?"

"I'm frightened," Anna says in a little girl's voice, speaking as her five-year-old twin sister. "I don't know where I am, and I'm scared."

"How about you, Elsa? Do you know why you're here?"

"Bloody oath, I do," says Anna, now speaking as her angry mother. "I tried to kill that harlot for what she did to my daughter, along with that bastard child she gave birth to." Her face distorts into a meshuga glower. "Can you believe that tart is trying to steal her bloke? I won't stand for it. Any decent mother would do the same thing. I was just protecting my daughter, and I would do it again!"

The doctors exchange looks. "And how do *you* feel about all this, Anna? Do you remember what happened?"

"I just want to go home," Anna sobs. "James, where are you? Sugar Bear, please, where are you?"

❦

Anna awoke the following day with a profound desiderate to run to Cassandra Fancy's garden. To lay among the surfeit of stunning flowers and stare up at the azure blue sky. Instead, she found herself in another small, dimly lit room, still heavily sedated, staring at the wall. Her straitjacket had been removed, but the door was locked. As the medication slowly wore off, she became aware of what had happened and why she was there—James and Rose had left her. Her husband no longer wanted her, and her best friend and cousin would no longer be living at Sugar Alexandria with her. Everything she knew was gone.

Her life had crumbled overnight.

Crushing her eyes shut, Anna moaned in pain over what she had done. "Mummy!" she screamed. "Mummy, I need you now!" Her scream ricocheted off the walls and absorbed back into her own skin, making her body shake.

Thoughts began to sail through her mind of lying next to James, feeling the warmth of his body, making him breakfast in the morning, and running the station together as a married couple. All those things were over now.

"James," she sobbed into her pillow, "please come back!" As she cried out to the white walls that confined her, she recalled the many times she had pushed him away, ignored his affections, dismissed his interests and music, or simply said an unkind word. She thought of how he would kiss her forehead before bed, and pull her small body into his until their breathing was in sync, hearts beating as one. Or how he would playfully slap her heinie to wake her in the morning. When she'd make him a nice dinner, he'd say, "Thanks a million, love." Too many times to count, she would look out the window and wave to him as he rode by on his horse Ireland, tipping his Akubra hat with a smile. She remembered him holding their twins, barechested, adoringly gazing down into their chubby faces. And she heard his last kind words to her: "Come lay with me, love. I miss your little body next to mine. Lovely Dawn misses you too."

"Oh, Sugar Bear, please come back!" she sobbed again, wringing her hair with her hands, her voice becoming hoarse. And then she felt something . . . The nurses had stripped and searched her for any jewelry or other objects, but they missed a bobby pin that managed to adhere to her scalp. She stopped crying for a moment and stared at the pin while her mind raced. Then she laughed. It was perfect. A mercy had been shown her, allowing her to escape her reality. All she had to do was remove the plastic tip, and the pin would become a weapon.

Her eyes flickered over to the door. No one was coming. As if a rat trying to free itself from a trap, she chewed off the protective plastic on the pin, then without hesitation dug it into her wrist until it bled. It was tough to get through the flesh at first, along with the intense pain that followed, but soon a lightheadedness came over her. She laid back on her bed and stared at the ceiling, waiting to pass out.

As Anna anticipated death, she thought of her cousin Rose, with her green, cat-like eyes and her quiet, yet charming demeanor. She thought of her husband James, always so grounded, so supportive, with his strong moral compass and his unconditional love. Then she imagined the two of them walking together hand in hand, their silhouettes so graceful, so alike. James and Rose kissed, then looked back at her, waving goodbye as the warm blood ran down her arms, pooling alongside her body like a scarlet halo.

"I love you, James. I love you, Rose," she whispered as her life force slowly left her soul . . .

The attendant bringing food and medication finds Anna and runs for help. Two nurses and a doctor immediately flock to her aid, trying to save her life. She fights them; she wants to die. When the needle dispenses its magic, sedation overcomes her like a possession.

She feels nothing.

With her wrists stitched and bound and the medication flowing through her veins, Anna hears someone murmur, "Poor girl. Her husband left her and she has a broken heart." She sees blurry shadows moving about the room and hears voices trailing off, fading into evanescent noises. Sleep finally arrives, as if a rolling wave coming in and taking her far away to sea. A friend to help her forget her suffering . . . Her mistakes . . . Rose.

"She's still not talking," Anna hears a nurse saying later that eve. "And the little she does, she's calling herself Rose Charlotte Moss. Poor thing. Poor, poor thing."

"Look at my eyes," Anna mumbles. "They're green like emeralds. And my skin, fair and smooth. My hair, dark and beautiful like the night sky. It's no wonder Sugar Bear loves me so . . ."

Anna's condition worsens, and she becomes phantasmal, calling herself Rose and demanding everyone else do the same. "Look at me!" she yells. "Look at my green eyes, my ivory skin, my raven hair! My name is Rose, not Anna!" she screams, scratching at her face. "I am beautiful, with shining green eyes! I am Rose, my son is Joshua, and my lover is James!"

The attendants run over, trying to grab her.

"Where's my baby!" Anna screams. "Where's my baby with dark hair and blue eyes! He's mine! Where is he! You have stolen him from me!" Falling to her knees, she sobs into her hands, moaning, "Where's my baby . . . Please give me back my child."

As the attendants subdue her, the nurse gives her another shot.

Anna's body numbs . . . Her mouth drools . . . She sees darkness.

Hours later she awakens, strapped to her bed, the aggressive nurse and attendants still there, demanding Anna properly identify herself.

"What is your name?" the nurse sternly asks, devoid of benevolence and mercy.

"Rose Charlotte Moss," says Anna, still delusional.

"No! That's your relative. Do you want us to take you to the ice room again?"

Anna shakes her head and shivers.

"Then I'll ask you one more time . . . What is your name?"

"What is my name?" Anna repeats, blinking hard.

The nurse doesn't answer.

"What's my name?" she asks again, louder, trying to reclaim her identity. Faint memories flash through her mind of Rose calling out to her in Cassandra Fancy's garden, and James calling her to come lie next to him in bed. Yet still her own name escapes her.

"What's my name!" Anna screams, trying to break free.

The nurse shakes her head; the attendants tighten her straps; they all leave the room.

"Anna May Shahan," she finally says to the walls, sobbing and sobbing as she remembers. "My name is Anna May Shahan."

⁓ᦂ⁓

James went to the hotel lobby and called the hospital to see how Anna was doing and let them know where he was staying. The receptionist put him straight through to Dr. Anderson, Chief Physician of Psychiatry, who wanted to get some background information on their new patient.

"How is she?" James asked.

"Right now she's sedated and sleeping," Dr. Anderson said. He opened Anna's file on his desk. "There's much we still need to observe and evaluate on your wife's condition, Mr. Shahan. Do you mind if I ask you a few questions about her past behavior? It would help."

"Of course."

They conversed at length about Anna's symptoms and odd proclivities over the years, with James relating in detail everything abnormal he had witnessed her say and do. He told the doctor all about her hallucinations—the woman dressed in black Victorian clothing, the Black Shuck, the bloodied man, the mysterious shadow people, the sudden bugs—and he described Anna's bizarre shrine she had made for her deceased mother and sister, along with her goose-feathered crown and wings. He related how Anna would talk to Elsa and Blessing and even talk as if she were them when she got angry, and how she would sometimes see them. It surprised James how composed he was as he spoke, listing off his wife's aberrant behaviors as if they were benign trivialities, having to deal with them for so long. But he wanted to give the doctor a clear and complete picture so they would be better able to help her.

"What do you think, Dr. Anderson? Have you seen people like Anna before? Will you be able to help her?"

The doctor paused. "I have treated many different patients and a variety of mental illnesses in my career, Mr. Shahan. Some have been so severe they never leave the hospital, while others improve and learn how to cope with it, despite the struggle."

"And where would you put Anna on that spectrum?"

"It's too early to tell. We just don't know right now. I'll be honest with you, though: In most cases like Anna's, the prognosis isn't good. It tends to get worse over time."

"But she was living a relativity normal life up till now."

"Was she, though? All these extraordinary behaviors, hallucinations, and other oddities say otherwise. You did an exceptional job managing it, but normal is not how I'd characterize this. Had your wife been with a less understanding and patient man, I don't think she'd have lasted as long as she did in the outside world. She'd likely have ended up here much sooner."

James appreciated the acknowledgment, thinking of the years he had tried carving out a normal life with Anna, ignoring her strange vagaries, catering to her ailments, sacrificing most of his own identity in the process. Once you're married, however, it's in sickness and in health. That is what he had been taught, what he believed, and what he lived.

"I'm going to assign Anna to a specialist here named Dr. Octavia," said Dr. Anderson. "She's incredibly knowledgeable on illnesses like this, and she's had a great deal of success with a number of other patients exhibiting similar behaviors. With some unique one-on-one treatment that Anna wouldn't get elsewhere, I'm confident Dr. Octavia will be able to help her too."

"Ta, Dr. Anderson."

The doctor closed Anna's file. "Mr. Shahan, thank you for the information you provided; it's been most helpful. I do, however, have to tell you some bad news . . . A few days ago, Anna attempted suicide."

Silence . . .

"Mr. Shahan, you there?"

"How?"

"She slit her wrists with a sharp bobby pin she had in her hair."

Again, silence . . .

"Mr. Shahan, are you still on the phone?"

"Yes. Please tell me she's all right."

"She's stable."

James paused. "Thank God. Please keep me notified of any changes, or if there's anything I can do."

"Of course. I'll connect you back to the receptionist so you can give us your contact information."

As James hung up the phone, he felt nauseated, his knees threatening to buckle. He chose not to tell Rose–it would greatly upset her–and immediately dialed his sister's number to break the news of everything that had happened over the last three years. Christian would want to know.

The phone rang several times. "Flame Tree Grill. Josephine speaking."

James took a deep breath "Hey sis, it's me." He clenched the telephone receiver. "Sit down. I have to tell you a few things . . ."

⚜

Anna is awake again, screaming. The bugs are everywhere. "Get them off me!" she cries out. "Where are they all coming from!" Frenetically she scratches at her skin–there are so many she can't keep them off–and soon she has ripped the bandages from her wrists.

"Hold her down before she rips out her stitches too," the nurse says to the male attendant, preparing the needle.

"Get them off me!" Anna continues to scream. "Get them off me! Oh God, why are there so many!"

The syringe administers its alchemy. Anna goes catatonic. The nurse redresses her wrists.

⚜

When Anna roused, she found herself robed in a housecoat, sitting outside in a wheelchair with the sunshine on her face. Heavily medicated and disoriented, her wrists ached, and she noticed they were bound. "Was I in some kind of accident?" she mumbled incoherently to no one. Confused, her mind wandered as she scanned the garden, and that's when she saw them . . . The shadow people! No longer were they just dark, faceless figures but shape-shifting beings she could clearly see.

Half human, half animal.

Swan people.

Black or white androgynous life forms, faces resembling the elegant aquatic birds within the genus Cygnus, but with human characteristics and bodies. Creepy yet fascinating. Even beautiful. One of the swan people came up to her, curious, inquisitively eyeing the new visitor. Anna almost screamed until she saw it was no threat. The white swan person inspected her head to toe, gracefully examining Anna as if a wonder to behold. Joined by a black one, they both stared at her until one of them spoke in her mind: "We are different beings, yet one and the same," it whispered. Then they all vanished.

Anna kept looking around for more of the creatures, but all she saw was a nurse approaching her. "Where am I?" she slurred, a disquieting sensation running through her body.

"You're at the Pleasant Skies Psychiatric Hospital," said the nurse.

"Why am I here?" asked Anna, her throat sore and hoarse from so much screaming and crying.

"Because you did something you shouldn't have." The nurse handed her a book—*Beowulf*. "Here, this should keep you occupied when you're fully coherent."

Anna stared at the cover and read the title aloud: "Beeeoowuulf."

"That's right. It's a famous Old English poem about a Scandinavian hero who slays the monster Grendel with his bare hands. Later he becomes a king and slays a fierce dragon, but is mortally wounded and dies." The nurse smirked. "Makes us consider the consequences of our choices, aye? We better be sure going into battle is worth it, because it could cost us our life."

Anna tried to process the story's meaning, then remembered why she was at the hospital and started to sob.

Apathetic, the nurse walked off.

When she had no more tears, Anna stared at the book cover again, imagining King Beowulf slaying the monster Grendel and the fierce dragon, then dying. He had won the battle, but suffered a heavy loss and paid with his life. Just like her. She had gotten her way with James giving Rose a baby, but in the process, lost everything. She thought of this until the sun died behind the horizon and the nurse came back, rolling her to her empty room.

Anna

A male patient tried to rape me tonight.
I bit his neck so hard he ran from my room, bleeding profusely.
They blamed me for attacking him and strapped me to my bed again.
I begged Genevieve to help me, to release me, to save me.
But all she did was pet the Black Shuck, and tell me she had tried to warn
me.

Shock therapy treatments came next for Anna, followed by hydrotherapy with ice water.

"Anna, bite down on the mouthpiece," the administering doctor ordered.

"Please don't do this to me again," she cried. "I'll be good; I promise." Anna tried to kick with her legs and pull away as the nurses strapped her in. "James, save me! Please save me!" she begged.

"Bite down, I said."

Closing her eyes, she bit down, just as the physician injected the Cardiazol to artificially induce the convulsions. A feeling of parlous terror enveloped her like a blanket–it happened every time–and moments later her small body began to shake violently. Uncontrollably. One nurse held her head against the pillow, another her thin arms, the third her tiny ankles. Still conscious and in pain, all she could do was wait for it to stop. For the relief to come when it was over.

"You must hate me, to do this!" she screamed.

The nurses gave no response. When finished, they mummified her in towels soaked in ice-cold water—another novel therapy that seemed more like punishment than panacea.

Anna thought of God: Is he watching this? Does he see what they are doing to me? Is he disciplining me because of what I have done, and what I allowed? "God has forgotten me!" she laughed deliriously. "He has forgotten my name!"

Anna

I broke out of my room and ran down the hallway, screaming for help.
"Where do I run to escape?" I begged one of the patients.
"You're in hell, doll. There is no place to run."

That very night is when the nightmares begin. Nightmares of witches trying to convince her to cross a broken bridge with snakes hissing at the bottom. Monsters lurching at her. Half dragon, half lion, snarling, teeth showing, seeking to consume her.

Hallucinations of a pack of Black Shucks appear at the end of her bed, with shiny black fur and glowing, bloodred eyes. They only stare at her, perhaps feeling pity, curiosity, or even gratification. Over the centuries from creation onward, the immortal beasts have witnessed the lives of all. Anna's is just another pearl, dropped into the abyss of flawed human existence.

Does seeing her suffer remind them of Eve? Eve's forbidden fruit was rebellion; Anna's forbidden fruit was Rose. And now the taste is rancorous. The sustenance, poison.

"All I wanted was to make her happy," Anna murmurs in and out of consciousness. "All I wanted was the love I never had from my mum and sister."

Ghostlike images continue to flash in front of her: Genevieve's face with Rose's eyes. Anna's twin sister, Blessing, grown and searching for her in Cassandra Fancy's garden. Her mother Elsa, frantically calling for her. Sugar Alexandria on fire, burning to the ground. She can hear baby Joshua crying and crying and crying, until she realizes it is she herself sobbing. Then the

Australian wind blows in her mind, taking pieces of her with it. I will only be bones soon, she thinks . . .

The wind will only leave my bones.

Genevieve

"Wipe your runny nose and be a big girl," the woman in the black Victorian dress bids the next morning, sitting on the corner of the bed.

Anna's eyes grow bright, always so grateful to see her lifelong companion. "I'm so afraid, Genevieve."

"Don't be, Sweet Pea. Like Yarra always says, you're a little Aussie battler. So straighten up and get ahold of yourself. You'll be home at Sugar Alexandria in no time."

"Anna, you need to dress and get ready," a nurse said, entering her room.

"Why?"

"You're being taken to the courthouse at ten o'clock." The nurse looked at her wristwatch. "That's an hour from now."

Anna rolled over in bed. "But I'm too weak, and I'm still recovering." She flashed her palms, displaying her bandaged wrists. "I'm in no condition to travel anywhere."

The nurse was not dissuaded. "Get up, take your medication, and get ready to go."

Anna did as she said, and an hour later an officer appeared, handcuffing and escorting her to the waiting patrol car.

As they drove to their destination, Anna pressed her forehead against the cool glass, staring out the window at the scenery passing by. Soon they were at the courthouse, and the officer led her into a courtroom, sitting her down in a boxed-in section for the accused. Scared and alone, she stared straight ahead. Yet she could feel something. A presence. Looking over her shoulder, she saw the swan people sitting at the back of the room, impeccably dressed in suits and ties, gazing at her with curiosity and intense interest over her fate. Genevieve, her mother and sister, and the bloodied man were there too, all awaiting to hear her sentence for what she had done.

The Honorable Chief Justice Sir Gerard Columcille emerged from his chambers. Sitting down on his imposing bench, he glanced up at Anna only once as he read the doctor's transcript. "Crikey, hard to believe such a small woman could be such trouble," he muttered to himself.

Anna heard him. "But it wasn't me who did any of those things!" she pleaded. "My mum and sister did! Ask them—they're sitting right over there!" she beseeched, pointing at Elsa and Blessing, both smirking. "Ask them!"

The judge ignored her.

A low murmur of excitement flooded the room, and Anna turned around to see James walk into the courtroom, hat in hand. She started to cry. "James, tell them it wasn't me!" she begged. "Tell them about Mummy and Blessing!"

"Your Honor, my wife's not well," James explained, deferentially approaching the bench. "She can't be held responsible for her actions because she's mentally ill."

The judge looked up from the transcript again, annoyed at James' lack of protocol. "From this moment onward, you'll address me as Your Honorable Chief Justice. Now sit down, Mr. Shahan. And speak only when spoken to."

James nodded and sat down in one of the front row seats.

"I read what happened," the judge said. "Pretty vicious attack on Miss Moss and her infant child. She came close to killing them both."

James remained silent, fearful the judge would be harsh.

"I also read what was going on at Sugar Alexandria," he continued, his eyes slowly moving back and forth between husband and wife. "Outrageous and perverse conduct."

The public who had shown up to watch the hearing began whispering behind James' back.

"You know, son, there are civilized laws in this country that are made for a reason. They're for the common good of all, and they apply to everyone—no exceptions." He looked disgusted. "Were you living in a polygamist relationship?"

"No," James answered. "I mean, yes. Well, not entirely. My relationship with my wife's cousin was originally only meant to give her a child."

A susurrus of shock ran through the crowd as people gasped.

"I should throw all three of you in jail for being so morally corrupt," the judge said, exchanging glances of disbelief with the bailiff.

James only stared down at the floor, holding tightly on to his hat. In that moment he recalled warning Anna of the trouble it could cause if they followed through with her verboten plan, having no idea just how disastrous it would become.

"Whose idea was it to allow such scandalous behavior?" the judge questioned. "What impoverished wisdom conceived this filth?"

"Your Honorable Chief Justice, my wife was only trying to facilitate her cousin having a baby."

"Why didn't she find a bloke of her own?"

Knowing the judge already had a preconceived moral verdict, James attempted to appeal to his empathetic side. "Because Rose has some physical deformities which made it . . . difficult for her."

"Such as?"

"She was born with a birth defect where the muscles in her leg are severely underdeveloped. She can walk, but not very far without her cane."

"So you both took pity on Miss Moss—is that it?"

James didn't reply.

"Mr. Shahan, you and your wife are a very unusual couple. I don't know what to think of these immoral misgivings; this promiscuous, unlawful behavior; but I find it abhorrent and appalling. And if this was your wife's idea, why in the good Lord's name did you go along with it?"

James looked over at Anna. He didn't want to say he was forced, or tricked, so he took the blame upon himself. "Because I love both women and wanted to make them happy."

The public gallery went wild with chaos, people standing and shouting and shaking their fists in self-righteous fury.

"Silence!" the judge bellowed, hammering his gavel on the desk. "There will be no disorder in my courtroom!"

The room quieted.

"Your Honorable Chief Justice," James pleaded, "when she found out that I had continued the infidelity with her cousin beyond that one night, she temporarily lost her sense of reality. That's why she acted out in a fit of rage."

"People get mad all the time. Doesn't give you license to attack someone with a knife," the judge rebuffed, "or threaten to throw a baby into a fire."

The small crowd of spectators gasped again.

"I beg of you, please be lenient with her. Don't sentence her to jail. No one was seriously injured, and prison would destroy her. We also have two three-year-old daughters who need their mother, and my wife owns a cattle station outside of Esperance that will not function for long if she is incarcerated. Please allow her to remain in the custody of the hospital until she gets well. They can give her the help she needs."

"James . . . ," Anna said, her eyes appearing wild like a trapped, injured animal. "Tell them it wasn't me."

He turned to his wife. "Anna, it *was* you. You attacked Rose and the baby." Never again would he lie to protect her from her own egregious actions.

"No! No! No!"

"Anna, stop. Just stop talking," he said, inwardly praying the judge would show her mercy and compassion.

The Honorable Chief Justice tapped his finger on the desk, adjudicating. "That child she threatened to harm—it's yours, I assume?"

James nodded.

"Son, you have gotten yourself into one nasty hornet's nest," he chuckled. The bailiff quietly laughed as well, and the audience either shared in their amusement or scowled at the morally debased man being questioned before them. Several people yelled out, "Adulterer! You're going straight to hell!"

The judge threw down his gavel again, and the room once more went silent. "Any more bloody outbursts from the gallery, and I'll have you all removed from my court." Turning his attention back to James, he asked, "Do you regret having an affair with this . . . ," looking down at the paperwork, "Ambrosia Charlotte Moss?"

James hesitated, not wanting to respond. He didn't want to further upset Anna.

"And will you and your wife try to reconcile once this matter is resolved?"

Again, no response.

"Mr. Shahan, you do understand you're in a court of law, aye? When I ask you a question, you are to answer it to the best of your ability without delay."

"No, I do not regret my relationship with Rose," James finally said. "I love her, and I love our newborn son, just as I love my daughters with my wife."

"Which woman will you be continuing a domestic relationship with?"

"I'd rather not say."

"Answer the question."

James touched his beard, thinking before speaking. Taking a deep breath, he said, "I'll be marrying Rose as soon as my divorce is granted."

A flurry of murmuring stirred up among the crowd again, and for a third time the judge slammed down his gavel, regaining control of his courtroom. He looked over at Anna, slumped in her chair, tears running down her cheeks. "Do you have anything to say for yourself, young lady?" he asked.

Anna began to cry.

"Reading over the doctor's notes, I see you're suffering from a few forms of mental illness, and from the recent event, experienced a severe psychotic episode. Nevertheless, the act was still reprehensible—attempted murder of a new mother and her child. You should be held accountable, regardless." The older man's eyes danced back and forth between James and Anna, pondering on a wise and just decision over Anna's atonement. "We'll recess until 1 p.m.," he said, "at which time I will render my decision."

As the judge stood up to return to his chambers, Anna found her voice again. "James," she said, fighting the effects of the medication to call out his name.

He turned to look at her, pain in his eyes, seeing her suffer. "Yes, Anna?"

"James, help me . . ." She showed him her handcuffs, and as she tried to stand, she stumbled and fell to the floor, screaming, thrashing about on the ground, wailing uncontrollably, "What have I done! What have I done! James, help me!"

He attempted to run to her, but one of the guards held him back. "Let me go!" he yelled.

"What have I done, James! I tried to kill Rose and Joshua!" she screamed in a moment of clarity. "How could I do that! God help me!" she cried out.

The judge, remaining still, observed with consternation as this young woman sobbed and wailed before him, scratching at her own face, pounding at her own body, as if to inflict her own punishment.

James bit down on his knuckles and helplessly watched as the other guard held down his hysterical wife while an attendant from the hospital gave her a shot. Slowly she subdued as the medication took effect, all the while calling out James' name.

⤞⧽✦⧼⤝

The townsfolk spew vitriol and fire at Anna as she is removed from the courtroom . . .

Criminal!
Scandalous!
Uncivilized!
Dastardly!
Abomination!
Witch!

⤞⧽✦⧼⤝

Anna was declared mentally unfit for trial and deemed not criminally responsible for her actions. Overnight, it was done. She would be held at the Pleasant Skies Psychiatric Hospital for evaluation and treatment until further notice.

James drove back to the hotel in a daze. Almost fourteen years later, it was really finally over, and he could now seek a divorce. The asperities of a life he did not want, shackled to the land, were rescinded; and the responsibilities of taking care of a mentally ill wife, who tricked him into marriage, were now in the hands of an institution. He was free to go on with life. His life, not Anna's.

In a miraculous and dramatic twist of fate, the pianist and teacher was no longer imprisoned by the grazier.

The keymaster had finally been found.

"She was committed to the hospital indefinitely," James said as he walked into the hotel room, taking off his fedora and tie. "There'll be no jail time or any more court dates. The judge could clearly see she is unwell. It's over."

Rose walked into his embrace and laid her head against his chest but said nothing. Breathing a modicum of relief, she was indeed thankful it was over. Yet she could not stop seeing Anna stabbing at her with a knife, and holding her baby over a fire, threatening to throw him in.

CHAPTER 45

"I'm here to see Anna Shahan," James said. It had been several days since Anna was committed to the mental hospital, and Dr. Anderson had finally told him he could visit his wife.

"One moment, please," the nurse replied. After checking her list, she buzzed him in.

James walked into the mental health facility, holding his hat in his hands while he followed the nurse to Anna's room. The atmosphere of the place unnerved him, and he was not prepared for what he would find. Thinking at first that his wife was peacefully sleeping, he quickly realized she was heavily sedated and strapped to the bed. "Anna," he softly said, stroking her hair. "It's me, love."

She gave no response.

"Crikey, why is she so drugged?" James asked the nurse. "And why is she strapped in like this?"

"It's a precaution," the nurse answered. "Whenever someone attempts suicide, we have to ensure they don't try to hurt themselves again."

James' heart dropped.

The nurse leaned over and gently shook her awake. "Anna, your husband is here."

She slowly opened her eyes. "James?"

"Yes, love, I'm right here," he replied.

Anna turned to him, her eyes bloodshot and glazed, her lips dry and cracked. She started to cry.

James held her hand.

After a moment, she said, "I know who they are now."

"Who, love?"

"The shadow people."

He exchanged glances with the nurse.

"They're magical beasts. Swans. There are nine of them, James. Nine swan people. I have counted them and there are nine."

"It's the medication," the nurse said.

"Black and white, they are. They follow me everywhere. Rose sent them to protect me."

"That's grouse, love. I bet they're a beauty."

"You know what else?"

"What, love?"

Anna became more animated. "I saw the stars in my eyes yesterday. They shined so brightly, so vivid. Such a beauty of a scene." Excitement started bubbling up in her as she slurred her words. "I flew into the night sky and met the sheila on the moon who makes them out of diamonds. She told me secrets and gave me a map to a treasure of souls. You want to come with me to meet her? We'll collect stardust on the way and sprinkle it on the suffering. We'll sprinkle it on Rose and Joshua, on Mummy and Blessing."

"Sure, Anna. If you want me to go with you, I will," he said, alarmed and afraid for his wife, choking back tears. "As soon as you're better."

"We'll take Ireland and ride in the carriage to where we need to go. Rose will be our guide through the constellations, and Yarra and the girls will join us. We'll all live up in the sky with the stars."

James nodded. He too wanted to cry.

Anna began to laugh through her tears, looking up into the bright light that hung above her bed. "We'll all go to the heavens and live there forever and ever and ever, where no wickedness, greed, or evil will ever touch us." Her laughter turned to cackling, sounding like a crow in distress.

James only stared at her, horrified and shocked at the sight of his wife and what she had become.

❧⚜☙

Before leaving the psychiatric hospital, James went to speak to Dr. Anderson.

"Mr. Shahan, after a thorough evaluation of your wife, we have come to the conclusion that she has a condition called schizophrenia, along with sporadic multiple personality disorder triggered as a coping mechanism to disconnect from stressful or traumatic situations. Both are mental illnesses, and we don't know what causes them. There appears to be some other personality disorder she suffers from as well, with respect to normal social interactions, but we don't have a formal diagnosis for it."

"All these years of her whispering and hallucinations, her tantrums and odd behaviors, you're saying are from these ailments?"

"Yes. She was clearly struggling, but also likely hiding the extent of her illness. I suspect what recently happened between you and her, combined with these underlying conditions, triggered the psychotic episode she suffered."

"Will she get better?"

"There's no cure for this, Mr. Shahan."

"Will she get worse?"

"Like I said during our initial conversation, we're not sure. Every case is different."

"What are you doing to help her?"

"Dr. Octavia will be trying different therapies and medications, hoping to gain control of it. But there are no guarantees."

"Ta, Dr. Anderson. I always knew there was something wrong; at least I have some answers now."

"Yes. We'll keep you informed on her progress."

James got up to leave. After seeing the piteous state Anna was in, and hearing the doctor's prognosis, the travail on his face was palpable.

"Mr. Shahan . . . ," Dr. Anderson said when James was at the door.

He looked back at him.

"This isn't your fault, mate. These illnesses are hereditary, and Anna's psychotic episode was bound to happen sooner or later."

"I should have gotten her the help she needed before this," James said, disappointed in himself. "Instead of catering to it, I should have fought for her to get help."

"Well, Anna is where she belongs now."

~⁂~

Sitting in his Ford Model T outside the mental hospital, James is unaware of the time passing by. He is traumatized by what he has witnessed, unable to shake the images in his head, still seeing Anna strapped to her bed, heavily sedated, crying, mumbling incoherently and slurring her words as she spoke of an Elysian ignis fatuus. Who is the woman I just saw, he asks himself? What have they done to Anna?

What have *I* done to her?

"The next visit will be better," the nurse had reassured. But will it? What if she remains this way?

With trembling hand, he lights a cigarette and wonders what will befall his soon-to-be ex-wife. She could remain committed in this mental institute for years. Perhaps even decades.

Rose had left her scarf on the seat next to him, and he grabs it to wipe the tears from his eyes. The sweet smell of her scent evaporates his moment of despair, and his deportment transforms to resolute. The truth is he was never in love with Anna, not the way a husband should be and the way a wife deserves. Though contrite about Anna's current condition, saddened and concerned for her well-being, he has no regrets about the end of a marriage he never wanted from the beginning.

No matter what, I'll make sure Anna is taken care of, he promises. Then he thinks of the woman waiting for him, their son she holds, and their unborn child she carries. But I still have to go on with my life, his internal dialogue continues, and I'll be doing that with Rose.

✧

James stopped at the grocery store to pick up a few things on the way home. He then went to a jeweler and sold the solid gold watch his grandfather had given him, using the money to buy something very special—a wedding ring for Rose.

Notwithstanding the stressful events beforehand, James noticed how refreshing it was to amble along in town, leisurely enjoying the day, doing as he wished. The harsh work under the blistering sun he had become accustomed to, with Anna micromanaging his every move, seemed so far away. Now all he had to do was take care of the woman he loved, along with their beautiful baby. The dichotomy between the two worlds was monumental.

When back at the hotel, James found the note Rose had left him and went downstairs to join her and Joshua for dinner. Rose stood and waved when she saw him, and when he got to the booth, he kissed her, almost picking her up off the floor. "I was away from you all day," he said, "and I could barely stand it. Thought about you all the way here."

Rose kissed him back. "Me too."

They scooted into the booth side by side, and he draped his arm around her. Minutes later, the waitress appeared, and they ordered a simple meal of hamburgers, fries, and Cokes.

Rose wanted to know how the visit with Anna went. "How was she, James?"

"It's going to take time, but Anna is a strong woman," was all he said. He wasn't going to share what he had witnessed, nor did he even want to think about it.

Unsatisfied, Rose wanted to know more about her dear cousin, but he stopped her short. "Don't worry, love, she's in good hands. Now tell me about your day."

Rose smiled. "It was wonderful. I put Joshua in the baby carriage, and we went window-shopping. Then we went to the park. A few people commented what a beautiful child he is, with his sterling blue eyes and curled lashes. I told them he has his father's eyes."

James looked over at his son with pride. "The little lad did take after me, aye? But he has your dark hair."

Baby Joshua seemed to know they were talking about him, a mouth full of pink gums showing as he smiled.

A man and his wife walked up to the table. "James Shahan—I knew that was you!" He grabbed James' hand and shook it. "Crikey, haven't seen you since we left Esperance!"

"Killian Kelly, how ya been?" James nervously greeted. "G'day, Mrs. Kelly," he said to the man's wife.

"Bonzer, mate," said Killian. He and his wife looked with curiosity at Rose.

"This is Anna's cousin Rose and her son Joshua."

"Where's Anna?" Mrs. Kelly asked.

"Well, she's aah . . . She's in the hospital right now."

"You don't say," said Killian, a look of genuine concern on his face.

"Is it serious?" Mrs. Kelly asked.

"She'll be all right. She just needs some rest, is all."

"Whatcha doin' all the way out here, anyway?" asked Killian. "Sugar Alexandria is hours away."

"We thought it would be grand to have dinner away from the station for once."

"Kinda far for dinner," he laughed. "You runnin' from the law or somethin'?"

"Nope. Just having dinner," James repeated.

As the conversation continued, Killian could sense the tension growing and decided to take his leave. "Anyhow, we'll let you finish your tucker, aye? Grouse seein' ya again, mate." He tipped his hat at Rose. "Nice to meet you, Miss Rose."

After the couple left, James leaned into Rose and said, "This is why we should leave Straya, not just Esperance. Make a fresh start elsewhere."

"Leave the country? Where would we go?"

"Ireland," said James, a glint in his eye. "It wouldn't be until everything is settled here, but my uncle in Cong is a wealthy bloke from owning one of the finest distilleries in County Galway. I'm sure he'll rent us the cottage he owns, and give me a job too. Once we're situated, I can then pursue my music career again."

"What about Scarlet and Mabel?"

"I can't rip them from the only home they've ever known and drag them halfway across the world right now. It's better I leave them at Sugar Alexandria for the time being. They'll be all right with Yarrajan, who truly is a grandmother to them, and my sister has agreed to take them on the weekends for as long as needed. Besides, I'll come back and visit them when I can."

"You talk like Anna is never getting out."

James thought of the pitiful and wretched state Anna was in when he saw her. "That's a real possibility, Rose. She could end up committed in that psychiatric hospital for the rest of her life, and we need to be prepared for that."

⁓ৎৢ৯⳩৫৶৶⁓

"She's got one of the hypodermic needles!" the nurse shouted, sounding the alarm.

Anna was throwing a tantrum, flipping her bed over and screaming to go home. She had had enough of the Pleasant Skies Psychiatric Hospital, and was more than ready to walk out the door, then walk all the way back to Sugar Alexandria if need be. Since being admitted, she had been subdued and sedated routinely, put through shock therapy, hydrotherapy, and other cruel therapies, and she couldn't take it anymore. This time she would fight back.

"Not again!" she screamed, cornered by the doctors and nurses closing in. "I can't stand when you bloody sedate me! Please, not again!" Suddenly she was keenly aware of what the cattle and sheep must feel when rounded up by the stockmen and ringers, and in that high-stress moment, she felt sorry for each and every one of them.

"Anna, hand the needle to the nurse," one of the doctors said calmly.

"If any of you dirty buggers touches me, I'll stab you!" she yelled, pointing it at them.

"Listen to my voice," said another doctor. "You're in control, Anna. All you have to do is hand over the medication."

Anna remembered what Yarrajan used to say to the chickens she would handpick for dinner, and it seemed apropos. "Which one of you is going down first!"

Sure enough, when a nurse tried to grab her wrist, Anna stabbed and injected her with the needle. Startled, the nurse staggered to the side, caught by one of the attendants.

"Fight them, Sweet Pea!" Genevieve cheered from the doorway. "Fight for your life!"

Anna put up her fists. "That's right! If you want me, you have to fight me!" she screamed.

The doctors grew tired of her antics and gave the order for the male attendants to subjugate her. Quickly she was overpowered and carried to her bed.

"Such rage in such a tiny sheila," the first doctor said to the other.

"As they say, it's not the size of the dog in the fight but the fight in the dog that matters." Both doctors laughed, watching as the attendants right-sided Anna's bed and strapped her down while she swung at the air, cursing and fighting to the end.

"Stop laughing at me!" she screamed, her eyes becoming heavy from the shot they gave her. "Stop laughing at me," slurring her words, sobbing, staring up into the group of medical staff holding her down. "Genevieve!" she cried out. "Please help me! . . . Somebody, please!"

The nurse locked the door as they left, leaving Anna to sleep it off. Struggling to open her eyes, Anna instantly saw the swan people sitting all around her.

Then it happened . . .

Velvety white wings broke through her skin, unfolding like a saffron crocus in the early morn. They spread out across the room, the wingspan so large and heavy the tips touched the walls. On witnessing the nonpareil event, the swan people erupted in a standing ovation, hailing the swan queen in veneration.

Tears flowed down Anna's cheeks. "My husband left me for a sheila with a crook leg," she cried, "but I'm the one with the wings to fly."

CHAPTER 46

Another week passed before James returned to Sugar Alexandria. The drive there was long, and as he traveled the familiar route, he scanned the vast, endless landscape, remembering the night before his wedding to Anna when it seemed as if the Australian red earth would swallow him whole. Ironically, it now felt hospitable and welcoming. Like curtains being drawn to expose a beautiful view.

When he caught sight of Sugar Alexandria, a strange ambience overwhelmed him. He was no longer James Shahan the station owner but a visitor—a man just stopping by another man's home—instead of the head of the household he was only a short time ago.

Yarrajan met him at the door, her dark eyes exuding great dismay, remaining quiet as if she were mute. James understood, knowing the Aboriginal woman had raised Anna from infancy and saw her as her own daughter, whom he had betrayed. He visited with his girls awhile, reassuring them that everything was all right despite their parent's recent absence, and Scarlet and Mabel appeared comforted by their father's presence. Soon they were playing with their toys as if nothing had changed.

Outside, James called the men together to speak to them, explaining the situation in both English and Nukunu, revealing that Anna would be away for a while and Moony would be in charge until her return. The men were nonpartisan, more concerned about keeping their jobs than anything else.

Back inside the farmhouse, James went into his den. That was the room he would escape to when he needed a break from his wife, from his life, and from the disappointment of unrealized dreams. Casting his eyes around the small sanctuary he had created, the sight and smell of his books immediately summoned memories both pleasant and distressing. For close to fourteen years, how many hours had he spent in there, seeking distraction and comfort from his treasured tomes? How many times did he lock the door and become lost in some captivating story or new learning, his books serving as friends, confidantes, mentors, and guardian angels?

Too many to count.

Spinning the copper globe on the corner of the luxurious cherrywood desk, James stared up at the impressive oil painting on the wall depicting a scene from *Moby Dick*. He then gathered some of his and Rose's love letters hidden away, and took only one book off the shelf–*The Time Machine*, by H.G. Wells. Shutting the door behind him, he smiled. Now he too felt as if he had all the time in the world.

Anna

I awake in the middle of the night, my eyes focusing on the clock high on the wall–3 a.m., the witching hour. Is Rose a witch, I wonder? Could this really be?

Brooding over the answer, I visualize her vomiting frogs and spiders, casting spells, and giving James her love potion. How else could this all have happened? James loves me and would never defy me or go against my wishes. What evil thing has taken ahold of my dear husband to betray me? What sinister, vile monster has crawled up inside him and made him leave me?

Then I look into the shadows and see the bloodied man, concealing himself as always. "I've tried being nice to you," I say. "I've tried talking to you. Yet all you do is stalk me." He doesn't answer, so I walk over to him, unafraid. Feeling brave, I poke at his chest where the blood is gushing. I can even smell the maroon liquid. "What is it that you want from me?"

"Please don't kill me," he begs, putting his hands up to protect himself. "Please don't kill me . . ."

There were moments in the mental hospital when total mayhem broke loose. When a patient had to be restrained and the other patients went wild, screaming, hollering, cheering for the person to fight back against their tormentor. Other times an eerie quiet settled in, like a thick brume drifting in from the sea at midnight.

Anna, drenched in sweat from despondency and wretchedness, eyes dark and lost, mouth dry, stared up at the ceiling in her hospital room one morning, ignoring the physician asking her questions.

"You need to start talking to me, Anna," Dr. Octavia said. "I can help you, but you have to tell me what's going on inside."

The doctor wouldn't leave, and after a short while, Anna finally gave in and slowly opened up, like the petals of a morning glory at first sign of light. Dr. Octavia listened carefully, empathetically, diligently taking notes. She cared, and that made Anna open up even more, no longer apprehensive over how crazy she must sound. Before she knew it, she was telling the psychiatrist everything, from the very beginning of her lonely childhood, to the wonderful summers she would spend with Rose, the voices and other hallucinations that became part of her life, and finally, the events that led to that catastrophic day she had her mental breakdown and almost killed two people she dearly loved.

At the end of it all, Anna's shoulders slumped. "What's wrong with me, Dr. Octavia?" she asked. "Honestly, why am I here? What's wrong with me?"

"Several things are at play," the doctor answered, "both cognitive and emotional. We believe the hallucinations you have are due to a condition called schizophrenia, and your intermittent identity dissociation triggered by extreme stress is called multiple personality disorder. A third condition manifests itself where you lack certain social aspects commonly found in others."

"What's that one called?"

"We don't have a name for it yet. It's a developmental disability characterized, in varying degrees, by difficulties in social interactions and relationships, as well as verbal and nonverbal communication and the ability to relate to others."

"I'm a mess, aren't I. A broken egg."

"You've suffered these conditions a long time, Anna, with no medical help. Give yourself some credit."

"It was all James."

"How's that?"

"He was always so understanding and caring. Patient with me, helping me with every crook issue I had."

"Well you're with us now, and we're going to help you in ways your husband could not."

"How?"

"Through therapeutics and medication."

"Will I be like this forever?"

The doctor gave her an honest look. "To some degree, yes. There's no cure, Anna."

Tears streamed down her face again. "Will it get worse?"

"We just don't know right now."

"I could end up never leaving here, aye? Please tell me the truth, Dr. Octavia."

The doctor closed her notebook. "Yes, Anna, there is a possibility of that. It all depends on how well you respond to the treatment protocols we administer."

And with those final, inauspicious words, Anna felt her entire world being swallowed down by the mouths of a minacious monster they called schizophrenia, a looming demon they called multiple personality disorder, and a concealed rapscallion yet to be named.

The Voices

The incantations come and go. First lightly, then violently, as real as hands grabbing her, pulling her into the abyss. "Anna, talk to us . . . Anna, talk to us . . . Anna, I said talk to us! Now!"

"I . . . I . . . I can't!"

"We miss you, Anna. Come talk to us." The voices begin to blend together, sounding instrumental in tone. Like numerous fairies speaking to her.

"Leave me alone! You're not real!"

"Anna, we love you."

"The medication will kick in soon, and when it does, you'll go back to where you came from. And good riddance! You have only caused me to be crook in the worst way."

"Anna . . . Anna . . . Anna . . . ," the voices keep chanting, only to drift into nothing.

She covers her ears and waits, begging them to leave her in peace. But then she hears Genevieve, whispering to her. Anna uncovers her ears. "What, Genevieve? What did you say?"

"Would you like me to read you a book, Sweet Pea? *The Secret Garden*, perhaps?"

Anna thinks of her cherished story. Rose, with her impaired leg, is like crippled Colin Craven who recovers in the garden, his legs remaining weak from long disuse. Liam, with his good nature and kind way toward animals, is like affable Dickon Sowerby. And she herself is Martha Lennox, whose mother died when she was young, just like hers. "Rose, Liam, and I used to play in Cassandra's garden, just like the children in that book," she says, her eyes welling with tears. "Our friendship was just as special."

"I know, dear," Genevieve replies, sitting beside Anna on the bed, opening the book.

"And when Rose returned to Sugar Alexandria, so did the magic of the garden."

"Yes, love."

With sincere, glossy eyes, Anna looks at the woman from the 1800s in the black Victorian dress. "I'm not supposed to talk to you, though. I've been told you're not real. But just for tonight, go ahead and read it to me, Genevieve. What could it hurt?"

Anna

D r. Octavia asked me if the hallucinations are still bothering me, now that I've been on the medication for a while. I told her they sometimes still do. She said to be patient, that eventually they will subside; and if not, she will change the dosage. Do I want them gone? No more conversations with Mummy and Blessing? Or Genevieve? If they disappear, whom else can I confide in?

No one–I am alone.

Everyone I love is gone.

I wish I were dead.

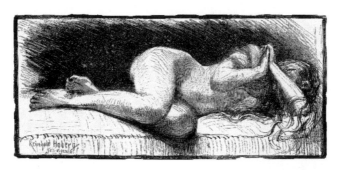

CHAPTER 47

A few weeks had passed. It surprised Rose how easily she and James had adjusted to their new world. Though their daily activities were simple—eating at the diner; strolling down the street, window-shopping; or driving through the city, sightseeing—it felt comfortable. It felt right. As if they had been together all along.

"Dadda!" Joshua chirped in his high chair.

James and Rose looked at each other. They were downstairs having dinner in the hotel restaurant again.

"Dadda! Dadda!" he repeated, kicking in his seat while reaching for his father.

James lifted him out of the chair and sat him on his knee. The baby kicked his legs again, happily smiling at him. "First time my son called me Dadda," James proudly announced, kissing the top of Joshua's head.

Rose smiled.

He pulled out a stuffed Dalmatian for his son, handing it to him. "Bought this in town earlier."

Joshua grabbed the toy and snuggled it close.

James put him back in his high chair and revealed a small box in his hand. "And I bought this for you," he said, grinning.

Rose's face lit up. She took the velvet-covered jewelry box and opened it. "Oh my God. James, it's beautiful," she said, staring down at a square-cut emerald on a slender gold band.

"Same color as your eyes, love." He got down on one knee and removed the promise ring he had given her over a decade ago at his sister's wedding, which she now wore on her ring finger. "Ambrosia Charlotte Moss, will you marry me?" he asked, replacing the old ring with the new.

Rose never smiled wider in her life.

"Whaddya say, Charlotte? Wanna give it a go?"

"Yes! Yes! Yes!" she squealed, looking up from the glorious, intricate ring.

The other patrons in the restaurant were watching and cheered in delight. Even the hotel owner was there. "Drinks are on the house tonight!" he yelled out as James and Rose embraced in a long, amorous kiss.

Later that night, with Joshua sleeping soundly, the engaged couple crawled under the cool, crisp sheets. Skin on skin, arms and legs intertwined, they kissed wildly, passionately, making love through the night.

No more hiding.

No more secrets.

No more love triangle.

The future theirs for the taking.

James

Everything in my life is moving, changing.
The cycle is starting over, but this time correcting itself.
First it was too quickly, after I met Anna.
Then it was too slowly, after I married her.
And now it is shifting again, after meeting Rose.
I can feel it.
After waiting over a decade, the liberation is overwhelming.
The excitement intoxicating.
The expectation of what's to come exhilarating.
I am grateful beyond words for a second chance.
A second chance to live the life I choose to live.

James went to visit Anna again. Instead of being in her room, heavily sedated and strapped to her bed, this time she was out in the courtyard of the mental health facility, painting a picture. James saw her from a distance, relief sweeping through his body. She looked good, he thought, considering. Much better than when he last visited.

"Anna," the nurse called out. "Your husband is here to see you."

She turned. As soon as she saw James, she immediately dropped her paintbrush and ran to him, throwing her arms around his neck. "I knew you would come for me!"

"Now Anna, you know that you're going to be here for a while," said the nurse. "This is just a visit."

"Can I have some privacy with her please?" James asked.

The nurse nodded and went back inside the clinic.

"Let's go sit by the garden, love. I saw a bench there," he said, staring at her wrists.

Anna grabbed his hand as they walked. "I'm so rapt to see you, James. And I have so much to tell you. You don't have to work so hard at the station anymore, and you can start teaching piano lessons any time you want."

James only listened.

"I promise life will be grand between us when I get home."

He forced a smile.

"And I know this will be hard for us, but I am sending Rose away. I have thought about it a lot, and it's the right thing to do," she said, tears streaming down her face.

James continued to hold her hand. "I just want you to get healthy, Anna. Don't worry about anything right now; it's going to be all right. Don't think about Rose or the station or anything else; just get better."

Anna stared deep into his crystal blue eyes. "I have missed you so much, Sugar Bear. You're my whole world. I'm sorry what I made you do."

James put his arm around her, and Anna cried on his shoulder until his shirt became damp from her tears. He remained still, allowing her to release her emotions, and they sat like that for a long while as the sun crossed the sky and began to sink below the earth. James was saying goodbye to Anna in his own way. There was no need to be harsh about this, or cruel. It would take time for her to work through. To let him go. He would give her the time she needed to heal.

"Remember when we used to ride on the tractor, and we would find a spot and pash?" she asked.

"I remember."

"I want to do that again. I want to find a beauty of a spot and just enjoy the day—you and me. Have some tucker and some grog, and watch the sunset."

"Sounds grouse, Anna."

"When I get back, I'm going to be the best wife and mum. You'll see."

He simply nodded, gently pulling her head onto his chest.

Before returning to the hotel, James went back to Sugar Alexandria to see his daughters. Yarrajan was a godsend, and he thanked her again for temporarily looking after his girls. He then paid the stockmen and ringers their wages, and checked with Moony how things were going.

Everything was still running smoothly.

Life was pushing forward.

Time stood still for no one.

CHAPTER 48

Anna

I think of the woman I have now allowed myself to hate . . .
Rose.
My beloved cousin who has forsaken me.

"Friendship is a single soul dwelling in two bodies," she had said to me once.

She lied.

Rose wants to be one soul with my husband James, not me.

I think of her hands, as I always do, as I always will. So painfully lovely with her long and slender fingers, flawless oval nail beds, and a pinkness in her fingertips as she plays her violin. I think of the blue veins that carry her blood from those fingertips all the way to her heart. Her shameful, selfish, evil heart.

Does she even have one?

I wonder if when she dies someday, when they open her up, if they'll find a vacant hole there. Maybe her blood only circulates through her body like a river with no beginning and no end, and if she were to be sliced at her extremities, she would bleed out for days, becoming weaker and weaker but never dying.

Unable to die because she is soulless.

James would find her in a pool of blood, flailing about in her own liquid, her white oleander skin saturated in scarlet red, her aqua green eyes all the more vivid and piercing. Then he would finally have regrets, leaving me for a woman who is inhuman.

A snake with no heart or soul.

Genevieve

"I have a secret to tell you," softly whispers in Anna's ear as she lies in bed. "A secret, a secret, a secret . . . ," the voice chants, fading into nothing.

Anna slowly wakes to see beautiful Genevieve standing at the foot of her bed, distraught-looking and pale. The Black Shuck is curled up in a ball, sleeping by her feet. "A secret?" she asks, rubbing her eyes.

"Yes, something they're not telling you."

Anna sits up in bed. "What are they not telling me?"

"That you were born here at Pleasant Skies."

"That's a lie!" Anna shouts, alarmed at what her friend just said.

"You were born here, and you've never known the outside world. Everything in your life, you've imagined. Sugar Alexandria, James, Scarlet and Mabel, Yarrajan, and yes, even your beloved cousin Rose. None of it is real. They are all hallucinations."

"No, that's not true!"

"Yes, Sweet Pea, it is. You created a world within a world to escape your life here in this dark place."

Anna panics. Can this really be so? She knows she does hallucinate at times, but has everything she's ever known and loved been an illusion all along? Running to the locked door, she bangs and bangs for someone to come, screaming, "Help! Somebody help me! Please, I'm losing my mind!"

"What's all the fuss, Anna?" Nurse Fletcher asked, annoyed as she opened the door.

Anna was in a desperate state, terrified at what Genevieve had told her. "Have I lived here my whole life! Have I! Tell me!"

"Calm down, calm down," the nurse said, taking her by the shoulders and leading her back to bed. "You were admitted here not long ago."

"Oh, thank God!" Anna exclaimed, clenching her hands together. "Thank you, God! Thank you!" she kept saying. She got down on her knees at her bedside and prayed. "Please help me, God. Please. My life has become a nightmare, and I don't know what is real anymore. Please have mercy and help me."

Nurse Fletcher pulled Anna up from the floor. "Your nervous system is all worked up, love. Your hallucinations won't go away until you learn how to control yourself. I've been working here long enough to know."

"I'm trying," Anna cried, "but it's so hard."

The nurse had no sympathy. "Quit your whingeing. I've seen much worse than you."

Anna looked up at her.

"That's right, honey. I've seen things in here you wouldn't believe." The nurse gave Anna her daily medication, along with a judgmental scowl. "By the way, I read in your file what happened. What you allowed."

Anna took the small blue and white pills and the cup of water. "What do you mean?"

"Having your own husband do the unspeakable to produce a bastard child for your cousin. You're lucky the townsfolk didn't set your station on fire."

Anna's face grew hot with embarrassment. "That's supposed to be private."

"Nothing's private here, cupcake."

"I have rights. I know I do."

Nurse Fletcher smirked. "The minute you try to slash someone's throat and kill their baby, you lose all your rights."

Anna stared up at the nurse with wide and distrusting eyes, realizing she wasn't the friendly kind. "You don't know the whole story."

"I know enough," the nurse said, folding her chubby arms across her chest, carefully surveying Anna. She was an intimidating woman.

"What is it?" Anna asked.

"Show me your tongue."

"What for?"

"To make sure you took the medication."

Anna stuck out her tongue, feeling childish as she did, just like her twin girls would do to show they had eaten their porridge.

"Good on ya," said the nurse, seeing that Anna had indeed swallowed the pills.

"I don't like the meds. They make me sleepy and nauseated and my mouth gets dry."

Nurse Fletcher walked toward the door. "Doesn't matter much what you like or don't like while you're in here. All that matters is you control yourself and don't hurt someone else again. Try not to be an animal anymore."

"I'm not an animal, and I will be out of here soon."

"Soon, aye?"

"Yes."

The nurse only laughed. She laughed all the way down the hall.

Anna

Genevieve brought me a gift today, apologizing for upsetting me. She gave me a beautiful spider named Eden. The spider weaved her intricate web in the windowsill, and I have fallen in love with my new friend.

How lovely she looks as she spins her silky threads. How peaceful she appears as she sleeps.

I catch bugs for her and drop them in her web, and she waves to me in return.

Eden has given me new hope . . .

"Why are you in here, anyway, love?"

Anna was painting a picture of Cassandra Fancy's garden. She turned to see where the voice was coming from. "Excuse me?"

"You don't look insane to me. Why did they send you here?" An older woman in her late sixties stood before her, with skinny legs, a wide middle, large bug eyes, and reddish hair teased into an incredible updo, giving her an extra six inches of height. She smoked from an opera length cigarette holder and blew the smoke out at Anna.

Anna coughed. "No, I am not insane. I mean . . . I don't think I'm insane. They say I have skizo something, and maybe more than one personality, but the conditions are only triggered through stress. Oh yeah, and apparently I'm not very social. Or something like that."

"Sounds fascinating. The name's Ruby Davis." She extended her hand–wrist limp and palm down–as if Anna should kiss it.

"My name's Anna Shahan."

Ruby walked in a circle around her, scanning her up and down. "How old are you, twenty-five?"

"I'm thirty-two," Anna replied, returning to her painting.

"You look younger. But don't worry, honey; time will fix that."

She just ignored the eccentric woman.

"I killed my husband. That's why I'm in here."

"If you killed your husband, why aren't you in prison?"

Ruby laughed. "Because rich people don't go to prison. Don't you know that?" By all accounts, she should have, but two very important variables worked in her favor. One, she was the richest woman in Kalgoorlie. And two, the judge on the case, unbeknownst to all, had been her good friend for many years.

"Why did you kill him?" Anna asked, unfazed, not taking her eyes off her work.

"He was my seventh husband, and the seventh bloke to cheat on me. I didn't even mean to kill the bloody bastard; I only wanted to shoot him in the leg. But I've never been a good shot."

"Where did you hit him?"

"In the groin. He bled out before the doc got to him," Ruby said, flicking ashes into the wind. "Kinda serves him right, though; don't you think?"

Anna didn't respond.

"When I was young, my mother told me to marry rich. She said life is hard–a rich man will make it easier. But rich men aren't always faithful men."

Anna remained focused on her painting, but something about the older lady intrigued her.

Ruby sat down in a chair nearby and watched Anna paint. After a moment, she tilted her face toward the sun and closed her eyes. "You ever gonna tell me why you're in here? You can trust Mummy Ruby; I'm here to listen."

Anna stopped painting and sat next to her. "My husband told me he's in love with my cousin, who was living with us. When I heard that, I had a breakdown and attacked her with a knife. That's why they put me in here."

Ruby opened her eyes and cackled. "What did you attack *her* for? You should have filleted *him*!"

Anna

I paint the sky to pass the time.
I paint the flowers on the hospital grounds.
I paint the birds I see in the trees.
I paint Sugar Alexandria, and my beautiful daughters.
But I am not an artist.
The paintings look runny, blotchy, a sad representation of what is real.
I wish I could paint as Rose does, where the paintings come to life.
I would paint a heavenly place . . . Cassandra Fancy's garden.
Then step inside and disappear.

CHAPTER 49

"I'm not like the other people in here, Christian. They're all mad," Anna cried, clutching her brother's hands. He had come to visit her and was now about to leave. "They torture me in here, you know." Glancing over at the supervising nurse, she lowered her voice. "They hold me down and inject me with something that feels like I'm being electrocuted, and they wrap me up in ice-cold sheets for hours. If I get upset, they stick me with needles and I go numb."

"Anna, I don't know what to say."

"Say you'll take me with you."

"Love, you know I can't. If I do, they'll send the authorities, and you'll end up back here anyway."

"I'm going to die in this place!"

Christian took her by the shoulders and looked deep into her eyes. *"Be strong,"* he urged in Danish. *"Be strong for those precious daughters of yours. They're waiting for you at home."*

Anna burrowed herself in her brother's embrace. *"Take me with you now!"* she sobbed into his chest. *"I'm begging you!"*

Christian held her tight, and his eyes watered, feeling her pain. He had to fight the adjuration to pick up his little sister's small body and run with it out the door. But he couldn't. Anna had stabbed Rose and threatened the life of an infant; she was lucky not to be in jail.

"I'm so heartbroken," Anna cried, rife with despair.

"Just do as they say, love, and you'll be released soon."

"I shouldn't have forced James to bed her." She clenched her fists, frantically looking up at her brother with wild, crazed eyes. "It was all a mistake. I just wanted to give her a baby so she'd stay. I never once thought they'd both leave me."

Christian took her small hands and kissed them, gently unclenching her fingers. "Don't think about it now. It's spilled milk. Just get better, love."

Again, she pleaded with him to take her home. Again, he said he couldn't.

The nurse reminded them that visiting hours were over. Christian picked up his sister and carried her to her room as she clung to him crying. He laid her on the bed, covered her with a blanket and tenderly kissed her forehead, then turned to leave.

"Look at me," Anna said, tears flowing down her cheeks, her face gaunt, her eyes doleful, her expression desperate, her hair messy, and her frame thin.

Christian observed his once salubrious, lively sister now forlorn and pitiful in appearance.

"Remember me as I was before this. When I was happy and living in a dream," she cried, sure that she was going to die in the institute. "Don't remember me as I am now. Promise me."

"I promise, love," he said, holding back his emotion. Shutting the door behind him, his own tears let loose.

Anna

In my dreams at night, the walls in the hospital are covered with Rose's art. All her paintings are there, and they come alive, each character stepping out of the frame to congregate in the halls of the mental institute, just as they did back at the farmhouse. Oh how lovely it is to visit with everyone in my sleep! Everything makes sense in that moment, and everything is grouse.

I long to see the same paintings when I am awake. To touch them, feel the texture of the canvas, and call the names of those I love to come out again and visit me, as they have so many times before.

Yes, it is a delusional world I live in.

But it gives me comfort and solace.

Even great joy.

And it is all mine.

Mine alone.

"If your bloke left you for another sheila, I don't understand why we can't be together," said Shaun Haven, another patient at the Pleasant Skies Psychiatric Hospital. He had fallen hard for Anna and wanted to marry her.

"I'm a grown sheila in my thirties," Anna replied. "I can't be with someone who's only twenty-three."

"Why not? What difference does age make?"

"A woman doesn't want a boy. She needs a man."

"I'm not a boy."

Anna looked at his pale skin, messy blond hair, blue eyes, and rosy cheeks. "Shaun, you're too young for me," she said. "Besides, this is no place to meet someone you wanna marry."

Tears started running down his face, but he made no noise.

"I'm sorry."

"You don't care for me at all?" he asked, his voice breaking.

"Just because I won't marry you, doesn't mean I don't care for you."

He gazed at her with a face so childlike and innocent. "I wish you loved me like I love you."

"Well I don't, Shaun. I don't love you, and I never will."

"What if I hang myself because you won't marry me?"

Anna's eyes widened with alarm. She slapped him. "Don't you say that! Don't you ever say that! You're going to find a wonderful girl someday who will love and cherish you!"

"I only want you, though."

"You don't want me, Shaun. You deserve way better than me."

He started to cry, burying his head in her chest. Anna allowed him. She rocked back and forth, humming a song that Yarrajan used to sing to her as a child. An old Aboriginal song about love and heartbreak.

The next morning, Anna found Shaun hanging from a ripped bedsheet attached to the back of his door. His eyes were closed, his shirt off, his arms dangling to the sides. Before she even touched his cold skin, Anna knew he was gone, but she frantically undid the makeshift noose anyway, releasing his body to the floor.

Sitting beside him, crying, she promised she would marry him as she shook his limp frame. But he didn't wake up. Then she screamed loudly. The nurses and male attendants ran into the room, pulling her off his body.

"I'll marry you, you stupid boy! I will marry you!" she cried over and over.

The attendants lifted Shaun onto the bed and covered his face with the sheet.

Anna continued to ululate uncontrollably. "I should have agreed to marry him!" she cried out. "But I told him I didn't love him! It's all my fault!"

They didn't listen to her. They only dragged her to her room, giving her a shot to sedate her.

Moments later, the medication worked its magic. "A face with no freckles is like a flower with no bloom," Anna slurred.

The nurse observed Anna's eyes closing. "That's right, love," she said, patting her on the shoulder. "You're a beauty with all those lovely freckles."

***

Late at night, heavily drugged, Anna gets out of bed and wanders the halls of the institute. She finds a pen on the floor and a piece of ripped construction paper and writes a letter to herself . . .

> *Shaun is gone.*
>
> *Another person has left me.*
>
> *As I walk the inside of these dark prison corridors and witness the lunacy here, it scares me. The people frighten me with their madness, their screams, their insanity. Why am I housed with such ones? Then my thoughts turn on me, as if betraying my own soul: Perhaps I am just like them.*
>
> *I look over at my reflection in the window, and my worst fears are confirmed. In my white hospital gown, with my pale face and shadowed eyes, I have become one of them. I press my forehead against the cool glass, and it soothes me. I press my hands against the glass, as well, and once more I am soothed. I remember stabbing my beloved cousin Rose, and instead of remorse, I feel a sense of accomplishment, wishing the knife had gone deeper. Wishing it had avenged my pain. I think of her flesh slicing open, her red blood seeping forth, and I smile.*
>
> *Yes, I belong here.*
>
> *I look over at the other patients trapped in this haunted hell with me—this endless maze—and I believe we are all snakes at the bottom of a hole. When I look up at the sky where the top of the snake hole should be, I indeed see a bright*

light, but it makes me laugh. I laugh until I start crying and fall to my knees. Until the attendants come and drag me to my room. When I look at them, they too are snakes.

Just like me.

The Black Shuck's bloodred eyes glowed in the darkness of Anna's room. "Why are you here?" she asked.

The wolf snarled and growled, baring its razor-sharp teeth. "I am desire incarnate," it replied in Anna's mind.

"Who are you, though?" Anna asked again. "Are you the bloodied man I see?"

The beast let out a bloodcurdling howl. "I am all of you! Each of you are a ravenous wolf who longed for what you could not have!"

"But I killed you," Anna said. "I shot you dead, and James buried you. How can you still visit me if you're dead and buried?"

"Woman, it wasn't me you killed. No, not I."

"Then who?"

"A man. You killed a man, not a wolf. Shot him thrice in cold blood."

"No! That's a lie! You're a bloody liar!" Anna screamed so hard the sound made her teeth ache. Her heart pounded and her mind raced. Did I shoot James, she wondered? Maybe that's why they put me in here. Maybe I shot my husband, and everything else afterward I have imagined. Maybe it's all part of a sick dreamworld I created, just as Genevieve said. "Oh, God! Help me! Please help me!"

CHAPTER 50

A few days after Shaun Haven's death, the hopelessness of her situation cut into Anna. Deep, like the edge of a razor blade against the softest of skin. And not just over Shaun, but everything. She had tried her best to pull herself from the heartache, yet found she was prostrated.

Ruby had given her a pair of dull scissors she had stolen from the front desk—"For protection against the male trolls with clammy hands," she said—and Anna retrieved them from the hiding spot in her room. She went crazy with the secateurs and started chopping off her locks erratically. It looked terrible. Different lengths; tufts sticking up; one side cropped more shambolic than the other.

Running her hands through her sheared hair, she felt as if she had hit the true depths of despair. Desperately she tried to remember the things that made her happy: Her daughters, life on the station, her friendship with Rose, Cassandra Fancy's garden.

Her beautiful kulning.

Anna began to sing the ancient, traditional forest opera. The sounds echoed off the walls and could be heard throughout the entire hospital. She was a Viking princess, calling her longship, leading it to safety through the treacherous fjords. All the patients quieted, listening to the evocative, haunting notes. Even the doctors, nurses, and attendants stood still, homing in on the melodious tune. Anna walked out into the hallway and continued to sing, and as she passed each room, all the patients slowly emerged, following her in awe, as if livestock beckoned home.

The following morning they gave Anna a decent haircut–little curls framing her face–and afterward she returned to her bed. For days she tried to stand up and get dressed, only to lie back down. The sun rose, then set, then rose again. She lost track of time. She informed the head nurse that she no longer wanted any visitors, and even when her brother Christian brought the twins, she refused to see them.

Dr. Octavia changed her medication and saw her daily now, instead of only once a week. The new regimen was working.

Slowly the storm was calming, the beast within starting to rest.

Anna

Today I received a wonderful surprise: Genevieve woke me with a lovely smile on her face, opening her arms and saying, "Sweet Pea, look around you!"

What a miracle! . . . Cassandra's garden was everywhere in my room!

Flowers blooming, sculptures coming to life, Mrs. Swan welcoming me home–I couldn't believe my eyes. So vibrant were the colors, so psychedelic, I danced in delight in my whilom sanctuary.

Ruby often visited Anna, uninvited and unannounced, barging into her room, a mask of thick makeup on her face, batting her false eyelashes while smoking long cigarettes and pointing her finger, asking, "How ya doin', kid?" one hand on her hip. "Mummy Ruby is here to help. Anything you need, doll, just ask."

Ruby supplied Anna with things she was either not allowed or couldn't get on a regular basis from her brother when he visited. Lipstick, chewing gum and candy, magazines, cigarettes and alcohol—both considered contraband by the hospital—and anything else she might fancy. The older woman took her in like a mother hen, treating her as a daughter, unleashing on anyone who dared to even look at Anna the wrong way. She was hard, acerbic, and crude. She cussed like a sailor. But she also taught Anna about life, about men, and even about women. Women like Rose.

"I think I might have killed my husband," Anna confessed one night.

"No, kid, that's impossible. I saw him visiting you, more than once."

"Are you sure?" Anna was trembling. "He's tall and lanky with dirty blond hair and a beard. Are you sure that's who you saw?"

"Yes, love. Stop worryin' that pretty head of yours. Unlike my cheatin' bastard, yours is still very much alive."

Anna looked up at the older woman, her face pale and distraught. "If it wasn't James, then it was someone else. I know I killed someone. But who?"

Anna

The days and weeks are passing by.
My medication is my crutch, and the treatments my distraction.
The doctors are all strangers, and the nurses too.
Ruby is my protector and a mother to me.
Genevieve and the swan people are my watchers.

"Anna, do you remember the wolf you shot and killed several years ago?" Dr. Octavia asked during their next session.

"Yes, the Black Shuck."

"And you now know you hallucinate that animal, right? It's not real."

"I killed a demon she-wolf," Anna replied.

"That's a folktale, love. A story created about a wolf that lived in England a long time ago. We don't even have wolves here in Australia."

Anna stared at the doctor, feeling as if the room were suddenly shrinking. "I shot a wolf," she insisted again. "James even buried it in the family burial plot."

The doctor paused, thinking how best to proceed. "You have a rare mental condition where you see things that your imagination creates. Like the bloodied man, for example. Who is that?"

"I don't know," Anna said, biting her nails.

"I think you do."

"Dr. Octavia, I have no idea who that is."

"Listen, love . . . I want you to try to remember that day. What happened right before you shot the wolf?"

Anna tried hard to recall the events of that fatal night. "I saw the Black Shuck sneak into the chicken coop," she said, "and all the hens were squawking. I grabbed the shotgun and went to confront it, and when I opened the door, the wolf was eating all the eggs."

"Look deeper, Anna. Try harder to remember what really happened . . . Was it a wolf? . . . Or a man?"

Anna closed her eyes and went deep into the recesses of her mind, conjuring up the past. "It . . . It was a man . . . A man eating raw eggs . . . He was starving and . . ."

"And what, Anna?"

"He was transitioning back and forth between a beast and a man."

"Tell me what he said before he changed back to the wolf."

Anna began to visibly shake. "He said . . . He said don't shoot me. Please don't kill me."

Suddenly Anna remembered that day, as if a light were switched on in a dark room. The entire deadly scene played out in her head, like watching a moving picture show . . . She follows the Black Shuck with razor-sharp teeth and bloodred eyes into the henhouse, loaded shotgun in hand. The beast is both a wolf and a man, begging for his life, and she shoots him three times in the chest. Seconds later, James bursts in, grabbing the gun from her, yelling at the top of his lungs as he drags her outside . . . "Anna, what have you done!" ricochets in her ears. "What have you done!"

Yes, now she remembered.

She had indeed killed an innocent man!

"Why are you cryin', kid?" Ruby asked. She had seen Anna run out of the doctor's office, upset and delirious.

"I've done something unforgivable!" cried Anna. "I'm going to hell, for sure!"

"What'd you do?"

"Remember when I told you I think I might have killed a bloke?"

"Yes. You thought it was your husband, but I told you it wasn't."

Anna shook her head in distress. "For years I thought it was something else. My mind plays tricks on me. But I did kill someone, Ruby. I killed a vagrant who was only looking for food." Tears streamed down her face. "The doctor wanted me to acknowledge it, and now I remember. I shot the man three times in the chest. James made a wood coffin for him, and he's buried at Sugar Alexandria." She started sobbing.

"Now, now, kid. It was a mistake; you didn't mean to do it," said Ruby, her motherly side trying to comfort Anna. "Did they say what's gonna happen to you?"

"No, but I've already been declared insane. I'll never be leaving this place."

Ruby sat on the edge of her bed, placing her hand on Anna's shoulder.

"What would I do without you?" Anna cried. "You're all the family I have left." The drifter she had shot, who had begged for his life, materialized clearly in her mind "I'm so sorry," she wailed. "I'm so sorry."

After that day, Anna never saw the hallucination of the bloodied man again.

Ruby introduced Anna to a woman her own age, named Aurora Vega. A skinny, shy girl, who was always reading a book. Aurora had wild and unruly, cardinal red hair, emerald eyes, freckles that covered every inch of her skin, and a quiet, secretive persona on a willowy frame that reminded Anna of Rose. The three women became inseparable, walking the halls each day, spending time outside in the courtyard, and eating their meals together. Anna would talk for hours, telling them all about her life and why she ended up at Pleasant Skies. She related everything that happened with James, Rose, and Joshua. She talked about Genevieve and the Black Shuck, the bloodied man, the shadow people who were now swan people in the hospital, and Rose's paintings that came to life for her, resurrecting her mother, sister, and grandmother. She spoke of her childhood secret room and Cassandra Fancy's garden, and everything else about her glorious life at Sugar Alexandria.

Ruby and Aurora listened sympathetically, empathetically, consolingly, supportively, lovingly.

Where Ruby was like a mother to Anna, Aurora replaced her cousin Rose. Anna was learning to trust people again. Learning to laugh again. Maybe all I needed from the beginning was some loyal cobbers to pull me through, Anna thought as the three women walked down the long hallway of the mental hospital.

⁓ᴄᴇᴏᴊᴇᴏᴏ⁓

Between the shock therapy, hydrotherapy, and other so-called innovative treatments, several doctors evaluate Anna during her stay at the Pleasant Skies Psychiatric Hospital. They all ask her the same questions over and over until she responds as expected. Gradually they are taking the veneer off her denial and sharpening her common sense, helping her cope with her conditions, ameliorating her pain, giving her the tools required to become a stronger woman among the adversities and vicissitudes of life. Anna is welcoming the transformation, seeing the reality of her new world, accepting the situation and viewing her circumstances in a different light.

She is slowly healing despite the insanity inside her. And around her.

The voices don't visit Anna as much as they used to due to the medication, and she now feels more lonely as a result. She thinks of what she was, what she is, and what she is becoming. Who am I, she wonders? What is the point of my existence now? Her pain, thick and heavy, gnaws at her with the rising sun as if a rat on a piece of cheese, then gorges on her with the rising moon as if a starving wolf devouring a deer.

Contemplating the things that Dr. Octavia has said, and what will happen next, she thinks of Moony and wishes she could speak with him. What would the pragmatic older stockman tell her? Most likely that life goes on. And what about Yarrajan, the Aboriginal nanny who had raised her like a daughter—what did she say about the white woman with snake eyes? "You should never have a single sheila with no children livin' with you. This will only cause trouble for you and Mister."

Yarra was right.

And now an immeasurable chasm exists between Anna and her once-beloved, so immense that if one fell into it they would continue to fall endlessly. No nostrum, catholicon, or theriac can ever heal it. To Anna, her cousin is as dead and buried as her sister, mother, and father.

As she ruminates over things, Anna stares out the window at the garden below and notices the flowers are blooming. But she feels nothing. "I will never be the same again," she mumbles to herself. "Not even a beautiful flower excites me anymore." And yet, she still goes out to the garden, picks several blossoms, and brings them to her room.

❧

"I have never met anyone else like you, Ruby," Anna said one night, smoking and drinking until the wee hours of morn. "Because of you, I'm gonna make it through this bloody nightmare."

"That a girl!" Ruby cackled. "We'll get through this together, kid!"

❧

"Where's Eden?" Anna asked, alarmed that her arachnid friend was nowhere in sight.

The nurse handed Anna her medication. "Who's Eden?"

Anna threw the pills on the floor. "Where is she!" she shouted.

"Stop that right now! If you throw another fit, you'll be sedated and strapped to your bed!"

Anna panicked, fearing that Eden had been killed by the cleaning staff. But then her eyes caught something moving in the corner above the window. "Oh, Eden!" she exclaimed. "Thank God you're still here!" She fell to her knees, crying, thankful her little companion was still alive.

That night, Anna put Eden on her hand, and the eight-legged creature crawled up and down her arm. It now trusted Anna, and Anna's adoration of the little bug grew. "You're precious to me, Eden," she whispered. "Please never scare me like that again." She returned the spider to its web, feeding it a fly she had caught earlier.

James called the hospital every week to check on Anna's status. The doctor always said the same thing—she was steadily improving, but not ready for any further jarring situation. Meaning the divorce papers should be held off. Though he was eager to finalize things, James respected the doctor's recommendations. He didn't want to cause Anna to regress, so he patiently waited until he received the news that she was strong enough for the certitude of their divorce. His life with Rose was on hold for the time being, until that Friday night when the phone rang.

"It's the hospital," Rose said, rubbing her growing abdomen.

He took the phone. "G'day, James here."

"How are you, Mr. Shahan? This is Dr. Octavia."

James' heartbeat increased. "Good, ta."

"I'm calling to give you an update on your wife. The last time we spoke, we talked about the timing of giving Anna your divorce papers. In my medical opinion, I believe she should see her cousin Rose first. No matter the outcome."

James hesitated. "Are you sure about that?"

"Yes. I think it's a necessary step for Anna to progress further. She may get angry, but this is the best controlled environment for her to be in when venting that anger. Releasing her pent-up emotions will actually be healthy for her."

"All right, Dr. Octavia. I'll let Rose know."

CHAPTER 51

"Hell is empty and all the devils are here."

– William Shakespeare

It was a cool day when Rose arrived at the Pleasant Skies Psychiatric Hospital. As she stepped out of the taxicab, she remained still a moment, leaning on her cane, staring at her surroundings. Two enormous marble lions sat right out front, flanking the gray stone steps as if guards, both holding solid spheres. A small patch of lush, green grass with several rosebushes decorated each side of the entrance. And hydrangea vines with clusters of white flowers climbed up the hospital's brick wall–a soft and arresting contrast to the darkness hidden within.

An older gentleman–the groundskeeper–noticed her while trimming the rosebushes. He handed her a long-stemmed rose and pointed at the mental health facility. "You have family here?" he asked, his eyes conveying concern.

"Thank you," said Rose, taking the flower. "Yes, my cousin is in there."

"That's too bad. Bunch of lost souls, they are."

A strong gust of chilly wind blew where they stood, tussling Rose's hair.

"When I work late, I hear the screams. Screams that don't sound human. Laughter, too, but wicked sounding. So terrible are the noises they prickle your skin and reach deep into your bones." He shook his head. "I won't go in there. No, I won't, not for nothin'."

Goose bumps formed on Rose's arms as she watched the groundskeeper return to trimming the foliage. She heard him murmur, "Roses are such a beauty, but there be thorns. There be many, sharp thorns."

Eager to get the visit over with, and hopefully, find closure for both herself and her cousin, Rose proceeded up the steps and entered the building.

"She's already waiting for you," the admissions nurse said, eyeing her up and down, having heard the lascivious talk bruited about by Anna.

Rose followed the nurse down the long, white hallway through the eerie, unfamiliar atmosphere, as if a sinister man had taken her by the hand, leading her to a haunted room. Patients shuffled by—a few appearing normal, most not. She searched their faces as they passed, feeling sorry for them all. And yet a few even scared her. "Screams that don't sound human. Laughter, too, but wicked sounding," echoed in her mind.

The entrance to the common area was straight ahead. Instantly Rose's mouth became dry, and her heart began to pound. Any moment now, she would be face-to-face with her cousin whom she hadn't seen since that tragic day. She said a silent prayer as the doors opened.

"Hello, Anna," Rose greeted with a shaky voice, already fighting back tears. She took a seat across the table from her.

"Lottie," Anna replied. She too was trembling, clammy, pale, a strange expression radiating from her face.

Anna was supposed to throw her arms around Rose, telling her how sorry she was for the things she had done—stabbing her with a knife in a fit of rage and threatening to toss her baby into the fire—and then they would weep together. Or perhaps Rose was supposed to throw her arms around Anna, apologizing for how it all ended between the three of them, begging for her forgiveness for taking away James. Yet at that moment, Rose's words evaded her. Seeing her cousin look so sickly, her hair in a messy, uneven bob, her eyes dark and lost, tore at her heart. She only cried where she sat, while Anna stared right through her, pondering that horrible, god-awful day the sky fell from the heavens and the sun lost its shine. The day her world had folded in on itself and collapsed.

"Min elskede," Anna scoffed in Danish. *"Hvorfor kom du?"* (*"My beloved. Why did you come?"*)

Rose wiped away her tears. "Because it was time."

"Time to clear your conscience?"

"Anna . . . ," she said, almost breathlessly.

"Isn't that why you are here?" Anna interrupted. "To make yourself feel better?"

"I came here to talk to you. To figure things out. To . . ."

"Stop," Anna interposed again. "There will be none of that today, trying to make me believe how devo you are over everything. You'll have to go to a priest for that."

"We're still cousins, Anna. We're still family."

"After what you have done, you call that family?"

"I'm sorry."

"Too right; you're real sorry."

An uncomfortable quiet passed between the two women. Rose took a moment to glance around the large room as Anna glared at her, thinking about that night in the windmill when Rose had reintroduced Anna's grand idea that became her undoing, saying it would be just one time. As her gaze penetrated through her disloyal cousin, she felt as if the personification of the picture Yarrajan had made her out of the colorful beads—a vulnerable rabbit left behind by two beautiful deer. She had always balked at the Aboriginal woman's uncanny ability to prognosticate the woe, and yet here she was, sitting in a mental institute with her cousin visiting her. "Are you still tasting the stars, love?" she sarcastically asked.

"No, Anna, I'm not tasting the stars."

Anna's countenance remained cold and contemptuous, believing her cousin had intended on stealing her husband from the beginning. A Machiavellian spider, waiting, waiting, waiting, with grace and beauty spinning her web, until the fly is enticed and trapped.

Rose tried to change the mood of the visit. "Hey, remember when I used to leave Sugar Alexandria at the end of each summer and go back to England? We never said goodbye to each other. Instead, I would say, 'Abyssinia, Kitten.' And you would say, 'Until then, Lottie Dottie. Have a bee's knees time back in London.' " Rose's throat choked with emotion. "Remember that? And then we would do the Charleston and laugh." She raised her hands, mimicking the dance, waving them from side to side.

"I remember many things," Anna replied, unmoved, her eyes boring into Rose's soul. "Like you stealing my husband away from me."

Rose frowned. "Anna, someday we're going to sit down and be able to talk about this, and you will understand more." She wanted to say so many things to her.

"I will, huh?" Anna smirked. "I highly doubt that." She shook her head in disgust. "So where are you two living now?"

"We're staying in a hotel," Rose replied.

"Apples–both of you get to live it up while I wallow here in this nut-house."

"You won't be in here forever, Anna."

"How do you know?"

"Because James and I wouldn't allow it." Rose forced a smile. "Soon you'll be back to drinking tea in your secret room, visiting Cassandra's garden, and managing your beautiful station at Sugar Alexandria."

"But you and James will be gone." Anna momentarily stared off into space, then narrowed her eyes at Rose, motioning at her neck. "I see your scars have healed well. Mine have too," she said, turning her palms up, showing the jagged cicatrices across her wrists.

James hadn't told Rose that Anna had attempted suicide. Immediately her eyes welled with tears.

"Don't you bloody cry again. Don't you do it. Those tears are for yourself, you rabid feral."

Rose's lip quivered, even as she desperately tried to control herself and keep her composure.

Sitting back in her chair, Anna methodically surveyed her once-beloved cousin. "You make quite a statement when you walk into a room. You know that? Without saying a word, you light it up. I see now that it's a talent. A charm. You charmed me, and you charmed James."

"No, Anna, it wasn't like that."

An intense hush followed as both women stared at each other in a proverbial dual. Rose, once the savior, now the sinner.

"Look at you, just staring at me, saying nothing. Why don't you have the guts to say it? Your entire plan was to get him right from the start." With her anger now boiling over, Anna stood and leaned across the table. "It wasn't *my* plan that worked; it was *your* plan that worked!" she yelled, her voice cracking with emotion. "Am I right!" She slapped Rose across the face. Hard. She slapped her again.

The male attendants immediately ran up to them, grabbing Anna by the wrist. "That's it. Visiting time is over."

Holding her cheek, Rose looked up at the men. "It's all right; I'm fine."

They hesitated.

"Please," she said. "It was only a misunderstanding. Everything's all right now."

The men released Anna. "Sit down, then. Any more outbursts and you're going back to your room for the rest of the day."

Anna obeyed, sitting back down in her chair, her gaze transitioning to her cousin's swollen abdomen—the progeny of her soon-to-be ex-husband.

Rose waited for the tension to subside. "There was no plan, Anna. I swear." Somewhere in the back of her mind was a memory of them as children, running through the ocean spray along the sandy shoreline, holding hands and laughing, their whole lives ahead of them. And then as adults, as recently as a few weeks ago, lying on the grass in Cassandra Fancy's garden, watching the sky turn colors from the splendiferous sunset.

"You're a bloody liar."

"I'm telling you the truth," Rose avowed. "I love you, and I will always love you."

Hearing those words softened Anna, causing a glimmer of who she once was to twinkle in her eyes. But just as swiftly as it came, she recrudesced to seething. "Poor, soft-spoken Lottie. Wouldn't harm a fly. How long were you in love with my husband? You at least owe me that. From the first day you arrived, or before?" Anna recalled Bowie Jenkins joking about seeing James and Rose kiss at Christian and Josephine's wedding. "You met him at my brother's wedding, didn't you. And then you came to the station with a plan to steal him."

"That's insane."

Anna laughed, lifting her arms in the air. "Maybe I am insane. Insane to ever trust you. You know what's happened to me in here? First I tried to end my life; then I was almost raped; and my sweet, young cobber committed suicide because of me. The suffering has been unbearable. I have walked with demons, and I still do, all because I tried to do a grouse deed for someone I loved."

Rose's baby kicked. She looked down, placing her hand on her belly.

Anna's eyes flickered there as well, as if she too had felt the child move inside her cousin's womb. "That's my husband's baby growing inside you."

The unborn child continued to move, and Rose protectively wrapped both arms around her stomach.

"Look, the baby's kicking you. It's upset. Even it knows what you have done to me," Anna hissed.

A sad darkness overtook Rose. She came here to make peace, hoping to salvage their friendship if possible, but clearly she had been overly sanguine. It was way too soon for any of that to happen, and it likely never would. "I shouldn't have come," she said, almost to herself.

"No, you shouldn't have. You're not my beloved cousin anymore. You're ugly to me. Horrible. A nasty witch who only cares about herself!" Anna yelled, reaching over and ripping off Rose's gold friendship locket. "You with your crook leg and face with no freckles. A face with no freckles is like a flower with no bloom!" she shouted. "A face with no freckles is like a flower with no bloom!"

Rose glanced over at the male attendants watching them, letting them know that everything was still ok.

Anna scowled at her, thinking of when her cousin had told her the story of *Swan Lake*, with the white swan and the black, one representing good and the other evil. For Anna it had a different simulacrum: The white swan was her compos mentis, the black swan her psychosis. She was sure Rose thought that too, and this made her hate her all the more. "And that story you told me—*Swan Lake*—it's not about good and evil, is it. It's about a woman with two personalities. Right?"

"No, it's not."

"That's what you think when you play that song: You think of me and my madness."

"No, Anna."

"I'm the white swan and the black!" she yelled. "And you're Charlotte the harlot!"

"Please stop," Rose begged.

"I put you on a throne, but you're no different from anyone else! You bleed, just like me! No different!"

Rose stood, still holding her distended stomach. The child inside had become active, kicking wildly. "Goodbye, Anna. *Jeg vil altid elske dig,*" she said in Danish, walking away, tears cascading down her cheeks. *("I will always love you.")*

Anna stood as well, following behind. "Wait! Please, I have to know! Please tell me! Did you only want a baby, or was your intention to steal my husband!" she yelled, her emotions fluctuating between supplication, desperation, and anger. "Please, have mercy! I deserve to know!"

Rose was almost running now.

"Tell me!" Anna screamed, pointing her finger at her. *"Jeg stolede på dig! Jeg stolede på dig!"* ("*I trusted you! I trusted you!*")

The two male attendants ran up and grabbed her, pulling her back on both sides. Anna fought them, letting out a long, harrowing caterwaul, collapsing to the floor. *"Jeg stolede på dig!"* she wailed incoherently. *"Jeg stolede på dig!"* ("*I trusted you! I trusted you!*")

Horrified, Rose dared not stop, not wanting to witness the attendants drag her cousin off.

"Hell is empty, Rose!" Anna screamed one last time, watching her once-beloved rush away. "And all the devils are here! Did you hear me! They're here!"

As she stepped through the double doors of the psychiatric hospital into the warmth of the sun, the fresh breeze caressed Rose's skin, and the birds sang a sweet melody. But in her mind, all she could hear were Anna's screams.

～ང⁂ᄋ～

Rose came home in tears; James held her while she cried.

"I should have gone with you," he said.

"No, that would have only made it worse."

He recalled what Dr. Octavia had said, that it was a necessary evil in Anna's recovery for her to see Rose. "Maybe, but I hate that you had to go through that."

"I'm just glad it's over," said Rose. "But you were right—I don't think Anna and I will be seeing each other again for a very long time."

The following day, James called Dr. Octavia to see how Anna was doing. The doctor said it was a significant breakthrough for Anna to see her cousin, despite her emotional outburst at the end, and the visit had been a success. Rather than having another psychotic episode, Anna talked about her feelings and reasoned on them, showing that her condition was improving and that she was using the tools given her. It was a phenomenal positive development in her case. As a result, Dr. Octavia gave James the clearance he was looking for to bring the divorce papers. She believed Anna was ready . . .

CHAPTER 52

"No good deed goes unpunished."

– Oscar Wilde

"Your husband is here," the nurse said, opening Anna's bedroom door without knocking. "He's waiting for you in the cafeteria." Anna hurriedly ran a brush through her hair, applied some lipstick, and darted down the hallway to meet him. She frowned when she didn't see Scarlet and Mabel.

"How are you, Anna?" James asked, setting his briefcase down, giving her a level gaze.

"You missed the last few Sundays."

"I know. I called you, though."

Anna inspected him. He was clean-shaven, wearing a tweed sweater, a bow tie, and his hair sleeked back. New reading glasses with a thick, black rim framed his face. She hardly recognized him. "You look different," she said, leaning back in her chair, biting her nails. "You don't look like a grazier anymore."

"I'm not a grazier anymore, Anna. I don't work at the station; you know that."

"Ruby was right–you look like a librarian. Like a dag."

James was unbothered by her rude comment. Not the least bit fazed.

"Ruby said that's why you fell for Rose, because you're both intellectual dags."

He only glanced down at his briefcase. Inside held the impetus for his final visit with his wife.

"Why didn't you bring Scarlet and Mabel? They're all right, aren't they?"

"Yes, Anna, they're doing grouse."

"So why didn't you bring them?"

"Your brother will later." Opening his briefcase, he handed her the documents.

"What's this?"

"Divorce papers."

Anna stared at him, emotion effusing from her body. Slowly she looked down at the paperwork, focusing on his signature at the bottom of the page. At one time she had admired the fluid curves of his penmanship; now they disturbed her, made her nauseated. She felt as if she had an itch, only to scratch it and find she had no skin. Her flesh had been cut from the bone.

"I would appreciate it if you signed it today while I'm here," James said with little expression.

"It's really over?" she asked in a small voice, trying to control her grief. "Our life together is really over?"

He nodded.

"So easy for you."

"Nothing about this is easy."

"I sign this and you get to be with her."

James' jaw tightened.

"Rose . . . ," Anna said, tears filling her eyes. "You and Rose." Her cousin's face appeared in her mind; baby Joshua's cry rang in her ears.

"If need be, the court will grant the divorce without your signature."

"Then why ask me?"

"Out of respect for you."

A pain tore through Anna's stomach as if being gutted. "What does a person become when everything they are is stripped away?" she asked, her voice quivering. "Who do they become?" She kept staring at her soon-to-be ex-husband, begging for answers. "Who am I now, if not James Shahan's wife?"

Her words did not affect him. He simply took out a pen and laid it on the paper.

"We had a life together, and now we don't. What does that mean?" she muttered, picking up the pen with a shaking hand. Thick tears fell onto the paper.

"I'm giving you my half of Sugar Alexandria. The farmhouse, the animals, the land–everything. They were only mine through marriage anyway, so I'm just giving them back. The Tin Lizzie, my piano, and the savings in my account I am keeping, but other than that, it's all yours." As he spoke, his eyes never wavered from her face. "You'll find the paperwork pretty simple, Anna. It's cut-and-dried."

"What about our daughters? Where do they fit in all this?"

"They will stay at Sugar Alexandria with Yarrajan until you get out. After that, we will work out some arrangement that suits everyone while I'm gone."

"Gone? Where are you going?"

"I think it's better for us if no one knew for the time being."

Anna was crying. "Us? . . . You mean you and Rose. Go ahead, say it: Rose, my lovely cousin."

"I'm sorry, Anna. I never wanted to hurt you. I know this is extremely hard right now, but you will survive without me. And I will always be in your life in some way, because we have two beautiful daughters together."

"All I wanted was for Rose to have a baby," she sobbed, "not to lose my family."

He said nothing.

"I feel like I'm dying, James. Do you know that? I feel like I'm dying. You and Rose have killed me."

He reached for her hand.

Pulling it away as if he had just burned her, she yelled, "No, don't touch me!"

James winced a little and glanced around the room. Other patients and visitors had begun to stare. "Can you please calm down?" he asked.

"Oh, are you embarrassed that people will know what happened!" Anna shouted. She looked over at the people staring. "My husband is leaving me for my cousin Rose. Isn't he a ripper?"

James lowered his head and ran his hand through his hair. He was afraid this would happen.

"Was I not pretty enough?" she whimpered. "Is that it?"

"That has nothing to do with anything, and you know it."

"Then help me understand, James. Give it a burl; explain to me why."

"You tricked me into marriage," he said in a low, controlled voice.

She looked up at him with wide, curious eyes, resembling a child being caught stealing candy.

"I was supposed to go to London to advance my studies, and then go on to have a career in music. You ended all that."

"All blokes marry sheilas when they get them pregnant."

"You were not pregnant, Anna, and you didn't get pregnant until ten years later."

"You took my virginity."

"And I paid dearly for that."

"You love me, and Rose is making you leave me."

"Anna . . . ." He shook his head in frustration. "Pay attention to what I am saying . . . I'm surprised I stayed as long as I did, even before Rose came to live with us. I was meant to have a life immersed in music, not working as a grazier on a cattle station."

Anna's body began to shake on the inside. "Then why didn't you leave years ago?"

"I'll tell you why . . . I felt sorry for you. I knew there was something not right with you, and I didn't want to abandon a woman with mental illness. Then our babies were born, and I was even more trapped."

Anna appeared dumbstruck. "Trapped?"

"That's right. You know how many times I had to pray for endurance to not just get up and leave and start the life I was intended to live? Too many times to even remember." He pushed his glasses up on the bridge of his nose. "You pressuring me to give Rose a child, I suppose only hurried a destiny that would have happened anyway."

"But you fought me on it," she said, still trying to understand. "You told me you didn't want to break your vows."

"What I was torn about is what would happen afterward. I was afraid of the vicious gossip, the station being boycotted because of the adultery within our family, and the repercussions of a baby born with no last name. That is where my true struggle was. But then you wouldn't give up. You pushed me into it. And once I was with her . . . fell in love with her . . . I couldn't go back to how it was before."

"And how was that?"

"Anna, aside from your illness and difficult behaviors, you don't like physical intimacy. You barely even let me touch you."

She didn't disagree.

"I had to painstakingly train myself how to love a woman who could not love me back—at least in a normal, healthy way—and it was slowly destroying me."

"I can love," Anna said, crying again.

"Emotionally you're missing an important part that's just not there, and I can't take it anymore. I don't want to endure it any longer. It's not just the fits you throw, or the hallucinations; it's something else. Something deep inside you. You're not capable of intimate human connection. Or empathy. At least not with me."

"No," Anna said, covering her ears and weeping louder. "We had a happy marriage until my cousin arrived."

James reached over and pulled her hands away from her face. "Anna, listen to me. I never wanted to marry you, and you know it. You stole fourteen years from me, and I'm asking you now to let me go."

Anna was desperate, clinging to his arm. "I'm crook. I need you to take care of me."

"I know you're crook, but the doctors assure me that with treatment and medication you can live a full, productive life on your own. You can do it without me, love. In fact, you have to." He placed her hands back on her lap.

"All those happy memories. We would eat tucker by the sea, and pash in the field. Remember? Don't tell me those weren't grand times."

"They were. I was making the most out of my life. But it still wasn't the life I wanted, and you know that."

Anna's skin grew sensitive, covering in a cold sweat. The fabric of her clothing bristled against her as goose bumps spread over her epidermis. "We can sell the station. We can leave and go anywhere you want," she said in one last attempt to save herself. "You and me, together."

"Anna . . . It's over."

The fight in her was quickly fading. "What happened to 'Till death do us part,' aye?" she pleaded. "That's what we always used to say to each other, remember?"

"It's over, Anna," he said again.

As she heard those words, her shoulders slumped. Defeated. "A face with no freckles is like a flower with no bloom," she sniveled. Looking up at him, her voice soft and her eyes sad, she added, "Rose has no freckles, wears glasses, and has a crook leg and finger."

"I love her, Anna. None of those things bother me. I want to spend the rest of my life with her."

"I gather after I sign this, you two will get married, aye?"

He didn't answer.

Anna wiped her eyes. "Remember that children's story, *East of the Sun and West of the Moon*? I was just thinking the other day how my life is like that tale. She didn't know she had a prince and gave him away to a wicked princess, and that's exactly what happened to me."

James remained silent.

"I only allowed this so Rose could have a baby, not so she could steal my husband and destroy my family."

There was no point in arguing, refuting, or defending, and even if there were, James knew it wasn't the time or the place.

Anna drummed her thumb on the paperwork, staring at him, then quickly signed it and pushed it back.

"Ta, Anna." He took the papers and got up to leave. In his hand was the key to a new life.

"I trusted both of you! I loved both of you!" she yelled as he walked away. "You both betrayed me!"

James motioned to the nurse to buzz the door open.

"Do you know which one of us was the wolf, James!" She stood and shouted at his back, "I thought it was Rose, buts it's not! It's all of us! The Black Shuck was in all of us because we each longed for something we could not have! Did you hear me! We're all ravenous wolves when it comes to what we desire!"

He did not stop.

He just kept walking.

Rose was bathing Joshua in the sink, just as she once had in the shallow waters of Indigo Bay. She poured warm water on his chubby, silky body, lathering him up, then rinsed and repeated. Absorbed in her task, feeling over his round cheeks, the fullness of his belly, and the intricacy of his tiny fingers and toes, the utter perfection of his small form fascinated her. Happiness filled her soul.

After she was done bathing him, she wrapped Joshua in a towel and took him to the bedroom to put on a clean diaper. Laying him flat on his back, she kissed his stomach and feet as he giggled in delight. To have no love at all for so long, only to overflow with it afterward, having both a child and the man of her dreams, was exhilarating.

When James got home, he found Rose sleeping in the bedroom, curled up to Joshua beside her. Gently he laid next to them.

She awoke. "How did it go? How's Anna?"

"Much better," he simply said. He didn't want to elaborate on Anna's sorrow over the divorce. "And she signed the papers. It's done."

Rose laid her head on his chest, remembering Anna as a little girl meeting her at the train station that first day she arrived in Esperance, jumping up and down in glee. "I love you, Lottie," she recalled her sweet cousin saying to her many a time since. "And I would do anything in the world for you. Just anything."

⁓⦅❦⦆⁓

Who was the black Shuck?

James and Rose were preparing to leave Australia and start their new life. But he had something he had to do first. Something his honor, duty, and moral accountability demanded . . . It was time to make peace with Anna's beast. Except, Anna hadn't killed a wolf. She killed a man named Callum McTavish–a bloke in James' platoon. The same bloke he had saved from that barbed wire fence during the war.

After returning home, Callum was unable to cope with his unspeakable experiences from the war and became addicted to opium, living as a vagrant on the street. Drifting aimlessly from place to place, he begged for food and stole what he could along the way. Another sad casualty of the Great War. Dead, though not from a bullet or a bomb.

James never in a million years thought that after saving the man's life his own mentally ill wife would take it from him, hallucinating the Black Shuck and emptying their shotgun into his chest. When he went to confess to Constable Higgins what Anna had done, the constable commended him for coming forward after all these years, then told James the drifter was trespassing in the night and stealing, both of which could be perceived as a threat. As far as Constable Higgins was concerned, it was self-defense and protection of property. "Besides," he said, patting James on the back, "poor Anna has already been committed to Pleasant Skies and will likely be there a long time. No need to add any more misery to an already tragic outcome."

After telling Rose the gruesome truth about who was buried in the unmarked grave at the Polston family burial plot, James went to the home Callum McTavish grew up in. The one he had visited in his youth, playing with Callum when they were children.

⁓⦅❦⦆⁓

"I'm sorry, Mrs. McTavish, but I was only protecting my wife," James

490

said, hat in hand, deep remorse reflecting in his eyes.

"Anna thought me grandson was a threat, aye? That he was gonna hurt her? And you were doin' what any bloke would do for his wife. Is that it?"

"She was hallucinating, Mrs. McTavish. Anna is a sick woman."

"I heard she tried to kill her cousin, too. And the sheila's baby. Ain't that right?"

"Yes, and that's why she's been committed to the Pleasant Skies Psychiatric Hospital."

Several great-grandchildren were sitting around the room, quietly playing, their ears perking up as the adults talked, curious over the strange man speaking about their uncle. "Do you know what Callum means in Gaelic, son?" She poured them both a glass of her husband's moonshine. Though Mr. McTavish had died of smallpox many years earlier, she had learned how to brew his recipe.

"Dove," James said.

The older woman nodded. "When you have a bairn, there's this blissful moment when you hold them right after they're born, and all is right in the world. Like you're holdin' the sun. That's what it was like for me with Callum's daddy." Her tired gray eyes welled with tears. "He died of consumption, God rest his soul. Callum's mum, too. And now Callum himself is gone." One of her great-grandchildren climbed onto her lap, and she picked the little girl up and cradled her. "The poor lad was never the same after the war," she said, a sadness in her voice. "He died there, and another bloke returned in his place. I'm just thankful his sufferin' has now ended."

"And his remains?" James asked.

Mrs. McTavish tossed back her moonshine. "Leave them undisturbed. I know Sugar Alexandria; it's a beauty of a place to rest in peace. His sister would agree."

James nodded and touched the woman's hand. "You're both welcome to visit the burial plot whenever you like. I will have a proper tombstone made for him, and a deaf young man who lives on the neighboring station always puts flowers on Callum's grave. He's resting in a beauty of a spot."

"You're an honorable soul, James Shahan," said the older woman, wiping her tears. She blinked, thinking a moment. "Do you know what Shahan means in Gaelic?"

James wasn't sure.

"It means king, my good man. It means king."

CHAPTER 53

James and Rose left for the land of Éire, embarking a ship destined for the tiny village of Cong straddling the borders of County Galway and County Mayo. With the divorce finalized, they could now start their new life together, getting married and raising a family.

Before they departed, James hired a lawyer to fight through the justice system on his ex-wife's behalf. True to his word, and unbeknownst to Anna, he intended to ensure she would not get lost in a system that permanently institutionalized those who had no voice.

As the ship set sail from Fremantle Harbour, James and Rose both stared at the country and continent they once called home. A torrent of memories flooded their minds, each for different reasons, each invoking a spate of emotions.

When they could no longer see land, he looked over at her, once again holding her chin in his hand, gazing deep into her iridescent green eyes. As always, an entire world he wanted reflected back at him.

✦

Now in Ireland, it was the day of James and Rose's wedding. A sacred union between two people who loved each other deeply, and against all odds, had found each other again. Even the heavens seemed to rejoice as the setting sun painted the sky a variety of colors—countless shades and hues revealing God's imagination.

Rose wore a white lace wedding dress with a long Irish veil. James wore a tartan kilt. As the bagpipes belted out their distinct and cherished sound, he waited for his bride to make her appearance. Everyone stood when she showed herself; James' breath caught in his lungs at her beauty.

Standing in a field among James' family, endless green extending out on all sides, they exchanged vows, both reading a personal pledge to each other.

"My husband . . . May you never lie, steal, or cheat. But if you must lie, lie with me all the nights of my life. If you must steal, steal away my sorrows. And if you must cheat, cheat death, because I could never live a day without you."

"My wife . . . You are blood of my blood, and bone of my bone. I give you my body that we might be one. I give you my spirit until my life is done."

The spectacular natural phenomenon across the Irish horizon exemplified the future waiting for them . . .

Vast and endless.

Full of hope and promise.

~·~·~

The celebratory reception was next. Gifts were exchanged, food and drink bountiful, laughter and dancing continuous. James played on an old piano owned by his aunt, and Rose brought out her violin.

"What a beautiful couple," Aunt Saoirse said in Gaelic to her husband Flanagan. *"All their children will look like angels from heaven."*

As the festive night continued, Rose walked up to James with a come-hither grin. "You look rather smart and dashing in that kilt," she said, slapping his behind.

He smiled. "I feel like a drongo, but I have to admit, it's growing on me."

She slid her hand into his. "That shouldn't be hard, having an Irishman's pedigree."

"Bloody oath."

Bagpipes and fiddles, sweet aromas of different foods, beer mugs cheering, and people chattering in Gaelic surrounded them. Rose would ask, "What did he say?", and James would translate in her ear, kissing her cheek with each translation. It felt amazing. Incredible. As if there had never been anyone but them. As if they had married soon after meeting at Christian and Josephine's wedding and had never been apart.

As if they had never known Sugar Alexandria.

The windmill.

Anna.

James and Rose stayed in the medieval cobblestone bungalow owned by his uncle, surrounded by emerald rolling hills with a crystal clear pond in the back. Sheep and goats scattered about like trees, and friendly townsfolk stopped by to chat, curious over the new guests. It was a magical time for them both, and they savored every blissful moment, spending joyous, languorous days as a family, embracing the Irish experience and delighting in the simple things available to them. Everything from bathing their son in a tiny metal tub in the backyard; having a picnic out in the lush, green field; peregrinating hand in hand through the old town; dining in the only restaurant; to having a pint with the locals in the pub.

At times they were so happy they could sing, catching themselves staring at each other, teary-eyed. How can this be, they both thought? We are together in Ireland with our son, and another baby on the way. What miracle in the universe has allowed this?

And so it was . . .

"This is quite the operation," James said, walking through the old distillery owned by his uncle Flanagan.

The short, older man, broad-shouldered with squinty eyes and thick brows, skin red as a berry and hair to match, smiled at his nephew. "You know I have seven girls, aye?" he said, putting his arm around James' shoulder. "Siobhan, bless her heart, wants to manage this place; but I need a son. You could be that bloke, lad. You would do a proper job of it, too, and that's no lie."

James looked around the two-hundred-year-old stone building that had been in his family for generations, breathing in the various aromas of the distillation process. "Become a master distiller, devoted to keeping the Shahan liquid gold flowing, aye?"

His uncle nodded. "Too right, me boy. Would do you good to work here, raisin' your family in the land of Éire where you belong."

"Ta, Uncle Flanagan. I do need a job, so I'll take you up on it. But eventually I'm going to pursue my music career again. It's what I've dreamed of my whole life, and I'm gonna make it happen."

"I figured as much. Teach Siobhan, and she'll take over when you leave," said the convivial man, winking at his nephew. He walked up to a small cabinet against the stone wall and pulled out a fancy-looking bottle, pouring two drams of his finest whiskey. With a sparkle in his eye, he said, "Try this, lad."

Both men examined the golden fluid as they would a beautiful woman, swirling it in his glass, admiring its color, clarity, and viscosity before slowly raising it to his nose. Breathing in deeply, they each closed their eyes and savored the olfactory delectations of a round, buttery undertone with aromas of baked apple, linseed and tea tree oils, honey and vanilla. Opening their eyes, they looked at each other and smiled, taking a mouthful and letting it sit on their palates before swallowing, relishing the piquant taste with hints of cocoa and orange-scented butterscotch on the finish.

"Uisce na beathe!" Uncle Flanagan whooped in Gaelic. *("The water of life!")*

"Mionn fuilteach!" replied James. *("Bloody oath!")*

The older man poured two more drams. "To James Ragnar Shahan, my favorite nephew, being back in his home country with his beauty of a wife and son!" he toasted, lifting his glass.

James laughed. "And to Ugly Agnes and her ace Irish whiskey!"

A candle is lit; a candle is burned. The cycle of life is continuous. What is taken away is sometimes added back in abundance, and as the cycle pushes forward, both life and death co-exist. In life, our road ahead is paved with choices that lead to triumphs and regrets. And in death, we return to the dust from which we came.

Three months later, Rose gave birth to James' second son. They named him Ragnar. Life was moving forward as it always does, giving and taking along the way.

CHAPTER 54

Anna spends her days planting flowers in the hospital garden, just as she once did at Cassandra Fancy's garden. She enjoys being outdoors in the sunshine, temporarily escaping the sadness inside Pleasant Skies.

Yearning for her past life, she thinks of Sugar Alexandria—the rolling hills, the crops and animals, and the haunting sound of kulning that she would sing to bring the livestock in from the pastures they've been masticating. She thinks of Yarrajan—the only mother she really had; the stockmen and ringers; and most of all, her sweet young daughters, Scarlet and Mabel. She wants to go home. She is finally ready to pick up the pieces of her life and move on.

As she plants another beautiful native iris—the flower symbolizing hope—Anna longs so badly to be on the other side of the institute walls again. Free, able to watch the Australian sunset while sitting on her porch with her girls by her side.

But will she be able to?

Will they ever let her go?

Anna

I am healing in spite of things.

Dr. Octavia has been my lifeline.

Ruby, witty and full of wisdom, has been my mentor.

Aurora has been my friend.

The medications are working, helping me cope with my conditions, and when the hallucinations sometimes return, I merely ignore them until they vanish.

I've been learning how to handle stress better, too.

How to express myself and react appropriately, behave in the correct way, and show concern and empathy when I should.

And now I have been thinking more about my life outside this place.

My life with my daughters.

My life back at Sugar Alexandria without James and Rose.

I can see myself in it, terrified yet desperate to move forward.

Yes, I can see the light at the end of the tunnel.

Walking toward that warm, anodyne, glowing light.

✦

Dr. Octavia reviewed Anna's progress with Dr. Anderson, Chief Physician of Psychiatry at the Pleasant Skies Psychiatric Hospital. They both agreed that though Anna had made great strides with her treatment and improved significantly, the psychotic episode she had that almost resulted in a double murder could not be easily dismissed. Nor could her attempted suicide. So much was still unknown about schizophrenia and multiple personality disorder that to release her would be tantamount to medical malpractice, especially if she then relapsed and tried to hurt someone else again. Or herself. She may have to remain at the hospital indefinitely.

"I heard you're helping out in the cafeteria now," Dr. Octavia said during one of their therapy sessions. "Doing a grand job too, they tell me."

Anna proudly nodded. "They let me help serve the food trays and wash the dishes. I'm not allowed to touch the knives, though," she added, somewhat offended by the restriction. Pausing, she displayed a pensive guise.

"What is it, love?" asked the doctor.

Anna sighed. "I was just thinking about washing dishes in my own kitchen at Sugar Alexandria. I really miss my home and my daughters. When will I be released, Dr. Octavia?"

The doctor, knowing it wasn't likely to happen any time soon, diverted the conversation: "Where's Ruby and Aurora? I asked you to bring them with you today."

"What are you talking about? They're sitting in the room with us," Anna said, pointing at the couch next to her. "I'm surprised you haven't told Ruby to put her durry out, smoking like a chimney in front of you."

"Anna, there's something you need to know about these two women. Something you won't like."

"What's that?"

"They're not being honest with you."

"They're not?"

"No, they're not."

"What do you mean?" Anna looked at Ruby who was puffing on her opera length cigarette holder while filing her red nails, and at Aurora who was eating black licorice while reading a book.

"There are no patients at this hospital named Ruby Davis or Aurora Vega," said the doctor.

Confused, Anna stared at her in shock. "Is this some kind of joke? I know when someone is real."

"Ask Ruby and Aurora to talk to me, then."

Anna looked at her mentor and friend. "Say something to her, Ruby."

"If I did, doll, she still wouldn't listen."

Anna got scared. "Aurora, talk to the doctor."

But Aurora only turned a page in her book.

"Like the shadow people, and the swan people, and Genevieve, and your loved ones who come out of your cousin's paintings at night, they are hallucinations that your mind has created."

"No," Anna said, visibly trembling. "Ruby is like a mother to me, and Aurora like a sister. They're real," she cried. "They have to be!"

"Think, Anna. Ruby is the mother figure you've always wanted, and she protects you and makes you feel secure here at Pleasant Skies. Aurora is your cobber who looks like Rose, replacing your friendship that was destroyed."

"You're wrong!" Anna insisted. Her denial would not let them go.

"Anna, there's no one in the room here but us. The mind is extremely powerful, and yours has tricked you again."

"Don't listen to her, kid," Ruby said, a smirk on her face as she sat smugly on the couch. "Just agree with her, and let's go back to your room and we'll drink some booze."

Aurora remained quietly absorbed in her book.

"But Ruby gives me all sorts of gifts," Anna said, trying to reason with the doctor, presenting proof of her own.

"All gifts were from your brother when he visited."

"And the attendants have seen me and Aurora plant flowers in the garden. They watch us."

"You planted those flowers by yourself."

"But, but . . . Ruby loves me and Aurora is my cobber and, and, and . . ."

"Anna," said the doctor, giving her an empathetic look. "Aurora is Rose with long red hair. Look at her."

"You're mad, just like the people in this hospital!"

"Rose's full name is Ambrosia, and you call this woman Aurora. She's a hallucination."

"She's trying to drive you insane, kid," Ruby said. "Grab the pen on her desk and stab her! Stab her now! It's your only chance to escape!"

"No, Ruby!" Anna yelled. "I would never do that!"

The doctor kept pressing forward, knowing this was a pivotal moment for her patient. "Look at Aurora, Anna. Really look at her closely."

Aurora glanced up from her book and smiled.

"What color are her eyes?"

"Green. Emerald green."

"What color are Rose's eyes?"

"Emerald green," said Anna, studying the woman sitting on the couch next to Ruby. She noticed her quiet, poised demeanor, then watched in horror as Aurora slowly lifted her skirt to expose a deformed right leg. It had changed and now looked like Rose's! Dr. Octavia was right! "Oh God, I'm insane!" Anna cried out. "I'm insane!"

The doctor came over and held her. "It's all right, love."

Anna wanted to run, but instead sobbed into Dr. Octavia's shoulder.

"We needed to do this. The first step is to recognize what's real and what's not. After that, like learning a new language, you can learn how to live with it., deciphering what's real from what's a hallucination."

"How? How do I even know *you're* real?"

"That's where the learning comes in. Through careful observation, concrete evidence, corroboration with others, and common sense, you'll be able to recognize details to differentiate fact from fiction, reality from fantasy. Take the swan people, for example, or the insects that sometimes crawl on you. No one else has seen them, aye? And common sense tells you there's no such thing as a half swan half human. The same is true about Rose's artwork–everyone knows paintings don't come to life."

"Couldn't I just be gifted? Seeing and hearing things others don't?"

"If you want a somewhat normal life, you will have to ignore the voices and visual hallucinations, reining them in and accepting the fact that this is an illness not a gift."

Anna calmed, listening to the doctor's logic.

"You're a strong woman with a strong mind and a strong will, Anna. You can do this. When you suspect something is not real, test it out. Soon you'll become good at it, and you'll trust your judgment."

Ruby and Aurora were listening on the couch. Ruby had the same disapproving smirk on her face, puffing on her opera length cigarette holder, and Aurora winked at Anna before returning to her book.

Anna closed her eyes and focused hard, even praying, trying to control the hallucination, telling herself it wasn't real. When she opened her eyes again, Ruby and Aurora were gone.

~c✦☙~

After discovering Ruby and Aurora are not real, Anna improves immensely, gaining a momentous measure of control over her illness. It makes her feel more powerful and confident.

She tries hard to ignore the voices when they come, and if any of the hallucinations appear, she stares them down until they go away. She gives them absolutely no attention, going about her day, eating her meals, reading books in the library about her condition, avoiding sugar, and getting plenty of fresh air and sunshine, her freckles turning from pink to brown. She even volunteers for additional minor duties inside the hospital, and assists the groundskeeper with maintaining the garden outside.

I can fight this, she thinks. I can overcome it. Using the same spunk, determination, and stubbornness I was born with, and the logic Dr. Octavia has enlightened me with, I can even beat it.

"I have great news for you, love," Dr. Octavia said one afternoon, a motherly smile gracing her lips as she opened Anna's file.

Anna got excited, sitting in the chair by the large window overlooking the hospital grounds—a consistent fixture in her therapy. "I'm going home?"

"Not just yet, but soon. Your ex-husband petitioned the court, giving strong testimony that what happened was uncharacteristic of your nature, and that you were fully capable of living on your own despite your illness, just as you had been for years before the attack."

Anna was completely surprised. "James did that for me?"

"Yes. He hired a top lawyer to pursue the case, and the judge authorized your release, as long as your supervising physician agreed it was safe to do so. I issued that statement of agreement last week."

A rush of emotions surged through Anna—hope, joy, relief, sadness, regret, repentance, forgiveness. "James fought for me," she cried.

"He did."

Fat, happy tears streamed down Anna's cheeks. "If it hadn't been for James, I'd probably have suffered much worse. He has the patience of a wise old tree, and the heart of an ocean." She smiled as she cried. "Oh, James. My sweet, tender James."

"He still cares about you, Anna. To fight so hard in court for your release like that shows a sense of loyalty and dedication to you, despite what happened in your marriage."

"Loyalty and dedication to a broken egg."

"You're not a broken egg, love. You just have some ailments that you need to be aware of and effectively deal with."

Anna stared at the ground. The weight of that reality often hit her without warning. "I am grateful I'm going home, but I still hear voices and see things that aren't there, Dr. Octavia. I'm scared I won't be able to hold things together."

The doctor closed Anna's file. "Do you know who Joan of Arc was?"

Anna shook her head.

"She was a fifteenth-century heroine who led the French army to victory over the English at Orléans during the Hundred Years' War, and became a martyr for France. They even canonized her as a saint. And yet, she also heard voices, just like you, and saw visions of things not real. A lot of doctors have since speculated that she suffered the same conditions as you."

That dulcified Anna, and suddenly she felt stronger, envisioning herself as a modern-day Joan of Arc, fighting the battle of her illnesses.

"In fact, there are many people with this condition, and they all fight the same war you do." The doctor pulled out another folder from her desk. "One of them was a person very near and dear to your heart, and I believe you're ready to know who that was. You're ready for the truth."

"The truth?"

Dr. Octavia handed her the folder. "I think this is going to play a large part in your ongoing recovery. By knowing your family history, you won't feel so alone over what's ahead."

Anna looked at the name on the cover and felt the earth move beneath her feet. It read, *Elsa Polston*. Wide-eyed, she opened the folder and scanned the first page . . .

Patient Name: Elsa Polston
Date of Birth: April 11, 1877
Diagnosis: Schizophrenia, Multiple Personality Disorder, Other Unknown
Severity: Acute
Prognosis: Poor
Status: Died June 29, 1911

Confused and in shock, Anna looked up at the doctor.

"Your mother was also a patient at Pleasant Skies," Dr. Octavia said. She explained how Elsa had suffered from severe mental illness and declining health for years, in and out of the hospital multiple times.

"I don't understand," said Anna. "It says here she died in 1911, but Mummy died giving birth to me and Blessing."

"No, Anna, she didn't. Your mother died here, ten years after you were born."

Anna was speechless.

"After delivering you and your sister, her mental health declined to the point where she had to be committed indefinitely."

"No, that's not true," Anna protested.

"Yes, love; it is."

Anna began to cry uncontrollably.

Dr. Octavia got up and hugged her, holding her tight.

"They lied to me," Anna said, sobbing. "Everyone lies to me."

"Your family thought they were protecting you."

"So I'm sick like she was? I have the same illnesses as Mummy?"

"Your ailments are nowhere near as bad as hers were. That's the good news, love. Your symptoms are much milder, and you can still live a functional life."

Anna sobbed into her shoulder. "How do you know, though? How do you know I won't get worse and end up here forever, just like my mum?"

"Because I've treated you for months, now, and I see the strength and determination in you. You've dealt with this your whole life without even knowing what it was, and that's remarkable. Now that you have the tools necessary, I'm certain your symptoms will subside and become manageable. And I will help you, too, even when you leave here. You just need to be a warrior like Joan of Arc and fight this. Avoid stress, stay calm, take your medication, and try to abstain from sugar where possible. You can control it, Anna. In your mother's case, it controlled her."

"I can't believe they never told me," Anna cried. "Oh, Mummy, I'm so sorry. I wish I could hug you now. I wish Blessing and I could be with you, to comfort you."

Dr. Octavia gently took hold of Anna's small shoulders and looked directly into her eyes. "Listen to me, love. You have two beautiful daughters as well. Right now they're waiting for you; they need their mummy home with them. You can be for your girls what your mum wasn't able to be for you."

Anna sobered at the doctor's assertion, wiping her eyes. "You're right. My girls need me," she said, elation passing through her as if the clouds were parting to let the sun shine through. At that moment, so many unanswered questions were now answered, and she felt closer to her mother than ever before. "I'm going to keep taking care of myself for my daughters," she continued with conviction. "No sugar, avoid stress, ignore the voices and other hallucinations if they return, and take my medication. I can be a warrior like Joan of Arc. I can fight this."

"Good girl, Anna. Good girl."

CHAPTER 55

One year to the day she was first admitted to the Pleasant Skies Psychiatric Hospital, Anna was finally released. Dr. Octavia once again reassured her that she had all the necessary tools and inner strength required to carve out a wonderful new life for herself, and encouraged her not to give up, even in the face of future challenges. With tears in her eyes, Anna thanked her, pledging to the doctor she would do her very best.

Outside, a stiff, chilly wind blew, and a single white butterfly glided in the breeze, unaware of its delicate and refined beauty. As Anna watched it, she recalled when Rose had gathered all the chrysalides from the yard at Sugar Alexandria, and the euphoria of witnessing them complete their metamorphosis into butterflies. The image of them flying all around her outside the windmill radiated in her mind, while Rose's words echoed: "Like butterflies, we are constantly transforming; we just don't always notice it. Through love we heal and through knowledge we become wiser, experiencing our own metamorphosis, so to speak, and it's an extraordinary thing."

Before Anna could go home, she had to live with Christian and Josephine for a while, under her brother's supervision and care. She couldn't be with her daughters unchaperoned, either, until the judge was satisfied she was no longer a threat to herself, to them, or to anyone. In the meantime, she worked at her brother's restaurant, went to sleep, then woke the next morning to do it all over again.

Days passed. Then weeks.

During this time, they told her James and Rose had moved to Ireland and soon after had their second child—a boy they named Ragnar. Another son, Anna pondered. And the world around her spun.

While waitressing at The Flame Tree Grill one morning, Anna waited on a customer named Flossy McKay, a neighboring station owner and widower who came to the restaurant for breakfast. A tall, burly man, he tipped his Akubra hat at Anna and sat down, then ordered practically everything on the menu. He was bossy with her, too, perhaps even a bit rude, and wouldn't call her by her nametag—he just called her Goldilocks. Goldilocks get me this; Goldilocks get me that. She didn't like it. She made a mental note that the next time he came in, she would have the other waitress serve him. Otherwise, she might give him a piece of her mind.

Every morning, the same man came in for breakfast and sat down in his usual booth, asking for his favorite waitress—he wouldn't give his order to anyone but her. Anna complied and served him breakfast each day, despite being ordered around. He chuckled when he saw her getting frustrated, but his tip was more than generous, so she endured.

At first Anna would only stand there with a deadpan face, avoiding eye contact with him as she took his order. But then she realized he was actually flirting with her, and her vacuous expression turned into a smile, the gap between her front teeth showing.

"Well look at that," he noticed, "you have a gap between your teeth.

That's about the most adorable thing I have ever seen."

Her smile grew larger, dimples popping.

Soon Anna looked forward to serving Flossy each morning, a funny sensation rising in her belly each time he walked through the door. She even surprised herself, finding she was attracted to his boyish face, with the dimple in his chin, his short nose, and his happy brown eyes that seemed to sparkle when they looked at her.

Flossy asked Anna if she'd go out for dinner with him, but Anna wasn't ready for that yet and declined. He wouldn't take no for an answer, though, and after a dozen more attempts to woo her, she finally accepted.

They went to an expensive high-end restaurant where Flossy told her to order anything her little heart desired. It surprised Anna how the somewhat presumptuous man she had come to know from the diner was also keenly witty and humorous, both of them laughing so hard her side hurt.

"What are you staring at, love?" he asked.

"Your hands."

"What's wrong with them?"

"They're just so different from my ex-husband's."

"Is that a good thing or bad?"

"Just different. His fingers were long and slender." Anna remembered how soft James' hands once were, and how they bled from the hard work he wasn't accustomed to. "He had the hands of a pianist; your hands look like a bunch of bananas," she laughed.

"Bananas! Oh, you!" Flossy said, tickling her until she begged him to stop. Then he took her hand and kissed the back of it. "And your hand is like a seashell, love. A seashell I want to hold for the rest of my days."

When they were finished eating, the conversation became more serious, and Anna shared her heartache—she told him about James and Rose. As she told her story, it amazed her that she could feel the pain wash over her, but she did not cry. Almost as if it were another woman's life story and not her own. Struck by how sad it sounded, she now felt embarrassed how she had allowed herself to be so wrapped up in her cousin's happiness that she ended up destroying her own. Flossy only shrugged and told her she was better off without them.

"I'm not like other sheilas, Flossy," Anna said, sipping on her drink. "I might not be good for you."

"How's that?"

"I have to take meds, and sometimes I still see and hear things that are not there."

"You worry too much, love," was all he said. "Let me decide what's good or bad for me."

After they left the restaurant, they went for a stroll and window-shopped, holding hands. Eventually they found themselves at a park, and that's when Flossy grabbed her and kissed her under a bridge.

"You looked like a girl who needed a kiss," he said, plucking a magnolia off a nearby bush and sticking it in her hair.

Anna closed her eyes, letting the cool night air buss her skin. The lovely scent of the flowers in bloom intoxicated her senses as she inhaled. "Can you kiss me again?" she asked, opening her eyes and gazing up at him.

He tilted his hat up and pulled her in close, kissing her long and hard. He kissed her until she shivered and became breathless, enmeshing his large hands into her hair, causing the white magnolia to fall to the ground, its delicate, white petals softly opening.

CHAPTER 56

Anna

Working at The Flame Tree Grill had been a necessary step for me, turning out to be a better experience than expected, but it was time for me to go home. Christian told me he had spoken with Dr. Octavia, and they both agreed I was ready to live on my own. As I packed my things, I realized it had been well over a year since I last saw Sugar Alexandria. A mix of emotions flooded my body.

Lovely Dawn was the first to run up and greet me, snorting at my feet and making me smile. Bluebelle, Catalou, and Beauty soon joined her, then scampered off chasing after the geese. Poka hopped across the stockyard, returning to the bush. The farmhouse looked the same, the barn did as well, and the three windmills still spun effortlessly in complete harmony, as if three wooden souls welcoming their guest. That's when it hit me I was actually home.

Yarra welcomed me at the door, tears in her eyes, and I gave her a big hug. I told her how much I missed and loved her, thanking her for all that she had done. She smiled and called me her pale little rabbit. And yet, behind her smile lurked a sadness.

Scarlet and Mabel excitedly ran up to me, and I dropped to my knees to hug them, squeezing their little bodies and kissing their rosy cheeks. "Look at you big girls," I cried. I was so happy to see them, and with my precious daughters in my arms, everything in the world was once again right.

Later that day, Yarra had a lovely surprise for me. She brought me outside where a dozen Aboriginal children patiently waited, and with her nod, they began to sing. Highs and lows, on key and off, each child sang different notes, yet collectively sounded beautiful.

"They be welcomin' you home, Miss Anna," said the only mother I've ever known.

～∽⤫∾～

Glenda TrufflePig stopped by, bringing along her famous peacock pecan pie. Anna invited Glenda in and served the pie with two glasses of goat milk, her face devoid of joy, her sparkle gone.

"Look at you with your sour face and bitterness," Glenda said, not having any of Anna's pouting. "Cheer up, girl."

"It's not that easy, Glenda. I have lost my husband and my best cobber. I doubt I'll ever be rapt again."

The older woman laughed. "Listen to ya whingeing. You live on the most beauty of a station in the entire Shire of Esperance, right by the bloody sea. Some of the best stockmen and ringers in all of Straya work for you. Your daughters are happy and healthy, and you're still a young sheila with plenty o' time to meet another bloke. Yet here you are, cryin' over an English tart and a skinny bogan who you tricked into marriage anyway."

Anna went to argue, but Glenda stopped her. "Shush, now! You know it's true, and that's no lie. Everyone in the whole bloody town knows how you tricked that poor bloke into being a station owner."

"You're right," Anna said remorsefully. "I shouldn't have done that."

"Aah, no worries, love. All spilt milk now."

"But who's gonna wanna marry me, Glenda? I'm not well. There's something different about me."

"Ha! There isn't a person on this earth who doesn't have quirks and oddities of some kind."

Anna smiled.

"There she is! There's that sheila I have always known. The girl with bloomin' cornflowers in her eyes and fire in her soul!" Glenda reached over and touched Anna's cheek. "Listen, child. All you need is a tablespoon of joy, and a big slice of sunshine. And I'll tell ya another thing—you need to find that girl who ran barefoot in the woods; climbed trees and danced in the rain; collected mushrooms, herbs, and spices for tucker; and sang that sweet opera to the animals. Where is that wild girl? Where'd she go? Bring her back, love."

"I'm still here," Anna said, remembering all those things the eccentric trapper said. Remembering who she once was, her eyes filling with tears. "I'm right here."

"God bless ya, little Anna! God bless ya!"

Anna

I did my Scandinavian kulning this morning for the first time since being back, and the cows and sheep sauntered toward me. It was a lonely feeling not having Rose by my side, playing her violin as she often did when I sang. But I continued on anyway, and soon all the animals were home.

Later in the day, I visited Cassandra Fancy's garden to release Eden, whom I had taken home from the hospital in a box. I found a beauty of a spot with lovely flowers and protective rocks, and the spider who had been my cherished cobber during a time of despair slowly crawled out, disappearing into her new abode. It was a sweet moment for me, and I smiled.

As I laid ruminating on the soft grass among the beautiful blossoms, the impressive statues, and the tranquil pond with Mrs. Swan, I realized that throughout my life I had created a dreamworld of sorts. Some of it was real, and some not. My childhood second nanny Genevieve, my secret room, the shrine I built for Mummy and Blessing, Cassandra's garden, Rose's windmill, and the hallucinations from the paintings were all part of this fantasy. So was the trinity I had created with James and Rose. Though we had all been one unit once, one family, like a splendid tree with its roots deep in the ground, the integrity of the soil proved fickle.

Lying on the grass in that magnificent garden on that beauty of a day, I reveled in the wonder of it all. Butterflies gently floated by, hummingbirds sought nectar from the flowers, Mrs. Swan glided serenely in the pond, and the sweet smell of cherry blossoms wafted through the air. In that moment, I felt total peace. I knew this was where I was meant to be, and my happiness depended on no one but me.

Like a reflection in still water, the land I was born on, that I grew up on, that I will die on, is an extension of me and the wild things I love. The things that feed my soul. Why I foolishly craved Rose's love and friendship so much that it nearly destroyed me, when the land was my true mother, sister, and friend, is beyond me. Knowing this now, however, I can breathe easy, as if the land has opened its arms to me, cleansed me, rebirthed me, rocking me like a baby.

Yes, Sugar Alexandria in the wild and wondrous Outback, with all her stupendous glory, has called me home.

CHAPTER 57

Flossy McKay picked up Anna every Friday night and took her out to dinner, shopping, or to the movies. It did not bother him that she had to take medication, nor was he worried that she sometimes saw or heard things that were not there. He even teased her about it, saying they were just small dents in the armor of a beautiful sheila.

Anna liked how tall and strong he was, and felt secure with his hand protectively encasing hers. When they conversed, he spoke about his love for the land, the station work, and the animals and crops. She shared her love of these things as well, and soon Flossy came to Sugar Alexandria regularly, helping her on the station wherever he could.

One enchanted evening, after months of courting, Flossy McKay got down on one knee. "Anna May Polston," he said, his kind eyes nervous yet sincere, "I have fallen in love with you somethin' awful, and I want you by my side for the rest of my life." Popping open the lid of a small velvet box, he presented her with a sparkling, heart-shaped diamond. "Will you marry me and make me the happiest bloke in all of Straya?"

In happy shock, Anna squealed. "Yes, I will marry you!" she exclaimed. "Yes, a thousand times yes!" jumping up and down.

Flossy picked her up and spun her around the room, kissing her lips. It was a deliriously blissful moment for them both. One of many to come.

Flossy and Anna were married in a large ceremony at Sugar Alexandria. All the other station owners around the Shire of Esperance were invited with their families, and the turnout was surprisingly spectacular. The most glorious wedding of the year. By then the scandalous gossip had died down, and most people agreed that Anna had suffered enough. Plus, their busybody curiosity to see Anna getting hitched was stronger than their self-righteous indignation.

Only once during the ceremony did Anna think of James and Rose. Her eyes swept among the guests, searching for their faces despite knowing they were not present. She envisioned them sitting side by side, holding hands, both babies in tow, one on each of their laps, smiling and happy for her on finding true love and moving on. But then Flossy walked up and put his arm around her, and his firm embrace made her feel as if James and Rose didn't exist.

Not long after the wedding, Flossy sold his land, and they joined forces to expand the operations of Sugar Alexandria, increasing their head of cattle, along with the sheep, ostriches, camels, wheat, and sugarcane. They hired more men, too, and built new living quarters for the stockmen and ringers next to the barn. Anna became absorbed in her own life—her husband, her girls, the station—and Sugar Alexandria thrived. Her memories of James and Rose gradually faded like colors on an old painting, going out of focus, seeping to the back of her mind.

As the sands of time continued to fall, her new life kept forging ahead. James and Rose's world kept moving forward too. Life, like ivy, thrives in ways you cannot explain, organically creating its own path, building its own structures, climbing up walls and growing in the direction of its heart's desire.

The clock ticked on. Anna continued to heal and learn how to cope with and manage her illnesses. More babies were born.

Seasons changed.

Years passed.

CHAPTER 58

Several Years Later . . .

Year after year, the emerald Irish spring turns into a golden summer, giving birth to amber autumn, fading away into gray winter before starting the cycle all over. This continual spinning of time takes no prisoners and gives no quarter, especially with respect to those we love . . .

James and Rose were still in Ireland, living in the quaint, medieval cottage in the village of Cong. They relished in exploring the land and the people, and every weekend James would take his family along the narrow, winding roads, cutting across endless emerald fields scattered with Galway sheep, sojourning in different towns where they would sightsee, immersing themselves in his Gaelic heritage.

They loved spending time in Kinsale, County Cork, a town famous for its scenic harbor, cramped streets with quaint, colorful shops, restaurants, and art galleries, and two seventeenth-century fortresses overlooking the River Bandon: the vast, star-shaped Charles Fort to the southeast, and the smaller James Fort on the river's opposite bank.

Or visiting Sean's Pub in the heart of Ireland, halfway between Dublin and Galway. The low-ceilinged, one-thousand-year-old watering hole with riverside garden, live music, and historical artifacts was the oldest pub in the country, and part of the life and soul of Athlone, County Westmeath.

The young family explored several of the over three thousand castles dotting the island, from cliff-side promontory to inland oasis, the ancient ruins displaying different architectural shapes and styles with Gothic windows, Celtic round towers, Norman keeps, and Romanesque arches. Like Dunluce Castle, the quintessential medieval Irish citadel looming over the sea atop a dark basalt outcrop, and once home to the feuding McQuillan and MacDonnell clans. Or Ballynahinch Castle, built over half a millennium ago, where some of the most infamous figures of Irish legend, including pirate queen and chieftain, Grace O'Malley, and the 'Ferocious O'Flaherty Clan', graced its halls.

They enjoyed hiking the Wicklow Mountains, with its stunning, wide-open vistas and fast-flowing streams descending into deep lakes in the wooded valleys. Or walking the top of the Cliffs of Moher—the fourteen-kilometer-long sea bluffs located at the southwestern edge of the Burren region in County Clare, known to many as the eighth wonder of the world.

The Shahans took long drives, like the one-hundred-seventy-nine-kilometer circular route along the Ring of Kerry in the Iveragh Peninsula of southwest Ireland's County Kerry, with its rugged and verdant coastal landscapes and rural seaside villages. And they visited countless other iconic landmarks, each with its own history and charm, singing the popular Irish song, *Molly Malone*, laughing and clapping along the way.

In all these places they visited, the happy family tried different eateries and foods, learned Goidelic history and culture, and participated in the traditional celebrations accompanied by the Celtic harp, the uillean pipes, and the dancers wearing kilts and ghillies. This was their life for the time being, loving everything their new world had to offer.

During this time, Rose gave birth to their third child—a beautiful baby girl: Ireland Anna Shahan. She was so small and fragile—quite different from her brothers. Rose knew it would be her last, so she endeavored to enjoy her new baby as much as she could, holding her often, kissing her until the infant squirmed, having the child sleep on her chest every night. James said she was spoiling her, but in truth, he spoiled her more. When he was home, he barely put her down. Two sons and a daughter, plus two twin girls who would visit during holidays and summer break—their family was complete.

James also made new, influential friends in the music world. He started out modestly, playing to enthusiastic audiences in the local church and theater, and that's when he met Chaste Nightingale, a French aristocrat married to an Irish politician. Refined and slightly pretentious, she was also a deliciously friendly woman and quite the social butterfly, calling everyone by their first name in such a warm fashion as if she had known them her entire life. Chaste happened to be visiting the village of Cong one evening when James was performing in the local theater, and after hearing him play, implored him to attend her yearly soiree at her mansion in Dublin to perform for her guests. James agreed, and there he put his musical talents on display. Mesmerizing many with his renditions of Mozart, Beethoven, Bach, Rachmaninoff, and several others, it led to an invitation to perform as a special guest with a prestigious symphony orchestra, and James accepted, starting a professional tour across Europe. After twenty-plus years in the waiting, the curtain call had finally arrived.

With the success of his acclaimed debut in the symphony orchestra, and the connections he made as a result, James was invited back to several venues for an encore recital. He took his family with him to Denmark, Finland, Switzerland, Germany, Austria, Czechoslovakia, Italy, and a host of other countries and cities where he was scheduled to play. When he laid his hands upon the ebony and ivory, his fingers embracing every key as if a precious gem, the grand piano sung. He played for his audience, for his children, for Rose. He played for God and His angels. He played for his own soul, exceedingly thankful for his dreams come true.

As his music career grew, James continued to perform as a solo pianist at many functions, fundraisers, and events. And then he was invited to tour Australia, playing for sold-out crowds in large auditoriums. He was known as the grazier who became a pianist, or perhaps the pianist who was once a grazier.

"He's the best I've ever heard, hands down," the audience would say afterward. "His ability is superb. That pianist has a gift from heaven."

But James had a secret. He knew the key to his exceptional skill was interwoven with his humble, grateful spirit. Because for so long, he had been held down, his wings tied.

After that sad day at the Pleasant Skies Psychiatric Hospital, Rose had never seen her Kitten again. She had hoped against hope that one day Anna would forgive her, triggering a reconciliation at last, but it never happened. It had been several years since they last spoke, and now that she was back in Australia with her husband, her optimism once again revived.

While James was scheduled to play several concerts in Perth, Fremantle, and Kalgoorlie, Rose's curiosity got the better of her, and three times she made the long drive out to Sugar Alexandria, observing from a distance the place she once called home. With her hair tied back in a scarf, wearing large sunglasses for disguise, she would take in the large Danish farmhouse, the three magnificent windmills, the sprawling land and the beautiful, enormous sunflowers bleeding out on both sides of the wrought iron gate like tall yellow wings.

She was never lucky enough to catch sight of her cousin, unfortunately, but Anna's children would sometimes run alongside her slow-moving car, waving and trying to race her as she inched along. They'd stick their tiny hands out to touch hers, each one bearing Anna's lovely freckles, each one laughing and giggling just as Rose remembered their mother had. "The stranger is here again!" they would squeal in delight, excited to see the mysterious visitor. "Who are you?" they would ask.

Rose would simply smile and keep driving, thinking but not saying, "Your mother was once my best cobber. My Kitten. And I was her beloved." In the rearview mirror, she'd watch their little bodies standing barefoot, wearing only overalls in the middle of that long dirt road, wondering who she was, and why she would only drive on by.

One afternoon while shopping in town, Anna came across a poster advertising James' next performance in Kalgoorlie. Just as her daughters had excitedly described, James Ragnar Shahan, the visiting Irish pianist, was scheduled to play at the Hummingbird Auditorium. She took down the poster and brought it back to her car, examining it closely. The photo only showed half of James' face; the other half was a grand piano. Across the image of the piano, a list of all the songs he was to perform was written in fancy cursive. Anna scanned the titles of his originals . . .

An Irishman's Tears
James, Her Muse
Sùilean Uaine (Green Eyes)
The Fire Dance
The Heart of the Ocean
Paintings Come to Life
The Consequence of Anna

Anna's eyes rested on the last title, *The Consequence of Anna*. At first anger bubbled up inside her, seeing that he had named a song after her suffering. But then the sensation cooled, and surprisingly she felt flattered. She liked the idea of once again being a part of James and Rose, even if only in the title of a song. She wondered what the music sounded like, and if it would take her back to the life she had once lived with them.

An esteemed classical music critic had written a review of James' last concerto, and it was included on the poster. As Anna read it, it was hard for her to imagine that he was speaking about her former husband . . .

"From an eerie stillness to a frenetic burst of music that exploded as loud as thunder. It was in that moment that the man became the piano. Two beings—one human, one machine—merging to produce a sound that was otherworldly. How on earth did this Irishman—once a grazier—learn to play with such genius! Unbridled passion, unprecedented showmanship, and unequaled talent mesmerized the theater, moving all to tears. The pianist played as if his life depended on it, his strangely elegant hands moving across the keys with impetuosity, his shoulders

swaying, head lolling, eyes on fire, an eidolon haunting his body. At the end I was numb. Emotionally exhausted. Tingling. I have never heard anyone play the piano like that before . . . and I doubt I ever will again."
– Pablo Delacroix

Anna shivered as she folded up the poster. I want to go see him play, she thought. No, I *must* go see him play. I will not rest until I have heard him once again.

On the day of the concert, Flossy watched the children while Anna went alone to Kalgoorlie to see her ex-husband perform. She sat at the very back, hidden in her black hat and coat, hidden in the crowd of people, hidden in the vastness of the auditorium, hidden in the darkness. Suddenly, the spotlight shined on James, and her heart pounded rapidly in her chest as the audience cheered. With a transitory introduction from the violins, he began to play.

The music was bold, incredible, enthralling, the sound touching Anna's soul. And as she listened, she cried. He was brilliant, conferring on her a sense of peace she had never felt before. Why had she never embraced his music when they were together, she pondered? Why had she ignored his desire to play, even putting him down for it? How could she have denied such a talent? Regret washed over her, knowing that she alone had kept this man from his gift for over a decade.

The last song, *The Consequence of Anna*, was the most powerful. Erratic, capricious, eerily emotional, thunderous and sad. But wholly beautiful, she concluded. As the sorrowful melody filled the auditorium, images and memories flashed through her mind. The song poignantly captured a part of her life that eventually turned tragic. Her life with James and Rose. It sang to her from the bowels of the grand piano played by her ex-husband, reminding her of times and seasons and experiences. She thought of when she had tricked James into marriage with a false pregnancy. She thought of running Sugar Alexandria together with him, and having children with him. She thought of her loving Rose, him loving Rose, and her losing them both. Her happiness that turned to denial and pain and suffering. It was all magically embedded into the notes, into the melody, into the chorus.

At the end of the song, Rose walked onstage and kissed her husband. Anna could not look away. "Lottie, I would do anything for you, just anything," she recalled always saying to her cousin. "Oh, Kitten, how I love you so," Rose would always reply.

Anna ripped her eyes away from the couple on stage and fled. As she exited the auditorium, wondrous reflections danced in her head. She knew the answer to the riddle: "That pianist was once my husband," she whispered proudly to herself, tears streaming. "And he wrote that song about us."

On the long drive home that night, Anna hummed the dramatic song James had written, inspired by her . . .

The Consequence of Anna.

The sun rises; the sun sets; and this cycle repeats itself endlessly. Life, when examined, is but a tree, with branches that continually grow and spread out, until the Maker brings you home . . .

PART FOUR

"Life appears to me too short to be spent in nursing animosity, or registering wrongs."

– Charlotte Brontë

CHAPTER 59

Decades Later . . .

James was neither asleep nor awake, lying in his bed somewhere in no-man's-land, half listening as his wife spoke on the phone in the kitchen. They had just returned from Switzerland where he had performed in a charitable concert, and now that he was home again, he realized extensive travels were no longer meant for him. After decades of traveling all over the world as a pianist and composer, his vigor and energy had now waned.

Closing his eyes, he began to reminisce over his life. Academic awards and accomplishments from his years of teaching filled him with pride, and countless memories and experiences from his performances as a professional pianist filled him with joy. He and Rose even had the pleasure of creating a foundation for the deaf, which turned into a school called Liam's Lyrics, teaching deaf children and adults how to play musical instruments through their novel technique of vibration and image association. The school became quite successful, too, picking up support from several other sponsors and philanthropists to expand across both Ireland and Australia.

James had more life mementos surrounding him than he could ever wish for. A life built by a miraculous twist of fate that poked its head up to intervene, correcting the discordance and removing the flaw. It changed the entire course of his history, his reality. Whereas once he had succumbed to cerebral ennui, now he was a man full of gratitude for the gifts God had given him.

"How was your nap?" Rose asked.

He blinked, reaching for his glasses as he tried to focus on his wife. "Grouse. Who was that on the phone?"

"Scarlet. She had sad news: Anna's husband passed away last night."

James frowned. "That's too bad. God rest his soul."

Rose sat down on the bed and held his hand. "I think about her quite often nowadays."

"I know. Me too," he replied, squeezing her hand in agreement.

"I wish it hadn't turned out so tragic back then," Rose said, her eyes tearing. "The way it all unfolded . . . The attack, her emotional pain, being committed . . . So dark."

James stared out the window. An image of a young Anna running to meet him as he walked across the stockyard at Sugar Alexandria flashed through his mind. He could see her face so clearly, smiling at him under a pure, unadulterated blue sky, a marmalade lollipop of a sun hanging low, peeking behind a feathery veil of evening clouds. "Rose," he said.

"Yes?"

"I have been thinking lately . . . about after I pass."

"Oh, don't say such things. You still have a ways to go."

"I know, but when I do, I think I would like to be laid to rest at Sugar Alexandria instead of my father's Irish burial plot, if Anna will allow it."

Rose looked at him with great surprise. "I don't understand. You had always longed to leave that place."

"I feel differently now. Sugar Alexandria was such a beauty of a place, right by the ocean, despite the arduous work it demanded. And I don't think I would have become the pianist and composer I am today without the experience of my marriage to Anna. In fact, in that little cabin in Indigo Bay—the Barracuda Hut—I composed some of my best work. Not to mention that I would have never met you again if it weren't for that place. So in many ways, Sugar Alexandria has made me who I am, and given me what I have."

Rose kissed the back of his hand, then laid down next to him. "If you are to be buried there, then so am I."

Life is such a funny, glorious, and tragic enigma, all at the same time, James found himself thinking. We begin with a blank canvas, and as the days spread out before us, we color our own world with the desires, ambitions, and circumstances we've been given. He had finally been able to paint his own authenticity as he wanted. Although he was remorseful that Anna had been hurt in the process, what he did was only take back his own life. The life he was meant to live. The life he so badly yearned for. But now, it was time to return to Australia, to the red earth, the open skies, and perhaps . . . even Sugar Alexandria.

Holding tightly on to his wife, James thought of the small wooden animals he used to whittle at the station when he craved his own freedom. In his mind's eye, he could see each and every bird he ever sculpted come alive and take flight into the shining heavens above. Then he saw Anna again, as she once was, running alongside his tractor, holding wildflowers in her hand and waving him home.

Sugar Alexandria had prospered for many years, as did Anna's family. But time waits for no one, and as the years layered one after the other like sediment cakes at the bottom of the sea, Anna found herself living alone as a widow. Flossy had passed away, and all her children were grown and married with lives and children of their own. Now with a crown of silver hair, she spent her days taking long walks by the shoreline, baking bickies for her grandchildren, or picking flowers from Cassandra Fancy's garden, placing them on the graves in the family burial plot, including Callum McTavish's.

With the ongoing help of Dr. Octavia, and the support of her husband, Anna had succeeded in gaining control of her schizophrenia and sporadic multiple personality disorder. She sought out answers for the third, unnamed disorder Dr. Octavia said she had, as well, receiving an official diagnosis of Asperger's syndrome, or high-functioning autism. Learning from the books the doctor recommended, she trained herself how to socially interact appropriately, how to recognize the feelings and emotions of others and display empathy when called for, and how to control her outbursts and tantrums, her nonstop rambling, and other idiosyncrasies. It wasn't easy, but the schizophrenia medication kept the hallucinations and trance-like whispering episodes at bay, and with a newfound awareness and understanding of the syndrome that previously had no name, she made great strides in coping with it. Flossy was her tower of strength, too, assisting her every step of the way. He truly loved Anna and gave everything he had to advocate for his wife, helping her with her conditions. It made all the difference in their relationship, and that's why it had lasted.

The life given to Anna was not what she had originally wanted, but it was what she needed. The years with Flossy had been like soft feathers to cushion her fall, and the new memories they created together were silver and gold.

With each day that ended with the sun absconding from the moon, Anna often found herself standing in front of one of the paintings in the farmhouse. Seeing herself as she once was, and Rose too, intensified her longing to see her cousin again. A craving to laugh as they once had. How wonderful it would be to walk through Cassandra's garden together, if only one last time before she died! She had forgotten her pain, and in doing so, her heart opened for the woman she once loved as a sister. I wonder, she asked herself, if I will ever see my beloved Rose again . . .

On one particular morning, Anna was assorting flowers from Cassandra Fancy's garden when she noticed she had subconsciously picked all the violets. Purple—such a beautiful color.

Rose's favorite color.

The scent of Chypre de Coty mixed with clove suddenly overwhelmed her senses, and the taste of black licorice settled on her tongue as Rose's image walking toward her through the fields of wheat filled her mind like a beacon of light. An image as intoxicating as it was haunting.

Walking to the window, she stared at the three Danish windmills proudly standing their ground in the yard. As their imposing blades spun, her eyes lingered on the center mill that had once been her beloved cousin's home. Becoming lost in the past, instantly—as if a mirage—she saw Rose standing in front of the windmill, her belly pregnant with Joshua. Rose smiled and waved, motioning for Anna to come outside and join her. Anna smiled at the illusion and lifted her hand, momentarily waving back at the ethereal image only she could see.

The knocking on the door broke Anna's trance, bringing her back to the present.

"Want me to get it, Miss Anna?" Allora called out from the other room. She had been working at the station ever since her grandmother, Yarrajan, had passed.

"No worries, love, I can get it." Grabbing her spectacles off the table, Anna got up and walked to the front door. Her arthritic hand curled around the doorknob and opened it; on the other side stood a tall man with a familiar face. He reminded Anna of someone, but she could not recall whom.

"G'day, Mrs. McKay," he said with a strong Irish accent and easygoing smile, removing his fedora. Dressed in a three-piece suit, clean-shaven with his hair sleeked back, his piercing eyes were magnetic.

Anna took in his appearance. "You're obviously not a stockman looking for work. You a reporter?" She smirked. "After all these years, there's still interest in that story, aye? Guess the sticky beaks never go away."

His smile widened. "No, I'm not a reporter. I'm a physician. But I did come here to talk to you."

"About what?"

"I'm James and Rose Shahan's son, Joshua. And the half brother of Scarlet and Mabel."

Anna blanched. Blinking hard, she tried to refocus her eyes on him, momentarily speechless. "You're baby Joshua?" she finally asked in disbelief.

He laughed. "Yes. Except, as you can see, I'm not a baby anymore."

Instantly Anna saw the newborn whom she had once cradled in her arms and kissed on his cheek. The very neonate she had helped bring into this world, thinking it would secure her lasting happiness at Sugar Alexandria. The same innocent child she had threatened to throw into a fire while suffering a psychotic episode, leading to a mental breakdown. His cries echoed in her head from that horrific day, and she panicked. "Sorry, not a good time," she said, attempting to shut the door.

He held it open. "Please, Mrs. McKay," he entreated, making direct eye contact with her. "Let me talk to you. I won't take much of your time; I promise."

Anna stared at him, his face and demeanor so much like James. Unmistakably, painfully similar. She had feared this day her entire life, and now here it was, catching her unprepared. And yet, in a bizarre flip of her dread of ever meeting this man standing right in front of her, she suddenly felt calm, no longer scared of him. Instead, she felt only love. Love for him. Love for his mother. Love for his father.

"May I please come in?" Joshua asked.

Anna opened the door the rest of the way. As he walked past, his masculine scent drifted into the air–the same scent of his father–and James' image materialized in her mind, her ex-husband holding her against his bare chest, kissing her. She pushed the image aside and directed her guest into the kitchen where they both sat down at the table.

"I know you weren't expecting me, and I apologize for just showing up like this. But I was afraid you'd say no if I called ahead first."

Handing him a glass of iced tea, Anna continued to examine her somewhat serendipitous visitor–a version of the man she had once called her husband. Her eyes scanned his every feature, seeking to find a glimmer of his mother.

"I've wanted to meet you for a long time now," Joshua continued. "My mum told me everything that happened between you, her, and my father–how I came into this world–and what ultimately destroyed your friendship in the end. Such a sad story. When we all moved back to Straya six months ago, I knew that, at the right time, I would see you. That I *had* to see you."

Tears filled Anna's eyes. She didn't know what to say, so she just listened.

"I don't blame you for any of it, Mrs. McKay. And I certainly didn't come here to judge anyone, drudge up the past, or make you feel bad about anything. I simply wanted to meet the special woman who initiated giving me life."

Anna could not contain her emotions any longer and began to weep. "You don't hate me, then?" she sniffled. "You don't think I'm evil for what I almost did to you and your mother when you were a baby?"

"Of course not," he said, handing her his handkerchief. "I'm here on this earth because of you, and you fulfilled my mother's lifelong dream."

Anna lowered her head. "I wasn't on any medication back then," she said, her voice cracking. "I didn't even know I had the mental conditions that I do, or how to cope with them. No one did."

He put his hand over hers. "I know, Mrs. McKay. I'm a doctor now, and I'm amazed you went as long as you did without any help. It's remarkable, in fact, and you shouldn't beat yourself over it."

She glanced at his hands–a carbon copy of James'–causing a pang to twist in her heart. Looking up at him, deep remorse etched across her face, she said, "I have no idea what came over me that day. I swear. Why I did that to you, or to your mother whom I loved dearly, has tormented me ever since."

"It's not your fault," he explained with genuine empathy. "It was the mental illness, not you."

"Even still, I've never been able to forgive myself for that," she said, her tears refusing to break.

Joshua kept holding her hand. "You must forgive yourself," he softly said, "because my mother has, and so have I."

After regaining her equanimity, Anna and Joshua visited with each other. He told her about his life growing up, his profession as a doctor, and his wife and children, proudly showing Anna pictures of them all. And Anna shared memories of the life she once lived with his parents–the beautiful troika that was her precious family for a few magical years. Reflections of James and Rose flashed through her mind as she spoke.

"How are your mum and dad doing?" she asked.

"Very well, ta."

"Over the years, I've cut out newspaper articles about your father's career as a professional pianist. They cover an entire board now, and I keep it in my daughters' old room."

"He was passionate about teaching, that's for sure. But his concerts gave him the most joy, I think."

Anna slowly nodded, lost in the past for a transient moment, thinking about that concert she had gone to at the Hummingbird Auditorium in Kalgoorlie where James electrified the audience. The powerful, poignant melody of *The Consequence of Anna* came back to her, and she once again teared up.

"What is it, Mrs. McKay?" asked Joshua.

"Oh, it's nothing," she said, wiping her eyes. "And call me Anna. You're family to me."

He smiled.

"Tell me something, Joshua . . . Why after all these years did you come? Why now?"

He paused, thinking on how to articulate his answer. "Until recently, my mum thought you might not be able to handle seeing me. She has always deeply regretted what happened to you, and she didn't want to cause you any more sorrow. My mum blames herself for everything."

Anna smiled—a coalition of love, pain, and regret. "I loved Rose so much it hurt," she said, the irony of her words not lost on either of them.

"She loved you too, Anna. Still does, very much."

"We were once like sisters, your mum and I. Closer than sisters, in fact." Anna looked at the strawberry heart-shaped birthmark on his wrist. "I was the first one to notice that, you know," she proudly stated, pointing at it. "I was holding you not long after you were born, and I said, 'Look at this. He was kissed by an angel and it left its mark.' At the time I thought it was . . ." She stopped.

"What, Anna? You thought it was what?"

"A sign from above that what we did was a good thing, not a sin," she said, her voice cracking again.

His eyebrows tensed, and for a moment his own expression mirrored hers. "That was quite something, what you allowed."

Anna locked eyes with him. "It was the biggest scandal Esperance has ever seen. Few women would have given such a gift, and although I paid dearly for it, the gift I do not regret." She put her hand on his. "Because look at you now, aye? What a glorious gift you turned out to be."

They moved into the living room where Anna showed Joshua the Shahan family portrait still mounted above the fireplace mantle. Standing before the impressive artwork, he marveled at his father as a young man, holding him as a baby, his stepsisters as young girls at his dad's feet, and his youthful mother and her cousin at his dad's side.

"Lovely, isn't it?" Anna asked. "Your father had a gift with the piano, and your mother with the violin and her paintings."

She took Joshua through the rest of the house to view all of Rose's work—twenty-two pieces in all. "There was a rumor that some of these images came to life for you," he said as they stared at the one of Anna's mother. "That they would visit and talk to you."

Anna smiled. "Maybe."

"Do they still?"

"Only if I don't take my medication, dear," she said with a twinkle in her eye. "You can take a painting with you, if you like. As many as you wish."

"No, that's all right. They belong here. My mum painted loads of them, and I already have several in my medical office as well as my home. Her work even hangs in restaurants and offices all over County Galway in Ireland. You should be proud—your image is well known in those parts because my mum painted many of you and her together in different scenes and settings at Sugar Alexandria."

"Rose continued to paint me?" Anna couldn't believe it.

"Yes. She always missed your friendship, and I think the paintings connected her to you in some way. Your friendship lived on through her art."

Anna felt so happy, so proud. "Can I hug you?" she asked.

"Of course, you can," he chuckled, opening his arms to her.

With the visit over, Anna followed him out to his car. As he was about to leave, she touched his arm resting on the doorframe of the open window. "Tell your mum to stop by sometime, will ya? And tell her to bring Lottie; I miss her terribly."

Joshua smiled. He knew that was Anna's endearing nickname for Rose, and it excited him to be able to tell his mother what she had just said. "I will, Anna. I certainly will. Hooroo!"

As she stepped away from the vehicle, Anna smiled and waved, watching Joshua drive off. *He looks like James, sounds like James, but has his mum's eyes,* she thought. *He has Rose's green eyes.*

CHAPTER 60

Two weeks later, Anna abruptly woke from her sleep. She did not have to be told that her ex-husband had died—she felt it in her bones. Confirmation of the sad news came that morning when Scarlet and Mabel called to tell her.

When the invitation to the wake arrived, Anna sat outside on the rear porch with the small envelope in her hand, gazing out at the three Danish windmills. All she ever had to do was stare at the large structures, and they would take her back, silently speaking to her about the tragic love triangle that happened all those years ago.

Feeling all alone, as if James had still been her husband all this time and now had passed, tears ran down like rain as the memories came flooding in. So much pain, so much suffering, caused by her mental illness and subsequent bad choices. Stubbornness, hardness, and decisions that unintentionally pushed the two people she loved the most together. She had loved Rose more than she loved her own husband, and ultimately lost them both as a result.

Wiping away her tears, she gazed up at the Australian sky, so vast and ever-changing. Low-hanging clouds traveled as soft as a whisper on the lips of a child, while the setting sun became a large, gold gem sinking into tomorrow. Spears of rays broke through the water vapor, sacrificing its light, causing prismatic images across the horizon.

Anna could see bright yellow and gold streaks in the sky that reminded her of the specks in Rose's green eyes. It made her ache. As if pages turned in a book, the passage of time had healed her wounds, and she eagerly awaited the day of her cousin's return . . .

～⚽～

James Ragnar Shahan was laid to rest on a Sunday afternoon. Family and friends–people from all walks of life–came to pay their last respects for the man they knew as a professional pianist and music professor. They came to acknowledge the legacy left behind from a life well lived.

Joshua gave the eulogy. He spoke eloquently about James, relating to the audience how his intelligence, inner strength, moral principles, and many kindnesses touched the lives of all who knew him. He talked about James' philanthropy within the Aboriginal community, and how he and Rose founded a musical school for the deaf. He praised James' dedication to his family, raising five children–Scarlet and Mabel; Joshua, Ragnar, and Ireland–and lastly, he talked about his love and respect for his father, and how he was proud to call him Dad.

"My father had a pure soul," Joshua said with strong emotion. "He lived the life he dreamed, a life he said was solid gold. But out of all his many accomplishments, his greatest was the love he had for his wife. He often said to my mum, 'Ambrosia Charlotte Shahan . . . you are the reason.' "

Anna did not go to James' funeral. On that day, she got up early and sat on her porch with her coffee, staring out into the stockyard, remembering . . . Oh, to remember! To once again taste the flavor of yesterday. Remnants of the past, like flecks of bright, golden embers burning in her mind. As the memories seized her, a mix of happy and sad tears began to run down her creased cheeks. "Did you bake any bickies for me, Tin Tin?" she could still hear James asking as he threw off his Akubra hat and pulled off his boots. "C'mere; lemme kiss ya, love. I missed you while I was out in the paddock all day." Oh, my sweet and gifted James, she thought. I'm sorry I tricked you into a life you did not want. I am happy Rose came into our lives and freed you.

Later in the evening, Anna went over to her liquor cabinet and poured herself a whiskey. It had been James' drink of choice. She put a record on the gramophone and retrieved an old shoebox containing photos from her previous life, sitting down to peruse through them. She wanted to continue reminiscing about the two people she had loved and lost so long ago.

Holding a picture of herself in her hands—a photo that Rose had taken of her sitting on the swing in Cassandra Fancy's garden—Anna recalled how young and naïve she had once been. An innocence so pure she could still feel its warmth, despite it having turned bitterly cold. She listened to the music coming from the gramophone, and as the melody filled the air, she hummed along, embracing the nostalgia that encompassed her. That's when she heard a car pulling into the driveway. She thought it was her daughters coming to visit after the funeral, but when she moved the curtain aside, the car looked unfamiliar to her.

Stepping onto the porch, Anna watched as an older woman with a cane got out of the vehicle and slowly walked toward her. The woman waved, and yet still Anna could not place the face. Shielding her eyes from the glare of the setting sun, she squinted to get a better look.

The woman smiled. "It's been a lifetime, but I was hoping you would still recognize me." Just then, the light caught in her eyes, revealing emerald green with a gold ring around her pupils. And her cane—it was the same one James had made from the lid prop of his piano . . .

Rose!

Anna hastily went out to meet her cousin as emotion surged through her body with such intensity it almost brought her to her knees. When they were standing arm's-length apart, she found she could not speak. All she could do was stare with thick tears in her eyes. Reaching out to Rose, she grabbed her hands.

"I know. It's been a long time," Rose said, her voice cracking and her eyes glistening.

"Min elskede . . . ," Anna cried in Danish. *"Min Lottie . . ."* (*"My beloved . . . My Lottie . . ."*) She could say nothing more. She tried, but the words were not there.

"Min søde Killing . . ." (*"My sweet Kitten . . ."*)

Anna touched Rose's face, not believing it was her. "Lottie . . . ," she said again.

"It's me, Anna. It's really me."

"I have missed you so much," Anna cried, her tears letting loose.

"I have missed you so much too," said Rose, reaching up to hold Anna's cheek.

They hugged each other, and once again, Anna felt the love of her mother, sister, and cousin all in one woman.

"I am so sorry about what I did that day," Anna said right away, as if it had happened only days ago instead of decades. "I don't know what came over me." She was sobbing now. "How could I do such a thing, attacking you and threatening your precious baby?"

"You were not well, Anna, and had been suffering, undiagnosed, for a long time." Rose gently squeezed her hand. "Things could have turned out far worse under the circumstances."

"I am truly sorry, though, Rose."

"Oh, hush, girl," she said, wiping away Anna's tears. "That was a long time ago. You've seen Joshua—that baby has grown up now and is a doctor with teenage children of his own. Besides, you're not that person anymore. With your medication, you've learned how to manage your illness."

Anna kept sobbing, unable to forgive herself all these years.

"Let's not talk of that day," Rose said, bringing little Anna in for another hug. "Let's never talk about it again."

Embracing tightly for the longest time, all the tears they had both stored up for decades, waiting for this very day, let loose. The two women then stepped back to look at each other again, still holding hands. A calm passed over them, as if a fever breaking. God himself muted the sounds around them; even the birds held their song. Both knew in that moment that the sisterly love they once shared had survived it all.

"Can you believe James is gone?" Rose asked. "The life we shared with him . . . All that love . . . All those children. Now it feels as if it all happened in the blink of an eye." She sighed. "I just can't believe he's gone, God rest his soul."

"Yes, God rest his soul," said Anna.

"I thought you might come to his funeral."

Anna's glossy eyes continued to stare at her cousin, afraid that if she looked away, Rose would vanish. "I thought about both of you all day."

The two women finally went into the house. Rose inspected all the artwork she had painted many moons ago; they looked exactly the same as the day she had created them. Anna had taken great care of each piece, always waxing the frames and cleaning the canvases with care.

"Precious moments in time," Rose said.

"Yes," replied Anna. "From a most happy period of our lives."

They found themselves in the kitchen, sitting at the same table where they used to eat together with James as a family, conversing at length about everything. They talked about Joshua's visit, how pleased Anna was to have met him, and how he looked like his father but had his mother's eyes. Rose agreed. They looked at pictures, drank Scotch, and shared stories about their lives, their children, and their grandchildren. They reminisced about the summers they used to spend together when they were teenagers. But they did not bring up the betrayal that ultimately separated them.

"You and James lived in Ireland all those years," Anna said, "and my daughters were always showing me all the photos you sent. What a beauty of a place! The castles, the history, all that lush, green land. James had always wanted to live there, and I'm rapt he finally did. I honestly couldn't believe it when my daughters told me you were moving back."

"Well, we did, and I'm here to stay," Rose said, putting her hand over Anna's.

Though advanced in years, both women felt young again. They laughed, cried, and chatted away endlessly like best of friends, as if no time had passed at all. Anna kept staring at Rose, searching her aged face. The years of life had left their lines behind, but her green eyes were still the same. There in her cousin's gaze was the woman she had loved so dearly.

"I missed laughing with you like this," Anna said. "We would always laugh so hard until it hurt."

"I know," said Rose. "You were the only one who could do that to me, too. Never had a friend again who could make me laugh like that."

"Me neither," said Anna. "Those days were ace. It was such a gift to have a cobber like you while it lasted."

Rose nodded.

An older man wearing spectacles and overalls walked in through the back door, holding and petting a small rabbit. He looked at Rose and smiled.

"Liam, you remember Rose, don't you?" Anna asked in sign language, waving him to the kitchen table. Over the years, she had learned how to use the visual gesticulations to communicate with her deaf friend.

He put the rabbit on the floor–it scampered under the hutch–then came and sat down with them. "You mean your cousin Lottie?" he signed.

Anna smiled. "Yes, my cousin Lottie."

He remained still a moment, then signed, "Cold is like a sad sound on the piano. Warm is like a beautiful, welcoming sound on the violin. Yellow is a lively vibration from a happy song, and red means thunderous and loud– the strongest vibration you can feel." Grinning, he added, "Of course I remember her."

Rose laughed. "It's so great to see you, Liam."

"It's been a long time," he signed. "Anna told me about Music Man. That makes me sad."

"He's resting now," signed Rose. She too had learned Australian sign language–enough to communicate–through her philanthropic involvement with her and James' foundation for the deaf.

"Before he moved to Ireland, he was my best mate."

"I know. He was very fond of you too, Liam."

"He started a school for the deaf named after me, and I got to go. It made me so rapt."

"Yes, you did–Liam's Lyrics. I was there the day you graduated."

"That was a good day."

"It was."

Liam lowered his head. "I shouldn't have been watching," he signed, his eyes tearing up. "All those years ago, I should have minded my own business. I ruined everything, and I'm sorry."

"No, no, no," Anna said, reaching over and gently lifting his chin. "You helped me to see things clearly," she signed. "I have learned so much from you."

Retrieving a handkerchief from his pocket, he wiped his eyes. "Friendship, love, happiness, sadness . . . Life . . . It all goes round and round, doesn't it?"

Both women agreed.

He gave Anna a concerned look, and signed, "Did you remember your medication today?"

Anna chuckled. "Yes, love," she signed back. Turning to Rose, she said, "He takes such good care of me."

"If she doesn't take it, she hears the voices."

Rose nodded, fully aware of Anna's lifelong condition.

"It was grouse seeing you again, Rose," Liam signed, a despondency still in his eyes. "I better get back to feeding the animals." He stood, kissed her on the cheek, then left outside.

"He lives in the windmill now," Anna said. "Has been for some time. After Cybill died, I took him in."

"That's lovely, Anna. Very kind of you." Rose gave her cousin a warm smile, seeing that Anna had indeed changed, displaying concern and empathy for the deaf and intellectually challenged now-older man.

The two of them continued their visit, moving to the living room where they had spent countless days before. Rose withdrew a photo album from her purse. "I brought you a prezzie," she said. "From when I was here at Sugar Alexandria."

Anna took the album and began flipping through the black-and-white photos—the halcyon days of their youth. "Seeing these is like going back in time," she said, sniffling as she flipped through the pages. "I remember me and James picking you up at the train station." Anna closed her eyes. "You were sitting on the bench, waiting, all dressed in black with a lace veil, Matilda in her carrier next to you."

"Yes, that's right. I remember that too."

Anna reopened her eyes. "I wanted so badly for you to stay with us forever."

"I did stay quite a long time."

"And we had such fun, didn't we? We'd stay up late in the windmill, drinking Yarrajan's blackberry wine, listening to records and talking. You'd tell me these marvelous tales about faraway lands, with kings and queens, warriors and gods, and exotic animals—they were mesmerizing. And often we would get dressed up and play with your makeup, doing the Charleston and Foxtrot as we drank spiked fizzies, or listen to late-night radio programs."

Rose laughed. "Sometimes James would even join us."

"What a ripper time we all had then. Memories to last a lifetime." Anna got up and retrieved a small box, handing it to Rose.

"All the postcards from Europe I sent you," Rose said upon removing the lid. "You kept them."

"I did. Whenever I received one, especially from Ireland, I imagined you and James and your children in that foreign land, visiting all these beautiful places, learning new things. Those cards have become sacred to me. Ta for sending them, Rose."

"I am so happy you kept them." As Rose sorted through each postcard, she told Anna everything about the place—where it was, what they did there after James' performances, things that happened—a new adventure with each one.

"And one last gift, Kitten." Rose pulled out four children's books: *East of the Sun and West of the Moon*, *Alice in Wonderland*, *The Secret Garden*, and *Emma*. They were originals in pristine condition.

"Oh, Lottie . . ."

"I read these books to you so often I practically memorized them," Rose chuckled.

Anna held the books close to her heart. "They were my favorites. I'll look through them tonight before bed. Ta, Lottie. Ta for all the prezzies."

The night passed by quickly, giving way to the early-morning hours. As the sun was rising, creating a pastel sky, they found themselves outside by Rose's car, still talking, still catching up. It was difficult to say goodbye.

"You come back and visit me again soon, Lottie," Anna said, her voice cracking.

"Of course I will, Kitten. There's still a lot of catching up to do."

"We should have all the children and grandchildren over here for a big barbie sometime."

Rose nodded. She had something on her mind, though. Something she still hadn't brought up, but wanted to. Searching for the right words, deep remorse evincing from her face, she said, "Anna, I swear on my life that I never meant to hurt you. I did not come to Australia to take James from you, but I did fall in love with him after we became friends. And I truly believe he was my soul mate."

Anna gave her cousin a look of absolution. "Took me a long time to acknowledge it, but I believe that too, Rose. James was a pianist, not a grazier. He felt trapped here with me, living the life of a station owner by my will. I was just thinking today, that in a lot of ways, you unchained him from this prison. You freed him from a place he never wanted to be."

"He loved you, Anna. And the girls."

"I know. But not with the kind of love he had for you. He deserved that kind of love. He deserved *you*, Rose. You were bloody grouse for him."

"Anna . . . ," Rose said, her eyes tearing up again. "James told me after we heard of Flossy's passing that he would like to be laid to rest at Sugar Alexandria, if you'll allow it."

Anna couldn't believe her ears. The one place James had always wanted to be free from was now his preferred burial site. How could this be?

"He said you were an important part of our younger lives, and that he still had fond memories from that time. I do too, and I'd like to be buried here as well."

Anna fought hard to maintain her composure. The trinity she had created that crumbled in life would soon come full circle, reunited in death. It took a long moment for her to regain her equilibrium. "Of course he can be laid here," she said. "And you too."

Rose squeezed her hand. "I wished you could have stayed in our lives all those years. I wish we could have figured this all out back then. Why did it take so long for us to reconcile?"

"Because the child in me loved you, and when that happened with you and James, the child died," Anna said, her voice melancholic as she spoke. "The woman I then became hated you, and I was that woman for a very long time." She paused before continuing. "As time went on, I hated myself for what I had done. And to not talk to you meant I didn't have to face that. It was better to just act like it never happened, as if you had never been in my life to begin with. As difficult as that was, that's how I survived it all."

Rose understood. She hugged Anna's small, fragile shoulders, kissing her forehead. "My sweet Kitten. Always and forever, my sweet little Kitten," she whispered.

"I never had another friendship again like we had, Rose. I had other cobbers, but nothing like the joy I shared with you."

"Likewise," said Rose. "I too never had that again."

"Oh goodness, wait! Here . . ." Anna had been wearing both their friendship lockets for decades now. Removing the one she had torn off of Rose in the mental institute, she replaced it back around her cousin's neck.

Rose put her hand over the heart-shaped pendant, pressing it into her chest.

The sun was completely up when Rose left Sugar Alexandria. Anna waved goodbye, watching through blurred, teary eyes as the car became a dot in the far-off distance. *"Min elskede . . . ,"* she whispered in Danish. *"Min elskede . . ."* (*"My beloved . . . My beloved . . ."*)

Time, fate, destiny.

Mistakes and consequences.

None of those things matter, because in the end, God always has the last word. He corrects all errors, straightens all paths, and mends all broken ties.

Anna pondered over this as she went back into the farmhouse. At one point in her existence, she was a walking, raw wound; but now her spirits were as wide as the deep blue sea.

And as serene.

Life is so similar to a song, she thought. Like a piece that is richer for its unresolved chords. A symphony of happiness, sadness, comedy, and even poetry. Sometimes it stabs you in the heart, and other times it thaws the ice and warms your bones, gracing you with its indelible charm. But no matter the circumstance, you listen to it to the very end until the notes fade. Once the song is over, there is only silence. Stillness. A person has no choice but to move on to see what lies beyond the music.

Anna went into her bedroom and opened her cedar hope chest, removing the sculpture James had carved of Rose all those years ago. The one she had ripped from his hands in the distillery that night, chastising him for creating it. She put the figurine on the vanity in front of her and stared at it in ardent wonder, thinking of how her ex-husband had carved it with no flaw. Two perfect legs. The meaning behind it was lost to her then, but not now. No, now she understood. James was in love with Rose mind, body, and soul—and her flawed limb was invisible to him. How fitting to bring it out in this moment, she thought. To gaze at it, hold it close, and reminisce about a most beautiful time in their lives. The relic represented all the wonderful stories the three of them shared when they were young.

Morning light flooded the room, illuminating everything in its path. Including Anna. Forgetting to take her medication, she only stood there, basking in the warmth of the glow, smiling as an excitement stirred in her old soul while a peace permeated through her body. Putting her hand on her heart, so grateful for the visit from her beloved Rose, she suddenly heard the whispers . . . Someone calling her name . . . The paintings began to move and speak to her!

Anna put her finger to her lips. "Shhhh," was all she said, grinning so big it hurt, dimples popping, gap between her teeth showing, the girlish spunk still shining through . . .

The End

Dear Reader,

We hope you enjoyed *The Consequence of Anna*. It took much effort and care to write this poignant yet beautiful story between James, Anna, and Rose, and if you have a moment, we would be very grateful if you left a rating/review on Amazon at:
https://www.amazon.com/review/create-review/?asin=B0CJM7J13L

Also, if you'd like to read a more nefarious ending of what could have happened had things gone terribly wrong, you can download it for free at:
https://katebirkinbooks.com/COA-alternative-ending

Lastly, join our exclusive Readers' Club mailing list to receive free give-aways and updates on our hot new releases at:
https://katebirkinbooks.com/subscribe-welcome

Thank you so much!
Kate & Mark

James and Rose Shahan

James Ragnar Shahan, The Pianist

My Dearest Anna,   August 12, 1935

Sometimes at the end of the day, holding baby Joshua in my arms, I watch the sunset and think of what you have given me, and my heart aches. Because of you, my life is so full now. It was a gift of love what you allowed, but a deep sin for me to accept. And yet look what I have — my precious, beautiful son Joshua.

I have this dreadful, painful fear, though, that I am dead to you now. Am I? Am I only a ghost whom you once loved as a sister? Oh, if only there were a way we could be friends again. Please, Kitten, I beg of you... forgive.

Remember how we were as children — two lionesses in a beautiful lair, playing in the wheat fields, my cane our magical wand, granting all our wishes? Remember the joy, the laughter, and the kinship we shared as adults, and our girls' nights in the windmill? We were unstoppable then, weren't we? We could be again.

Your Beloved, always...
Rose

April 15, 1933

Rose,

Last night I walked through the farmhouse in the darkness, soundlessly, and the rooms all felt foreign to me. If not evil. I don't belong here, I thought. I never did. Instantly I wanted to leave and crawl into bed beside you in the windmill, hold you in my arms, feel the warmth of your body, and wake up to your smile. But of course, I could not. Instead, I made myself get back into bed with Anna, drape my arm across her, and imagine it was you.

Soon, though... Soon we will leave — you, me, Joshua, and our child you now carry. When I think of it, an excitement stirs in my body, despite the obvious repercussions neither of us wanted. When the truth is told, we will finally be together as we should have been from the start. What a glorious future we have in store, and it is fast approaching.

I love you,
James

AFTERWORD

The character of Anna May Shahan suffered from three undiagnosed mental disorders: schizophrenia; dissociative identity disorder, previously known as multiple personality disorder; and Asperger's syndrome, a disorder without medical recognition until the mid-1940s. Because of her conditions, and especially when under stress, she hallucinated, hearing and seeing things not there; she adopted the imagined thoughts, perceptions, and occasionally, persona, of her deceased mother and sister; and she lacked certain emotional and cognitive abilities that most people take for granted, manifesting others that puzzled and sometimes upset those around her. Including those she most loved. Questionable choices, actions, and words, though not meant to harm or offend, often did exactly that. In the end, they became her undoing, having dire consequences for her, destroying the utopian world she so desperately tried to maintain.

Irrespective of Anna's delusional behaviors brought on by schizophrenia and dissociative identity disorder, her inability to empathize with her husband James, being completely removed from his feelings, desires, and goals, is a common trait in those who suffer from Asperger's syndrome. Unless it directly affects their own happiness, such ones cannot see or recognize the plight of others. Rose, on the other hand, filled a deep emotional hole for Anna, who never knew her mother, and lost her twin sister at five years of age. She made Anna happy in a way James could not; therefore, Anna would do anything for her, manipulating any situation to keep her beloved cousin with her at Sugar Alexandria. It clouded her judgment, blurred her moral compass, and drove her to go so far as to control, badger, and coerce her loyal husband into finally conceding to her will, whilst against his own, agreeing to father her cousin's child.

Anna did not know how to love the way others love—with kindness, consideration, and selflessness. She loved only through ownership. She owned her land, she owned her children, and she believed she owned her husband and cousin, not loving them as family members but as possessions, going to great lengths to keep her paradise exactly as she had created it. Virtues, principles, mainstream norms of right and wrong abandoned, the result was disastrous for her. James and Rose suffered too, albeit in different ways than Anna. A broken marriage, the loss of a dear friend, children of divorce, the scorn of the town, and lifelong guilt—all remnants of the tragic aftermath of their love triangle.

In retrospect, would Anna Shahan have fallen into this state of euphoric delusion, conjuring up such a preposterous idea in the belief that it would secure everyone's lasting happiness at Sugar Alexandria, if she had not suffered from these three debilitating mental illnesses? Most likely not. She believed, in the deepest part of her soul, that she was doing something for the greater good of them all, completely unaware of how James and Rose already had intense feelings for each other, despite keeping them at bay. Strong-willed, unable to relate to, acknowledge, or even recognize another person's sentiments and desires when they conflicted with her own, Anna did not mean to be dismissive of her husband, obsessive over her cousin, or unprincipled and morally defunct. She simply wanted to be happy. And yet, because of her disorders, she paid the ultimate price in the end, losing everything she loved, simultaneously becoming both the grievous perpetrator and the heartbroken victim.

Poor, sweet Anna . . . Innocent and culpable at the same time.

Some would say Rose was the perpetrator, not Anna. Some would contend that she was the one who egregiously manipulated things to her own benefit, lacking empathy and concern for everyone else when she agreed to Anna's plan for gifting her a child through Anna's husband James. After all, she loved James; perhaps she wanted to steal him away for herself, regretful over letting him go many years earlier when they first met at his sister's wedding. Did she take advantage of her sweet, naïve cousin, knowing that Anna had not the mental acuity to fully understand what she was proposing? Knowing that Anna would do anything for her, desperate to keep her at Sugar Alexandria? And yet, as already stated, Rose too suffered from the repercussions of what they did. Her insatiable desire to have her own child, although fulfilled, brought with it decades of sadness over the cost.

Lastly, there was James Shahan. Suffering in his own way long before

Rose came back to Australia, tricked into marriage to a woman he did not love but felt responsible for, robbed of his lifelong dream of becoming a professional pianist and music professor. Was he the only one blameless in this ordeal? Granted, he was against the whole idea from the start, rebuking his wife at the very notion of it, resisting until the end . . .

Until he didn't.

What happened to the man of integrity? What happened to the man who believed in the sanctity of his marriage vows before God? Perhaps he saw it as an opportunity to escape the life of a grazier that he so loathed. His intellect and musical talent wasting at the station, Rose may have been the keymaster to finally set him free. Did he escape unscathed? No, he did not. To his dying day he would remember the haunting pain in his wife's eyes, her attempted suicide, the pitiful endeavors to win him back, and the distress he forced upon his innocent little girls who lost the security and togetherness of growing up in a loving family.

"The heart is more treacherous than anything else and is desperate. Who can know it?"

Penned by the ancient prophet Jeremiah in the Holy Bible, never were truer words spoken. Anna was desperate to keep her beloved Rose with her at Sugar Alexandria forever. Rose was desperate to at last have her own child. And James was desperate to finally escape a life he did not want. Yes indeed! . . . The heart is more treacherous than anything else and is desperate. Who can know it!

Spotlight on Schizophrenia, Dissociative Identity Disorder, and Asperger's Syndrome

Note: The ensuing discussion is not always true in all cases of these three serious mental disorders. We cannot categorically stereotype or generalize every person who suffers them, only reference those characteristics that are commonly shared. Similarly, each symptom or behavior, if and when present, can vary in intensity and frequency.

Schizophrenia

The term schizophrenia was first coined by the Swiss psychiatrist Eugen Bleuler in 1908, during a lecture given at a psychiatric conference in Berlin, Germany. He described it as the separation of function between personality, thinking, memory, and perception–the "splitting" of the mind–denoting the loss of contact with reality through indulgence in bizarre fantasy, and the coexistence of mutually exclusive contradictions within the psyche.

Schizophrenia is a heartbreaking and debilitating mental disorder, and not just for those suffering it but also for those who love and care for them. It is a serious disease of the mind in which people interpret reality abnormally. In some cases the condition remains latent or is not fully expressed until certain circumstances are met, suggesting that derangements of thought processes are specific rather than general. Most people with schizophrenia are not any more dangerous or violent than the general population, and onset tends to occur earlier in men than women.

Schizophrenia may manifest via some combination of hallucinations–especially hearing voices and seeing things in the absence of an external stimulus–delusions, chaotic thinking, anomalous behavior, disorganized speech, inappropriate actions and feelings, emotional disturbances, withdrawal from personal relationships, and a sense of mental fragmentation. There is no cure, and people with schizophrenia require lifelong care. Early diagnosis and treatment may help bring symptoms under control before serious complications develop, and may help improve the long-term outlook. Today over twenty million people worldwide are affected.

Famous people who have been diagnosed with schizophrenia include Zelda Fitzgerald, the writer, artist, and 1920s fashion symbol married to famous author F. Scott Fitzgerald. Bettie Page, the "Queen of Pinups" who pushed boundaries in the 1950s with risqué photos that made her a modeling icon. Syd Barrett, the British musician and founding member of rock band Pink Floyd. John Nash Jr., one of the world's most brilliant mathematicians and 1994 Nobel Prize winner in Economic Sciences. Eduard Einstein, the youngest child of German physicist Albert Einstein. And debatably, Vincent van Gogh, one of history's greatest artists, whose behavior some scholars say stemmed from this crippling disease.

Dissociative Identity Disorder

Dissociative identity disorder (previously known as multiple personality disorder) is a complex illness that is thought to stem from a combination of factors, most notably severe trauma during early childhood. It is an acute form of mental separation characterized by the presence of two or more distinct or split identities–referred to as personality states–each having power over the individual's behavior. The dissociative aspect serves as a psychological coping mechanism, whereby the person literally shuts off or dissociates themselves from a situation or experience that is too violent, traumatic, or painful to assimilate with their conscious self, compartmentalizing the trauma by breaking off and creating other personalities that don't have the problem.

Not everyone with dissociative personality disorder experiences these "alters" the same way. For some, the different identities have their own age, sex, or race, and their own postures, gestures, and distinct way of speaking. Often they are imaginary people, and sometimes even animals. As each personality reveals itself through environmental triggers or life events, controlling the individual's comportment and thoughts, it's called "switching". This can take seconds to minutes to days.

Usually there is a host personality within the individual, identifying with the person's real name, and often the distinct personalities have no memory of what went on when the others were in charge, having no awareness that they even exist.

While there is no cure for dissociative identity disorder, long-term treatment can be helpful. Psychotherapy is the mainstay of clinical protocol, designed to help "fuse" the separate dissociated states into one consolidated personality that can control the problematic triggers.

There are a number of famous, sensational cases of dissociative identity disorder well-documented in the annals of psychiatric literature. While this disease is rare, it can be extremely difficult to live with. It has long been suspected that Marilyn Monroe, the 1950s American actress, model, and singer, notoriously known as one of the world's biggest and most enduring sex symbols, was suffering from dissociative identity disorder. Heisman Trophy winner, professional football star, and Olympian Herschel Walker, too, suffered this illness, writing about his struggle managing multiple personalities in his book, *Breaking Free.*

Asperger's Syndrome

Asperger's syndrome is a form of high-functioning autism. People who have this condition can be highly intelligent, successful, and even great leaders, but there is an element of emotional and social understanding that is often missing—the fundamental ability to empathize with others, recognize and acknowledge their feelings, or respond appropriately to them. They may miss social cues that are obvious, like body language or the expressions on someone's face, and yet demonstrate intellectual awareness in many other ways. Obsessive interests or traits, repetitive or restrictive patterns of behavior, aversion to change, and many other conditions may also manifest themselves to varying degrees.

In their personal lives, people with Asperger's syndrome often lack satisfying relationships because of these difficulties they may have in socially connecting with others. Romantic companions often express frustration over their Asperger partner's robotic behavior, creating sadness, loneliness, and a feeling of rejection and emotional abandonment.

Asperger's syndrome affects males more often than females, and females are typically diagnosed at a later age. The syndrome was named after the Austrian pediatrician, Hans Asperger, who, in 1944, described children in his care who were clumsy and lacking in nonverbal communication skills and understanding of others' feelings. The modern conception of Asperger's syndrome came into existence in 1981 and went through a period of popularization. It became a standardized diagnosis in the early 1990s. Many questions and controversies remain, and there is doubt about whether it is distinct from high-functioning autism. Partly because of this, the percentage of people affected is not firmly established. Nonetheless, it has been estimated that over thirty-seven million people currently live with Asperger's syndrome around the globe.

Famous people who have long been considered to be somewhere on the autism spectrum include: Michelangelo, Wolfgang Amadeus Mozart, Sir Isaac Newton, Nikola Tesla, Albert Einstein, Thomas Jefferson, Benjamin Banneker, Charles Darwin, Hans Christian Andersen, William Butler Yeats, and Steve Jobs.

BOOK CLUB

*T*he Consequence of Anna is a story with multiple themes and issues relevant to today's society. Some are timeless, like love, friendship, infidelity, heartache, and sacrifice; while others are just now receiving the attention they deserve due to changing norms, attitudes, and social stigmas regarding mental illness and its treatments. As such, the authors of this poignant tale inspired by true events felt *The Consequence of Anna* was perfect for book clubs, and took the liberty to generate a list of questions to facilitate interesting discussion . . .

General Questions About the Book

1. What did you like most about the book? What did you like the least?
2. Was this a page-turner for you, or did it take you a while to finish?
3. Did the book's pace seem appropriate for the story?
4. Did the story strike you as original and unique?
5. How well do you think the authors conveyed the setting, time period, and world in which the characters lived?
6. What do you think of the book's title in relation to the story? Would you have given it a different title, and if yes, what would it be?
7. What do you think of the book's cover and how well it conveys what the story is about?
8. What do you think of the images in the book? Were they a nice touch or just a distraction?
9. What did you think of the length of the book? If it's too long, what would you cut?
10. What did you think of the writing style, and are there any standout sentences/paragraphs?

11. Did you reread, highlight, or bookmark any passages, and if so, which ones and why?

12. Which chapter or scene stuck with you the most, and why?

13. What were the central themes and issues of the book? How well do you think the authors explored them?

14. What symbolism caught your attention, and how well did the authors use it?

15. How did the story impact you? What emotions did it evoke? Do you think you'll remember it in a few months or years?

16. How thought-provoking did you find the book? Did it change your opinion about anything, or did you learn something new from it? If so, what?

17. What surprised you most about the book, and why?

18. Was there any part of the plot or aspects of the characters that frustrated or upset you? If so, why?

19. Are there any lingering questions you're still thinking about?

20. How did you feel about the ending? How might you change it?

21. Would you ever consider re-reading it? Why or why not?

22. Who do you most want to read this book, and why?

23. Are there any books you would compare this one to? If yes, describe the connection.

24. If you could ask the authors anything, what would it be?

25. Rate this book on a scale of 1 to 10, with 10 being the highest. Why did you give that rating? Did any part of this book club discussion change your rating from what it was after finishing the book?

General Questions About the Characters

1. Who was your favorite character, and why?

2. Were there any characters you disliked, and why?

3. Did the characters seem believable to you? Were they thoroughly fleshed out? Did they remind you of anyone?

4. Which character or moment prompted the strongest emotional reaction for you, and why?

5. Which character did you identify with, relate to, or empathize with most?

6. What were the power dynamics between the characters, and how did

that affect their interactions?

7. Were there times you disagreed with a character's actions? If yes, what would you have done differently?

8. How does the way the characters see themselves differ from the way others see them?

9. How have the characters changed by the end of the book?

10. Were there any secondary characters you would have liked to know more about?

11. Which character would you most like to meet in real life?

12. If you were making a movie of this book, who would you cast for each role?

Specific Questions About Anna, James, and Rose

1. In one sentence, how would you describe Anna, James, and Rose?

2. If you could meet Anna, James, and Rose, what would you say to each of them?

3. Did Anna truly love James and Rose, or did she only view them as possessions?

4. Aside from her loneliness due to the loss of her mother and sister, why was Anna's sisterly love for Rose so intense?

5. If Anna had not suffered from mental illness and had bonded with James emotionally and intimately, would the love triangle have still transpired?

6. Should James and Rose have disclosed to Anna right away that they had met before at Christian and Josephine's wedding? Why or why not?

7. Should Rose have left Sugar Alexandria as soon as she realized the feelings between her and James were still very strong?

8. Who was ultimately to blame for the love triangle–Anna, James, or Rose–and why?

9. Was it more wrong of James and Rose to capitulate to Anna's plan knowing she was mentally ill?

10. Why do you think Anna hallucinated a woman from the 1800s in a black Victorian dress, and where might she have gotten Genevieve's name?

11. Why do you think Anna hallucinated the shadow people, and who

or what do you think they were?

12. Why do you think Anna hallucinated the Black Shuck when she knew it was a folklore tale?

13. Why do you think Anna hallucinated Callum McTavish as being the Black Shuck before she killed him?

14. Should Anna have gone to prison for killing Callum McTavish, or was her suffering in the mental institution punishment enough?

15. Should James have been held accountable for protecting his mentally ill wife by covering up her murder of Callum McTavish?

16. Should Anna have agreed to see her beloved Rose long before she did, rather than waiting decades until they were old?

17. If you were Joshua, would you have visited Anna, knowing she had almost killed you and your mother when you were a baby?

18. Was it wrong for James to start his life over in Ireland with Rose, leaving his twin daughters behind?

19. On hearing James' play his moving composition, *The Consequence of Anna*, should Anna have been upset instead of honored?

20. If Anna had known from the start that her mother had suffered the same mental illnesses as her, and died in the Pleasant Skies Psychiatric Hospital, do you think it would have facilitated Anna getting help sooner?

21. What do you think of James' reasoning for wanting to be buried at Sugar Alexandria instead of his father's Irish burial plot, when for so many years he loathed his life there?

22. Why do you think Anna kept the figurine James had carved of Rose, despite what happened between the three of them?

23. At the end of the book after Rose's visit, Anna forgets to take her medication, and the paintings begin to move and speak to her. She shushes them and grins. What do you think that means?

Made in United States
North Haven, CT
08 July 2024

54524532R00340